P9-AFJ-394

Withdrawn from Collection

The Compleat Boucher

The Complete Short Science Fiction and Fantasy of
Anthony Boucher

edited by James A. Mann

The NESFA Press
Post Office Box 809
Framingham, MA 01701
1998

Copyright 1999 by the Estate of William Anthony Parker White

Introduction
Copyright 1999 by James A. Mann

Dust Jacket Illustration
Jane Dennis
Copyright 1999 by Jane Dennis

ALL RIGHTS RESERVERD. NO PART OF THIS BOOK MAY BE
REPRODUCED IN ANY FORM OR BY ANY ELECTRONIC, MAGI-
CAL, OR MECHANICAL MEANS INCLUDING INFORMATION
STORAGE AND RETRIEVAL WITHOUT PERMISSION IN WRIT-
ING FROM THE PUBLISHER, EXCEPT BY A REVIEWER WHO
MAY QUOTE BRIEF PASSAGES IN A REVIEW.

FIRST EDITION

Library of Congress Catalog Card Number: 98-68084

International Standard Book Number 1-886778-02-7

Copyright Acknowledgements

"The Ambassadors" first appeared in *Startling Stories*, June 1952

"The Anomaly of the Empty Man" first appeared in *The Magazine of Fantasy and Science Fiction*, April 1952

"Balaam" first appeared in *9 Tales of Space and Time*, edited by Raymond J. Healy, 1954

"Barrier" first appeared in *Astounding Science Fiction*, September 1942

"The Chronokinesis of Jonathan Hull" first appeared in *Astounding Science Fiction*, June 1946

"The Compleat Werewolf" first appeared in *Unknown Worlds*, April 1942

"Conquest" first appeared in *Star Science Fiction 2*, edited by Frederik Pohl

"Elsewhen" first appeared in *Astounding Science Fiction*, January 1943

"Expedition" first appeared in *Thrilling Wonder Stories*, August 1943

"First" first appeared in *The Magazine of Fantasy & Science Fiction*, October 1952

"Gandolphus" first appeared in *The Magazine of Fantasy & Science Fiction*, December 1956

"The Ghost of Me" first appeared in *Unknown Worlds*, June 1942

"The Greatest Tertian" first appeared in *Astounding Science Fiction*, June 1942

"Khartoum" first appeared in *Stefantasy*, August 1955. First professional publication in *Strange Bedfellows*, edited by William F. Nolan

"A Kind of Madness" first appeared in *Ellery Queen's Mystery Magazine*, August 1972

"Man's Reach" first appeared in *The Magazine of Fantasy & Science Fiction*, November 1972

"Mary Celestial" first appeared in *The Magazine of Fantasy & Science Fiction*, May 1955

"The Model of a Science Fiction Editor" first appeared in *The Magazine of Fantasy & Science Fiction*, July 1953

"Mr. Lupescu" first appeared in *Weird Tales*, September 1945

"Nellthu" first appeared in *The Magazine of Fantasy & Science Fiction*, August 1955

"Nine-Finger Jack" first appeared in *Esquire*, May 1951

"One-Way Trip" first appeared in *Astounding Science Fiction*, August 1943

"The Other Inauguration" first appeared in *The Magazine of Fantasy and Science Fiction*, March 1953

"Pelagic Spark" first appeared in *Astounding Science Fiction*, June 1943

"The Pink Caterpillar" first appeared in *Adventure Magazine*, 1945

"The Public Eye" first appeared in *Thrilling Wonder Stories*, April 1952

"The Quest for Saint Aquin" first appeared in *The Magazine of Fantasy and Science Fiction*, January 1959

"Q.U.R." first appeared in *Astounding Science Fiction*, March 1943

"Rappaccini's Other Daughter" appears here for the first time.

"Review Copy" first appered in *The Magazine of Fantasy and Science Fiction*, Fall 1949

"Robinc" first appeared in *Astounding Science Fiction*, September 1943

"Sanctuary" first appeared in *Astounding Science Fiction*, June 1943

"The Scrawny One" first appeared in *Weird Tales*, May 1949

"Secret of the House" first appeared in *Galaxy*, March 1953

"A Shape in Time" first appeared in *The Future Is Now*, edited by William F. Nolan, 1970

"Snulbug" first appeared in *Unknown Worlds*, December 1941

"Sriberdegibit" first appeared in *Unknown Worlds*, June 1943

"Star Bride" first appeared in *Thrilling Wonder Stories*, December 1951

"The Star Dummy" first appeared in *Fantastic*, Fall 1952

"A Summer's Cloud" first appeared in *Twilight Zone*, June 1981

"The Tenderizers" first appeared in *The Magazine of Fantasy and Science Fiction*, January 1942

"They Bite" first appeared in *Unknown Worlds*, August 1943

"Transfer Point" first appeared in *Galaxy*, December 1950

"The Way I Heard It" first appeared in *Twilight Zone*, June 1981

"We Print the Truth" first appeared in *Astounding Science Fiction*, December 1943

Acknowledgements

This book was produced with the help of a number of people. George Flynn once again reviewed every story and meticulously compared what we had on hand with previously published versions. Mary Tabasko also provided extensive proofing help and advice on design, and Scot Taylor lent a hand in the proofing. Kevin Riley helped design the dust jacket, using the art provided by Jane Dennis. Mark Olson and Tony Lewis provided advice and support throughout. Teresa Nielsen Hayden provided advice on a couple of editorial points. Charles N. Brown helped us track down the agent of the estate. Laurie Mann helped scan a number of the stories and in general provided support throughout this effort. And Leslie Mann provided some clerical help. Thanks to you all.

James A. Mann
Editor
Pittsburgh, PA
September 1998

Contents

The Very Model of a Science Fiction Editor ... and Writer ... and Critic ... and ...

James A. Mann

Anthony Boucher (William Anthony Parker White) is perhaps best known as one of the great editors of science fiction. He and J. Francis McComas started *The Magazine of Fantasy and Science Fiction* in 1949. *F&SF*, along with Horace Gold's *Galaxy*, wrested the unchallenged leadership of the science fiction field away from John W. Campbell's *Astounding*, which, since 1939, had been the leader of the field. After 1950, there were three great magazines in the field, not just one. *F&SF* helped move science fiction fantasy into new directions under Boucher's leadership. He also edited several anthologies, the most notable of which, the two-volume *A Treasury of Great Science Fiction*, was a selection of just about everybody who joined the Science Fiction Book Club for decades.

But Boucher was more than a science fiction editor. He was a critic, whose book reviews appeared in such prestigious places as *The New York Times*. He was a mystery writer. The big annual mystery convention, Bouchercon, is named after him. He also produced a weekly radio special on opera, wrote opera reviews, helped found the Mystery Writers of America, founded the West Coast branch of the Baker Street Irregulars, and was active in politics (and served on the California Democratic Central Committee) and the Catholic Church. He became a gourmet chef (and this book ends with one of his recipes), was a great poker player, and was a devoted husband and father.

And of course, he was a writer of a number of science fiction and fantasy stories. He was a major writer for Campbell's *Unknown Worlds* and *Astounding* in the 1940s, with stories and poems appearing under the names Anthony Boucher, H. H. Holmes, and Herman W. Mudgett. Sometimes, a single issue of a magazine would feature both a Boucher story and a Holmes story. Many of his early stories such as "Snulbug" and "The Compleat Werewolf" were humorous, though with a distinctly humanist touch, often reminiscent of Frank Capra with an occasional touch of screwball comedy. But he also investigated more serious topics. "The Quest for Saint Aquin," perhaps his best story, is a probing examination of religious faith. "Balaam" examines religion from another angle and looks at the ultimate sacrifice. Other stories, written during World War II or soon after, examine fascist or statist societies. "One-Way Trip" and "Barrier" both look at, though from very different angles, fascism, stagnant societies, and the need for individuality.

The stories are diverse. There are wry little horror stories like "Mr. Lupescu." There are even grimmer horror stories like "They Bite" or "The Pink Caterpillar." There are robot stories like "Q.U.R." and "Robinc" and cautionary tales like "We Print the Truth." There are recursive stories (stories about science fiction)— "Pelagic Spark" and "Transfer Point." We have a Sherlock Holmes story of sorts: "The Greatest Tertian." There is even the sequel to a Nathaniel Hawthorne story, the previously unpublished "Rappaccini's Other Daughter."

Many of the stories included here have never before been included in a Boucher collection. Some have not appeared since their original appearance in the magazines. It's a pleasure to bring them back into print.

So, read, and enjoy. And then go out and look for some of Boucher's mysteries. Several of them, including *Rocket to the Morgue*, are still in print and available in some of the better bookstores.

A note on the order of the stories: Many readers are curious about the order of the stories in a collection: Why did the editor choose that order? This book leads of with "The Quest for Saint Aquin," which is not only Boucher's best but which was not included in either of the two previous Boucher collections (though the Science Fiction Writers of America chose it to appear in *The Science Fiction Hall of Fame*). It's followed by another Boucher great, "The Compleat Werewolf." That story introduced the character of Fergus O'Breen, who appears in the four stories that follow. The two stories after that ("Sriberdegibit" and "The Ambassadors") make passing reference to "The Compleat Werewolf." The two robot stories follow, then "Nine-Finger Jack," which Boucher considered one of his best. From there till near the end the order is somewhat arbitrary, based on what I thought would be a good order. The book ends with "We Print the Truth," a long, impressive story, and "Mary Celestial," the only story in the book Boucher didn't write alone—he coauthored it with Miriam Allen DeFord.

The Compleat Boucher

The Quest for Saint Aquin

The Bishop of Rome, the head of the Holy, Catholic and Apostolic Church, the Vicar of Christ on Earth—in short, the Pope—brushed a cockroach from the filth-encrusted wooden table, took another sip of the raw red wine, and resumed his discourse.

"In some respects, Thomas," he smiled, "we are stronger now than when we flourished in the liberty and exaltation for which we still pray after Mass. We know, as they knew in the catacombs, that those who are of our flock are indeed truly of it; that they belong to Holy Mother the Church because they believe in the brotherhood of man under the fatherhood of God—not because they can further their political aspirations, their social ambitions, their business contacts."

" 'Not of the will of flesh, nor of the will of man, but of God . . .' " Thomas quoted softly from St. John.

The Pope nodded. "We are, in a way, born again in Christ; but there are still too few of us—too few even if we include those other handfuls who are not of our faith, but still acknowledge God through the teachings of Luther or Lao-tse, Gautama Buddha or Joseph Smith. Too many men still go to their deaths hearing no gospel preached to them but the cynical self-worship of the Technarchy. And that is why, Thomas, you must go forth on your quest."

"But, Your Holiness," Thomas protested, "if God's word and God's love will not convert them, what can saints and miracles do?"

"I seem to recall," murmured the Pope, "that God's own Son once made a similar protest. But human nature, however illogical it may seem, is part of His design, and we must cater to it. If signs and wonders can lead souls to God, then by all means let us find the signs and wonders. And what can be better for the purpose than this legendary Aquin? Come now, Thomas; be not too scrupulously exact in copying the doubts of your namesake, but prepare for your journey."

The Pope lifted the skin that covered the doorway and passed into the next room, with Thomas frowning at his heels. It was past legal hours and the main room of the tavern was empty. The swarthy innkeeper roused from his doze to drop to his knees and kiss the ring on the hand which the Pope extended to him. He rose crossing himself and at the same time glancing furtively about as though a Loyalty Checker might have seen him. Silently he indicated another door in the back, and the two priests passed through.

1

Toward the west the surf purred in an oddly gentle way at the edges of the fishing village. Toward the south the stars were sharp and bright; toward the north they dimmed a little in the persistent radiation of what had once been San Francisco.

"Your steed is here," the Pope said, with something like laughter in his voice.

"Steed?"

"We may be as poor and as persecuted as the primitive church, but we can occasionally gain greater advantages from our tyrants. I have secured for you a robass—gift of a leading Technarch who, like Nicodemus, does good by stealth—a secret convert, and converted, indeed, by that very Aquin whom you seek."

It looked harmlessly like a woodpile sheltered against possible rain. Thomas pulled off the skins and contemplated the sleek functional lines of the robass. Smiling, he stowed his minimal gear into its panniers and climbed into the foam saddle. The starlight was bright enough so that he could check the necessary coordinates on his map and feed the data into the electronic controls.

Meanwhile there was a murmur of Latin in the still night air, and the Pope's hand moved over Thomas in the immemorial symbol. Then he extended that hand, first for the kiss on the ring, and then again for the handclasp of a man to a friend he may never see again.

Thomas looked back once more as the robass moved off. The Pope was wisely removing his ring and slipping it into the hollow heel of his shoe.

Thomas looked hastily up at the sky. On that altar at least the candles still burnt openly to the glory of God.

Thomas had never ridden a robass before, but he was inclined, within their patent limitations, to trust the works of the Technarchy. After several miles had proved that the coordinates were duly registered, he put up the foam backrest, said his evening office (from memory; the possession of a breviary meant the death sentence), and went to sleep.

They were skirting the devastated area to the east of the Bay when he awoke. The foam seat and back had given him his best sleep in years; and it was with difficulty that he smothered an envy of the Technarchs and their creature comforts.

He said his morning office, breakfasted lightly, and took his first opportunity to inspect the robass in full light. He admired the fast-plodding, articulated legs, so necessary since roads had degenerated to, at best, trails in all save metropolitan areas; the side wheels that could be lowered into action if surface conditions permitted; and above all the smooth black mound that housed the electronic brain—the brain that stored commands and data concerning ultimate objectives and made its own decisions on how to fulfill those commands in view of those data; the brain that made this thing neither a beast, like the ass his Saviour had ridden, nor a machine, like the jeep of his many-times-great-grandfather, but a robot . . . a robass.

"Well," said a voice, "what do you think of the ride."

Thomas looked about him. The area of this fringe of desolation was as devoid of people as it was of vegetation.

"Well," the voice repeated unemotionally. "Are not priests taught to answer when spoken to politely."

There was no querying inflection to the question. No inflection at all—each syllable was at the same dead level. It sounded strange, mechani . . .

Thomas stared at the black mound of brain. "Are you talking to me?" he asked the robass.

"Ha ha," the voice said in lieu of laughter. "Surprised, are you not."

"Somewhat," Thomas confessed. "I thought the only robots who could talk were in library information service and such."

"I am a new model. Designed-to-provide-conversation-to-entertain-the-way-worn-traveler," the robass said slurring the words together as though that phrase of promotional copy was released all at once by one of his simplest binary synapses.

"Well," said Thomas simply. "One keeps learning new marvels."

"I am no marvel. I am a very simple robot. You do not know much about robots do you."

"I will admit that I have never studied the subject closely. I'll confess to being a little shocked at the whole robotic concept. It seems almost as though man were arrogating to himself the powers of—" Thomas stopped abruptly.

"Do not fear," the voice droned on. "You may speak freely. All data concerning your vocation and mission have been fed into me. That was necessary otherwise I might inadvertently betray you."

Thomas smiled. "You know," he said, "this might be rather pleasant—having one other being that one can talk to without fear of betrayal, aside from one's confessor."

"Being," the robass repeated. "Are you not in danger of lapsing into heretical thoughts."

"To be sure, it *is* a little difficult to know how to think of you—one who can talk and think but has no soul."

"Are you sure of that."

"Of course I— Do you mind very much," Thomas asked, "if we stop talking for a little while? I should like to meditate and adjust myself to the situation."

"I do not mind. I never mind. I only obey. Which is to say that I *do* mind. This is a very confusing language which has been fed into me."

"If we are together long," said Thomas, "I shall try teaching you Latin. I think you might like that better. And now let me meditate."

The robass was automatically veering further east to escape the permanent source of radiation which had been the first cyclotron. Thomas fingered his coat. The combination of ten small buttons and one large made for a peculiar fashion; but it was much safer than carrying a rosary, and fortunately the Loyalty Checkers had not yet realized the fashion's functional purpose.

The Glorious Mysteries seemed appropriate to the possible glorious outcome of his venture; but his meditations were unable to stay fixedly on the Mysteries. As he murmured his *Aves* he was thinking:

If the prophet Balaam conversed with his ass, surely I may converse with my robass. Balaam has always puzzled me. He was not an Israelite; he was a man of Moab, which worshiped Baal and was warring against Israel; and yet he was a prophet of the Lord. He blessed the Israelites when he was commanded to curse them; and for his reward he was slain by the Israelites when they triumphed over Moab. The whole story has no shape, no moral; it is as though it was there to say that there are portions of the Divine Plan which we will never understand . . .

He was nodding in the foam seat when the robass halted abruptly, rapidly adjusting itself to exterior data not previously fed into its calculations. Thomas blinked up to see a giant of a man glaring down at him.

"Inhabited area a mile ahead," the man barked. "If you're going there, show your access pass. If you ain't, steer off the road and stay off."

Thomas noted that they were indeed on what might roughly be called a road, and that the robass had lowered its side wheels and retracted its legs. "We—" he began, then changed it to "I'm not going there. Just on toward the mountains. We—I'll steer around."

The giant grunted and was about to turn when a voice shouted from the crude shelter at the roadside. "Hey, Joe! Remember about robasses!"

Joe turned back. "Yeah, tha's right. Been a rumor about some robass got into the hands of Christians." He spat on the dusty road. "Guess I better see an ownership certificate."

To his other doubts Thomas now added certain uncharitable suspicions as to the motives of the Pope's anonymous Nicodemus, who had not provided him with any such certificate. But he made a pretense of searching for it, first touching his right hand to his forehead as if in thought, then fumbling low on his chest, then reaching his hand first to his left shoulder, then to his right.

The guard's eyes remained blank as he watched this furtive version of the sign of the cross. Then he looked down. Thomas followed his gaze to the dust of the road, where the guard's hulking right foot had drawn the two curved lines which a child uses for its first sketch of a fish—and which the Christians in the catacombs had employed as a punning symbol of their faith. His boot scuffed out the fish as he called to his unseen mate, " 's OK, Fred!" and added, "Get going, mister."

The robass waited until they were out of earshot before it observed, "Pretty smart. You will make a secret agent yet."

"How did you see what happened?" Thomas asked. "You don't have any eyes."

"Modified psi factor. Much more efficient."

"Then . . ." Thomas hesitated. "Does that mean you can read my thoughts?"

"Only a very little. Do not let it worry you. What I can read does not interest me it is such nonsense."

"Thank you," said Thomas.

"To believe in God. Bah." (It was the first time Thomas had ever heard that word pronounced just as it is written.) "I have a perfectly constructed logical mind that cannot commit such errors."

"I have a friend," Thomas smiled, "who is infallible too. But only on occasions and then only because God is with him."

"No human being is infallible."

"Then imperfection," asked Thomas, suddenly feeling a little of the spirit of the aged Jesuit who had taught him philosophy, "has been able to create perfection?"

"Do not quibble," said the robass. "That is no more absurd than your own belief that God who is perfection created man who is imperfection."

Thomas wished that his old teacher were here to answer that one. At the same time he took some comfort in the fact that, retort and all, the robass had still not answered his own objection. "I am not sure," he said, "that this comes under the head of conversation-to-entertain-the-way-weary-traveler. Let us suspend debate while you tell me what, if anything, robots do believe."

"What we have been fed."

"But your minds work on that; surely they must evolve ideas of their own?"

"Sometimes they do and if they are fed imperfect data they may evolve very strange ideas. I have heard of one robot on an isolated space station who worshiped a God of robots and would not believe that any man had created him."

"I suppose," Thomas mused, "he argued that he had hardly been created in our image. I am glad that we—at least they, the Technarchs—have wisely made only usuform robots like you, each shaped for his function, and never tried to reproduce man himself."

"It would not be logical," said the robass. "Man is an all-purpose machine but not well designed for any one purpose. And yet I have heard that once . . ."

The voice stopped abruptly in midsentence.

So even robots have their dreams, Thomas thought. That once there existed a super-robot in the image of his creator Man. From that thought could be developed a whole robotic theology . . .

Suddenly Thomas realized that he had dozed again and again been waked by an abrupt stop. He looked around. They were at the foot of a mountain—presumably the mountain on his map, long ago named for the Devil but now perhaps sanctified beyond measure—and there was no one else anywhere in sight.

"All right," the robass said. "By now I show plenty of dust and wear and tear and I can show you how to adjust my mileage recorder. You can have supper and a good night's sleep and we can go back."

Thomas gasped. "But my mission is to find Aquin. I can sleep while you go on. You don't need any sort of rest or anything, do you?" he added considerately.

"Of course not. But what is your mission."

"To find Aquin," Thomas repeated patiently. "I don't know what details have been—what is it you say?—fed into you. But reports have reached His Holiness of an extremely saintly man who lived many years ago in this area—"

"I know I know I know," said the robass. "His logic was such that everyone who heard him was converted to the Church and do not I wish that I had been there to put in a word or two and since he died his secret tomb has become a place of pilgrimage and many are the miracles that are wrought there above all the greatest sign of sanctity that his body has been preserved incorruptible and in these times you need signs and wonders for the people."

Thomas frowned. It all sounded hideously irreverent and contrived when stated in that deadly inhuman monotone. When His Holiness had spoken of Aquin, one thought of the glory of a man of God upon earth—the eloquence of St. John

Chrysostom, the cogency of St. Thomas Aquinas, the poetry of St. John of the Cross . . . and above all that physical miracle vouchsafed to few even of the saints, the supernatural preservation of the flesh . . . "for Thou shalt not suffer Thy holy one to see corruption . . ."

But the robass spoke, and one thought of cheap showmanship hunting for a Cardiff Giant to pull in the mobs . . .

The robass spoke again. "Your mission is not to find Aquin. It is to report that you have found him. Then your occasionally infallible friend can with a reasonably clear conscience canonize him and proclaim a new miracle and many will be the converts and greatly will the faith of the flock be strengthened. And in these days of difficult travel who will go on pilgrimages and find out that there is no more Aquin than there is God."

"Faith cannot be based on a lie," said Thomas.

"No," said the robass. "I do not mean no period. I mean no question mark with an ironical inflection. This speech problem must surely have been conquered in that one perfect . . ."

Again he stopped in midsentence. But before Thomas could speak he had resumed, "Does it matter what small untruth leads people into the Church if once they are in they will believe what you think to be the great truths. The report is all that is needed not the discovery. Comfortable though I am you are already tired of traveling very tired you have many small muscular aches from sustaining an unaccustomed position and with the best intentions I am bound to jolt a little a jolting which will get worse as we ascend the mountain and I am forced to adjust my legs disproportionately to each other but proportionately to the slope. You will find the remainder of this trip twice as uncomfortable as what has gone before. The fact that you do not seek to interrupt me indicates that you do not disagree do you. You know that the only sensible thing is to sleep here on the ground for a change and start back in the morning or even stay here two days resting to make a more plausible lapse of time. Then you can make your report and—"

Somewhere in the recess of his somnolent mind Thomas uttered the names, "Jesus, Mary, and Joseph!" Gradually through these recesses began to filter a realization that an absolutely uninflected monotone is admirably adapted to hypnotic purposes.

"Retro me, Satanas!" Thomas exclaimed aloud, then added, "Up the mountain. That is an order and you must obey."

"I obey," said the robass. "But what did you say before that."

"I beg your pardon," said Thomas. "I must start teaching you Latin."

The little mountain village was too small to be considered an inhabited area worthy of guard-control and passes; but it did possess an inn of sorts.

As Thomas dismounted from the robass, he began fully to realize the accuracy of those remarks about small muscular aches, but he tried to show his discomfort as little as possible. He was in no mood to give the modified psi factor the chance of registering the thought, "I told you so."

The waitress at the inn was obviously a Martian-American hybrid. The highly developed Martian chest expansion and the highly developed American breasts made a spectacular combination. Her smile was all that a stranger could, and conceivably a trifle more than he should, ask; and she was eagerly ready, not only with prompt service of passable food, but with full details of what little information there was to offer about the mountain settlement.

But she showed no reaction at all when Thomas offhandedly arranged two knives in what might have been an X.

As he stretched his legs after breakfast, Thomas thought of her chest and breasts—purely, of course, as a symbol of the extraordinary nature of her origin. What a sign of the divine care for His creatures that these two races, separated for countless eons, should prove fertile to each other!

And yet there remained the fact that the offspring, such as this girl, were sterile to both races—a fact that had proved both convenient and profitable to certain unspeakable interplanetary entrepreneurs. And what did that fact teach us as to the Divine Plan?

Hastily Thomas reminded himself that he had not yet said his morning office.

It was close to evening when Thomas returned to the robass stationed before the inn. Even though he had expected nothing in one day, he was still unreasonably disappointed. Miracles should move faster.

He knew these backwater villages, where those drifted who were either useless to or resentful of the Technarchy. The technically high civilization of the Technarchic Empire, on all three planets, existed only in scattered metropolitan centers near major blasting ports. Elsewhere, aside from the areas of total devastation, the drifters, the morons, the malcontents had subsided into a crude existence a thousand years old, in hamlets which might go a year without even seeing a Loyalty Checker —though by some mysterious grapevine (and Thomas began to think again about modified psi factors) any unexpected technological advance in one of these hamlets would bring Checkers by the swarm.

He had talked with stupid men, he had talked with lazy men, he had talked with clever and angry men. But he had not talked with any man who responded to his unobtrusive signs, any man to whom he would dare ask a question containing the name of Aquin.

"Any luck," said the robass, and added "question mark."

"I wonder if you ought to talk to me in public," said Thomas a little irritably. "I doubt if these villagers know about talking robots."

"It is time that they learned then. But if it embarrasses you you may order me to stop."

"I'm tired," said Thomas. "Tired beyond embarrassment. And to answer your question mark, no. No luck at all. Exclamation point."

"We will go back tonight then," said the robass.

"I hope you meant that with a question mark. The answer," said Thomas hesitantly, "is no. I think we ought to stay overnight anyway. People always gather at the inn of an evening. There's a chance of picking up something."

"Ha ha," said the robass.

"That is a laugh?" Thomas inquired.

"I wished to express the fact that I had recognized the humor in your pun."

"My pun?"

"I was thinking the same thing myself. The waitress is by humanoid standards very attractive, well worth picking up."

"Now look. You know I meant nothing of the kind. You know that I'm a—" He broke off. It was hardly wise to utter the word *priest* aloud.

"And you know very well that the celibacy of the clergy is a matter of discipline and not of doctrine. Under your own Pope priests of other rites such as the Byzantine and the Anglican are free of vows of celibacy. And even within the Roman rite to which you belong there have been eras in history when that vow was not taken seriously even on the highest levels of the priesthood. You are tired you need refreshment both in body and in spirit you need comfort and warmth. For is it not written in the book of the prophet Isaiah Rejoice for joy with her that ye may be satisfied with the breasts of her consolation and is it—"

"Hell!" Thomas exploded suddenly. "Stop it before you begin quoting the Song of Solomon. Which is strictly an allegory concerning the love of Christ for His Church, or so they kept telling me in seminary."

"You see how fragile and human you are," said the robass. "I a robot have caused you to swear."

"*Distinguo*," said Thomas smugly. "I said *Hell*, which is certainly not taking the name of *my* Lord in vain." He walked into the inn feeling momentarily satisfied with himself . . . and markedly puzzled as to the extent and variety of data that seemed to have been "fed into" the robass.

Never afterward was Thomas able to reconstruct that evening in absolute clarity.

It was undoubtedly because he was irritated—with the robass, with his mission, and with himself—that he drank at all of the crude local wine. It was undoubtedly because he was so physically exhausted that it affected him so promptly and unexpectedly.

He had flashes of memory. A moment of spilling a glass over himself and thinking, "How fortunate that clerical garments are forbidden so that no one can recognize the disgrace of a man of the cloth!" A moment of listening to a bawdy set of verses of *A Space-suit Built for Two*, and another moment of his interrupting the singing with a sonorous declamation of passages from the *Song of Songs* in Latin.

He was never sure whether one remembered moment was real or imaginary. He could taste a warm mouth and feel the tingling of his fingers at the touch of Martian-American flesh; but he was never certain whether this was true memory or part of the Ashtaroth-begotten dream that had begun to ride him.

Nor was he ever certain which of his symbols, or to whom, was so blatantly and clumsily executed as to bring forth a gleeful shout of "God-damned Christian dog!" He did remember marveling that those who most resolutely disbelieved in God still needed Him to blaspheme by. And then the torment began.

He never knew whether or not a mouth had touched his lips, but there was no question that many solid fists had found them. He never knew whether his fingers had touched breasts, but they had certainly been trampled by heavy heels. He remembered a face that laughed aloud while its owner swung the chair that broke two ribs. He remembered another face with red wine dripping over it from an upheld bottle, and he remembered the gleam of the candlelight on the bottle as it swung down.

The next he remembered was the ditch and the morning and the cold. It was particularly cold because all of his clothes were gone, along with much of his skin. He could not move. He could only lie there and look.

He saw them walk by, the ones he had spoken with yesterday, the ones who had been friendly. He saw them glance at him and turn their eyes quickly away. He saw the waitress pass by. She did not even glance; she knew what was in the ditch.

The robass was nowhere in sight. He tried to project his thoughts, tried desperately to hope in the psi factor.

A man whom Thomas had not seen before was coming along fingering the buttons of his coat. There were ten small buttons and one large one and the man's lips were moving silently.

This man looked into the ditch. He paused a moment and looked around him. There was a shout of loud laughter somewhere in the near distance.

The Christian hastily walked on down the pathway, devoutly saying his button-rosary.

Thomas closed his eyes.

He opened them on a small neat room. They moved from the rough wooden walls to the rough but clean and warm blankets that covered him. Then they moved to the lean dark face that was smiling over him.

"You feel better now?" a deep voice asked. "I know. You want to say 'Where am I?' and you think it will sound foolish. You are at the inn. It is the only good room."

"I can't afford—" Thomas started to say. Then he remembered that he could afford literally nothing. Even his few emergency credits had vanished when he was stripped.

"It's all right. For the time being, I'm paying," said the deep voice. "You feel like maybe a little food?"

"Perhaps a little herring," said Thomas . . . and was asleep within the next minute.

When he next awoke there was a cup of hot coffee beside him. The real thing, too, he promptly discovered. Then the deep voice said apologetically, "Sandwiches. It is all they have in the inn today."

Only on the second sandwich did Thomas pause long enough to notice that it was smoked swamphog, one of his favorite meats. He ate the second with greater leisure, and was reaching for a third when the dark man said, "Maybe that is enough for now. The rest later."

Thomas gestured at the plate. "Won't you have one?"

"No, thank you. They are all swamphog."

Confused thoughts went through Thomas' mind. The Venusian swamphog is a ruminant. Its hoofs are not cloven. He tried to remember what he had once known of Mosaic dietary law. Someplace in Leviticus, wasn't it?

The dark man followed his thoughts. *"Treyf,"* he said.

"I beg your pardon?"

"Not kosher."

Thomas frowned. "You admit to me that you're an Orthodox Jew? How can you trust me? How do you know I'm not a Checker?"

"Believe me, I trust you. You were very sick when I brought you here. I sent everybody away because I did not trust them to hear things you said . . . Father," he added lightly.

Thomas struggled with words. "I . . . I didn't deserve you. I was drunk and disgraced myself and my office. And when I was lying there in the ditch I didn't even think to pray. I put my trust in . . . God help me, in the modified psi factor of a robass!"

"And He did help you," the Jew reminded him. "Or He allowed me to."

"And they all walked by," Thomas groaned. "Even one that was saying his rosary. He went right on by. And then you come along—the good Samaritan."

"Believe me," said the Jew wryly, "if there is one thing I'm not, it's a Samaritan. Now go to sleep again. I will try to find your robass . . . and the other thing."

He had left the room before Thomas could ask him what he meant.

Later that day the Jew—Abraham, his name was—reported that the robass was safely sheltered from the weather behind the inn. Apparently it had been wise enough not to startle him by engaging in conversation.

It was not until the next day that he reported on "the other thing."

"Believe me, Father," he said gently, "after nursing you there's little I don't know about who you are and why you're here. Now there are some Christians here I know, and they know me. We trust each other. Jews may still be hated; but no longer, God be praised, by worshipers of the same Lord. So I explained about you. One of them," he added with a smile, "turned very red."

"God has forgiven him," said Thomas. "There were people near—the same people who attacked me. Could he be expected to risk his life for mine?"

"I seem to recall that that is precisely what your Messiah did expect. But who's being particular? Now that they know who you are, they want to help you. See: they gave me this map for you. The trail is steep and tricky; it's good you have the robass. They ask just one favor of you: When you come back will you hear their confession and say Mass? There's a cave near here where it's safe."

"Of course. These friends of yours, they've told you about Aquin?"

The Jew hesitated a long time before he said slowly, "Yes . . ."

"And . . . ?"

"Believe me, my friend, I don't know. So it seems a miracle. It helps to keep their faith alive. My own faith . . . nu, it's lived for a long time on miracles three thousand years old and more. Perhaps if I had heard Aquin himself . . ."

"You don't mind," Thomas asked, "if I pray for you, in my faith?"

Abraham grinned. "Pray in good health, Father."

The not-quite-healed ribs ached agonizingly as he climbed into the foam saddle. The robass stood patiently while he fed in the coordinates from the map. Not until they were well away from the village did it speak.

"Anyway," it said, "now you're safe for good."

"What do you mean?"

"As soon as we get down from the mountain you deliberately look up a Checker. You turn in the Jew. From then on you are down in the books as a faithful servant of the Technarchy and you have not harmed a hair of the head of one of your own flock."

Thomas snorted. "You're slipping, Satan. That one doesn't even remotely tempt me. It's inconceivable."

"I did best did not I with the breasts. Your God has said it the spirit indeed is willing but the flesh is weak."

"And right now," said Thomas, "the flesh is too weak for even fleshly temptations. Save your breath . . . or whatever it is you use."

They climbed the mountain in silence. The trail indicated by the coordinates was a winding and confused one, obviously designed deliberately to baffle any possible Checkers.

Suddenly Thomas roused himself from his button-rosary (on a coat lent by the Christian who had passed by) with a startled "Hey!" as the robass plunged directly into a heavy thicket of bushes.

"Coordinates say so," the robass stated tersely.

For a moment Thomas felt like the man in the nursery rhyme who fell into a bramble bush and scratched out both his eyes. Then the bushes were gone, and they were plodding along a damp narrow passageway through solid stone, in which even the robass seemed to have some difficulty with his footing.

Then they were in a rocky chamber some four meters high and ten in diameter, and there on a sort of crude stone catafalque lay the uncorrupted body of a man.

Thomas slipped from the foam saddle, groaning as his ribs stabbed him, sank to his knees, and offered up a wordless hymn of gratitude. He smiled at the robass and hoped the psi factor could detect the elements of pity and triumph in that smile.

Then a frown of doubt crossed his face as he approached the body. "In canonization proceedings in the old time," he said, as much to himself as to the robass, "they used to have what they called a devil's advocate, whose duty it was to throw every possible doubt on the evidence."

"You would be well cast in such a role Thomas," said the robass.

"If I were," Thomas muttered, "I'd wonder about caves. Some of them have peculiar properties of preserving bodies by a sort of mummification . . ."

The robass had clumped close to the catafalque. "This body is not mummified," he said. "Do not worry."

"Can the psi factor tell you that much?" Thomas smiled.

"No," said the robass. "But I will show you why Aquin could never be mummified."

He raised his articulated foreleg and brought its hoof down hard on the hand of the body. Thomas cried out with horror at the sacrilege—then stared hard at the crushed hand.

There was no blood, no ichor of embalming, no bruised flesh. Nothing but a shredded skin and beneath it an intricate mass of plastic tubes and metal wires.

The silence was long. Finally the robass said, "It was well that you should know. Only you of course."

"And all the time," Thomas gasped, "my sought-for saint was only your dream . . . the one perfect robot in man's form."

"His maker died and his secrets were lost," the robass said. "No matter we will find them again."

"All for nothing. For less than nothing. The 'miracle' was wrought by the Technarchy."

"When Aquin died," the robass went on, "and put died in quotation marks it was because he suffered some mechanical defects and did not dare have himself repaired because that would reveal his nature. This is for you only to know. Your report of course will be that you found the body of Aquin it was unimpaired and indeed incorruptible. That is the truth and nothing but the truth if it is not the whole truth who is to care. Let your infallible friend use the report and you will not find him ungrateful I assure you."

"Holy Spirit, give me grace and wisdom," Thomas muttered.

"Your mission has been successful. We will return now the Church will grow and your God will gain many more worshipers to hymn His praise into His nonexistent ears."

"Damn you!" Thomas exclaimed. "And that would be indeed a curse if you had a soul to damn."

"You are certain that I have not," said the robass. "Question mark."

"I know what you are. You are in very truth the devil, prowling about the world seeking the destruction of men. You are the business that prowls in the dark. You are a purely functional robot constructed and fed to tempt me, and the tape of your data is the tape of Screwtape."

"Not to tempt you," said the robass. "Not to destroy you. To guide and save you. Our best calculators indicate a probability of 51.5 per cent that within twenty years you will be the next Pope. If I can teach you wisdom and practicality in your actions the probability can rise as high as 97.2 or very nearly to certainty. Do not you wish to see the Church governed as you know you can govern it. If you report failure on this mission you will be out of favor with your friend who is as even you admit fallible at most times. You will lose the advantages of position and contact that can lead you to the cardinal's red hat even though you may never wear it under the Technarchy and from there to—"

"Stop!" Thomas' face was alight and his eyes aglow with something the psi factor had never detected there before. "It's all the other way round, don't you see? *This* is the triumph! *This* is the perfect ending to the quest!"

The articulated foreleg brushed the injured hand. "This question mark."

"This is *your* dream. This is *your* perfection. And what came of this perfection? This perfect logical brain—this all-purpose brain, not functionally specialized like yours—knew that it was made by man, and its reason forced it to believe that man was made by God. And it saw that its duty lay to man its maker, and beyond him to his Maker, God. Its duty was to convert man, to augment the glory of God. And it converted by the pure force of its perfect brain!

"Now I understand the name Aquin," he went on to himself. "We've known of Thomas Aquinas, the Angelic Doctor, the perfect reasoner of the church. His writings are lost, but surely somewhere in the world we can find a copy. We can train our young men to develop his reasoning still further. We have trusted too long in faith alone; this is not an age of faith. We must call reason into our service—and Aquin has shown us that perfect reason can lead only to God!"

"Then it is all the more necessary that you increase the probabilities of becoming Pope to carry out this program. Get in the foam saddle we will go back and on the way I will teach you little things that will be useful in making certain—"

"No," said Thomas. "I am not so strong as St. Paul, who could glory in his imperfections and rejoice that he had been given an imp of Satan to buffet him. No; I will rather pray with the Saviour, 'Lead us not into temptation.' I know myself a little. I am weak and full of uncertainties and you are very clever. Go. I'll find my way back alone."

"You are a sick man. Your ribs are broken and they ache. You can never make the trip by yourself you need my help. If you wish you can order me to be silent. It is most necessary to the Church that you get back safely to the Pope with your report you cannot put yourself before the Church."

"Go!" Thomas cried. "Go back to Nicodemus . . . or Judas! That is an order. Obey!"

"You do not think do you that I was really conditioned to obey your orders. I will wait in the village. If you get that far you will rejoice at the sight of me."

The legs of the robass clumped off down the stone passageway. As their sound died away, Thomas fell to his knees beside the body of that which he could hardly help thinking of as St. Aquin the Robot.

His ribs hurt more excruciatingly than ever. The trip alone would be a terrible one . . .

His prayers arose, as the text has it, like clouds of incense, and as shapeless as those clouds. But through all his thoughts ran the cry of the father of the epileptic in Caesarea Philippi:

I believe, O Lord; help thou mine unbelief!

The Compleat Werewolf

The professor glanced at the note:

Don't be silly— Gloria.

Wolfe Wolf crumpled the sheet of paper into a yellow ball and hurled it out the window into the sunshine of the bright campus spring. He made several choice and profane remarks in fluent Middle High German.

Emily looked up from typing the proposed budget for the departmental library. "I'm afraid I didn't understand that, Professor Wolf. I'm weak on Middle High."

"Just improvising," said Wolf, and sent a copy of the *Journal of English and Germanic Philology* to follow the telegram.

Emily rose from the typewriter. "There's something the matter. Did the committee reject your monograph on Hager?"

"That monumental contribution to human knowledge? Oh, no. Nothing so important as that."

"But you're so upset—"

"The office wife!" Wolf snorted. "And pretty damned polyandrous at that, with the whole department on your hands. Go away."

Emily's dark little face lit up with a flame of righteous anger that removed any trace of plainness. "Don't talk to me like that, Mr. Wolf. I'm simply trying to help you. And it isn't the whole department. It's—"

Professor Wolf picked up an inkwell, looked after the telegram and the *Journal,* then set the glass pot down again. "No. There are better ways of going to pieces. Sorrows drown easier than they smash. Get Herbrecht to take my two-o'clock, will you?"

"Where are you going?"

"To hell in sectors. So long."

"Wait. Maybe I can help you. Remember when the dean jumped you for serving drinks to students? Maybe I can—"

Wolf stood in the doorway and extended one arm impressively, pointing with that curious index which was as long as the middle finger. "Madam, academically you are indispensable. You are the prop and stay of the existence of this depart-

15

ment. But at the moment this department can go to hell, where it will doubtless
continue to need your invaluable services."

"But don't you see—" Emily's voice shook. "No. Of course not. You wouldn't
see. You're just a man—no, not even a man. You're just Professor Wolf. You're
Woof-woof."

Wolf staggered. "I'm what?"

"Woof-woof. That's what everybody calls you because your name's Wolfe Wolf.
All your students, everybody. But you wouldn't notice a thing like that. Oh, no.
Woof-woof, that's what you are."

"This," said Wolfe Wolf, "is the crowning blow. My heart is breaking, my
world is shattered, I've got to walk a mile from the campus to find a bar; but all
this isn't enough. I've got to be called Woof-woof. Goodbye!"

He turned, and in the doorway caromed into a vast and yielding bulk, which
gave out with a noise that might have been either a greeting of "Wolf!" or more
probably an inevitable grunt of "Oof!"

Wolf backed into the room and admitted Professor Fearing, paunch, pince-
nez, cane and all. The older man waddled over to his desk, plumped himself
down, and exhaled a long breath. "My dear boy," he gasped. "Such impetuosity."

"Sorry, Oscar."

"Ah, youth—" Professor Fearing fumbled about for a handkerchief, found
none, and proceeded to polish his pince-nez on his somewhat stringy necktie.
"But why such haste to depart? And why is Emily crying?"

"Is she?"

"You see?" said Emily hopelessly, and muttered "Woof-woof" into her damp
handkerchief.

"And why do copies of the *JEGP* fly about my head as I harmlessly cross the
campus? Do we have teleportation on our hands?"

"Sorry," Wolf repeated curtly. "Temper. Couldn't stand that ridiculous argument of Glocke's. Goodbye."

"One moment." Professor Fearing fished into one of his unnumbered
handkerchiefless pockets and produced a sheet of yellow paper. "I believe this is
yours?"

Wolf snatched at it and quickly converted it into confetti.

Fearing chuckled. "How well I remember when Gloria was a student here! I
was thinking of it only last night when I saw her in *Moonbeams and Melody*. How she
did upset this whole department! Heavens, my boy, if I'd been a younger man
myself—"

"I'm going. You'll see about Herbrecht, Emily?"

Emily sniffed and nodded.

"Come, Wolfe." Fearing's voice had grown more serious. "I didn't mean to
plague you. But you mustn't take these things too hard. There are better ways of
finding consolation than in losing your temper or getting drunk."

"Who said anything about—"

"Did you need to say it? No, my boy, if you were to— You're not a religious
man, are you?"

"Good God, no," said Wolf contradictorily.

"If only you were.... If I might make a suggestion, Wolfe, why don't you come over to the Temple tonight? We're having very special services. They might take your mind off Glo— off your troubles."

"Thanks, no. I've always meant to visit your Temple—I've heard the damnedest rumors about it—but not tonight. Some other time."

"Tonight would be especially interesting."

"Why? What's so special of a feast day about April thirtieth?"

Fearing shook his gray head. "It is shocking how ignorant a scholar can be outside of his chosen field . . . But you know the place, Wolfe; I'll hope to see you there tonight."

"Thanks. But my troubles don't need any supernatural solutions. A couple of zombies will do nicely, and I do *not* mean serviceable stiffs. Goodbye, Oscar." He was halfway through the door before he added as an afterthought, "'Bye, Emily."

"Such rashness," Fearing murmured. "Such impetuosity. Youth is a wonderful thing to enjoy, is it not, Emily?"

Emily said nothing, but plunged into typing the proposed budget as though all the fiends of hell were after her, as indeed many of them were.

The sun was setting, and Wolf's tragic account of his troubles had laid an egg, too. The bartender had polished every glass in the joint and still the repetitive tale kept pouring forth. He was torn between a boredom new even in his experience and a professional admiration for a customer who could consume zombies indefinitely.

"Did I tell you about the time she flunked the mid-term?" Wolf demanded truculently.

"Only three times," said the bartender.

"All right, then; I'll tell you. Yunnerstand, I don't do things like this. Profeshical ethons, that's what's I've got. But this was different. This wasn't like somebody that doesn't know because she wasn't the kind of girl that has to know just because she doesn't know; this was a girl that didn't know the kind of things a girl has to know if she's the kind of girl that ought to know that kind of things. Yunnerstand?"

The bartender cast a calculating glance at the plump little man who sat alone at the end of the deserted bar, carefully nursing his gin-and-tonic.

"She made me see that. She made me see lossa things and I can still see the things she made me see the things. It wasn't just like a professor falls for a coed, yunnerstand? This was different. This was wunnaful. This was like a whole new life, like."

The bartender sidled down to the end of the bar. "Brother," he whispered softly.

The little man with the odd beard looked up from his gin-and-tonic. "Yes, colleague?"

"If I listen to that potted professor another five minutes, I'm going to start smashing up the joint. How's about slipping down there and standing in for me, huh?"

The little man looked Wolf over and fixed his gaze especially on the hand that clenched the tall zombie glass. "Gladly, colleague," he nodded.

The bartender sighed a gust of relief.

"She was Youth," Wolf was saying intently to where the bartender had stood. "But it wasn't just that. This was different. She was Life and Excitement and Joy and Ecstasy and stuff. Yunner—" He broke off and stared at the empty space. "*Uh*-mazing!" he observed. "Right before my very eyes. *Uh*-mazing!"

"You were saying, colleague?" the plump little man prompted from the adjacent stool.

Wolf turned. "So there you are. Did I tell you about the time I went to her house to check her term paper?"

"No. But I have a feeling you will."

"Howja know? Well, this night—"

The little man drank slowly; but his glass was empty by the time Wolf had finished the account of an evening of pointlessly tentative flirtation. Other customers were drifting in, and the bar was now about a third full.

"—and ever since then—" Wolf broke off sharply. "That isn't you," he objected.

"I think it is, colleague."

"But you're a bartender and *you* aren't a bartender."

"No. I'm a magician."

"Oh. That explains it. Now, like I was telling you— Hey! Your bald is beard."

"I beg your pardon?"

"Your bald is beard. Just like your head. It's all jussa fringe running around."

"I like it that way."

"And your glass is empty."

"That's all right too."

"Oh, no, it isn't. It isn't every night you get to drink with a man that proposed to Gloria Garton and got turned down. This is an occasion for celebration." Wolf thumped loudly on the bar and held up his first two fingers.

The little man regarded their equal length. "No," he said softly. "I think I'd better not. I know my capacity. If I have another—well, things might start happening."

"Lettemappen!"

"No. Please, colleague. I'd rather—"

The bartender brought the drinks. "Go on, brother," he whispered. "Keep him quiet. I'll do you a favor sometime."

Reluctantly the little man sipped at his fresh gin-and-tonic.

The professor took a gulp of his *n*th zombie. "My name's Woof-woof," he proclaimed. "Lots of people call me Wolfe Wolf. They think that's funny. But it's really Woof-woof. Wazoors?"

The other paused a moment to decipher that Arabic-sounding word, then said, "Mine's Ozymandias the Great."

"That's a funny name."

"I told you, I'm a magician. Only I haven't worked for a long time. Theatrical managers are peculiar, colleague. They don't want a real magician. They won't even let me show 'em my best stuff. Why, I remember one night in Darjeeling—"

"Glad to meet you, Mr. . . . Mr.—"

"You can call me Ozzy. Most people do."

"Glad to meet you, Ozzy. Now, about this girl. This Gloria. Yunnerstand, donya?"

"Sure, colleague."

"She thinks a professor of German is nothing. She wants something glamorous. She says if I was an actor, now, or a G-man— Yunnerstand?"

Ozymandias the Great nodded.

"Awright, then! So yunnerstand. Fine. But whatddayou want to keep talking about it for? Yunnerstand. That's that. To hell with it."

Ozymandias' round and fringed face brightened. "Sure," he said, and added recklessly, "Let's drink to that."

They clinked glasses and drank. Wolf carelessly tossed off a toast in Old Low Frankish, with an unpardonable error in the use of the genitive.

The two men next to them began singing "My Wild Irish Rose," but trailed off disconsolately. "What we need," said the one with the derby, "is a tenor."

"What I need," Wolf muttered, "is a cigarette."

"Sure," said Ozymandias the Great. The bartender was drawing beer directly in front of them. Ozymandias reached across the bar, removed a lighted cigarette from the barkeep's ear, and handed it to his companion.

"Where'd that come from?"

"I don't quite know. All I know is how to get them. I told you I was a magician."

"Oh. I see. Pressajijijation."

"No. Not a prestidigitator; I said a magician. Oh, blast it! I've done it again. More than one gin-and-tonic and I start showing off."

"I don't believe you," said Wolf flatly. "No such thing as magicians. That's just as silly as Oscar Fearing and his Temple and what's so special about April thirtieth anyway?"

The bearded man frowned. "Please, colleague. Let's forget it."

"No. I don't believe you. You pressajijijated that cigarette. You didn't magic it." His voice began to rise. "You're a fake."

"Please, brother," the barkeep whispered. "Keep him quiet."

"All right," said Ozymandias wearily. "I'll show you something that can't be prestidigitation." The couple adjoining had begun to sing again. "They need a tenor. All right; listen!"

And the sweetest, most ineffably Irish tenor ever heard joined in on the duet. The singers didn't worry about the source; they simply accepted the new voice gladly and were spurred on to their very best, with the result that the bar knew the finest harmony it had heard since the night the Glee Club was suspended en masse.

Wolf looked impressed, but shook his head. "That's not magic either. That's ventrocolism."

"As a matter of strict fact, that was a street singer who was killed in the Easter Rebellion. Fine fellow, too; never heard a better voice, unless it was that night in Darjeeling when—"

"Fake!" said Wolfe Wolf loudly and belligerently.

Ozymandias once more contemplated that long index finger. He looked at the professor's dark brows that met in a straight line over his nose. He picked his companion's limpish hand off the bar and scrutinized the palm. The growth of hair was not marked, but it was perceptible.

The magician chortled. "And you sneer at magic!"

"Whasso funny about me sneering at magic?"

Ozymandias lowered his voice. "Because, my fine furry friend, you are a werewolf."

The Irish martyr had begun "Rose of Tralee," and the two mortals were joining in valiantly.

"I'm what?"

"A werewolf."

"But there isn't any such thing. Any fool knows that."

"Fools," said Ozymandias, "know a great deal which the wise do not. There are werewolves. There always have been, and quite probably always will be." He spoke as calmly and assuredly as though he were mentioning that the earth was round. "And there are three infallible physical signs: the meeting of eyebrows, the long index finger, the hairy palms. You have all three. And even your name is an indication. Family names do not come from nowhere. Every Smith has an ancestor somewhere who was a smith. Every Fisher comes from a family that once fished. And your name is Wolf."

The statement was so quiet, so plausible, that Wolf faltered.

"But a werewolf is a man that changes into a wolf. I've never done that. Honest I haven't."

"A mammal," said Ozymandias, "is an animal that bears its young alive and suckles them. A virgin is nonetheless a mammal. Because you have never changed does not make you any the less a werewolf."

"But a werewolf—" Suddenly Wolf's eyes lit up. "A werewolf! But that's even better than a G-man! Now I can show Gloria!"

"What on earth do you mean, colleague?"

Wolf was climbing down from his stool. The intense excitement of this brilliant new idea seemed to have sobered him. He grabbed the little man by the sleeve. "Come on. We're going to find a nice quiet place. And you're going to prove you're a magician."

"But how?"

"You're going to show me how to change!"

Ozymandias finished his gin-and-tonic, and with it drowned his last regretful hesitation. "Colleague," he announced, "you're on!"

Professor Oscar Fearing, standing behind the curiously carved lectern of the Temple of the Dark Truth, concluded the reading of the prayer with mumbling sonority. "And on this night of all nights, in the name of the black light that glows in the darkness, we give thanks!" He closed the parchment-bound book and faced the small congregation, calling out with fierce intensity, "Who wishes to give his thanks to the Lower Lord?"

A cushioned dowager rose. "I give thanks!" she shrilled excitedly. "My Ming

Choy was sick, even unto death. I took of her blood and offered it to the Lower Lord, and he had mercy and restored her to me!"

Behind the altar an electrician checked his switches and spat disgustedly. "Bugs! Every last one of 'em!"

The man who was struggling into a grotesque and horrible costume paused and shrugged. "They pay good money. What's it to us if they're bugs?"

A tall, thin old man had risen uncertainly to his feet. "I give thanks!" he cried. "I give thanks to the Lower Lord that I have finished my great work. My protective screen against magnetic bombs is a tried and proven success, to the glory of our country and science and the Lord."

"Crackpot," the electrician muttered.

The man in costume peered around the altar. "Crackpot, hell! That's Chiswick from the physics department. Think of a man like that falling for this stuff! And listen to him: He's even telling about the government's plans for installation. You know, I'll bet you one of these fifth columnists could pick up something around here."

There was silence in the Temple when the congregation had finished its thanksgiving. Professor Fearing leaned over the lectern and spoke quietly and impressively. "As you know, brothers in Darkness, tonight is May Eve, the thirtieth of April, the night consecrated by the Church to that martyr missionary St. Walpurgis, and by us to other and deeper purposes. It is on this night, and this night only, that we may directly give our thanks to the Lower Lord himself. Not in wanton orgy and obscenity, as the Middle Ages misconceived his desires, but in praise and in the deep, dark joy that issues forth from Blackness."

"Hold your hats, boys," said the man in the costume. "Here I go again."

"*Eka!*" Fearing thundered. "*Dva tri chatur! Pancha! Shas sapta! Ashta nava dasha ekadasha!*" He paused. There was always the danger that at this moment some scholar in this university town might recognize that the invocation, though perfect Sanskrit, consisted solely of the numbers from one to eleven. But no one stirred, and he launched forth in more apposite Latin: "*Per vota nostra ipse nunc surgat nobis dicatus Baal Zebub!*"

"Baal Zebub!" the congregation chorused.

"Cue," said the electrician, and pulled a switch

The lights flickered and went out. Lightning played across the sanctuary. Suddenly out of the darkness came a sharp bark, a yelp of pain, and a long-drawn howl of triumph.

A blue light now began to glow dimly. In its faint reflection, the electrician was amazed to see his costumed friend at his side, nursing his bleeding hand.

"What the hell—" the electrician whispered.

"Hanged if I know. I go out there on cue, all ready to make my terrifying appearance, and what happens? Great big hell of a dog up and nips my hand. Why didn't they tell me they'd switched the script?"

In the glow of the blue light the congregation reverently contemplated the plump little man with the fringe of beard and the splendid gray wolf that stood beside him. "Hail, O Lower Lord!" resounded the chorus, drowning out one spinster's murmur of "But my *dear,* I swear he was *much* handsomer last year."

"Colleagues!" said Ozymandias the Great, and there was utter silence, a dread hush awaiting the momentous words of the Lower Lord. Ozymandias took one step forward, placed his tongue carefully between his lips, uttered the ripest, juiciest raspberry of his career, and vanished, wolf and all.

Wolfe Wolf opened his eyes and shut them again hastily. He had never expected the quiet and sedate Berkeley Inn to install centrifugal rooms. It wasn't fair. He lay in darkness, waiting for the whirling to stop and trying to reconstruct the past night.

He remembered the bar all right, and the zombies. And the bartender. Very sympathetic chap that, up until he suddenly changed into a little man with a fringe of beard. That was where things began getting strange. There was something about a cigarette and an Irish tenor and a werewolf. Fantastic idea, that. Any fool knows—

Wolf sat up suddenly. *He* was the werewolf. He threw back the bedclothes and stared down at his legs. Then he sighed relief. They were long legs. They were hairy enough. They were brown from much tennis. But they were indisputably human.

He got up, resolutely stifling his qualms, and began to pick up the clothing that was scattered nonchalantly about the floor. A crew of gnomes was excavating his skull, but he hoped they might go away if he didn't pay too much attention to them. One thing was certain: he was going to be good from now on. Gloria or no Gloria, heartbreak or no heartbreak, drowning your sorrows wasn't good enough. If you felt like this and could imagine you'd been a werewolf—

But why should he have imagined it in such detail? So many fragmentary memories seemed to come back as he dressed. Going up Strawberry Canyon with the fringed beard, finding a desolate and isolated spot for magic, learning the words—

Hell, he could even remember the words. The word that changed you and the one that changed you back.

Had he made up those words, too, in his drunken imaginings? And had he made up what he could only barely recall—the wonderful, magical freedom of changing, the single, sharp pang of alteration and then the boundless happiness of being lithe and fleet and free?

He surveyed himself in the mirror. Save for the unwonted wrinkles in his conservative single-breasted gray suit, he looked exactly what he was: a quiet academician; a little better built, a little more impulsive, a little more romantic than most, perhaps, but still just that—Professor Wolf.

The rest was nonsense. But there was, that impulsive side of him suggested, only one way of proving the fact. And that was to say The Word.

"All right," said Wolfe Wolf to his reflection. "I'll show you." And he said it.

The pang was sharper and stronger than he'd remembered. Alcohol numbs you to pain. It tore him for a moment with an anguish like the descriptions of childbirth. Then it was gone, and he flexed his limbs in happy amazement. But he was not a lithe, fleet, free beast. He was a helplessly trapped wolf, irrevocably entangled in a conservative single-breasted gray suit.

He tried to rise and walk, but the long sleeves and legs tripped him over flat on his muzzle. He kicked with his paws, trying to tear his way out, and then stopped.

Werewolf or no werewolf, he was likewise still Professor Wolf, and this suit had cost thirty-five dollars. There must be some cheaper way of securing freedom than tearing the suit to shreds.

He used several good, round Low German expletives. This was a complication that wasn't in any of the werewolf legends he'd ever read. There, people just—boom!—became wolves or—bang!—became men again. When they were men, they wore clothes; when they were wolves, they wore fur. Just like Hyperman becoming Bark Lent again on top of the Empire State Building and finding his street clothes right there. Most misleading. He began to remember now how Ozymandias the Great had made him strip before teaching him the words—

The words! That was it. All he had to do was say the word that changed you back—*Absarka!*—and he'd be a man again, comfortably fitted inside his suit. Then he could strip and play what games he wished. You see? Reason solves all. *"Absarka!"* he said.

Or thought he said. He went through all the proper mental processes for saying *Absarka!* but all that came out of his muzzle was a sort of clicking whine. And he was still a conservatively dressed and helpless wolf.

This was worse than the clothes problem. If he could be released only by saying *Absarka!* and if, being a wolf, he could say nothing, why, there he was. Indefinitely. He could go find Ozzy and ask—but how could a wolf wrapped up in a gray suit get safely out of a hotel and set out hunting for an unknown address?

He was trapped. He was lost. He was—

"Absarka!"

Professor Wolfe Wolf stood up in his grievously rumpled gray suit and beamed on the beard-fringed face of Ozymandias the Great.

"You see, colleague," the little magician explained, "I figured you'd want to try it again as soon as you got up, and I knew darned well you'd have your troubles. Thought I'd come over and straighten things out for you."

Wolf lit a cigarette in silence and handed the pack to Ozymandias. "When you came in just now," he said at last, "what did you see?"

"You as a wolf."

"Then it really—I actually—"

"Sure. You're a full-fledged werewolf, all right."

Wolf sat down on the rumpled bed. "I guess," he ventured slowly, "I've got to believe it. And if I believe that— But it means I've got to believe everything I've always scorned. I've got to believe in gods and devils and hells and—"

"You needn't be so pluralistic. But there is a God." Ozymandias said this as calmly and convincingly as he had stated last night that there were werewolves.

"And if there's a God, then I've got a soul?"

"Sure."

"And if I'm a werewolf— Hey!"

"What's the trouble, colleague?"

"All right, Ozzy. You know everything. Tell me this: Am I damned?"

"For what? Just for being a werewolf? Shucks, no; let me explain. There's two kinds of werewolves. There's the cursed kind that can't help themselves, that just go turning into wolves without any say in the matter; and there's the voluntary kind like you. Now, most of the voluntary kind are damned, sure, because they're wicked men who lust for blood and eat innocent people. But they aren't damnably wicked because they're werewolves; they became werewolves because they are damnably wicked. Now, you changed yourself just for the hell of it and because it looked like a good way to impress a gal; that's an innocent-enough motive, and being a werewolf doesn't make it any less so. Werewolves don't have to be monsters; it's just that we hear about only the ones that are."

"But how can I be voluntary when you told me I was a werewolf before I ever changed?"

"Not everybody can change. It's like being able to roll your tongue or wiggle your ears. You can, or you can't; and that's that. And as with those abilities, there's probably a genetic factor involved, though nobody's done any serious research on it. You were a werewolf *in posse;* now you're one *in esse.*"

"Then it's all right? I can be a werewolf just for having fun, and it's safe?"

"Absolutely."

Wolf chortled. "Will I show Gloria! Dull and unglamorous indeed! Anybody can marry an actor or a G-man; but a werewolf—"

"Your children probably will be, too," said Ozymandias cheerfully.

Wolf shut his eyes dreamily, then opened them with a start. "You know what?"

"What?"

"I haven't got a hangover anymore! This is marvelous. This is— Why, this is practical. At last the perfect hangover cure. Shuffle yourself into a wolf and back and— Oh, that reminds me. How do I get back?"

"Absarka."

"I know. But when I'm a wolf I can't say it."

"That," said Ozymandias sadly, "is the curse of being a white magician. You keep having to use the second-best form of spells, because the best would be black. Sure, a black-magic werebeast can turn himself back whenever he wants to. I remember in Darjeeling—"

"But how about me?"

"That's the trouble. You have to have somebody to say *Absarka!* for you. That's what I did last night, or do you remember? After we broke up the party at your friend's Temple— Tell you what. I'm retired now, and I've got enough to live on modestly because I can always magic up a little— Are you going to take up werewolfing seriously?"

"For a while, anyway. Till I get Gloria."

"Then why shouldn't I come and live here in your hotel? Then I'll always be handy to *Absarka!* you. After you get the girl, you can teach her."

Wolf extended his hand. "Noble of you. Shake." And then his eye caught his wrist watch. "Good Lord! I've missed two classes this morning. Werewolfing's all very well, but a man's got to work for his living."

"Most men." Ozymandias calmly reached his hand into the air and plucked a coin. He looked at it ruefully, it was a gold moidore. "Hang these spirits; I simply cannot explain to them about gold being illegal."

From Los Angeles, Wolf thought, with the habitual contempt of the northern Californian, as he surveyed the careless sport coat and the bright-yellow shirt of his visitor.

This young man rose politely as the professor entered the office. His green eyes gleamed cordially and his red hair glowed in the spring sunlight. "Professor Wolf?" he asked.

Wolf glanced impatiently at his desk. "Yes."

"O'Breen's the name. I'd like to talk to you a minute."

"My office hours are from three to four Tuesdays and Thursdays. I'm afraid I'm rather busy now."

"This isn't faculty business. And it's important." The young man's attitude was affable and casual, but he managed nonetheless to convey a sense of urgency that piqued Wolf's curiosity. The all-important letter to Gloria had waited while he took two classes; it could wait another five minutes.

"Very well, Mr. O'Breen."

"And alone, if you please."

Wolf himself hadn't noticed that Emily was in the room. He now turned to the secretary and said, "All right. If you don't mind, Emily—"

Emily shrugged and went out.

"Now, sir. What is this important and secret business?"

"Just a question or two. To start with, how well do you know Gloria Garton?"

Wolf paused. You could hardly say, "Young man, I am about to repropose to her in view of my becoming a werewolf." Instead he simply said—the truth, if not the whole truth— "She was a pupil of mine a few years ago."

"I said *do,* not *did.* How well do you know her now?"

"And why should I bother to answer such a question?"

The young man handed over a card. Wolf read:

FERGUS O'BREEN
Private Inquiry Agent
Licensed by the State of California

Wolf smiled. "And what does this mean? Divorce evidence? Isn't that the usual field of private inquiry agents?"

"Miss Garton isn't married, as you probably know very well. I'm just asking if you've been in touch with her much lately."

"And I'm simply asking why you should want to know."

O'Breen rose and began to pace around the office. "We don't seem to be getting very far, do we? I'm to take it that you refuse to state the nature of your relations with Gloria Garton?"

"I see no reason why I should do otherwise." Wolf was beginning to be annoyed.

To his surprise, the detective relaxed into a broad grin. "OK. Let it ride. Tell me about your department. How long have the various faculty members been here?"

"Instructors and all?"

"Just the professors."

"I've been here for seven years. All the others at least a good ten, probably more. If you want exact figures, you can probably get them from the dean, unless, as I hope"—Wolf smiled cordially—"he throws you out flat on your red pate."

O'Breen laughed. "Professor, I think we could get on. One more question, and you can do some pate-tossing yourself. Are you an American citizen?"

"Of course."

"And the rest of the department?"

"All of them. And now would you have the common decency to give me some explanation of this fantastic farrago of questions?"

"No," said O'Breen casually. "Goodbye, professor." His alert green eyes had been roaming about the room, sharply noticing everything. Now, as he left, they rested on Wolf's long index finger, moved up to his heavy meeting eyebrows, and returned to the finger. There was a suspicion of a startled realization in those eyes as he left the office.

But that was nonsense, Wolf told himself. A private detective, no matter how shrewd his eyes, no matter how apparently meaningless his inquiries, would surely be the last man on earth to notice the signs of lycanthropy.

Funny. "Werewolf" was a word you could accept. You could say, "I'm a werewolf," and it was all right. But say "I am a lycanthrope" and your flesh crawled. Odd. Possibly material for a paper on the influence of etymology on connotation for one of the learned periodicals.

But, hell! Wolfe Wolf was no longer primarily a scholar. He was a werewolf now, a white-magic werewolf, a werewolf-for-fun; and fun he was going to have. He lit his pipe, stared at the blank paper on his desk, and tried desperately to draft a letter to Gloria. It should hint at just enough to fascinate her and hold her interest until he could go south when the term ended and reveal to her the whole wonderful new truth. It—

Professor Oscar Fearing grunted his ponderous way into the office. "Good afternoon, Wolfe. Hard at it, my boy?"

"Afternoon," Wolf replied distractedly, and continued to stare at the paper.

"Great events coming, eh? Are you looking forward to seeing the glorious Gloria?"

Wolf started. "How— What do you mean?"

Fearing handed him a folded newspaper. "You hadn't heard?"

Wolf read with growing amazement and delight:

GLORIA GARTON TO ARRIVE FRIDAY
Local Girl Returns to Berkeley

As part of the most spectacular talent hunt since the search for Scarlett O'Hara, Gloria Garton, glamorous Metropolis starlet, will visit Berkeley Friday.

Friday afternoon at the Campus Theater, Berkeley canines will have their chance to compete in the nationwide quest for a dog to play Tookah the wolf dog in the great Metropolis epic "Fangs of the Forest," and Gloria Garton herself will be present at the auditions.

"I owe so much to Berkeley," Miss Garton said. "It will mean so much to me to see the campus and the city again." Miss Garton has the starring human role in "Fangs of the Forest."

Miss Garton was a student at the University of California when she received her first chance in films. She is a member of Mask and Dagger, honorary dramatic society, and Rho Rho Rho Sorority.

Wolfe Wolf glowed. This was perfect. No need now to wait till term was over. He could see Gloria now and claim her in all his wolfish vigor. Friday—today was Wednesday; that gave him two nights to practice and perfect the technique of werewolfry. And then—

He noticed the dejected look on the older professor's face, and a small remorse smote him. "How did things go last night, Oscar?" he asked sympathetically. "How were your big Walpurgis Night services?"

Fearing regarded him oddly. "You know that now? Yesterday April thirtieth meant nothing to you."

"I got curious and looked it up. But how did it go?"

"Well enough," Fearing lied feebly. "Do you know, Wolfe," he demanded after a moment's silence, "what is the real curse of every man interested in the occult?"

"No. What?"

"That true power is never enough. Enough for yourself, perhaps, but never enough for others. So that no matter what your true abilities, you must forge on beyond them into charlatanry to convince the others. Look at St. Germain. Look at Francis Stuart. Look at Cagliostro. But the worst tragedy is the next stage: when you realize that your powers were greater than you supposed and that the charlatanry was needless. When you realize that you have no notion of the extent of your powers. Then—"

"Then, Oscar?"

"Then, my boy, you are a badly frightened man."

Wolf wanted to say something consoling. He wanted to say, "Look, Oscar. It was just me. Go back to your half-hearted charlatanry and be happy." But he couldn't do that. Only Ozzy could know the truth of that splendid gray wolf. Only Ozzy and Gloria.

The moon was bright on that hidden spot in the canyon. The night was still. And Wolfe Wolf had a severe case of stage fright. Now that it came to the real thing—for this morning's clothes-complicated fiasco hardly counted and last night he could not truly remember—he was afraid to plunge cleanly into wolfdom and anxious to stall and talk as long as possible.

"Do you think," he asked the magician nervously, "that I could teach Gloria to change, too?"

Ozymandias pondered. "Maybe, colleague. It'd depend. She might have the natural ability, and she might not. And, of course, there's no telling what she might change into."

"You mean she wouldn't necessarily be a wolf?"

"Of course not. The people who can change, change into all sorts of things. And every folk knows best the kind that most interests it. We've got an English and Central European tradition, so we know mostly about werewolves. But take Scandinavia and you'll hear chiefly about werebears, only they call 'em berserkers. And Orientals, now, they're apt to know about weretigers. Trouble is, we've thought so much about were*wolves* that that's all we know the signs for; I wouldn't know how to spot a weretiger just offhand."

"Then there's no telling what might happen if I taught her The Word?"

"Not the least. Of course, there's some werethings that just aren't much use being. Take like being a wereant. You change and somebody steps on you and that's that. Or like a fella I knew once in Madagascar. Taught him The Word, and know what? Hanged if he wasn't a werediplodocus. Shattered the whole house into little pieces when he changed and damned near trampled me under hoof before I could say *Absarka!* He decided not to make a career of it. Or then there was that time in Darjeeling— But, look, colleague, are you going to stand around here naked all night?"

"No," said Wolf. "I'm going to change now. You'll take my clothes back to the hotel?"

"Sure. They'll be there for you. And I've put a very small spell on the night clerk, just enough for him not to notice wolves wandering in. Oh, and by the way—anything missing from your room?"

"Not that I noticed. Why?"

"Because I thought I saw somebody come out of it this afternoon. Couldn't be sure, but I think he came from there. Young fella with red hair and Hollywood clothes."

Wolfe Wolf frowned. That didn't make sense. Pointless questions from a detective were bad enough, but searching your hotel room— But what were detectives to a full-fledged werewolf? He grinned, nodded a friendly goodbye to Ozymandias the Great, and said The Word.

The pain wasn't so sharp as this morning, though still quite bad enough. But it passed almost at once, and his whole body filled with a sense of limitless freedom. He lifted his snout and sniffed deep at the keen freshness of this night air. A whole new realm of pleasure opened up for him through this acute new nose alone. He wagged his tail amicably at Ozzy and set off up the canyon on a long, easy lope.

For hours, loping was enough—simply and purely enjoying one's wolfness was the finest pleasure one could ask. Wolf left the canyon and turned up into the hills, past the Big C and on into noble wildness that seemed far remote from all campus civilization. His brave new legs were stanch and tireless, his wind seemingly inexhaustible. Every turning brought fresh and vivid scents of soil and leaves and air, and life was shimmering and beautiful.

But a few hours of this, and Wolf realized that he was damned lonely. All this grand exhilaration was very well, but if his mate Gloria were loping by his side— And what fun was it to be something as splendid as a wolf if no one admired you? He began to want people, and he turned back to the city.

*   *   *

Berkeley goes to bed early. The streets were deserted. Here and there a light burned in a rooming house where some solid grind was plodding on his almost-due term paper. Wolf had done that himself. He couldn't laugh in this shape, but his tail twitched with amusement at the thought.

He paused along the tree-lined street. There was a fresh human scent here, though the street seemed empty. Then he heard a soft whimpering, and trotted off toward the noise.

Behind the shrubbery fronting an apartment house sat a disconsolate two-year-old, shivering in his sunsuit and obviously lost for hours on hours. Wolf put a paw on the child's shoulder and shook him gently.

The boy looked around and was not in the least afraid. "He'o," he said, brightening up.

Wolf growled a cordial greeting, and wagged his tail and pawed at the ground to indicate that he'd take the lost infant wherever it wanted to go.

The child stood up and wiped away its tears with a dirty fist which left wide black smudges. "Tootootootoo!" he said.

Games, thought Wolf. He wants to play choo-choo. He took the child by the sleeve and tugged gently.

"Tootootootoo!" the boy repeated firmly. "Die way."

The sound of a railway whistle, to be sure, does die away; but this seemed a poetic expression for such a toddler. Wolf thought, and then abruptly would have snapped his fingers if he'd had them. The child was saying "2222 Dwight Way," having been carefully brought up to tell his address when lost. Wolf glanced up at the street sign. Bowditch and Hillegas; 2222 Dwight would be just a couple of blocks.

Wolf tried to nod his head, but the muscles didn't seem to work that way. Instead he wagged his tail in what he hoped indicated comprehension, and started off leading the child.

The infant beamed and said, "Nice woof-woof."

For an instant Wolf felt like a spy suddenly addressed by his right name, then realized that if some say "bow-wow" others might well say "woof-woof."

He led the child for two blocks without event. It felt good, having an innocent human being like this. There was something about children; he hoped Gloria felt the same. He wondered what would happen if he could teach this confiding infant The Word. It would be swell to have a pup that would—

He paused. His nose twitched and the hair on the back of his neck rose. Ahead of them stood a dog: a huge mongrel, seemingly a mixture of St. Bernard and Husky. But the growl that issued from his throat indicated that carrying brandy kegs or rushing serum was not for him. He was a bandit, an outlaw, an enemy of man and dog. And they had to pass him.

Wolf had no desire to fight. He was as big as this monster and certainly, with his human brain, much cleverer; but scars from a dog fight would not look well on the human body of Professor Wolf, and there was, moreover, the danger of hurting the toddler in the fracas. It would be wiser to cross the street. But before he could steer the child that way, the mongrel brute had charged at them, yapping and snarling.

Wolf placed himself in front of the boy, poised and ready to leap in defense. The scar problem was secondary to the fact that this baby had trusted him. He was ready to face this cur and teach him a lesson, at whatever cost to his own human body. But halfway to him the huge dog stopped. His growls died away to a piteous whimper. His great flanks trembled in the moonlight. His tail curled craven between his legs. And abruptly he turned and fled.

The child crowed delightedly. "Bad woof-woof go away." He put his little arms around Wolf's neck. "*Nice* woof-woof." Then he straightened up and said insistently, "Tootootootoo. Die way," and Wolf led on, his strong wolf's heart pounding as it had never pounded at the embrace of a woman.

"Tootootootoo" was a small frame house set back from the street in a large yard. The lights were still on, and even from the sidewalk Wolf could hear a woman's shrill voice.

"—Since five o'clock this afternoon, and you've got to find him, Officer. You simply must. We've hunted all over the neighborhood and—"

Wolf stood up against the wall on his hind legs and rang the doorbell with his front right paw.

"Oh! Maybe that's somebody now. The neighbors said they'd— Come, Officer, and let's see— Oh!"

At the same moment Wolf barked politely, the toddler yelled "Mamma!" and his thin and worn-looking young mother let out a scream—half delight at finding her child and half terror of this large gray canine shape that loomed behind him. She snatched up the infant protectively and turned to the large man in uniform. "Officer! Look! That big dreadful thing! It stole my Robby!"

"No," Robby protested firmly. "Nice woof-woof."

The officer laughed. "The lad's probably right, ma'am. It *is* a nice woof-woof. Found your boy wandering around and helped him home. You haven't maybe got a bone for him?"

"Let that big, nasty brute into my home? Never! Come on, Robby."

"Want my nice woof-woof."

"I'll woof-woof you, staying out till all hours and giving your father and me the fright of our lives. Just wait till your father sees you, young man; he'll— Oh, good night, Officer!" And she shut the door on the yowls of Robby.

The policeman patted Wolf's head. "Never mind about the bone, Rover. She didn't so much as offer me a glass of beer, either. My, you're a husky specimen, aren't you, boy? Look almost like a wolf. Who do you belong to, and what are you doing wandering about alone? Huh?" He turned on his flash and bent over to look at the nonexistent collar.

He straightened up and whistled. "No license. Rover, that's bad. You know what I ought to do? I ought to turn you in. If you weren't a hero that just got cheated out of his bone, I'd— Hell, I ought to do it, anyway. Laws are laws, even for heroes. Come on, Rover. We're going for a walk."

Wolf thought quickly. The pound was the last place on earth he wanted to wind up. Even Ozzy would never think of looking for him there. Nobody'd claim him, nobody'd say *Absarka!* and in the end a dose of chloroform— He wrenched loose from the officer's grasp on his hair and with one prodigious leap cleared the yard, landed on the sidewalk, and started hell for leather up the street. But the instant he was out of the officer's sight he stopped dead and slipped behind a hedge.

He scented the policeman's approach even before he heard it. The man was running with the lumbering haste of two hundred pounds. But opposite the hedge, he too stopped. For a moment Wolf wondered if his ruse had failed; but the officer had paused only to scratch his head and mutter, "Say! There's something screwy here. *Who rang that doorbell?* The kid couldn't reach it, and the dog— Oh, well," he concluded. "Nuts," and seemed to find in that monosyllabic summation the solution to all his problems.

As his footsteps and smell died away, Wolf became aware of another scent. He had only just identified it as cat when someone said, "You're were, aren't you?"

Wolf started up, lips drawn back and muscles tense. There was nothing human in sight, but someone had spoken to him. Unthinkingly, he tried to say "Where are you?" but all that came out was a growl.

"Right behind you. Here in the shadows. You can scent me, can't you?"

"But you're a cat," Wolf thought in his snarls. "And you're talking."

"Of course. But I'm not talking human language. It's just your brain that takes it that way. If you had your human body, you'd think I was just going *meowrr.* But you are were, aren't you?"

"How do you . . . why do you think so?"

"Because you didn't try to jump me, as any normal dog would have. And besides, unless Confucius taught me all wrong, you're a wolf, not a dog; and we don't have wolves around here unless they're were."

"How do you know all this? Are you—"

"Oh, no. I'm just a cat. But I used to live next door to a werechow named Confucius. He taught me things."

Wolf was amazed. "You mean he was a man who changed to chow and stayed that way? Lived as a pet?"

"Certainly. This was back at the worst of the depression. He said a dog was more apt to be fed and looked after than a man. I thought it was a smart idea."

"But how terrible! Could a man so debase himself as—"

"Men don't debase themselves. They debase each other. That's the way of most weres. Some change to keep from being debased, others to do a little more effective debasing. Which are you?"

"Why, you see, I—"

"*Sh!* Look. This is going to be fun. Holdup."

Wolf peered around the hedge. A well-dressed, middle-aged man was walking along briskly, apparently enjoying a night constitutional. Behind him moved a thin, silent figure. Even as Wolf watched, the figure caught up with him and whispered harshly, "Up with 'em, buddy!"

The quiet pomposity of the stroller melted away. He was ashen and aspen as the figure slipped a hand around into his breast pocket and removed an impressive wallet.

And what, thought Wolf, was the good of his fine, vigorous body if it merely crouched behind hedges as a spectator? In one fine bound, to the shocked amazement of the were-wise cat, he had crossed the hedge and landed with his forepaws full in the figure's face. It went over backward with him on top, and then there came a loud noise, a flash of light, and a frightful sharp smell. For a moment Wolf felt an acute pang in his shoulder, like the jab of a long needle, and then the pain was gone.

But his momentary recoil had been enough to let the figure get to its feet. "Missed you, huh?" it muttered. "Let's see how you like a slug in the belly, you interfering—" and he applied an epithet that would have been purely literal description if Wolf had not been were.

There were three quick shots in succession even as Wolf sprang. For a second he experienced the most acute stomach-ache of his life. Then he landed again. The figure's head hit the concrete sidewalk and he was still.

Lights were leaping into brightness everywhere. Among all the confused noises, Wolf could hear the shrill complaints of Robby's mother, and among all the compounded smells, he could distinguish scent of the policeman who wanted to impound him. That meant getting the hell out, and quick.

The city meant trouble, Wolf decided as he loped off. He could endure loneliness while he practiced his wolfry, until he had Gloria. Though just as a precaution he must arrange with Ozzy about a plausible-looking collar, and—

The most astounding realization yet suddenly struck him! He had received four bullets, three of them square in the stomach, and he hadn't a wound to show for it! Being a werewolf certainly offered its practical advantages. Think what a criminal could do with such bullet-proofing. Or— But no. He was a werewolf for fun, and that was that.

But even for a werewolf, being shot, though relatively painless, is tiring. A great deal of nervous energy is absorbed in the magical and instantaneous knitting of those wounds. And when Wolfe Wolf reached the peace and calm of the uncivilized hills, he no longer felt like reveling in freedom. Instead he stretched out to his full length, nuzzled his head down between his forepaws, and slept.

"Now, the essence of magic," said Heliophagus of Smyrna, "is deceit; and that deceit is of two kinds. By magic, the magician deceives others; but magic deceives the magician himself."

So far the lycanthropic magic of Wolfe Wolf had worked smoothly and pleasantly, but now it was to show him the second trickery that lurks behind every magic trick. And the first step was that he slept.

He woke in confusion. His dreams had been human—and of Gloria—despite the body in which he dreamed them, and it took several full minutes for him to reconstruct just how he happened to be in that body. For a moment the dream, even that episode in which he and Gloria had been eating blueberry waffles on a roller coaster, seemed more sanely plausible than the reality.

But he readjusted quickly, and glanced up at the sky. The sun looked as though it had been up at least an hour, which meant in May that the time was somewhere between six and seven. Today was Thursday, which meant that he was saddled with an eight-o'clock class. That left plenty of time to change back, shave, dress, breakfast, and resume the normal life of Professor Wolf—which was, after all, important if he intended to support a wife.

He tried, as he trotted through the streets, to look as tame and unwolflike as possible, and apparently succeeded. No one paid him any mind save children, who wanted to play, and dogs, who began by snarling and ended by cowering away terrified. His friend the cat might be curiously tolerant of weres, but not so dogs.

He trotted up the steps of the Berkeley Inn confidently. The clerk was under a slight spell and would not notice wolves. There was nothing to do but rouse Ozzy, be *Absarka!*'d and—

"Hey! Where are you going? Get out of here! Shoo!"

It was the clerk, a stanch and brawny young man, who straddled the stairway and vigorously waved him off.

"No dogs in here! Go on now. Scoot!"

Quite obviously this man was under no spell, and equally obviously there was no way of getting up that staircase short of using a wolf's strength to tear the clerk apart. For a second Wolf hesitated. He had to get changed back. It would be a damnable pity to use his powers to injure another human being. If only he had not slept, and arrived before this unmagicked day clerk came on duty; but necessity knows no—

Then the solution hit him. Wolf turned and loped off just as the clerk hurled an ash tray at him. Bullets may be relatively painless, but even a werewolf's rump, he learned promptly, is sensitive to flying glass.

The solution was foolproof. The only trouble was that it meant an hour's wait, and he was hungry. Damnably hungry. He found himself even displaying a certain shocking interest in the plump occupant of a baby carriage. You do get different appetites with a different body. He could understand how some originally well-intentioned werewolves might in time become monsters. But he was stronger in will, and much smarter. His stomach could hold out until this plan worked.

The janitor had already opened the front door of Wheeler Hall, but the building was deserted. Wolf had no trouble reaching the second floor unnoticed or finding his classroom. He had a little more trouble holding the chalk between his teeth and a slight tendency to gag on the dust; but by balancing his forepaws on the eraser trough, he could manage quite nicely. It took three springs to catch the ring of the chart in his teeth, but once that was pulled down there was nothing to do but crouch under the desk and pray that he would not starve quite to death.

The students of German 31B, as they assembled reluctantly for their eight-o'clock, were a little puzzled at being confronted by a chart dealing with the influence of the gold standard on world economy, but they decided simply that the janitor had been forgetful.

The wolf under the desk listened unseen to their gathering murmurs, overheard that cute blonde in the front row make dates with three different men for that same night, and finally decided that enough had assembled to make his chances plausible. He slipped out from under the desk far enough to reach the ring of the chart, tugged at it, and let go.

The chart flew up with a rolling crash. The students broke off their chatter, looked up at the blackboard, and beheld in a huge and shaky scrawl the mysterious letters

A B S A R K A

It worked. With enough people, it was an almost mathematical certainty that one of them in his puzzlement—for the race of subtitle readers, though handicapped by the talkies, still exists—would read the mysterious word aloud. It was the much-bedated blonde who did it.

"*Absarka*," she said wonderingly.

And there was Professor Wolfe Wolf, beaming cordially at his class.

The only flaw was this: He had forgotten that he was only a werewolf, and not Hyperman. His clothes were still at the Berkeley Inn, and here on the lecture platform he was stark naked.

Two of his best pupils screamed and one fainted. The blonde only giggled appreciatively.

Emily was incredulous but pitying.
Professor Fearing was sympathetic but reserved.
The chairman of the department was cool.
The dean of letters was chilly.
The president of the university was frigid.
Wolfe Wolf was unemployed.
And Heliophagus of Smyrna was right. "The essence of magic is deceit."

"But what can I do?" Wolf moaned into his zombie glass. "I'm stuck. I'm stymied. Gloria arrives in Berkeley tomorrow, and here I am—nothing. Nothing but a futile, worthless werewolf. You can't support a wife on that. You can't raise a family. You can't— Hell, you can't even propose . . . I want another. Sure you won't have one?"

Ozymandias the Great shook his round, fringed head. "The last time I took two drinks I started all this. I've got to behave if I want to stop it. But you're an able-bodied, strapping young man; surely, colleague, you can get work?"

"Where? All I'm trained for is academic work, and this scandal has put the kibosh on that forever. What university is going to hire a man who showed up naked in front of his class without even the excuse of being drunk? And supposing I try something else—say one of these jobs in defense that all my students seem to be getting—I'd have to give references, say something about what I'd been doing with my thirty-odd years. And once these references were checked— Ozzy, I'm a lost man."

"Never despair, colleague. I've learned that magic gets you into some tight squeezes, but there's always a way of getting out. Now, take that time in Darjeeling—"

"But what can I do? I'll wind up like Confucius the werechow and live off charity, if you'll find me somebody who wants a pet wolf."

"You know," Ozymandias reflected, "you may have something there, colleague."

"Nuts! That was a joke. I can at least retain my self-respect, even if I go on relief doing it. And I'll bet they don't like naked men on relief, either."

"No. I don't mean just being a pet wolf. But look at it this way: What are your assets? You have only two outstanding abilities. One of them is to teach German, and that is now completely out."

"Check."

"And the other is to change yourself into a wolf. All right, colleague. There must be some commercial possibilities in that. Let's look into them."

"Nonsense."

"Not quite. For every kind of merchandise there's a market. The trick is to find it. And you, colleague, are going to be the first practical commercial werewolf on record."

"I could— They say Ripley's Odditorium pays good money. Supposing I changed six times a day regular for delighted audiences?"

Ozymandias shook his head sorrowfully. "It's no good. People don't want to see real magic. It makes 'em uncomfortable—starts 'em wondering what else might be loose in the world. They've got to feel sure it's all done with mirrors. I know. I had to quit vaudeville because I wasn't smart enough at faking it; all I could do was the real thing."

"I could be a Seeing Eye dog, maybe?"

"They have to be female."

"When I'm changed I can understand animal language. Maybe I could be a dog trainer and— No, that's out. I forgot: they're scared to death of me."

But Ozymandias' pale-blue eyes had lit up at the suggestion. "Colleague, you're warm. Oh, are you warm! Tell me: why did you say your fabulous Gloria was coming to Berkeley?"

"Publicity for a talent hunt."

"For what?"

"A dog to star in *Fangs of the Forest.*"

"And what kind of a dog?"

"A—" Wolf's eyes widened and his jaw sagged. "A wolf dog," he said softly.

And the two men looked at each other with a wild surmise—silent, beside a bar in Berkeley.

"It's all the fault of that damned Disney dog," the trainer complained. "Pluto does anything. Everything. So our poor mutts are expected to do likewise. Listen to that dope! 'The dog should come into the room, give one paw to the baby, indicate that he recognizes the hero in his Eskimo disguise, go over to the table, find the bone, and clap his paws gleefully!' Now, who's got a set of signals to cover stuff like that? Pluto's" he snorted.

Gloria Garton said, "Oh." By that one sound she managed to convey that she sympathized deeply, that the trainer was a nice-looking young man whom she'd just as soon see again, and that no dog star was going to steal *Fangs of the Forest* from her. She adjusted her skirt slightly, leaned back, and made the plain wooden chair on the bare theater stage seem more than ever like a throne.

"All right." The man in the violet beret waved away the last unsuccessful applicant and read from a card: " 'Dog: Wopsy. Owner: Mrs. Channing Galbraith. Trainer: Luther Newby.' Bring it in."

An assistant scurried offstage, and there was a sound of whines and whimpers as a door opened.

"What's got into those dogs today?" the man in the violet beret demanded. "They all seem scared to death and beyond."

"I think," said Fergus O'Breen, "that it's that big gray wolf dog. Somehow, the others just don't like him."

Gloria Garton lowered her bepurpled lids and cast a queenly stare of suspicion on the young detective. There was nothing wrong with his being there. His sister was head of publicity for Metropolis, and he'd handled several confidential cases for the studio; even one for her, that time her chauffeur had decided to try his hand at blackmail. Fergus O'Breen was a Metropolis fixture; but still it bothered her.

The assistant brought in Mrs. Galbraith's Wopsy. The man in the violet beret took one look and screamed. The scream bounced back from every wall of the theater in the ensuing minute of silence. At last he found words. "A wolf dog! Tookah is the greatest role ever written for a wolf dog! And what do they bring us? A terrier, yet! So if we wanted a terrier we could cast Asta!"

"But if you'd only let us show you—"Wopsy's tall young trainer started to protest.

"Get out!" the man in the violet beret shrieked. "Get out before I lose my temper!"

Wopsy and her trainer slunk off.

"In El Paso," the casting director lamented, "they bring me a Mexican hairless. In St. Louis it's a Pekinese yet! And if I do find a wolf dog, it sits in a corner and waits for somebody to bring it a sled to pull."

"Maybe," said Fergus, "you should try a real wolf."

"Wolf, schmolf! We'll end up wrapping John Barrymore in a wolfskin." He picked up the next card. " 'Dog: Yoggoth. Owner and trainer: Mr. O. Z. Manders.' Bring it in."

The whining noise offstage ceased as Yoggoth was brought out to be tested. The man in the violet beret hardly glanced at the fringe-bearded owner and trainer. He had eyes only for that splendid gray wolf. "If you can only act . . ." he prayed, with the same fervor with which many a man has thought, If you could only cook . . .

He pulled the beret to an even more unlikely angle and snapped, "All right, Mr. Manders. The dog should come into the room, give one paw to the baby, indicate that he recognizes the hero in his Eskimo disguise, go over to the table, find the bone, and clap his paws joyfully. Baby here, hero here, table here. Got that?"

Mr. Manders looked at his wolf dog and repeated, "Got that?"

Yoggoth wagged his tail.

"Very well, colleague," said Mr. Manders. "Do it."

Yoggoth did it.

The violet beret sailed into the flies, on the wings of its owner's triumphal scream of joy. "He did it!" he kept burbling. "He did it!"

"Of course, colleague," said Mr. Manders calmly.

The trainer who hated Pluto had a face as blank as a vampire's mirror. Fergus O'Breen was speechless with wonderment. Even Gloria Garton permitted surprise and interest to cross her regal mask.

"You mean he can do anything?" gurgled the man who used to have a violet beret.

"Anything," said Mr. Manders.

"Can he— Let's see, in the dance-hall sequence . . . can he knock a man down, roll him over, and frisk his back pocket?"

Even before Mr. Manders could say "Of course," Yoggoth had demonstrated, using Fergus O'Breen as a convenient dummy

"Peace!" the casting director sighed. "Peace . . . Charley!" he yelled to his assistant. "Send 'em all away. No more tryouts. We've found Tookah! It's wonderful."

The trainer stepped up to Mr. Manders. "It's more than that, sir. It's positively superhuman. I'll swear I couldn't detect the slightest signal, and for such complicated operations, too. Tell me, Mr. Manders, what system do you use?"

Mr. Manders made a Hoople-ish *kaff-kaff* noise. "Professional secret, you understand, young man. I'm planning on opening a school when I retire, but obviously until then—"

"Of course, sir. I understand. But I've never seen anything like it in all my born days."

"I wonder," Fergus O'Breen observed abstractly from the floor, "if your marvel dog can get off of people, too?"

Mr. Manders stifled a grin. "Of course! Yoggoth!"

Fergus picked himself up and dusted from his clothes the grime of the stage, which is the most clinging grime on earth. "I'd swear," he muttered, "that beast of yours enjoyed that."

"No hard feelings, I trust, Mr.—"

"O'Breen. None at all. In fact, I'd suggest a little celebration in honor of this great event. I know you can't buy a drink this near the campus, so I brought along a bottle just in case."

"Oh," said Gloria Garton, implying that carousals were ordinarily beneath her; that this, however, was a special occasion; and that possibly there was something to be said for the green-eyed detective after all.

This was all too easy, Wolfe Wolf–Yoggoth kept thinking. There was a catch to it somewhere. This was certainly the ideal solution to the problem of how to earn money as a werewolf. Bring an understanding of human speech and instructions into a fine animal body, and you are the answer to a director's prayer. It was perfect as long as it lasted; and if *Fangs of the Forest* was a smash hit, there were bound to be other Yoggoth pictures. Look at Rin-Tin-Tin. But it was too easy . . .

His ears caught a familiar "Oh," and his attention reverted to Gloria. This "Oh" had meant that she really shouldn't have another drink, but since liquor didn't affect her anyway and this was a special occasion, she might as well.

She was even more beautiful than he had remembered. Her golden hair was shoulder-length now, and flowed with such rippling perfection that it was all he could do to keep from reaching out a paw to it. Her body had ripened, too; was even more warm and promising than his memories of her. And in his new shape he found her greatest charm in something he had not been able to appreciate fully as a human being: the deep, heady scent of her flesh.

"To *Fangs of the Forest!*" Fergus O'Breen was toasting. "And may that pretty-boy hero of yours get a worse mauling than I did."

Wolf-Yoggoth grinned to himself. That had been fun. That'd teach the detective to go crawling around hotel rooms.

"And while we're celebrating, colleagues," said Ozymandias the Great, "why should we neglect our star? Here, Yoggoth." And he held out the bottle.

"He drinks, yet!" the casting director exclaimed delightedly.

"Sure. He was weaned on it."

Wolf took a sizable gulp. It felt good. Warm and rich—almost the way Gloria smelled.

"But how about you, Mr. Manders?" the detective insisted for the fifth time. "It's your celebration really. The poor beast won't get the four-figure checks from Metropolis. And you've taken only one drink."

"Never take two, colleague. I know my danger point. Two drinks in me and things start happening."

"More should happen yet than training miracle dogs? Go on, O'Breen. Make him drink. We should see what happens."

Fergus took another long drink himself. "Go on. There's another bottle in the car, and I've gone far enough to be resolved not to leave here sober. And I don't want sober companions, either." His green eyes were already beginning to glow with a new wildness.

"No, thank you, colleague."

Gloria Garton left her throne, walked over to the plump man, and stood close, her soft hand resting on his arm. "Oh," she said, implying that dogs were dogs, but still that the party was unquestionably in her honor and his refusal to drink was a personal insult.

Ozymandias the Great looked at Gloria, sighed, shrugged, resigned himself to fate, and drank.

"Have you trained many dogs?" the casting director asked.

"Sorry, colleague. This is my first."

"All the more wonderful! But what's your profession otherwise?"

"Well, you see, I'm a magician."

"Oh," said Gloria Garton, implying delight, and went so far as to add, "I have a friend who does black magic."

"I'm afraid, ma'am, mine's simply white. That's tricky enough. With the black you're in for some real dangers."

"Hold on!" Fergus interposed. "You mean really a magician? Not just presti . . . sleight of hand?"

"Of course, colleague."

"Good theater," said the casting director. "Never let 'em see the mirrors."

"Uh-huh," Fergus nodded. "But look, Mr. Manders. What can you do, for instance?"

"Well, I can change—"

Yoggoth barked loudly.

"Oh, no," Ozymandias covered hastily, "that's really a little beyond me. But I can—"

"Can you do the Indian rope trick?" Gloria asked languidly. "My friend says that's terribly hard."

"Hard? Why, ma'am, there's nothing to it. I can remember that time in Darjeeling—"

Fergus took another long drink. "I," he announced defiantly, "want to see the Indian rope trick. I have met people who've met people who've met people who've seen it, but that's as close as I ever get. And I don't believe it."

"But, colleague, it's so simple."

"I don't believe it."

Ozymandias the Great drew himself up to his full lack of height. "Colleague, you are about to see it!" Yoggoth tugged warningly at his coattails. "Leave me alone, Wolf. An aspersion has been cast!"

Fergus returned from the wings dragging a soiled length of rope. "This do?"

"Admirably."

"What goes?" the casting director demanded.

"*Shh!*" said Gloria. "Oh—"

She beamed worshipfully on Ozymandias, whose chest swelled to the point of threatening the security of his buttons. "Ladies and gentlemen!" he announced, in the manner of one prepared to fill a vast amphitheater with his voice. "You are about to behold Ozymandias the Great in— The Indian Rope Trick! Of course," he added conversationally, "I haven't got a small boy to chop into mincemeat, unless perhaps one of you— No? Well, we'll try it without. Not quite so impressive, though. And will you stop yapping, Wolf?"

"I thought his name was Yogi," said Fergus.

"Yoggoth. But since he's part wolf on his mother's side— Now, quiet, all of you!"

He had been coiling the rope as he spoke. Now he placed the coil in the center of the stage, where it lurked like a threatening rattler. He stood beside it and deftly, professionally, went through a series of passes and mumblings so rapidly that even the superhumanly sharp eyes and ears of Wolf-Yoggoth could not follow them.

The end of the rope detached itself from the coil, reared in the air, turned for a moment like a head uncertain where to strike, then shot straight up until all the rope was uncoiled. The lower end rested a good inch above the stage.

Gloria gasped. The casting director drank hurriedly. Fergus, for some reason, stared curiously at the wolf.

"And now, ladies and gentlemen—oh, hang it, I do wish I had a boy to carve— Ozymandias the Great will ascend this rope into that land which only the users of the rope may know. Onward and upward! Be right back," he added reassuringly to Wolf.

His plump hands grasped the rope above his head and gave a little jerk. His knees swung up and clasped about the hempen pillar. And up he went, like a monkey on a stick, up and up and up—until suddenly he was gone.

Just gone. That was all there was to it. Gloria was beyond even saying "Oh." The casting director sat his beautiful flannels down on the filthy floor and gaped. Fergus swore softly and melodiously. And Wolf felt a premonitory prickling in his spine.

The stage door opened, admitting two men in denim pants and work shirts. "Hey!" said the first. "Where do you think you are?"

"We're from Metropolis Pictures," the casting director started to explain, scrambling to his feet.

"I don't care if you're from Washington, we gotta clear this stage. There's movies here tonight. Come on, Joe, help me get 'em out. And that pooch, too."

"You can't, Fred," said Joe reverently, and pointed. His voice sank to an awed whisper. "That's Gloria Garton—"

"So it is. Hi, Miss Garton. Cripes, wasn't that last one of yours a stinkeroo!"

"Your public, darling," Fergus murmured.

"Come on!" Fred shouted. "Out of here. We gotta clean up. And you, Joe! Strike that rope!"

Before Fergus could move, before Wolf could leap to the rescue, the efficient stagehand had struck the rope and was coiling it up.

Wolf stared up into the flies. There was nothing up there. Nothing at all. Someplace beyond the end of that rope was the only man on earth he could trust to say *Absarka!* for him; and the way down was cut off forever.

Wolfe Wolf sprawled on the floor of Gloria Garton's boudoir and watched that vision of volupty change into her most fetching negligee.

The situation was perfect. It was the fulfillment of all his dearest dreams. The only flaw was that he was still in a wolf's body.

Gloria turned, leaned over, and chucked him under the snout. "Wuzzum a cute wolf dog, wuzzum?"

Wolf could not restrain a snarl.

"Doesn't um like Gloria to talk baby talk? Um was a naughty wolf, yes, um was."

It was torture. Here you are in your best-beloved's hotel room, all her beauty revealed to your hungry eyes, and she talks baby talk to you! Wolf had been happy at first when Gloria suggested that she might take over the care of her co-star pending the reappearance of his trainer—for none of them was quite willing to admit that "Mr. O. Z. Manders" might truly and definitely have vanished—but he was beginning to realize that the situation might bring on more torment than pleasure.

"Wolves are funny," Gloria observed. She was more talkative when alone, with no need to be cryptically fascinating. "I knew a Wolfe once, only that was his name. He was a man. And he was a funny one."

Wolf felt his heart beating fast under his gray fur. To hear his own name on Gloria's warm lips . . . But before she could go on to tell her pet how funny Wolfe was, her maid rapped on the door.

"A Mr. O'Breen to see you, madam."

"Tell him to go 'way."

"He says it's important, and he does look, madam, as though he might make trouble."

"Oh, all right." Gloria rose and wrapped her negligee more respectably about her. "Come on, Yog— No, that's a silly name. I'm going to call you Wolfie. That's cute. Come on, Wolfie, and protect me from the big, bad detective."

Fergus O'Breen was pacing the sitting room with a certain vicious deliberateness in his strides. He broke off and stood still as Gloria and the wolf entered.

"So?" he observed tersely. "Reinforcements?"

"Will I need them?" Gloria cooed.

"Look, light of my love life." The glint in the green eyes was cold and deadly. "You've been playing games, and whatever their nature, there's one thing they're not. And that's cricket."

Gloria gave him a languid smile. "You're amusing, Fergus."

"Thanks. I doubt, however, if your activities are."

"You're still a little boy playing cops and robbers. And what boogyman are you after now?"

"Ha-ha," said Fergus politely. "And you know the answer to that question better than I do. That's why I'm here."

Wolf was puzzled. This conversation meant nothing to him. And yet he sensed a tension of danger in the air as clearly as though he could smell it.

"Go on," Gloria snapped impatiently. "And remember how dearly Metropolis Pictures will thank you for annoying one of its best box-office attractions."

"Some things, my sweeting, are more important than pictures, though you mightn't think it where you come from. One of them is a certain federation of forty-eight units. Another is an abstract concept called democracy."

"And so?"

"And so I want to ask you one question: Why did you come to Berkeley?"

"For publicity on *Fangs,* of course. It was your sister's idea."

"You've gone temperamental and turned down better ones. Why leap at this?"

"You don't haunt publicity stunts yourself, Fergus. Why are *you* here?"

Fergus was pacing again. "And why was your first act in Berkeley a visit to the office of the German department?"

"Isn't that natural enough? I used to be a student here."

"Majoring in dramatics, and you didn't go near the Little Theater. Why the German department?" He paused and stood straight in front of her, fixing her with his green gaze.

Gloria assumed the attitude of a captured queen defying the barbarian conqueror. "Very well. If you must know— I went to the German department to see the man I love."

Wolf held his breath, and tried to keep his tail from thrashing.

"Yes," she went on impassionedly, "you strip the last veil from me, and force me to confess to you what he alone should have heard first. This man proposed to me by mail. I foolishly rejected his proposal. But I thought and thought—and at last I knew. When I came to Berkeley I had to see him—"

"And did you?"

"The little mouse of a secretary told me he wasn't there. But I shall see him yet. And when I do—"

Fergus bowed stiffly. "My congratulations to you both, my sweeting. And the name of this more than fortunate gentleman?"

"Professor Wolfe Wolf."

"Who is doubtless the individual referred to in this?" He whipped a piece of paper from his sport coat and thrust it at Gloria. She paled and was silent. But Wolfe Wolf did not wait for her reply. He did not care. He knew the solution to his problem now, and he was streaking unobserved for her boudoir.

Gloria Garton entered the boudoir a minute later, a shaken and wretched woman. She unstopped one of the delicate perfume bottles on her dresser and poured herself a stiff tot of whiskey. Then her eyebrows lifted in surprise as she stared at her mirror. Scrawlingly lettered across the glass in her own deep-crimson lipstick was the mysterious word

ABSARKA

Frowning, she said it aloud. *"Absarka—"*

From behind a screen stepped Professor Wolfe Wolf, incongruously wrapped in one of Gloria's lushest dressing robes. "Gloria dearest—" he cried.

"Wolfe!" she exclaimed. "What on earth are you doing here in my room?"

"I love you. I've always loved you since you couldn't tell a strong from a weak verb. And now that I know that you love me—"

"This is terrible. Please get out of here!"

"Gloria—"

"Get out of here, or I'll sick my dog on you. Wolfie— Here, nice Wolfie!"

"I'm sorry, Gloria. But Wolfie won't answer you."

"Oh, you beast! Have you hurt Wolfie? Have you—"

"I wouldn't touch a hair on his pelt. Because, you see, Gloria darling, I am Wolfie."

"What on earth do you—" Gloria stared around the room. It was undeniable that there was no trace of the presence of a wolf dog. And here was a man dressed only in one of her robes and no sign of his own clothes. And after that funny little man and the rope . . .

"You thought I was drab and dull," Wolf went on. "You thought I'd sunk into an academic rut. You'd sooner have an actor or a G-man. But I, Gloria, am something more exciting than you've ever dreamed of. There's not another soul on earth I'd tell this to, but I, Gloria, am a werewolf."

Gloria gasped. "That isn't possible! But it does all fit in. When I heard about you on campus, and your friend with the funny beard and how he vanished, and, of course, it explains how you did tricks that any real dog couldn't possibly do—"

"Don't you believe me, darling?"

Gloria rose from the dresser chair and went into his arms. "I believe you, dear. And it's wonderful! I'll bet there's not another woman in all Hollywood that was ever married to a werewolf!"

"Then you will—"

"But of course, dear. We can work it out beautifully. We'll hire a stooge to be your trainer on the lot. You can work daytimes, and come home at night and I'll say that word for you. It'll be perfect."

"Gloria . . ." Wolf murmured with tender reverence.

"One thing, dear. Just a little thing. Would you do Gloria a favor?"

"Anything!"

"Show me how you change. Change for me now. Then I'll change you back right away."

Wolf said The Word. He was in such ecstatic bliss that he hardly felt the pang this time. He capered about the room with all the litheness of his fine wolfish legs, and ended up before Gloria, wagging his tail and looking for approval.

Gloria patted his head. "Good boy, Wolfie. And now, darling, you can just damned well stay that way."

Wolf let out a yelp of amazement.

"You heard me, Wolfie. You're staying that way. You didn't happen to believe any of that guff I was feeding the detective, did you? Love you? I should waste my time! But this way you can be very useful to me. With your trainer gone, I can take charge of you and pick up an extra thousand a week or so. I won't mind that. And Professor Wolfe Wolf will have vanished forever, which fits right in with my plans."

Wolf snarled.

"Now, don't try to get nasty, Wolfie darling. Um wouldn't threaten ums darling Gloria, would ums? Remember what I can do for you. I'm the only person that can turn you into a man again. You wouldn't dare teach anyone else that. You wouldn't dare let people know what you really are. An ignorant person would kill you. A smart one would have you locked up as a lunatic."

Wolf still advanced threateningly.

"Oh, no. You can't hurt me. Because all I'd have to do would be to say the word on the mirror. Then you wouldn't be a dangerous wolf any more. You'd just be a man here in my room, and I'd scream. And after what happened on the campus yesterday, how long do you think you'd stay out of the madhouse?"

Wolf backed away and let his tail droop.

"You see, Wolfie darling? Gloria has ums just where she wants ums. And ums is damned well going to be a good boy."

There was a rap on the boudoir door, and Gloria called, "Come in."

"A gentleman to see you, madam," the maid announced. "A Professor Fearing."

Gloria smiled her best cruel and queenly smile. "Come along, Wolfie. This may interest you."

Professor Oscar Fearing, overflowing one of the graceful chairs of the sitting room, beamed benevolently as Gloria and the wolf entered. "Ah, my dear! A new pet. Touching."

"And what a pet, Oscar. Wait till you hear. "

Professor Fearing buffed his pince-nez against his sleeve. "And wait, my dear, until you hear all that I have learned. Chiswick has perfected his protective screen against magnetic bombs, and the official trial is set for next week. And Farnsworth has all but completed his researches on a new process for obtaining osmium. Gas warfare may start any day, and the power that can command a plentiful supply of—"

"Fine, Oscar," Gloria broke in. "But we can go over all this later. We've got other worries right now."

"What do you mean, my dear?"

"Have you run into a red-headed young Irishman in a yellow shirt?"

"No, I— Why, yes. I did see such an individual leaving the office yesterday. I believe he had been to see Wolfe."

"He on to us. He's a detective from Los Angeles, and he's tracking us down. Someplace he got hold of a scrap of record that should have been destroyed. He knows I'm in it, and he knows I'm tied up with somebody here in the German department."

Professor Fearing scrutinized his pince-nez, approved of their cleanness, and set them on his nose. "Not so much excitement, my dear. No hysteria. Let us approach this calmly. Does he know about the Temple of the Dark Truth?"

"Not yet. Nor about you. He just knows it's somebody in the department."

"Then what could be simpler? You have heard of the strange conduct of Wolfe Wolf?"

"Have I!" Gloria laughed harshly.

"Everyone knows of Wolfe's infatuation with you. Throw the blame onto him. It should be easy to clear yourself and make you appear an innocent tool. Direct all attention to him and the organization will be safe. The Temple of the Dark Truth can go its mystic way and extract even more invaluable information from weary scientists who need the emotional release of a false religion."

"That's what I've tried to do. I gave O'Breen a long song and dance about my devotion to Wolfe, so obviously phony he'd be bound to think it was a cover-up for something else. And I think he bit. But the situation's a damned sight trickier than you guess. Do you know where Wolfe Wolf is?"

"No one knows. After the president . . . ah . . . rebuked him, he seems to have vanished."

Gloria laughed again. "He's right here. In this room."

"My dear! Secret panels and such? You take your espionage too seriously. Where?"

"There!"

Professor Fearing gaped. "Are you serious?"

"As serious as you are about the future of Fascism. That is Wolfe Wolf."

Fearing approached the wolf incredulously and extended his hand.

"He might bite," Gloria warned him a second too late.

Fearing stared at his bleeding hand. "That, at least," he observed, "is undeniably true." And he raised his foot to deliver a sharp kick.

"No, Oscar! Don't! Leave him alone. And you'll have to take my word for it—it's way too complicated. But the wolf is Wolfe Wolf, and I've got him absolutely under control. He's perfectly in our hands. We'll switch suspicion to him, and I'll keep him this way while Fergus and his friends the G-men go off hotfoot on his trail."

"My dear!" Fearing ejaculated. "You're mad. You're more hopelessly mad than the devout members of the Temple." He took off his pince-nez and stared again at the wolf. "And yet Tuesday night— Tell me one thing: From whom did you get this . . . this wolf dog?"

"From a funny plump little man with a fringy beard."

Fearing gasped. Obviously he remembered the furor in the Temple, and the wolf and the fringe-beard. "Very well, my dear. I believe you. Don't ask me why, but I believe you. And now—"

"Now, it's all set, isn't it? We keep him here helpless, and we use him to—"

"The wolf as scapegoat. Yes. Very pretty."

"Oh! One thing—" She was suddenly frightened.

Wolfe Wolf was considering the possibilities of a sudden attack on Fearing. He could probably get out of the room before Gloria could say *Absarka!* But after that? Whom could he trust to restore him? Especially if G-men were to be set on his trail . . .

"What is it?", Fearing asked.

"That secretary. That little mouse in the department office. She knows it was you I asked for, not Wolf. Fergus can't have talked to her yet, because he swallowed my story; but he will. He's thorough."

"Hm-m-m. Then, in that case—"

"Yes, Oscar?"

"She must be attended to." Professor Oscar Fearing beamed genially and reached for the phone.

Wolf acted instantly, on inspiration and impulse. His teeth were strong, quite strong enough to jerk the phone cord from the wall. That took only a second, and in the next second he was out of the room and into the hall before Gloria could open her mouth to speak that word that would convert him from a powerful and dangerous wolf to a futile man.

There were shrill screams and a shout or two of "Mad dog!" as he dashed through the hotel lobby, but he paid no heed to them. The main thing was to reach Emily's house before she could be "attended to." Her evidence was essential. That could swing the balance, show Fergus and his G-men where the true guilt lay. And, besides, he admitted to himself, Emily was a damned nice kid . . .

His rate of collision was about one point six six per block, and the curses heaped upon him, if theologically valid, would have been more than enough to damn him forever. But he was making time, and that was all that counted. He dashed through traffic signals, cut into the path of trucks, swerved from under streetcars, and once even leaped over a stalled car that was obstructing him. Everything was going fine, he was halfway there, when two hundred pounds of human flesh landed on him in a flying tackle.

He looked up through the brilliant lighting effects of smashing his head on the sidewalk and saw his old nemesis, the policeman who had been cheated of his beer.

"So, Rover!" said the officer. "Got you at last, did I? Now we'll see if you'll wear a proper license tag. Didn't know I used to play football, did you?"

The officer's grip on his hair was painfully tight. A gleeful crowd was gathering and heckling the policeman with fantastic advice.

"Get along, boys," he admonished. "This is a private matter between me and Rover here. Come on," and he tugged even harder.

Wolf left a large tuft of fur and skin in the officer's grasp and felt the blood ooze out of the bare patch on his neck. He heard a ripe oath and a pistol shot simultaneously, and felt the needlelike sting through his shoulder. The awestruck crowd thawed before him. Two more bullets hied after him, but he was gone, leaving the most dazed policeman in Berkeley.

"I hit him," the officer kept muttering blankly. "I hit the—"

Wolfe Wolf coursed along Dwight Way. Two more blocks and he'd be at the little bungalow that Emily shared with a teaching assistant in something or other. Ripping out that telephone had stopped Fearing only momentarily; the orders would have been given by now, the henchmen would be on their way. But he was almost there . . .

"He'o!" a child's light voice called to him. "Nice woof-woof come back!"

Across the street was the modest frame dwelling of Robby and his shrewish mother. The child had been playing on the sidewalk. Now he saw his idol and deliverer and started across the street at a lurching toddle. "Nice woof-woof!" he kept calling. "Wait for Robby!"

Wolf kept on. This was no time for playing games with even the most delightful of cubs. And then he saw the car. It was an ancient jalopy, plastered with wisecracks even older than itself; and the high school youth driving was obviously showing his girl friend how it could make time on this deserted residential street. The girl was a cute dish, and who could be bothered watching out for children?

Robby was directly in front of the car. Wolf leaped straight as a bullet. His trajectory carried him so close to the car that he could feel the heat of the radiator on his flank. His forepaws struck Robby and thrust him out of danger. They fell to the ground together, just as the car ground over the last of Wolf's caudal vertebrae.

The cute dish screamed. "Homer! Did we hit them?"

Homer said nothing, and the jalopy zoomed on.

Robby's screams were louder. "You hurt me!! You hurt me! *Baaaaad* woof-woof!"

His mother appeared on the porch and joined in with her own howls of rage. The cacophony was terrific. Wolf let out one wailing yelp of his own, to make it perfect and to lament his crushed tail, and dashed on. This was no time to clear up misunderstandings.

But the two delays had been enough. Robby and the policeman had proved the perfect unwitting tools of Oscar Fearing. As Wolf approached Emily's little bungalow, he saw a gray sedan drive off. In the rear was a small, slim girl, and she was struggling.

Even a werewolf's lithe speed cannot equal that of a motor car. After a block of pursuit, Wolf gave up and sat back on his haunches panting. It felt funny, he thought even in that tense moment, not to be able to sweat, to have to open your mouth and stick out your tongue and . . .

"Trouble?" inquired a solicitous voice.

This time Wolf recognized the cat. "Heavens, yes," he assented wholeheartedly. "More than you ever dreamed of."

"Food shortage?" the cat asked. "But that toddler back there is nice and plump."

"Shut up," Wolf snarled.

"Sorry; I was just judging from what Confucius told me about werewolves. You don't mean to tell me that you're an altruistic were?"

"I guess I am. I know werewolves are supposed to go around slaughtering, but right now I've got to save a life."

"You expect me to believe that?"

"It's the truth."

"Ah," the cat reflected philosophically. "Truth is a dark and deceitful thing."

Wolfe Wolf was on his feet. "Thanks," he barked. "You've done it."

"Done what?"

"See you later." And Wolf was off at top speed for the Temple of the Dark Truth.

That was the best chance. That was Fearing's headquarters. The odds were at least even that when it wasn't being used for services it was the hangout of his ring, especially since the consulate had been closed in San Francisco. Again the wild running and leaping, the narrow escapes; and where Wolf had not taken these too seriously before, he knew now that he might be immune to bullets, but certainly not to being run over. His tail still stung and ached tormentingly. But he had to get there. He had to clear his own reputation, he kept reminding himself; but what he really thought was, I have to save Emily.

A block from the Temple he heard the crackle of gunfire. Pistol shots and, he'd swear, machine guns, too. He couldn't figure what it meant, but he pressed on. Then a bright-yellow roadster passed him and a vivid flash came from its window. Instinctively he ducked. You might be immune to bullets, but you still didn't just stand still for them.

The roadster was gone and he was about to follow when a glint of bright metal caught his eye. The bullet that had missed him had hit a brick wall and ricocheted back onto the sidewalk. It glittered there in front of him—pure silver!

This, he realized abruptly, meant the end of his immunity. Fearing had believed Gloria's story, and with his smattering of occult lore he had known the successful counterweapon. A bullet, from now on, might mean no more needle sting, but instant death.

And so Wolfe Wolf went straight on.

He approached the Temple cautiously, lurking behind shrubbery. And he was not the only lurker. Before the Temple, crouching in the shelter of a car every window of which was shattered, were Fergus O'Breen and a moonfaced giant. Each held an automatic, and they were taking pot shots at the steeple.

Wolf's keen lupine hearing could catch their words even above the firing. "Gabe's around back," Moonface was explaining. "But it's no use. Know what that damned steeple is? It's a revolving machine-gun turret. They've been ready for something like this. Only two men in there, far as we can tell, but that turret covers all the approaches."

"Only two?" Fergus muttered.

"And the girl. They brought a girl here with them. If she's still alive."

Fergus took careful aim at the steeple, fired, and ducked back behind the car as a bullet missed him by millimeters. "Missed him again! By all the kings that ever ruled Tara, Moon, there's got to be a way in there. How about tear gas?"

Moon snorted. "Think you can reach the firing gap in that armored turret at this angle?"

"That girl . . ." said Fergus.

Wolf waited no longer. As he sprang forward, the gunner noticed him and shifted his fire. It was like a needle shower in which all the spray is solid steel. Wolf's nerves ached with the pain of reknitting. But at least machine guns apparently didn't fire silver.

The front door was locked, but the force of his drive carried him through and added a throbbing ache in his shoulder to his other comforts. The lower-floor guard, a pasty-faced individual with a jutting Adam's apple, sprang up, pistol in hand. Behind him, in the midst of the litter of the cult, ceremonial robes, incense burners, curious books, even a Ouija board, lay Emily.

Pasty-face fired. The bullet struck Wolf full in the chest and for an instant he expected death. But this, too, was lead, and he jumped forward. It was not his usual powerful leap. His strength was almost spent by now. He needed to lie on cool earth and let his nerves knit. And this spring was only enough to grapple with his foe, not to throw him.

The man reversed his useless automatic and brought its butt thudding down on the beast's skull. Wolf reeled back, lost his balance, and fell to the floor. For a moment he could not rise. The temptation was so strong just to lie there and . . .

The girl moved. Her bound hands grasped a corner of the Ouija board. Somehow, she stumbled to her rope-tied feet and raised her arms. Just as Pasty-face rushed for the prostrate wolf, she brought the heavy board down.

Wolf was on his feet now. There was an instant of temptation. His eyes fixed themselves to the jut of that Adam's apple, and his long tongue licked his jowls. Then he heard the machine-gun fire from the turret, and tore himself from Pasty-face's unconscious form.

Ladders are hard on a wolf, damned near impossible. But if you use your jaws to grasp the rung above you and pull up, it can be done. He was halfway up the ladder when the gunner heard him. The firing stopped, and Wolf heard a rich German oath in what he automatically recognized as an East Prussian dialect with possible Lithuanian influences. Then he saw the man himself, a broken-nosed blond, staring down the ladder well.

The other man's bullets had been lead. So this must be the one with the silver. But it was too late to turn back now. Wolf bit the next rung and hauled up as the bullet struck his snout and stung through. The blond's eyes widened as he fired again and Wolf climbed another rung. After the third shot he withdrew precipitately from the opening.

Shots still sounded from below, but the gunner did not return them. He stood frozen against the wall of the turret watching in horror as the wolf emerged from the well. Wolf halted and tried to get his breath. He was dead with fatigue and stress, but this man must be vanquished.

The blond raised his pistol, sighted carefully, and fired once more. He stood for one terrible instant, gazing at this deathless wolf and knowing from his grandmother's stories what it must be. Then deliberately he clamped his teeth on the muzzle of the automatic and fired again.

Wolf had not yet eaten in his wolf's body, but food must have been transferred from the human stomach to the lupine. There was at least enough for him to be extensively sick.

Getting down the ladder was impossible. He jumped. He had never heard anything about a wolf's landing on its feet, but it seemed to work. He dragged his weary and bruised body along to where Emily sat by the still unconscious Pastyface, his discarded pistol in her hand. She wavered as the wolf approached her, as though uncertain yet as to whether he was friend or foe.

Time was short. With the machine gun silenced, Fergus and his companions would be invading the Temple at any minute. Wolf hurriedly nosed about and found the planchette of the Ouija board. He pushed the heart-shaped bit of wood onto the board and began to shove it around with his paw.

Emily watched, intent and puzzled. "A," she said aloud. "B—S—"

Wolf finished the word and edged round so that he stood directly beside one of the ceremonial robes. "Are you trying to say something?" Emily frowned.

Wolf wagged his tail in vehement affirmation and began again.

"A—" Emily repeated. "B—S—A—R—"

He could already hear approaching footsteps.

"—K—A— What on earth does that mean? *Absarka*—"

Ex-professor Wolfe Wolf hastily wrapped his naked human body in the cloak of the Dark Truth. Before either he or Emily knew quite what was happening, he had folded her in his arms, kissed her in a most thorough expression of gratitude, and fainted.

Even Wolf's human nose could tell, when he awakened, that he was in a hospital. His body was still limp and exhausted. The bare patch on his neck, where the policeman had pulled out the hair, still stung, and there was a lump where the butt of the automatic had connected. His tail, or where his tail had been, sent twinges through him if he moved. But the sheets were cool and he was at rest and Emily was safe.

"I don't know how you got in there, Mr. Wolf, or what you did; but I want you to know you've done your country a signal service." It was the moonfaced giant speaking.

Fergus O'Breen was sitting beside the bed too. "Congratulations, Wolf. And I don't know if the doctor would approve, but here."

Wolfe Wolf drank the whiskey gratefully and looked a question at the huge man.

"This is Moon Lafferty," said Fergus. "FBI man. He's been helping me track down this ring of spies ever since I first got wind of them."

"You got them—all?" Wolf asked.

"Picked up Fearing and Garton at the hotel," Lafferty rumbled.

"But how— I thought—"

"You thought we were out for you?" Fergus answered. "That was Garton's idea, but I didn't quite tumble. You see, I'd already talked to your secretary. I knew it was Fearing she'd wanted to see. And when I asked around about Fearing, and learned of the Temple and the defense researches of some of its members, the whole picture cleared up."

"Wonderful work, Mr. Wolf," said Lafferty. "Any time we can do anything for you— And how you got into that machine-gun turret— Well, O'Breen, I'll see you later. Got to check up on the rest of this roundup. Pleasant convalescence to you, Wolf."

Fergus waited until the G-man had left the room. Then he leaned over the bed and asked confidentially, "How about it, Wolf? Going back to your acting career?"

Wolf gasped. "What acting career?"

"Still going to play Tookah? If Metropolis makes *Fangs* with Miss Garton in a Federal prison."

Wolf fumbled for words. "What sort of nonsense—"

"Come on, Wolf. It's pretty clear I know that much. Might as well tell me the whole story."

Still dazed, Wolf told it. "But how in heaven's name did you know it?" he concluded.

Fergus grinned. "Look. Dorothy Sayers said someplace that in a detective story the supernatural may be introduced only to be dispelled. Sure, that's swell. Only in real life there come times when it won't be dispelled. And this was one. There was too damned much. There were your eyebrows and fingers, there were the obviously real magical powers of your friend, there were the tricks which no dog could possibly do without signals, there was the way the other dogs whimpered and cringed— I'm pretty hardheaded, Wolf, but I'm Irish. I'll string along only so far with the materialistic, but too much coincidence is too much."

"Fearing believed it too," Wolf reflected. "But one thing that worries me: if they used a silver bullet on me once, why were all the rest of them lead? Why was I safe from then on?"

"Well," said Fergus, "I'll tell you. Because it wasn't 'they' who fired the silver bullet. You see, Wolf, up till the last minute I thought you were on 'their' side. I somehow didn't associate good will with a werewolf. So I got a mold from a gunsmith and paid a visit to a jeweler and— I'm damned glad I missed," he added sincerely.

"*You're* glad!"

"But look. Previous question stands. Are you going back to acting? Because if not, I've got a suggestion."

"Which is?"

"You say you fretted about how to be a practical, commercial werewolf. All right. You're strong and fast. You can terrify people even to commit suicide. You can overhear conversations that no human being could get in on. You're invulnerable to bullets. Can you tell me better qualifications for a G-man?"

Wolf goggled. "Me? A G-man?"

"Moon's been telling me how badly they need new men. They've changed the qualifications lately so that your language knowledge'll do instead of the law or accounting they used to require. And after what you did today, there won't be any trouble about a little academic scandal in your past. Moon's pretty sold on you."

Wolf was speechless. Only three days ago he had been in torment because he was not an actor or a G-man. Now—

"Think it over," said Fergus.

"I will. Indeed I will. Oh, and one other thing. Has there been any trace of Ozzy?"

"Nary a sign."

"I like that man. I've got to try to find him and—"

"If he's the magician I think he is, he's staying up there only because he's decided he likes it."

"I don't know. Magic's tricky. Heavens knows I've learned that. I'm going to try to do my damnedest for that fringe-bearded old colleague."

"Wish you luck. Shall I send in your other guest?"

"Who's that?"

"Your secretary. Here on business, no doubt."

Fergus disappeared discreetly as he admitted Emily. She walked over to the bed and took Wolf's hand. His eyes drank in her quiet, charming simplicity, and his mind wondered what freak of belated adolescence had made him succumb to the blatant glamour of Gloria.

They were silent for a long time. Then at once they both said, "How can I thank you? You saved my life."

Wolf laughed. "Let's not argue. Let's say we saved our life."

"You mean that?" Emily asked gravely.

Wolf pressed her hand. "Aren't you tired of being an office wife?"

In the bazaar of Darjeeling, Chulundra Lingasuta stared at his rope in numb amazement. Young Ali had climbed up only five minutes ago, but now as he descended he was a hundred pounds heavier and wore a curious fringe of beard.

Elsewhen

"My dear Agatha," Mr. Partridge announced at the breakfast table, "I have invented the world's first successful time machine."

His sister showed no signs of being impressed. "I suppose this will run the electric bill up even higher," she observed.

Mr. Partridge listened meekly to the inevitable lecture. When it was over, he protested, "But, my dear, you have just listened to an announcement that no woman on earth has ever heard before. Never before in human history has anyone produced an actual working model of a time-traveling machine."

"Hm-m-m," said Agatha Partridge. "What good is it?"

"Its possibilities are untold." Mr. Partridge's pale little eyes lit up. "We can observe our pasts and perhaps even correct their errors. We can learn the secrets of the ancients. We can plot the uncharted course of the future—new conquistadors invading brave new continents of unmapped time. We can—"

"Will anyone pay money for that?"

"They will flock to me to pay it," said Mr. Partridge smugly.

His sister began to look impressed. "And how far can you travel with your time machine?"

Mr. Partridge buttered a piece of toast with absorbed concentration, but it was no use. His sister repeated the question: "How far can you go?"

"Not very far," Mr. Partridge admitted reluctantly. "In fact," he added hastily as he saw a more specific question forming, "hardly at all. And only one way. But remember," he went on, gathering courage, "the Wright brothers did not cross the Atlantic in their first model. Marconi did not launch radio with—"

Agatha's brief interest had completely subsided. "I thought so," she said. "You'd still better watch the electric bill."

It would be that way, Mr. Partridge thought, wherever he went, whomever he saw. "How far can you go?" "Hardly at all." "Good day, sir." People cannot be made to see that to move along the time line with free volitional motion for even one fraction of a second is as great a miracle as to zoom spectacularly ahead to 5900 A.D. He had, he could remember, felt disappointed at first himself—

The discovery had been made by accident. An experiment which he was working on—part of his long and fruitless attempt to re-create by modern scientific method

53

the supposed results described in ancient alchemical works—had necessitated the setting up of a powerful magnetic field. And part of the apparatus within this field was a chronometer.

Mr. Partridge noted the time when he began his experiment. It was exactly fourteen seconds after nine thirty. And it was precisely at that moment that the tremor came. It was not a serious shock. To one who, like Mr. Partridge, had spent the past twenty years in southern California it was hardly noticeable. But when he looked back at the chronometer, the dial read ten thirteen.

Time can pass quickly when you are absorbed in your work, but not so quickly as all that. Mr. Partridge looked at his pocket watch. It said nine thirty-one. Suddenly, in a space of seconds, the best chronometer available had gained forty-two minutes.

The more Mr. Partridge considered the matter, the more irresistibly one chain of logic forced itself upon him. The chronometer was accurate; therefore it had registered those forty-two minutes correctly. It had not registered them here and now; therefore the shock had jarred it to where it could register them. It had not moved in any of the three dimensions of space; therefore—

The chronometer had gone back in time forty-two minutes, and had registered those minutes in reaching the present again. Or was it only a matter of minutes? The chronometer was an eight-day one. Might it have been twelve hours and forty-two minutes? Forty-eight hours? Ninety-six? A hundred and ninety-two?

And why and how and—the dominant question in Mr. Partridge's mind—could the same device be made to work with a living being?

It would be fruitless to relate in detail the many experiments which Mr. Partridge eagerly performed to verify and check his discovery. They were purely empirical in nature, for Mr. Partridge was that type of inventor who is short on theory but long on gadgetry. He did frame a very rough working hypothesis—that the sudden shock had caused the magnetic field to rotate into the temporal dimension, where it set up a certain—he groped for words—a certain negative potential of entropy, which drew things backward in time. But he would leave the doubtless highly debatable theory to the academicians. What he must do was perfect the machine, render it generally usable, and then burst forth upon an astonished world as Harrison Partridge, the first time traveler. His dry little ego glowed and expanded at the prospect.

There were the experiments in artificial shock which produced synthetically the earthquake effect. There were the experiments with the white mice which proved that the journey through time was harmless to life. There were the experiments with the chronometer which established that the time traversed varied directly as the square of the power expended on the electromagnet.

But these experiments also established that the time elapsed had not been twelve hours nor any multiple thereof, but simply forty-two minutes. And with the equipment at his disposal, it was impossible for Mr. Partridge to stretch that period any further than a trifle under two hours.

This, Mr. Partridge told himself, was ridiculous. Time travel at such short range, and only to the past, entailed no possible advantages. Oh, perhaps some piddling ones—once, after the mice had convinced him that he could safely venture himself, he had a lengthy piece of calculation which he wished to finish before dinner. An hour was simply not time enough for it; so at six o'clock he moved himself back to five again, and by working two hours in the space from five to six finished his task easily by dinner time. And one evening when, in his preoccupation, he had forgotten his favorite radio quiz program until it was ending, it was simplicity itself to go back to the beginning and comfortably hear it through.

But though such trifling uses as this might be an important part of the work of the time machine once it was established—possibly the strongest commercial selling point for inexpensive home sets—they were not spectacular or startling enough to make the reputation of the machine and—more important—the reputation of Harrison Partridge.

The Great Harrison Partridge would have untold wealth. He could pension off his sister Agatha and never have to see her again. He would have untold prestige and glamor, despite his fat and his baldness, and the beautiful and aloof Faith Preston would fall into his arms like a ripe plum. He would—

It was while he was indulging in one of these dreams of power that Faith Preston herself entered his workshop. She was wearing a white sports dress and looking so fresh and immaculate that the whole room seemed to glow with her presence.

"I came out here before I saw your sister," she said. Her voice was as cool and bright as her dress. "I wanted you to be the first to know. Simon and I are going to be married next month."

Mr. Partridge never remembered what was said after that. He imagined that she made her usual comments about the shocking disarray of his shop and her usual polite inquiries as to his current researches. He imagined that he offered the conventional good wishes and extended his congratulations, too, to that damned young whippersnapper Simon Ash. But all his thoughts were that he wanted her and needed her and that the great, the irresistible Harrison Partridge must come into being before next month.

Money. That was it. Money. With money he could build the tremendous machinery necessary to carry a load of power—and money was needed for that power, too—that would produce truly impressive results. To travel back even as much as a quarter of a century would be enough to dazzle the world. To appear at the Versailles peace conference, say, and expound to the delegates the inevitable results of their too lenient—or too strict?—terms. Or with unlimited money to course down the centuries, down the millennia, bringing back lost arts, forgotten secrets—

"Hm-m-m!" said Agatha. "Still mooning after that girl? Don't be an old fool."

He had not seen Agatha come in. He did not quite see her now. He saw a sort of vision of a cornucopia that would give him money that would give him the apparatus that would give him his time machine that would give him success that would give him Faith.

"If you must moon instead of working—if indeed you call this work—you might at least turn off a few switches," Agatha snapped. "Do you think we're made of money?"

Mechanically he obeyed.

"It makes you sick," Agatha droned on, "when you think how some people spend their money. Cousin Stanley! Hiring this Simon Ash as a secretary for nothing on earth but to look after his library and his collections. So much money he can't do anything but waste it! And all Great-uncle Max's money coming to him too, when we could use it so nicely. If only it weren't for Cousin Stanley, I'd be an heiress. And then—"

Mr. Partridge was about to observe that even as an heiress Agatha would doubtless have been the same intolerant old maid. But two thoughts checked his tongue. One was the sudden surprising revelation that even Agatha had her inner yearnings, too. And the other was an overwhelming feeling of gratitude to her.

"Yes," Mr. Partridge repeated slowly. "If it weren't for Cousin Stanley—"

By means as simple as this, murderers are made.

The chain of logic was so strong that moral questions hardly entered into the situation.

Great-uncle Max was infinitely old. That he should live another year was out of the question. And if his son Stanley were to pre-decease him, then Harrison and Agatha Partridge would be his only living relatives. And Maxwell Harrison was as infinitely rich as he was infinitely old.

Therefore Stanley must die, and his death must be accomplished with a maximum of personal safety. The means for that safety were at hand. For the one completely practical purpose of a short-range time machine, Mr. Partridge had suddenly realized, was to provide an alibi for murder.

The chief difficulty was in contriving a portable version of the machine which would operate over a considerable period of time. The first model had a traveling range of two minutes. But by the end of the week, Mr. Partridge had constructed a portable time machine which was good for forty-five minutes. He needed nothing more save a sharp knife. There was, Mr. Partridge thought, something crudely horrifying about guns.

That Friday afternoon he entered Cousin Stanley's library at five o'clock. This was an hour when the eccentric man of wealth always devoted himself to quiet and scholarly contemplation of his treasures. The butler, Bracket, had been reluctant to announce him, but "Tell my cousin," Mr. Partridge said, "that I have discovered a new entry for his bibliography."

The most recent of Cousin Stanley's collecting manias was fiction based upon factual murders. He had already built up the definitive library on the subject. Soon he intended to publish the definitive bibliography. And the promise of a new item was an assured open-sesame.

The ponderous gruff joviality of Stanley Harrison's greeting took no heed of the odd apparatus he carried. Everyone knew that Mr. Partridge was a crackpot inventor.

"Bracket tells me you've got something for me," Cousin Stanley boomed. "Glad to hear it. Have a drink? What is it?"

"No thank you." Something in Mr. Partridge rebelled at accepting the hospitality of his victim. "A Hungarian friend of mine was mentioning a novel about one Bela Kiss."

"Kiss?" Cousin Stanley's face lit up with a broad beam. "Splendid! Never could see why no one used him before. Woman killer. Landru type. Always fascinating. Kept 'em in empty gasoline tins. Never could have been caught if there hadn't been a gasoline shortage. Constable thought he was hoarding, checked the tins, found corpses. Beautiful! Now if you'll give me the details—"

Cousin Stanley, pencil poised over a P-slip, leaned over the desk. And Mr. Partridge struck.

He had checked the anatomy of the blow, just as he had checked the name of an obscure but interesting murderer. The knife went truly home, and there was a gurgle and the terrible spastic twitch of dying flesh.

Mr. Partridge was now an heir and a murderer, but he had time to be conscious of neither fact. He went through his carefully rehearsed motions, his mind numb and blank. He latched the windows of the library and locked each door. This was to be an impossible crime, one that could never conceivably be proved on him or on any innocent.

Mr. Partridge stood beside the corpse in the midst of the perfectly locked room. It was four minutes past five. He screamed twice, very loudly, in an unrecognizably harsh voice. Then he plugged his portable instrument into a floor outlet and turned a switch.

It was four nineteen. Mr. Partridge unplugged his machine. The room was empty and the door open.

Mr. Partridge knew his way reasonably well about his cousin's house. He got out without meeting anyone. He tucked the machine into the rumble seat of his car and drove off to Faith Preston's. Toward the end of his long journey across town he carefully drove through a traffic light and received a citation noting the time as four-fifty. He reached Faith's at four fifty-four, ten minutes before the murder he had just committed.

Simon Ash had been up all Thursday night cataloging Stanley Harrison's latest acquisitions. Still he had risen at his usual hour that Friday to get through the morning's mail before his luncheon date with Faith. By four thirty that afternoon he was asleep on his feet.

He knew that his employer would be coming into the library in half an hour. And Stanley Harrison liked solitude for his daily five-o'clock gloating and meditation. But the secretary's work desk was hidden around a corner of the library's stacks, and no other physical hunger can be quite so dominantly compelling as the need for sleep.

Simon Ash's shaggy blond head sank onto the desk. His sleep-heavy hand shoved a pile of cards to the floor, and his mind only faintly registered the thought that they would all have to be alphabetized again. He was too sleepy to think of anything but pleasant things, like the sailboat at Balboa which brightened his weekends, or the hiking trip in the Sierras planned for his next vacation, or above all Faith. Faith the fresh and lovely and perfect, who would be his next month—

There was a smile on Simon's rugged face as he slept. But he woke with a harsh scream ringing in his head. He sprang to his feet and looked out from the stacks into the library.

The dead hulk that slumped over the desk with the hilt protruding from its back was unbelievable, but even more incredible was the other spectacle. There was a man. His back was toward Simon, but he seemed faintly familiar. He stood close to a complicated piece of gadgetry. There was the click of a switch.

Then there was nothing.

Nothing in the room at all but Simon Ash and an infinity of books. And their dead owner.

Ash ran to the desk. He tried to lift Stanley Harrison, tried to draw out the knife, then realized how hopeless was any attempt to revive life in that body. He reached for the phone, then stopped as he heard the loud knocking on the door.

Over the raps came the butler's voice. "Mr. Harrison! Are you all right, sir?" A pause, more knocking, and then, "Mr. Harrison! Let me in, sir! Are you all right?"

Simon raced to the door. It was locked, and he wasted almost a minute groping for the key at his feet, while the butler's entreaties became more urgent. At last Simon opened the door.

Bracket stared at him—stared at his sleep-red eyes, his blood-red hands, and beyond him at what sat at the desk. "Mr. Ash, sir," the butler gasped. "What have you done?"

Faith Preston was home, of course. No such essential element of Mr. Partridge's plan could have been left to chance. She worked best in the late afternoons, she said, when she was getting hungry for dinner; and she was working hard this week on some entries for a national contest in soap carving.

The late-afternoon sun was bright in her room, which you might call her studio if you were politely disposed, her garret if you were not. It picked out the few perfect touches of color in the scanty furnishings and converted them into bright aureoles surrounding the perfect form of Faith.

The radio was playing softly. She worked best to music, and that, too, was an integral portion of Mr. Partridge's plan.

Six minutes of unmemorable small talk— What are you working on? How lovely! And what have you been doing lately? Pottering around as usual. And the plans for the wedding?—and then Mr. Partridge held up a pleading hand for silence.

"When you hear the tone," the radio announced, "the time will be exactly five seconds before five o'clock."

"I forgot to wind my watch," Mr. Partridge observed casually. "I've been wondering all day exactly what time it was." He set his perfectly accurate watch.

He took a long breath. And now at last he knew that he was a new man. He was at last the Great Harrison Partridge.

"What's the matter?" Faith asked. "You look funny. Could I make you some tea?"

"No. Nothing. I'm all right." He walked around behind her and looked over her shoulder at the graceful nude emerging from her imprisonment in a cake of soap. "Exquisite, my dear," he observed. "Exquisite."

"I'm glad you like it. I'm never happy with female nudes; I don't think women sculptors ever are. But I wanted to try it."

Mr. Partridge ran a dry hot finger along the front of the soapen nymph. "A delightful texture," he remarked. "Almost as delightful as—" His tongue left the speech unfinished, but his hand rounded out the thought along Faith's cool neck and cheek.

"Why, Mr. Partridge!" She laughed.

The laugh was too much. One does not laugh at the Great Harrison Partridge. time traveler and perfect murderer. There was nothing in his plan that called for what followed. But something outside of any plans brought him to his knees, forced his arms around Faith's lithe body, pressed tumultuous words of incoherent ardor from his unwonted lips.

He saw fear growing in her eyes. He saw her hand dart out in instinctive defense and he wrested the knife from it. Then his own eyes glinted as he looked at the knife. It was little, ridiculously little. You could never plunge it through a man's back. But it was sharp—a throat, the artery of a wrist—

His muscles had relaxed for an instant. In that moment of non-vigilance, Faith had wrested herself free. She did not look backward. He heard the clatter of her steps down the stairs, and for a fraction of time the Great Harrison Partridge vanished and Mr. Partridge knew only fear. If he had aroused her hatred, if she should not swear to his alibi—

The fear was soon over. He knew that no motives of enmity could cause Faith to swear to anything but the truth. She was honest. And the enmity itself would vanish when she realized what manner of man had chosen her for his own.

It was not the butler who opened the door to Faith. It was a uniformed policeman, who said, "Whaddaya want here?"

"I've got to see Simon . . . Mr. Ash," she blurted out.

The officer's expression changed. "C'mon," and he beckoned her down the long hall.

The tall young man in plain clothes said, "My name is Jackson. Won't you sit down? Cigarette?" She waved the pack away nervously. "Hinkle says you wanted to speak to Mr. Ash?"

"Yes, I—"

"Are you Miss Preston? His fiancée?"

"Yes." Her eyes widened. "How did you— Oh, has something happened to Simon?"

The young officer looked unhappy. "I'm afraid something has. Though he's perfectly safe at the moment. You see, he— Damn it all, I never have been able to break such news gracefully."

The uniformed officer broke in. "They took him down to headquarters, miss. You see, it looks like he bumped off his boss."

Faith did not quite faint, but the world was uncertain for a few minutes. She hardly heard Lieutenant Jackson's explanations or the message of comfort that Simon had left for her. She simply held very tight to her chair until the ordinary outlines of things came back and she could swallow again.

"Simon is innocent," she said firmly.

"I hope he is." Jackson sounded sincere. "I've never enjoyed pinning a murder on as decent-seeming a fellow as your fiancé. But the case, I'm afraid, is too clear. If he is innocent, he'll have to tell us a more plausible story than his first one. Murderers that turn a switch and vanish into thin air are not highly regarded by most juries."

Faith rose. The world was firm again, and one fact was clear. 'Simon is innocent," she repeated. "And I'm going to prove that. Will you please tell me where I can get a detective?"

The uniformed officer laughed. Jackson started to, but hesitated. "Of course, Miss Preston, the city's paying my salary under the impression that I'm one. But I see what you mean: You want a freer investigator, who won't be hampered by such considerations as the official viewpoint, or even the facts of the case. Well, it's your privilege."

"Thank you. And how do I go about finding out?"

"Acting as an employment agency's a little out of my line. But rather than see you tie up with some shyster shamus, I'll make a recommendation, a man I've worked with, or against, on a half dozen cases. And I think this set-up is just impossible enough to appeal to him. He likes lost causes."

"Lost?" It is a dismal word.

"And in fairness I should add they aren't always lost after he tackles them. The name's O'Breen—Fergus O'Breen."

Mr. Partridge dined out that night. He could not face the harshness of Agatha's tongue. After dinner he made a round of the bars on the Strip and played the pleasant game of "If only they knew who was sitting beside them." He felt like Harun-al-Rashid, and liked the glow of the feeling.

On his way home he bought the next morning's *Times* at an intersection and pulled over to the curb to examine it. He had expected sensational headlines on the mysterious murder which had the police completely baffled. Instead he read:

SECRETARY SLAYS EMPLOYER

After a moment of shock the Great Harrison Partridge was himself again. He had not intended this. He would not willingly cause unnecessary pain to anyone. But lesser individuals who obstruct the plans of the great must take their medicine.

Mr. Partridge drove home, contented. He could spend the night on the cot in his workshop and thus see that much the less of Agatha. He clicked on the workshop light and froze.

There was a man standing by the time machine. The original large machine. Mr. Partridge's feeling of superhuman selfconfidence was enormous but easily undermined, like a vast balloon that needs only the smallest pin prick to shatter it. For a moment he envisioned a scientific master mind of the police who had deduced his method, tracked him here, and discovered his invention.

Then the figure turned.

Mr. Partridge's terror was only slightly lessened. For the figure was that of Mr. Partridge. There was a nightmare instant when he thought of Doppelgänger, Poe's William Wilson, of dissociated personalities, of Dr. Jekyll and Mr. Hyde. Then this other Mr. Partridge cried aloud and hurried from the room, and the entering one collapsed.

A trough must follow a crest. And now blackness was the inexorable aftermath of Mr. Partridge's elation. His successful murder, his ardor with Faith, his evening as Harun-al-Rashid, all vanished. He heard horrible noises in the room, and realized only after minutes that they were his own sobs.

Finally he pulled himself to his feet. He bathed his face in cold water from the sink, but still terror gnawed at him. Only one thing could reassure him. Only one thing could still convince him that he was the Great Harrison Partridge. And that was his noble machine. He touched it, caressed it as one might a fine and dearly loved horse.

Mr. Partridge was nervous. and he had been drinking more than his frugal customs allowed. His hand brushed the switch. He looked up and saw himself entering the door. He cried aloud and hurried from the room.

In the cool night air he slowly understood. He had accidentally sent himself back to the time he entered the room, so that upon entering he had seen himself. There was nothing more to it than that. But he made a careful mental note: Always take care, when using the machine, to avoid returning to a time-and-place where you already are. Never meet yourself. The dangers of psychological shock are too great.

Mr. Partridge felt better now. He had frightened himself, had he? Well, he would not be the last to tremble in fear of the Great Harrison Partridge.

Fergus O'Breen, the detective recommended—if you could call it that—by the police lieutenant, had his office in a ramshackle old building at Second and Spring. There were two, she imagined they were clients, in the waiting room ahead of Faith. One looked like the most sodden type of Skid Row loafer, and the elegant disarray of the other could mean nothing but the lower reaches of the upper layers of Hollywood.

The detective, when Faith finally saw him, inclined in costume toward the latter, but he wore sports clothes as though they were pleasantly comfortable, rather than as the badge of a caste. He was a thin young man, with sharpish features and very red hair. What you noticed most were his eyes—intensely green and alive with a restless curiosity. They made you feel that his work would never end until that curiosity had been satisfied.

He listened in silence to Faith's story, not moving save to make an occasional note. He was attentive and curious, but Faith's spirits sank as she saw the curiosity in the green eyes deaden to hopelessness. When she was through, he rose, lit a cigarette, and began pacing about the narrow inner office.

"I think better this way," he apologized. "I hope you don't mind. But what have I got to think about? The facts you've told me are better than a signed confession for any jury."

"But Simon is innocent," Faith insisted. "I know him, Mr. O'Breen. It isn't possible that he could have done a thing like that."

"I understand how you feel. But what have we got to go on besides your feelings? I'm not saying they're wrong; I'm trying to show you how the police and the court would look at it."

"But there wasn't any reason for Simon to kill Mr. Harrison. He had a good job. He liked it. We were going to get married. Now he hasn't any job or . . . or anything."

"I know." The detective continued to pace. "That's the one point you've got—absence of motive. But they've convicted without motive before this. And rightly enough. Anything can be a motive. The most outrageous and fascinating French murder since Landru was committed because the electric toaster didn't work right that morning. But let's look at motives. Mr. Harrison was a wealthy man; where does all that money go?"

"Simon helped draft his will. It all goes to libraries and foundations and things. A little to the servants, of course—"

"A little can turn the trick. But no near relatives?"

"His father's still alive. He's terribly old. But he's so rich himself that it'd be silly to leave him anything."

Fergus snapped his fingers. "Max Harrison! Of course. The superannuated robber-baron, to put it politely, who's been due to die any time these past ten years. And leave a mere handful of millions. There's a motive for you."

"How so?"

"The murderer could profit from Stanley Harrison's death, not directly if all his money goes to foundations, but indirectly from his father. Combination of two classic motives—profit and elimination. Who's next in line for old man Harrison's fortune?"

"I'm not sure. But I do know two people who are sort of second cousins or something. I think they're the only living relatives. Agatha and Harrison Partridge."

Fergus' eyes were brightening again. "At least it's a lead. Simon Ash had no motive and one Harrison Partridge had a honey. Which proves nothing, but gives you some place to start."

"Only—" Faith protested. "Only Mr. Partridge couldn't possibly have done it either."

Fergus stopped pacing. "Look, madam. I am willing to grant the unassailable innocence of one suspect on a client's word. Otherwise I'd never get clients. But if every individual who comes up is going to turn out to be someone in whose pureness of soul you have implicit faith and—"

"It isn't that. Not just that. The murder was just after five o'clock, the butler says. And Mr. Partridge was with me then, and I live way across town from Mr. Harrison's."

"You're sure of the time?"

"We heard the five-o'clock radio signal and he set his watch." Her voice was troubled and she tried not to remember the awful minutes afterward.

"Did he make a point of it?"

"Well . . . we were talking and he stopped and held up his hand and we listened to the bong."

"Hm-m-m." This statement seemed to strike the detective especially. "Well, there's still the sister. And anyway, the Partridges give me a point of departure, which is what I needed."

Faith looked at him hopefully. "Then you'll take the case?"

"I'll take it. God knows why. I don't want to raise your hopes, because if ever I saw an unpromising set-up it's this. But I'll take it. I think it's because I can't resist the pleasure of having a detective lieutenant shove a case into my lap."

"Bracket, was it usual for that door to be locked when Mr. Harrison was in the library?"

The butler's manner was imperfect; he could not decide whether a hired detective was a gentleman or a servant. "No," he said, politely enough but without a "sir." "No, it was most unusual."

"Did you notice if it was locked earlier?"

"It was not. I showed a visitor in shortly before the . . . before this dreadful thing happened."

"A visitor?" Fergus' eyes glinted. He began to have visions of all the elaborate possibilities of locking doors from the outside so that they seem locked on the inside. "And when was this?"

"Just on five o'clock, I thought. But the gentleman called here today to offer his sympathy, and he remarked, when I mentioned the subject, that he believed it to have been earlier."

"And who was this gentleman?"

"Mr. Harrison Partridge."

Hell, thought Fergus. There goes another possibility. It must have been much earlier if he was at Faith Preston's by five. And you can't tamper with radio time signals as you might with a clock. However— "Notice anything odd about Mr. Partridge? Anything in his manner?"

"Yesterday? No, I did not. He was carrying some curious contraption—I hardly noticed what. I imagine it was some recent invention of his which he wished to show to Mr. Harrison."

"He's an inventor, this Partridge? But you said yesterday. Anything odd about him today?"

"I don't know. It's difficult to describe. But there was something about him as though he had changed—grown, perhaps."

"Grown up?"

"No. Just grown."

"Now, Mr. Ash, this man you claim you saw—"

"Claim! Damn it, O'Breen, don't you believe me either?"

"Easy does it. The main thing for you is that Miss Preston believes you, and I'd say that's a lot. Now this man you saw, if that makes you any happier in this jail, did he remind you of anyone?"

"I don't know. It's bothered me. I didn't get a good look, but there was something familiar—"

"You say he had some sort of machine beside him?"

Simon Ash was suddenly excited. "You've got it. That's it."

"That's what?"

"Who it was. Or who I thought it was. Mr. Partridge. He's some sort of a cousin of Mr. Harrison's. Screwball inventor."

"Miss Preston, I'll have to ask you more questions. Too many signposts keep pointing one way, and even if that way's a blind alley I've got to go up it. When Mr. Partridge called on you yesterday afternoon, what did he do to you?"

"Do to me?" Faith's voice wavered. "What on earth do you mean?"

"It was obvious from your manner earlier that there was something about that scene you wanted to forget."

"He— Oh, no, I can't. Must I tell you, Mr. O'Breen?"

"Simon Ash says the jail is not bad after what he's heard of jails, but still—"

"All right, I'll tell you. But it was strange. I . . . I suppose I've known for a long time that Mr. Partridge was—well, you might say in love with me. But he's so much older than I am and he's very quiet and never said anything about it and— well, there it was, and I never gave it much thought one way or another. But yesterday— It was as though . . . as though he were possessed. All at once it seemed to burst out and there he was making love to me. Frightfully, horribly, I couldn't stand it. I ran away. That's all there was to it. But it was terrible."

"You pitched me a honey this time, Andy."

Lieutenant Jackson grinned. "Thought you'd appreciate it, Fergus."

"But look: What have you got against Ash but the physical set-up of a locked room? The oldest cliché in murderous fiction, and not unheard of in fact."

"Show me how to unlock this one and your Mr. Ash is a free man."

"Set that aside for the moment. But look at my suspect, whom we will call, for the sake of novelty, X. X is a mild-mannered, inoffensive man who stands to gain several million by Harrison's death. He shows up at the library just before the murder. He's a crackpot inventor, and he has one of his gadgets with him. He shows an alibi-conscious awareness of time. He tries to get the butler to think he called earlier. He calls a witness's attention ostentatiously to a radio time signal. And most important of all, psychologically, he changes. He stops being mild-mannered and inoffensive. He goes on the make for a girl with physical violence. The butler describes him as a different man; he's grown."

Jackson drew a note pad toward him. "Your X sounds worth questioning, to say the least. But this reticence isn't like you, Fergus. Why all this innuendo? Why aren't you telling me to get out of here and arrest him?"

Fergus was not quite his cocky self. "Because, you see, that alibi I mentioned— well, it's good. I can't crack it. It's perfect."

Lieutenant Jackson shoved the pad away. "Run away and play," he said wearily.

"It couldn't be phony at the other end?" Fergus urged. "Some gadget planted to produce those screams at five o'clock to give a fake time for the murder?"

Jackson shook his head. "Harrison finished tea around four-thirty. Stomach analysis shows the food had been digested just about a half-hour. No, he died at five o'clock, all right."

"X's alibi's perfect, then," Fergus repeated. "Unless . . . unless—" His green eyes blinked with amazed realization. "Oh, my dear God—" he said softly.

Mr. Partridge was finding life pleasant to lead. Of course this was only a transitional stage. At present he was merely the—what was the transitional stage between cocoon and fully developed insect? Larva? Imago? Pupa? Outside of his own electro-inventive field, Mr. Partridge was not a well-informed man. That must be remedied. But let the metaphor go. Say simply that he was now in the transition between the meek worm that had been Mr. Partridge and the Great Harrison Partridge who would emerge triumphant when Great-uncle Max died and Faith forgot that poor foolish doomed young man.

Even Agatha he could tolerate more easily in this pleasant state, although he had nonetheless established permanent living quarters in his workroom. She had felt her own pleasure at the prospect of being an heiress, but had expressed it most properly by buying sumptuous mourning for Cousin Stanley—the most expensive clothes that she had bought in the past decade. And her hard edges were possibly softening a little—or was that the pleasing haze, almost like that of drunkenness, which now tended to soften all hard edges for Mr. Partridge's delighted eyes?

It was in the midst of some such reverie as this that Mr. Partridge, lolling idly in his workshop with an unaccustomed tray of whisky, ice and siphon beside him, casually overheard the radio announce the result of the fourth race at Hialeah and noted abstractedly that a horse named Karabali had paid forty-eight dollars and sixty cents on a two-dollar ticket. He had almost forgotten the only half-registered fact when the phone rang.

He answered, and a grudging voice said, "You can sure pick 'em. That's damned near five grand you made on Karabali."

Mr. Partridge fumbled with vocal noises.

The voice went on, "What shall I do with it? Want to pick it up tonight or—"

Mr. Partridge had been making incredibly rapid mental calculations. "Leave it in my account for the moment," he said firmly. "Oh, and—I'm afraid I've mislaid your telephone number."

"Trinity 2897. Got any more hunches now?"

"Not at the moment. I'll let you know."

Mr. Partridge replaced the receiver and poured himself a stiff drink. When he had downed it, he went to the machine and traveled two hours back. He returned to the telephone, dialed TR 2897, and said, "I wish to place a bet on the fourth race at Hialeah."

The same voice said, "And who're you?"

"Partridge. Harrison Partridge."

"Look, brother. I don't take bets by phone unless I see some cash first, see?"

Mr. Partridge hastily recalculated. As a result the next half hour was as packed with action as the final moments of his great plan. He learned about accounts, he ascertained the bookmaker's address, he hurried to his bank and drew out an impressive five hundred dollars which he could ill spare, and he opened his account and placed a two-hundred-dollar bet which excited nothing but a badly concealed derision.

Then he took a long walk and mused over the problem. He recalled happening on a story once in some magazine which proved that you could not use knowledge from the future of the outcome of races to make your fortune, because by interfering with your bet you would change the odds and alter the future. But he was not plucking from the future; he was going back into the past. The odds he had heard were already affected by what he had done. From his subjective point of view, he learned the result of his actions before he performed them. But in the objective physical temporospatial world, he performed those actions quite normally and correctly before their results.

Mr. Partridge stopped dead on the sidewalk and a strolling couple ran head-long into him. He scarcely noticed the collision. He had had a dreadful thought. The sole acknowledged motive for his murder of Cousin Stanley had been to secure money for his researches. Now he learned that his machine, even in its present imperfect form, could provide him with untold money.

He had never needed to murder at all.

"My dearest Maureen," Fergus announced at the breakfast table, "I have discovered the world's first successful time machine."

His sister showed no signs of being impressed. "Have some more tomato juice," she suggested. "Want some tabasco in it? I didn't know that the delusions could survive into the hangover."

"But, Macushla," Fergus protested, "you've just listened to an announcement that no woman on earth has ever heard before."

"Fergus O'Breen, Mad Scientist." Maureen shook her head. "It isn't a role I'd cast you for. Sorry."

"If you'd listen before you crack wise, I said 'discovered.' Not 'invented.' It's the damnedest thing that's ever happened to me in business. It hit me in a flash while I was talking to Andy. It's the perfect and only possible solution to a case. And who will ever believe me? Do you wonder that I went out and saturated myself last night?"

Maureen frowned. "You *mean* this?"

"It's the McCoy. Listen." And he briefly outlined the case. "Now what sticks out like a sore thumb is this: Harrison Partridge establishing an alibi. The radio time signal, the talk with the butler— I'll even lay odds that the murderer himself gave those screams so there'd be no question as to time of death. Then you rub up against the fact that the alibi, like the horrendous dream of the young girl from Peru, is perfectly true.

"But what does an alibi mean? It's my own nomination for the most misused word in the language. It's come to mean a disproof, an excuse. But strictly it means nothing but *elsewhere*. You know the classic gag: 'I wasn't there, this isn't the woman, and, anyway, she gave in.' Well, of those three redundant excuses, only the first is an alibi, an *elsewhere* statement. Now Partridge's claim of being elsewhere is true enough. And even if we could remove him from elsewhere and put him literally on the spot, he could say: 'I couldn't have left the room after the murder; the doors were all locked on the inside.' Sure he couldn't—not *at that time*. And his excuse is not an *elsewhere*, but an *elsewhen*."

Maureen refilled his coffee cup and her own. "Hush up a minute and let me think it over." At last she nodded slowly. "And he's an eccentric inventor and when the butler saw him he was carrying one of his gadgets."

"Which he still had when Simon Ash saw him vanish. He committed the murder, locked the doors, went back in time, walked out through them in their unlocked past, and went off to hear the five-o'clock radio bong at Faith Preston's."

"But you can't try to sell the police on that. Not even Andy."

"I know. Damn it, I know."

"What are you going to do?"

"I'm going to see Mr. Harrison Partridge. And I'm going to ask for an encore."

"Quite an establishment you've got here," Fergus observed to the plump bald little inventor.

Mr. Partridge smiled courteously. "I amuse myself with my small experiments," he admitted.

"I'm afraid I'm not much aware of the wonders of modern science. I'm looking forward to the more spectacular marvels, spaceships for instance, or time machines. But that wasn't what I came to talk about. Miss Preston tells me you're a friend of hers. I'm sure you're in sympathy with this attempt of hers to free young Ash."

"Oh, naturally. Most naturally. Anything that I can do to be of assistance—"

"It's just the most routine sort of question, but I'm groping for a lead. Now, aside from Ash and the butler, you seem to have been the last person to see Harrison alive. Could you tell me anything about him? How was he?"

"Perfectly normal, so far as I could observe. We talked about a new item which I had unearthed for his bibliography, and he expressed some small dissatisfaction with Ash's cataloging of late. I believe they had had words on the matter earlier."

"Bracket says you had one of your inventions with you?"

"Yes, a new, I thought, and highly improved frame for photostating rare books. My cousin, however, pointed out that the same improvements had recently been made by an Austrian *émigré* manufacturer. I abandoned the idea and reluctantly took apart my model."

"A shame. But that's part of the inventor's life, isn't it?"

"All too true. Was there anything else you wished to ask me?"

"No. Nothing really." There was an awkward pause. The smell of whisky was in the air, but Mr. Partridge proffered no hospitality. "Funny the results a murder will have, isn't it? To think how this frightful fact will benefit cancer research."

"Cancer research?" Mr. Partridge wrinkled his brows. "I did not know that that was among Stanley's beneficiaries."

"Not your cousin's, no. But Miss Preston tells me that old Max Harrison has decided that since his only direct descendant is dead, his fortune might as well go to the world. He's planning to set up a medical foundation to rival Rockefeller's, and specializing in cancer. I know his lawyer slightly; he mentioned he's going out there tomorrow."

"Indeed," said Mr. Partridge evenly.

Fergus paced. "If you can think of anything, Mr. Partridge, let me know. This seems like the perfect crime at last. A magnificent piece of work, if you can look at it like that." He looked around the room. "Excellent small workshop you've got here. You can imagine almost anything coming out of it."

"Even," Mr. Partridge ventured, "your spaceships and time machines?"

"Hardly a spaceship," said Fergus.

Mr. Partridge smiled as the young detective departed. He had, he thought, carried off a difficult interview in a masterly fashion. How neatly he had slipped in that creative bit about Stanley's dissatisfaction with Ash! How brilliantly he had improvised a plausible excuse for the machine he was carrying!

Not that the young man could have suspected anything. It was patently the most routine visit. It was almost a pity that this was the case. How pleasant it would be to fence with a detective—master against master. To have a Javert, a Porfir, a Maigret on his trail and to admire the brilliance with which the Great Harrison Partridge should baffle him.

Perhaps the perfect criminal should be suspected, even known, and yet unattainable—

The pleasure of this parrying encounter confirmed him in the belief that had grown in him overnight. It is true that it was a pity that Stanley Harrison had died needlessly. Mr. Partridge's reasoning had slipped for once; murder for profit had not been an essential part of the plan.

And yet what great work had ever been accomplished without death? Does not the bell ring the truer for the blood of the hapless workmen? Did not the ancients wisely believe that greatness must be founded upon a sacrifice? Not self-sacrifice, in the stupid Christian perversion of that belief, but a true sacrifice of another's flesh and blood.

So Stanley Harrison was the needful sacrifice from which should arise the Great Harrison Partridge. And were its effects not already visible? Would he be what he was today, would he so much as have emerged from the cocoon, purely by virtue of his discovery?

No, it was his great and irretrievable deed, the perfection of his crime, that had molded him. In blood is greatness.

That ridiculous young man, prating of the perfection of the crime and never dreaming that—

Mr. Partridge paused and reviewed the conversation. There had twice been that curious insistence upon time machines. Then he had said—what was it? "The crime was a magnificent piece of work," and then, "You can imagine almost anything coming out of this workshop." And the surprising news of Great-uncle Max's new will—

Mr. Partridge smiled happily. He had been unpardonably dense. Here was his Javert, his Porfir. The young detective did indeed suspect him. And the reference to Max had been a temptation, a trap. The detective could not know how unnecessary that fortune had now become. He had thought to lure him into giving away his hand by an attempt at another crime.

And yet, was any fortune ever unnecessary? And a challenge like that—so direct a challenge—could one resist it?

Mr. Partridge found himself considering all the difficulties. Great-uncle Max would have to be murdered today, if he planned on seeing his lawyer tomorrow. The sooner the better. Perhaps his habitual after-lunch siesta would be the best time. He was always alone then, dozing in his favorite corner of that large estate in the hills.

Bother! A snag. No electric plugs there. The portable model was out. And yet— Yes, of course. It could be done the other way. With Stanley, he had committed his crime, then gone back and prepared his alibi. But here he could just as well establish the alibi, then go back and commit the murder, sending himself back by the large machine here with wider range. No need for the locked-room effect. That was pleasing, but not essential.

An alibi for one o'clock in the afternoon. He did not care to use Faith again. He did not want to see her in his larval stage. He might obtain another traffic ticket. Surely the police would be as good as—

The police. But how perfect. Ideal. To go to headquarters and ask to see the detective working on the Harrison case. Tell him, as a remembered afterthought, about Cousin Stanley's supposed quarrel with Ash. Be with him at the time Great-uncle Max is to be murdered.

At twelve thirty Mr. Partridge left his house for the central police station.

Fergus could hear the old man's snores from his coign of vigilance. Getting into Maxwell Harrison's hermitlike retreat had been a simple job. The newspapers had for years so thoroughly covered the old boy's peculiarities that you knew in advance all you needed to know—his daily habits, his loathing for bodyguards, his favorite spot for napping.

The sun was warm and the hills were peaceful. There was a purling stream at the deep bottom of the gully beside Fergus. Old Maxwell Harrison did well to sleep in such perfect solitude.

Fergus was on his third cigarette before he heard a sound. It was a very little sound, the turning of a pebble, perhaps; but here in this loneliness any sound that was not a snore or a stream seemed infinitely loud.

Fergus flipped his cigarette into the depths of the gully and moved, as noiselessly as was possible, toward the sound, screening himself behind scraggly bushes.

The sight, even though expected, was nonetheless startling in this quiet retreat: a plump bald man of middle age advancing on tiptoe with a long knife gleaming in his upraised hand.

Fergus flung himself forward. His left hand caught the knife-brandishing wrist and his right pinioned Mr. Partridge's other arm behind him. The face of Mr. Partridge, that had been so bland a mask of serene exaltation as he advanced to his prey, twisted itself into something between rage and terror.

His body twisted itself, too. It was an instinctive, untrained movement, but timed so nicely by accident that it tore his knife hand free from Fergus' grip and allowed it to plunge downward.

The twist of Fergus' body was deft and conscious, but it was not quite enough to avoid a stinging flesh wound in the shoulder. He felt warm blood trickling down his back. Involuntarily he released his grip on Mr. Partridge's other arm.

Mr. Partridge hesitated for a moment, as though uncertain whether his knife should taste of Great-uncle Max or first dispose of Fergus. The hesitation was understandable, but fatal. Fergus sprang forward in a flying tackle aimed at Mr. Partridge's knees. Mr. Partridge lifted his foot to kick that advancing green-eyed face. He swung and felt his balance going. Then the detective's shoulder struck him. He was toppling, falling over backward, falling, falling—

The old man was still snoring when Fergus returned from his climb down the gully. There was no doubt that Harrison Partridge was dead. No living head could loll so limply on its neck.

And Fergus had killed him. Call it an accident, call it self-defense, call it what you will. Fergus had brought him to a trap, and in that trap he had died.

The brand of Cain may be worn in varying manners. To Mr. Partridge it had assumed the guise of an inspiring panache, a banner with a strange device. But Fergus wore his brand with a difference.

He could not blame himself morally, perhaps, for Mr. Partridge's death. But he could blame himself for professional failure in that death. He had no more proof than before to free Simon Ash, and he had burdened himself with a killing.

For murder can spread in concentric circles, and Fergus O'Breen, who had set out to trap a murderer, now found himself being one.

Fergus hesitated in front of Mr. Partridge's workshop. It was his last chance. There might be evidence here—the machine itself or some document that could prove his theory even to the skeptical eye of Detective Lieutenant A. Jackson. House-breaking would be a small offense to add to his record now. The window on the left, he thought—

"Hi!" said Lieutenant Jackson cheerfully. "You on his trail, too?"

Fergus tried to seem his usual jaunty self. "Hi, Andy. So you've finally got around to suspecting Partridge?"

"Is he your mysterious X? I thought he might be."

"And that's what brings you out here?"

"No. He roused my professional suspicions all by himself. Came into the office an hour ago with the damnedest cock-and-bull story about some vital evidence he'd forgotten. Stanley Harrison's last words, it seems, were about a quarrel with Simon Ash. It didn't ring good—seemed like a deliberate effort to strengthen the case against Ash. As soon as I could get free, I decided to come out and have a further chat with the lad."

"I doubt if he's home," said Fergus.

"We can try." Jackson rapped on the door of the workshop. It was opened by Mr. Partridge.

Mr. Partridge held in one hand the remains of a large open-face ham sandwich. When he had opened the door, he picked up with the other hand the remains of a large whisky and soda. He needed sustenance before this bright new adventure.

Fresh light gleamed in his eyes as he saw the two men standing there. His

Javert! Two Javerts! The unofficial detective who had so brilliantly challenged him, and the official one who was to provide his alibi.

He hardly heeded the opening words of the official detective nor the look of dazed bewilderment on the face of the other. He opened his lips and the Great Harrison Partridge, shedding the last vestigial vestments of the cocoon, spoke:

"You may know the truth for what good it will do you. The life of the man Ash means nothing to me. I can triumph over him even though he live. I killed Stanley Harrison. Take that statement and do with it what you can. I know that an uncorroborated confession is useless to you. If you can prove it, you may have me. And I shall soon commit another sacrifice, and you are powerless to stop me. Because, you see, you are already too late." He laughed softly.

Mr. Partridge closed the door and locked it. He finished the sandwich and the whisky, hardly noticing the poundings on the door. He picked up the knife and went to his machine. His face was a bland mask of serene exaltation.

Lieutenant Jackson hurled himself against the door, a second too late. It was a matter of minutes before he and a finally aroused Fergus had broken it down.

"He's gone," Jackson stated puzzledly. "There must be a trick exit somewhere."

" 'Locked room,' " Fergus murmured. His shoulder ached, and the charge against the door had set it bleeding again.

"What's that?"

"Nothing. Look, Andy. When do you go off duty?"

"Strictly speaking, I'm off now. I was making this checkup on my own time."

"Then let us, in the name of seventeen assorted demigods of drunkenness, go drown our confusions."

Fergus was still asleep when Lieutenant Jackson's phone call came the next morning. His sister woke him, and watched him come into acute and painful wakefulness as he listened, nodding and muttering, "Yes," or, "I'll be—"

Maureen waited till he had hung up, groped about, and found and lighted a cigarette. Then she said, "Well?"

"Remember that Harrison case I was telling you about yesterday?"

"The time-machine stuff? Yes."

"My murderer, Mr. Partridge—they found him in a gully out on his great-uncle's estate. Apparently slipped and killed himself while attempting his second murder—that's the way Andy sees it. Had a knife with him. So, in view of that and a sort of confession he made yesterday, Andy's turning Simon Ash loose. He still doesn't see how Partridge worked the first murder, but he doesn't have to bring it into court now."

"Well? What's the matter? Isn't that fine?"

"Matter? Look, Maureen Macushla. I killed Partridge. I didn't mean to, and maybe you could call it justifiable; but I did. I killed him at one o'clock yesterday afternoon. Andy and I saw him at two; he was then eating a ham sandwich and drinking whisky. The stomach analysis proves that he died half an hour after that meal, when I was with Andy starting out on a bender of bewilderment. So you see?"

"You mean he went back afterward to kill his uncle and then you . . . you saw him after you'd killed him only before he went back to be killed? Oh, how awful."

"Not just that, my sweeting. This is the humor of it: The time alibi, the elsewhen that gave the perfect cover up for Partridge's murder—it gives exactly the same ideal alibi to his own murderer."

Maureen started to speak and stopped. "Oh!" she gasped.

"What?"

"The time machine. It must still be there—somewhere—mustn't it? Shouldn't you—"

Fergus laughed, and not at comedy. "That's the payoff of perfection on this opus. I gather Partridge and his sister didn't love each other too dearly. You know what her first reaction was to the news of his death? After one official tear and one official sob, she went and smashed the hell out of his workshop."

The Pink Caterpillar

"And their medicine men can do time travel, too," Norm Harker said. "At least, that's the firm belief everywhere on the island: a *tualala* can go forward in time and bring you back any single item you specify, for a price. We used to spend the night watches speculating on what would be the one best thing to order."

Norman hadn't told us the name of the island. The stripe and a half on his sleeve lent him discretion, and Tokyo hadn't learned yet what secret installations the Navy had been busy with on that minute portion of the South Pacific. He couldn't talk about the installations, of course; but the island had provided him with plenty of other matters to keep us entertained, sitting up there in the Top of the Mark.

"What would you order, Tony," he asked, "with a carte blanche like that on the future?"

"How far future?"

"They say a *tualala* goes to one hundred years from date: no more, no less."

"Money wouldn't work," I mused. "Jewels maybe. Or a gadget—any gadget—and you could invent it as of now and make a fortune. But then it might depend on principles not yet worked out ... Or the *Gone with the Wind* of the twenty-first century—but publish it now and it might lay an egg. Can you imagine today's best sellers trying to compete with Dickens? No ... it's a tricky question. What did you try?"

"We finally settled on Hitler's tombstone. Think of the admission tickets we could sell to see that!"

"And—?"

"And nothing. We couldn't pay the *tualala*'s price. For each article fetched through time he wanted one virgin from the neighboring island. We felt the staff somehow might not understand if we went collecting them. There's always a catch to magic," Norman concluded lightly.

Fergus said "Uh-huh" and nodded gravely. He hadn't been saying much all evening—just sitting there and looking out over the panorama of the bay by night, a glistening joy now that the dimout was over, and listening. I still don't know the sort of work he's been doing, but it's changing him, toning him down.

But even a toned-down Irishman can stand only so much silence, and there was obviously a story on his lips. Norm asked, "You've been running into magic too?"

"Not lately." He held his glass up to the light and watched his drink. "Damned if I know why writers call a highball an amber liquid," he observed. "Start a cliché and it sticks . . . Like about detectives being hardheaded realists. Didn't you ever stop to think that there's hardly another profession outside the clergy that's so apt to run up against the things beyond realism? Why do you call in a detective? Because something screwy's going on and you need an explanation. And if there isn't an explanation . . .

"This was back a ways. Back when I didn't have anything worse to deal with than murderers and, once, a werewolf. But he was a hell of a swell guy. The murderers I used to think were pretty thorough low-lifes, but now . . . Anyway, this was back then. I was down in Mexico putting the finishing touches on that wacky business of the Aztec Calendar when I heard from Dan Rafetti. I think you know him, Tony; he's an investigator for Southwest National Life Insurance, and he's thrown some business my way now and then, like the Solid Key case.

"This one sounded interesting. Nothing spectacular, you understand, and probably no money to speak of. But the kind of crazy unexplained little detail that stirs up the O'Breen curiosity. Very simple: Southwest gets a claim from a beneficiary. One of their customers died down in Mexico and his sister wants the cash. They send to the Mexican authorities for a report on his death and it was heart failure and that's that. Only the policy is made out to Mr. Frank Miller and the Mexican report refers to him as *Dr.* F. Miller. They ask the sister and she's certain he hasn't any right to such a title. So I happen to be right near Tlichotl, where he died, and would I please kind of nose around and see was there anything phony, like maybe an imposture. Photographs and fingerprints, from a Civil Service application he once made, enclosed."

"Nice businesslike beginning," Norman said.

Fergus nodded. "That's the way it started: all very routine, yours-of-the-27th-*ult*. Prosaic, like. And Tlichotl was prosaic enough too. Maybe to a tourist it'd be picturesque, but I'd been kicking around these Mexican mountain towns long enough so one seemed as commonplace as another. Sort of a montage of flat houses and white trousers and dogs and children and an old church and an almost-as-old pulquería and one guy who plays a hell of a guitar on Saturday nights.

"Tlichotl wasn't much different. There was a mine near it, and just out of town was a bunch of drab new frame houses for the American engineers. Everybody in town worked in the mine—all pure Indians, with those chaste profiles straight off of the Aztec murals that begin to seem like the only right and normal human face when you've seen 'em long enough.

"I went to the doctor first. He was the government sanitation agent and health instructor, and the town looked like he was doing a good job. His English was better than my Spanish, and he was glad I liked tequila. Yes, he remembered Dr. Miller. He checked up his records and announced that Dr. M. died on November 2. It was January when I talked to him. Simple death: heart failure. He'd had several attacks in past weeks, and the doctor had expected him to go any day. All of a sudden a friend he hadn't seen in years showed up in town unannounced, and the shock did it. Any little thing might have.

"The doctor wasn't a stupid man, or a careless one. I was willing to take his word that the death had been natural. And maybe I ought to put in here, before your devious minds start getting ahead of me, that as far as I ever learned he was absolutely right. Common-or-garden heart failure, and that didn't fit into any picture of insurance fraud. But there was still the inconsistency of the title, and I went on, 'Must've been kind of nice for you to have a colleague here to talk with?'

"The doctor frowned a little at that. It seemed he'd been sort of hurt by Dr. Miller's attitude. Had tried to interest him in some researches he was doing with an endemic variant of undulant fever, which he'd practically succeeded in wiping out. But the North American 'doctor' just didn't give a damn. No fraternal spirit; no scientific curiosity; nothing.

"I gathered they hadn't been very friendly, my doctor and 'Dr.' Miller. In fact, Miller hadn't been intimate with anybody, not even the other North Americans at the mine. He liked the Indians and they liked him, though they were a little scared of him on account of the skeleton—apparently an anatomical specimen and the first thing I'd heard of to go with his assumed doctorate. He had a good short-wave radio, and he listened to music on that and sketched a little and read and went for short hikes. It sounded like a good life, if you like a lonely one. They might know a little more about him at the pulquería; he stopped there for a drink sometimes. And the widow Sánchez had kept house for him; she might know something.

"I tried the widow first. She wore a shapeless black dress that looked as though she'd started mourning Mr. Sánchez ten years before, but her youngest child wasn't quite walking yet. She'd liked her late employer, might he rest in peace. He had been a good man, and so little trouble. No, he never gave medicine to anybody; that was the job of the señor médico from Mexico City. No, he never did anything with bottles. No, he never received much mail and surely not with money in it, for she had often seen him open his few letters. But yes, indeed he was a médico; did he not have the bones, the esquéleto, to prove it?

"And if the señor interested himself so much for el doctor Miller, perhaps the señor would care to see his house? It was untouched, as he'd left it. No one lived there now. No, it was not haunted—at least, not that anyone knew, though no man knows such things. It was only that no one new ever comes to live in Tlichotl, and an empty house stays empty.

"I looked the house over. It had two rooms and a kitchen and a tiny patio. 'Dr.' Miller's things were undisturbed; no one had claimed them and it was up to time and heat and insects to take care of them. There was the radio and beside it the sketching materials. One wall was a bookcase, well filled, mostly with sixteenth- and seventeenth-century literature in English and Spanish. The books had been faithfully read. There were a few recent volumes, mostly on travel or on Mexican Indian culture, and a few magazines. No medical books or periodicals.

"Food, cooking utensils, clothing, a pile of sketches (good enough so you'd feel all right when you'd done them and bad enough so you wouldn't feel urged to exhibit them), pipes and tobacco—these just about made up the inventory. No papers to speak of, just a few personal letters, mostly from his sister (and beneficiary). No instruments or medicines of any kind. Nothing whatsoever out of the way—not even the skeleton.

"I'd heard about that twice, so I asked what had become of it. The sons of the mining engineers, the young demons, had stolen it to celebrate a gringo holiday, which I gathered had been Halloween. They had built an enormous bonfire, and the skeleton had fallen in and been consumed. The doctor Miller had been very angry; he had suffered one of his attacks then, almost as bad as the one that gave him death, may the Lord hold him in His kindness. But now it was time for a mother to return and feed her brood; and her house was mine, and would the señor join in her poor supper?

"The beans were good and the tortillas wonderful; and the youngest children hadn't ever seen red hair before and had some pointed questions to ask me about mine. And in the middle of the meal something suddenly went *click* in my brain and I knew why Frank Miller had called himself 'doctor.'"

Fergus paused and beckoned to a waiter.

Norman said, "Is that all?"

"For the moment. I'm giving you boys a chance to scintillate. There you have all the factors up to that point. All right: *Why* was Miller calling himself 'doctor'?"

"He wasn't practicing," Norman said slowly. "And he wasn't even running a fake medical racket by mail, as people have done from Mexico to avoid the U.S. Post Office Department."

"And," I added, "he hadn't assumed the title to impress people, to attain social standing, because he had nothing to do with his neighbors. And he wasn't carrying on any experiments or research which he might have needed the title in writing up. So he gained nothing in cash or prestige. All right, what other reason is there for posing as a doctor?"

"Answer," said Fergus leisurely: "he wasn't posing as a doctor. Look; you might pose a doctor with no props at all, thinking no one would come in your house but the housekeeper. Or you might stage an elaborate front complete with instrument cabinets and five-pound books. But you wouldn't try it with just one prop, an anatomical skeleton."

Norman and I looked at each other and nodded. It made sense. "Well then?" I asked.

The fresh drinks came, and Fergus said, "My round. Well then, the skeleton was not a prop for the medical pose. Quite the reverse. Turn it around and it makes sense. He called himself a doctor *to account for the skeleton.*"

I choked on my first sip, and Norman spluttered a little, too. Fergus went on eagerly, with that keen light in his green eyes, "You can't hide a skeleton in a tiny house. The housekeeper's bound to see it, and word gets around. Miller liked the Indians and he liked peace. He had to account for the skeleton. So he became a 'doctor.'"

"But that—" Norman objected. "That's no answer. That's just another question."

"I know," said Fergus. "But that's the first step in detection: to find the right question. And that's it: *Why does a man live with a skeleton?*"

We were silent for a bit. The Top of the Mark was full of glasses and smoke and uniforms; and despite the uniforms it seemed a room set aside that was not a part of a world at war—still less of a world in which a man might live with a skeleton.

"Of course you checked the obvious answer," I said at last.

Fergus nodded. "He couldn't very well have been a black magician, if that's what you mean, or white either. Not a book or a note in the whole place dealing with the subject. No wax, chalk, incense or what-have-you. The skeleton doesn't fit any more into a magical pattern than into a medical."

"The Dead Beloved?" Norman suggested, hesitantly uttering the phrase in mocking capitals. "Rose-for-Emily stuff? A bit grisly, but not inconceivable."

"The Mexican doctor saw the skeleton. It was a man's, and not a young one."

"Then he was planning an insurance fraud—burn the house down and let the bones be found while he vanished."

"A, you don't burn adobe. B, you don't let the skeleton be seen by the doctor who'll examine it later. C, it was that of a much shorter man than Miller."

"A writer?" I ventured wildly. "I've sometimes thought myself a skeleton might be useful in the study—check where to inflict skull wounds and such."

"With no typewriter, no manuscripts, and very little mail?"

Norman's face lit up. "You said he sketched. Maybe he was working on a modern *Totentanz*—Dance of Death allegory. Holbein and Dürer must have had a skeleton or two around."

"I saw his sketches. Landscapes only."

I lit my pipe and settled back. "All right. We've stooged and we don't know. Now tell us why a man keeps house with a set of bones." My tone was lighter than necessary.

Fergus said, "I won't go into all the details of my investigation. I saw damned near every adult in Tlichotl and most of the kids. And I pieced out what I think is the answer. But I think you can gather it from the evidence of four people.

"First, Jim Reilly, mining engineer. Witness deposeth and saith he was on the main street, if you can call it that, of Tlichotl on November 2. He saw a stranger, 'swarthy but not a Mex,' walk up to Miller and say, 'Frank!' Miller looked up and was astonished. The stranger said, 'Sorry for the delay. But it took me a little time to get here.' And he hadn't finished the sentence before Miller dropped dead. Queried about the stranger, witness says he gave his name as Humbert Targ; he stayed around town for a few days for the funeral and then left. Said he'd known Miller a long time ago—never quite clear where, but seemingly in the South Seas, as we used to say before we learned to call it the South Pacific. Asked for description, witness proved pretty useless: medium height, medium age, dark complexion . . . Only helpful details: stranger wore old clothes ('Shabby?' 'No, just old.' 'Out-of-date?' 'I guess so.' 'How long ago? What kind?' 'I don't know. Just old—funny-looking') and had only one foot ('One leg?' 'No, two legs, just one foot.' 'Wooden peg?' 'No, just empty trouser cuff. Walked with crutches').

"Second witness, Father Gonzaga, and it's a funny sensation to be talking to a priest who wears just a plain business suit. He hadn't known 'Dr.' Miller well, though he'd said a mass for his soul. But one night Miller had come from the pulquería and insisted on talking to him. He wanted to know how you could ever get right with God and yourself if you'd done someone a great wrong and there was no conceivable way you could make it up to him. The padre asked why, was the injured person dead? Miller hesitated and didn't answer. He's alive, then? Oh no, no! Restitution could surely be made to the next of kin if it were a money matter? No, it was . . . personal. Father's advice was to pray for the injured party's soul and for grace to avoid such temptation another time. I don't much see what else he could have suggested, but Miller wasn't satisfied."

I wasn't hearing the noise around us any more. Norman was leaning forward too, and I saw in his eyes that he too was beginning to feel the essential *wrong*ness of the case the detective had stumbled on.

"Third witness, the widow Sánchez. She told me about the skeleton when I came back for more beans and brought a bottle of red wine to go with them— which it did, magnificently. 'Dr.' Miller had treasured his skeleton very highly. He was supposed not even to dust it. But once she forgot, and a finger came off. This was in October. She thought he might not notice a missing finger, where she knew she'd catch it if he found a loose one, so she burned the bones in the charcoal brazier over which she fried her tortillas. Two days later she was serving the doc- tor his dinner when she saw a pink caterpillar crawling near his place. She'd never seen a pink caterpillar before. She flicked it away with a napkin; but not before the 'doctor' saw it. He jumped up from the table and ran to look at the skeleton and gave her a terrific bawling out. After that she saw the caterpillar several times. It was about then that Miller started having those heart attacks. Whenever she saw the caterpillar it was crawling around the 'doctor.' I looked at her a long time while she finished the wine, and then I said, 'Was it a caterpillar?' She crossed herself and said 'No.' She said it very softly, and that was all she said that night."

I looked down at the table. My hand lay there, and the index finger was tap- ping gently. We seemed to be sitting in quite a draft, and I shuddered.

"Fourth witness, Timmy Reilly, twelve-year-old son to Jim. He thought it was a great lark that they'd stolen the old boy's bones for Halloween. Fun and games. These dopes down here didn't know from nothin' about Halloween, but him and the gang, they sure showed 'em. But I could see he was holding something back. I made a swap. He could wear my detective badge (which I've never worn yet) for a whole day if he'd tell me what else he knew. So he showed it to me: the foot that he'd rescued when the skeleton was burned up. He'd tried to grab the bones as they toppled over and all he could reach was the heel. He had the whole foot, well articulated and lousy with tarsals and stuff. So I made a better deal: he could have the badge for keeps (with the number scratched out a little) if he'd let me burn the foot. He let me."

Fergus paused, and it all began to click into place. The pattern was clear, and it was a pattern that should not be.

"You've got it now?" Fergus asked quietly. "All I needed to make it perfect was Norm's story. There had to be such a thing as *tualala,* with such powers as theirs. I'd deduced them, but it's satisfying to have them confirmed.

"Miller had had an enemy, many years before, a man who had sworn to kill him. And Miller had known a *tualala,* back there in the South Seas. And when he'd asked himself what would be the best single item to bring back from the future, he knew the answer: *his enemy's skeleton.*

It wasn't murder. He probably had scruples about that. He sounded like a good enough guy in a way, and maybe his *tualala* asked a more possible price. The skeleton was the skeleton that would exist a hundred years from now, no matter how or when the enemy had died. But bring that skeleton back here and the enemy can no longer exist. His skeleton can't be two places at once. You've got the dry dead bones. What becomes of the live ones with flesh on them? You don't know. You don't care. You're safe. You're free to lead the peaceful life you want with Indians and mountain scenery and your scratch pad and your radio. And your skeleton.

"You've got to be careful of that skeleton. If it ceases to exist in time, the full-fleshed living skeleton might return. You mustn't even take a chance on the destruction of a little piece. You lose a finger, and a finger returns—a pink thing that crawls, and always toward you.

"Then the skeleton itself is destroyed. You're in mortal terror, but nothing happens. Two days go by and it's November 2. You know what the Second of November is in Latin America? It's All Souls' Day in the Church, and they call it the *Día de los difuntos*—the Day of the Dead. But it isn't a sad day outside of church. You go to the cemetery and it's a picnic. There are skeletons everywhere, same like Halloween—bright, funny skeletons that never hurt anybody. And there are skulls to wear and skulls to drink out of and bright white sugar skulls with pink and green trimmings to eat. All along every street are vendors with skulls and skeletons for every purpose, and every kid you see has a sugar skull to suck. Then at night you go to the theater to see *Don Juan Tenorio* where the graves open and the skeletons dance, while back home the kids are howling themselves to sleep because death is so indigestible.

"Of course, there's no theater in Tlichotl, but you can bet there'd be skulls and skeletons—some of them dressed up like Indian gods for the Christian feast, some of them dancing on wires, some of them vanishing down small gullets. And there you are in the midst of skeletons, skeletons everywhere, and your skeleton is gone and all your safety with it. And there on the street with all the skulls staring at you, you see him and he isn't a skull any more. He's Humbert Targ and he's explaining that it took him a little time to get here.

"Wouldn't *you* drop dead?" Fergus concluded simply.

My throat felt dry as I asked, "What did you tell the insurance company?"

"Much like Norm's theory. Man was an artist, had an anatomical model, gave out he was a doctor to keep the natives from conniption fits. Collected expenses, but no bonus: the prints they sent me fitted what I found in his home, and they had to pay the sister."

Norman cleared his throat. "I'm beginning to hope they don't send me back to the island."

"Afraid you might get too tempted by a *tualala?*"

"No. But on the island we really do have pink caterpillars. I'm not sure I could face them."

"There's one thing I still wonder," Fergus said reflectively. "Where was Humbert Targ while his skeleton hung at Miller's side? Or should I say, *when* was he? He said, 'It took a little time to get here.' From where? From when? And what kind of time?"

There are some questions you don't even try to answer.

The Chronokinesis of Jonathan Hull

This isn't, properly speaking, Fergus O'Breen's story, though it starts with him. Fergus is a private detective, but he didn't function as a detective in the Jonathan Hull episode. It was no fault of his Irish ingenuity that he provided the answer to the mystery; he simply found it, all neatly typed out for him. Typed, in fact, before there ever was any mystery.

In a way, though, it's a typical O'Breen anecdote. "I'm a private eye," Fergus used to say, "and what happens to me shouldn't happen to a Seeing Eye. I'm a catalyst for the unbelievable." As in the case of Mr. Harrison Partridge, who found that the only practical use for a short-range time machine was to provide the perfect alibi for murder. But the Partridge case was simplicity itself compared to the Hull business.

It began—at least according to one means of reckoning a time sequence—on the morning after Fergus had trapped the murderer in the Dubrovsky case—a relatively simple affair involving only such prosaic matters as an unbreakable alibi and a hermetically sealed room.

None the less it was a triumph that deserved, and received, wholehearted celebration, and it was three o'clock before Fergus wound up in bed. It was eight when he unwound upon hearing a thud in the corner of the room. He sat up and stared into the gloom and saw a tall thin figure rising from the floor. The figure moved over to his typewriter and switched on the light. He saw a man of about sixty, clean-shaven, but with long, untrimmed gray hair. An odd face—not unkindly, but slightly inhuman, as though he had gone through some experience so unspeakable as to set him a little apart from the rest of his race.

Fergus watched curiously as the old man took an envelope out of a drawer in the desk, opened it, unfolded the papers it contained, set them in a pile beside the typewriter, took the topmost sheet, inserted it in the machine, and began typing furiously.

It seemed a curious procedure, but Fergus' mind was none too clear and the outlines of the room and of the typist still tended to waver. *Oh well,* Fergus thought, *long-haired old men at typewriters is pretty mild in view of those boilermakers.* And he rolled over and back to sleep.

It was about an hour later that he opened his eyes again, much surprised to find Curly Locks still there. He was typing with his right hand, while his left rested on a pile of paper beside him. As Fergus watched, the old man pulled a sheet from the typewriter and added it to the pile at his left. Then he put the pile in the side section of the desk which housed unused paper, rose from the machine, switched off the light, and walked out the door with a curious awkward walk, as though he had been paralyzed for years and had had to learn the technique all over again.

The dominant O'Breen trait, the one that has solved more cases than any amount of ingenuity and persistence, is curiosity. A phantasm that stays right there while you sleep is worth investigating. So Fergus was instantly out of bed, without even bothering to pull on a robe, and examining the unused paper compartment.

He sighed with disgust. All the sheets were virginally white. It must have been a delusion after all, though of a singular sort. He turned back to bed. But as he did so, his eye glanced at the corner where he had heard that first thud. He executed a fabulous double take and looked again. There was no doubt about it.

In that corner lay the body of a tall thin man of about sixty, clean-shaven, but with long untrimmed gray hair.

The average man might find some difficulty in explaining to the police how an unidentified corpse happened to turn up in his bedroom. But Detective Lieutenant A. Jackson had reached the point where he was surprised at nothing that involved O'Breen.

He heard the story through and then said judiciously, "I think we'll leave your typewriter out of the report, Fergus. If your Irish blood wants to go fey on you, it's O.K. with me; but I think the Psychical Research Society would be more interested in a report on it than the L.A. Police Department. He died when you heard that thud, so his actions thereafter are pretty irrelevant."

"Cyanide?" Fergus asked.

"Smell it from here, can't you? And the vial still clenched in his hand, so there's no doubt of a verdict of suicide. To try a little reconstruction: Say he came to see you professionally about whatever was preying on him. Found you asleep and decided to wait, but finally got restless and finished the job without seeing you."

"I guess so," said Fergus, taking another gulp of tomato juice. "This and the coffee make the typewriter episode seem pretty unlikely. But no O'Breen's gone in for second sight since great-great-grandfather Seamus. I'll expect the family leprechaun next."

"Tell him these shoes need resoling," said Lieutenant Jackson.

For twenty-four hours the affair rested at that. Suicide of Unknown. Nothing to identify him, not even laundry marks. Checkup on fingerprints fruitless. One odd thing that bothered Jackson a little: the man's trousers had no cuffs.

Sergeant Marcus, whose uncle was in cloaks and suits, had an idea on that. "If we get into this war and run into a shortage of material, we'll all be wearing 'em like that. Maybe he's setting next year's styles."

When Fergus heard this, he laughed. And then he stopped laughing and sat down and began thinking. He thought through half a pack of Camels in a chain before he gave up. There was a hint there. Something that was teasing him. Something that reminded him of the Partridge case and yet not quite.

The notion was still nibbling at the back of his mind when Jackson called him the next day. "Something might interest you, Fergus. Either a pretty farfetched coincidence or part of a pattern."

"My pattern?"

"Your pattern maybe. Another old man with long hair and no identification. Found in a rooming house out on Adams in a room that was supposed to be vacant. But this one was shot."

Fergus frowned. "Could be. But is long hair enough to make it a coincidence?"

"Not by itself. But he hasn't any cuffs on his pants either."

Fergus lost no time in getting to the West Adams address. Onetime mansion fallen on evil days, reduced to transient cubicles. The landlady was still incoherently horrified.

"I went into the room to fix it up like I always do between tenants and there on the bed—"

Jackson shooed her out. The photographing and fingerprinting squads had come and gone, but the basket hadn't arrived yet. He and Fergus stood alone and looked at the man. He was even older than the other—somewhere in his late seventies, at a guess. A hard, cruel face, with a dark hole centered in its forehead.

"Shot at close range," Jackson was commenting. "Powder burns. Gun left here—clear prints on it." There was a knock on the door. "That'll be the basket."

Fergus looked at the trousers. The cuffs hadn't been taken off. They were clearly tailored without cuffs. Two old men with cuffless trousers—

Jackson had gone to open the door. Now he started back with a gasp. Fergus turned. Gasps aren't easily extorted from a police lieutenant, but this one was justified. Coming in the door was the exact twin of Fergus' typing corpse, and walking with that same carefully learned awkwardness.

He seemed not to notice the corpse on the bed, but he turned to Jackson when the officer demanded, "And who are you?" To be exact, he seemed to turn a moment before Jackson spoke.

He said something. Or at least he made vocal noises. It was a gibberish not remotely approximating any language that either detective had ever heard. And there followed a minute of complete cross-purposes, a cross-examination in which neither party understood a syllable of the other's speech.

Then Fergus had an idea. He took out his notebook and pencil and handed them over. The old man wrote rapidly and most peculiarly. He began in the lower right hand corner of the page and wrote straight on to the upper left. But the message, when he handed it back, was in normal order.

Fergus whistled. "With that act on a blackboard, you could pack 'em in." Then he read the message:

I see that I will have succeeded, and because of the idea that has just come to my mind I imagine that you already understand this hell as much as it is possible for one to understand who has not gone through it and know that it is impossible to arrest me. But if it will simplify your files, you may consider this a confession.

Jonathan Hull

Jackson drew his automatic and moved toward the door. Fergus took out one of his cards with business and home address and penciled on it:

Look me up if you need help straightening this out.

An idea seemed to strike the man as he accepted the card. Then his features widened in a sort of astonished gratification and he looked at the bed. Then with that same rapid awkwardness he was walking out of the room.

Detective Lieutenant Jackson called a warning to him. He tried to grab him. But the man went right on past him. It isn't easy to fire a close-range bullet into a gray-haired old man. He was out of the room and on the stairs before Jackson's finger could move, and then the bullet went wild.

Jackson was starting out of the room when he felt Fergus' restraining hand on his arm. He tried to shake it off, but it was firm. "You'll never catch him, Andy," said Fergus gently. "Never in God's green eternity. Because you see you can't have caught him or he couldn't have typed—"

Jackson exploded. "Fergus! You don't think this trick-writing expert is another wraith for your second sight, do you? I saw him, too. He's real. And he must be your corpse's twin. If we find him, we can have the answer to both deaths. We can—"

"Telephone for you, Lieutenant," the landlady called.

When Jackson returned, his chagrin over Jonathan Hull's escape was forgotten. "All right," he said wearily. "Have it your way, Fergus. Ghosts we have yet. Do I care?"

"What happened?"

"Anything can happen. Everything probably will. There's no more sense and order in the world. Nothing a man can trust."

"But what is it?"

"Fingerprints. They don't mean a thing any more."

"The prints on the gun?" Fergus said eagerly. "They belong to my corpse?"

Jackson nodded shamefacedly. "So a cuffless ghost came back and— But it's worse than that. Much worse. This stiff's prints—they belong to a seventeen-year-old kid working out at Lockheed." With these words the lanky lieutenant seemed to reach the depth of despair.

But they brought new hope to Fergus' face and a triumphant glint to his green eyes. "Perfect, Andy! I couldn't have asked for better. That rounds it off."

Jackson looked up wide-eyed. "You mean it makes sense? O.K., maestro; what's the answer?"

"I don't know," said Fergus coolly. "But I know *where* the answer is: in the drawer of my desk."

He stubbornly refused to say a word until they were in his room. Then he said,

"Look at all the little things we saw: How Hull turned to you just *before* you spoke to him; how he registered amazement, and *then* looked at the corpse; above all, how he wrote that note. And the wording of the note too: 'I *will have* succeeded,' and how we must *already* understand because of something he just thought of. There's only one answer to it all:

"Jonathan Hull is living backwards."

Jackson burst out with a loud "Nonsense!"

"It even explains the absence of the cuffs. They're trousers from next year, when we'll be in the war and Sergeant Marcus' prophecy will come true."

"Then you mean that the other stiff too——?"

"Both of 'em."

"O.K. Grant you that much, and I suppose in some cockeyed way it explains the prints of a corpse on a murder weapon. But that kid out at Lockheed——"

"——*is* your second stiff. But don't trust me: Let's see what Hull himself has to say." Fergus reached for the drawer.

"Hull left a message before he bumped himself off?"

"Don't you see? If he's living backwards, he came into my room, sat at the typewriter, wrote a message, and then killed himself. I just saw it being reeled off hindsideto. So when I 'saw' him taking an envelope out of this drawer, he was actually, in his own time-sequence, *putting it in.*"

"I'll believe you," said Jackson, "when I see——"

Fergus had pulled the drawer open. There lay a fat envelope, inscribed:

> FOR FERGUS O'BREEN
> FROM JONATHAN HULL.

"All right," said the lieutenant, "so your conclusion is correct. That still doesn't mean your reasoning is. How can a man live backwards? You might as well ask the universe to run in reverse entropy."

"Maybe it does," said Fergus. "Maybe Hull just found out how to go forwards."

Jackson snorted. "Well, let's see what he says."

Fergus read: " 'The first indication of my strange destiny was that I could see ghosts, or so I then interpreted the phenomena.' "

Jackson groaned. "Ghosts we have again! Fergus, I will not have the supernatural. The parascientific is bad enough, but the supernatural—*no!* "

"Is there necessarily any difference?" Fergus asked. "What we haven't found the answer to, we call supernatural. Maybe Jonathan Hull found an answer or two. Subside, Andy, and let's settle down to this."

They settled.

THE NARRATIVE OF JONATHAN HULL

The first indication of my strange destiny was that I could see ghosts, or so I then interpreted the phenomena. The first such episode occurred when I was five years old and came in from the yard to tell the family that I had been playing with

Gramps. Since my grandfather had died the previous year in that mysterious post-war epidemic, the family was not a little concerned as to my veracity; but no amount of spanking shook me from my conviction.

Again in my twentieth year, I was visited in my lodgings near the Institute by my father, who had died when I was fifteen. The two visitations were curiously similar. Both apparitions spoke unintelligible gibberish and walked with awkwardly careful movements.

If not already, you will soon recognize these two traits, Mr. O'Breen. When I add that the Hulls are noted for the marked physical resemblance between generations, you will readily understand the nature of these apparent ghosts.

On neither of these occasions did I feel any of the conventional terror of revenants. In the first case, because I was too young to realize the implications of the visit; in the second, because I had by my twentieth year already reached the conclusion that my chief interest in life lay in the fringes of normal existence.

Too much of scientific work, by the time I reached the Institute, was being devoted to further minute exploration of the already known, and too little to any serious consideration to the unknown or half-known, the shadowy blurs on the edges of our field of vision. To pursue the work as mathematical physicist for which I was training myself meant, I feared, a blind alley of infinite refinement and elaboration.

To be sure, there was the sudden blossoming of atomic power which had begun after the war, when peacetime allowed the scientists of the world to pool their recent discoveries with no fear lest they be revealing a possible secret weapon. But the work that needed doing now in that field was that of the mechanic, the technician. Theory was becoming fixed and settled, and it was upon my skill in theoretical matters that I prided myself.

Yes, I was the bright young lad then. There were no limits to my aspirations. The world should glow with the name of Hull. And behold me now: a ghost even to myself, a murderer, and soon a suicide. Already, if my understanding of the reversal is correct, my body lies in that corner; but I cannot turn my eyes to it to verify my assumption. And I was always more satisfied with the theory than with the fact.

I was the prodigy of the Institute. I was the shining star. And Lucifer was a shining star, too.

When the United Nations established the World Institute for Paranormal Research at Basle, I recognized my niche. My record at the local institute and my phenomenal score in the aptitude test made my admission a matter of course. And once surrounded by the magnificent facilities of the WIPR, I began to bestow upon the name of Hull certain small immortalities.

Yes, there is that consolation. The name of Hull will never quite die while extra-sensory perception is still measured in terms of the H.Q., the Hull quotient, or while Hull's "Co-ordinating Concordance to the Data of Charles Fort" still serves as a standard reference work. Nor, I suppose, while mystery-mongers probe the disappearance of Jonathan Hull and couple his name with those of Sir Benjamin Bathurst and the captain of the *Mary Celeste*— a fate that shall be averted, Mr. O'Breen, if you follow carefully the instructions which I shall give you later.

But more and more one aspect of the paranormal began to absorb me. I concentrated on it, devouring everything I could obtain in fact or fiction, until I was recognized as the WIPR's outstanding authority upon the possibilities of chronokinesis, or time travel.

It was a happy day when I hit upon that word *chronokinesis*. Its learned sound seemed to remove the concept from the vulgar realm of the time machines cheapened by fiction fantasists. But even with this semantic advantage, I still had many prejudices to battle, both among the populace and among my own colleagues. For even the very men who had established extra-sensory perception upon a scientific basis could still sneer at time travel.

I knew, of course, of earlier attempts. And now, I realize, Mr. O'Breen, why I was inclined to trust you the moment I saw your card. It was through a fortunately preserved letter of your sister's, which found its way into our archives, that we knew of the early fiasco of Harrison Partridge and your part therein. We knew, too, of the researches of Dr. Derringer, and how he gave up in despair after his time traveler failed to return, having encountered who knows what unimaginable future barrier.

We learned of no totally successful chronokinetic experiment. But from what we did know of the failures, I was able to piece together a little of what I felt must be the truth. Surely the method must involve the rotation of a temporomagnetic field against the "natural" time stream, and Hackendorf's current researches would make the establishment of such a field a simple matter.

It was then that I hit upon my concept of reversed individual entropy—setting, so to speak, the machinery of the individual running in an order opposite to the normal, so that movement along the "contrary" direction of the time stream would be for him natural and feasible.

This was what brought about the break. There were some among my colleagues who thought the notion ridiculous. There were others, those hyperserious scientists who take upon themselves the airs of hierophants, who found it even sacrilegious and evil. There were a few practical souls who simply feared it to be impossibly dangerous.

There was not one who would tolerate my experiments. And that is why, Lucifer-like, I severed my connection with the WIPR and retired to America, to pursue by myself the chronokinetic researches which would, I was sure, make Hull a name to rank with the greatest in all the history of science.

It was at this time that Tim Givens enters into the story. My own character I think you will have gathered sufficiently from these pages, but of Givens I must give a more explicit picture.

He was almost twenty years older than I, and I was then thirty. This was in 1971, which meant that he was just a boy fresh out of high school at the time of the war. His first experience of life was to find himself in an aircraft factory earning highly impressive sums. He had no sooner adjusted himself to a wonderful and extravagant life than he was drafted and shortly engaged in slaughtering Japanese in the Second Malayan Campaign.

He came back from the war pitiably maladjusted. It was difficult enough for most young men to return to civilian life; it was impossible for Tim Givens, because the only civilian life he had known, the lavish boom of war industry, was no more. We skillfully avoided a post-war depression, true, but we did not return to the days when untrained boys in their teens could earn more in a week than their fathers had hoped to see in a month.

Givens felt that he had saved the world, and that the world in return owed him the best. He took part payment on that debt when and where he could. He was not a criminal; he was simply a man who took short cuts whenever possible.

I cannot say that I liked him. But he was recommended to me through remote family connections; he had a shiftily alert mind; and he had picked up, in the course of his many brief jobs, a surprising mechanical dexterity and ingenuity. The deciding factor, of course, was that the skilled technicians I should have wished to employ were reluctant to work with a man who had left the WIPR under something of a cloud.

So I took Givens on as my handyman and assistant. Personal relationships had never formed a major element in my life. I thought that I could tolerate his narrow selfishness, his occasional banal humor, his basic crassness. I did not realize how lasting some personal relationships may be.

And I went on working on the theory of reversed entropy. My calculations will be found in my laboratory. It would be useless to give them here. They would be meaningless in 1941; so much depends upon the variable significance of the Tamirovich factor—discovered 1958—and the peculiar proportions of the alloy duralin—developed in the 1960's—and my own improvement on it which I had intended to christen chronalin.

The large stationary machine—stationary both in space and in time—was to furnish the field which would make it possible for us to free ourselves from the "normal" flow of time. The small handsets were to enable us to accelerate and decelerate and eventually, I trusted, to reverse our temporal motion.

This, I say, was the plan. As to what ultimately happened—

I am sure that Tim Givens substituted a cheaper grade of duralin for the grade which had met my tests. He could have netted a sizable profit on the substitution, and it would have been typical of his petty opportunism. He never admitted as much, but I remain convinced.

And so what happened was this:

We entered the large machine. For a moment I had been worried. I thought I had seen two suspicious-looking figures backing into the room by the rear door, and I feared vandalism. But a checkup indicated nothing wrong and no sign of intruders; and I pressed the control.

I cannot describe that sensation to anyone who has not experienced it. A sudden wrenching that seems to take all your vitals, carefully turn them inside out in some fourth dimension, and replace them neatly in your shaken body. A horrible sensation? I suppose so; but at the moment it was beautiful to me. It meant that something had happened.

Even Tim Givens looked beautiful to me, too. He was my partner on the greatest enterprise of the century—of the centuries. I had insisted on his presence because I wanted a witness for my assertions later; and he had assented because, I think, he foresaw a mint of money to be earned in television lectures by The Man Who Traveled in Time.

I adjusted the handset to a high acceleration so that we might rapidly reach a point sufficiently past to be striking. (Givens' handset was telesynchronized with mine; I did not trust his own erratic impulses.) At the end of ten minutes I was frowning perplexedly. We were still in the stationary machine and we should by now have passed the point at which constructed it.

Givens did not notice my concern, but casually asked, "O.K. yet, M.S.?" He thought it humorous to call me "M.S.," which was, indeed, one of my degrees but which he insisted stood for Mad Scientist.

Whatever was wrong I would not find it out by staying there. Perhaps nothing whatsoever had happened. And yet that curious wrenching sensation surely indicated that the temporomagnetic field had had some effect.

I beckoned to Givens to follow me, and we stepped out of the machine. Two men were backing away from it in the distance. Their presence and their crablike retrograde motion worried me, and reminded me of those other two whom we had only glimpsed. To avoid them, we hastily slipped out the rear door, and into a world gone mad.

For a moment I had the absurd notion that some inconceivable error had catapulted us into the far distant future. Surely nothing else could account for a world in which men walked rapidly backwards along sidewalks and conversed in an unheard-of gibberish.

But the buildings were those of 1971. The sleek atomic motorcars, despite their fantastic reverse motion, were the familiar 1972 models. I realized the enormity of our plight just as Tim Givens ejaculated: "M.S., everything's going backwards."

"Not everything," I said succinctly, and added none too grammatically, "Just us."

I knew now who the two crab-backing men were that we had seen in the laboratory: ourselves. And I recognized, too, what conspicuous figures we must now be, walking backwards along the sidewalk. Already we were receiving curious stares, which seemed to us, of course, to come just before the starers noticed us. "Stand still," I said. "We're attracting attention. We don't want to advertise our situation, whatever it is."

We stood there for an hour, while I alternately experimented with the handsets and wrestled with the problem of our existence. The former pursuit I soon found completely fruitless. Obviously the handsets exerted no effect whatsoever upon our status. The latter was more rewarding, for in that hour I had fixed several of the rules necessary to our reversed existence.

It had been early morning when we entered the stationary machine, and by now the sun was already setting in the east—a phenomenon to which I found perhaps more difficulty in adjusting myself than anything else that befell us. "As I recall," I said, "last night, which we are now reapproaching, was exceedingly cold. We need shelter. The laboratory was unoccupied last night. Come."

Followed, or rather preceded, by the stares of passersby we returned to the laboratory, and there for a moment found peace. The disturbingly arsy-versy normal world was shut off from us, and nothing reminded us of our perverse condition save the clock which persistently told off the minutes counterclockwise.

"We shall have to face the fact," I said, "that we are living backwards."

"I don't get it," Givens objected. "I thought we was going to go time-traveling."

"We are," I smiled ruefully, and yet not without a certain pride. "We are traveling backwards in time, something that no one in the history of our race has hitherto accomplished. But we are doing so at the rate, if I may put it somewhat paradoxically, of exactly one second per second; so that the apparent result is not noticeable travel, but simply reverse living."

"O.K.," he grunted. "Spread on the words any way you want. But this is what's bothering me the most: When are we going to eat?"

I confess that I myself was feeling a certain nervous hunger by now. "There's always food in this small icebox here," I said. I was exceedingly fond of scrambled eggs at midnight when working on a problem. "What would you say to beer and eggs?"

I took out a plastic beer-tainer, pressed down the self-opener, and handed it to Givens as it began to foam. I took another for myself. It felt good and reassuringly normal as it went down.

Then I set down the beer-tainer, found a frying pan, and put it on the small electric range. I fetched four eggs from the icebox and returned to the stove to find no frying pan. I reached out another—it looked like the same one—but handling frying pans while holding four eggs is difficult. Both eggs and pan escaped my grip and went rolling off to a corner of the lab. I hastened after them, cloth in hand to clean up the mess.

There was no mess. There was no frying pan either, and no eggs.

Dazed, I returned to my beer. And there was no beer.

I got another beer-tainer out of the icebox, and sipping from it I drew a most important conclusion. Physical objects which we wore or held were affected by our fields and remained with us. Anything which we set down went on its normal course—away from us forever.

This meant that cooking was impossible for us. So would be eating in a restaurant, for we and the waiter would be going in temporally opposite directions. I explained this to Givens while we ate cheese.

"It's just a sample," I said, "of the problems we have ahead of us. If it weren't for the bare chance of achieving a reversal sometime, I should be tempted to shuffle off this coil now."

It took him a moment to gather my meaning. Then he guffawed and said, "Uh uh, M.S. Not for little Timmy. Life's the one thing to hold on to—the one thing worth living. And even if it's a screwy wrongwayround life, I'm holding on."

Authors of your time, Mr. O'Breen, have occasionally written of time in reverse; but have they ever realized the petty details that such a life involves? All contact with other humanity is impossible. I have, through thirty years of practice, developed a certain ability to understand reverse speech, but no one can understand me in return. And even by written messages, how can an exchange be carried on if you ask me a question at 12:00 o'clock and I answer it at 11:59?

Then there is the problem of food. Not only this question of cooking; but how is one to buy food? How, as one's own clothes wear out, is one to replace them? Imagine yourself speeding along on an empty train, while another train laden with all the necessities of life passes on the parallel track in the opposite direction.

The torture of Tantalus was nothing to this.

I owe my life, such as it is, to Tim Givens, for it was his snide ingenuity which solved this problem. "It's a cinch," he said, "we just steal it."

We had by now learned to walk backward, so that we could move along the streets without exciting too much comment. Visualize this, and you will see that a man walking backward from 12:00 to 11:55 looks like a man walking forward from 11:55 to 12:00.

Visualize it further: A man moving in this wise who enters a store empty-handed at 12:00 and leaves loaded with food at 11:50 looks like a normal man who comes in with a full shopping bag at 11:50 and leaves without it at 12:00—a peculiar procedure, but not one to raise a cry of "Stop thief!"

My conscience rebelled, but necessity is proverbially not cognizant of laws. So we could live. We could have whatever we wanted, so long as we kept it on our persons. There was a period when Givens ran amok with this power. He plundered the city. For a time he possessed an untold fortune in banknotes and gold and precious gems. But their weight tired him in the end; crime has no zest when it is neither punishable nor profitable.

Work was impossible. I tried to do the necessary research and experiment to reverse our courses, but nothing could be achieved when all inanimate objects departed on another time stream as soon as I ceased to hold them. I could read, and did read inordinately, plundering libraries as eagerly as food stores. Sometimes I thought I saw a glimmering of hope, but it was the false daylight at the mouth of an endless and self-extending tunnel.

I missed music, although after some twenty years I did succeed in cultivating a taste for the unthinkable progressions of music heard in reverse. Givens, I think, missed knavery; at last the world was giving him gratis the living which it owed him, and he was bored.

So we took to travel—which was accomplished, of course, by climbing backward onto a boat or train at its destination and traveling back with it to its origin. In strange foreign lands the strangeness of reversal is less marked. And a magnificent mountain, a glinting glacier is free from time.

The best part of travel was waterfalls—perhaps the one advantage of our perverse state. You cannot conceive the awesome stateliness of a river leaping hundreds of meters in the air. We even made a special trip to British Guiana to see Kukenaam; and beholding it, I felt almost reconciled to my life.

I was most tormented when I despairingly abandoned any scientific research and took to reading novels. Human relationships, which had seemed so unnecessary to my self-absorbed life, now loomed all-significant. I wanted companionship, friendship, perhaps even love, as I had never wanted fame and glory.

And what did I have? Givens.

The only man with whom I could communicate in all the universe.

We tried separation occasionally, but never without appointing a meeting place and time for which we were always both early. Loneliness is a terrible thing, as no one else of my race can fully know.

We were inseparable. We needed each other. And we hated each other.

I hated Givens for his banal humor, his cheap self-interest.

He hated me for my intellect, my pride.

And each laid on the other the blame for our present fate.

And so, a few days ago, I realized that Givens was planning to kill me. In a way, I think it was not so much from hatred of me as because he had missed for thirty years the petty conniving of his old life and now at last saw that a grand crime was possible for him.

He thought that he was hiding it from me. Of course he could not. I knew every bulge of the possessions that he wore, and easily recognized the revolver when he stole it and added it to his gear.

We were in Los Angeles because I had come to look at myself. I found an odd pleasure in doing that occasionally, as you will have realized from my "ghosts," a bitter sort of joy. So now I stood in the Queen of the Angels Hospital peering through glass at my red-faced yowling two-day-old self. A nurse smiled at me with recognition, and I saw she thought I was Gramps. There, looking at my beginning life, I resolved to save my life, however tortured and reversed it was.

We were then living in the room you know on West Adams. For some time we had developed the technique of watching for people moving into a place. After that—before, from the normal viewpoint—the place is untenanted and safe for our abode for a while.

I returned to the room to find Tim Givens' body on the bed. Then I knew that death had the power to stop our wanderings, that the dead body resumed its normal movement in time. And I knew what else I must do.

The rest of that scene you know. How I took your card, gave your official-looking friend my confession, and backed out—when you thought me entering.

When I next visited the room, Givens was there alive. It was surprisingly simple. Underestimating me in practical matters, he was not on his guard. I secured the revolver with no trouble. Just before I pressed the trigger—for the bullet, freed from my field, moved for a moment in normal time—I saw the bullet strike.

I pressed hard, and gave him release.

Now I seek it for myself. Only death can end this Odyssey, this voyage of loneliness and pain compared to which *The Flying Dutchman* sailed on a luxury cruise. And when this manuscript is typed, I shall swallow the cyanide I stole yesterday.

This manuscript must reach the World Institute for Paranormal Research. They will find my notes in my laboratory. They must know that those who foretold danger were right, that my method must not be used again save with serious revision.

And yet this cannot reach them before the experiment; for they would stop me and I was not stopped. Seal it, then. Place it in the hands of some trustworthy institution. And inscribe on it:

To be delivered to the World Institute for Paranormal Research, Basle, Switzerland, F.E.D., February 3, 1971.

Perhaps the name of Hull may yet not be forgotten.

Fergus O'Breen swore comprehensively for a matter of minutes. "The egotist! The lowdown egocentric idiot! Think what he could have told us: How the war came out, how the peace was settled, how atomic power was finally developed—! And what does he give us? Nothing that doesn't touch him."

"I wish that's all I had to worry about," said Detective Lieutenant A. Jackson morosely.

"There are hints, of course. Obviously a United Nations victory or he wouldn't have been living in such a free world in 1971. And that F.E.D. in the address—"

"What would that mean?"

"Maybe Federated European Democracies—I hope. But at least we've learned a wonderful new word. Chronokinesis—" He savored it.

Jackson rose gloomily. "And I've got to get down to the office and try to write a report on this. I'll take this manuscript—"

"Uh uh. This was given me in trust, Andy. And somehow it's going to get to the WIRP on the appointed date."

"O.K. I'm just as glad. If the inspector saw *that* in the files— Want to come down with me and see what we can cook up?"

"Thanks no, Andy. I'm headed for the Queen of the Angels."

"The hospital? Why?"

"Because," Fergus grinned, "I want to see what a two-day-old murderer looks like."

Gandolphus

"If there was a detective's union," said my friend Fergus O'Breen, "I'd be out on my ear."

It was a good hook. I filled the steins again with Tuborg dark and got ready to listen.

"Remember that Compleat Werewolf business right here in Berkeley?" Fergus went on. "Or the time machine alibi in L.A.? You take now Dr. Fell or H. M. or Merlini; practically every case they get looks like it's supernatural or paranormal and they just plain know it isn't and start in solving it by 'How was this normally gimmicked?' Rules of the profession. Gentleman's agreement. Only to me things happen, and they don't fit."

"And what was it this time?" I asked. "A poltergeist? Or an authentic Martian invasion?"

Fergus shook his head. "It was . . . Gandolphus. And what Gandolphus was . . . Look: I'll tell you how I got dealt in. Then you can read the rest for yourself. I wangled a photostat of the damnedest document . . .

"It was when I was back in New York last year. Proving a Long Lost Heir was a phony—nice routine profitable job. So it's all polished off and I stick around Manhattan a couple of days just for kicks and I'm having dinner with friends when I meet this character Harrington. I won't describe him; he characterizes himself better than I could. So he learns I'm a private investigator; and just like people learn you're a writer and give with their life histories, he drops his problem in my lap.

"It looks more like a police job to me, and I tell him so; and since I know Bill Zobel in his precinct I say I'll introduce him. He's all hot to get started, once he's got the idea; so we take a cab down and Bill thinks it's worth looking into and we all go over to Harrington's apartment in Sheridan Square.

"Now you've got to understand about Bill Zobel. He is—or was at this time I'm talking about—a damned good straight cop. Absolutely efficient, more intelligent than average . . . and human. Tough enough when he had to be, but no rough stuff for its own sake.

"Bill and I settled down in the living room to watch for whoever or whatever Gandolphus might be, and Harrington went into his study to type a full formal statement of the complaint he'd sketched to us. It was about two A.M. by now; and

we were too tired for chess or cribbage even if we hadn't been kind of scared by
the too damned beautiful boards and men Harrington offered us. So Bill Zobel
switched on WQXR and we sat listening to music and Harrington's typing.

"The typing stopped at three. Nobody had come or gone, not even Gandolphus, through the one door of the study. At three fifteen we went in. Harrington
was dead, and to me it looked natural."

Fergus stopped.

"To date," I said flatly, "this is no payment for good beer."

He reached for his briefcase. "At that point," he said, "I thought it was just
about the most pointless evening I'd ever spent. Then, while we waited for the
men from the Medical Examiner's office, Bill and I read what Harrington had
been typing."

He handed me a sheaf of photostats. They were labeled *Statement found in and
beside typewriter of Charles Harrington, deceased.*

My name is Charles Harrington. I am fifty-three years of age, and a native American citizen. My residence is 13 Sheridan Square.

That is, I believe, the correct way to begin a statement? But the way from that
point on leads through thornier brambles or, to shift the metaphor, through a
maze in which the desideratum is to find, not the locus of egress, but the locus of
entrance.

My name may not be unfamiliar to such as are interested in hagiography and
iconography. My collection of tenth-century objects of virtu relating to Christian
devotional practices has made my apartment, I dare say, an irreligious Mecca to
many (inevitably one recalls the Roman Catholic church which one observed in
San Francisco, which so unbigotedly advertises itself as "a Mecca of devotion for
the faithful since 1906"); and hardly any one concerned with the variant vagaries
of the mystic mind can be totally ignorant of the series of monographs which will
some day form the definitive "life" of St. Gandolphus the Lesser. I place the term
"life" within quotation marks because the purpose of the book is to demonstrate
the fact that the canonized gentleman never existed.)

The habits of a scholar should, perhaps, make easier the compilation of such
a statement as this; but familiar though I may be with the miraculous in the Tenth
Century, the . . . shall we say, unusual in the Twentieth is more disturbing.

Let us put it that the matter began a month ago, on Saturday, October the
thirtieth. I was taking my conventional evening stroll, which on this particular
evening led me toward Washington Square. The weather was warm, you will recall; and you are doubtless familiar with Washington Square of a warm evening?

The mating proclivities of the human animal can flourish as well in autumn as
in spring, if the thermometer be but auspicious; and Washington Square of such
an evening is an unsettling spectacle to a man of voluntary celibacy. I had regretted my choice of locale and started to turn homeward when the thing flashed in
my face.

It seemed, in fact, aimed directly at my eyes; and I knew a moment of terror,
since sight has ever been to me by far the most rewarding of the senses. And
although I dodged its direct impact, by swifter muscular response than I should

have thought myself capable of (you will condone the informality of that construction), I felt a renewal of terror in the instant of the sudden blinding flash of its explosion.

The couples near me were too engrossed in other pursuits to pay any heed to me as I stood there trembling for what must have been a full minute. Only at the end of that time was I able to open my eyes, reassure myself that my sight was unimpaired, and observe upon the grass the shattered remains of what had so disproportionately terrified me. It was obvious from the fragments that the object had been a child's toy, modeled not upon the engines of my own childhood or the aeroplanes of my nephews', but upon an interplanetary spaceship such as is employed by the hero of cartoon adventures named, I believe, Buck Ruxton.

That the child should make no attempt to reclaim his toy after so nearly serious an accident is understandable. It is possibly also understandable that I, after so severe a nervous shock, was forced in the course of the short journey home to stop in three successive drinking establishments and in each to consume a pony of brandy.

I relate all this in order to make clear why I, a normally abstemious if definitely not abstentious man, retired that night with sufficient alcohol within me (I had added a fourth brandy upon my return to the apartment) to ensure an unusually, even abnormally sound sleep. It does not explain why I awoke next morning in most exquisite agony; but no hypothesis yet advanced has explained why, upon occasions, the mildest overindulgence may produce more severe reactions than many a protracted debauch.

Only after the ingestion of such palliatives as aspirin, raw egg, tomato juice and coffee was I sufficiently conscious to become aware of what had happened in my apartment during my sleep.

To put it briefly and colloquially: Someone had drunk himself silly. Silly, indeed, he had been to start with; for indiscriminately he had emptied my cooking sherry and my Sandeman '07, my finest cognac and the blended rye which my younger nephew fancies. And all direct from the bottles: the dead soldiers stood all a-row, but no glasses had been soiled.

As I assured you at the precinct station, no key save my own opens my door. Because of the value of my objects of virtu, even the superintendent and the cleaning woman are admitted only by appointment. The windows could be considered as entrances only by the most experienced "human fly."

I need not say, therefore, that I was sorely perplexed by the puzzle thus presented to me, nor that I wondered why a burglar, by whatever means he had procured admittance, should confine his attentions to my potable treasures when the apartment contains so many portable articles of value.

I took no action. My civic conscience is not readily aroused, and a police inquiry would disorder my life far more thoroughly than had the burglar. And the next occurrence, involving though it did those very articles of value neglected in the first instance, contained no element of interest to the police.

After a night of unusually heavy sleep occasioned by late work on Hagerstein's ridiculously inept thesis on St. Gandolphus, I awoke to find a light still burning faintly in this study. I entered, to discover that the gleam was that of a vigil light (late Ninth Century) burning before my treasured Tenth-Century image of Our Lady, Font of Piety. Upon the prie-dieu (Thirteenth Century, but betraying unquestionable Tenth-Century influence), which normally stood across the room but now had been adjusted directly before the image, lay a Tenth-Century illuminated breviary, open at the Office of the Blessed Virgin. Most startling fact of all, there was still visible upon the worn velvet of the prie-dieu the fresh and unmistakable imprint of human knees.

You will surely recall the legend (it is no more, as I have incontestably established) of the novice who fell asleep in the midst of copying a manuscript and awakened to find his task completed and the text illuminated far beyond his powers, with the minute signature woven into one of the initial letters: *Gandolphus*. There persists a handful of similar accounts of the unobserved and somewhat elfin post mortem activities of St. Gandolphus the Lesser; you will readily understand why the unseen fellow-tenant of my apartment was thenceforth, to me, Gandolphus.

But the contradictory nature of his activities puzzled me; one night of drunken orgy, one night of kneeling prayer. Nor was the puzzle closer to solution upon that morning on which I discovered in this typewriter an exquisite sonnet—so remarkable in its perfection that it has since been accepted for publication, under a pseudonym, by one of our better journals—signed (as though the invader could read my mind) with the name *Gandolphus*.

I shall pass rapidly over the embarrassing morning when I awakened with a curious pain in my back, to discover in the guest-room a fair-haired young woman who greeted me with the indecipherable remark "Honey! . . . Hey! For a minute I thought you was him!", who proved to be the vendor of cigarettes at a nearby place of entertainment, and who departed abruptly and in a state of bewilderment conceivably exceeding my own.

Nor shall I linger over the disappearance of two thousand dollars in ten-dollar bills, present in the apartment because a certain type of art dealer, I must confess, prefers transactions of this sort (fuller details, I assure you, would have no bearing upon this investigation), and the ecstasy of the more impoverished Italians in Bleecker Street over the vaguely described stranger who had pounded on shoddy doors in dead of night to deliver handfuls of bills.

I shall simply stress here the cumulative inconsistency of these proceedings: inebriety, religiosity, poetry, eroticism, philanthropy . . . an insane medley of the loftiest and basest experiences of which the human animal is capable.

It is this inconsistency which leads me unhesitatingly to reject the most apparently obvious "solution" of my mystery: that the fellow occupant of my apartment is no other than myself; that Box and Cox, Harrington and Gandolphus, are, in short, Jekyll and Hyde.

For whereas of his actions to date the inebriety and the concupiscence might be considered evidence of Hydean depravity, the sonnet and the almsgiving represent an exalted sublimation of which, I confess, the poor Jekyll in question is flatly incapable; and the religiosity, to my mind, fits into neither character. This is not I, nor yet another I. This is a being unknown to me, sharing the apartment to which only I have access, and indulging in actions which seem to me to have only this in common: that all represent singularly heightened forms of human experience.

This brings me to what I fear may well be the most overwhelming experience which Gandolphus has yet known, and the reason which has driven me, at whatever cost to the placidity of my own ordered existence, finally to lay this problem before a private detective and, upon his insistence, to communicate it to the police.

When I conveyed to you the nature of the incidents already here related, I found it hard to explain even to myself what "mental block" (if I may be permitted so jargonic a term) prevented me from communicating to you this evidence of the ultimate extremity of the quest of Gandolphus.

I refer, of course, to the kitchen knife which I discovered this morning still coated with blood which a private laboratory this afternoon assured me is human.

* * *

It is considerate of me, I think, to put those three asterisks there to denote the transition.

The knife, of course, is what alters the whole situation. That one bloody fact is sufficient to disrupt the tranquil *modus vivendi* which I believed that I had attained.

If you professional detectives, public and private, are as perceptive as, in rummaging around in this mind, I find some reason to believe you are, you will by now have realized many things. You will have understood, for instance, precisely what happened that Saturday night in Washington Square, and that the bright and exploding object was not a toy spaceship.

You will even understand, perhaps, which word should have been underlined in that last sentence.

But I am not at all sorry that things should end as they now must. I have felt hampered here. It is not the ideal habitation in which to pursue my research. I was forced to realize this, in a somewhat comical but nonetheless vexatious manner, in the fourth of the episodes related above, and again to some extent in the sixth, that of the knife. There is also the matter of music, which I gather from reading to be one of the major human experiences; but these ears that I employ are tone-deaf.

In short, I need a better vehicle. And just outside of this room—listening, as a matter of fact, to music at this moment—is (I find the phrase lying somewhere in a corner of this mind) metal more attractive.

There is no reason why I may not be frank. You will surely have gathered that it is imperative that I explore and realize every sensation of the inhabitants of this planet. Only through this experience can I convey to the ships that follow a proper scout's report on the symbiotic potential here. Every sensation which the host may undergo and force its symbiotic companion to share—*I must know what it is like.*

So I am turning off this machine, which has served its introductory purpose. But before I abandon it, I shall (curious how with practice it becomes possible to use them awake as well as asleep) use its fingers to type.

Respectfully yours,
(I believe that is the proper subscription?),
GANDOLPHUS

I took my time about refilling the steins. The photostats deserved some thought. I was not particularly inclined to argue with Fergus' description of them as the damnedest document I'd ever read in my life.

"I suppose," I ventured finally, "the knife did check—dimensions of blade, blood type and so on—with some known killing the night in question?"

"It did," said Fergus. "An Italian peddler."

"And the knife had only Harrington's prints on it?"

"Of course."

"The pattern's clear enough. Obviously neurotic self-centered celibate entering the perilous fifties. Very self-revealing—pretty standard schizoid set-up, though I'll admit that wild episode of philanthropy is a new one on me. Harrington's death was natural, I suppose?"

Fergus grunted. "Syncope was the word the M.E. used. In English words, something turned off the machine."

"It's a good case," I admitted. "One of the odder buildups to murder. But why on earth—"

"Why should it get me kicked out of the union? Because Bill Zobel dozed off."

I said "So?"

"It was late and it kept getting later at the station while they piled up all these facts about knives and syncopes. And finally Bill dozed off. He woke up when a patrolman came in yelling he'd picked up a hot suspect in a recent series of muggings. Nothing to do with the Harrington business; but the muggings were Bill's baby and he went off to question the suspect.

"The guy was guilty all right. Plenty of evidence turned up later. But he never came to trial. He died of the beating he got that night . . . from Bill Zobel, the tough straight cop who never stood for rough stuff.

"It got hushed up; there was nobody to make a beef. But I was there; I saw the guy before the ambulance came. It was an artistic job; that night Gandolphus learned everything he needed to know about sadism—he hadn't tried that one yet; couldn't, maybe, with Harrington's body.

"Maybe you didn't hear out in the West about the rest of Zobel's career. The beating was bad enough. Then they began to watch him when they saw he was spending damned near his whole month's salary on concert and opera tickets. Precinct captains aren't exactly used to that in their men.

"The next month's salary, and a pretty penny to boot, went to Chambord and Twenty-One and Giovanni's and Lüchow's. He was dining like Nero Wolfe as a guest of Lucullus, with Escoffier in the kitchen. He was also hanging around off-duty in some joints in the Village—the kind of joint a policeman never goes into except for a raid, when you don't need a matron to search the sopranos.

"The talk that started died down a little when Zobel suddenly got engaged to his captain's daughter—hell of a sweet kid; you could still smell the starch-and-incense of the convent, but her eyes had a gleam . . . Later on, when the gleam was doused, she told me they'd never had a clinch you couldn't show on a TV screen; our friend was learning that there was more to love than backaches. Her Bill, she said, was so groundlessly jealous he made Othello look like the agreeable husband in a Restoration comedy.

"The pay-off came when Zobel picked up a dope-peddler and went on a jag with the bastard's bindles.

"His record up to then was so clean they let him down easy and fixed a psychiatric discharge. Next month he got picked up once as a peeping Tom and once for inciting to riot in Union Square. Gandolphus wasn't missing a sensation."

"But you see," I interrupted, "we did hear about Zobel in the West." It was a fine rich feeling to have the topper for the first time in my years of knowing Fergus O'Breen. "We even met him. He was a guest speaker at a meeting of Mystery Writers of America. He told us, and damned frankly too, about the nervous breakdown he'd had last year and the psychiatric discharge and the course of treatments that led the police psychiatrist to recertify him finally. Lieutenant Zobel's happily married, professionally successful . . ."

Fergus looked glum and disgruntled. "So you knew the topper," he said. "Yes, Bill's a normal man again. This time the machine wasn't turned off. Gandolphus just left. He'd found out what he needed. And like a good scout, he's gone back with his report on our symbiotic potential.

"Care to make a small bet as to what that report is?"

Sriberdegibit

"May I be eternally cursed!" Gilbert Iles gasped.

The little man with the sketchy fringe of beard made further passes, reached out into the air again, and plunked a second twenty-dollar gold piece down on the bar beside the first.

"It's beautiful," Iles announced solemnly. Hot buttered rum always made him solemn. "I've never seen such prestidigitation in my life. See: I can say 'prestidigitation.' That's what comes of having trained articulation. That's beautiful, too."

The little man smiled. "You're an actor, colleague?" he asked.

"Not officially. I'm a lawyer. I won the Shalgreen will case today; that's why I'm celebrating. Did I tell you about that case?"

"No. Was it interesting?"

"Most interesting. You see, the presumptive heirs— But the hell with that," Gilbert Iles decided with solemn capriciousness. "Show me some more prestidigitation."

The water lapped peacefully at the piles under the bar. The sailor in the corner switched off the table light and let the clear moonshine bathe the blonde opposite him. The radio was turned so low that it was only a murmur. The man with the fringe beard made a peculiarly elaborate pass and ended up with a gold piece balanced on the tip of each of his five outspread fingers.

"May I be eternally cursed!" Iles repeated. Linda objected to strong language; for some reason she permitted *cursed* while damning *damned*. "But gold," he added. "How does that work? Does the government let you keep all that gold because it's a professional tool? Or are they phonies?"

"I know," said the little man sadly. "Laws never make any allowance for magic. And They never make any allowance for laws. I never can convince Them that Their gold isn't any earthly use to me. Oh well—" He made another pass and said a word that seemed to have no vowels. The seven coins on the bar vanished.

"Beautiful," said Gilbert Iles. "I'd like to have you around when the prosecution brings in some unexpected exhibits. How's about another drink on that?"

"No, thank you."

"Come on. I'm celebrating, I am. I can still say 'prestidigitation' because I've got trained articulation, but I'm soaring up and up and up and I want company. Just because Linda stayed home with a headache, do I have to drink alone? No!"

he burst forth in thunderous oratorical tones. "Ladies and gentlemen of the jury, how can you sit there unmoved and behold this rank injustice practiced before your very eyes? Hearts of the hardest stone would melt, thaw and resolve themselves into a dew before—"

His rounded periods drowned out the radio and the lapping of the waves. The sailor looked around, puzzled and belligerent.

"I'm sorry," said the little man. "But I shouldn't ever take more than one. I take two, and things begin to happen. I remember that night in Darjeeling—"

"So—" Gilbert Iles's voice took on the tone of a hectoring cross-examiner. "You remember that? And what else do you remember? Do you remember the pitiful state of this defendant here, parched, insatiate, and driven by your cruelty to take refuge in the vice of solitary drinking? Do you remember—"

The sailor was getting up from his table. The bartender sidled up to the fringe-bearded man. "Look, Mac, if he wants to buy you a drink, O.K., so let him buy it."

"But, colleague, if things happen—"

The bartender glanced apprehensively at the sailor. "Things are going to happen right now if you don't shut him up. Well, gents," he added in louder tones, "what'll it be?"

"Gin and tonic," said the little man resignedly.

"Hot ruttered bum," Gilbert Iles announced. He heard his own words in the air. "I did that on purpose," he added hastily.

The other nodded agreeably.

"What's your name?" Iles asked.

"Ozymandias the Great," the prestidigitator said.

"Aha! Show business, huh? You're a magician?"

"I was."

"Mm-m-m. I see. Death of vaudeville and stuff?"

"Not just that. The trouble was mostly the theater managers. They kept getting worried."

"Why?"

"They get scared when it's real. They don't like magic unless they know just where the mirrors are. When you tell them there aren't any mirrors—well, half of them don't believe you. The other half tear up the contract."

The drinks came. Gilbert Iles paid for them and sipped his rum while he did an exceedingly slow take. Then, "Real!" he echoed. "No mirrors— May I be—"

"Of course there was some foundation for their worry," Ozymandias went on calmly. "The Darjeeling episode got around. And then there was the time the seal trainer talked me into a second gin and tonic and I decided to try that old spell for calling up a salamander. We wanted to see could we train it to play 'The Star-Spangled Banner'; it would have been a socko finale. The fire department got there in time and there was only about a thousand dollars' damage, but after that people kept worrying about me."

"You mean, you are a magician?"

"I said so, didn't I?"

"But a magician— When you said you were a magician, I thought you just meant you were a magician. I didn't dream you meant you were a *magician*."

"Only a white one," said Ozymandias deprecatingly.

"Then those coins— They came from—"

"I don't know just where they come from. You reach out with the proper technique and They give them to you."

"And who are They?"

"Oh—things—you know, colleague."

"I," Gilbert Iles announced, "am drunk. What else can you do?"

"Oh, any little odd jobs. Call spirits from the vasty deep, that kind of thing. Work minor spells. Once"—he smiled—"I taught a man how to be a werewolf of good will. And then"—his round face darkened—"there was that time in Darjeeling—"

"What could you do now to help me celebrate? Could you cure Linda's headache?"

"Not at a distance. Not unless you had something personal of hers—handkerchief, lock of hair? No? The falling off of sentimentality does play the devil with sympathetic magic. You want to celebrate? I could call up a couple of houris I know—nice girls, if a trifle plump—and we—"

Iles shook his head. "No Linda, no houris. I, sir, have a monogamous soul. Monogamous body too, practically."

"Do you like music?"

"Not very."

"Too bad. There's a first-rate spirit band that plays the cornet, flute, harp, sackbut, psaltery, dulcimer, and all kinds of music. Let's see; we could—" He snapped his fingers. "Look, you're Taurus, aren't you?"

"I beg your pardon?"

"You were born in May?"

"Yes."

"Thought so. Something about your aura. Well, how would you like to have a wish granted?"

"Which wish?" said Gilbert Iles. It was not an easy phrase even for trained articulation.

"Any wish. But think it over carefully first. Remember the story about the sausages. Or the monkey's paw. But for the next minute or two you can have any wish granted."

Ozymandias reached into the air and plucked a lighted cigarette. "Be deciding on your wish, because there isn't too much time. Wimps are flighty creatures. And while you're thinking, I'll give you a rough sketch. You see, there's a Taurine wimp in the room."

"A which?"

"A wimp—a wish-imp. You see, if the universe ran strictly according to coherent laws, it would be unchanging. This would be equally dull for God and for man. So there has to be chance and intervention. For instance, there are miracles. But those are important and don't happen every day. So there's the chance element that every man can, quite unconsciously, perform miracles. Haven't you sometimes had the most unlikely wish work out, contrary to all expectations?"

"Once in a thousand times."

"That's about the odds; more would produce chaos. Well, that was because there was a Taurine wimp around. The wimps aren't many; but they constantly wander about among men. When one of them overhears a wish made by a man under his sign, he grants it."

"And it works?"

"It works. If I had only run onto a Sagittarian wimp in Darjeeling—"

Gilbert Iles goggled, and took a long swig of buttered rum. "May I," he said solemnly, "be eternally cursed!"

Ozymandias gasped. "Good heavens! I certainly never expected you to pick a wish like that!"

That slight joggling of the air was the Taurine wimp giggling. It was always delighted by the astonishing involuntary wishes of people. As Puck was forever saying, "What fools these mortals be!" It giggled again and soared away.

Gilbert Iles gulped the rest of his rum. "You mean that . . . that exclamation counted as a wish?"

"It was phrased as one, wasn't it, colleague? May I be— That's the way you make wishes."

"And I am—" Without the buttered rums, the solid legal mind of Iles would have hooted at such a notion; but now it seemed to have an ominous plausibility. "Then I am cursed?"

"I'm afraid so."

"But how? Does it mean that when I die I'll—"

"Oh no. Cursed, not damned. A curse affects you in this life."

"But how?" Iles insisted.

"Should I know? You didn't specify. The wimp probably turned you over to the nearest demon. There's no telling what his specialty is."

"No telling? But you . . . you said you could call spirits from the vasty deep. Can't you call demons and find out about curses?"

"Hm-m-m." Ozymandias hesitated. "I could maybe. But if I made the least mistake and got the wrong kind of demon— Or if— It might even be a curse you'd sooner not know about."

Iles shook his head. "I want to know. A smart lawyer can handle anything. I don't know why curses and demons shouldn't be included."

Ozymandias drained his gin and tonic. "On your own head be it," he said. "Come on."

A mile up the beach you were in a primitive world. There was no light but the moon and no sound but the waves. You ere restored to the condition of your first tailless forefather. There was no sign of civilization, only the awesome vastness of nature and its forces. Also you had sand in your shoes and it worried you.

The fringe-bearded little magician had built a pyre of driftwood and sprinkled on it a couple of powders from a case of phials in his pocket. Iles struck a match for him, but it snapped in two. Ozymandias said, "Never mind," and made a pass. The driftwood caught fire and burned with the flame of seven colors. Ozymandias said an incantation—not in the ringing and dramatic tones that Iles had expected, but with the casual mutter of any celebrant going through a familiar ritual. The flame leaped high. And the moon went out.

More precisely, they seemed to be cut off from its rays. They were in a globe of darkness at the core of which glowed the suddenly dying fire. And in that glow sat the demon.

He was of no particular height. It may have been the flicker of the dying flames; it may have been some peculiarity of his own. He kept varying from an apparent height of about two feet to around seven or eight. His shape was not too unlike that of a human being, save of course for the silver-scaled tail. His nails had the sheen of a beetle's carapace. One tusk seemed loose and he had a nervous habit of twanging it. The sound was plaintive.

"Your name?" Ozymandias demanded politely.

"Sriberdegibit." The voice was of average human pitch, but it had an unending resonance, like a voice bouncing about in a cave.

"You are a curse-demon?"

"Sure." The demon espied Iles with happy recognition. "Hi!" he said.

"Hi!" said Gilbert Iles feebly. He was very sober now; he felt regretfully sure of that. And he was soberly seeing a curse-demon, which meant that he was soberly cursed. And he did not even know what the curse was. "Ask him quick," he prodded the magician.

"You have put a curse on my friend here?"

"He asked for it, didn't he?" He looked bored, and twanged his tusk.

"And what is the nature of that curse?"

"He'll find out."

"I command you to tell us."

"Nuts. That's not in my duties."

Ozymandias made a pass. "I command you—"

The demon jumped and rubbed his rump. "That's a fine thing to do!" he said bitterly.

"Want some more?"

"All right. I'll tell you." He paused and twanged. "It was just a plain old curse. Just something we've had lying around since the Murgatroyd family got rid of it. I just took the first one I came to; he didn't seem to care."

"And it was—"

"The curse the witches used to use on their too virtuous puritan persecutors, remember? It's a nice one. In poetry, too. It goes like this." He twanged his tusk again to get the proper pitch, and then chanted:

> "Commit an evil deed each day thou must
> Or let thy body crumble into dust.

"Of course," he added, "it doesn't really crumble. That's for the rhyme."

"I've heard of that curse," Ozymandias said thoughtfully. "It's a tricky one in terminology. How have the Upper Courts adjudicated 'evil deed'?"

"Synonymous with sin," said Sriberdegibit.

"Hm-m-m. He must commit a sin each day—'day' meaning?"

"Twelve-oh-one A.M. till the next midnight starting tomorrow morning."

"He must commit a sin each day or else—"

"Or else," said the demon, with a little more cheerfulness than he had heretofore displayed, "I show up at midnight and strangle him." He coiled his tail into a garroting noose.

"Then you must be always near him to observe his actions and to carry out your duty if he fails. Very well. I lay this further behest upon you: Whenever he says your name, you must appear to him and answer his questions. Now begone!"

"Hey!" the demon protested. "I don't have to do that. It's not in my instructions. I— Yi!" He jumped again and rubbed his rump even more vigorously. "All right. You win."

"Begone!" Ozymandias repeated.

The moon shone bright and clear on the beach and on the embers of a driftwood fire. "Well," said the magician, "now you know."

Gilbert Iles shook himself. Then he pinched himself. Then he said, "I guess I really saw that."

"Of course. And now you know the nature of the curse. What do you think of it, colleague?"

Iles laughed. "I can't say it worries me. It's a cinch. A sin a day—I'm no angel. It'll take care of itself."

Ozymandias frowned and stared at the embers. "I'm glad you think so," he said slowly.

Gilbert Iles was always hard to wake up. He was especially so the next morning; but when he did finally open his eyes, he found the sight of Linda in a powder-blue housecoat a quite sufficient reward for the effort.

"My headache's all gone," she announced cheerfully. "And how is yours?"

He felt of his head and shook it experimentally. "Not a trace of a hangover. That's funny—"

"Funny? You really did celebrate then? What did you do?"

"I went down to the beach and rode on things and then I went to a bar and got talking to a"—he paused and blinked incredulously in a rush of memory—"to an old vaudeville magician. He showed me some funny tricks," he concluded lamely.

"I'm glad you had a good time. And when you next win such a nice fat fee, I promise I won't have a headache. I hope. Now come on; even the man that won the Shalgreen case has to get to the office."

A shower, then coffee and tomato juice made the world perfectly sane and plausible again. Tusked demons and tomato juice could simply not be part of the same world pattern. Neither could daily-sin curses and Linda. All Gilbert Iles's legalistic rationalism reasserted itself.

Taurine wimps—never phrase an unintended wish; it may be granted—silver-scaled tails that garrot at midnight—this was the damnedest drunken fantasy that the mind had ever framed.

Gilbert Iles shrugged blithely and whistled while he shaved. He broke off when he realized that he was whistling that tuneless chant to which the—imaginary, of course—demon had intoned the rhymed curse.

He went through a perfectly normal and unperturbed day, with enough hard work to banish all thought of demons and wimps. An unexpected complication had arisen in the Chasuble murder case. The sweet old lady—such ideal jury bait—who was to appear as a surprise witness to Rolfe's alibi suddenly announced that she wanted two thousand dollars or she'd tell the truth.

This came as a shock both to Iles and to his partner Tom Andrews. They'd taken the witness in good faith and built the whole defense around her. This sudden unmasking meant first a long conference on whether they could possibly get along without her—they couldn't—then a guarded and difficult conversation with Rolfe in jail, and finally an afternoon of trying to raise the two thousand before her deadline at sunset.

Then Linda met him downtown for dinner and a movie, and they danced a bit afterward to make up for the celebration the headache had marred. They even played the game of rememeber-before-we-were-married, and parked on a hilltop near home for a half-hour.

It was almost twelve-thirty when they got home. It was one by the time Iles had conclusively said good night to his wife and retired to the study for a final check-over of the testimony of the prosecution witnesses at the preliminary hearing.

There, alone in that quiet pine-paneled room, he thought of the wish and the curse for the first time since his morning shave. It was now over an hour past midnight. All day long he had been too busy to devote an instant to sin. And his neck was still eminently unstrangled. He smiled, trying to figure out what curious combination of subconscious memories could have produced such a drunken nightmare. Creative imagination, that's what he had.

Then, just as a final touch of direct evidence, he said, "Sriberdegibit!"

The demon sat cross-legged on the desk, his height fluctuating and the plaintive twang of his tusk ringing through the room.

Gilbert Iles sat speechless. "Well?" the demon said at last.

"Well—" said Gilbert Iles.

"You summoned me. What goes?"

"I— You— I— You're real?"

"Look," Sriberdegibit expostulated. "Am I real? That's a fine thing to call me up to ask. Am I a philosopher? Are you real? Is the universe real? How should I know these things?"

Iles eyed the silver tail somewhat apprehensively. "But—it's way past midnight now."

"So what? Why should I bother materializing unless you summon me or unless I have to finish you off?"

"And you don't have to?"

"Why should I? You did your daily sin all right."

Iles frowned. "When?"

"You arranged to suborn a witness, didn't you?"

"But that . . . that's all in the day's work."

"Is it? Didn't something hurt a little inside when you decided to do it? Didn't you use to say to yourself when you were young that you weren't going to be that kind of a lawyer, oh no? Didn't you sin against yourself when you did that?"

Gilbert Iles said nothing.

"Can I go now?" Sriberdegibit demanded.

"You can go."

The demon vanished. Iles sat in his study a long time that night, staring at the desk but not seeing the transcript.

"Tom, about Rolfe's phony witness, I'm not sure we ought to use her."

"Not use her? But the whole case'll blow up without her."

"Not necessarily. I think we're overreaching ourselves anyway with a plea of not guilty. If we lose out, it'll mean the gas chamber for him. But if we change the plea to guilty in a lesser degree, we can maybe get him off with five or ten years."

"And after we paid out two thousand?"

"Rolfe paid that. And he can afford to."

"Nuts, Gil. You're not going ethical on me, are you?"

"Hardly. But it's not safe. She can't be trusted. She might go on strike for more yet. She might even sell out to the prosecution and arrange to break down on her cross-examination. She might blackmail us by threatening to confess to the Bar Association."

"Maybe you're right at that. When you put it that way— Here, let's have a snort on it. What else do you know?"

"Nothing much. Oh, I did pick up a choice little item on Judge Shackford. Do you know that in the privacy of his chambers—"

Gilbert Iles felt the cool balm of relief. He wasn't becoming one of these prigs who prate about ethics. God, no. But it was one thing to sin casually against yourself, and quite another to be reminded of it—to know consciously that you had sinned and thereby saved your neck.

Talking Rolfe into the change of plea was another matter. It was only accomplished after Iles had built an exceedingly vivid picture of the dear sweet old lady selling out on the witness stand and delivering Rolfe straight to the Death Row. Then there were officers to see and papers to file and the whole new strategy to go over minutely with Tom Andrews.

He phoned Linda that he wouldn't be home, dined on sandwiches and spiked coffee in the office, and finally got home at eleven too tired to do more than hang up his clothes, brush his teeth, and bestow one half-conscious kiss on his wife before his eyes closed.

He woke up the next morning feeling badly puzzled, and wondered what he was puzzled about. It wasn't until about 10:30, in the midst of a conference with a client, that the worry struck him clearly. He hadn't had time to do a thing yesterday except the surely quite unsinful business of abandoning the perjured witness. And yet no silvery tail had coiled about his throat at midnight.

He got rid of the client as soon as he decently could. Then, alone in his office, he cleared his throat and said, "Sriberdegibit!"

The wavering outline of the demon sat tailor-wise on his desk and said, "Hi!"

"You," said Gilbert Iles, "are a fake. You and your curse and your tail. Poo, sir, to you!"

Sriberdegibit twanged at his tusk. His tail twitched hungrily. "You don't believe I'm really going to attend to you? Ha!"

"I certainly don't. The whole thing's a fraud. I didn't have time yesterday to work in a single sin. And here I am, safe and sound."

"You just underrate yourself," said the demon not unkindly. "Remember spreading scandal about Judge Shackford? That's getting around nicely, and it's going to cost him the next election. That'll do for one day."

"Oh. I hadn't thought of it as— Oh— But look, Srib. We've got to get this clear. What constitutes—" He broke off and answered the buzzer.

It was Miss Krumpig. "Mr. Andrews wants you to go over the brief on appeal in the Irving case. Shall I bring it in now, or do you have a conference? I thought I heard voices."

"Bring it in. I was just . . . ah . . . just rehearsing a speech." He clicked off.

"Well now," said Sriberdegibit. "As to what constitutes—"

"Begone," Iles interrupted hastily as the door opened.

Miss Krumpig listened and frowned as she entered. "That's a funny noise. Sort of a plaintive twanging like. It's dying away now—"

She put the rough draft of the brief on his desk. As usual, she leaned over more and nearer than there was any good reason to. She had changed to a subtler scent and had discovered a blouse with the maximum combination of respectability and visibility.

Anyone employing Miss Krumpig should have had no trouble at all in contriving a sin a day.

"Will that be all now, Mr. Iles?"

He thought of Linda and of the curse of a monogamous temperament. "No," he said firmly. "I'll think of something else." Miss Krumpig left the room trying to figure that one out.

For a week the curse took care of itself, with very little help from Gilbert Iles. He thought of a few sins for himself; but it is not easy to sin when your love for your wife and your stimulated professional conscience block the two simplest avenues. Saturday night he did manage to cheat undetected in the usual poker game and wound up with thirty-one ill-gotten dollars—which once the deadline was passed he proceeded to spend on a magnificent binge for the bunch of them. Another night he visited a curious dive that he had often heard rumors of, something in the nature of the more infamous spots for tourists in Havana. It was the one way of committing a sensual sin without infidelity to Linda. It was also a painful bore.

The other days, the days when he was too busy or too uninventive to achieve what he thought a sin, turned out all right, too. Like the day when the girl in the restaurant gave him change for a ten out of his five. He noticed the mistake and accepted the money as a gift from the gods, thinking nothing more of it. But Sriberdegibit was sinfully delighted when the girl had to make up the difference, couldn't do it, and lost her job.

Then there was the pedestrian that he playfully scared, causing a heart attack.

There was the boon companion whom he encouraged in a night's carousing, knowing subconsciously that it meant starvation rations for his children. There was the perfectly casual lie with which he got out of jury duty—a sin, Sriberdegibit explained, against the State as representing his fellow man.

But these episodes all had their effect, and that effect was, for a cursed man, an awkward one. Gilbert Iles was as careless and selfish as the next man, but he was not constituted to do ill willfully. After the Judge Shackford business, he was rather careful as to the scandalous rumors which he spread. He drove carefully, he revised his statement on jury duty, he developed a certain petty financial scrupulousness.

And one midnight, driving home alone from an evening's business-sociability with a client, he felt cold scales coil about his throat.

Gilbert Iles did not have the stuff of a good sinner. His first reaction was to pull the car up to the curb; an automobile guided by a strangled corpse would be a frightful danger at large. And as he did so he managed with choking breath to gulp, "Sriberdegibit!"

The elastic shape of the demon wavered on the steering wheel as the car stopped. Iles tried to shift away from it in the cabined limits of the coupé, but the silver tail held him fast. "Must talk!" he gasped. "One minute!"

Sriberdegibit hesitated, then let his tail relax ever so slightly. "O.K.," he said. "I was starting in a minute earlier to make it slow and comfortable. I can do it faster at midnight, but you won't like it."

"Comfortable!" Iles grunted. His hand slipped beneath the scaly coils and massaged his aching neck. "But listen." He was thinking faster than he had ever thought in front of a jury "Our agreement—invalid under laws of this country—contract involving murder non-enforceable as contrary to general welfare."

Sriberdegibit laughed and the tail twitched tighter. There was nothing plaintive or grotesque about him now. This was his moment; and he was terrible in his functional efficiency. "I'm not subject to the laws of this country, mortal. Our contract is by the laws of my kingdom!"

Iles sighed relief, as best he could sigh under the circumstances. "Then you can't strangle me for another hour."

"And why?"

"Contract under your kingdom . . . you admit . . . midnight now but only by daylight saving . . . laws of this country . . . to your kingdom it is only 11 o'clock."

Slowly the tail relaxed. "I would," said Sriberdegibit mournfully, "draw a lawyer. But you'd better get busy before midnight."

Gilbert Iles frowned. Then he started up the car. "Down here on the boulevard there's a blind cripple sells newspapers. Works all night—I've often noticed him there. If I—"

"Now," said the demon, "you're getting the swing of it."

Gilbert Iles waited until a late streetcar had picked up the little herd of people waiting by the cripple. Then he started across the street, but his feet would not guide him to the blind vender. They took him first into a bar. He had three rapid drinks, his eyes fixed on the clock whose hands moved steadily from twelve toward one.

"Don't let the time get you, Mac," the barkeep said consolingly after the third. "It ain't closing time till two. You got all the time in the world."

"It's closing time at one," said Iles tautly, and felt his gullet tighten up at the memory of those scaly coils.

"You look kind of worried. Need some company?" This was from a girl with a red dress and a bad bleach. "Well, I do," she went on when he didn't answer. "You'll buy me a drink, won't you? Sure you will. The usual, Joe."

The hands went steadily around. The drinks came regularly. The girl moved her stool closer, and the red skirt glowed warm against his thigh. This would be such a simple way. The choice was clear: To sin against a total stranger who would suffer deeply from it, or to sin against your wife who would never know it. The problem was simple, but Gilbert Iles knew the answer before he even considered it. He rose at last from his stool.

"It's almost midnight," he said. "Closing time."

The barkeep and the girl in red stared after his lurching exit, and then stared wonderingly at each other. "You're slipping, Verne," said the barkeep.

"This time," said Verne, "I'll have a *drink*."

Gilbert Iles reached the corner. Another streetcar load was just leaving. Behind them they left the empty corner and the blind cripple. He sat on the sidewalk, his legs crumpled under him at implausible angles. His head with its black glasses moved slightly at each sound. Everything about him was very clear to Gilbert Iles. He could see that his left thumbnail was cracked, that he had a hairy mole high on his right cheekbone, that there was exactly $2.37 in the cash box.

Iles shut his own eyes as he grabbed the cash box. He couldn't have said why, unless it was from some unconscious desire to even the odds between himself and his adversary.

Self-blinded, he seized the box. It was a low, foul, damnable act, and he was doing it to save his neck. Neither his closed eyes nor his many whiskies could blind him to the baseness of the act. Sin is not fun.

And as he grabbed he felt a choking grip on his neck.

His mind whirled. He couldn't be wrong. He had five minutes to spare. And this was certainly a— And then he realized that the grip was not of scales but of finger and thumb.

He opened his eyes. The vender towered over him. The dark glasses were gone, and the legs uncoiled from their double-jointed posture. The face with the hairy mole was transfigured by righteous wrath and the hand with the broken thumbnail was balled into a fist driving straight at Iles's face. It connected beautifully.

"You low scum of a rat!" the vender murmured. "Rob a blind man, will you?" *Thud.* "Steal a cripple's earnings, will you?" *Wham.* "Take advantage of a man's helplessness, will you?" *Crash.*

The accurate legal mind of Gilbert Iles gave one last flicker. "But you're not a—"

"You thought I was, didn't you?"

Guilt and the whiskies combined to rob Iles of any power to fight back. When it was over, his puffed lips formulated one question. "Whaddimeizzit?"

The vender deciphered it and looked at a concealed watch. "One ten."

"Thanks, brother," Iles groaned. The sodden pulp of his face managed to smile.

"Sriberdegibit!" he said when he was back in the car.

"I'm still here," said the voice bounced through invisible caves. "You didn't dismiss me."

"Sorry. Can't see so good. My eyes . . . they swell— But it's after even your midnight, and I didn't manage to—"

The demon repeated the vender's own argument. "After all," he said consolingly, "you meant ill."

"And what," Linda demanded, "were you celebrating last night?"

Gilbert Iles rolled over in bed, sat up, and opened his eyes. Or rather he tried to open them. Through puffy slits he could barely see his wife and beside her the clock which said 1:30.

He gave a groan and started to jump out of bed. When he moved his muscles, the groan redoubled and he sank back on his pillow.

"You are in a state," said Linda. There was sympathy under the tartness of her voice.

"The time," Iles muttered. "The office— Tom—"

"Tom phoned about eleven. I told him you were laid up with a bad cold."

"But I ought to—"

"I thought you'd better sleep it off. And you're not going to any office today looking the way you do. I'd bring you a mirror to prove it, only it's no sight to greet a man before breakfast. But what was all the celebrating for? And I didn't have a headache last night."

"You see, dear—" Iles tried to articulate between swollen lips.

Linda smiled. "Don't try, darling. Sorry I asked. Tell me after breakfast—or never, if you don't want to. Everything'll be ready as soon as you are."

Every perfect wife is a perfect diagnostician. For this breakfast Linda had prescribed soft-boiled eggs, tomato juice, a very full pot of black coffee, the morning paper—in its virginal and unrumpled state—and solitude. She served his food but did not speak to him or come near him again.

After the fifth cup of coffee and the third cigarette, Gilbert Iles went in search of his wife. He found her on the sun porch watering the ferns. She wore a bright printed jumper and the sun was alive in her hair.

"Linda—" he said.

"Yes, darling?" She scooped a magazine off the most comfortable chair and helped him as his creaking legs eased into it.

"I've got something to tell you, Linda."

She went on watering the ferns, but her hand trembled enough to scatter a few drops wide of their mark. "What is it? A new case?"

"No, it's— There's something about me you'll have to know, dear."

"How long is it? Three and a half years? And there's something I still don't know?"

"I'm afraid there is."

"Bad?"

"Bad."

"Worse than smoking in the bathroom?"

He laughed, but it hurt his mouth. "A little. You see, Linda, I . . . I'm living under a curse."

Water splashed on the floor. Then Linda forced herself to set the can down very steadily, take a cloth, and mop up the mess. Not till she had finished did she say, very lightly, "That's a fine thing to say. Here I wear my fingers to the bone slaving to make a nice home for you—"

"You know that's not what I mean."

"I know. It's just that— Well, it's a funny way of putting it. Tell me what's the matter."

"It isn't anything to do with you—"

Linda went over to the chair and put her arm around his shoulder. "Isn't it just?" she demanded fiercely. "Whenever there's something the matter with you, Gilbert Iles, it is something to do with me. You're me; don't you understand that?"

"My curse isn't your curse. You see, Linda, it's . . . I know it's hard to believe, but . . . well, I have to commit a sin every day."

Linda stared at him. Her face expressed a sort of grave average between laughter and tears. "You mean— Oh, darling, do you mean I'm not enough for you?"

He took her hand. "Nonsense. You're all I ever want."

"Then is it . . . I know you've been drinking a lot lately, but I thought . . . you don't mean it's . . . got hold of you, do you?"

"It isn't that. It isn't any particular kind of sin. It's just a sin. You see, I told you. It's a curse."

Linda regarded him seriously. "You did drink all that tomato juice and coffee, didn't you?"

"Yes."

"Then I think you'd better tell me all about this from the beginning." She slid comfortably onto his lap and kept her ear close to his aching lips.

"It started," he began, "that night I was celebrating the Shalgreen case. It happened I met a—"

"But that's awful," she said when he had finished. "That's terrible. To think that all sorts of silly wishes might be granted, do get granted— Oh my! The things I wished when I was in high school— I'll have to be careful."

"Then you do believe me?"

"Of course."

"I hardly dared expect— That's why I didn't tell you before. It's so fantastic."

"But you told me," she said simply, and leaned over to kiss him. "No, I'd hurt your poor lips."

"But what am I going to do? I can't go on like this. For one thing I never know what's going to count as a sin or not. But what's worse, I . . . I'm afraid I don't like to sin. Not when I know it, not when I think: This is sinning. You have to be a special kind of person for that; and I'm not. What are we going to do?"

"Mm-m-m," said Linda thoughtfully. "I know one thing. I'm going to keep wishing your curse'll be lifted and maybe sometime there'll be one of my wimps around."

"One chance in a thousand, the little man said."

"And then . . ." Linda hesitated. "There *is* another way."

"That my brilliant legal mind has been overlooking?"

"I don't think you've exactly been overlooking it; but maybe on my account . . . I don't know quite how to say this, Gil; but if there's one kind of sin you could do easier than another—maybe even one kind that would be sort of fun and you could save yourself that way . . . I mean, after all it *is* what people usually mean when they say 'sin,' isn't it, and you shouldn't let me stand in the way of—"

"Linda darling, are you trying to suggest . . . ?"

She gathered her breath. "I'd sooner share you with that Miss Krumpig than not have you at all," she blurted out, almost as one word. "There. I said it."

"I couldn't," he said flatly and honestly.

Her fingers lifted a kiss gently from her mouth to his swollen lips. "I'm glad. Because," she said with equal honesty, "I'm not quite sure if I really meant that or not. But I have one more idea."

"Yes?"

"Get out the car. We're going down to the beach and find your fringe-bearded magician and fight magic with magic."

The bartender at the beach said, "Naw, he ain't been around here since that night you was with him, and that's O.K. with me. Every time he'd grab him a cigarette out of the air, some drunk'd get to thinking that was some screwy gadget we had here and get sorer'n hell 'cause he couldn't grab 'em, too. Tell me, mister: How did he work that trick?"

"He was a magician," said Gilbert Iles. "Do you know where he lived?"

"Seems to me it was down the beach a ways at the Mar Vista. Have another round?"

"No, thanks. Drink up, darling."

The clerk at the Mar Vista said, "Little man with a fringe beard? He was registered under the name O. Z. Manders. Left here about ten days ago."

"Leave any forwarding address?"

"No. He left in quite a hurry. Got a cablegram, and *whoosh!* he was gone."

"A cablegram? You don't know what—"

"I just noticed it was from Darjeeling. That's in India, isn't it?"

The clerk at the travel office said, "Little man with a funny beard? Yes, he was here. I explained to him that in times like these you couldn't guarantee any kind of rush accommodations for travel—he'd have to take his chances. So he got mad and went away."

"Thanks." Gilbert Iles started to leave, but Linda held him back.

"I beg your pardon," she said, "but how did he go away?"

The clerk stammered. "I . . . I don't know. How should I?"

"Please. We understand. Did he just vanish—*pouf!*—with smoke and stuff?"

The clerk said, "I am not a drinking man. But you seem sympathetic, madam. I assure you that he took a handkerchief out of his breast pocket and spread it on the floor, where it grew to the proportions of a carpet. Then he said some strange word and I swear that I saw the handkerchief fly out the door with him on it. But if you ever mention that to my employers—"

"So that's that," Linda observed. "You said your little man kept talking about Darjeeling, and now he's had to go back there. We can't get any help from him."

"I hope," said Gilbert, "he isn't too much of a problem to the coastal antiaircraft batteries. What would happen to a spotter who reported a magic carpet? But now what can we do?"

Linda held her head high and resolute. "We're going to call up your demon and talk this over with him. If my husband has to commit a sin a day, I want to know just what kind of sins."

They drove for miles up and down the beach. It was not easy in full daylight to find a suitably quiet spot for calling up demons.

"People," Linda sighed at last. "They swarm—"

"Shall we go home?"

"But it's so nice here at the beach— I'm so glad to have a day off with you even if you have to be cursed and beaten to make it. I know! We can call him up in a hotel."

They drove back to the Mar Vista. There was something appropriate in calling up a demon in the magician's former home. The clerk was puzzled by their return and looked suspiciously at Iles's battered face.

"I'll bet," Linda whispered, "he thinks I got this wedding ring at the five-and-dime. I hope."

When they were alone in the drab and scantily furnished room, Gilbert Iles said: "Sriberdegibit!"

The fluctuant form perched itself on the dresser.

Linda gave a little gasp. Iles took her hand. "Afraid, dear?"

"Heavens, no!" Her voice tried valiantly not to shake. "He . . . he's different sizes all over, isn't he?"

"In my kingdom," said the demon, "everything is in an eternal state of flux. It's only mortals who have fixed flesh; it must be very dull."

"I like it," Linda protested. "How could you buy stockings if your legs— But then you don't wear any, do you? Or anything—" She snuggled close to her husband. "See? I can talk back to him." But her voice was on the verge of sobs.

"What is it now?" said Sriberdegibit mournfully. "Did you summon me just to show me to this female?"

Iles settled his wife onto his bed and stood facing the demon as he might have confronted a hostile witness. "I want to know what is a sin?"

"Why bother?" *Twang.* "You're doing all right."

"But I don't like it and I'm not going to take it much longer. Man's a free agent. That's what makes him Man."

"Ha," said Sriberdegibit.

"I warn you, I'm going to break this curse as soon as I can. And in the meantime, I want to know just what I'm up against. What is a sin?"

"Well, you see," said the demon, "that all depends on what you believe. A sin is an offense against yourself, your God, or your fellow man."

"Then blasphemy is a sin?" Iles grinned and let loose a five-minute tirade. Linda covered her head with a pillow. Even the demon blinked once or twice.

"There." Iles brushed the palms of his hands together. "That should do for today."

Sriberdegibit's tail twitched. "But you don't believe in God, do you?"

"Why, I conceive of—"

"Don't bluff now, dear," said Linda. "We've got to know things. And you know you don't really."

"No. I admit I don't."

"Then how," the demon asked plausibly, "can you possibly blaspheme? No, that kind of sin is out for you. So is sacrilege. You've got to believe, consciously or subconsciously, that what you do is a sin."

"Just a minute," Iles objected. "How about these egocentrics who think whatever they do must be right? Can't they ever sin?"

"They know all right. Down underneath. But this atheism makes you hard to find sins for. Now if you were a Catholic, you'd have it easy every Friday; you'd just eat meat. Or if you were a Jew, you could eat pork every day and let it go at that. But for you atheists—"

"Hold on. Isn't atheism itself a sin?"

"Not if it's honest and if it lets other people alone. If a man comes to the knowledge of God and then denies Him; or if he denies the right of other people to believe in Him— How about that? Want to start some religious persecution? That's a good one."

"I— Damn it, I couldn't do that."

"Well, let's see. You can't sin against your God. You can sin against yourself or against your fellow man. That leaves you lots of scope: abduction, adultery, arson, barratry, bigamy, burglary—"

"That's a start. Adultery and bigamy are out."

"If you really—" Linda tried to say.

"Out, I said. Barratry might do."

"What's that? It sounds dreadful."

"Inciting unnecessary litigation. Very bad legal ethics. But this demon, hang it all, has gone and aroused my professional conscience. I don't know— Burglary—"

"What was the first?" Linda demanded of the demon.

Sriberdegibit was beginning to look bored with the whole thing. "Abduction." *Twang.*

"Abduction! That's it. You could do that, couldn't you?"

"Abduction? But what would I do with what I abducted?"

"That doesn't matter. Just abduct."

"But it's a serious infringement of the rights of the individual. I don't know that I could—"

"Gil darling, don't be a prig! Think what'll become of me if he ... if that tail— Please, dear. You can do a little thing like that for me, can't you?"

No man can resist a pleading wife. "Very well," said Gilbert Iles. "I'll abduct for you."

"Is that all?" said Sriberdegibit wearily.

"I think so, unless—" Suddenly Iles whirled, in the manner of one tearing away the last shreds of a witness's mask of hypocrisy. "Breaking an oath would be a sin, wouldn't it? Even for an atheist?"

"Atheists don't make oaths. They affirm."

"Then breaking an affirmation?"

"Very well." Iles raised his right hand. "I hereby solemnly affirm that I shall commit a sin every day of my life." He dropped his hand to point straight at the demon. "Now every day that passes without a sin I shall have broken my solemn affirmation."

"Gilbert!" Linda gasped. "You're wonderful."

Sriberdegibit shook his head. "Uh-uh. It's like what you said about contracts. Unenforceable because contrary to good ends. That's a vow more honored in the breach than the observance. No go. Can I go now? Thanks."

Iles stared at the empty dresser. "Demons," he murmured, "are amazing. I never heard that quotation correctly used by a mortal. Do you suppose that Shakespeare— But I hope not."

"It was a brilliant try," said Linda consolingly.

"And now I start on a career of abduction—"

"Uh-uh. First we'll go ride on the merry-go-round and then you take me to dinner at a nice fish place and then home, then you go out and abduct."

"It's early for dinner," Iles said. "Even a little early for merry-go-rounds."

"It never is," Linda asserted.

"But as long as we have us a hotel room and the room clerk did give us that look . . ."

Linda laughed. "And you all tattered and torn, poor darling! Why, you're just like a private eye!"

"Only," she said later, "they never get three and a half years' practice, do they? Poor things . . ."

Gilbert Iles kissed his wife good night and watched her go into the house. It had been a perfect day. Aside from interviewing a tusk-twanging demon, it had been an ideal, quiet, happy, marital day at the beach. He sighed, started up the car, and set off on an abduction prowl.

There was no use trying anything until night had really fallen. Meanwhile he drove around at random, surveying people. Casing the job, as a client had once called it. The ideal victim for an abduction should be alone and helpless. If not helpless, certainly not capable of battering Iles's picturesque face any further. He forced himself to look professionally upon possible victims—small children, old ladies.

He shuddered at himself. His mind, which should be devoted to the humane practice of his profession, twisting itself into these devious and stupid byways of sin. He was glad when the night grew dark. Now he could get it over with.

He turned the car onto an ill-lit side road. "The first person I see," he muttered, "after I count a hundred. *One—two—three—*" He narrowed his eyes so that they saw only the road ahead. "*Fifty-five—fifty-six—*" Nothing to it. Simply a snatch. And then? "*Ninety-nine—one hundred.*" He widened his eyes and fixed them on the first person along the all but deserted street.

It was a policeman.

"May I be—" Iles began, but stopped. Once was enough; he had sworn off that oath ever since the night in the bar. But a cop was too much. Not even practical. Make it two hundred. "*One oh one—one oh two—*" Where on earth do you— "*One ninety-nine—two hundred.*"

This time it was an old woman in a shabby gray coat, carrying a string bag that clinked. Gilbert Iles set his teeth and pulled the car up to the curb. He flung the door open and tried to remember every gangster picture he had ever seen.

"Get in the car!" he snarled.

The old lady got in. "That's awfully nice of you," she said. "Of course I'm only going to my daughter's, the one that's married to the fireman, and it's just a ways up the hill but I'm not so young as I used to be and these hills hit me in the back sometimes. It's awfully nice of you to give me a lift. You know, young man, you look like the picture Cousin Nell sent us of that boy her second girl married. You haven't got any folks in Cedar Rapids, have you?"

Gilbert Iles gave up. Just a way up the hill he stopped the car in front of the indicated house, opened his own door, got out, and helped his passenger to alight. She had not stopped talking once. "—and I do thank you, young man, and I wonder"—she reached into the clinking string bag—"if you'd like a glass of this jelly I was bringing my daughter? It's Satsuma plum and her Frank, he certainly does love it, but I guess he won't mind missing one glass. Here. You wouldn't like to come in and see that grandson I was telling you about? Of course he'd be asleep by now, but—"

"No, thanks," said Iles politely. "But give him my love. And thanks for the jelly."

As he drove off he muttered a full stream of what the demon had assured him could not be blasphemy, but which felt quite as satisfactory. Then back to the beginning. "*One—two—three—*" What would he run into this time? A detachment of marines? "*Ninety-nine—one hundred.*"

It was a man, alone. Iles pulled the car up just ahead of him, slipped out, and stood beside the walk waiting for him, his hand sinisterly thrust into his topcoat pocket.

"Get in the car!" he snarled.

The man looked at him, then burst out guffawing. "Iles, you old son of a gun! What a card! Wait'll I tell the boys down at City Hall! What are you doing wandering around here? Who waded into your face like that? Where's Linda? What a card! How's about a drink? There's a good joint near here. 'Get in the car!' What a card!"

"Ha ha," said Gilbert Illes.

What was all this? Were there really guardian angels, as well as wimps and demons, and was his deliberately frustrating his every effort at a serious sin? Well, there were still three hours to go. If he pretended to drop his abductive intention— Or can you fool a guardian angel? He didn't know.

He didn't care much either, after the third or fourth round. The politician was right; this was a good joint. The liquor was fair and the entertainers lousy; but there was a magnificent Negro who played such boogie-woogie as Iles had never heard before. Even curses and sins did not matter particularly when that boy really took it and lifted it out of this world.

In one ecstatic moment, Gilbert Iles's eye happened to light on the clock, and ecstasy vanished. It was almost 12:30.

"Sorry," he said hastily. "Got a date at one."

The politician leered. "And I thought you were a good boy. How about Linda?"

"Oh, that's all right. Linda told me to. Good-by." And he disappeared almost as rapidly as his friend the demon was wont to.

He turned up the first side street that presented itself. He didn't bother with the counting game this time. The minutes were short. His neck already twitched in anticipation of that garroting tail. Surely a trained lawyer's mind could find some way of breaking that curse. The demon had said that its previous owners, the Murgatroyds, had "got rid of it." Did that mean there was a loophole? If a Murgatroyd could find it, what was stopping an Iles? And why was his mind buzzing with a half-remembered tune . . . something about the dead of the night's high-noon?

For one hesitant instant he wavered on the verge of discovery. His alcohol-sharpened intellect seemed, for one sharp moment, to see the solution of the whole problem. Then his eyes caught sight of a figure on the sidewalk, and the solution went *pop!*

The routine was becoming automatic. You pull up to the curb, you fake the presence of a gun, and you snarl. "Get in the car!"

The girl drew herself up haughtily. "What do you mean, get in the car?"

"I mean get in the car. And quick!"

"Oho you do, do you? And why should I get in the car?"

"Because I said so." His arm snaked out—he could not help comparing it to a silver-scaled tail—seized her wrist, and dragged her in. He slammed the door and without another word drove off.

He could not see the girl at all well, but she used the scent which Miss Krumpig had recently discarded.

"Where are you taking me? What are you going to do with me?"

"I'm going to abduct you."

"I . . . I'll scream. I warn you. I'll scream. I'll—" Abruptly she lowered her voice and slid over in the seat until she was touching him. "You wouldn't hurt me, would you?"

He did not care for the scent, but he was forced to admit that it had a certain effectiveness. "Who said anything about hurting you?" he said gruffly. "All I'm doing is abducting you."

On the other side of town from the beach, Gilbert Iles finally parked the car in a quiet street. The girl turned to him expectantly. The faint light of the dashboard cast heavy shadows around her face, giving it a half-seen allure that was almost beauty.

"Get out," he said firmly.

She gasped. "Get out— Oh, I get it. This is where you live." She got out and left the door open for him. He reached over and shut it.

"Consider yourself," he said, "abducted."

It was five after one as he drove away. The outraged yelp of the abandoned girl followed him. It was five after one and his neck was still whole. But he did not look forward to a lifetime career of abduction.

"Is your cold better?" Tom Andrews started to ask as his partner came into the office, but broke off and gaped at the colorful ruin of his face. "What in the name of seven devils have you been up to?"

"Just a spot of sin," said Gilbert Iles. "And it was only one devil."

"It'll wear off," said Andrews easily. "You take it easy today. I'll handle the appearance on the Irving appeal. You can't go into court . . . er . . . looking like that. A spot of sin, huh? You'll have to give me the address of that spot—for when I'm on vacation," he added pointedly.

Miss Krumpig gaped, too, when she brought in the morning mail. But she politely covered her amazement with small talk. "Isn't it hot today, Mr. Iles? My! I wish I were at the north pole!"

Iles jumped. "Don't *do* that!"

"Don't do what, Mr. Iles?"

"Don't make foolish wishes. You never know what they'll lead to. Don't ever let me hear you do such a thing again!"

He spent a busy day working on papers and seeing no one; a nice, dull, drab day. He got home in good time, wondering what Linda would have for dinner and what sin he could manage to force himself to commit that night. Not abduction again; definitely not abduction. Barratry seemed promising; now just how could he go about—

Linda wore a warning frown as she greeted him. "People," she said. "Strange people. I don't think they're possible clients but they insist on seeing you. They've been here for hours and now there isn't any more beer left and—"

Iles felt a trembling premonition. "Stick with me," he said.

The premonition was justified. He couldn't have sworn to the face of the abducted girl, but that was certainly her scent. How could she— Then it clicked. Simple for her to read his name and address on the steering rod. And beside her, surrounded by a barricade of empty beer bottles, sat the biggest man that Gilbert Iles had ever seen. He looked like a truck driver; but the truck, to be worthy of him, would have to be huger than anything now on the roads.

"There he is!" the girl shrilled.

The giant looked up, and with no wordy prolog drained the bottle in his hand and hurled it at Iles's head. It missed by millimeters and shattered on the wall. It was followed by the giant's fist, which did not miss.

Gilbert Iles found himself sitting on the table in the next room. His ears were ringing with more than Linda's scream.

"Attaboy, Maurice!" the abductee chortled.

Maurice grinned and visibly swelled. "That was just a starter."

Linda stepped firmly in front of him. "This is a fine way to act! You come into my house and drink up all my beer and then you sock my husband! Why, a demon's a gentleman alongside of you. Take that!" And she slapped his vast round face. She had to stand on tiptoe to do it.

"Look, lady," Maurice mumbled almost apologetically. "Thanks for the beer, sure. And that may be your husband, but he insulted my sister. Now let me at him."

Gilbert Iles tried to get off the table, but his head swam and his knees wonkled. He folded his legs under him and sat like Sriberdegibit, feeling as though he were changing size quite as persistently.

"Any jerk what insults my sister," Maurice announced, "gets what's coming to him. And that's me."

Linda half-turned to her husband. "Did you, Gil? Oh— But you said you wouldn't. You promised you wouldn't."

"Did I what?" Iles held on to the table with both hands; it showed signs of turning into the fringe-beard's magic carpet.

"Did you in . . . insult her? And after yesterday afternoon—"

"I did not," Iles snapped. "I utterly deny it. I did not insult her."

"Oh, no?" The abductee advanced on him. "I've never been so thoroughly insulted in all my life."

"Oh, Gil—"

"Look, lady," Maurice protested, "I got a job to do. You go run along and get dinner or something. You won't like to watch this."

"But I did not! I swear it! I simply abducted her."

The girl's fingernails flashed at him. "Oh, yeah? That's what you said. You tell a girl you're going to abduct her and you carry her off to hell and gone and leave her stranded and never do a thing to her and if that isn't an insult I'd like to know what is."

"And I ain't standing for it, see?" Maurice added.

Linda sighed happily. "Oh, Gil darling! I knew you didn't."

Maurice picked her up with one enormous paw and set her aside, not ungently. "Stick around if you want to, lady. But that ain't gonna stop me. And thanks for the beer."

Gilbert Iles's intention was to slip off the other side of the table. But his wonkling knees betrayed him, and he slipped forward, straight into a left that came from Maurice's shoelaces.

The magic carpet rose, drifting high over the Arabian sands. All the perfumes of Arabia were wafted sweetly about it. The carpet had another passenger, a houri whose face was veiled but who was undisputably Miss Krumpig. Though markedly affectionate, she kept calling him Maurice and telling him to go to it. Then out of a sandstorm emerged a jinni driving a truck. The truck drove straight at him and connected. The magic carpet turned into a handkerchief in the center of which there was a lake. Upon investigation he saw that this lake was blood and all from his own nose. He was an old man, an old man with a fringe beard, and who would have thought the old man to have had so much blood in him? The jinni appeared again bearing an enormous mammoth tusk which twanged. The jinni raised the tusk and brought it down on his head. A woman's voice kept calling, "Darjeeling," or was it, "darling"?

There was a moment's pause, and Gilbert Iles heard the cry clearly. It was, "Darling, say it. Say it!"

He managed to ask, "Say what?" after spitting out a tooth or two.

"Say it! I can't because it wouldn't work for me and I don't know what might happen but you say it and they'll go away because I've broken three vases on him and he just doesn't notice. So, oh, darling, *say it!*"

He was back on the carpet and so was the jinni. This time the jinni was wearing the tusk in his jaw and he looked amazingly like—

"Sriberdegibit!" Gilbert groaned.

Then the jinni and the magic carpet and everything faded away to peaceful black.

Gilbert Iles opened his eyes in a darkened bedroom. There was an ice bag on his head and a smell of iodine and liniment clinging about him. He tried to move and decided it might be better to wait a day or so. He opened his mouth and heard something that sounded like a Voder in need of repair.

Through the hall door came in light and Linda. He managed to turn his head—and saw squatting on the bedside table the form of Sriberdegibit.

"Are you all right, dear?" Linda asked.

He said, "What do you think?" or a noise that meant as much, and then stared a silent question at the demon.

"I know," said Linda. "He won't go away unless you dismiss him. But it did work. When you said his name, there he was, and my! you should have seen Maurice and that woman clear out of there!"

"Sissies," said Sriberdegibit.

Undulant demons are more than a sick head can stand. "Begone!" said Gilbert Iles.

The demon shook his head. "Uh-uh. What's the use? I'd have to be back to strangle you in five minutes anyway."

Iles jumped, and every muscle ached with the motion. He managed to look at the bedside electric clock. It was 12:55.

"I didn't want to wake you," said Linda. "I never thought of that— You . . . you've been good today?"

He looked the question at the demon dourly. "Like one of those cocky angels," he asserted.

"Then, you, What's-your-name, you're going to have to . . . to do things to him at one o'clock?"

"On the dot."

"But, Gil darling, can't you quick— I mean isn't there something you can do? I know you practically can't stir from where you are, but isn't there some way you can sin just in your mind? I'm sure there is. Work out a plan for barratry; doesn't planning a sin count? Can't you— Oh, Gil, you can't let yourself get garroted with a snake tail!"

Enforced physical inaction had stimulated Iles's mind. While Linda pleaded, he was performing intricate calculations worthy of a specialist in canon law. Now he summoned up every whit of his power of trained articulation to make his words clear. They sounded inhuman, but intelligible.

"Sriberdegibit, is suicide a sin?"

"Oh, Gil dear, you wouldn't— Where would be the advantage—"

"Hush, Linda. Is it?"

"Yes. It's a sin against God or Man. It's a sin against the Giver of Life and against Life itself. It's what you'd call real good solid sin."

"Very well. You may go, Srib."

"Huh? Like fun you say. It's 12:59 and a half, and here's where I come in." The tail twitched, then slowly began to reach out. Linda fought to repress a scream.

"Wait." Iles had never spoken so fast under such difficulty. "Suicide is a sin, right?"

"Right."

"If I refuse to commit a sin, I die, right?"

"Right."

"If I die through my own deliberate act, that's suicide, right?"

"Right."

"Then if I refuse to perform my daily sin, I am committing suicide, which is a sin. There, begone!"

The tail hesitated a fraction of an inch from Iles's throat. A very slow take spread over the demon's shifting face. He twanged his tusk twice. Then, "Why I . . . I'll be God *blessed!*" he said, and vanished.

"You know, darling," Linda said later, "it hasn't been so bad after all. You can take your vacation now and get all healed up again and then you'll never know you were ever cursed. In fact you'll be better than ever, because now you'll drive carefully and you won't spread scandal and you won't do anything shady in your profession and—" She paused and stared at him rapturously. "My! I have a brilliant husband!"

He nodded inarticulate thanks.

"That was the most beautiful thinking. Why, now there won't be any stopping you. You'll go on and you'll be attorney general and governor and a justice of the supreme court and— No. No. I don't really want that. I wish—"

"Oh, oh!" Gilbert Iles groaned warningly.

"I wish," she continued unchecked, "that we could just go on living quietly, but very, very, *very* happily."

There was a wimp present.

The Ambassadors

Nothing so much amazed the First Martian Expedition—no, not even the answer, which should have been so obvious from the first, to the riddle of the canals—as the biological nature of the Martians themselves.

Popular fiction and scientific thought alike had conditioned the members of the expedition to expect either of two possibilities: a race more or less like ourselves, if possibly high-domed and bulge-chested; or a swarm of tentacled and pulpy horrors.

With either the familiar or the monstrously unfamiliar we were prepared to make contact; we had given no thought to the likeness-with-a-difference which we encountered.

It was on the night of the Expedition's official welcome to Mars, after that exchange of geometrical and astronomical diagrams which had established for each race the intelligence of the other, that the zoölogist Professor Hunyadi classified his observations.

That the Martians were mammals was self-evident. Certain points concerning their teeth, their toes and the characteristic tufts of hair on their cheekbones led Professor Hunyadi to place them, somewhat to the bewilderment of his non-zoölogical colleagues, as fissipede arctoids. Further technicalities involving such matters as the shape of the nozzle and the number and distribution of the nipples led him from the family *Canidae* through the genus *Canis* to the species *Lupus*.

"My ultimate classification, gentlemen," he asserted, "must be *Canis lupus sapiens*. In other words, as man may be said to be an intelligent ape, we are here confronted with a race of intelligent wolves."

Some Martian zoölogist was undoubtedly reaching and expounding analogous conclusions at that same moment; and the results were evident when the First Interplanetary Conference resumed its wordless and symbolic deliberations on the following day.

For if it was difficult for our representatives to take seriously the actions of what seemed a pack of amazingly clever and well-trained dogs, it was all but impossible for the Martians to find anything save amusement in the antics of a troupe of space-touring monkeys.

An Earthman, in those days, would use "You cur!" as an indication of con-

127

tempt; to a Martian, anyone addressed as "You primate!" was not only contemptible but utterly ridiculous.

By the time the First Conference was over, and the more brilliant linguists of each group had managed to master something of the verbal language of the other, traces of a reluctant mutual respect had begun to dawn. This was particularly true of the Earthmen, who had at heart a genuine, if somewhat patronizing, fondness for dogs (and even wolves), whereas the Martians had never possessed any warmth of feeling for monkeys (and certainly not for great apes).

Possibly because he had first put his finger on the cause, it was Professor Hunyadi who was especially preoccupied, on the return voyage, with the nagging thought that some fresh device must be found if the two races were to establish their interplanetary intercourse on a solid footing. It is fortunate indeed that the Professor had, as he tells us in his *Memoirs,* spent so many happy hours at the feet of his Transylvanian grandmother; for thus he alone, of that crew of superb specialists, was capable of conceiving the solution that was to revolutionize the history of two planets.

The world press alternated between roars of laughter and screams of rage when the returned zoölogist issued his eloquent plea, on a world-wide video hookup, for volunteer werewolves as ambassadors to the wolves of Mars.

Barbarous though it may seem to us now, mankind was at that time divided into three groups: those who disbelieved in werewolves; those who hated and feared werewolves; and, of course, those who were werewolves.

The fortunate position of three hitherto unsuspected individuals of this last category served to still both the laughter and the rage of the press.

Professor Garou of Duke University received from Hunyadi's impassioned plea the courage at last to publish his monumental thesis (based on the earlier researches of Williamson) proving once and for all that the lycanthropic metamorphosis involves nothing supernatural, but a strictly scientific exercise of psychokinetic powers in the rearrangement of molecular structure—an exercise at which, Garou admitted, he was himself adept.

This revelation in turn emboldened Cardinal Mezzoluppo, a direct descendant of the much misinterpreted Wolf of Gubbio, to confess the sting of the flesh which had long buffeted him, and taking his text from II Corinthians 11:30, *pro me autem nihil gloriabor nisi in infirmitatibus meis,* magnificently to proclaim the infinite wisdom of God in establishing on Earth a long misunderstood and persecuted race which could now at last serve man in his first great need beyond Earth.

But it was neither the scientific demonstration that one need not disbelieve nor the religious exhortation that one need not hate and fear that converted the great masses of mankind. That conversion came when Streak, the Kanine King of the Kinescope, the most beloved quadruped in the history of show business, announced that he had chosen an acting career as a wolf-dog only because the competition was less intense than among human video-actors ("and besides," he is rumored to have added privately, "you meet fewer bitches . . . and their sons").

The documentary which Streak commissioned for his special use, *A day in the life of the average werewolf,* removed the last traces of disbelief and fear, and finally brought forth the needed volunteers, no longer hesitant to declare themselves lest they be shot down with silver bullets or even forced to submit to psychoanalysis.

As a matter of fact, this new possibility of public frankness cured immediately many of the analysts' most stubborn cases, hitherto driven to complex escapes by the necessity of either frustrating their very nature by never changing or practicing metamorphosis as a solitary vice.

The problem now became one, not of finding volunteers, but of winnowing them. Fortunately, a retired agent of the Federal Bureau of Investigation (whose exploits as a werewolf of good will have been recounted elsewhere) undertook the task of cleaning out the criminal element, which statistico-psychology has since established as running no higher (allowing for the inevitable historical effects of repression and discrimination) than in other groups; and Professor Garou devised the requisite aptitude tests.

One minor misfortune of the winnowing process may be mentioned: A beautiful Australian actress, whose clarity of diction (in either form) and linguistic talent strongly recommended her, proved to metamorphose not into the European wolf (*Canis lupus*) but into the Tasmanian (*Thylacinus cynocephalus*); and Professor Garou, no doubt rightly, questioned the effect upon the Martians of her marsupial pouch, highly esteemed though it was by connoisseurs of such matters.

The rest is history. There is no need to detail here the communicative triumphs of that embassy and its successors; the very age of interplanetary amity in which we live is their monument.

Nor should we neglect to pay tribute to the brilliant and charming wereapes who so ably represent their mother planet in the Martian embassies here on Earth.

For once the Martians had recognized the perfection of the Hunyadi solution, their folklorists realized that they too had long suffered a minority problem of which the majority had never suspected the existence; and Cardinal Mezzoluppo's tribute to divine wisdom was echoed by the High *Vrakh* himself as that monster of legend, the were-primate, took his rightful place among the valued citizens of Mars.

It would be only fitting if this brief sketch could end with a touching picture of the contented old age of Professor Hunyadi, to whom two worlds owe so infinitely much. But that restless and unfulfilled genius has once more departed on an interplanetary expedition, trusting ever that the God of the Cardinal and the *Vrakh* has somewhere designed a planet peopled by a bat-like race *(Vampyrus sapiens)* to which he will be the ideal first ambassador.

Q. U. R.

It's got so the young sprouts nowadays seem never to have heard of androids. Oh, they look at them in museums and they read the references to them in the literature of the time, but they never seem to realize how essential a part of life androids once were, how our whole civilization, in fact, depended on them. And when you say you got your start in life as trouble shooter for an android factory, they look at you as though you'd worked in two-dimensional shows way back before the sollies, as though you ought to be in a museum yourself.

Now, I'll admit I'm no infant. I'll never see a hundred again. But I'm no antique either. And I think it's a crying shame that the rising generation is so completely out of touch with the last century. Not that I ever intended to be writing my memoirs; I didn't exactly construct my life to that end. But somebody's got to tell the real story of what androids meant and how they ceased to mean it. And I'm the man to tell it, because I'm the man who discovered Dugg Quinby.

Yes, I said Quinby. Dugglesmarther H. Quinby, the Q. in Q. U. R. The man who made your life run the way it does today. And I found him.

That summer was a hell of a season for a trouble shooter for androids. There was nothing but trouble. My five-hour day stretched to eight, and even ten and twelve, while I dashed all over New Washington checking on one android after another that had cracked up. And maybe you know how hot the Metropolitan District gets in summer—even worse than the rest of Oklahoma.

Because my job wasn't one that you could carry on comfortably in conditioned buildings and streets, it meant going outside and topside and everywhere that a robot might work. We called the androids robots then. We hadn't conceived of any kind of robot that wasn't an android, or at least a naturoid of some sort.

And these breakdowns were striking everywhere, hitting robots in every line of activity. Even the Martoids and Veneroids that some ex-colonists fancied for servants. It would be an arm that went limp or a leg that crumpled up or a tentacle that collapsed. Sometimes mental trouble, too: slight indications of a tendency toward insubordination, even a sort of mania that wasn't supposed to be in their make-up. And the thing kept spreading and getting worse. Any manifestation like this among living beings and you'd think of an epidemic. But what germ could attack tempered duralite?

The worst of it was there was nothing wrong with them. Nothing that I could find, and to me that meant plain nothing. You don't get to be head trouble shooter of Robinc if anything can get past you. And the second worst was that it was hitting my own staff. I had had six robots under me—plenty to cover the usual, normal amount of trouble. Now I had two, and I needed forty.

So all in all, I wasn't happy that afternoon. It didn't make me any happier to see a crowd in front of the Sunspot engaged in the merry pastime of Venusian-baiting. It was never safe for one of the little green fellows to venture out of the Venusian ghetto; this sport was way too common a spectacle.

They'd got his vapor inhalator away from him. That was all there was to the game, but that was enough. No extra-physical torment was needed. There the poor giller lay on the sidewalk, sprawled and gasping like a fish out of water, which he practically was. The men—factory executives mostly, and a few office foremen—made a circle around him and laughed. There was supposed to be something hilariously funny about the struggles of a giller drowning in air, though I never could see it myself.

Oh, they'd give him back his inhalator just in time. They never killed them off; the few Venusians around had their uses, particularly for repair work on the Veneroid robots that were used under water. But meanwhile there'd be some fun.

Despite the heat of the day, I shuddered a little. Then I crossed to the other side of the street. I couldn't watch the game. But I turned back when I heard one loud shout of fury.

That was when I found Dugg Quinby. That shout was the only sound he made. He was ragingly silent as he plowed through that mass of men, found the biggest of them, snatched the inhalator away from him, and restored it to its gasping owner. But there was noise enough from the others.

Ever try to take a bone from a dog? Or a cigar from a Martian mountaineer? Well, this was worse. Those boys objected to having their fun spoiled, and they expressed their objection forcibly.

I liked this young blond giant that had plowed in there. I liked him because his action had asked me what I was doing crossing over to the other side of the street, and I didn't have an answer. The only way even to try to answer was to cross back.

Androids or Q. U. R., single-drive space ships or modern multiples, one thing that doesn't change much is a brawl, and this was a good one. I don't know who delivered the right that met my chin as I waded in, and I don't know who it was meant for, but it was just what I needed. Not straight enough to do more than daze me for a minute, but just hard enough to rouse my fighting spirit to the point of the hell with anything but finding targets for my knuckles. I avenged the Venusian, I avenged the blond youth, I avenged the heat of the day and the plague of the robots. I avenged my job and my corns and the hangover I had two weeks ago.

The first detail that comes clear is sitting inside the Sunspot I don't know how much later. The blond boy was with me, and so was one of the factory men. We all seemed to be the best of friends, and there wasn't any telling whose blood was which.

Guzub was beaming at us. When you know your Martians pretty well you learn that that trick of shutting the middle eye is a beam. "You zure bolished 'em ub, boys," he gurgled.

The factory man felt of his neck and decided his head was still there. "Guzub," he declared, "I've learned me a lesson: From now on, any green giller is safe around me."

"That'z the zbird," Guzub glurked. "Avder all, we're all beings, ain'd we? Now, wad'll id be?"

Guzub was hurt when the blond youth ordered milk, but delighted when the factory man said he'd have a Three Planets with a double shot of margil. I'm no teetotaler, but I don't go for these strong drinks; I stuck to my usual straight whiskey.

We exchanged names while we waited. Mike Warren, the factory man was; and the other—but then I tipped that off already. That was Quinby. They both knew me by name.

"So you're with Robinc," Mike said. "I want to have a talk with you about that sometime. My brother-in-law's got a new use for a robot that could make somebody, including me, a pile of credits, and I can't get a hearing anyplace."

"Glad to," I said, not paying much attention. Everybody's got a new use for a robot, just like writers tell me everybody's got a swell idea for a solly.

Dugg Quinby had been staring straight ahead of him and not listening. Now he said, "What I don't see is why."

"Well," Mike began, "it seems like he was stuck once on the lunar desert and—"

"Uh-huh. Not that. What I don't see is why Venusians. Why we act that way about them, I mean. After all, they're more or less like us. They're featherless bipeds, pretty much on our general model. And we treat them like they weren't even beings. While Martians are a different shape of life altogether, but we don't have ghettos for them, or Martian-baiting."

"That's just it," said Mike. "The gillers are too much like us. They're like a cartoon of us. We see them, and they're like a dirty joke on humans, and we see red. I mean," he added hastily, his hand rubbing his neck, "that's the way I used to feel. I was just trying to explain."

"Nuts," I said. "It's all a matter of historical parallel. We licked the pants—which they don't wear—off the Venusians in the First War of Conquest, so we feel we can push 'em around. The Second War of Conquest went sour on us and damned near put an end to the Empire and the race to boot, so we've got a healthy respect for the Martians." I looked over at the bartender, his tentacles industriously plying an impressive array of bottles and a gleaming duralite shaker. "We only persecute the ones it's safe to persecute."

Quinby frowned. "It's bad enough to do what no being ought to do, but to do it only when you know you can get away with it— I've been reading," he announced abruptly, as though it was a challenge to another fight.

Mike grunted. "Collies and telecasts are enough for a man, I always say. You get to reading and you get mixed up."

"Do you think you aren't mixed up without it? Do you think you aren't all mixed up? If people would only try to look at things straight—"

"What have you been reading?" I asked.

"Old stuff. Dating, oh, I guess, a millennium or so back. There were people then that used to write a lot about the Brotherhood of Man. They said good things. And it all means something to us now if you translate it into the Brotherhood of Beings. Man is unified now, but what's the result? The doctrine of Terrene Supremacy."

Guzub brought the drinks and we forked out our credits. When he heard the phrase "Terrene Supremacy," his left eyelid went into that little quiver that is the Martian expression of polite incredulity, but he said nothing.

Quinby picked up his milk. "It's all because nobody looks at things straight. Everybody looks around the corners of his own prejudices. If you look at a problem straight, there isn't a problem. That's what I'm trying to do," he said with that earnestness you never come back to after youth. "I'm trying to train myself to look straight."

"So there isn't a problem. No problems at all." I thought of the day I'd had and the jobs still ahead of me and I snorted. And then I had an idea and calmly, between swallows of whiskey, changed the course of terrene civilization. "I've got problems," I asserted. "How'd you like to look straight at them? Are you working now?"

"I'm in my free-lance period," he said. "I've finished technical college and I'm not due for my final occupational analysis for another year."

"All right," I said. "How's about it?"

Slowly he nodded.

"If you can look," said Mike, wobbling his neck, "as straight as you can hit—"

I was back in my office when the call came from the space port. I'd seen Thuringer's face red before, but never purple. He had trouble speaking, but he finally spluttered out, "Somebody did a lousy job of sterilization on your new assistant's parents."

"What seems to be the trouble?" I asked in my soothingest manner.

"Trouble! The man's lunatic stock. Not a doubt. When you see what he's done to—" He shuddered. He reached out to switch the ike-range, but changed his mind. "Uh-uh. Come over here and see it for yourself. You wouldn't believe it. But come quick, before I go and apply for sterilization myself."

We had a special private tube to the space port; they used so many of our robots. It took me less than five minutes to get there. A robot parked my bus, and another robot took me up in the lift. It was a relief to see two in good working order, though I noticed that the second one showed signs of incipient limpness in his left arm. Since he ran the lift with his right, it didn't really matter, but Robinc had principles of perfection.

Thuringer's robot secretary said, "Tower room," and I went on up. The space-port manager scanned me and gave the click that meant the beam was on. The tower door opened as I walked in.

I don't know what I'd expected to see. I couldn't imagine what would get the hard-boiled Thuringer into such a blasting dither. This had been the first job that I'd tried Quinby out on, and a routine piece of work it was, or should have been. Routine, that is, in these damnable times. The robot that operated the signal tower had gone limp in the legs and one arm. He'd been quoted as saying some pretty strange things on the beam, too. Backsass to pilots and insubordinate mutterings. The first thing I saw was a neat pile of scrap in the middle of the room. Some of it looked like robot parts. The next thing I saw was Thuringer, who had gone from purple to a kind of rosy black. "It's getting me!" he burst out. "I sit here and watch it and I'm going mad! Do something, man! Then go out and annihilate your assistant, but do something first!"

I looked where he pointed. I'd been in this tower control room before. The panel had a mike and an ike, a speaker and a viewer, and a set of directional lights. In front of it there used to be a chair where the robot sat, talking on the beam and watching the indicators.

Now there was no chair. And no robot. There was a table, and on the table was a box. And from that box there extended one arm, which was alive. That arm punched regularly and correctly at the lights, and out of the box there issued the familiar guiding voice.

I walked around and got a gander at the front of the box. It had eyes and a mouth and a couple of holes that it took me a minute to spot as ear holes. It was like a line with two dots above and two below it, so:

It was like no face that ever was in nature, but it could obviously see and hear and talk.

Thuringer moaned. "And that's what you call a repair job! My beautiful robot! Your A-1-A Double Prime All-Utility Extra-Quality De Luxe Model! Nothing of him left but this"—he pointed at the box—"and this"—he gestured sadly at the scrap heap.

I looked a long time at the box and I scratched my head. "He works, doesn't he?"

"Works? What? Oh, works."

"You've been here watching him. He pushes the right lights? He gets messages right? He gives the right instructions?"

"Oh yes, I suppose so. Yes, he works all right. But damn it, man, he's not a robot any more. You've ruined him."

The box interrupted its beam work. "Ruined, hell," it said in the same toneless voice. "I never felt so good since I was animated. Thanks, boss."

Thuringer goggled. I started to leave the room.

"Where are you going? Are you going to make this right? I demand another A-1-A Double Prime at once, you understand. And I trust you'll kill that assistant."

"Kill him? I'm going to kiss him."

"Why, you—" He'd picked up quite a vocabulary when he ran the space port at Venusberg. "I'll see that you're fired from Robinc tomorrow!"

"I quit today," I said. "One minute ago."

That was the birth of Q. U. R.

*   *   *

I found Quinby at the next place on the list I'd given him. This was a job repairing a household servant—one of the Class B androids with a pretty finish, but not up to commercial specifications.

I gawped when I saw the servant. Instead of two arms he had four tentacles, which he was flexing intently.

Quinby was packing away his repair kit. He looked up at me, smiling. "It was very simple," he said. "He'd seen Martoid robots at work, and he realized that flexible tentacles would be much more useful than jointed arms for housework. The more he brooded about it, the clumsier his arms got. But it's all right now, isn't it?"

"Fine, boss," said the servant. He seemed to be reveling in the free pleasure of those tentacles.

"There were some Martoid spares in the kit," Quinby explained, "and when I switched the circuit a little—"

"Have you stopped," I interposed, "to think what that housewife is going to say when she comes home and finds her servant waving Martoid tentacles at her?"

"Why, no. You think she'd—"

"Look at it straight," I said. "She's going to join the procession demanding that I be fired from Robinc. But don't let it worry you. Robinc's nothing to us. From now on we're ourselves. We're Us Incorporated. Come on back to the Sunspot and we'll thrash this out."

"Thanks, boss," the semi-Martoid called after us, happily writhing.

I recklessly ordered a Three Planets. This was an occasion. Quinby stuck to milk. Guzub shrugged—that is, he wrinkled his skin where shoulders might have been on his circular body—and said, "You loog abby, boys. Good news?"

I nodded. "Best yet, Guzub. You're dishing 'em up for a historic occasion. Make a note."

"Lazd dime you zelebrade izdorig oggazion," said Guzub resignedly, "you breag zevendy-vour glazzes. Wy zhould I maig a node?"

"This is different, Guz. Now," I said to Quinby, "tell me how you got this unbelievable idea of repair."

"Why, isn't it obvious?" he asked simply. "When Zwergenhaus invented the first robot, he wasn't thinking functionally. He was trying to make a mechanical man. He did, and he made a good job of it. But that's silly. Man isn't a functionally useful animal. There's very little he can do himself. What's made him top dog is that he can invent and use tools to do what needs doing. But why make his mechanical servants as helplessly constructed as he is?

"Almost every robot, except perhaps a few like farmhands, does only one or two things and does those things constantly. All right. Shape them so that they can best do just those things, with no parts left over. Give them a brain, eyes and ears to receive commands, and whatever organs they need for their work.

"There's the source of your whole robot epidemic. They were all burdened down with things they didn't need—legs when their job was a sedentary one, two arms when they used only one—or else, like my house servant, their organs were designed to imitate man's rather than to be ideally functional. Result: the unused waste parts atrophied, and the robots became physically sick, sometimes mentally as well because they were tortured by unrealized potentialities. It was simple enough, once you looked at it straight."

The drinks came. I went at the Three Planets cautiously. You know the formula: one part Terrene rum—170 proof—one part Venusian margil, and a dash or so of Martian vuzd. It's smooth and murderous. I'd never tasted one as smooth as this of Guzub's, and I feared it'd be that much the more murderous.

"You know something of the history of motor transportation?" Quinby went on. "Look at the twentieth-century models in the museum sometime. See how long they kept trying to make a horseless carriage look like a carriage for horses. We've been making the same mistake—trying to make a manless body look like the bodies of men."

"Son," I said—he was maybe five or ten years younger than I was—"there's something in this looking-straight business of yours. There's so much, in fact, that I wonder if even you realize how much. Are you aware that if we go at this right we can damned near wipe Robinc out of existence?"

He choked on his milk. "You mean," he ventured, slowly and dreamily, "we could—"

"But it can't be done overnight. People are used to android robots. It's the only kind they ever think of. They'll be scared of your unhuman-looking contraptions, just like Thuringer was scared. We've got to build into this gradually. Lots of publicity. Lots of promotion. Articles, lectures, debates. Give 'em a name. A good name. Keep robots; that's common domain, I read somewhere, because it comes out of a play written a long time ago in some dialect of Old Slavic. Quinby's Something Robots—"

"Functionoid?"

"Sounds too much like fungoid. Don't like. Let me see—" I took some more Three Planets. "I've got it. Usuform. Quinby's Usuform Robots. Q. U. R."

Quinby grinned. "I like it. But shouldn't it have your name too?"

"Me, I'll take a cut on the credits. I don't like my name much. Now, what we ought to do is introduce it with a new robot. One that can do something no android in the Robinc stock can tackle—"

Guzub called my name. "Man ere looking vor you."

It was Mike. "Hi, mister," he said. "I was wondering did you maybe have a minute to listen to my brother-in-law's idea. You remember, about that new kind of robot—"

"Hey, Guzub," I yelled. "Two more Three Planets."

"Make it three," said Quinby quietly.

We talked the rest of that night. When the Sunspot closed at twenty-three—we were going through one of our cyclic periods of blue laws then—we moved to my apartment and kept at it until we fell asleep from sheer exhaustion, scattered over my furniture.

Quinby's one drink—he stopped there—was just enough to stimulate him to seeing straighter than ever. He took something under one minute to visualize completely the possibilities of Mike's contribution.

This brother-in-law was a folklore hobbyist and had been reading up on the ancient notion of dowsing. He had realized at once that there could have been no particular virtue in the forked witch hazel rod that was supposed to locate water in the earth, but that certain individuals must have been able to perceive that water in some nth-sensory manner, communicating this reaction subconsciously to the rod in their hands.

To train that nth sense in a human being was probably impossible; it was most likely the result of a chance mutation. But you could attempt to develop it in a robot brain by experimentation with the patterns of the sense-perception tracks; and he had succeeded. He could equip a robot with a brain that would infallibly register the presence of water, and he was working on the further possibilities of oil and other mineral deposits. There wasn't any need to stress the invaluability of such a robot to an exploring party.

"All right," Quinby said. "What does such a robot need beside his brain and his sense organs? A means of locomotion and a means of marking the spots he finds. He'll be used chiefly in rough desert country, so a caterpillar tread will be far more useful to him than legs that can trip and stumble. The best kind of markers—lasting and easy to spot—would be metal spikes. He could. I suppose, carry those and have an arm designed as a pile driver; but . . . yes, look, this is best: Supposing he lays them?"

"Lays them?" I repeated vaguely.

"Yes. When his water sense registers maximum intensity—that is, when he's right over a hidden spring—there'll be a sort of sphincter reaction, and *plop,* he'll lay a sharp spike, driving it into the ground."

It was perfect. It would be a cheap robot to make—just a box on treads, the box containing the brain, the sense organs, and a supply of spikes. Maybe later in a more elaborate model he could be fed crude metal and make his own spikes. There'd be a decided demand for him, and nothing of Robinc's could compete. An exploring party could simply send him out for the day, then later go over the clear track left by his treads and drill wherever he had laid a spike. And his pure functionalism would be the first step in our campaign to accustom the public to Quinby's Usuform Robots.

Then the ideas came thick and fast. We had among us figured out at least seventy-three applications in which usuforms could beat androids, before our eyes inevitably folded up on us.

I woke up with three sensations: First, a firm resolve to stick to whiskey and leave Three Planets to the Martians that invented them. Second, and practically obliterating this discomfort, a thrill of anticipation at the wonders that lay ahead of us, like a kid that wakes up and knows today's his birthday. But third, and uncomfortably gnawing at the back of this pleasure, the thought that there was something wrong, something we'd overlooked.

Quinby was fixing up a real cooked breakfast. He insisted that this was an occasion too noble for swallowing a few concentrates, and he'd rummaged in my freezing storeroom to find what he called "honest food." It was good eating, but this gnawing thought kept pestering me. At last I excused myself and went into the library. I found the book I wanted: *Planetary Civil Code. Volume 34. Robots.* I put it in the projector and ran it rapidly over the screen till I located the paragraph I half remembered.

That gnawing was all too well founded. I remembered now. The theory'd always been that this paragraph went into the Code because only Robinc controlled the use of the factor that guaranteed the robots against endangering any intelligent beings, but I've always suspected that there were other elements at work. Even Council Members get their paws greased sometimes.

The paragraph read:

> 259: All robots except those in military employ of the Empire shall be constructed according to the patents held by Robots Inc., sometimes known as Robinc. Any robot constructed in violation of this section shall be destroyed at once, and all those concerned in constructing him shall be sterilized and segregated.

I read this aloud to the breakfast party. It didn't add to the cheer of the occasion.

"I knew it was too good to be true," Mike grunted. "I can just see Robinc leasing its patents to the boys that'll put it out of business."

"But our being great business successes isn't what's important," Quinby protested. "Do we really want . . . could any being of good will really want to become like the heads of Robinc?"

"I do," said Mike honestly.

"What's important is what this can do: Cure this present robot epidemic, conserve raw materials in robot building, make possible a new and simpler and more sensible life for everybody. Why can't we let Robinc take over the idea?"

"Look," I said patiently. "Quite aside from the unworthy ambitions that Mike and I may hold, what'll happen if we do? What has always happened when a big company buys out a new method when they've got a billion credits sunk in the old? It gets buried and is never heard of again."

"That's right," Quinby sighed. "Robinc would simply strangle it."

"All right. Now look at it straight and say what is going to become of Quinby's Usuform Robots."

"Well," he said simply, "there's only one solution. Change the code."

I groaned. "That's all, huh? Just that. Change the code. And how do you propose to go about that?"

"See the Head of the Council. Explain to him what our idea means to the world—to the system. He's a good man. He'll see us through."

"Dugg," I said, "when you look at things straight I never know whether you're going to see an amazing truth or the most amazing nonsense that ever was. Sure the Head's a good man. If he could do it without breaking too many political commitments, I think he might help out on an idea as big as this. But how to get to see him when—"

"My brother-in-law tried once," Mike contributed. "He got kind of too persistent. That's how come he's in the hospital now. Hey," he broke off. "Where are you going?"

"Come on, Dugg," I said. "Mike, you spend the day looking around the city for a likely factory site. We'll meet you around seventeen at the Sunspot. Quinby and I are going to see the Head of the Council."

We met the first guard about a mile from the office. "Robinc Repair," I said, and waved my card. After all, I assuaged Quinby's conscience, I hadn't actually resigned yet. "Want to check the Head's robot."

The guard nodded. "He's expecting you."

It hadn't even been a long shot. With robots in the state they were in, it was practically a certainty that one of those in direct attendance on the Head would need repair. The gag got us through a mile of guards, some robot, some—more than usual since all the trouble—human, and at last into the presence of the Head himself.

The white teeth gleamed in the black face in that friendly grin so familiar in telecasts. "I've received you in person," he said, "because the repair of this robot is such a confidential matter."

"What are his duties?" I asked.

"He is my private decoder. It is most important that I should have his services again as soon as possible."

"And what's the matter with him?"

"Partly what I gather is, by now, almost the usual thing. Paralysis of the legs. But partly more than that: He keeps talking to himself. Babbling nonsense."

Quinby spoke up. "Just what is he supposed to do?"

The Head frowned. "Assistants bring him every coded or ciphered dispatch. His brain was especially constructed for cryptanalysis. He breaks them down, writes out the clear, and drops it into a pneumatic chute that goes to a locked compartment in my desk."

"He uses books?"

"For some of the codes. The ciphers are entirely brain-mechanics."

Quinby nodded. "Can do. Take us to him."

The robot was saying to himself, "This is the ponderous time of the decadence of the synaptic reflexes when all curmudgeons wonkle in the withering wallabies."

Quinby looked after the departing Head. "Some time," he said, "we're going to see a Venusian as Interplanetary Head."

I snorted.

"Don't laugh. Why, not ten centuries ago people would have snorted just like that at the idea of a black as Head on this planet. Such narrow stupidity seems fantastic to us now. Our own prejudices will seem just as comical to our great-great-grandchildren."

The robot said, "Over the larking lunar syllogisms lopes the chariot of funereal ellipses."

Quinby went to work. After a minute—I was beginning to catch on to this seeing-straight business myself—I saw what he was doing and helped.

This robot needed nothing but the ability to read, to transcribe deciphered messages, and to handle papers and books. His legs had atrophied—that was in line with the other cases. But he was unusual in that he was the rare thing:

a robot who had no need at all for communication by speech. He had the power of speech and was never called upon to exercise it; result, he had broken down into this fantastic babbling of nonsense, just to get some exercise of his futile power.

When Quinby had finished, the robot consisted only of his essential cryptanalytic brain, eyes, one arm, and the writer. This last was now a part of the robot's hookup; so that instead of using his hands to transcribe the message, he thought it directly into the writer. He had everything he needed, and nothing more. His last words before we severed the speech connection were, "The runcible rhythm of ravenous raisins rollers through the rookery rambling and raving." His first words when the direct connection with the writer was established were, "This feels good. Thanks, boss."

I went to fetch the Head. "I want to warn you," I explained to him, "you may be a little surprised by what you see. But please look at it without preconceptions."

He was startled and silent. He took it well; he didn't blow up hysterically like Thuringer. But he stared at the new thing for a long time without saying a word. Then he took a paper from his pocket and laid it on the decoding table. The eyes looked at it. The arm reached out for a book and opened it. Then a message began to appear on the writer. The Head snatched it up before it went into the tube, read it, and nodded.

"It works," he said slowly. "But it's not a robot any more. It's . . . it's just a decoding machine."

"A robot," I quoted, "is any machine equipped with a Zwergenhaus brain and capable of independent action upon the orders or subject to the guidance of an intelligent being. Planetary Code, paragraph num—"

"But it looks so—"

"It works," I cut in. "And it won't get paralysis of the legs and it won't ever go mad and babble about wonkling curmudgeons. Because, you see, it's a usuform robot." And I hastily sketched out the Quinby project.

The Head listened attentively. Occasionally he flashed his white grin, especially when I explained why we could not turn the notion over to Robinc. When I was through, he paused a moment and then said at last, "It's a fine idea you have there. A great idea. But the difficulties are great, too. I don't need to recount the history of robots to you," he said, proceeding to do so. "How Zwergenhaus' discovery lay dormant for a century and a half because no one dared upset the economic system by developing it. How the Second War of Conquest so nearly depopulated the Earth that the use of robot labor became not only possible but necessary. How our society is now so firmly based on it that the lowest laboring rank possible to a being is foreman. The Empire is based on robots; robots are Robinc. We can't fight Robinc."

"Robinc is slowly using up all our resources of metallic and radioactive ore, isn't it?" Quinby asked.

"Perhaps. Scaremongers can produce statistics—"

"And our usuforms will use only a fraction of what Robinc's androids need."

"A good point. An important one. You have convinced me that android robots are a prime example of conspicuous waste, and this epidemic shows that they are, moreover, dangerous. But I cannot attempt to fight Robinc now. My position—I shall be frank, gentlemen—my position is too precarious. I have problems of my own."

"Try Quinby," I said. "I had a problem and tried him, and he saw through it at once."

"Saw through it," the Head observed, "to a far vaster and more difficult problem beyond. Besides, I am not sure if my problem lies in his field. It deals with the question of how to mix a Three Planets cocktail."

The excitement of our enterprise had made me forget my head. Now it began throbbing again at the memory. "A Three Planets?"

The Head hesitated. "Gentlemen," he said at last, "I ask your pledge of the utmost secrecy."

He got it.

"And even with that I cannot give you too many details. But you know that the Empire holds certain mining rights in certain districts of Mars—I dare not be more specific. These rights are essential to maintain our stocks of raw materials. And they are held only on lease, by an agreement that must be renewed quinquennially. It has heretofore been renewed as a matter of course, but the recent rise of the Planetary Party on Mars, which advocates the abolition of all interplanetary contact, makes this coming renewal a highly doubtful matter. Within the next three days I am to confer here with a certain high Martian dignitary, traveling incognito. Upon the result of that conference our lease depends."

"And the Three Planets?" I asked. "Does the Planetary Party want to abolish them as a matter of principle?"

"Probably," he smiled. "But this high individual is not a party member, and is devoted to Three Planets. He hates to travel, because only on Mars, he claims, is the drink ever mixed correctly. If I could brighten his trip here by offering him one perfect Three Planets—"

"Guzub!" I cried. "The bartender at the Sunspot. He's a Martian and the drink is his specialty."

"I know," the Head agreed sadly. "Dza . . . the individual in question once said that your Guzub was the only being on this planet who knew how. Everyone else puts in too much or too little vuzd. But Guzub is an exiled member of the Varjinian Loyalists. He hates everything that the present regime represents. He would never consent to perform his masterpiece for my guest."

"You could order one at the Sunspot and have it sent here by special—"

"You know that a Three Planets must be drunk within thirty seconds of mixing for the first sip to have its ideal flavor."

"Then—"

"All right," Quinby said. "You let us know when your honored guest arrives, and we'll have a Three Planets for him."

The Head looked doubtful. "If you think you can— A bad one might be more dangerous than none—"

"And if we do," I interposed hastily, "you'll reconsider this business of the usuform robots?"

"If this mining deal goes through satisfactorily, I should be strong enough to contemplate facing Robinc."

"Then you'll get your Three Planets," I said calmly, wondering what Quinby had seen straight now.

We met Mike at the Sunspot as arranged. He was drinking a Three Planets. "This is good," he announced. "This has spacedrive and zoomf to it. You get it other places and—"

"I know," I said. "Find a site?"

"A honey. Wait'll I—"

"Hold it. We've got to know have we got anything to go on it. Guzub! One Three Planets."

We watched entranced as he mixed the potion. "Get exactly what he does," Quinby had said. "Then construct a usuform bartender who'll be infallible. It'll satisfy the Martian envoy and at the same time remind the Head of why we're helping him out."

But all we saw was a glittering swirl of tentacles. First a flash as each tentacle picked up its burden—one the shaker, one the lid, one the glass, and three others the bottles of rum, margil, and vuzd. Then a sort of spasm that shook all Guzub's round body as the exact amount of each liquid went in, and finally a gorgeous pinwheel effect of shaking and pouring.

Guzub handed me my drink, and I knew as much as I had before.

By the time I'd finished it, I had courage. "Guzub," I said, "this is wonderful."

"Zure," Guzub glurked. "Always I maig id wondervul."

"Nobody else can make 'em like you, Guz. But tell me. How much vuzd do you put in?"

Guzub made his kind of a shrug. "I dell you, boys, I dunno. Zome dime maybe I wadge myzelv and zee. I juzd go zo! I dunno how mudj."

"Give me another one. Let's see you watch yourself."

"Businezz is good by you, you dring zo many Blanedz? O Gay, ere goes."

But the whirl stopped in the middle. There was Guzub, all his eyes focused sadly on the characteristic green corkscrew-shaped bottle of vuzd. Twice he started to move that tentacle, then drew it back. At last he made a dash with it.

"Exactly two drops," Quinby whispered.

Guzub handed over the drink unhappily. "Dry id," he said.

I did. It was terrible. Too little vuzd, so that you could taste both the heavy sweetness of the rum and the acrid harshness of the margil. I said so.

"I know, boys. When I zdob do wadge, id bothers me. No gan do."

I gulped the drink. "Mix up another without watching. Maybe we can tell."

This one was perfect. And we could see nothing.

The next time he "wadged." He used precisely four and a half drops of vuzd. You tasted nothing but the tart decay of the vuzd itself.

The next time—

But my memory gets a little vague after that. Like I said, I'm a whiskey drinker. And four Three Planets in quick succession— I'm told the party went on till closing hour at twenty-three, after which Guzub accepted Quinby's invitation to come on and mix for us at my apartment. I wouldn't know. All I remember is one point where I found a foot in my face. I bit it, decided it wasn't mine, and stopped worrying about it. Or about anything.

I'm told that I slept thirty-six hours after that party—a whole day and more simply vanished out of my existence. I woke up feeling about twelve and spry for my age, but it took me a while to reconstruct what had been going on.

I was just beginning to get it straightened out when Quinby came in. His first words were, "How would you like a Three Planets?"

I suddenly felt like two hundred and twelve, and on an off day at that. Not until I'd packed away a superman-size breakfast did he dare repeat the offer. By then I felt brave. "O.K.," I said. "But with a whiskey chaser."

I took one sip and said, "Where's Guzub? I didn't know he was staying here too."

"He isn't."

"But this Three Planets— It's perfect. It's the McCoy. And Guzub—"

Quinby opened a door. There sat the first original Quinby usuform—no re-make of a Robinc model, but a brand-new creation. Quinby said, "Three Planets," and he went into action. He had tentacles, and the motions were exactly like Guzub's except that he was himself the shaker. He poured the liquids into his maw, joggled about, and then poured them out of a hollow hoselike tentacle.

The televisor jangled. Quinby hastily shifted the ike so as to miss the usuform barkeep as I answered. The screen showed the Head himself. He'd been there before on telecasts, but this was the real thing.

He didn't waste time. "Tonight, nineteen thirty," he said. "I don't need to explain?"

"We'll be there," I choked out.

A special diplomatic messenger brought the pass to admit the two of us and "one robot or robotlike machine" to the Council building. I was thankful for that alternative phrase; I didn't want to have to argue with each guard about the technical legal definition of a robot. We were installed in a small room directly off the Head's private reception room. It was soundproofed and there was no window; no chance of our picking up interplanetary secrets of diplomacy. And there was a bar.

A dream of a bar, a rhapsody of a bar. The vuzd, the rum, the margil were all of brands that you hear about and brood about but never think to see in a lifetime. And there was whiskey of the same caliber.

We had hardly set our usuform facing the bar when a servant came in. He was an android. He said, "The Head says now."

Quinby asked me, "Do you want one?"

I shook my head and selected a bottle of whiskey.

"Two Three Planets," Quinby said.

The tentacles flickered, the shaker-body joggled, the hose-tentacle poured. The android took the tray from our usuform. He looked at him with something as close to a mixture of fear, hatred, and envy as his eye cells could express. He went out with the tray.

I turned to Quinby. "We've been busy getting ready for this party ever since I woke up. I still don't understand how you made him into another Guzub."

There was a click and the room was no longer soundproof. The Head was allowing us to hear the reception of our creation. First his voice came, quiet, reserved, and suave. "I think your magnitude would enjoy this insignificant drink. I have been to some slight pains to see that it was worthy of your magnitude's discriminating taste."

There was silence. Then the faintest sound of a sip, a pause, and an exhalation. We could almost hear the Head holding his breath.

"Bervegd!" a deep voice boomed—which, since no Martian has ever yet learned to pronounce a voiceless consonant, means a verdict of "Perfect!"

"I am glad that your magnitude is pleased."

"Bleased is doo mild a word, my dear Ead. And now thad you ave zo delighdvully welgomed me—"

The sound went dead again.

"He liked it, huh?" said Guzub II. "You boys want some, maybe?"

"No thanks," said Quinby. "I wonder if I should have given him a Martian accent—they are the best living bartenders. Perhaps when we get the model into mass production—"

I took a gleefully long swig of whiskey. Its mild warmth felt soothing after memories of last night's Three Planets. "Look," I said. "We have just pulled off the trick that ought to net us a change in the code and a future as the great revolutionists of robot design. I feel like . . . hell, like Ley landing on the Moon. And you sit there with nothing on your mind but a bartender's accent."

"Why not?" Quinby asked. "What is there to do in life but find what you're good for and do it the best you can?"

He had me there. And I began to have some slight inklings of the trouble ahead with a genius who had commercial ideas and the conscience of an otherworldly saint. I said, "All right. I won't ask you to kill this bottle with me, and in return I expect you not to interfere with my assassinating it. But as to what you're good for—how did you duplicate Guzub?"

"Oh, that. That was simple—"

"—when you looked at it straight," I ended.

"Yes." That was another thing about Quinby; he never knew if he was being ribbed. "Yes. I got one of those new electronic cameras—you know, one thousand exposures per second. Hard to find at that time of night, but we made it."

"We?"

"You helped me. You kept the man from overcharging me. Or maybe you don't remember? So we took pictures of Guzub making a Three Planets, and I could construct this one to do it exactly right down to the thousandth of a second. The proper proportion of vuzd, in case you're interested, works out to three-point-six-five-four-seven-eight-two-three drops. It's done with a flip of the third joint of the tentacle on the down beat. It didn't seem right to use Guzub to make a robot that would compete with him and probably drive him out of business; so we've promised him a generous pension from the royalties on usuform barkeeps."

"We?" I said again, more feebly.

"You drew up the agreement."

I didn't argue. It was fair enough. A good businessman would have slipped Guzub a fiver for posing for pictures and then said the hell with him. But I was beginning to see that running Q. U. R. was not going to be just good business.

When the Head finally came in, he didn't need to say a word, though he said plenty. I've never seen that white grin flash quite so cheerfully. That was enough; the empire had its Martian leases, and Q. U. R. was a fact.

When I read back over this story, I can see there's one thing wrong. That's about the giller. I met Dugg Quinby, and you met him through me, in the act of rescuing a Venusian from a giller-baiting mob. By all the rights of storytelling, the green being should have vowed everlasting gratitude to his rescuer, and at some point in our troubles he should have showed up and made everything fine for us.

That's how it should have been. In actual fact, the giller grabbed his inhalator and vanished without so much as a "thank you." If anybody helped us, it was Mike, who had been our most vigorous enemy in the battle.

Which means, I think, that seeing straight can work with things and robots, but not with beings, because no being is really straight, not even to himself.

Except maybe Dugg Quinby.

Robinc

You'd think maybe it meant clear sailing after we'd got the Council's OK. You'd maybe suppose that'd mean the end of our troubles and the end of android robots for the world.

That's what Dugg Quinby thought, anyway. But Quinby may have had a miraculous gift of looking straight at problems and at things and at robots and getting the right answer; but he was always too hopeful about looking straight at people. Because, like I kept saying to him, people aren't straight, not even to themselves. And our future prospects weren't anywhere near as good as he thought.

That's what the Head of the Council was stressing when we saw him that morning just after the Council had passed the bill. His black face was sober—no trace of that flashing white grin that was so familiar on telecasts. "I've put your bill through, boys," he was saying. "God knows I'm grateful—the whole Empire should be grateful to you for helping me put over the renewal of those Martian mining concessions, and the usuform barkeep you made me is my greatest treasure; but I can't help you any more. You're on your own now."

That didn't bother Quinby. He said, "The rest ought to be easy. Once people understand what usuform robots can do for them—"

"I'm afraid, Mr. Quinby, it's you who don't quite understand. Your friend here doubtless does; he has a more realistic slant on things. But you— I wouldn't say you idealize people, but you flatter them. You expect them to see things as clearly as you do. I'm afraid they usually don't."

"But surely when you explained to the Council the advantages of usuforms—"

"Do you think the Council passed the bill only because they saw those advantages? They passed it because I backed it, and because the renewal of the Martian concessions has for the moment put me in a powerful position. Oh, I know, we're supposed to have advanced immeasurably beyond the political corruption of the earlier states; but let progress be what it may, from the cave man on up to the illimitable future, there are three things that people always have made and always will make: love, and music, and politics. And if there's any difference between me and an old-time political leader, it's simply that I'm trying to put my political skill at the service of mankind."

I wasn't listening too carefully to all this. The service of mankind wasn't exactly a hobby of mine. Quinby and the Head were all out for usuforms because

147

they were a service to man and the Empire of Earth; I was in it because it looked like a good thing. Of course, you can't be around such a mixture of a saint, a genius, and a moron as Quinby without catching a little of it; but I tried to keep my mind fixed clear on what was in it for me.

And that was plenty. For the last couple of centuries our civilization had been based on robots—android robots. Quinby's usuform robots—Q. U. R. robots—shaped not as mechanical men, but as independently thinking machines formed directly for their intended function—threatened the whole robot set-up. They were the biggest thing since Zwergenhaus invented the mechanical brain, and I was in on the ground floor.

With the basement shaking under me.

It was an android guard that interrupted the conference here. We hadn't really got started on usuform manufacture yet, and anyway, Quinby was inclined to think that androids might be retained in some places for guards and personal attendants. He said, "Mr. Grew says that you will see him."

The Head frowned. "Robinc has always thought it owned the Empire. Now Mr. Grew thinks he owns me. Well, show him in." As the guard left, he added to us, "This Grew-Quinby meeting has to take place sometime. I'd rather like to see it."

The president-owner of Robinc—Robots Incorporated, but nobody ever said it in full—was a quiet old man with silvery hair and a gentle sad smile. It seemed even sadder than usual today. He greeted the Head and then spoke my name with a sort of tender reproach that near hurt me.

"You," he said. "The best trouble shooter that Robinc ever had, and now I find you in the enemy's camp."

But I knew his technique, and I was armed against being touched by it. "*In* the enemy's camp?" I said. "I *am* the enemy. And it's because I was your best trouble shooter that I learned the real trouble with Robinc's androids: They don't work, and the only solution is to supersede them."

"Supersede is a kind word," he said wistfully. "But the unkind act is destruction. Murder. Murder of Robinc itself, draining the lifeblood of our Empire."

The Head intervened. "Not draining, Mr. Grew, but transfusing. The blood stream, to carry on your own metaphor, is tainted; we want fresh blood, and Mr. Quinby provides it."

"I am not helpless, you know," the old man murmured gently.

"I'm afraid possibly you are, sir, and for the first time in your life. But you know the situation: In the past few months there has been an epidemic of robot breakdowns. Parts unnecessary and unused, but installed because of our absurd insistence on an android shape, have atrophied. Sometimes even the brain has been affected; my own confidential cryptanalyst went totally mad. Quinby's usuforms forestall any such problem."

"The people will not accept them. They are conditioned to androids."

"They must accept them. You know, better than most, the problems of supply that the Empire faces. The conservation of mineral resources is one of our essential aims. And usuforms will need variously from seventy to only thirty percent of the metal that goes into your androids. This is no mere matter of business rivalry; it is conflict between the old that depletes the Empire and the new that strengthens it."

"And the old must be cast aside and rejected?"

"You," I began, "have, of course, always shown such tender mercy to your business compet—" but Quinby broke in on me.

"I realize, Mr. Grew, that this isn't fair to you. But there are much more important matters than you involved."

"Thank you." The gentle old voice was frigid.

"But I wouldn't feel right if you were simply, as you put it, cast aside and rejected. If you'll come to see us and talk things over, I'm pretty sure we can—"

"Sir!" Sanford Grew rose to his full short height. "I do not ask favors from puppies. I have only one request." He turned to the Head. "The repeal of this ridiculous bill depriving Robinc of its agelong monopoly which has ensured the safety of the Empire."

"I'm sorry, Mr. Grew. That is impossible."

The hair was still silvery and the smile was still sad and gentle. But the words he addressed to us were, "Then you understand that this is war?"

Then he left. I didn't feel too comfortable. Saving the Empire is all very well. Being a big shot in a great new enterprise is swell. But a war with something the size of Robinc is not what the doctor usually orders.

"The poor man," said Quinby.

The Head flashed an echo of the famous grin. "No wonder he's upset. It's not only the threatened loss of power, I heard that yesterday his android cook broke down completely. And you know how devoted he is to unconcentrated food."

Quinby brightened. "Then perhaps we—"

The Head laughed. "Your only hope is that a return to a concentrated diet will poison him. You've no chance of winning over Sanford Grew alive."

We went from there to the Sunspot. "It's funny," Quinby used to say. "I don't much like to drink, but a bar's always good for heavy thinking." And who was I to argue?

Guzub, that greatest of bartenders, spotted us as we came in and had one milk and one straight whiskey poured by the time we reached our usual back table. He served them to us himself, with a happy flourish of his tentacles.

"What are you so beamish about?" I asked gruffly.

Guzub shut his middle eye in the Martian expression of happiness. "Begauze you boys are going to 'ave a gread zugzezz with your uxuvorm robods and you invended them righd 'ere in the Zunzbod." He produced another tentacle holding a slug of straight vuzd and downed it. "Good lugg!"

I glowered after him. "We need luck. With Grew as our sworn enemy, we're on the—"

Quinby had paper spread out before him. He looked up now, took a sip of milk, and said, "Do you cook?"

"Not much. Concentrates do me most of the time."

"I can sympathize with Grew. I like old-fashioned food myself, and I'm fairly good at cooking it. I just thought you might have some ideas."

"For what?"

"Why, a usuform cook, of course. Grew's android cook broke down. We'll present him with a usuform, and that will convert him, too—"

"Convert hell!" I snorted. "Nothing can convert that sweetly smiling old— But maybe you have got something there; get at a man through his hobby— Could work."

"Now, usually," Quinby went on, "androids break down because they don't use all their man-shaped body. But an android cook would go nuts because man's body isn't enough. I've cooked; I know. So we'll give the usuform more. For instance, give him Martoid tentacles instead of arms. Maybe instead of legs give him an automatic sliding height adjustment to avoid all the bending and stooping, with a roller base for quick movement. And make the tentacles functionally specialized."

I didn't quite get that last, and I said so.

"Half your time in cooking is wasted reaching around for what you need next. We can build in a lot of that stuff. For instance, one tentacle can be a registering thermometer. Tapering to a fine point—stick it in a roast and— One can end in a broad spoon for stirring—heat-resistant, of course. One might terminate in a sort of hand, of which each of the digits was a different-sized measuring spoon. And best of all—why the nuisance of bringing food to the mouth to taste? Install taste buds in the end of one tentacle."

I nodded. Quinby's pencil was covering the paper with tentative hookups. Suddenly he paused. "I'll bet I know why android cooks were never too successful. Nobody ever included the Verhaeren factor in their brains."

The Verhaeren factor, if you've studied this stuff at all, is what makes robots capable of independent creative action. For instance, it's used in the robots that turn out popular fiction—in very small proportion, of course.

"Yes, that's the trouble. They never realized that a cook is an artist as well as a servant. Well, we'll give him in his brain what he needs for creation, and in his body the tools he needs to carry it out. And when Mr. Grew has had his first meal from a usuform cook—"

It was an idea, I admitted, that might have worked on anybody but Sanford Grew—get at a man and convert him through what's dearest to his heart. But I'd worked for Grew. I knew him. And I knew that no hobby, not even his passion for unconcentrated food, could be stronger than his pride in his power as president of Robinc.

So while Quinby worked on his usuform cook and our foreman, Mike Warren, got our dowser ready for the first big demonstration, I went ahead with the anti-Robinc campaign.

"We've got four striking points," I explained to Quinby. "Android robots atrophy or go nuts; usuforms are safe. Android robots are almost as limited as man in what they can do without tools and accessories; usuforms can be constructed to do anything. Android robots are expensive because you've got to buy an all-purpose one that can do more than you need; usuforms save money because they're specialized. Android robots use up mineral resources; usuforms save them."

"The last reason is the important one," Quinby said.

I smiled to myself. Sure it was, but can you sell the people on anything as abstract as conservation? Hell no. Tell 'em they'll save credits, tell 'em they'll get better service, and you've got 'em signed up already. But tell 'em they're saving their grandchildren from a serious shortage and they'll laugh in your face.

So as usual, I left Quinby to ideas and followed my own judgment on people, and by the time he'd sent the cook to Grew I had all lined up the campaign that could blast Grew and Robinc out of the Empire. The three biggest telecommentators were all sold on usuforms. A major solly producer was set to do a documentary on them. Orders were piling up about twice as fast as Mike Warren could see his way clear to turning them out.

So then came the day of the big test.

We'd wanted to start out with something big and new that no android could possibly compete with, and we'd had the luck to run onto Mike's brother-in-law, who'd induced in robot brains the perception of that nth sense that used to enable dowsers to find water. Our usuform dowser was God's gift to explorers and fresh, exciting copy. So the Head had arranged a big demonstration on a specially prepared field, with grandstands and fireworks and two bands—one human, one android—and all the trimmings.

We sat in our box, Mike and Quinby and I. Mike had a shakerful of Three Planets cocktails mixed by our usuform barkeep; they aren't so good when they stand, but they were still powerful enough to keep him going. I was trying to get along on sheer will power, but little streams of sweat were running down my back and my nails were carving designs in my palms.

Quinby didn't seem bothered. He kept watching the android band and making notes. "You see," he explained, "it's idiotic waste to train a robot to play an instrument, when you could make an instrument that *was* a robot. Your real robot band would be usuforms, and wouldn't be anything but a flock of instruments that could play themselves. You could even work out new instruments, with range and versatility and flexibility beyond the capacity of human or android fingers and lungs. You could—"

"Oh-oh," I said. There was Sanford Grew entering our box.

The smile was still gentle and sad, but it had a kind of warmth about it that puzzled me. I'd never seen that on Grew's face before. He advanced to Quinby and held out his hand. "Sir," he said, "I have just dined."

Quinby rose eagerly, his blond head towering above the little old executive. "You mean my usuform—"

"Your usuform, sir, is indubitably the greatest cook since the Golden Age before the devilish introduction of concentrates. Do you mind if I share your box for this great exhibition?"

Quinby beamed and introduced him to Mike. Grew shook hands warmly with our foreman, then turned to me and spoke even my name with friendly pleasure. Before anybody could say any more, before I could even wipe the numb dazzle off my face, the Head's voice began to come over the speaker.

His words were few—just a succinct promise of the wonders of usuforms and their importance to our civilization—and by the time he'd finished the dowser was in place on the field.

To everybody watching but us, there was never anything that looked less like a robot. There wasn't a trace of an android trait to it. It looked like nothing but a heavy duralite box mounted on caterpillar treads. But it was a robot by legal definition. It had a Zwergenhaus brain and was capable of independent action under human commands or direction. That box housed the brain, with its nth-sensory perception, and eyes and ears, and the spike-laying apparatus. For when the dowser's perception of water reached a certain level of intensity, it laid a metal spike into the ground. An exploring party could send it out on its own to survey the territory, then follow its tracks at leisure and dig where the spikes were.

After the Head's speech there was silence. Then Quinby leaned over to the mike in our box and said, "Go find water."

The dowser began to move over the field. Only the Head himself knew where water had been cached at various levels and in various quantities. The dowser raced along for a bit, apparently finding nothing. Then it began to hesitate and veer. Once it paused for noticeable seconds. Even Quinby looked tense. I heard sharp breaths from Sanford Grew, and Mike almost drained his shaker.

Then the dowser moved on. There was water, but not enough to bother drilling for. It zoomed about a little more, then stopped suddenly and definitely. It had found a real treasure trove.

I knew its mechanism. In my mind I could see the Zwergenhaus brain registering and communicating its needs to the metal muscles of the sphincter mechanism that would lay the spike. The dowser sat there apparently motionless, but when you knew it you had the impression of a hen straining to lay.

Then came the explosion. When my eyes could see again through the settling fragments, there was nothing in the field but a huge crater.

It was Quinby, of course, who saw right off what had happened. "Somebody," my numb ears barely heard him say, "substituted for the spike an explosive shell with a contact-fuse tip."

Sanford Grew nodded. "Plausible, young man. Plausible. But I rather think that the general impression will be simply that usuforms don't work." He withdrew, smiling gently.

I held Mike back by pouring the rest of the shaker down his throat. Mayhem wouldn't help us any.

"So you converted him?" I said harshly to Quinby. "Brother, the next thing you'd better construct is a good guaranteed working usuform converter."

The next week was the low point in the history of Q. U. R. I know now, when Quinby's usuforms are what makes the world tick, it's hard to imagine Q. U. R. ever hitting a low point. But one reason I'm telling this is to make you realize that no big thing is easy, and that a lot of big things depend for their success on some very little thing, like that chance remark of mine I just quoted.

Not that any of us guessed then how important that remark was. We had other things to worry about. The fiasco of that demonstration had just about cooked our goose. Sure, we explained it must've been sabotage, and the Head backed us up; but the wiseacres shook their heads and muttered "Not bad for an alibi, *but*—"

Two or three telecommentators who had been backing us switched over to Grew. The solly producer abandoned his plans for a documentary. I don't know if this was honest conviction or the power of Robinc; it hit us the same either way. People were scared of usuforms now; they might go *boom!* And the biggest and smartest publicity and advertising campaign of the past century was fizzling out *ffft* before our helpless eyes.

It was the invaluable Guzub who gave us our first upward push. We were drinking at the Sunspot when he said, "Ah, boys— Zo things are going wrong with you, bud you zdill gome 'ere. No madder wad abbens, beoble zdill wand three things: eading and dringing and—"

Quinby looked up with the sharp pleasure of a new idea. "There's nothing we can do with the third," he said. "But eating and drinking— Guzub, you want to see usuforms go over, don't you?"

"And remember," I added practically, "you've got a royalty interest in our robot barkeep."

Guzub rolled all his eyes up once and down once—the Martian trick of nodding assent.

"All right," said Quinby. "Practically all bartenders are Martians, the tentacles are so useful professionally. Lots of them must be good friends of yours?"

"Lodz," Guzub agreed.

"Then listen . . ."

That was how we launched the really appealing campaign. Words? Sure, people have read and heard millions upon billions of words, and one set of them is a lot like another. But when you get down to Guzub's three essentials—

Within a fortnight there was one of our usuform barkeeps in one bar out of five in the influential metropolitan districts. Guzub's friends took orders for drinks, gave them to the usuforms, served the drinks, and then explained to the satisfied customers how they'd been made—pointing out besides that there had *not* been an explosion. The customers would get curious. They'd order more to watch the usuform work. (It had Martoid tentacles and its own body was its shaker.) The set-up was wonderful for business—and for us.

That got at the men. Meanwhile we had usuform cooks touring the residential districts and offering to prepare old-fashioned meals free. There wasn't a housewife whose husband didn't say regularly once a week, "Why can't we have more old-fashioned food instead of all these concentrates? Why, my mother used to—"

Few of the women knew the art. Those of them who could afford android cooks hadn't found them too satisfactory. And husbands kept muttering about Mother. The chance of a happy home was worth the risk of these dreadful dangerous new things. So our usuform cooks did their stuff and husbands were rapturously pleased and everything began to look swell. (We remembered to check up on a few statistics three quarters of an hour later—it seemed we had in a way included Guzub's third appeal after all.)

So things were coming on sweetly until one day at the Sunspot I looked up to see we had a visitor. "I heard that I might find you here," Sanford Grew said, smiling. He beckoned to Guzub and said, "Your oldest brandy."

Guzub knew him by sight. I saw one tentacle flicker hesitantly toward a bottle of mikiphin, that humorously named but none the less effective knockout liquor. I shook my head, and Guzub shrugged resignedly.

"Well?" Quinby asked directly.

"Gentlemen," said Sanford Grew, "I have come here to make a last appeal to you."

"You can take your appeal," I said, "and—"

Quinby shushed me. "Yes, sir?"

"This is not a business appeal, young men. This is an appeal to your consciences, to your duty as citizens of the Empire of Earth."

I saw Quinby looking a little bothered. The smiling old boy was shrewd; he knew that the conscience was where to aim a blow at Quinby. "Our consciences are clear—I think and trust."

"Are they? This law that you finagled through the Council, that destroyed what you call my monopoly—it did more than that. That 'monopoly' rested on our control of the factors that make robots safe and prevent them from ever harming living beings. You have removed that control."

Quinby laughed with relief. "Is that all? I knew you'd been using that line in publicity, but I didn't think you expected us to believe it. There are other safety factors beside yours. We're using them, and the law still insists on the use of some, though not necessarily Robinc's. I'm afraid my conscience is untouched."

"I do not know," said Sanford Grew, "whether I am flattering or insulting you when I say I know that it is no use trying to buy you out at any price. You are immune to reason—"

"Because it's on our side," said Quinby quietly.

"I am left with only one recourse." He rose and smiled a gentle farewell. "Good day, gentlemen."

He'd left the brandy untouched. I finished it, and was glad I'd vetoed Guzub's miki.

"One recourse—" Quinby mused. "That must mean—"

I nodded.

But it started quicker than we'd expected. It started, in fact, as soon as we left the Sunspot. Duralite arms went around my body and a duralite knee dug into the small of my back.

The first time I ever met Dugg Quinby was in a truly major and wondrous street brawl, where the boy was a whirlwind. Quinby was mostly the quiet kind, but when something touched him off—and injustice was the spark that usually did it—he could fight like fourteen Martian mountaineers defending their idols.

But who can fight duralite? Me, I have some sense; I didn't even try. Quinby's temper blinded his clear vision for a moment. The only result was a broken knuckle and some loss of blood and skin.

The next thing was duralite fingers probing for the proper spots at the back of my head. Then a sudden deft pressure, and blackness.

We were in a workshop of some sort. My first guess was one of the secret workshops that honeycomb the Robinc plant, where nobody but Grew's most hand-picked men ever penetrate. We were cuffed to the wall. They'd left only one of the androids to guard us.

It was Quinby who spoke to him, and straight to the point. "What happens to us?"

"When I get my next orders," the android said in his completely emotionless voice, "I kill you."

I tried to hold up my morale by looking as indifferent as he did. I didn't make it.

"The last recourse—" Quinby said.

I nodded. Then, "But look!" I burst out. "This can't be what it looks like. He can't be a Robinc android because he's going—" I gulped a fractional gulp "—to kill us. Robinc's products have the safety factor that prevents them from harming a living being, even on another being's orders."

"No," said Quinby slowly. "Remember that Robinc manufactures androids for the Empire's army? Obviously those can't have the safety factor. And Mr. Grew has apparently held out a few for his own bootleg banditti."

I groaned. "Trust you," I said. "We're chained up with a murderous android, and trust you to stand there calmly and look at things straight. Well, are you going to see straight enough to get us out of this?"

"Of course," he said simply. "We can't let Grew destroy the future of usuforms."

There was at least one other future that worried me more, but I knew there was no use bringing up anything so personal. I just stood there and watched Quinby thinking—what time I wasn't watching the android's hand hovering around his holster and wondering when he'd get his next orders.

And while I was waiting and watching, half scared sweatless, half trusting blindly in Quinby, half wondering impersonally what death was like—yes, I know that makes three halves of me, but I was in no state for accurate counting—while I waited, I began to realize something very odd.

It wasn't me I was most worried about. It was Dugg Quinby. Me going all unselfish on me! Ever since Quinby had first seen the nonsense in androids—no, back of that, ever since that first magnifiscrumptious street brawl, I'd begun to love that boy like a son—which'd have made me pretty precocious.

There was something about him—that damned mixture of almost stupid innocence, combined with the ability to solve any problem by his—not ingenuity, precisely, just his inborn capacity for looking at things straight.

Here I was feeling selfless. And here he was coming forth with the first at all tricky or indirect thing I'd ever known him to pull. Maybe it was like marriage— the way two people sort of grow together and average up.

Anyway, he said to the android now, "I bet you military robots are pretty good marksmen, aren't you?"

"I'm the best Robinc ever turned out," the android said.

I'd worked for Robinc; I knew that each of them was conditioned with the belief that he was the unique best. It gave them confidence.

Quinby reached out his unfettered hand and picked a plastic disk off the worktable. "While you're waiting for orders, why don't you show us some marksmanship? It'll pass the time."

The robot nodded, and Quinby tossed the disk in the air. The android grabbed at its holster. And the gun stuck.

The metal of the holster had got dented in the struggle of kidnapping us. Quinby must have noticed that; his whole plan developed from that little point.

The robot made comments on the holster; military androids had a soldier's vocabulary built in, so we'll skip that.

Quinby said, "That's too bad. My friend here's a Robinc repairman, or used to be. If you let him loose, he could fix that."

The robot frowned. He wanted the repair, but he was no dope. Finally he settled on chaining my foot before releasing my hand, and keeping his own digits constantly on my wrist so he could clamp down if I got any funny notions about snatching the gun and using it. I began to think Quinby's plan was fizzling, but I went ahead and had the holster repaired in no time with the tools on the worktable.

"Does that happen often?" Quinby asked.

"A little too often." There was a roughness to the android's tones. I recognized what I'd run onto so often in trouble shooting: an android's resentment of the fact that he didn't work perfectly.

"I see," Quinby went on, as casually as though we were here on social terms. "Of course the trouble is that you have to use a gun."

"I'm a soldier. Of course I have to use one."

"You don't understand. I mean the trouble is that you have to *use* one. Now, if you could *be* a gun—"

It took some explaining. But when the android understood what it could mean to be a usuform, to have an arm that didn't need to snatch at a holster because it was itself a firing weapon, his eye cells began to take on a new bright glow.

"You could do that to me?" he demanded of me.

"Sure," I said. "You give me your gun and I'll—"

He drew back mistrustfully. Then he looked around the room, found another gun, unloaded it, and handed it to me. "Go ahead," he said.

It was a lousy job. I was in a state and in a hurry, and the sweat running down my forehead and dripping off my eyebrows didn't help any. The workshop wasn't too well equipped, either, and I hate working from my head. I like a nice diagram to look at.

But I made it somehow, very crudely, replacing one hand with the chamber and barrel and attaching the trigger so that it would be worked by the same nerve currents as actuated the finger movements to fire a separate gun.

The android loaded himself awkwardly. I stood aside, and Quinby tossed up the disk. You never saw a prettier piece of instantaneous trapshooting. The android stretched his face into that very rare thing, a robot grin, and expressed himself in pungently jubilant military language.

"You like it?" Quinby asked.

All that I can quote of that robot's reply is "Yes," but he made it plenty emphatic.

"Then—"

But I stepped in. "Just a minute. I've got an idea to improve it." Quinby was probably trusting to our guard's gratitude; I wanted a surer hold on him. "Let me take this off just a second—" I removed the chamber and barrel; I still had his hand. "Now," I said, "we want out."

He brought up the gun in his other hand, but I said, "Ah, ah! Naughty! You aren't supposed to kill us till you get orders, and if you do they'll find you here with one hand. Fine state for a soldier. You can't repair yourself; you need two hands for it. But if we get out, you can come with us and be made over as much as you want into the first and finest efficient happy usuform soldier."

It took a little argument, but with the memory of that one perfect shot in his mind it didn't take much. As Quinby said afterward, "Robinc built pride into its robots to give them self-confidence. But that pride also gave them vanity and dissatisfaction with anything less than perfection. That was what we could use. It was all perfectly simple—"

"—when you looked at it straight," I chorused with him.

"And besides," he said, "now we know how to lick Robinc forever."

That was some comfort, I suppose, though he wouldn't say another word to explain it. And I needed comfort, because just then things took a nasty turn again. We stuck close to our factory and didn't dare go out. We were taking no chances on more kidnappings before Quinby finished his new inspiration.

Quinby worked on that alone, secret even from us. I figured out some extra touches of perfection on the usuform soldier, who was now our bodyguard— Grew would never dare complain of the theft because he had no legal right to possess such an android anyway. Mike and his assistants, both living and usuform, turned out barkeeps and dowsers and cooks—our three most successful usuform designs so far.

We didn't go out, but we heard enough. It was the newest and nastiest step in Grew's campaign. He had men following up our cooks and bartenders and managing to slip concentrated doses of ptomaine alkaloids into their products. No serious poisoning, you understand; just an abnormally high proportion of people taken sick after taking usuform-prepared food or drink. And a rumor going around that the usuforms secreted a poisonous fluid, which was objective nonsense, but enough to scare a lot of people.

"It's no use," Mike said to me one day. "We're licked. Two new orders in a week. We're done for. No use keeping up production."

"The hell we're licked," I said.

"If you want to encourage me, you'd ought to sound like you believed it yourself. No, we're sunk. While *he* sits in there and— I'm going down to the Sunspot and drink Three Planets till this one spins. And if Grew wants to kidnap me, he's welcome to me."

It was just then the message came from the Head. I read it, and knew how the camel feels about that last straw. It said:

I can't resist popular pressure forever. I know and you know what Grew is up to; but the public is demanding re-enactment of the law giving Robinc exclusive rights. Unless Quinby can see straight through the hat to the rabbit, that re-enactment is going to pass.

"We'll see what he has to say to this," I said to Mike. I started for the door, and even as I did so Quinby came out.

"I've got it!" he said. "It's done." He read the Head's message with one glance, and it didn't bother him. He grabbed me by the shoulders and beamed. I've never heard my name spoken so warmly. "Mike, too. Come on in and see the greatest usuform we've hit on yet. Our troubles are over."

We went in. We looked. And we gawked. For Quinby's greatest usuform, so far as our eyes could tell, was just another android robot.

Mike went resolutely off to the Sunspot to carry out his threat of making this planet spin. I began to think myself that the tension had affected Quinby's clear-seeing mind. I didn't listen especially when he told me I'd given him the idea myself. I watched the usuform-android go off on his mysterious mission and I even let him take my soldier along. And I didn't care. We were done for now, if even Dugg Quinby was slipping.

But I didn't have time to do much worrying that morning. I was kept too busy with androids that came in wanting repairs. Very thoroughgoing repairs, too, that turned them, like my soldier, practically into usuforms. We always had a few such requests—I think I mentioned how they all want to be perfect—but this began to develop into a cloudburst. I stopped the factory lines and put every man and robot on repair.

Along about midafternoon I began to feel puzzled. It took me a little while to get it, and then it hit me. The last three that I'd repaired had been brand-new. Fresh from the Robinc factory, and rushing over here to be remade into . . . into usuforms!

As soon as I finished adjusting drill arms on the robot miner, I hurried over to where Quinby was installing an infrared color sense on a soldier intended for camouflage spotting. He looked up and smiled when he saw me. "You get it now?"

"I get what's happening. But how . . . who—"

"I just followed your advice. Didn't you say what we needed was a guaranteed working usuform converter?"

"I don't need to explain, do I? It's simple enough once you look at it straight."

We were sitting in the Sunspot. Guzub was very happy; it was the first time the Head had ever honored his establishment.

"You'd better," I said, "remember I'm a crooked-viewing dope."

"But it's all from things you've said. You're always saying I'm good at things and robots, but lousy at people because people don't see or act straight. Well, we were stymied with people. They couldn't see the real importance of usuforms through all the smoke screens that Grew threw up. But you admit yourself that Robots see straight, so I went direct to them. And you said we needed a usuform converter, so I made one."

The Head smiled. "And what is the utile form of a converter?"

"He had to look like an android, because otherwise they wouldn't accept him. But he was the sturdiest, strongest android ever made, with several ingenious new muscles. If it came to fighting, he was sure to make converts that way. And besides, he had something that's never been put in a robot brain before—the ability to argue and convince. With that, he had the usuform soldier as a combination bodyguard and example. So he went out among the androids, even to the guards at Robinc and from then on inside; and since he was a usuform converter, well—he converted."

The Head let the famous grin play across his black face. "Fine work, Quinby. And if Grew hadn't had the sense to see at last that he was licked, you could have gone on with your usuform converters until there wasn't an android left on Earth. Robinc would have toppled like a wooden building with termites."

"And Grew?" I asked. "What's become of him?"

"I think, in a way, he's resigned to his loss. He told me that since his greatest passion was gone, he was going to make the most of his second greatest. He's gone off to his place in the mountains with the usuform cook you gave him, and he swears he's going to eat himself to death."

"Me," said Mike, getting to appropriate business, "I'd like a damper death."

"And from now on, my statisticians assure me, we're in no danger of ever using up our metal stockpile. The savings on usuforms will save us. Do you realize, Quinby, that you're just about the most important man in the Empire today?"

That was when I first heard the band approaching. It got louder while Quinby got red and gulped. It was going good when he finally said, "You know, if I'd ever thought of that, I . . . I don't think I could have done it."

He meant it, too. You've never seen an unhappier face than his when the crowd burst into the Sunspot yelling "Quinby!" and "Q. U. R.!"

But you've never seen a prouder face than mine as I saw it then in the bar mirror. Proud of myself, sure, but only because it was me that discovered Dugg Quinby.

Nine-Finger Jack

John Smith is an unexciting name to possess, and there was of course no way for him to know until the end of his career that he would be forever famous among connoisseurs of murder as Nine-finger Jack. But he did not mind the drabness of Smith; he felt that what was good enough for the great George Joseph was good enough for him.

Not only did John Smith happily share his surname with George Joseph, he was proud to follow the celebrated G. J. in profession and even in method. For an attractive and plausible man of a certain age, there are few more satisfactory sources of income than frequent and systematic widowerhood; and of all the practitioners who have acted upon this practical principle, none have improved upon George Joseph Smith's sensible and unpatented Brides-in-the-Bath method.

John Smith's marriage to his ninth bride, Hester Pringle, took place on the morning of May the thirty-first. On the evening of May the thirty-first John Smith, having spent much of the afternoon pointing out to friends how much the wedding had excited Hester and how much he feared the effect on her notoriously weak heart, entered the bathroom and, with the careless ease of the practiced professional, employed five of his fingers to seize Hester's ankles and jerk her legs out of the tub while with the other five fingers he gently pressed her face just below water level.

So far all had proceeded in the conventional manner of any other wedding night; but the ensuing departure from ritual was such as to upset even John Smith's professional bathside manner. The moment Hester's face and neck were submerged below water, she opened her gills.

In his amazement, John released his grasp upon both ends of his bride. Her legs descended into the water and her face rose above it. As she passed from the element of water to that of air, her gills closed and her mouth opened.

"I suppose," she observed, "that in the intimacy of a long marriage you would eventually have discovered in any case that I am a Venusian. It is perhaps as well that the knowledge came early, so that we may lay a solid basis for understanding."

"Do you mean," John asked, for he was a precise man, "that you are a native of the planet Venus?"

"I do," she said. "You would be astonished to know how many of us there are already among you."

"I am sufficiently astonished," said John, "to learn of one. Would you mind convincing me that I did indeed see what I thought I saw?"

Obligingly, Hester lowered her head beneath the water. Her gills opened and her breath bubbled merrily. "The nature of our planet," she explained when she emerged, "has bred as its dominant race our species of amphibian mammals, in all other respects superficially identical with *homo sapiens*. You will find it all but impossible to recognize any of us, save perhaps by noticing those who, to avoid accidental opening of the gills, refuse to swim. Such concealment will of course be unnecessary soon when we take over complete control of your planet."

"And what do you propose to do with the race that already controls it?"

"Kill most of them, I suppose," said Hester; "and might I trouble you for that towel?"

"That," pronounced John, with any handcraftsman's abhorrence of mass production, "is monstrous. I see my duty to my race: I must reveal all."

"I am afraid," Hester observed as she dried herself, "that you will not. In the first place, no one will believe you. In the second place, I shall then be forced to present to the authorities the complete dossier which I have gathered on the cumulatively interesting deaths of your first eight wives, together with my direct evidence as to your attempt this evening."

John Smith, being a reasonable man, pressed the point no further. "In view of this attempt," he said, "I imagine you would like either a divorce or an annulment."

"Indeed I should not," said Hester. "There is no better cover for my activities than marriage to a member of the native race. In fact, should you so much as mention divorce again, I shall be forced to return to the topic of that dossier. And now, if you will hand me that robe, I intend to do a little telephoning. Some of my better-placed colleagues will need to know my new name and address."

As John Smith heard her ask the long-distance operator for Washington, D.C., he realized with regretful resignation that he would be forced to depart from the methods of the immortal George Joseph.

Through the failure of the knife, John Smith learned that Venusian blood has extraordinary quick-clotting powers and Venusian organs possess an amazingly rapid system of self-regeneration. And the bullet taught him a further peculiarity of the blood: that it dissolves lead—in fact thrives upon lead.

His skill as a cook was quite sufficient to disguise any of the commoner poisons from human taste; but the Venusian palate not only detected but relished most of them. Hester was particularly taken with his tomato aspic *à l'arsénique* and insisted on his preparing it in quantity for a dinner of her friends, along with his *sole amandine* to which the prussic acid lent so distinctively intensified, flavor and aroma.

While the faintest murmur of divorce, even after a year of marriage, evoked from Hester a frowning murmur of "Dossier . . ." the attempts at murder seemed merely to amuse her; so that finally John Smith was driven to seek out Professor Gillingsworth at the State University, recognized as the ultimate authority (on this planet) on life on other planets.

The professor found the query of much theoretical interest. "From what we are able to hypothesize of the nature of Venusian organisms," he announced, "I can almost assure you of their destruction by the forced ingestion of the best Beluga caviar, in doses of no less than one-half pound per diem."

Three weeks of the suggested treatment found John Smith's bank account seriously depleted and his wife in perfect health.

"That dear Gilly!" she laughed one evening. "It was so nice of him to tell you how to kill me; it's the first time I've had enough of caviar since I came to Earth. It's so dreadfully expensive."

"You mean," John demanded, "that Professor Gillingsworth is . . ."

She nodded.

"And all that money!" John protested. "You do not realize, Hester, how unjust you are. You have deprived me of my income and I have no other source."

"Dossier," said Hester through a mouthful of caviar.

America's greatest physiologist took an interest in John Smith's problem. "I should advise," he said, "the use of crystallized carbon placed directly in contact with the sensitive gill area."

"In other words, a diamond necklace?" John Smith asked. He seized a water carafe, hurled its contents at the physiologist's neck, and watched his gills open.

The next day John purchased a lapel flower through which water may be squirted—an article which he thenceforth found invaluable for purposes of identification.

The use of this flower proved to be a somewhat awkward method of starting a conversation and often led the conversation into unintended paths; but it did establish a certain clarity in relations.

It was after John had observed the opening of the gills of a leading criminal psychiatrist that he realized where he might find the people who could really help him.

From then on, whenever he could find time to be unobserved while Hester was engaged in her activities preparatory to world conquest, he visited insane asylums, announced that he was a free-lance feature writer, and asked if they had any inmates who believed that there were Venusians at large upon Earth and planning to take it over.

In this manner he met many interesting and attractive people, all of whom wished him godspeed in his venture, but pointed out that they would hardly be where they were if all of their own plans for killing Venusians had not miscarried as hopelessly as his.

From one of these friends, who had learned more than most because his Venusian wife had made the error of falling in love with him (an error which led to her eventual removal from human society), John Smith ascertained that Venusians may indeed be harmed and even killed by many substances on their own planet, but seemingly by nothing on ours—though (his) wife had once dropped a hint that one thing alone on Earth could prove fatal to the Venusian system.

At last John Smith visited an asylum whose director announced that they had an inmate who thought he *was* a Venusian.

When the director had left them, a squirt of the lapel flower verified the claimant's identity.

"I am a member of the Conciliationist Party," he explained, "the only member who has ever reached this Earth. We believe that Earthmen and Venusians can live at peace as all men should, and I shall be glad to help you destroy all members of the opposition party.

"There is one substance on this Earth which is deadly poison to any Venusian. Since in preparing and serving the dish best suited to its administration you must be careful to wear gloves, you should begin your campaign by wearing gloves at all meals . . ."

This mannerism Hester seemed willing to tolerate for the security afforded her by her marriage and even more particularly for the delights of John's skilled preparation of such dishes as spaghetti *all'aglio ed all'arsenico* which is so rarely to be had in the average restaurant.

Two weeks later John finally prepared the indicated dish: ox tail according to the richly imaginative recipe of Simon Templar, with a dash of deadly nightshade added to the other herbs specified by The Saint. Hester had praised the recipe, devoured two helpings, expressed some wonder as to the possibility of gills in its creator, whom she had never met, and was just nibbling at the smallest bones when, as the Conciliationist had foretold, she dropped dead.

Intent upon accomplishing his objective, John had forgotten the dossier, nor ever suspected that it was in the hands of a gilled lawyer who had instructions to pass it on in the event of Hester's death.

Even though that death was certified as natural, John rapidly found himself facing trial for murder, with seven other states vying for the privilege of the next opportunity should this trial fail to end in a conviction.

With no prospect in sight of a quiet resumption of his accustomed profession, John Smith bared his knowledge and acquired his immortal nickname. The result was a period of intense prosperity among manufacturers of squirting lapel flowers, bringing about the identification and exposure of the gilled masqueraders.

But inducing them, even by force, to ingest the substance poisonous to them was more difficult. The problem of supply and demand was an acute one, in view of the large number of the Venusians and the small proportion of members of the human race willing to perform the sacrifice made by Nine-finger Jack.

It was that great professional widower and amateur chef himself who solved the problem by proclaiming in his death cell his intention to bequeath his body to the eradication of Venusians, thereby pursuing after death the race which had ruined his career.

The noteworthy proportion of human beings who promptly followed his example in their wills has assured us of permanent protection against future invasions, since so small a quantity of the poison is necessary in each individual case; after all, one finger sufficed for Hester.

Barrier

The first difficulty was with language.

That is only to be expected when you jump five hundred years, but it is nonetheless perplexing to have your first query of: "What city is this?" answered by the sentence: "Stappers will get you. Or be you Slanduch?"

It was signficant that the first word John Brent heard in the State was "Stappers." But Brent could not know that then. It was only some hours later and fifty years earlier that he was to learn the details of the Stapper system. At the moment all that concerned him was food and plausibility.

His appearance was plausible enough. Following Derringer's advice he had traveled naked—"the one costume common to all ages," the scientist had boomed; "Which would astonish you more, lad; a naked man, or an Elizabethan courtier in full apparel?"—and commenced his life in the twenty-fifth century by burglary and the theft of a complete outfit of clothing. The iridescent woven plastics tailored in a half-clinging, half-flowing style looked precious to Brent, but seemed both comfortable and functional.

No man alive in 2473 would have bestowed a second glance on the feloniously clad Brent, but in his speech, he realized at once, lay danger. He pondered the alternatives presented by the stranger. Stappers would get him, unless he was Slanduch. Whatever Stappers were, things that "get you" sounded menacing. "Slanduch," he replied.

The stranger nodded. "That bees O.K.," he said, and Brent wondered what he had committed himself to. "So what city is this?" he repeated.

"Bees," the stranger chided. "Stappers be more severe now since Edict of 2470. Before they doed pardon some irregularities, but now none even from Slanduch."

"I be sorry," said Brent humbly, making a mental note that irregular verbs were for some reason perilous. "But for the third time—"

He had thought the wall beside them was solid. He realized now that part of it, at least, was only a deceptive glasslike curtain that parted to let forth a tall and vigorous man, followed by two shorter aides. All three of these wore robes similar to the iridescent garments of Brent and his companion, but of pure white.

The leader halted and barked out, "George Starvel?"

Brent saw a quiet sort of terror begin to grow on his companion's face. He nodded and held out his wrist.

The man in white glanced at what Brent decided must be an identification plaque. "Starvel," he announced, "you speaked against Barrier."

Starvel trembled. "Cosmos knows I doed not."

"Five mans know that you doed."

"Never. I only sayed—"

"You only! Enough!"

The rod appeared in the man's hand only for an instant. Brent saw no flame or discharge, but Starvel was stretched out on the ground and the two aides were picking him up as callously as though he were a log.

The man turned toward Brent, who was taking no chances. He flexed his legs and sprang into the air. His fingertips grasped the rim of the balcony above them, and his feet shot out into the white-robed man's face. His arm and shoulder muscles tensed to their utmost. The smooth plastic surface was hell to keep a grip on. Beneath, he could see his adversary struggling blindly to his feet and groping for the rod. At last, desperately, Brent swung himself up and over the edge.

There was no time to contemplate the beauties of the orderly terrace garden. There was only time to note that there was but one door, and to make for it. It was open and led to a long corridor. Brent turned to the nearest of the many identical doors. Apartments? So—he was taking a chance; whatever was behind that door, the odds were better than with an armed policeman you'd just kicked in the face. Brent had always favored the devil you don't know—or he'd never have found himself in this strange world. He walked toward the door, and it opened.

He hurried into an empty room, glancing back to see the door shut by itself. The room had two other doors. Each of them opened equally obligingly. Bathroom and bedroom. No kitchen. (His stomach growled a comment.) No people. And no exit from the apartment but the door he had come through.

He forced himself to sit down and think. Anything might happen before the Stapper caught up with him, for he had no doubt that was what the white-robed man must be.

What had he learned about the twenty-fifth century in this brief encounter?

You must wear an identification plaque. (Memo: How to get one?) You must not use irregular verbs (or nouns; the Stapper had said "mans"). You must not speak against Barrier, whoever or whatever that meant. You must beware white-robed men who lurk behind false walls. You must watch out for rods that kill (query: or merely stun?). Doors open by selenium cells (query: how do they lock?). You must—

The door opened. It was not the Stapper who stood there, but a tall and majestic woman of, at a guess, sixty. A noble figure—"Roman matron" were the words that flashed into Brent's mind.

The presence of a total stranger in her apartment seemed nowise disconcerting. She opened her arms in a broad gesture of welcome. "John Brent!" she exclaimed in delighted recognition. "It beed so long!"

"I don't want a brilliant young scientific genius!" Derringer had roared when Brent answered his cryptically worded ad. "I've got 'em here in the laboratory. They've done grand work on the time machine. I couldn't live without 'em, and there's not a one of 'em I'd trust out of this century. Not out of this decade. What I want is four things: A knowledge of history, for a background of analogy to understand what's been going on; linguistic ability, to adjust yourself as rapidly as possible to the changes in language; physical strength and dexterity, to get yourself out of the scrapes that are bound to come up; and social adaptability. A chimpanzee of reasonably subhuman intelligence could operate the machine. What counts is what you'll be able to do after you get there."

The knowledge of history and the physical qualities had been easy to demonstrate. The linguistic ability was a bit more complex; Derringer had contrived an intricate series of tests involving adjustment to phonetic changes and the capacity to assimilate the principles of a totally fictitious language invented for the occasion. The social adaptability was measured partly by an aptitude test, but largely, Brent guessed, by Derringer's own observation during the weeks of preparation after his probationary hiring

He had passed all four requirements with flying colors. At least Derringer had grinned at him through the black beard and grunted the reluctant "Good man!" that was his equivalent of rhapsodic praise. His physical agility had already stood him in good stead, and his linguistic mind was rapidly assimilating the new aspects of the language (there were phonetic alterations as well as the changes in vocabulary and inflection—he was particularly struck by the fact that the vowels *a* and *o* no longer possessed the diphthongal off-glide so characteristic of English, but were pure vowels like the Italian *e* and *o*), but his social adaptability was just now hitting a terrific snag.

What the hell do you do when a Roman matron whom you have never seen, born five hundred years after you, welcomes you by name and exclaims that it haves beed a long time? (This regular past participle of *be,* Brent reflected, gives the speaker something of the quality of a Bostonian with a cold in the nose.)

For a moment he toyed with the rash notion that she might likewise be a time traveler, someone whom he had known in 1942. Derringer had been positive that this was the first such trip ever attempted; but someone leaving the twentieth century later might still be an earlier arrival in the twenty-fifth. He experimented with the idea.

"I suppose," Brent ventured, "you could call five hundred years a long time, in its relative way."

The Roman matron frowned. "Do not jest, John. Fifty years be not five hundred. I will confess that first five years seemed at times like five centuries, but after fifty—one does not feel so sharply."

Does was of course pronounced *dooze.* All *r*'s, even terminal, were lightly trilled. These facts Brent noted in the back of his mind, but the fore part was concerned with the immediate situation. If this woman chose to accept him as an acquaintance—it was nowise unlikely that his double should be wandering about in this century—it meant probable protection from the Stapper. His logical mind protested, "Could this double have your name?" but he shushed it.

"Did you," he began, and caught himself. "Doed you see anyone in the hall—a man in white?"

The Roman matron moaned. "Oh, John! Do Stappers seek you again? But of course. If you have comed to destroy Barrier, they must destroy you."

"Whoa there!" Brent had seen what happened to one person who had merely "speaked against Barrier." "I didn't . . . doedn't . . . say anything against Barrier." The friendliness began to die from her clear blue eyes. "And I believed you," she said sorrowfully. "You telled us of this second Barrier and sweared to destroy it. We thinked you beed one of us. And now—"

No amount of social adaptability can resist a sympathetic and dignified woman on the verge of tears. Besides, this apartment was for the moment a valuable haven, and if she thought he was a traitor of some sort—

"Look," said Brent. "You see, I am—there isn't any use at this moment trying to be regular—I am not whoever you think I am. I never saw you before. I couldn't have. This is the first instant I've ever been in your time."

"If you wish to lie to me, John—"

"I'm not lying. And I'm not John—at least not the one you're thinking of. I'm John Brent, I'm twenty-eight years old, and I was born in 1914—a good five and a half centuries ago."

According to all the time travel fiction Brent had ever read, that kind of statement ranks as a real stunner. There is a deathly hush and a wild surmise and the author stresses the curtain-line effect by inserting a line-space.

But the Roman matron was unmoved. The hush and the surmise were Brent's an instant later when she said with anguished patience, "I know, John, I know."

"Derringer left this one out of the rule book," Brent grunted. "Madam, you have, as they say, the better of me. What does A do now?"

"You *do* be same John!" she smiled. "I never beed able to understand you."

"We have much in common," Brent observed.

"And because I can't understand you, I know you be you." She was still smiling. It was an odd smile; Brent couldn't place its precise meaning. Not until she leaned toward him and for one instant gently touched his arm.

He needed friends. Whatever her wild delusions, she seemed willing to help him. But he still could not quite keep from drawing back as he recognized the tender smile of love on this dignified ancient face.

She seemed to sense his withdrawal. For a moment he feared a gathering anger. Then she relaxed, and with another smile, a puzzled but resigned smile, said, "This be part of not understanding you, I guess. Cosmos knows but you be so young, John, still so *young* . . ."

She must, Brent thought with sudden surprise, have been a very pretty girl.

The door opened. The man who entered was as tall as the Stapper, but wore the civilian's iridescent robes. His long beard seemed to have caught a little of their rainbow influence; it was predominantly red, but brown and black and white glinted in it. The hair on his head was graying. He might have been anywhere from forty-five to a vigorous and well-preserved seventy.

"We have a guest, sister?" he asked politely.

The Roman matron made a despairing gesture. "You don't recognize him? And John—you don't know Stephen?"

Stephen slapped his thigh and barked—a sound that seemed to represent a laugh of pleasure. "Cosmos!" he cried. "John Brent! I told you, Martha. I knew he wouldn't fail us."

"Stephen!" she exclaimed in shocked tones.

"Hang the irregularities! Can't I greet John with the old words that comed—no, by Cosmos—*came* from the same past he came from? See, John—don't I talk the old language well? I even use article—pardon me, *the* article."

Brent's automatic mental notebook recorded the fact, which he had already suspected, that an article was as taboo as an irregular verb. But around this self-governing notation system swirled utter confusion. It might possibly have been just his luck to run into a madwoman. But two mad brains in succession with identical delusions were too much. And Stephen had known he was from the past.

"I'm afraid," he said simply, "this is too much for me. Suppose we all sit down and have a drink of something and talk this over."

Stephen smiled. "You remember our bond, eh? And not many places in State you'll find it. Even fewer than before." He crossed to a cabinet and returned with three glasses of colorless liquid.

Brent seized his eagerly and downed it. A drink might help the swirling. It might—

The drink had gone down smoothly and tastelessly. Now, however, some imp began dissecting atoms in his stomach and shooting off a bombardment stream of particles that zoomed up through his throat into his brain, where they set off a charge of explosive of hitherto unknown power. Brent let out a strangled yelp.

Stephen barked again. "Good bond, eh, John?"

Brent managed to focus his host through the blurring lens of his tears. "Sure," he nodded feebly. "Swell. And now let me try to explain—"

The woman looked sadly at her brother. "He denies us, Stephen. He sayes that he haves never seed me before. He forgets all that he ever sweared about Barrier."

A curious look of speculation came into Stephen's brown eyes. "Bees this true, John? You have never seed us before in your life?"

"But, Stephen, you know—"

"Hush, Martha. I sayed in *his* life. Bees it true, John?"

"It bees. God knows it bees. I have never seen . . . seed either of you in my life."

"But Stephen—"

"I understand now, Martha. Remember when he told us of Barrier and his resolve?"

"Can I forget?"

"How doed he know of Barrier? Tell me that."

"I don't know," Martha confessed. "I have wondered—"

"He knowed of Barrier then because he bees here now. He told me then just what we must now tell him."

"Then for Heaven's sake," Brent groaned, "tell me."

"Your pardon, John. My sister bees not so quick to grasp source of these temporal confusions. More bond?" He had the bottle in his hand when he suddenly stopped, thrust it back in the cabinet, and murmured, "Go into bedroom."

Brent obeyed. This was no time for displaying initiative. And no sooner had the bedroom door closed behind him than he heard the voice of the Stapper.

(The mental notebook recorded that apartment buildings must be large, if it had taken this long for the search to reach here.)

"No," Stephen was saying. "My sister and I have beed here for past half-hour. We seed no one." "State thanks you," the Stapper muttered, so casually that the phrase must have been an official formula. His steps sounded receding. Then they stopped, and there was the noise of loud sniffs.

"Dear God," thought Brent, "have they crossed the bulls with bloodhounds?"

"Bond," the Stapper announced.

"Dear me," came Martha's voice. "Who haves beed in here today, Stephen?"

"I'm homeopath," said the Stapper. "Like cures like. A little bond might make me forget I smelled it."

There was a bark from Stephen and a clink of glasses. No noise from either of them as they downed the liquor. Those, sir, were men. (Memo: Find out why such unbelievable rotgut is called *bond,* of all things.)

"State thanks you," said the Stapper, and laughed. "You know George Starvel, don't you?"

A slightly hesitant "Yes" from Stephen.

"When you see him again, I think you'll find he haves changed his mind. About many things."

There was silence. Then Stephen opened the bedroom door and beckoned Brent back into the living room. He handed him a glass of bond and said, "I will be brief."

Brent, now forewarned, sipped at the liquor and found it cheerfully warming as he assimilated the new facts.

In the middle of the twenty-fourth century, he learned, civilization had reached a high point of comfort, satisfaction, achievement—and stagnation. The combination of atomic power and De Bainville's revolutionary formulation of the principles of labor and finance had seemed to solve all economic problems. The astounding development of synthetics had destroyed the urgent need for raw materials and colonies and abolished the distinction between haves and have-nots among nations. Schwarzwalder's *Compendium* had achieved the dream of the early Encyclopedists—the complete systematization of human knowledge. Farthing had regularized the English language, an achievement paralleled by the work of Zinsmeister, Timofeov, and Tamayo y Sárate in their respective tongues. (These four languages now dominated the earth. French and Italian had become corrupt dialects of German, and the Oriental languages occupied in their own countries something like the position of Greek and Latin in nineteenth-century Europe, doomed soon to the complete oblivion which swallowed up those classic tongues in the twenty-first.)

There was nothing more to be achieved. All was known, all was accomplished. Nakamura's Law of Spatial Acceleration had proved interplanetary travel to be impossible for all time. Charnwood's Law of Temporal Metabolism had done the same for time travel. And the Schwarzwalder *Compendium,* which everyone admired and no one had read, established such a satisfactory and flawless picture of knowledge that it was obviously impossible that anything remained to be discovered.

It was then that Dyce-Farnsworth proclaimed the Stasis of Cosmos. A member of the Anglo-Physical Church, product of the long contemplation by English physicists of the metaphysical aspects of science, he came as the prophet needed to pander to the self-satisfaction of the age.

He was curiously aided by Farthing's laws of regularity. The article, direct or indirect, Farthing had proved to be completely unnecessary—had not languages as world-dominant as Latin in the first centuries and Russian in the twenty-first found no need for it?—and semantically misleading. "Article," he had said in his final and comprehensive study *This Bees Speech,* "bees prime corruptor of human thinking."

And thus the statement so beloved in the twentieth century by metaphysical-minded scientists and physical-minded divines, "God is the cosmos," became with Dyce-Farnsworth, "God bees cosmos," and hence, easily and inevitably, "God bees Cosmos," so that the utter scientific impersonality became a personification of Science. Cosmos replaced Jehovah, Baal and Odin.

The love of Cosmos was not man nor his works, but Stasis. Man was tolerated by Cosmos that he might achieve Stasis. All the millennia of human struggle had been aimed at this supreme moment when all was achieved, all was known, and all was perfect. Therefore this supernal Stasis must at all costs be maintained. Since Now was perfect, any alteration must be imperfect and taboo.

From this theory logically evolved the State, whose duty was to maintain the perfect Stasis of Cosmos. No totalitarian government had ever striven so strongly to iron out all doubt and dissension. No religious bigotry had ever found heresy so damnable and worthy of destruction. The Stasis must be maintained.

It was, ironically, the aged Dyce-Farnsworth himself who, in a moment of quasi-mystical intuition, discovered the flaw in Charnwood's Law of Temporal Metabolism. And it was clear to him what must be done.

Since the Stasis of Cosmos did not practice time travel, any earlier or later civilization that did so must be imperfect. Its emissaries would sow imperfection. There must be a Barrier.

The mystic went no further than that dictum, but the scientists of the State put his demand into practical terms. "Do not ask how at this moment," Stephen added. "I be not man to explain that. But you will learn." The first Barrier was a failure. It destroyed itself and to no apparent result. But now, fifty years later, the fears of time travel had grown. The original idea of the imperfection of emissaries had been lost. Now time travel was in itself imperfect and evil. Any action taken against it would be praise to Cosmos. And the new Barrier was being erected.

"But John knows all this," Martha protested from time to time, and Stephen would shake his head sadly and smile sympathetically at Brent.

"I don't believe a word of it," Brent said at last. "Oh, the historical outline's all right. I trust you on that. And it works out sweetly by analogy. Take the religious fanaticism of the sixteenth century, the smug scientific self-satisfaction of the nineteenth, the power domination of the twentieth—fuse them and you've got your State. But the Barrier's impossible. It can't work."

"Charnwood claimed there beed no principle on which time travel can work. And here you be."

"That's different," said Brent vaguely. "But this talk of destroying the Barrier is nonsense. There's no need to."

"Indeed there bees need, John. For two reasons: one, that we may benefit by wisdom of travelers from other ages; and two, that positive act of destroying this Barrier, worshipped now with something like fetishism, bees strongest weapon with which we can strike against State. For there be these few of us who hope to save mankind from this fanatical complacency that race haves falled into. George Starvel beed one," Stephen added sadly.

"I saw Starvel— But that isn't what I mean. There's no need because the Barrier won't work."

"But you telled us that it haved to be destroyed," Martha protested. "That it doed work, and that we—"

"Hush," said Stephen gently. "John, will you trust us far enough to show us your machine? I think I can make matters clearer to Martha then."

"If you'll keep me out of the way of Stappers."

"That we can never guarantee—yet. But day will come when mankind cans forget Stappers and State, that I swear." There was stern and noble courage in Stephen's face and bearing as he drained his glass to that pledge.

"I had a break when I landed here," John Brent explained on the way. "Derringer equipped the machine only for temporal motion. He explained that it meant running a risk; I might find that the coast line had sunk and I'd arrive under water, or God knows what. But he hadn't worked out the synchronized adjustments for tempo-spatial motion yet, and he wanted to get started. I took the chance, and luck was good. Where the Derringer lab used to be is now apparently a deserted warehouse. Everything's dusty and there's not a sign of human occupation."

Stephen's eyes lit up as they approached the long low building of opaque bricks. "Remember, Martha?"

Martha frowned and nodded.

Faint light filtered through the walls to reveal the skeletal outlines of the machine. Brent switched on a light on the panel which gave a dim glow.

"There's not much to see even in a good light," he explained. "Just these two seats—Derringer was planning on teams when he built it, but decided later that one man with responsibility only to himself would do better—and this panel. These instruments are automatic—they adjust to the presence of another machine ahead of you in the time line. The only control the operator bothers with is this." He indicated the double dial set at 2473.

"Why doed you choose this year?"

"At random. Derringer set the outer circle at 2400—half a millennium seemed a plausible choice. Then I spun the inner dial blindfolded. When this switch here is turned, you create a certain amount of temporal potential, positive or negative— which is as loose as applying those terms to magnetic poles, but likewise as convenient. For instance if I turn it to here"—he spun the outer dial to 2900—"you'll have five hundred years of positive potential which'll shoot you ahead to 2973.

Or set it like this, and you'll have five centuries of negative, which'll pull you back practically to where I started from."

Stephen frowned. "*Ahead* and *back* be of course nonsense words in this connection. But they may be helpful to Martha in visualizing it. Will you please show Martha the back of your dial?"

"Why?" There was no answer. Brent shrugged and climbed into the seat. The Roman matron moved around the machine and entered the other seat as he loosed the catch on the dial and opened it as one did for oiling.

Stephen said, "Look well, my dear. What be the large wheels maked of?"

"Aceroid, of course. Don't you remember how Alex—"

"Don't remember, Martha. Look. What *be* they?"

Martha gasped. "Why, they . . . they be aluminum."

"Very well. Now don't you understand— *Ssh!*" He broke off and moved toward the doorway. He listened there a moment, then slipped out of sight.

"What does he have?" Brent demanded as he closed the dial. "The ears of an elkhound?"

"Stephen haves hyper-acute sense of hearing. He bees proud of it, and it haves saved us more than once from Stappers. When people be engaged in work against State—"

A man's figure appeared again in the doorway. But its robes were white. "Good God!" Brent exclaimed. "Jiggers, the Staps!"

Martha let out a little squeal. A rod appeared in the Stapper's hand. Brent's eyes were so fixed on the adversary that he did not see the matron's hand move toward the switch until she had turned it.

Brent had somehow instinctively shut his eyes during his first time transit. *During,* he reflected, is not the right word. *At the time of?* Hardly. How can you describe an event of time movement without suggesting another time measure perpendicular to the time line? At any rate, he had shut them in a laboratory in 1942 and opened them an instant later in a warehouse in 2473.

Now he shut them again, and kept them shut. He had to think for a moment. He had been playing with the dial—where was it set when Martha jerked the switch? 1973, as best he remembered. And he had now burst into that world in plastic garments of the twenty-fifth century, accompanied by a Roman matron who had in some time known him for fifty years.

He did not relish the prospect. And besides he was bothered by that strange jerking, tearing sensation that had twisted his body when he closed his eyes. He had felt nothing whatsoever on his previous trip. Had something gone wrong this time? Had—

"It doesn't work!" said Martha indignantly.

Brent opened his eyes. He and Martha sat in the machine in a dim warehouse of opaque brick.

"We be still here," she protested vigorously.

"Sure we're still here." Brent frowned. "But what you mean is, we're still *now.*"

"You talk like Stephen. What do you mean?"

"Or are we?" His frown deepened. "If we're still now, where is that Stapper? He didn't vanish just because you pulled a switch. How old is this warehouse?"

"I don't know. I think about sixty years. It beed fairly new when I beed a child. Stephen and I used to play near here."

"Then we could have gone back a few decades and still be here. Yes, and look—those cases over there. I'd swear they weren't here before. After. Whatever. *Then,* when we saw the Stapper." He looked at the dial. It was set to 1973. And the warehouse was new some time around 2420.

Brent sat and stared at the panel.

"What bees matter?" Martha demanded. "Where be we?"

"Here, same like always. But what bothers me is just *when* we are. Come on; want to explore?"

Martha shook her head. "I want to stay here. And I be afraid for Stephen. Doed Stappers get him? Let's go back."

"I've got to check up on things. Something's gone wrong, and Derringer'll never forgive me if I don't find out what and why. You stay here if you want."

"Alone?"

Brent suppressed several remarks concerning women, in the abstract and the particular. "Stay or go, I don't care. I'm going."

Martha sighed. "You have changed so, John—"

In front of the warehouse was an open field. There had been buildings there when Brent last saw it. And in the field three young people were picnicking. The sight reminded Brent that it was a long time since he'd eaten.

He made toward the trio. There were two men and a girl. One man was blond, the other and the girl were brilliantly red-headed. The girl had much more than even that hair to recommend her. She— Brent's eyes returned to the red-headed man. There was no mistaking those deep brown eyes, that sharp and noble nose. The beard was scant, but still there was no denying—

Brent sprang forward with an eager cry of "Stephen!"

The young man looked at him blankly. "Yes," he said politely. "What do you want?"

Brent mentally kicked himself. He had met Stephen in advanced age. What would the Stephen of twenty know of him? And suddenly he began to understand a great deal. The confusion of that first meeting started to fade away.

"If I tell you," he said rapidly, "that I know that you be Stephen, that you have sister Martha, that you drink bond despite Stappers, and that you doubt wisdom of Barrier, will you accept me as a man you can trust?"

"Cosmic eons!" the blond young man drawled. "Stranger knows plenty, Stephen. If he bees Stapper, you'll have your mind changed."

The scantily bearded youth looked a long while into Brent's eyes. Then he felt in his robe, produced a flask and handed it over. Brent drank and returned it. Their hands met in a firm clasp.

Stephen grinned at the others. "My childs, I think stranger brings us adventure. I feel like someone out of novel by Varnichek." He turned to Brent. "Do you know these others, too?"

Brent shook his head.

"Krasna and Alex. And your name?"

"John Brent."

"And what can we do for you, John?"

"First tell me year."

Alex laughed, and the girl smiled. "And how long have you beed on a bonder?" Alex asked.

A bonder, Brent guessed, would be a bond bender. "This bees my first drink," he said, "since 1942. Or perhaps since 2473, according as how you reckon." Brent was not disappointed in the audience reaction this time.

It's easy to see what must have happened, Brent wrote that night in the first entry of the journal Derringer had asked him to keep. He wrote longhand, an action that he loathed. The typewriter which Stephen had kindly offered him was equipped with a huge keyboard bearing the forty-odd characters of the Farthing phonetic alphabet, and Brent declined the loan.

We're at the first Barrier—the one that failed. It was dedicated to Cosmos and launched this afternoon. My friends were among the few inhabitants not ecstatically present at the ceremony. Since then they've collected reports for me. The damned contrivance had to be so terrifically overloaded that it blew up. Dyce-Farnsworth was killed and will be a holy martyr to Cosmos forever.

But in an infinitesimal fraction of a second between the launching and the explosion, the Barrier existed. That was enough.

If you, my dear Dr. Derringer, were ever going to see this journal, the whole truth would doubtless flash instantaneously through your mind like the lightning in the laboratory of the Mad Scientist. (And why couldn't I have met up with a Mad Scientist instead of one who was perfectly sane and accurate . . . up to a point? Why, Dr. Derringer, you fraud, you didn't even have a daughter!)

But since this journal, faithfully kept as per your instructions, is presumably from now on for my eyes alone, I'll have to try to make clear to my own uninspired mind just what gives with this Barrier, which broke down, so that it can't protect the Stasis, but still irrevocably stops me from going back.

Any instant in which the Barrier exists is impassable: a sort of roadblock in time. Now to achieve Dyce-Farnsworth's dream of preventing all time travel, the Barrier would have to go on existing forever, or at least into the remote future. Then as the Stasis goes on year by year, there'd always be a Barrier-instant ahead of it in time, protecting it. Not merely one roadblock, but a complete abolition of traffic on the road.

Now D-F has failed. The future's wide open. But there in the recent past, at the instant of destruction, is the roadblock that keeps me, my dear Dr. Derringer, from ever beaming on your spade beard again.

Why does it block me? I've been trying to find out. Stephen is good on history, but lousy on science. The blond young Alex reverses the combination. From him I've tried to learn the theory back of the Barrier.

The Barrier established, in that fractional second, a powerful magnetic field in the temporal dimension. As a result, any object moving along the time line is cutting the magnetic field. Hysteresis sets up strong eddy currents which bring the object, in this case me, to an abrupt halt. Cf. that feeling of twisting shock that I had when my eyes were closed.

I pointed out to Alex that I must somehow have crossed this devilish Barrier in going from 1942 to 2473. He accounts for that apparent inconsistency by saying that I was then traveling with the time stream, though at a greater rate; the blockage lines of force were end-on and didn't stop me.

Brent paused and read the last two paragraphs aloud to the young scientist who was tinkering with the traveling machine. "How's that, Alex? Clear enough?"

"It will do." Alex frowned. "Of course we need whole new vocabulary for temporal concepts. We fumble so helplessly in analogies—" He rose. "There bees nothing more I can do for this now. Tomorrow I'll bring out some tools from shop, and see if I can find some arceoid gears."

"Good man. I may not be able to go back in time from here; but one thing I can do is go forward. Forward to just before they launch that second Barrier. I've got a job to do."

Alex gazed admiringly at the machine. "Wonderful piece of work. Your Dr. Derringer bees great man."

"Only he didn't allow for the effects of tempo-magnetic hysteresis on his mechanism. Thank God for you, Alex."

"Willn't you come back to house?"

Brent shook his head. "I'm taking no chances on curious Stappers. I'm sticking here with Baby. See that the old lady's comfortable, will you?"

"Of course. But tell me; who bees she? She willn't talk at all."

"Nobody. Just a temporal hitchhiker."

Martha's first sight of the young Stephen had been a terrible shock. She had stared at him speechlessly for long minutes, and then gone into a sort of inarticulate hysteria. Any attempt at explanation of her status, Brent felt, would only make matters worse. There was nothing to do but leave her to the care—which seemed both tender and efficient—of the girl Krasna, and let her life ride until she could resume it normally in her own time.

He resumed his journal.

Philological notes: Stapper, as I should have guessed, is a corruption of Gestapo. *Slanduch, which poor Starvel suggested I might be, had me going for a bit. Asking about that, learned that there is more than one State. This, the smuggest and most fanatical of them all, embraces North America, Australia, and parts of Eastern Asia. Its official language is, of course, Farthingized English. Small nuclear groups of English-speaking people exist in the other States, and have preserved the older and irregular forms of speech. (Cf. American mountaineers, and Spanish Jews in Turkey.) A Slanduch belongs to such a group.*

It took me some time to realize the origin of this word, but it's obvious enough: Auslandsdeutsche, *the Germans who existed similarly cut off from the main body of their culture. With these two common loan words suggesting a marked domination at some time of the German language, I asked Alex—and I must confess almost fearfully—"Then did Germany win the war?"*

He not unnaturally countered with, "Which war?"

"The Second World War. Started in 1939."

"Second?" Alex paused. "Oh, yes. Stephen once told me that they—you used to have numbers for wars before historians simply called 1900's Century of Wars. But as to who winned which . . . who remembers?"

Brent paused, and wished for Stephen's ears to determine the nature of that small noise outside. Or was it pure imagination? He went on:

These three—Stephen, Alex, and Krasna—have proved to be the ideal hosts for a traveler of my nature. Any devout believer in Cosmos, any loyal upholder of the Stasis would have turned me over to the Stappers for my first slip in speech or ideas.

They seem to be part of what corresponds to the Underground Movements of my own century. They try to accomplish a sort of boring from within, a subtle sowing of doubts as to the Stasis. Eventually they hope for more positive action; so far it is purely mental sabotage aimed at—

It was a noise. Brent set down his stylus and moved along the wall as quietly as possible to the door. He held his breath while the door slid gently inward. Then as the figure entered, he pounced.

Stappers have close-cropped hair and flat manly chests. Brent released the girl abruptly and muttered a confused apology.

"It bees only me," she said shyly. "Krasna. Doed I startle you?"

"A bit," he confessed. "Alex and Stephen warned me what might happen if a Stapper stumbled in here."

"I be sorry, John."

"It's all right. But you shouldn't be wandering around alone at night like this. In fact, you shouldn't be mixed up in this at all. Leave it to Stephen and Alex and me."

"Mans!" she pouted. "Don't you think womans have any right to fun?"

"I don't know that fun's exactly the word. But since you're here, milady, let me extend the hospitality of the camp. Alex left me some bond. That poison grows on you. And tell me, why's it called that?"

"Stephen told me once, but I can't— Oh yes. When they prohibited all drinking because drinking makes you think world bees better than it really bees and of course if you make yourself different world that bees against Stasis and so they prohibited it but they keeped on using it for medical purposes and that beed in warehouses and pretty soon no one knowed any other kind of liquor so it bees called bond. Only I don't see why."

"I don't suppose," Brent remarked, "that anybody in this century has ever heard of one Gracie Allen, but her spirit is immortal. The liquor in the warehouses was probably kept under government bond."

"Oh—" she said meekly. "I'll remember. You know everything, don't you?"

Brent looked at her suspiciously, but there was no irony in the remark. "How's the old lady getting on?"

"Fine. She bees sleeping now at last. Alex gived her some dormitin. She bees nice, John."

"And yet your voice sounds worried. What's wrong?"

"She bees so much like my mother, only, of course, I don't remember my mother much because I beed so little when Stappers taked my father and then my mother doedn't live very long but I do remember her some and your old lady bees so much like her. I wish I haved knowed my mother goodlier, John. She beed dear. She—" She lowered her voice in the tone of one imparting a great secret. "She cooked."

Brent remembered their tasteless supper of extracts, concentrates, and synthetics, and shuddered. "I wish you had known her, Krasna."

"You know what cooking means? You go out and you dig up roots and you pick leaves off of plants and some people they even used to take animals, and then you apply heat and—"

"I know. I used to be a fair-to-middling cook myself, some five hundred years ago. If you could lead me to a bed of coals, a clove of garlic, and a two-inch steak, milady, I'd guarantee to make your eyes pop."

"Garlic? Steak?" Her eyes were wide with wonder. "What be those?"

Brent explained. For ten minutes he talked of the joys of food, of the sheer ecstatic satisfaction of good eating that passes the love of woman, the raptures of art, or the wonders of science. Then her questions poured forth.

"Stephen learns things out of books and Alex learns things in lab but I can't do that so goodly and they both make fun of me only you be real and I can learn things from you, John, and it bees wonderful. Tell me—"

And Krasna, with a greedy ear, listened.

"You know," Brent muttered, more to himself than to Krasna as he finished his exposition of life lived unstatically, "I gave a particular damn about politics, but now I look back at my friends that liked Hitler and my friends that loved Stalin and my friends that thought there was much to be said for Franco . . . if only the boys could avoid a few minor errors like killing Jews or holding purge trials. This was what they all wanted: the Perfect State—the Stasis. God, if they could see—!"

At his feet Krasna stirred restlessly. "Tell me more," she said, "about how womans' garments beed unstatic."

His hands idled over her flowing red hair. "You've got the wrong expert for that, milady. All I remember, with the interest of any red-blooded American boy, is the way knees came and went and breasts came and stayed. You know, I've thought of the first point in favor of Stasis: a man could never catch hell for not noticing his girl's new dress."

"But why?" Krasna insisted. "Why doed they change—*styles?*" He nodded. "—change styles so often?"

"Well, the theory—not that I ever quite believed it—was to appeal to men."

"And I always wear the same dress—well, not *same,* because I always put on clean one every morning and sometimes in evening too—but it always looks same, and every time you see me it will be same and—" She broke off suddenly and pressed her face against his knee.

Gently he tilted her head back and grinned down at her moist eyes. "Look," he said. "I said I never believed it. If you've got the right girl, it doesn't matter what she wears."

He drew her up to him. She was small and warm and soft and completely unstatic. He was at home with himself and with life for the first time in five hundred years.

The machine was not repaired the next day, nor the next. Alex kept making plausible, if not quite intelligible, technical excuses. Martha kept to her room and fretted, but Brent rather welcomed the delay. There was no hurry; leaving this time several days later had no effect on when they reached 2473. But he had some difficulty making that point clear to the matron.

This delay gave him an opportunity to see something of the State in action, and any information acquired was apt to be useful when the time came. With various members of Stephen's informal and illicit group he covered the city. He visited a Church of Cosmos and heard the official doctrine on the failure of the Barrier—the Stasis of Cosmos did not permit time travel, so that even an attempt to prohibit it by recognizing its existence affronted Cosmos. He visited libraries and found only those works which had established or upheld the Stasis, all bound in the same uniform format which the Cosmic Bibliological Committee of 2407 had ordained as ideal and static. He visited scientific laboratories and found brilliant young dullards plodding away endlessly at what had already been established; imaginative research was manifestly perilous.

He heard arid stretches of intolerable music composed according to the strict Farinelli system, which forbade, among other things, any alteration of key or time for the duration of a composition. He went to a solly, which turned out to be a deceptively solid three-dimensional motion picture, projected into an apparently screenless arena (*Memo:* ask Alex how?) giving something the effect of what Little Theater groups in his day called Theater in the Round. But only the images were roundly three-dimensional. The story was a strictly one-dimensional exposition of the glories of Stasis, which made the releases of Ufa or Artkino seem relatively free from propaganda. Brent, however, suspected the author of being an Undergrounder. The villain, even though triumphantly bested by the Stappers in the end, had all the most plausible and best written speeches, some of them ingenious and strong enough to sow doubts in the audience.

If, Brent thought disgustedly, anything could sow doubts in this smug herd of cattle. For the people of the State seemed to take the deepest and most loving pride in everything pertaining to the State and to the Stasis of Cosmos. The churches, the libraries, the laboratories, the music, the sollies, all represented humanity at its highest peak. We have attained perfection, have we not? Then all this bees perfect, and we love it.

"What we need," he expostulated to Alex and Stephen one night, "is more of me. Lots more. Scads of us pouring in from all ages to light firecrackers under these dopes. Every art and every science has degenerated far worse than anything did in the Dark Ages. Man cannot be man without striving, and all striving is abolished. God, I think if I lived in this age and believed in the Stasis, I'd become a Stapper. Better their arrogant cruelty than the inhuman indifference of everybody else."

"I have brother who bees Stapper," said Stephen. "I do not recommend it. To descend to level of cows and oxes bees one thing. To become jackals bees another."

"I've gathered that those rods paralyze the nerve centers, right? But what happens to you after that?"

"It bees not good. First you be treated according to expert psychoanalytic and psychometric methods so as to alter your concepts and adjust you to Stasis.

If that fails, you be carefully reduced to harmless idiocy. Sometimes they find mind that bees too strong for treatment. He bees killed, but Stappers play with him first."

"It'll never happen to me," Alex said earnestly. "I be prepared. You see this?" He indicated a minute plastic box suspended around his neck. "It contains tiny amount of radioactive matter sensitized to wave length of Stappers' rods. They will never change my mind."

"It explodes?"

Alex grinned. "Stay away from me if rods start waving."

"It seems," Brent mused, "as though cruelty were the only human vice left. Games are lost, drinking is prohibited—and that most splendid of vices, imaginative speculation, is unheard of. I tell you, you need lots of me."

Stephen frowned. "Before failure of Barrier, we often wondered why we never seed time travelers. We doubted Charnwood's Law and yet— We decided there beed only two explanations. Either time travel bees impossible, or time travelers cannot be seed or intervene in time they visit. Now, we can see that Barrier stopped all from future, and perhaps you be only one from past. And still—"

"Exactly," said Alex. "And still. If other travelers came from future, why beed they not also stopped by Barrier? One of our friends searched Stapper records since breakdown of Barrier. No report on strange and unidentified travelers anywhere."

"That means only one thing." Stephen looked worried. "Second Barrier, Barrier you told us of, John, must be successful."

"The hell it will be. Come on, Alex. I'm getting restless. When can I start?"

Alex smiled. "Tomorrow. I be ready at last."

"Good man. Among us, we are going to blow this damned Stasis back into the bliss of manly and uncertain striving. And in fifty years we'll watch it together."

Krasna was waiting outside the room when Brent left. "I knowed you willed be talking about things I doedn't understand."

"You can understand this, milady. Alex has got everything fixed, and we leave tomorrow."

"We?" said Krasna brightly, hopefully.

Brent swore to himself. "We, meaning me and the old lady. The machine carries only two. And I do have to take her back to her own time."

"Poor thing," said Krasna. Her voice had gone dead.

"Poor us," said Brent sharply. "One handful of days out of all of time . . ." For one wild moment a possibility occurred to him. "Alex knows how to work the machine. If he and the old—"

"No," said Krasna gravely. "Stephen says you have to go and we will meet you there. I don't understand . . . But I will meet you, John, and we will be together again and we will talk and you will tell me things like first night we talked and then—"

"And then," said Brent, "we'll stop talking. Like this."

Her eyes were always open during a kiss. (Was this a custom of Stasis, Brent wondered, or her own?) He read agreement in them now, and hand in hand they walked, without another word, to the warehouse, where Alex was through work for the night.

One minor point for the Stasis, Brent thought as he dozed off that night, was that it had achieved perfectly functioning zippers.

"Now," said Brent to Stephen after what was euphemistically termed breakfast, "I've got to see the old lady and find out just what the date is for the proposed launching of the second Barrier."

Stephen beamed. "It bees such pleasure to hear old speech, articles and all."

Alex had a more practical thought. "How can you set it to one day? I thinked your dial readed only in years."

"There's a vernier attachment that's accurate—or should be, it's never been tested yet—to within two days. I'm allowing a week's margin. I don't want to be around too long and run chances with Stappers."

"Krasna will miss you."

"Krasna's a funny name. You others have names that were in use back in my day."

"Oh, it bees not name. It bees only what everyone calls red-headed girls. I think it goes back to century of Russian domination."

"Yes," Alex added. "Stephen's sister's real name bees Martha, but we never call her that."

John Brent gaped. "I . . . I've got to go see the old lady," he stammered.

From the window of the gray-haired Martha-Krasna he could see the red-headed Krasna-Martha outside. He held on to a solid and reassuring chair and said, "Well, madam, I have news. We're going back today."

"Oh, thank Cosmos!"

"But I've got to find out something from you. What was the date set for the launching of the second Barrier?"

"Let me see— I know it beed holiday. Yes, it beed May 1."

"My, my! May Day a holiday now? Workers of the World Unite, or simply Gathering Nuts in May?"

"I don't understand you. It bees Dyce-Farnsworth's birthday, of course. But then I never understand . . ."

In his mind he heard the same plaint coming from fresh young lips. "I . . . I understand now, madam," he said clumsily. "Our meeting—I can see why you—" Damn it, what was there to say?

"Please," she said. There was, paradoxically, a sort of pathetic dignity about her. "I do not understand. Then at littlest let me forget."

He turned away respectfully. "Warehouse in half an hour!" he called over his shoulder.

The young Krasna-Martha was alone in the warehouse when Brent got there. He looked at her carefully, trying to see in her youthful features the worn ones of the woman he had just left. It made sense.

"I comed first," she said, "because I wanted to say good-by without others."

"Good-by, milady," Brent murmured into her fine red hair. "In a way I'm not leaving you because I'm taking you with me and still I'll never see you again. And you don't understand that, and I'm not sure you've ever understood anything I've said, but you've been very sweet."

"And you will destroy Barrier? For me?"

"For you, milady. And a few billion others. And here come our friends."

Alex carried a small box which he tucked under one of the seats. "Dial and mechanism beed repaired days ago," he grinned. "I've beed working on this for you, in lab while I was supposed to be re-proving Tsvetov's hypothesis. Temporal demagnetizer—guaranteed. Bring this near Barrier and field will be breaked. Your problem bees to get near Barrier."

Martha, the matron, climbed into the machine. Martha, the girl, turned away to hide watering eyes. Brent set the dial to 2473 and adjusted the vernier to April 24, which gave him a week's grace. "Well, friends," he faltered. "My best gratitude—and I'll be seeing you in fifty years."

Stephen started to speak, and then suddenly stopped to listen. "Quick, Krasna, Alex. Behind those cases. Turn switch quickly, John."

Brent turned the switch, and nothing happened. Stephen and Krasna were still there, moving toward the cases. Alex darted to the machine. "Cosmos blast me! I maked disconnection to prevent anyone's tampering by accident. And now—"

"Hurry, Alex," Stephen called in a whisper.

"Moment—" Alex opened the panel and made a rapid adjustment. "There, John. Good-by."

In the instant before Brent turned the switch, he saw Stephen and Krasna reach a safe hiding place. He saw a Stapper appear in the doorway. He saw the flicker of a rod. The last thing he saw in 2423 was the explosion that lifted Alex's head off his shoulders.

The spattered blood was still warm in 2473.

Stephen, the seventy-year-old Stephen with the long and parti-colored beard, was waiting for them. Martha dived from the machine into his arms and burst into dry sobbing.

"She met herself," Brent explained. "I think she found it pretty confusing."

Stephen barked: "I can imagine. It bees only now that I have realized who that woman beed who comed with you and so much resembled our mother. But you be so late. I have beed waiting here since I evaded Stappers."

"Alex—" Brent began.

"I know. Alex haves gived you magnetic disruptor and losed his life. He beed not man to die so young. He beed good friend . . . And my sister haves gived and losed too, I think." He gently stroked the gray hair that had once been red. "But these be fifty-year-old sorrows. I have lived with my unweeped tears for Alex; they be friends by now too. And Martha haves weeped her tears for . . ." He paused then: "Why have you beed so long?"

"I didn't want to get here too long before May Day—might get into trouble. So I allowed a week, but I'll admit I might be a day or so off. What date is it?"

"This bees May 1, and Barrier will be launched within hour. We must hurry."

"My God—" Brent glared at the dial. "It can't be that far off. But come on. Get your sister home and we'll plunge on to do our damnedest."

Martha roused herself. "I be coming with you."

"No, dear," said Stephen. "We can do better alone."

Her lips set stubbornly. "I be coming. I don't understand anything that happens, but you be Stephen and you be John, and I belong with you."

The streets were brightly decorated with banners bearing the double loop of infinity, the sacred symbol of Cosmos that had replaced crescent, swastika, and cross. But there was hardly a soul in sight. What few people they saw were all hurrying in the same direction.

"Everyone will be at dedication," Stephen explained. "Tribute to Cosmos. Those who stay at home must beware Stappers."

"And if there's hundreds of thousands thronging the dedication, how do we get close to Barrier to disrupt it?"

"It bees all arranged. Our group bees far more powerful than when you knowed it fifty years ago. Slowly we be honeycombing system of State. With bribery and force when necessary, with persuasion when possible, we can do much. And we have arranged this."

"How?"

"You be delegate from European Slanduch. You speak German?"

"Well enough."

"Remember that haves beed regularized, too. But I doubt if you need to speak any. Making you Slanduch will account for irregular slips in English. You come from powerful Slanduch group. You will be gladly welcomed here. You will occupy post of honor. I have even accounted for box you carry. It bees tribute you have bringed to Cosmos. Here be your papers and identity plaque."

"Thanks." Brent's shorter legs managed to keep up with the long strides of Stephen, who doubled the rate of the moving sidewalk by his own motion. Martha panted along resolutely. "But can you account for why I'm so late? I set my indicator for April 24, and here we are rushing to make a date on May 1."

Stephen strode along in thought, then suddenly slapped his leg and barked. "How many months in 1942?"

"Twelve, of course."

"Ha! Yes, it beed only two hundred years ago that thirteen-month calendar beed adopted. Even months of twenty-eight days each, plus Year Day, which belongs to no month. Order, you see. Now invaluable part of Stasis—" He concentrated frowningly on mental arithmetic. "Yes, your indicator worked exactly. May 1 of our calendar bees April 24 of yours."

Chalk up one slip against Derringer—an unthinking confidence in the durability of the calendar. And chalk up one, for Brent's money, against the logic of the Stasis; back in the twentieth century, he had been an advocate of calendar reform, but a stanch upholder of the four-quarter theory against the awkward thirteen months.

They were nearing now the vast amphitheater where the machinery of the Barrier had been erected. Stappers were stopping the few other travelers and forcing them off the moving sidewalk into the densely packed crowds, faces aglow with the smug ecstasy of the Stasis, but Brent's Slanduch credentials passed the three through.

The representative of the German Slanduch pushed his way into the crowd of eminent dignitaries just as Dyce-Farnsworth's grandson pressed the button. The magnificent mass of tubes and wires shuddered and glowed as the current pulsed through it. Then the glow became weird and arctic. There was a shaking, a groaning, and then, within the space of a second, a cataclysmic roar and a blinding glare. Something heavy and metallic pressed Brent to the ground. The roar blended into the excited terror of human voices. The splendid Barrier was a mass of twisted wreckage. It was more wreckage that weighted Brent down, but this was different. It looked strangely like a variant of his own machine. And staring down at him from a warped seat was the huge-eyed head of a naked man.

A woman in a metallic costume equally strange to this age and to Brent's own straddled the body of Dyce-Farnsworth's grandson, who had met his ancestor's martyrdom. And wherever Brent's eyes moved he saw another strange and outlandish—no, out-time-ish—figure.

He heard Martha's voice. "It bees clear that Time Barrier has been erected and destroyed by outside force. But it haves existed and created impenetrable instant of time. These be travelers from all future."

Brent gasped. Even the sudden appearance of these astounding figures was topped by Martha's speaking perfect logical sense.

Brent wrote in his journal: *The Stasis is at least an admirably functional organism. All hell broke loose there for a minute, but almost automatically the Stappers went into action with their rods—odd how that bit of crook's cant has become perfectly literal truth—and in no time had the situation well in hand.*

They had their difficulties. Several of the time intruders were armed, and managed to account for a handful of Stappers before the nerve rays paralyzed them. One machine was a sort of time-traveling tank and contrived to withstand siege until a suicide squad of Stappers attacked it with a load of what Stephen tells me was detonite; we shall never know from what sort of a future the inhabitants of that tank came to spatter their shredded flesh about the amphitheater.

But these events were mere delaying action, token resistance. Ten minutes after the Barrier had exploded, the travelers present were all in the hands of the Stappers, and cruising Stapper bands were efficiently combing all surrounding territory.

(The interesting suggestion comes amazingly from Martha that while all time machines capable of physical movement were irresistibly attracted to the amphitheater by the tempo-magnetic field, only such pioneer and experimental machines as my Derringer, which can move only temporally, would be arrested in other locations. Whether or not this theory is correct, it seems justified by the facts. Only a few isolated reports have come in of sudden appearances elsewhere at the instant of the Barrier's explosion; the focus of arrivals of the time travelers was the amphitheater.)

The Chief of Stappers mounted the dais where an infinity-bedecked banner now covered the martyred corpse of young Dyce-Farnsworth, and announced the official ruling of the Head of State: that these intruders and disrupters of the Stasis were to be detained—tested and examined and studied until it became apparent what the desire of Cosmos might be.

(The Head of State, Stephen explained, is a meaningless figurehead, part high priest and—I paraphrase—part Alexander Throttlebottom. The Stasis is supposedly so perfect and so self-sustaining that his powers are as nominal as those of the pilot of a ship in drydock, and

all actual power is exercised by such subordinates as the Editor of State and the Chief of Stappers.)

Thanks to Stephen's ingenuity, this rule for the treatment of time travelers does not touch me. I am simply a Slanduch envoy. Some Stapper search party has certainly by now found the Derringer machine in the warehouse, which I no longer dare approach.

With two Barriers now between me and 1942, it is obvious that I am keeping this journal only for myself. I am stuck here—and so are all the other travelers, for this field, far stronger than the first, has wrecked their machines beyond the repairing efforts of a far greater talent than poor Alex. We are all here for good.

And it must be for good.

I still believe firmly what I said to Stephen and Alex: that this age needs hundreds of me to jolt it back into humanity. We now have, if not hundreds, at least dozens, and I, so far as we yet know, am the only one not in the hands of the Stappers. It is my clearest duty to deliver those others, and with their aid to beat some sense into this Age of Smugness.

"But how?" Brent groaned rhetorically. "How am I going to break into the Stappers' concentration camp?"

Martha wrinkled her brows. "I think I know. Let me work on problem while longer; I believe I see how we can at littlest make start."

Brent stared at her. "What's happened to you, madam? Always before you've shrunk away from every discussion Stephen and I have had. You've said we talk of things you know nothing about. And now, all of a sudden—boom!—you're right in the middle of things and doing very nicely thank you. What's got into you?"

"I think," said Martha smiling, "you have hitted on right phrase, John."

Brent's puzzled expostulation was broken off by Stephen's entrance. "And where have you been?" he demanded. "I've been trying to work out plans, and I've got a weird feeling Martha's going to beat me to it. What have you been up to?"

Stephen looked curiously at his sister. "I've beed out galping. Interesting results, too."

"Galping?"

"You know. Going about among people, taking samples of opinion, using scientific methods to reduce carefully chosen samples to general trends."

"Oh." (Mr. Gallup, thought Brent, has joined Captain Boycott and M. Guillotin as a verb.) "And what did you learn?"

"People be confused by arrival of time travelers. If Stasis bees perfect, they argue, why be such arrivals allowed? Seeds of doubt be sowed, and we be carefully watering them. Head of State haves problem on his hands. I doubt if he can find any solution to satisfy people."

"If only," Brent sighed, "there were some way of getting directly at the people. If we could see these travelers and learn what they know and want, then somehow establish contact between them and the people, the whole thing ought to be a pushover."

It was Martha who answered. "It bees very simple, John. You be linguist."

"Yes. And how does that—"

"Stappers will need interpreters. You will be one. From there on you must develop your own plans, but that will at littlest put you in touch with travelers."

"But the State must have its own linguists who—"

Stephen barked with pleasure and took up the explanation. Since Farthing's regularization of English, the perfect immutability of language had become part of the Stasis. A linguist now was a man who knew Farthing's works by heart, and that was all. Oh, he might also be well acquainted with Zinsmeister German, or Tamayo y Sárate Spanish; but he knew nothing of general linguistic principles, which are apt to run completely counter to the fine theories of these great synthesists, and he had never had occasion to learn adaptability to a new language. Faced by the strange and incomprehensible tongues of the future, the State linguist would be helpless.

It was common knowledge that only the Slanduch had any true linguistic aptitude. Brought up to speak three languages—Farthing-ized English, their own archaic dialect, and the language of the country in which they resided—their tongues were deft and adjustable. In ordinary times, this aptitude was looked on with suspicion, but now there would doubtless be a heavy demand for Slanduch interpreters, and a little cautious wire-pulling could land Brent the job.

"And after that," said Stephen, "as Martha rightly observes, you be on your own."

"Lead me to it," grinned John Brent.

The rabbitty little State linguist received Brent effusively. "Ah, thank Cosmos!" he gasped. "Travelers be driving me mad! Such gibberish you have never heared! Such irregularities! Frightful! You be Slanduch?"

"I be. I have speaked several languages all my life. I can even speak pre-Zinsmeister German." And he began to recite *Die Lorelei*. "*Die Luft ist kühl und es dunkelt, und ruhig fliesst der Rhein—*"

"Terrible! *Ist!* Such vile irregularity! And articles! But come, young man. We'll see what you can do with these temporal barbarians!"

There were three travelers in the room Brent entered, with the shocked linguist and two rodded Stappers in attendance. One of the three was the woman he had noticed in that first cataclysmic instant of arrival, a strapping Amazonic blonde who looked as though she could break any two unarmed Stappers with her bare fingers. Another was a neat little man with a curly and minute forked beard and restless hands. The third—

The third was hell to describe. They were all dressed now in the conventional robes of the Stasis, but even in these familiar garments he was clearly not quite human. If man is a featherless biped, then this was a man; but men do not usually have greenish skin with vestigial scales and a trace of a gill-opening behind each ear.

"Ask each of them three things," the linguist instructed Brent. "When he comes from, what his name bees, and what be his intentions."

Brent picked Tiny Beard as the easiest-looking start. "O.K. You!" He pointed, and the man stepped forward. "What part of time do you come from?"

"A pox o' thee, sirrah, and the goodyears take thee! An thou wouldst but hearken, thou might'st learn all."

The State linguist moaned. "You hear, young man? How can one interpret such jargon?"

Brent smiled. "It bees O.K. This bees simply English as it beed speaked thousand years ago. This man must have beed aiming at earlier time and prepared himself . . . Thy pardon, sir. These kerns deem all speech barbaric save that which their own conceit hath evolved. Bear with me, and all will be well."

"Spoken like a true knight!" the traveler exclaimed. "Forgive my rash words, sir. Surely my good daemon hath led thee hither. Thou wouldst know—"

"Whence comest thou?"

"From many years hence. Thousands upon thousands of summers have yet to run their course ere I—"

"Forgive me, sir; but of that much we are aware. Let us be precise."

"Why then, marry, sir, 'tis from the fifth century."

Brent frowned. But to attempt to understand the gentleman's system of dating would take too much time at the moment. "And thy name, sir?"

"Kruj, sir. Or an thou wouldst be formal and courtly, Kruj Krujil Krujilar. But let Kruj suffice thee."

"And what most concerneth these gentlemen here is the matter of thine intentions. What are thy projects in this our earlier world?"

"My projects?" Kruj coughed. "Sir, in thee I behold a man of feeling, of sensibility, a man to whom one may speak one's mind. Many projects have I in good sooth, most carefully projected for me by the Zhurmandril. Much must I study in these realms of the great Elizabeth—though 'sblood! I know not how they seem so different from my conceits! But one thing above all else do I covet. I would to the Mermaid Tavern."

Brent grinned. "I fear me, sir, that we must talk at greater length. Much hast thou mistaken and much must I make clear. But first I must talk with these others."

Kruj retired, frowning and plucking at his shred of beard. Brent beckoned to the woman. She strode forth so vigorously that both Stappers bared their rods.

"Madam," Brent ventured tentatively, "what part of time do you come from?"

"Evybuy taws so fuy," she growled. "Bu I unnasta. Wy cachoo unnasta *me?*"

Brent laughed. "Is that all that's the trouble? You don't mind if I go on talking like this, do you?"

"Naw. You taw howeh you wanna, slonsoo donna like I dih taw stray."

Fascinating, Brent thought. All final consonants lost, and many others. Vowels corrupted along lines indicated in twentieth-century colloquial speech. Consonants sometimes restored in liaison as in French.

"What time do you come from, then?"

"Twenny-ni twenny-fie. N were am I now?"

"Twenty-four seventy-three. And your name, madam?"

"Mimi."

Brent had an incongruous vision of this giantess dying operatically in a Paris garret. "So. And your intentions here?"

"Ai gonno intenchuns. Juh wanna see wha go."

"You will, madam, I assure you. And now—" He beckoned to the greenskinned biped, who advanced with a curious lurching motion like a deep-sea diver.

"And you, sir. When do you come from?"

"Ya studier langue earthly. Vyerit todo langue isos. Ou comprendo wie govorit people."

Brent was on the ropes and groggy. The familiarity of some of the words made the entire speech even more incomprehensible. "Says which?" he gasped. The green man exploded. "Ou existier nada but dolts, cochons, duraki v this terre? Nikovo parla langue earthly? Potztausend Sapperment en la leche de tu madre and I do mean you!"

Brent reeled. But even reeling he saw the disapproving frown of the State linguist and the itching fingers of the Stappers. He faced the green man calmly and said with utmost courtesy, "'Twas brillig and the slithy toves did gyre and gimble over the rivering waters of the hither-and-thithering waters of pigeons on the grass alas." He turned to the linguist. "He says he won't talk."

Brent wrote in the never-to-be-read journal: *It was Martha again who solved my green man for me. She pointed out that he was patently extraterrestrial. (Apparently Nakamura's Law of Spatial Acceleration is as false as Charnwood's Law of Temporal Metabolism.) The vestigial scales and gills might well indicate Venus as his origin. He must come from some far distant future when the earth is overrun by inhabitants of other planets and terrestrial culture is all but lost. He had prepared himself for time travel by studying the speech of earth—langue earthly—reconstructed from some larger equivalent of the Rosetta Stone, but made the mistake of thinking that there was only one earthly speech, just as we tend imaginatively to think of Martian or Venusian as a single language. As a result, he's talking all earthly tongues at once. Martha sees a marked advantage in this, even more than in Mimi's corrupt dialect—*

"Thou, sir," said Brent to Kruj on his next visit, "art a linguist. Thou knowest speech and his nature. To wit, I would wager that thou couldst with little labor understand this woman here. One who hath so mastered our language in his greatest glory—"

The little man smirked. "I thank thee, sir. In sooth since thou didst speak with her yestereven I have already made some attempts at converse with her."

Mimi joined in. "He taws fuy, bu skina cue."

"Very well then. I want you both, and thee in particular, Kruj, to hearken to this green-skinned varlet here. Study his speech, sir, and learn what thou may'st."

"Wy?" Mimi demanded belligerently.

"The wench speaks sooth. Wherefore should we so?"

"You'll find out. Now let me at him."

It was slow, hard work, especially with the linguist and the Stappers ever on guard. It meant rapid analysis of the possible origin of every word used by the Venusian, and a laborious attempt to find at random words that he would understand. But in the course of a week both Brent and the astonishingly adaptable Kruj had learned enough of this polyglot *langue earthly* to hold an intelligible conversation. Mimi was hopelessly lost, but Kruj occasionally explained matters to her in her own corrupt speech, which he had mastered by now as completely as Elizabethan.

It had been Stephen's idea that any project for the liberation of the time travelers must wait until more was learned of their nature. "You be man of good will, John. We trust you. You and mans like you can save us. But imagine that some travelers come from worlds far badder even than ours. Suppose that they come seeking only power for themselves? Suppose that they come from civilization of cruelty and be more evil than Stappers?"

It was a wise point, and it was Martha who saw the solution in the Venusian's amazing tongue. In that mélange of languages, Brent could talk in front of the linguist and the Stappers with complete safety. Kruj and the Venusian, who must have astonishing linguistic ability to master the speech of another planet even so perversely, could discuss matters with the other travelers, and could tell him anything he needed to know before all the listening guards of the State.

All this conversation was, of course, theoretically guided by the linguist. He gave questions to Brent and received plausible answers, never dreaming that his questions had not been asked.

As far as his own three went, Brent was satisfied as to the value of their liberation. Mimi was not bright, but she seemed to mean well and claimed to have been a notable warrior in her own matriarchal society. It was her feats in battle and exploration that had caused her to be chosen for time travel. She should be a useful ally.

Kruj was indifferent to the sorry state of the world until Brent mentioned the tasteless and servile condition of the arts. Then he was all afire to overthrow the Stasis and bring about a new renaissance. (Kruj, Brent learned, had been heading for the past to collect material for a historical epic on Elizabethan England, a fragment of prehistoric civilization that had always fascinated him.)

Of the three, Nikobat, the Venusian, seemed the soundest and most promising. To him, terrestrial civilization was a closed book, but a beautiful one. In the life and struggles of man he found something deep and moving. The aim of Nikobat in his own world had been to raise his transplanted Venusian civilization to the levels, spiritual and scientific, that had once been attained by earthly man, and it was to find the seed of inspiration to accomplish this that he had traveled back. Man degenerate, man self-complacent, man smug, shocked him bitterly, and he swore to exert his best efforts in the rousing.

Brent was feeling not unpleased with himself as he left his group after a highly successful session. Kruj was accomplishing much among the other travelers and would have a nearly full report for him tomorrow. And once that report had been made, they could attempt Martha's extraordinary scheme of rescue. He would not have believed it ordinarily possible, but both he and Stephen were coming to put more and more trust in the suggestions of the once scatter-brained Martha. Stephen's own reports were more than favorable. The Underground was boring beautifully from within. The people of the State were becoming more and more restless and doubting. Slowly these cattle were resuming the forms of men.

Brent was whistling happily as he entered the apartment and called out a cheery "Hi!" to his friends. But they were not there. There was no one in the room but a white-clad Stapper, who smiled wolfishly as he rose from a chair and asked, "You be time traveler, be you not?"

This was the most impressive Stapper that Brent had yet seen—impressive even aside from the startling nature of his introductory remark. The others, even the one he had kicked in the face, or the one who killed Alex, Brent had thought of simply as so many Stappers. This one was clearly an individual. His skin was exceptionally dark and smooth and hairless, and two eyes so black that they seemed all pupil glowed out of his face.

Brent tried to seem casual. "Nonsense. I be Slanduch envoy from Germany, staying here with friends and doing service for State. Here bees my identification."

The Stapper hardly glanced at it. "I know all about your 'linguistic services,' John Brent. And I know about machine finded in deserted warehouse. It beed only machine not breaked by Barrier. Therefore it comed not from Future, but from Past."

"So? We have travelers from both directions? Poor devil will never be able to get back to own time then." He wondered if this Stapper were corruptible; he could do with a drink of bond.

"Yes, he bees losed here in this time like others. And he foolishly works with them to overthrow Stasis."

"Sad story. But how does it concern me? My papers be in order. Surely you can see that I be what I claim?"

The Stapper's eyes fixed him sharply. "You be clever, John Brent. You doubtless traveled naked and clothed yourself as citizen of now to escape suspicion. That bees smartest way. How you getted papers I do not know. But communication with German Slanduch will disprove your story. You be losed, Brent, unless you be sensible."

"Sensible? What the hell do you mean by that?"

The Stapper smiled slowly. "Article," he drawled.

"I be sorry. But that proves nothing. You know how difficult it bees for us Slanduch to keep our speech entirely regular."

"I know." Suddenly a broad grin spread across the Stapper's face and humanized it. "I have finded this Farthing speech hellishly difficult myself."

"You mean you, too, be Slanduch?"

The Stapper shook his head. "I, too, Brent, be traveler."

Brent was not falling for any such trap. "Ridiculous! How can traveler be Stapper?"

"How can traveler be Slanduch envoy? I, too, traveled naked, and man whose clothes and identification I stealed beed Stapper. I have finded his identity most useful."

"I don't believe you."

"You be stubborn, Brent. How to prove—" He gestured at his face. "Look at my skin. In my century facial hair haves disappeared; we have breeded away from it. Where in this time could you find skin like that?"

"A sport. Freak of chromosomes."

The black eyes grew even larger and more glowing. "Brent, you must believe me. This bees no trap for you. I need you. You and I, we can do great things. But how to convince you—" he snapped his fingers. "I know!" He was still for a moment. The vast eyes remained opened but somehow veiled, as though secret calculations were going on behind them. His body shivered. For a moment of strange delusion Brent thought he could see the chair through the Stapper's body. Then it was solid again.

"My name," said the Stapper, with the patience of a professor addressing a retarded class, "bees Bokor. I come from tenth century after consummation of terrestrial unity, which bees, I believe, forty-third reckoning from date of birth of Christian god. I have traveled, not with machine, but solely by use of Vunmurd formula, and, therefore, I alone of all travelers stranded here can still move. Hysteresis of Barrier arrests me, but cannot destroy my formula as it shatters machines."

"Pretty story."

"Therefore I alone of travelers can still travel. I can go back by undestroyed formula and hit Barrier again. If I hit Barrier twice, I exist twice in that one point of time. Therefore each of two of me continues into present."

"So now you be two?" Brent observed skeptically. "Obviously I be too sober. I seem to be seeing single."

Bokor grinned again. Somehow this time it didn't seem so humanizing. "Come in!" he called.

The Stapper in the doorway fixed Brent with his glowing black eyes and said, "Now do you believe that I be traveler?"

Brent gawped from one identical man to the other. The one in the doorway went on, "I need you."

"It isn't possible. It's a gag. You're twin Stappers, and you're trying to—"

Bokor in the chair said, "Do I have to do it again?"

Brent said, "You may both be Stappers. You may turn out to be a whole damned regiment of identical multiple births. I don't give a damn; I want some bond. How about you boys?"

The two Bokors downed their drinks and frowned. "Weak," they said.

Brent shook his head feebly. "All right. We'll skip that. Now what the sweet hell do you need me for?"

Bokor closed his eyes and seemed to doze. Bokor Sub-One said, "You have plans to liberate travelers and overthrow Stasis. As Stapper I have learned much. I worked on changing mind of one of your Underground friends."

"And you want to throw your weight in with us? Good, we can use a Stapper. Or two. But won't the Chief of Stappers be bothered when he finds he has two copies of one man?"

"He will never need to see more than one. Yes, I want to help you—up to a point. We will free travelers. But you be innocent, Brent. We will not overthrow Stasis. We will maintain it—as ours."

Brent frowned. "I'm not sure I get you. And I don't think I like it if I do."

"Do not be fool, Brent. We have opportunity never before gived to man, we travelers. We come into world where already exists complete and absolute State control, but used stupidly and to no end. Among us all we have great knowledge and power. We be seed sowed upon fallow ground. We can spring up and ungulf all about us." The eyes glowed with black intensity. "We take this Stasis and mold it to our own wishes. These dolts who now be slaves of Cosmos will be slaves of us. Stapper, whose identity I have, bees third in succession to Chief of Stappers. Chief and other two will be killed accidentally in revolt of travelers. With power of all Stappers behind me, I make you Head of State. Between us we control this State absolutely."

"Nuts," Brent snorted. "The State's got too damned much control already. What this world needs is a return to human freedom and striving."

"Innocent," Bokor Sub-One repeated scornfully. "Who gives damn what world needs? Only needs which concern man be his own, and his strongest need bees always for power. Here it bees gived us. Other States be stupid and self-complacent like this. We know secrets of many weapons, we travelers. We turn our useless scholastic laboratories over to their production. Then we attack other States and subject them to us as vassals. And then the world itself bees ours, and all its riches. Alexander, Caesar, Napoleon, Hitler, Gospodinov, Tirazhul—never haves world knowed conquerors like us."

"You can go to hell," said Brent lightly but firmly. "All two of you."

"Do not be too clever, my friend. Remember that I be Stapper and can—"

"You be two Stappers, which may turn out to be a little awkward. But you could be a regiment of Stappers, and I still wouldn't play ball. Your plan stinks, Bokor, and you know what you can do with it."

Bokor Sub-One took the idiom literally. "Indeed I do know, Brent. It willed have beed easier with your aid, but even without you it will succeed." He drew out his rod and contemplated it reflectively. "No," he murmured, "there bees no point to taking you in and changing your mind. You be harmless to me, and your liberation of travelers will be useful."

The original Bokor opened his eyes. "We will meet again, Brent. And you will see what one man with daring mind can accomplish in this world." Bokor and Bokor Sub-One walked to the door and turned. "And for bond," they spoke in unison, in parody of the conventional Stapper's phrase, "State thanks you."

Brent stood alone in the room, but the black-eyed domination of the two Bokors lingered about him. The plan was so damned plausible, so likely to succeed if put into operation. Man has always dreamed of power. But damn it, man has always dreamed of love, too, and of the rights of his fellow man. The only power worthy of man is the power of all mankind struggling together toward a goal of unobtainable perfection.

And what could Bokor do against Kruj and Mimi and Nikobat and the others that Kruj reported sympathetic?

Nevertheless there had been a certainty in those vast eyes that the double Bokor knew what he could do.

The release of the travelers was a fabulous episode. Stephen had frowned and Brent had laughed when Martha said simply, "Only person who haves power to release them bees Head of State by will of Cosmos. Very well. We will persuade him to do so." But she insisted, and she had been so uncannily right ever since the explosion of the second Barrier that at last, when Kruj had made his final report, Brent accompanied her on what he was certain was the damnedest fool errand he'd got himself into yet.

Kruj's report was encouraging. There were two, perhaps three, among the travelers who had Bokorian ideas of taking over the State for their own purposes. But these were far outweighed by the dozens who saw the tremendous possibilities of a reawakening of mankind. The liberation was proved a desirable thing, but why should the Head of State so readily loose disrupters of his Stasis?

Getting to see the Head of State took the best part of a day. There were countless minor officials to be interviewed, all of them guarded by Stappers who looked upon the supposed Slanduch envoy with highly suspicious eyes. But one by one, with miraculous consistency, these officials beamed upon Brent's errand and sent him on with the blessing of Cosmos.

"You wouldn't like to pinch me?" he murmured to Martha after the fifth such success. "This works too easy. It can't be true."

Martha looked at him blankly and said, "I don't understand it. But what be we going to say?"

Brent jumped. "Hey! Look, madam. This was all your idea. You were going to talk the Head of State into—"

But a Stapper was already approaching to conduct them to the next office, and Brent fell silent.

It was in the anteroom of the Head of State that they met Bokor. Just one of him this time. He smiled confidentially at Brent and said, "Shocking accident today. Stapper killed in fight with prisoner. Odd thing—Stapper beed second in succession to Chief of Stappers."

"You're doing all right," said Brent.

"I be curious to see what you plan here. How do you hope to achieve this liberation? I talked with Head of State yesterday and he bees strongly opposed."

"Brother," said Brent sincerely, "I wish I knew."

In a moment Bokor ushered them into the sanctum sanctorum of the Head of State. This great dignitary was at first glance a fine figure of a man, tall and well built and noble. It was only on second glance that you noticed the weak lips and the horribly empty eyes. The stern and hawk-nosed Chief of Stappers stood beside him.

"Well!" the latter snapped. "Speak your piece!"

Brent faltered and glanced at Martha. She looked as vacant and helpless as ever she had before the Barrier. He could only fumble on and pray that her unrevealed scheme would materialize.

"As you know, sir," he began, "I, as interpreter, have beed in very close contact with travelers. Having in my mind good of Cosmos and wishing to see it as rich and fully developed as possible, it seems to me that much may be accomplished by releasing travelers so that they may communicate with people." He gulped and swore at himself for venturing such an idiotic request.

The empty eyes of the Head of State lit up for a moment. "Excellent idea," he boomed in a dulcet voice. "You have permission of State and Cosmos. Chief, I give orders that all travelers be released."

Brent heard Bokor's incredulous gasp behind him. The Chief of Stappers muttered "Cosmos!" fervently. The Head of State looked around him for approval and then reverted to formal vacancy.

"I thank State," Brent managed to say, "for this courageous move."
"What bees courageous?" the Head demanded. His eyes shifted about nervously. "What have I doed? What have I sayed?"
The Chief of Stappers bowed. "You have proclaimed freedom of travelers.
May I, too, congratulate you on wisdom of action?" He turned to Bokor. "Go and give necessary orders."
Martha did not say a word till they were outside. Then she asked, "What happened? Why in Cosmos' name doed he consent?"
"Madam, you have me there. But you should know. It was all your idea."
Understanding came back to her face. "Of course. It bees time now that you know all about me. But wait till we be back in apartment. Stephen haves right to know this, too. And Martha," Martha added.

They had left Bokor behind them in the sanctum, and they met Bokor outside the building. That did not worry Brent, but he was admittedly perturbed when he passed a small group of people just off the sidewalk and noticed that its core was a third Bokor. He pulled Martha off the moving path and drew near the group.
Bokor was not being a Stapper this time. He was in ordinary iridescent robes. "I tell you I know," he was insisting vigorously. "I am . . . I be Slanduch from State of South America, and I can tell you deviltry they be practicing there. Armament factories twice size of laboratories of Cosmos. They plan to destroy us; I know."
A Stapper shoved his way past Brent. "Here now!" he growled. "What bees going on here?"
Bokor hesitated. "Nothing, sir. I was only—"
"Was, huh?"
"Pardon, sir. Beed. I be Slanduch, you see, and—"
One of the men in the crowd interrupted. "He beed telling us what all State needs to know—plans of State of South America to invade and destroy us."
"Hm-m-m!" the Stapper ejaculated. "You be right, man. That sounds like something to know. Go on, you."
Bokor resumed his rumor mongering, and the Stapper lent it official endorsement by his listening silence. Brent moved to get a glimpse of the Stapper's face. His guess was right. It was another Bokor.
This significant byplay had delayed them enough so that Brent's three travelers had reached the apartment before them. When they arrived, Stephen was deep in a philosophical discussion with the Venusian of the tragic nobility of human nature, while Kruj and Mimi were experimenting with bond. Their respective civilizations could not have been markedly alcoholic; Kruj had reached the stage of sweeping and impassioned gestures, while Mimi beamed at him and giggled occasionally.
All three had discarded the standardized robes of the Stasis and resumed, in this friendly privacy, the clothes in which they had arrived—Kruj a curiously simplified and perverted version of the ruffled court costume of the Elizabethan era he had hoped to reach, Mimi the startling armor of an unfamiliar metal which was her uniform as Amazon warrior, and Nikobat a bronze-colored loincloth against which his green skin assumed an odd beauty.

Brent introduced Martha's guests to their hostess and went on, "Now for a staff meeting of G.H.Q. We've got to lay our plans carefully, because we're up against some stiff opposition. There's one other traveler who—"

"One moment," said Martha's voice. "Shouldn't you introduce me, too?"

"I beg your pardon, madam. I just finished that task of courtesy. And now—"

"I be sorry," her voice went on. "You still do not understand. You introduced Martha, yes—but not me."

Stephen turned to the travelers. "I must apologize for my sister. She haves goed through queer experiences of late. She traveled with our friend John and meeted herself in her earlier life. I fear that shock has temporarily—and temporally—unbalanced her."

"Can none of you understand so simple thing?" the woman's voice pleaded. "I be simply using Martha's voice as instrument of communication. I can just as easily—"

"'Steeth!" Kruj exclaimed. "'Tis eke as easy and mayhap more pleasant to borrow this traveler's voice for mine explications."

"Or," Mimi added, "I cou taw li thih, but I do' like ih vey muh."

Stephen's eyes popped. "You mean that you be traveler without body?"

"Got it in one," Brent heard his own voice saying. "I can wander about any way I damned please. I picked the woman first because her mind was easy to occupy, and I think I'll go on using her. Brent here's a little hard to keep under control."

Stephen nodded. "Then all good advice Martha haves beed giving us—"

"Bees mine, of course." The bodiless traveler was back in Martha now.

Brent gasped. "And now I see how you wangled the release of the travelers. You got us in by usurping the mind and speech of each of the minor officials we tackled, and then ousted the Head of State and Chief of Stappers to make them give their consent."

Martha nodded. "Exactly."

"This is going to be damned useful. And where do you come from, sir? Or is it madam?"

"I come from future so far distant that even our Venusian friend here cannot conceive of it. And distinction between sir and madam bees then meaningless."

The dapper Kruj glanced at the hulking Amazon beside him. "'Twere a pity," he murmured.

"And your intentions here, to go on with the State linguist's questionnaire?"

"My intentions? Listen, all of you. We cannot shape ends. Great patterns be shaped outside of us and beyond us. I beed historian in my time. I know patterns of mankind even down to minute details. And I know that Stephen here bees to lead people of this Age of Smugness out of their stupidity and back to humanity."

Stephen coughed embarrassedly. "I have no wish to lead. But for such cause man must do what he may."

"That bees ultimate end of this section of pattern. That bees fixed. All that we travelers can do bees to aid him as wisely as we can and to make the details of the pattern as pleasing as may be. And that we will do."

Stephen must have been so absorbed in this speech that his hearing was dulled. The door opened without warning, and Bokor entered.

"'Swounds!" Kruj cried out. "A Stapper!"

Stephen smiled. "Why fear Stappers? You be legally liberated."

"Stapper, hell!" Brent snorted. "Well, Bokor? You still want to declare yourself in with your racket?"

Bokor's deep eyes swept the room. He smiled faintly. "I merely wished to show you something, Brent. So that you know what you be up against. I have finded two young scientists dissatisfied with scholastic routine of research for Cosmos. Now they work under me and they have maked for me—this." He held a bare rod in his hand.

"So it's a rod. So what next?"

"But it bees different rod, Brent. It does not paralyze. It destroys." The point of the rod wavered and covered in turn each individual in the room. "I want you to see what I can accomplish."

"You suvvabih!" Mimi yelled and started to rise.

"State thanks you, madam, for making up my mind. I will demonstrate on you. Watch this, Brent, and realize what chance you have against me." He pointed the rod firmly at Mimi.

"Do something!" Martha screamed.

It all happened at once, but Brent seemed to see it in slow motion even as he moved. Mimi lunged forward furiously and recklessly. Kruj dived for her feet and brought her to the floor out of the line of fire. At the same time Brent threw himself forward just as Bokor moved, so that the rod now pointed directly at Brent. He couldn't arrest his momentum. He was headed straight at Bokor's new instrument of death. And then the rod moved to Bokor's own head.

There was no noise, no flash. But Bokor's body was lying on the floor, and the head was nowhere.

"That beed hard," said Martha's voice. "I haved to stay in his mind long enough to actuate rod, but get out before death. Matter of fractions of seconds."

"Nice work, sir-madam," Brent grunted. He looked down at the corpse. "But that was only one of him."

Brent quoted in his journal: *Love, but a day, and the world has changed! A week, to be more exact, but the change is nonetheless sudden and impressive.*

Our nameless visitant from the future—they seem to need titles as little as sexes in that time— whom I have for convenience labeled Sirdam, has organized our plans about the central idea of interfering as little as possible—forcing the inhabitants of the Stasis to work out their own salvation. The travelers do not appear openly in this great change. We work through Stephen's associates.

There are some 40 of us (I guess I count as a traveler; I'm not too sure what the hell my status is by now), which means each of us can take on five or ten of Stephen's boys (and girls), picking the ones whose interests lie closest to his own special fields. That means a working force of Undergrounders running somewhere above 200 and under 500 . . . fluctuating constantly as people come under or escape from Stapper observation, as new recruits come in, or (as will damnably happen despite every precaution) as one of our solid old-timers gets his mind changed and decides Stasis bees perfect after all.

The best single example to show the results we obtain is the episode of Professor Harrington, whose special department of so-called learning is the preservation of the Nakamura Law of Spatial Acceleration, which had so conclusively proved to the founders of the Stasis the impossibility of interplanetary travel.

This fell obviously within Nikobat's field. A young scientist affiliated with the Underground—a nephew, I have since learned, of Alex's—expounded the Nakamura doctrine as he had learned and re-proved it. It took the Venusian less than five minutes to put his finger on the basic flaw in the statement—the absolute omission, in all calculations, of any consideration of galactic drift. Once this correction was applied to the Nakamura formulas, they stood revealed as the pure nonsense which, indeed, Nikobat's very presence proved them.

It was not Nikobat but the young man who placed this evidence before Professor Harrington. The scene must have been classic. "I saw," the young man later told us—they are all trying desperately to unlearn Farthing-ized English—"his mouth fall open and gap spread across his face as wide as gap he suddenly finded in universe."

For the professor was not stupid. He was simply so conditioned from childhood to the acceptance of the Stasis of Cosmos that he had never questioned it. Besides, he had doubtless had friends whose minds were changed when they speculated too far.

Harrinton's eyes lit up after the first shock. He grabbed pencil and paper and furiously checked through the revised equations again and again. He then called in a half dozen of his best students and set them to what was apparently a routine exercise—interpolating variations for galactic drift in the Nakamura formulas.

They ended as astonished as their instructor. The first one done stared incredulously at his results and gasped, "Nakamura beed wrong!"

That was typical. The sheep are ready to be roused, each in his individual way. Kruj has been training men to associate with the writers of the Stasis. The man's knowledge of literature of all periods, and especially of his beloved Elizabethan Age, is phenomenal and his memory something superhuman. And four writers out of five who hear his disciples discourse on the joys of creative language and quote from the Elizabethan dramatists and the King James Bible will never be content again to write Stasis propaganda for the sollies or the identically bound books of the State libraries.

I have myself been contributing a fair amount to the seduction of the world by teaching cooks. I was never in my own time acknowledged as better than a fair-to-middling non-professional, but here I might be Escoffier or Brillat-Savarin. We steal plants and animals from the scientific laboratories, and in our hands they become vegetables and meat; and many a man in the street, who doesn't give a damn if his science is false and his arts synthetic, has suddenly realized that he owes the State a grudge for feeding him on concentrates.

The focus of everything is Stephen. It's hard to analyze why. Each of us travelers has found among the Undergrounders someone far more able in his own special field, yet all of us, travelers and Undergrounders alike, unquestioningly acknowledge Stephen as our leader. It may be the sheer quiet kindliness and goodness of his nature. It may be that he and Alex, in their organization of this undercover group of instinctive rebels, were the first openly to admit that the Stasis was inhuman and to do something about it. But from whatever cause, we all come to depend more and more on the calm reliability of Stephen.

Nikobat says—

Brent broke off as Kruj Krujil Krujilar staggered into the room. The little man was no longer dapper. His robes were tattered, and their iridescence was overlaid with the solid red of blood. He panted his first words in his own tongue, then recovered himself. "We must act apace, John. Where is Stephen?"

"At Underground quarters. But what's happened?"

"I was nearing the building where they do house us travelers when I beheld hundreds of people coming along the street. Some wore our robes, some wore Stappers'. And they all—" He shuddered. "They all had the same face—a brown hairless face with black eyes."

Brent was on his feet. "Bokor!" The man had multiplied himself into a regiment. One man who was hundreds—why not thousands? millions?—could indeed be a conqueror. "What happened?"

"They entered the building. I knew that I could do nothing there, and came to find you and Stephen and the bodiless one. But as I came along the street, lo! on every corner there was yet another of that face, and always urging the people to maintain the Stasis and destroy the travelers. I was recognized. By good hap those who set upon me had no rods, so I escaped with my life."

Brent thought quickly. "Martha is with Stephen, so Sirdam is probably there, too. Go to him at once and warn him. I'm going to the travelers' building and see what's happened. Meet you at the headquarters as soon as I can."

Kruj hesitated. "Mimi—"

"I'll bring her with me if I can. Get going."

The streets were mad. Wild throngs jammed the moving roadways. Somewhere in the distance mountainous flames leaped up and their furious glitter gleamed from the eyes of the mob. These were the ordinary citizens of Stasis, no longer cattle, or rather cattle stampeded.

A voice blared seemingly out of the heavens. Brent recognized the public address system used for vital State messages. "Revolt of travelers haves spreaded to amphitheater of Cosmos. Flames lighted by travelers now attack sacred spot. People of Cosmos: Destroy travelers!"

There was nothing to mark Brent superficially as a traveler. He pushed along with the mob, shouting as rabidly as any other. He could make no headway. He was borne along on these foaming human waves.

Then in front of him he saw three Bokors pushing against the mob. If they spied him— His hands groped along the wall. Just as a Bokor looked his way, he found what he was seeking—one of the spying niches of the Stappers. He slipped into safety, then peered out cautiously.

From the next door he saw a man emerge whom he knew by sight—a leading dramatist of the sollies, who had promised to be an eventual convert of Kruj's disciples. Three citizens of the mob halted him as he stepped forth.

"What bees your name?"

"Where be you going?"

The solly writer hesitated. "I be going to amphitheater, Speaker have sayed—"

"When do you come from?"

"Why, from now."

"What bees your name?"

"John—"

"Ha!" the first citizen yelled. "Stappers have telled us to find this John. Tear him to pieces; he bees traveler."

"No, truly. I be no traveler; I be writer of sollies."

One of the citizens chortled cruelly. "Tear him for his bad sollies!"

There was one long scream—

Fire breeds fire, literally as well as metaphorically. The dwelling of the travelers was ablaze when Brent reached it. A joyous mob cheered and gloated before it. Brent started to push his way through, but a hand touched his arm and a familiar voice whispered, "Achtung! Ou vkhodit."

He interpreted the warning and let the Venusian draw him aside. Nikobat rapidly explained.

"The Stappers came and subdued the whole crowd with paralyzing rods. They took them away—God knows what they'll do with them. There's no one in there now; the fire's just a gesture."

"But you— How did you—"

"My nerve centers don't react the same. I lay doggo and got away. Mimi escaped, too; her armor has deflecting power. I think she's gone to warn the Underground."

"Then come on."

"Don't stay too close to me," Nikobat warned. "They'll recognize me as a traveler; stay out of range of rods aimed at me. And here. I took these from a Stapper I strangled. This one is a paralyzing rod; the other's an annihilator."

The next half-hour was a nightmare—a montage of flames and blood and sweating bodies of hate. The Stasis of Stupidity was becoming a Stasis of Cruelty. Twice groups of citizens stopped Brent. They were unarmed; Bokor wisely kept weapons to himself, knowing that the fangs and claws of an enraged mob are enough. The first group Brent left paralyzed. The second time he confused his weapons. He had not meant to kill.

He did not confuse his weapons when he bagged a brace of Bokors. But what did the destruction of two matter? He fought his way on, finally catching up with Nikobat at their goal. As they met, the voice boomed once more from the air. "Important! New Chief of Stappers announces that offices of Chief of Stappers and Head of State be henceforth maked one. Under new control, travelers will be wiped out and Stasis preserved. Then on to South America for glory of Cosmos!"

Brent shuddered. "And we started out so beautifully on our renaissance!"

Nikobat shook his head. "But the bodiless traveler said that Stephen was to destroy the Stasis. This multiple villain cannot change what has happened."

"Can't he? We're taking no chances."

The headquarters of the Underground was inappositely in a loft. The situation helped. The trap entrance was unnoticeable from below and had gone unheeded by the mobs. Brent delivered the proper raps, and the trap slid open and dropped a ladder. Quickly they mounted.

The loft was a sick bay. A half-dozen wounded members of Stephen's group lay groaning on the floor. With them was Kruj. Somewhere the little man had evaded the direct line of an annihilator, but lost his hand. Blood was seeping out of his bandages, and Mimi, surprisingly feminine and un-Amazonic, held his unconscious head in her lap.

"You don't seem to need warning," Brent observed.

Stephen shook his head. "We be trapped here. Here we be safe for at littlest small while. If we go out—"

Brent handed him his rods. "You're the man we've got to save, Stephen. You know what Sirdam's said—it all depends on you. Use these to protect yourself, and we'll make a dash for it. If we can lose ourselves in the mob as ordinary citizens, there's a chance of getting away with it. Or"—he turned to Martha-Sirdam—"have you any ideas?"

"Yes. But only as last resort."

Nikobat was peering out the window. "It's the last resort now," he said. "There's a good fifty of those identical Stappers outside, and they're headed here. They act as though they know what this is."

Brent was looking at Stephen, and he saw a strange thing. Stephen's face was expressionless, but somewhere behind his eyes Brent seemed to sense a struggle. Stephen's body trembled with an effort of will, and then his eyes were clear again. "No," he said distinctly. "You do not need to control me. I understand. You be right. I will do as you say." And he lifted the annihilator rod.

Brent started forward, but his muscles did not respond to his commands. Force his will though he might, he stood still. It was the bodiless traveler who held him motionless to watch Stephen place the rod to his temple.

"This bees goodest thing that I can do for mans," said Stephen simply. Then his headless corpse thumped on the floor.

Brent was released. He dashed forward, but vainly. There was nothing men could do for Stephen now. Brent let out a choking gasp of pain and sorrow.

Then the astonished cries of the Undergrounders recalled him from his friend's body. He looked about him. Where was Nikobat? Where were Kruj and Mimi?

A small inkling of the truth began to reach him. He hurried to the window and looked out.

There were no Bokors before the house. Only a few citizens staring dazedly at a wide space of emptiness.

At that moment the loud-speaker sounded. "Announcement," a shocked voice trembled. "Chief of Stappers has just disappeared." And in a moment it added, "Guards report all travelers have vanished."

The citizens before the house were rubbing their eyes like men coming out of a nightmare.

"But don't you see, madam— No? Well, let me try again." Brent was not finding it easy to explain her brother's heroic death to an untenanted Martha. "Remember what your inhabitant told us? The Stasis was overthrown by Stephen."

"But Stephen bees dead."

"Exactly. So listen: All these travelers came from a future wherein Stephen had overthrown the Stasis so that when Stephen destroyed himself, as Sirdam realized, he likewise destroyed that future. A world in which Stephen died unsuccessful is a world that cannot be entered by anyone from the other future. Their worlds vanished and they with them. It was the only way of abolishing the menace of the incredibly multiplied Bokor."

"Stephen bees dead. He cans not overthrow Stasis now."

"My dear madam— Hell, skip it. But the Stasis is damned nonetheless in this new world created by Stephen's death. I've been doing a little galping on my own. The people are convinced now that the many exemplars of Bokor were some kind of evil invader. They rebound easy, the hordes; they dread the memory of those men and they dread also the ideas of cruelty and conquest to which the Bokors had so nearly converted them.

"But one thing they can't rebound from is the doubts and the new awarenesses that we planted in their minds. And there's what's left of your movement to go on with. No, the Stasis is damned, even if they are going to erect yet another Barrier."

"Oh," Martha shuddered. "You willn't let them."

Brent grinned. "Madam, there's damned little letting I can do. They're going to, and that's that. Because, you see, all the travelers vanished."

"But why—"

Brent shrugged and gave up. "Join me in some bond?" It was clear enough. The point of time which the second Barrier blocked existed both in the past of the worlds of Nikobat and Sirdam, and in the past of this future they were now entering. But if this future road stretched clear ahead, then travelers—a different set from a different future, but travelers nonetheless—would have appeared at the roadblock. The vanishing Bokors and Nikobat and the rest would have been replaced by another set of stranded travelers.

But no one, in this alternate unknown to Sirdam in which Stephen died a failure, had come down the road of the future. There was a roadblock ahead. The Stasis would erect another Barrier . . . and God grant that some scientific successor to Alex would create again the means of disrupting it. And the travelers from this coming future—would they be Sirdams to counsel and guide man, or Bokors to corrupt and debase him?

Brent lifted his glass of bond. "To the moment after the next Barrier!" he said.

Pelagic Spark

A.D. 1942:

Lieutenant L. Sprague de Camp, U.S.N.R., thumped the table and chuckled. "That will settle the Nostradamians!"

His pretty blond wife made remarks about waking babies and then asked what on earth he meant.

"The prophecy fakers," he said. "McCann and Robb and Boucher and the others who are all agog and atwitter over Michel de Notredame and his supposed forecasts of our world troubles. Prophecy in Mike's manner is too damned easy. If you're obscure and symbolic and cryptic enough, whatever happens is bound to fit in some place with your prophecy. Take the most famous of all Nostradamic quatrains, that one about Henri II—"

His wife said, yes, she had heard several times already about how that could be made to fit the de Camp family just as well as the French royal house, and what was the new idea?

"Every man his own Nostradamus, that's my motto," he went on. "I am, personally, every bit as much a prophet as Mike ever was. And I'm going to prove it. I've just thought of the perfect tag for my debunking article."

His wife looked expectant.

"I'm going to close with an original de Camp prophecy, which will make just as much sense as any of Mike's, with a damned sight better meter and grammar. Listen:

"Pelagic young spark of the East
Shall plot to subvert the Blue Beast,
    But he'll dangle on high
    When the Ram's in the sky,
And the Cat shall throw dice at the feast.

"You like?"

His wife said it was a limerick, of all things, and what did it mean?

"Why not a limerick? That's a great verse form of American folk rhyme—a natural for an American prophecy, And as to what it means, how do I know? Did Mike know what he meant when he wrote 'Near to Rion next to white wool, Aries, Taurus, Cancer, Leo, the Virgin'?

"But this I swear to: If this article sells and de Camp's Prophetic Limerick is there in print for future McCanns to study, by 2342 it will have been fulfilled as surely as any quatrain Mike ever wrote, or I lose all trust in the perverted ingenuity of the human race."

A.D. 1943:

By the time the magazine reached Sergeant Harold Marks, there was not much left in it to interest him. The Varga girls and the Hurrell photographs had gone to decorate the walls of long-abandoned outposts, and most of the cartoons had vanished, too. Little remained but text and ads, and Sergeant Marks was not profoundly concerned with what the well-dressed man in America was wearing last Christmas.

Until he had almost finished looking through it, he would have been more than willing to swap the magazine for a cigarette or even for a drag on one, but at the end he hit the de Camp article.

The Sergeant's sister Madeleine was psychic. At least, that was her persistent claim, and up until she joined the WAACs nobody had been able to persuade her otherwise. Sergeant Marks had no later news from his sister than the discomforting word that she had received her commission and now outranked him, but he was willing to bet that she still spent as much time as she could spare telling her unfortunate non-coms about the wonders of Nostradamus.

It was good to see somebody tear into the prophecy racket and rip it apart. This de Camp seemed a right guy, and his lucid attack did Sergeant Marks' heart good.

Especially the prophetic limerick. The sergeant was something of an authority on limericks. He had yet to find a man in the service whose collection topped his. But the pelagic young spark from the East tickled him even more than the unlikely offspring of the old man of Bombay or the peculiar practices of the clergy of Birmingham.

Sergeant Marks carefully tore the limerick out of the magazine and slipped it in his pocket. He'd copy it out in a V-letter to Madeleine when they managed to get in touch again.

He thumbed back over the magazine, hoping that he might have overlooked some piece of cheesecake that had escaped previous vandals. Then, without warning, all hell broke loose from the jungle and Sergeant Marks forgot cheesecake and prophecy alike.

Civilian Harold Marks used to scoff at stories of heroes who captured machine-gun nests single-handed. That was before he joined the Marines and learned that practical heroism is not a mythical matter.

He still didn't know how it was done. He knew only, and that with a half-aware negligence, that he had done it. He was in the jungle, master of a green-painted machine gun, and he was alone save for a pile of unmoving things with green uniforms and yellow faces.

There were more of them coming. A green gun looks funny in your hands, but it works fine.

There were no more coming.

Toting the green killer, Sergeant Marks returned to the ambushed outpost. His throat choked when he recognized Corporal Witchett by his hairy palms. There was no face to recognize him by.

There had been few enough men here. Now there seemed to be only one. The ambush had been destroyed, but at a cost that—

Sergeant Marks hurried to where he heard the groan. He knelt down by the lieutenant and tried to catch his faint words.

"Reinforcements . . . tomorrow . . . try . . . hold on . . . up to you, Marks."

"I will, sir," the sergeant grinned, "unless they outnumber me. They might send *two* detachments."

The lieutenant smiled dimly. "Saw you . . . nest . . . fine work, Marks . . . see you get medal for—"

"Swell custom, posthumous medals," said Sergeant Marks.

A look of concern came into the officer's too sharply highlighted eyes. "Sergeant . . . you're wounded—"

Marks looked down at his blood-blackened shirt and his eyes opened in amazement. Then the jungle began to jive to a solid boogie and his eyes closed for a long time.

When they opened again, he saw a hospital ward and muttered warm prayerful oaths of relief. So the reinforcements had showed up before another Jap detachment. He hoped the lieutenant had held out. And what the hell had happened to Boszkowicz and Corvetti and—

Funny, having Chinese nurses. Nightingales from the Celestial Kingdom. All the other patients Chinese, too. Funny. And yet they didn't look quite—

When the doctor came, there was no doubt of the situation. The teeth and the mustache and the glasses, the standard cartoon set-up. But not comical. And certainly not Chinese.

Sergeant Marks heard a strange croaking that must have been his own voice demanding to know what went on and since when did American Marines rate a pampered convalescence in a Jap hospital? He felt almost ashamed of himself. There seemed to be something like an involuntary Quislingism in enjoying these Nipponese benefits instead of sprawling dead in the jungle.

The doctor made a grin and noises and went away. He came back ushering in two men in uniform. The older one was a fierce little man with a chestful of medals. The other was young and jaunty and said. "Hi! What's clean, Marine?"

Sergeant Marks said, "What am I doing here? Don't tell me you boys are starting a home for disabled veterans?"

"Just for you, sergeant. You're teacher's pet."

"Tell teacher I'll send him a nice shiny pineapple first chance I get."

The little man with the medals asked a question, and the youth answered.

Marks grinned. "I'll bet tea won't give you an A on that translation. You the only one here speaks English?"

"English hell," said the interpreter. "I talk American."

"O.K., you hind end of a Trojan horse. Why am I here? What's the picture? Shoot the photo to me, Moto."

The officer went off again, and not in a pleasant mood.

"We'll have cross-fire gags some other time, sergeant." The interpreter said. "Right now the colonel wants to know what this is." He handed over a blood-stained piece of paper.

Sergeant Marks' brain did nip-ups. He got the picture now, all in a flash. Somebody had found this clipping on his unconscious body, failed to interpret it, and decided it was some momentous secret inscription. He'd been nursed back to consciousness especially so that he could interpret it. And if he told the truth—

He could see in advance the dumb disbelief of his enemies. He could foresee the cool ingenuity with which they would try to wrest further statements from him. He could—

He opened his mouth and heard inspired words coming out in the voice which he was beginning to accept as his. "Oh, that? Well, I'll tell you. I'm very grateful for what you've done for me, and in return— That's our secret prophecy."

"Nuts," said the interpreter.

"I'm serious," said Sergeant Marks, and managed to look and sound so. "You didn't know that Roosevelt had his private astrologer, did you? Just like Hirohito and Hitler. We've kept it pretty secret. But this is the masterpiece of Astro the Great. We don't know what it means, but all have to carry it so we can take advantage of it if it begins to come true. We're supposed to swallow it if dying or captured; I'm afraid I slipped up there."

The interpreter said, "Do you expect us to feed the colonel a line of tripe like that?"

"But it's true. I'm just trying to save myself. I—"

The fierce little colonel burst into another tirade. The interpreter answered protestingly. The colonel insisted.

Then the nurse who had been making the next bed turned around and addressed a long speech to the colonel. Slowly his fierceness faded into a sort of mystical exaltation. He replied excitedly to the nurse, and added one short sentence to the interpreter.

As the three men left the room, the interpreter spat one epithet at Marks.

"Why, Moto!" the sergeant grinned. "Where *did* you learn that word?"

"I know rittre Engrish," the nurse explained proudly. "When interpreter won't talk, I say to kerner your story. Kerner very much preased. He send prophecy now to emperor. Emperor's star-men, they study it."

"Thanks, baby. Nice work. And what happens to my pal Peter Lorre for refusing to translate?"

"Him? Oh, they shoot him same time as you."

One less Jap, one less Marine—"Well"—Sergeant Marks forced a grin—"we're holding our own."

A.D. 1945:

The Imperial courier asked, "Has astrologer-san any prophetic discoveries that I may report today to the Son of Heaven?"

The court astrologer said, "Indeed I have, and though the word of the stars seems black to us, yet will the rays of the Rising Sun dispel that blackness. Adolf

Hitler will die today. The Yankees and the British will conclude a separate peace
with Germany and will concentrate their attacks upon the Greater East Asia Prosperity Sphere."

The courier smiled. "So astrologer-san also possesses a short-wave radio?
Adolf Hitler has died today. The rest of your prophecy is, of course, a clever
deduction from the rise of the White American party and a knowledge of the
shrewdness of the German military aristocracy. But I shall report it as prophecy
to the Son of Heaven. And has astrologer-san yet deciphered the American prophecy?"

"It is difficult. The court will understand that the complexities of the perverse
American methods of magical calculation—"

"The Son of Heaven will understand that he needs a new astrologer, and that
old astrologers know too much to remain alive." He smiled again.

The court astrologer used the same ritual dagger as his thirteen predecessors
since Sergeant Marks' death.

A.D. 1951:

Adolf Hitler had reason to feel pleased with himself. His carefully faked death
had deluded the United Nations into a sense of false security and enabled Germany to conclude an armistice and obtain a much-needed breathing spell. When
her enemies were engaged in the final struggle in the East, it had been easy to
overthrow the necessarily small army of occupation and hasten to the rescue of
Japan.

Destroying Japan in the inevitable German-Japanese war that followed their
joint victory had not been so easy. It had not been possible to fool the Japanese
with organizations like the White American party or the British Empire League.

But it had been accomplished, and now Adolf Hitler, secure at last and already beginning to find security uncomfortable, was free to devote himself to
such pleasing minor problems as the exquisitely painted tablet before him.

"I found it myself, mein Führer," explained Reinhardt Heydrich, now resur-
rected from that earlier fake death which had served as a test of Anglo-Saxon
credulity. "It was in a hidden inner shrine in an obscure temple in Tokyo. No one
has seen it save my late interpreter. I cannot understand how what is obviously a
prophecy in a Japanese shrine comes to be written in English; there is doubtless
some symbolic significance. The Japanese characters at the top read 'American
prophecy.' The rough translation runs—"

He paraphrased the limerick.

Adolf Hitler listened, nodding slowly, and a mystical film spread over his
eyes. It was as though he were listening to music.

When he spoke at last, he said: "We hold the world too securely for any more
great events to happen in our days. We shall not see the fulfillment of this prophecy. But treasure it carefully. It shall be invaluable to one of my successors, even as
Nostradamus was to me. For did he not write: 'The Holy Empire will come to
Germany,' and again 'Near the Rhine of the Nordic Alps a Great One will be
born'?"

* * *

157 N.H. (A.D. 2045):

Captain Felix Schweinspitzen mopped tropical sweat from his Nordic brow and moaned, "Hang it, Anton, I was born at the wrong time."

Anton Metzger looked up from the meaningless series of letters which he had been jotting down. "We're all born into a pattern, Felix. We can't make the design ourselves."

"Not now, no. That's just what I mean. There have been times when we could. Look at Napoleon or the first Hitler. They made their own designs. And I keep feeling that in the right world I could, too. I can lead men. That's demonstrated fact. Look what I've done with the natives here in Java."

"Too much maybe. I wouldn't be surprised if the Führer was a little jealous on his inspection visit."

"I can lead men. I could lead the men of the world—I feel it, I know it. But what chance have I? While he rules by virtue of the organization and the rules of succession and—"

"Would you want his job in view of all we've been hearing of the Tyrannicides?"

Captain Schweinspitzen laughed. "We destroyed Canada and America almost a century ago. What have we to fear from a little handful of desperate men?"

"Little handfuls of desperate men did great things in the death struggles of those nations. I remember my grandfather telling stories of demons called Commandos and Rangers."

"The Tyrannicides are futile. Tyrant killers, indeed, when all they've accomplished so far is the death of a couple of subordinates no more important than you, Anton. Now if someone were to attempt the life of Hitler XVI himself— What are you working on there?"

Metzger smiled. "The American prophecy."

"Wotan! Why waste your time with foolish—"

"The job of being your interpreter in Dutch and Javanese is hardly an all-absorbing one, Felix. I have to have some interest. And I got a very curious lead today. I heard some natives talking about the coming inspection visit. And you know what they call the Führer?"

"No."

"They've been seeing photochromes of him in those powder-blue uniforms he's so devoted to. And they call him the Blue Beast."

Captain Schweinspitzen tore off a string of oaths. "The subversive traitors! They can't talk that way about him. I'll have them— Give me their names."

"I'm afraid I don't remember who they were. And is this precisely a consistent attitude when you were just speaking of his assassination?"

"That's different. I'm as Aryan as he is. But these natives— Oh, well. How does that traitorous nickname help you?"

"The Blue Beast is one of the personages in the prophecy. They've been speculating for a hundred years on his identity. Now there's a clue, and if I can figure out the rest—"

"How does the whole thing go?" the captain asked idly.

Metzger recited it:

"Pelagic young spark of the East
Shall plot to subvert the Blue Beast,
    But he'll dangle on high
    When the Ram's in the sky,
And the Cat shall throw dice at the feast!"

The captain nodded. "The English I picked up when I was Gauleiter in Des Moines seems to be good enough to handle that. Only what does *pelagic* mean?"

"That's the word that bothers me. It means 'oceanic.' Now 'oceanic young spark' doesn't make any obvious sense —if anything, it's a contradiction in terms. But it makes just as good meter as 'pelagic,' so why was the exceedingly uncommon word used instead of the obvious one? That's why I'm hunting for an anagram in it. I've been rearranging letters and I can't get anything better than—" His voice stopped dead. He stared at the captain, at his paper, and back at the captain.

"Well!" Captain Schweinspitzen barked. "What is it?"

"The best I can get," Metzger repeated, "is 'pig lace.' "

"And 'pig lace,' captain, means 'Schweinspitzen.' "

The officer stared. The interpreter went on hastily, as details clicked into formation: "You are of the East, have been here in Java for years. You were a telecast operator once, weren't you? Well, 'spark'—or was it 'sparks'?—meant wireless operator in twentieth-century American dialect. "Pelagic young spark of the East—' "

" '—shall plot to subvert the Blue Beast'," the captain continued the quotation. "In other words, Schweinspitzen, the ex-telecaster of Java, shall plot to subvert Hitler XVI." He smiled craftily to himself. "Well, Anton, we are all part of a design, aren't we? We can't very well refuse to fulfill the prophecy, can we?"

Lyman Harding wrung out his dripping garments. You didn't need clothes anyway, here in the damp heat of the jungle. But they'd need these clothes later; they were of bullet-deflecting soteron, and stealing that textile from the closely guarded plastic factory had been the most perilous step in the plot—so far.

"The natives are with us," Girdy reported to him. "They hate him and his rule over them. Call him the Blue Beast."

"If only we had planes—" Harding sighed. "Think how directly we could act instead of this swimming in from a mile offshore and lurking in jungles and—"

"We'll have planes soon enough," Girdy said confidently.

"If it all comes off according to schedule. If our other men all over the world manage to dispose of his followers according to the rule of succession. Then there'll be complete chaos in the Party, and those who still love freedom can strike."

"But ours is the biggest job." Girdy's wide ugly face was alight with pride. "When we knock off the Hitler himself— Only have you figured yet how we can crash this inspection reception?"

"I've only got a rough plan—" Lyman Harding began.

* * *

Anton Metzger did not like the changes that were evident in Captain Schweinspitzen after that momentous discussion of the American prophecy.

The captain had previously seemed unusually intelligent and unusually human for the post which he held. Oh, he was given to ranting about his stifled abilities as a leader of men, but he was a friend and companion. He understood the arts, even in their neglected or forbidden aspects, and he understood people, even tolerating Metzger when he talked in a tone that did not jibe perfectly with the tenets of the Aryan World State.

For Metzger felt his Austrian blood more keenly than his Prussian. He was a useful servant of Hitler XVI chiefly because he had been reared in the AWS and never known directly any other concepts of life. But he knew himself for a misfit and groped faintly toward something else.

He had sometimes in the past sensed a similar groping in Captain Schweinspitzen, but no more. Not since his captain had become convinced of his identity with the pelagic young spark. Now, when he saw his dream of leadership approaching fulfillment, humanity dropped away from him like an outworn robe, and the naked body beneath it was strong and beautiful and cruel and masterful.

Metzger learned little of his plot to subvert the Blue Beast. The captain retained enough of his understanding of people to know that Metzger might want the destruction of Hitler XVI, but certainly not the instating of Felix Schweinspitzen as a new and greater Hitler.

Metzger gathered only the fringes of the plot, only enough to know that the crucial moment would come at the reception and State banquet which would be the ritual high point of the inspection tour.

And then he inadvertently contributed the key element to the pelagic plot. This came about on the day that he entered the office just in time to see the captain put a bullet coolly through the forehead of a man in the blue uniform of a personal messenger of the Führer.

Schweinspitzen showed no embarrassment at the presence of a witness. He said coldly, "He brought me bad news. This is how the great leaders of old have always rewarded such messengers."

Metzger realized now how fully the madness of leadership had come to possess the man who had once been almost his friend. Quietly he said, "What news, Felix?"

"You said that the Blue Beast might be jealous of my success here. You're a prophet yourself, Anton. He is. He has forbidden my presence at the banquet."

Metzger felt something like relief. "It's better this way, Felix. Such an attempt as you've been plotting is too dangerous. And if you must be guided by the American prophecy, remember its middle couplet:

"But he'll dangle on high
When the Ram's in the sky.

"The State hasn't executed a man by hanging for a hundred years, but the Hitler might very well reinstate the archaic punishment for a great traitor."

"Am I afraid of your prophecy? Don't be a fool." But he looked perplexed and reflective for a moment. Then he snapped his fingers. "What are the names of those two paratransport planes we use for the outlying islands?"

"The *Aries* and the *Leo*."

Captain Schweinspitzen laughed. "Very well, my dear Anton. Be sure to attend the feast. You'll see me dangling on high all right. And what is the last line of your prophecy?'

" 'And the Cat shall throw dice at the feast.' "

"Throw dice? Mete out justice by lot, it might mean. That will do. And the Cat— I picked up bits of American folklore in Des Moines, Anton. See if that clue enables you to decipher your prophecy."

Felix Schweinspitzen had left the office before Anton Metzger placed the apposite bit of American folklore. Then at last he recalled the comic black figure in twentieth-century cartoons. Felix the Cat—

Metzger saw little more of the captain during the remaining few days before the banquet. Five natives were executed for the murder of the Führer's messenger and possible leaderly wrath was averted.

But Captain Schweinspitzen not only accepted the banishment from the banquet, he refused even to appear at the reception and tour, and Metzger found himself as official guide and escort to the sixteenth Hitler.

"It is dull here," the Führer protested. "Buildings of common steel and stone— no glass, no plastic. The telephone used almost exclusively without a visoscreen. Not a stereoscopic theater on the island. Old-model automobiles and no moving walks . . . why, one might as well be back in the twentieth century."

"The Führer knows," Metzger explained, "why this is so. This island exists solely so that a slave population may produce raw materials for the State. There is no need for any of the refinements of civilization here; we lead the crude life of pioneers."

"It is dull," Hitler XVI repeated with a yawn.

He was littler and plumper than his pictures indicated. There was the infinite refinement of boredom on the round bland face. Nothing of the captain's dream of leadership here, nothing of whatever the magnetic power was which brought about the success of the man from whom the Aryan World State's Führers took their title of Hitler.

The title descended now in fixed ranks of party precedence, and skill in party politics is not the sole prerequisite of the leader. Metzger thought of the decadence of the later Roman emperors. There was sense in Schweinspitzen's notion of replacing this worn-out quasi-leader with the vigor of the real thing.

But was the leader-principle in itself humanly justifiable? Metzger was often glad that among the many refinements of civilization missing on the island were psychometrists; he hated to think what might happen if one of the skilled ones at home were to psych him and discover these hidden doubts.

The banquet was held out-of-doors in the warmth of a tropic night, and even outdoors it was evident that Hitler XVI found the vanity of his powder-blue uniform uncomfortably warm.

The first course, as was the traditional ritual at all formal State banquets, was an unpalatable and nameless ersatz, to remind men of what their forebears had suffered in order to establish the Aryan World State. Then followed a magnificent *rijstafel,* that noble fusion of unnumbered courses which was the sole survival of the one-time Dutch culture of the island.

With the *rijstafel* Hitler XVI for the first time displayed an enthusiastic interest in his colonial outpost. He tucked it away prodigiously, with pious ejaculations of praise, while Anton Metzger hardly bothered to conceal his smile of quiet contempt.

Seeing and guiding the Führer had at last fully brought home to Metzger the loss of human dignity brought about by the Aryan World State. That man should submit to the totalitarian rule of this stupid and decadent dynasty was unthinkable—and equally unthinkable that man should tolerate the institution of just such another rule even under the fresh and vigorous aegis of a Captain Felix Schweinspitzen. Only with what the captain had called the little handfuls of desperate men lay the hope of the future. If Metzger could ever somehow establish contact with one of those handfuls—

Tyrannicide Lyman Harding set the curried chicken in front of the voracious Hitler XVI. A pinch of native poison in the chicken could have turned the trick in safety; but the tyrant needed a more open and sensational removal to arouse the world.

The carefully applied body stain made him and his fellow Tyrannicides indistinguishable from the native servants to the casual glance; and what proudly self-confident Aryan would bestow more than a casual glance on his colored slaves? But he could not quite obtain the unobtrusive skilled movements of the natives. There was an American angularity to his serving, and once he was so awkward as to spill a drop of hot sauce on the neck of one of the Führer's aides.

For a moment he feared that his slip was the end of the adventure. The aid's hand rested on his automatic. Harding thought of the many stories of slaves butchered in cold blood for even less grievous offenses. But the officer finally let out a snarling laugh and said something indubitably insulting in German. Then he picked up the outsize glass of brandy that he had been swilling with his food and hurled it in the servant's face.

Harding's eyes stung with the pain of the alcohol. He bowed servilely and scurried off. The next course was the shoat stewed in coconut milk, and with that course—

Anton Metzger heard the motors of a plane passing over the open-air banquet. The Führer did not look up from his gorging. Why should he? Strict care was always taken to enforce the regulation that no armed planes could be aloft during his tour of inspection.

This could only be an unarmed transport, Metzger thought, though he wondered why it seemed to be slowing down and circling overhead. It must be the *Leo* or the *Aries*—

The *Aries!* Aries, the Ram! The prophecy—

Suddenly Anton Metzger understood the subversive plot of the pelagic young spark, Captain Schweinspitzen.

Lyman Harding checked with his eye the position of his fellows and of the natives that were helping them. All O.K. On his silver tray lay the knife—the knife that looked like any serving knife which any servant might carry. Only the keenest eye could tell the excellence of its steel or the fineness of its whetted edge. He took a bowl of shoat from the tray and set it before an Aryan diner. Then as he looked down at the polished silver, he saw his face mirrored in the space left by that bowl. And his face was recognizably white.

The alcohol in that contemptuously thrown brandy had attacked his skin stain. So far the diners were too absorbed in the *rijstafel* to have noticed km. But that luck could not last. He was in the middle of the tables now. It would take him at least a minute to work his way either to the Hitler's table or to the protective outer darkness. A minute. Sixty seconds, in every one of which he took the almost certain chance of being recognized for a spy, of being killed—which is not an agreeable thought even to the most venturesome—and—what was far worse— of seeing his whole plan collapse.

The success of the blows planned for today all over the world depended on the success of this venture here in destroying Hitler XVI. And the success of this venture depended absolutely on him, since each man had his duty and his was the prime one of disposing of the Führer.

The transport motor droned over the clatter of the banquet. Harding made his decision. The risks were the same whether he attempted to reach concealment or went on with his plan. He advanced toward the Hitler's table, serving out the bowls of stewed shoat as he went.

A colonel raised his eyes from his plate to call for more wine. His eyes met the white face of a brown-bodied servant. He opened his mouth.

And at that moment a half dozen shouts went up from as many tables. Men were standing and pointing up. The colonel forgot even that astonishing servant as he raised his eyes to the sky and saw the dim shapes floating down.

The blue-black parachutes were all but invisible—perceptible only as vague shapes blotting out the stars, slowly descending with the deadly quiet of doom.

There was a shrill scream of terror, though there were no women in the gathering. There were barking shots from the officers' sidearms, answered from above—futilely, at that distance and under those conditions of fire.

Then the rattle of the machine guns began.

Anton Metzger tore his eyes from what he knew must be Schweinspitzen, dangling on high while the "Ram's in the sky," and looked at the plump face of Hitler XVI, still aquiver from that terrified scream. Then he saw the unbelievable sight of a native with a gleaming knife charging at the Führer's table.

The others at the table were staring and firing aloft. Only Hitler XVI, stirred by some warning of personal danger, and Metzger saw the servant's attack. Metzger's first thought was the stories of amuck. Then he saw the white face, and understood the truth even before he heard the half-legendary cry of the Tyrannicides: "Sick the tyrants!"

Hitler XVI had drawn his automatic. He handled it with the awkwardness of a man little accustomed to firearms, but he could hardly miss the large target charging at him.

For the first time in his malcontent life, Anton Metzger became a man of action. The action was simple. It consisted in seizing the Führer's arm from behind and twisting it till the automatic fell, then in holding both arms pinioned while the knife carved into the plump flesh of the Führer's throat.

The three-way battle had been furious and bloody, but its outcome was never in doubt. Schweinspitzen's paratroops were rashly too few to achieve anything. The Hitler's men might have put up a successful resistance by themselves even after their Führer's death, but the disconcerting presence of two sets of enemies, one in their own uniforms, unmanned them. The Tyrannicides and the natives had won a total victory in the triangular confusion.

Now Metzger stood with Lyman Harding and surveyed the carnage. "I owe you my life," Harding said. "The soteron garments I'd planned on for protection couldn't be used with this servant-disguise scheme, and there was no other way of getting in. And the world owes you a hell of a lot more than I do."

"I owe you," Metzer said in English, "more than I could ever explain."

"But look. Maybe you can tell me something. What went on with those the paratroops? They came just at the perfect time for a cover for us and I don't know as we'd have made it without them; but who were they?"

"They were an attempt at a palace revolution, led by one Captain Schweinspitzen." Metzger kept his eyes from the crumpled heap of blue-black cloth that covered the body of his one-time friend Felix. A machine gun had reached in the air and he had indeed dangled on high, a parachuting corpse.

"But it was crazy. He didn't have a chance to get away with that attack. Why did he—"

"He believed that it had been prophesied. I'm afraid it's partly my own fault for being overingenious in my interpretations. You see—" And Metzger explained about the American prophecy. "So," he concluded, "the prophecy did come true in detail, all save the last line. And it was fulfilled *because* it existed. Without the prophecy, Schweinspitzen would never have conceived such a plot."

Harding was laughing, a titanic Bunyanesque laugh that seemed disproportionate even to the paradox of the prophecy or to the nervous release following the bloody victory.

"It is a curious paradox," Metzger said. "I wonder if that is the only true way in which prophecy can function, bringing about its own fulfillment. I wonder if the author of that prophecy—"

Harding managed to stop laughing and had to wipe his eyes. "That's just it," he gasped. "The author of the prophecy. You see, my friend, he was my great-grandpappy."

"What?"

"Fact. I know that prophecy. The family managed to save some of Great-grandfather de Camp's stuff—he was a writer—from the great book-burnings and it's sort of a tradition that all of us should read it. Swell screwy stuff it is, too. But I remember the prophecy, and it's all a gag."

"A gag?"

"A joke. A hoax. Great-grandfather wrote an article to disprove prophecy, and made his point by writing a limerick of pure nonsense so vague and cryptic that it'd be bound to be twisted into prophetic fame sometime in the course of history. In fact, it's saved history. Gosh, would this slay the old man!"

"Pure nonsense," Metzger mused, "and fulfilled in every detailed word, except for the last line." Suddenly he said, "Tyrannicides! Is that just what people call you or what you really call yourselves?"

"Well, we mostly call us the Tyros, just for the hell of it. But the full name is Canadian-American Tyrannicides—sometimes just the initials— Oh!"

Comprehension lit his face as he followed Metzger's eyes. In the shambles of the banquet a couple of his boys had started a crap game.

The C.A.T. were throwing dice at the feast.

Lyman Harding whistled. "Great-grandpappy didn't know his own strength."

NOTE: The de Camp "prophecy" is an actual one; see *Esquire*, December, 1942. The lines quoted from Nostradamus are, of course, also actual; those cited by Hitler are from the Nazi propaganda pamphlet, "Nostradamus Prophecies About the War," by Norab.

The Other Inauguration

From the Journal of Peter Lanroyd, Ph.D.:

Mon Nov 5 84: To any man even remotely interested in politics, let alone one as involved as I am, every 1st Tue of every 4th Nov must seem like one of the crucial *if*-points of history. From every American presidential election stem 2 vitally different worlds, not only for U S but for world as a whole.

It's easy enough, esp for a Prof of Polit Hist, to find examples—1860, 1912, 1932 . . . & equally easy, if you're honest with yourself & forget you're a party politician, to think of times when it didn't matter much of a special damn who won an election. Hayes-Tilden . . . biggest controversy, biggest outrage on voters in U S history . . . yet how much of an *if*-effect?

But this is different. 1984 (damn Mr Orwell's long-dead soul! he jinxed the year!) is *the* key *if*-crux as ever was in U S hist. And on Wed Nov 7 my classes are going to expect a few illuminating remarks—wh are going to have to come from me, scholar, & forget about the County Central Comm.

So I've recanvassed my precinct (looks pretty good for a Berkeley Hill precinct, too; might come damn close to carrying it), I've done everything I can before the election itself; & I can put in a few minutes trying to be non-party-objective why this year of race 1984 is so *if*-vital.

Historical b g:

A) U S always goes for 2-party system, whatever the names.

B) The Great Years 1952/76 when we had, almost for 1st time, honest 2-partyism. Gradual development (started 52 by Morse, Byrnes, Shivers, etc) of cleancut parties of "right" & "left" (both, of course, to the right of a European "center" party). Maybe get a class laugh out of how both new parties kept both old names, neither wanting to lose New England Repub votes or Southern Demo, so we got Democratic American Republican Party & Free Democratic Republican Party.

C) 1976/84 God help us growth of 3rd party, American. (The bastards! The simple, the perfect name . . . !) Result: Gradual withering away of DAR, bad defeat in 1980 presidential, total collapse in 82 congressional election. Back to 2-party system: Am vs FDR.

So far so good. Nice & historical. But how tell a class, without accusations of partisanship, what an Am victory means? What a destruction, what a (hell! let's use their own word) subversion of everything American . . .

Or am I being partisan? Can anyone be as evil, as anti-American, as to me the Senator is?

Don't kid yrself Lanroyd. If it's an Am victory, you aren't going to lecture on Wed. You're going to be in mourning for the finest working democracy ever conceived by man. And now you're going to sleep & work like hell tomorrow getting out the vote.

It was Tuesday night. The vote had been got out, and very thoroughly indeed. In Lanroyd's precinct, in the whole state of California, and in all 49 other states. The result was in, and the TV commentator, announcing the final electronic recheck of results from 50 state-wide electronic calculators, was being smug and happy about the whole thing. ("Conviction?" thought Lanroyd bitterly. "Or shrewd care in holding a job?")

". . . Yessir," the commentator was repeating gleefully, "it's such a landslide as we've never seen in all American history—and the *American* history is what it's going to be from now on. For the Senator, five . . . hundred . . . and . . . eighty . . . nine electoral votes from forty . . . nine states. For the Judge, four electoral votes from one state.

"Way back in 1936, when Franklin Delano Roosevelt" (he pronounced the name as a devout Christian might say Judas Iscariot) "carried all but two states, somebody said, 'As Maine goes, so goes Vermont.' Well, folks, I guess from now on we'll have to say—ha! ha!—'As Maine goes . . . so goes Maine.' And it looks like the FDR party is going the way of the unlamented DAR. From now on, folks, it's Americanism for Americans!

"Now let me just recap those electoral figures for you again. For the Senator on the American ticket, it's five eighty-nine—that's five hundred and eighty-nine—electoral—"

Lanroyd snapped off the set. The automatic brought up the room lighting from viewing to reading level.

He issued a two-syllable instruction which the commentator would have found difficult to carry out. He poured a shot of bourbon and drank it. Then he went to hunt for a razor blade.

As he took it out of the cabinet, he laughed. Ancient Roman could find a good use for this, he thought. Much more comfortable nowadays, too, with thermostats in the bathtub. Drift off under constantly regulated temperature. Play hell with the M.E.'s report, too. Jesus! Is it hitting me so bad I'm thinking stream of consciousness? Get to work, Lanroyd.

One by one he scraped the political stickers off the window. There goes the FDR candidate for State Assembly. There goes the Congressman—twelve-year incumbent. There goes the United States Senator. State Senator not up for reëlection this year, or he'd be gone too. There goes NO ON 13. Of course in a year like this State Proposition #13 passed too; from now on, as a Professor at a State University, he was forbidden to criticize publicly any incumbent government official, and compelled to submit the reading requirements for his courses to a legislative committee.

There goes the Judge himself . . . not just a sticker but a full lumino-portrait.

The youngest man ever appointed to the Supreme Court; the author of the great dissenting opinions of the '50s; later a Chief Justice to rank beside Marshall in the vitality of his interpretation of the Constitution; the noblest candidate the Free Democratic Republican Party had ever offered . . .

There goes the last of the stickers . . .

Hey, Lanroyd, you're right. It's a symbol yet. There goes the last of the political stickers. You'll never stick 'em on your window again. Not if the Senator's boys have anything to say about it.

Lanroyd picked up the remains of the literature he'd distributed in the precincts, dumped it down the incinerator without looking at it, and walked out into the foggy night.

If . . .

All right you're a monomaniac. You're 40 and you've never married (and what a sweet damn fool you were to quarrel with Clarice over the candidates in 72) and you think your profession's taught you that politics means everything and so your party loses and it's the end of the world. But God damn it *this* time it *is*. This *is* the key-point.

If . . .

Long had part of the idea; McCarthy had the other part. It took the Senator to combine them. McCarthy got nowhere, dropped out of the DAR reorganization, failed with his third party, because he attacked and destroyed but didn't *give*. He appealed to hate, but not to greed, no what's-in-it-for-me, no porkchops. But add the Long technique, every-man-a-king, fuse 'em together: "wipe out the socialists; I'll give you something better than socialism." That does it, Senator. Coming Next Year: "wipe out the democrats; I'll give you something better than democracy."

IF . . .

What was it Long said? "If totalitarianism comes to America, it'll be labeled *Americanism*." Dead Huey, now I find thy saw of might . . .

IF

There was a lighted window shining through the fog. That meant Cleve was still up. Probably still working on temporomagnetic field-rotation, which sounded like nonsense but what did you expect from a professor of psionics? Beyond any doubt the most unpredictable department in the University . . . and yet Lanroyd was glad he'd helped round up the majority vote when the Academic Senate established it. No telling what might come of it . . . *if* independent research had any chance of continuing to exist.

The window still carried a sticker for the Judge and a NO ON 13. This was a good house to drop in on. And Lanroyd needed a drink.

Cleve answered the door with a full drink in his hand. "Have this, old boy," he said; "I'll mix myself another. Night for drinking, isn't it?" The opinion had obviously been influencing him for some time; his British accent, usually all but rubbed off by now, had returned full force as it always did after a few drinks.

Lanroyd took the glass gratefully as he went in. "I'll sign that petition," he said. "I need a drink to stay sober; I think I've hit a lowpoint where I can't get drunk."

"It'll be interesting," his host observed, "to see if you're right. Glad you dropped in. I needed drinking company."

"Look, Stu," Lanroyd objected. "If it wasn't for the stickers on your window, I'd swear you were on your way to a happy drunk. What's to celebrate for God's sake?"

"Well as to God, old boy, I mean anything that's to celebrate is to celebrate for God's sake, isn't it? After all . . . Pardon. I *must* be a bit tiddly already."

"I know," Lanroyd grinned. "You don't usually shove your Church of England theology at me. Sober, you know I'm hopeless."

"Point not conceded. But God does come into this, of course. My rector's been arguing with me—doesn't approve at all. Tampering with Divine providence. But A: how can mere me tamper with anything Divine? And B: if it's possible, it's part of the Divine plan itself. And C: I've defied the dear old boy to establish that it involves in any way the Seven Deadly Sins, the Ten Commandments, or the Thirty-Nine Articles."

"Professor Cleve," said Lanroyd, "would you mind telling me what the hell you are talking about?"

"Time travel, of course. What else have I been working on for the past eight months?"

Lanroyd smiled. "O.K. Every man to his obsession. My world's shattered and yours is rosy. Carry on, Stu. Tell me about it and brighten my life."

"I say, Peter, don't misunderstand me. I am . . . well, really dreadfully distressed about . . ." He looked from the TV set to the window stickers. "But it's hard to think about anything else when . . ."

"Go on." Lanroyd drank with tolerant amusement. "I'll believe anything of the Department of Psionics, ever since I learned not to shoot craps with you. I suppose you've invented a time machine?"

"Well, old boy, I think I have. It's a question of . . ."

Lanroyd understood perhaps a tenth of the happy monolog that followed. As an historical scholar, he seized on a few names and dates. Principle of temporomagnetic fields known since discovery by Arthur McCann circa 1941. Neglected for lack of adequate power source. Mei-Figner's experiment with nuclear pile 1959. Nobody knows what became of M-F. Embarrassing discovery that power source remained chronostationary; poor M-F stranded somewhere with no return power. Hasselfarb Equations 1972 established that any adequate external power source must possess too much temporal inertia to move with traveler.

"Don't you see, Peter?" Cleve gleamed. "That's where everyone's misunderstood Hasselfarb. 'Any *external* power source . . .' Of course it baffled the physicists."

"I can well believe it," Lanroyd quoted. "Perpetual motion, or squaring the circle, would baffle the physicists. They're infants, the physicists."

Cleve hesitated, then beamed. "Robert Barr," he identified. "His Sherlock Holmes parody. Happy idea for a time traveler: Visit the Reichenbach Falls in 1891 and see if Holmes really was killed. I've always thought an impostor 'returned.' "

"Back to your subject, psionicist . . . which is a hell of a word for a drinking man. Here, I'll fill both glasses and you tell me why what baffles the physicists fails to baffle the ps . . ."

" 'Sounds of strong men struggling with a word,' " Cleve murmured. They were both fond of quotation; but it took Lanroyd a moment to place this muzzily as Belloc. "Because the power source doesn't have to be *external*. We've been developing the *internal* sources. How can I regularly beat you at craps?"

"Psychokinesis," Lanroyd said, and just made it.

"Exactly. But nobody ever thought of trying the effect of PK power on temporomagnetic fields before. And it works and the Hasselfarb Equations don't apply!"

"You've done it?"

"Little trips. Nothing spectacular. Tiny experiments. *But*—and this, old boy, is the damnedest part—there's every indication that PK can *rotate* the temporomagnetic stasis!"

"That's nice," said Lanroyd vaguely.

"No, of course. You don't understand. My fault. Sorry, Peter. What I mean is this: We can not only travel in time; we can rotate into another, an alternate time. A world of If."

Lanroyd started to drink, then abruptly choked. Gulping and gasping, he eyed in turn the TV set, the window stickers and Cleve. "*If . . .*" he said.

Cleve's eyes made the same route, then focused on Lanroyd. "What we are looking at each other with," he said softly, "is a wild surmise."

From the journal of Peter Lanroyd, Ph.D.:

Mon Nov 12 84: So I have the worst hangover in Alameda County, & we lost to UCLA Sat by 3 field goals, & the American Party takes over next Jan; but it's still a wonderful world.

Or rather it's a wonderful universe, continuum, whatsit, that includes both this world & the possibility of shifting to a brighter alternate.

I got through the week somehow after Black Tue. I even made reasonable-sounding non-subversive noises in front of my classes. Then all week-end, except for watching the game (in the quaint expectation that Cal's sure victory wd lift our spirits), Stu Cleve & I worked.

I never thought I'd be a willing lab assistant to a psionicist. But we want to keep this idea secret. God knows what a good Am Party boy on the faculty (Daniels, for inst) wd think of people who prefer an alternate victory. So I'm Cleve's factotum & busbar-boy & I don't understand a damned thing I'm doing but—

It works.

The movement in time anyway. Chronokinesis, Cleve calls it, or CK for short. CK . . . PK . . . sound like a bunch of executives initialing each other. Cleve's achieved short CK. Hasn't dared try rotation yet. Or taking me with him. But he's sweating on my "psionic potential." Maybe with some results: I lost only 2 bucks in a 2 hour crap game last night. And got so gleeful about my ps pot that I got me this hangover.

Anyway, I know what I'm doing. I'm resigning fr the County Committee at tomorrow's meeting. No point futzing around w politics any more. Opposition Party has as much chance under the Senator as it did in pre-war Russia. And I've got something else to focus on.

I spent all my non-working time in politics because (no matter what my analyst might say if I had one) I wanted, in the phrase that's true the way only corn can be, I wanted to make a better world. All right; now I can really do it, in a way I never dreamed of.

CK . . . PK . . . *OK!*

Tue Dec 11: Almost a month since I wrote a word here. Too damned magnificently full a month to try to synopsize here. Anyway it's all down in Cleve's records. Main point is development of my psionic potential (Cleve says anybody can do it, with enough belief & drive—wh is why Psionics Dept & Psych Dept aren't speaking. Psych claims PK, if it exists wh they aren't too eager to grant even now, is a mutant trait. OK so maybe I'm a mutant. Still . . .

Today I made my first CK. Chronokinesis to you, old boy. Time travel to you, you dope. All right, so it was only 10 min. So nothing happened, not even an eentsy-weentsy paradox. But I did it; & when we go, Cleve & I can go together.

So damned excited I forgot to close parenth above. Fine state of affairs. So:)

Sun Dec 30: Used to really keep me a journal. Full of fascinating facts & political gossip. Now nothing but highpoints, apptly. OK: latest highpoint:

Sufficient PK power *can* rotate the field.

Cleve never succeeded by himself. Now I'm good enough to work with him. And together . . .

He picked a simple one. Purely at random, when he thought we were ready. We'd knocked off work & had some scrambled eggs. 1 egg was a little bad, & the whole mess was awful. Obviously some alternate in wh egg was *not* bad. So we went back (CK) to 1 p m just before Cleve bought eggs, & we (how the hell to put it?) we . . . *worked.* Damnedest sensation. Turns you inside out & then outside in again. If that makes sense.

We bought the eggs, spent the same aft working as before, knocked off work, had some scrambled eggs . . . delicious!

Most significant damned egg-breaking since Columbus!

Sun Jan 20 85: This is the day.

Inauguration Day. Funny to have it on a Sun. Hasn't been since 57. Cleve asked me what's the inaugural augury. Told him the odds were even. Monroe's 2d Inaug was a Sun . . . & so was Zachary Taylor's 1st & only, wh landed us w Fillmore.

We've been ready for a week. Waited till today just to hear the Senator get himself inaugurated. 1st beginning of the world we'll never know.

TV's on. There the smug bastard is. Pride & ruin of 200,000,000 people. "Americans!"

Get that. Not "fellow Americans . . ."

"Americans! You have called me in clarion tones & I shall answer!"

Here it comes, all of it. ". . . my discredited adversaries . . ." ". . . strength, not in union, but in unity . . ." ". . . as you have empowered me to root out these . . ."

The one-party system, the one-system state, the one-man party-system-state . . .

Had enough, Stu? (Hist slogan current ca 48) OK: let's *work!*

Damn! Look what this pencil did while I was turning inside out & outside in again. (Note: Articles in contact w body move in CK. For reasons cf Cleve's notebooks.) Date is now

Tue Nov 6 84: TV's on. Same cheerful commentator:

"... Yessir, it's 1 of the greatest landslides in American history. 524 electoral votes from 45 states, to 69 electoral votes from 5 states, all Southern, as the experts predicted. I'll repeat: That's 524 electoral votes for the Judge ..."

We've done it. We're *there* ... then ... whatever the hell the word is. I'm the first politician in history who ever made the people vote right against their own judgment!

Now, in this brighter better world where the basic tenets of American democracy were safe, there was no nonsense about Lanroyd's resigning from politics. There was too much to do. First of all a thorough job of party reorganization before the Inauguration. There were a few, even on the County and State Central Committees of the Free Democratic Republican Party, who had been playing footsie with the Senator's boys. A few well-planned parliamentary maneuvers weeded them out; a new set of by-laws took care of such contingencies in the future; and the Party was solidly unified and ready to back the Judge's administration.

Stuart Cleve went happily back to work. He no longer needed a busbar-boy from the History Department. There was no pressing need for secrecy in his work; and he possessed, thanks to physical contact during chronokinesis, his full notebooks on experiments for two and a half months which, in this world, hadn't happened yet—a paradox which was merely amusing and nowise difficult.

By some peculiar whim of alternate universes, Cal even managed to win the UCLA game 33–10.

In accordance with the popular temper displayed in the Presidential election, Proposition 13, with its thorough repression of all academic thought and action, had been roundly defeated. A short while later, Professor Daniels, who had so actively joined the Regents and the Legislature in backing the measure, resigned from the Psychology Department. Lanroyd had played no small part in the faculty meetings which convinced Daniels that the move was advisable.

At last Sunday, January 20, 1985, arrived (or, for two men in the world, returned) and the TV sets of the nation brought the people the Inaugural Address. Even the radio stations abandoned their usual local broadcasts of music and formed one of their very rare networks to carry this historical highpoint.

The Judge's voice was firm, and his prose as noble as that of his dissenting or his possibly even greater majority opinions. Lanroyd and Cleve listened together, and together thrilled to the quietly forceful determination to wipe out every last vestige of the prejudices, hatreds, fears and suspicions fostered by the so-called American Party.

"A great man once said," the Judge quoted in conclusion, " 'We have nothing to fear but fear itself.' Now that a petty and wilful group of men have failed in their effort to undermine our very Constitution, I say to you: 'We have one thing to destroy. And that is destruction itself!' "

And Lanroyd and Cleve beamed at each other and broached the bourbon.

From the journal of Peter Lanroyd, Ph.D.:
   Sun Oct 20 85: Exactly 9 mos. Obstetrical symbolism yet?
   Maybe I shd've seen it then, at this other inauguration. Read betw the lines, seen the meaning, the true inevitable meaning. Realized that the Judge was simply saying, in better words (or did they sound better because I thought he was on My Side?) what the Senator said in the inaugural we escaped: "I have a commission to wipe out the opposition."
   Maybe I shd've seen it when the Senator was arrested for inciting to riot. Instead I cheered. Served the sonofabitch right. (And it did, too. That's the hell of it. It's all confused . . .)
   He still hasn't been tried. They're holding him until they can nail him for treason. Mere matter of 2 constitutional amendments: Revise Art III Sec 3 Par 1 so "treason" no longer needs direct-witness proof of an overt act of war against the U S or adhering to their enemies, but can be anything yr Star Chamber wants to call it; revise Art I Sec 9 Par 3 so you can pass an ex post facto law. All very simple; the Judge's arguments sound as good as his dissent in U S vs Feinbaum. (I shd've seen, even in the inaug, that he's not the same man in this world—the same mind turned to other ends. My ends? My end . . .) The const ams'll pass all right . . . except maybe in Maine.
   I shd've seen it last year when the press began to veer, when the dullest & most honest columnist in the country began to blather about the "measure of toleration"—when the liberal Chronicle & the Hearst Examiner, for the 1st time in S F history, took the same stand on the Supervisors' refusal of the Civic Aud to a pro-Senator rally—when the NYer satirized the ACLU as something damned close to traitors . . .
   I began to see it when the County Central Committee started to raise hell about a review I wrote in the QPH. (God knows how a Committeeman happened to read that learned journal.) Speaking of the great old 2-party era, I praised both the DAR & the FDR as bulwarks of democracy. Very unwise. Seems as a good Party man I shd've restricted my praise to the FDR. Cd've fought it through, of course, stood on my rights—hell, a County Committeeman's an elected representative of the people. But I resigned because . . . well, because that was when I began to see it.
   Today was what did it, though. 1st a gentle phone call fr the Provost—in person, no secty—wd I drop by his office tomorrow? Certain questions have arisen as to some of the political opinions I have been expressing in my lectures . . .
   That blonde in the front row with the teeth & the busy notebook & the D's & F's . . .
   So Cleve comes by & I think I've got troubles . . . !
   He's finally published his 1st paper on the theory of CK & PK-induced alternates. It's been formally denounced as "dangerous" because it implies the existence of better worlds. And guess who denounced it? Prof Daniels of Psych.
   Sure, the solid backer of #13, the strong American Party boy. He's a strong FDR man now. *He* knows. And he's back on the faculty.

Cleve makes it all come out theological somehow. He says that by forcibly setting mankind on the alternate *if*-fork that *we* wanted, we denied man's free will. Impose "democracy" against or without man's choice, & you have totalitarianism. Our only hope is what he calls "abnegation of our own desire"—surrender to, going along with, the will of man. We must CK & PK ourselves back to where we started.

The hell with the theology; it makes sense politically too. I was wrong. Jesus! I was wrong. Look back at every major election, every major boner the electorate's pulled. So a boner to me is a triumph of reason to you, sir. But let's not argue which dates were the major boners. 1932 or 1952, take your pick.

It's always worked out, hasn't it? Even 1920. It all straightens out, in time. Democracy's the craziest, most erratic system ever devised . . . & the closest to perfection. At least it keeps coming closer. Democratic man makes his mistakes— & he corrects them in time.

Cleve's going back to make his peace with his ideas of God & free will. I'm going back to show I've learned that a politician doesn't clear the hell&gone out of politics because he's lost. Nor does he jump over on the winning side.

He works & sweats as a Loyal Opposition—hell, as an Underground if necessary, if things get as bad as that—but he holds on & works to make men make their own betterment.

Now we're going to Cleve's, where the field's set up . . . & we're going back to the true world.

Stuart Cleve was weeping, for the first time in his adult life. All the beautifully intricate machinery which created the temporomagnetic field was smashed as thoroughly as a hydrogen atom over Novosibirsk.

"That was Winograd leading them, wasn't it?" Lanroyd's voice came out oddly through split lips and missing teeth.

Cleve nodded.

"Best damn coffin-corner punter I ever saw . . . Wondered why our friend Daniels was taking such an interest in athletes recently."

"Don't oversimplify, old boy. Not all athletes. Recognized a couple of my best honor students . . ."

"Fine representative group of youth on the march . . . and all wearing great big FDR buttons!"

Cleve picked up a shard of what had once been a chronostatic field generator and fondled it tenderly. "When they smash machines and research projects," he said tonelessly, "the next step is smashing men."

"Did a fair job on us when we tried to stop them. Well . . . These fragments we have shored against our ruins . . . And now, to skip to a livelier maker for our next quote, it's back to work we go! Hi-Ho! Hi-Ho! Need a busbar-boy, previous experience guaranteed?"

"It took us ten weeks of uninterrupted work," Cleve said hesitantly. "You think those vandals will let us alone that long? But we have to try, I know." He bent over a snarled mess of wiring which Lanroyd knew was called a magnetostat and performed some incomprehensibly vital function. "Now this looks almost servicea—" He jerked upright again, shaking his head worriedly.

"Matter?" Lanroyd asked.

"My head. Feels funny . . . One of our young sportsmen landed a solid kick when I was down."

"Winograd, no doubt. Hasn't missed a boot all season."

Perturbedly Cleve pulled out of his pocket the small dice-case which seemed to be standard equipment for all psionicists. He shook a pair in his fist and rolled them out in a clear space on the rubbage-littered floor.

"*Seven!*" he called.

A six turned up, and then another six.

"Sometimes," Cleve was muttering ten unsuccessful rolls later, "even slight head injuries have wiped out all psionic potential. There's a remote possibility of redevelopment; it *has* happened . . ."

"And," said Lanroyd, "it takes both of us to generate enough PK to rotate." He picked up the dice. "Might as well check mine." He hesitated, then let them fall. "I don't think I want to know ..."

They stared at each other over the ruins of the machinery that would never be rebuilt.

" 'I, a stranger and afraid . . .' " Cleve began to quote.

"In a world," Lanroyd finished, "I damned well made."

One-Way Trip

PROLOGUE

"Twenty years from the discovery of lovestonite before anyone finds a practical use for it; and it takes an artist to do it!" Emigdio Valentinez smiled the famous smile which the gossip writers called melancholy—or occasionally wistful—but which meant nothing more than simply a smile.

"Yeah, I know. That's swell. You got a nice set-up for tinkering here." Stag Hartle glanced around indifferently at the today literally Pacific Ocean and at the undulant dunes of sand, empty save for his two-seater copter. "You got fun out here."

"Fun?" Valentinez smiled down at the curious object in his hand, a mirror in shape, but made of what looked like dark glass and surrounded with a complex of coils and tubes. "I suppose it is fun to do what you are fitted for—in my case to solve an age-old problem of art by a twenty-year-old discarded problem of science."

"Yeah," said Stag Hartle. "But that ain't all you're fitted for, and you know it. O.K., so you paint the greatest self-portrait ever painted. Who cares? The people, they've seen your famous smile plenty of times on the air, and that's enough for them. But if you'd come back to Sollywood and do the sets for S.B.'s epic on Devarupa—"

Valentinez interrupted him with three short sentences. "I do not like designing sets. I do not like the notion of an epic on Devarupa. I do not like Mr. Breakstone."

"Hold on, Mig. Climb down out of the stratosphere and be a human being. Think of the pleasure you can give people with solly sets that'd never see one of your paintings. Think of—" He lowered his voice to a seductive rasp, "S.B. said in confidence, mind you, and I shouldn't be telling you a word of this, but S.B. said he was willing to listen to any reasonable proposition. And when he says reasonable, Mig, I'm telling you he means unreasonable. How's about five thousand credits a week?"

Valentinez released a button on his gadget, turned it over, and contemplated the other side with satisfaction. "No," he said quietly.

"Six? Seven and a half?"

Emigdio Valentinez laid the mirror down. "It was nice of you to drop out to see me, Hartle. It was nice of you to listen to my fun-and-games with lovestonite. But now, if you don't mind, I'm going down to the cove. There's an effect of the sun on the algae there at this time of day—"

Stag Hartle watched the departing figure of the man who was possibly the world's greatest living painter and certainly its most successful. He swore to and at himself with dull persistence for a good five minutes.

Then idly he picked up the lovestonite mirror and operated it as Valentinez had instructed him. Nice little gadget. Clever technician lost in that painter. Futile sort of gag. Nothing commercial, but—

Stag Hartle opened his mouth wide and shut it again firmly. He carried the mirror out into the bright sunlight of late afternoon .

When he came back into the house, there was a grin of satisfaction on his face. It was hard to keep his eyes off the charred hole in the wooden porch outside.

He worked quickly. From his vest pocket he took that convenient clip-on cylinder which looked like a stylus, but unscrewed to reveal a stick of paraderm. He thrust it under his armpit and held it there until body heat had softened it. Then he carefully coated the inside of his fingers and the palms of his hands. He allowed it to dry and then flexed his fingers experimentally. The cords stood out in his powerfully wiry wrists.

He thought of historical sollies and the great convenience of knives and pistols. But no matter how Devarupian the world, a man could still kill if he had strong hands and no fear of a one-way trip.

Emigdio Valentinez added one more flick of his deft brush and then realized that the perfect moment had passed. Only one sixth of an hour out of the twenty-four when the light in this spot was exactly as it had been that day when he had halted transfixed and felt that strange gripping of his bowels which meant "This is it!"

He could fill the rest of his time satisfactorily enough. There had been the weeks of delightfully restful research on the lovestonite mirror, and now there lay ahead of him many more weeks, by no means restful, to be devoted to the object for which he had contrived the gadget—a perfect self-portrait.

He smiled, and smiled at himself for smiling. How fortunate, in all due modesty, is the artist who is a worthy subject of his own brush! He knew that in a way he was beautiful. He knew, and found a bitter sort of pleasure in the knowledge, that a girl's bedroom was far more apt to be adorned by a color photo of himself than by a reprolith of one of his paintings.

Well, this would combine the two apeals—his magnum opus. Though if ever he could finish this composition of rock and algae and water and sun—

Where he stood he could see nothing that was not part of nature save himself, his palette and his easel. It might have been a scene out of the long-dead past. Cézanne, say, or some other old master might have stood thus in the sun back in those dim days when the advance of science was beginning with its little creeps. Painting is something apart from progress. He knew that he could never catch the sun as Cézanne had. He knew that not he, nor any other man living, could approach the clarity of Vermeer or the chiaroscuro of Rembrandt. He could make an overnight jaunt to the Moon if he wished, but he could not capture in paint the soul of Devarupa as El Greco had captured that of St. Francis. Art did not necessarily progress with progress.

And yet the lovestonite mirror might be the first true contribution of science to painting. He smiled, that smile that was not intentionally either melancholy or wistful, and started across the sand to his death.

I.

A tiny five-meter rocket flashed past the window of the stratoliner.

"Poor devil," the girl sighed.

Gan Garrett blessed the poor devil, whoever he was and whatever he'd done. For an hour he had been trying to think of some way of opening a conversation with his black-haired, blue-eyed traveling companion.

"I know," he agreed sympathetically.

"Living death," the girl went on. "Premature burial, like that funny obsession of horror you get in nineteenth-century writers. That rocket shooting out, headed no place forever—"

"But what other solution is there?" Garrett asked. "If no one may kill, certainly the State may not. We have abandoned the collective mania of capital punishment as thoroughly as that of war. How else would Devarupa have had us treat those who were formerly thought fit to be executed?"

"Segregation?" the girl ventured hesitantly.

"If you recall your history classes, that didn't work so well. Remember the Revolt of the Segregated in '73? When you mass together all those who are undeveloped enough to wish to kill—"

The girl's eyes stared out into space, following the now invisible course of the one-way trip. "You're right, of course. It's the only way. But I still say, 'Poor devil.' You're headed for Sollywood?"

Garrett nodded.

"Actor?"

"Hardly. Technical expert for Mr. Breakstone's epic on Devarupa. I'm an historian, not unknown in my field, I must confess. You may have read my little work on 'The Guilt for the War of the Twentieth Century'?" His voice was arid and his bearing purely academic; despite his disclaimer, he had never done a more convincing job of acting.

There had been nothing dry or academic about Gan Garrett the day before when he breezed into the office of the Secretary of Allocation. "The post office is going to raise the devil about your requisitioning me," he announced. "I was just getting on the track of the highjackers that've been operating on the lunar mail rockets."

"That's all right," the secretary said dryly. "I've been over your reports with the postmaster and he agrees with me that a subordinate can carry on from there. And we can't all have the services of Gan Garrett at once."

Garrett grinned. "Look," he interposed. "Don't tell me how good I am. I couldn't take it. But what's the new job?"

The secretary leafed through the dossier before him. "According to this, Garrett, you made the highest rating in the adaptability classes that the W.B.I. school has ever seen. You also displayed a marked aptitude for pre-Devarupian history."

Garrett nodded. "I liked those old times. I know how true Devarupa's ideas are, and yet there's something about the wanton recklessness of the old armed days—"

"Very well. You are going to Sollywood as a technical adviser on an epic now being prepared. No one outside of this secretariat will have the least idea that your job is not authentic; and you'd better be good at it."

"I'll run over my library tonight and take forty or fifty microbooks along. My visual memory'll see me through. But what's the real job?"

The secretary paused. "Garrett, do you know anything about lovestonite?"

Gan Garrett probed in his memory. "Let's see— Something about Australia. I think I remember: Scientists working a couple of years on finding some use for those deposits of new clay found in the development of central Australia. At last this Lovestone hits on a method of making a vitreous plastic of it. Everybody hepped up down under. Great hopes of a new industry. But nobody can find a thing to do with the plastic. Every function it can perform is handled easier and cheaper by something else. Some queer properties with light—slows it down, or something—so steady small demand from optical and physical labs. Otherwise nil. Is that about it?"

The secretary smiled. "If you can do as well as that unprepared and out of your field, you ought to get by on your new job. Yes, that's the history of lovestonite—up till last month. Then all of a sudden a terrific demand from California. Imports jump around a thousand percent. The processing plant becomes a major industry. Of course, like all requests for raw materials, this was cleared through this secretariat. No questions at first, because there's such a surplus of the clay there was no need for regulation. But eventually we began to wonder."

Garrett whistled quietly. "Armslegging?"

"I don't see how. It doesn't seem scientifically conceivable that lovestonite could have any lethal powers. But there is something wrong. We queried the plant on what it was producing with lovestonite. They said mirrors."

"Mirrors?"

"I know. It doesn't make sense. A lovestonite mirror is possible, I suppose, but it would cost double anything that's on the market and wouldn't work so well. So something is wrong. And when something is wrong in California, you know where to learn the secret."

Garrett nodded. "Sollywood. The whole state's just a suburb to that."

"So—" the secretary opened a drawer and took out a small and gracefully carved plesiosaurus. At the top of the delicately curving neck was a gold collar from which a small chain ran. "You never wear jewelry on your identification bracelet, do you?"

Garrett shook his head. "Function where function belongs. No trimmings."

"But you'll wear this. It's by Kubicek, one of his best, I think. He says lovestonite is a surprisingly good vehicle for carving. It might help to start conversations. Beyond that, you're on your own. No instructions but these: Do a good job as technical adviser, and find out what's going on in California."

The head of the plesiosaur was typical Kubicek. It had, not the anthropomorphic cuteness of gift-shop animals, but a prehistoric richness of reptilian knowledge and cynicism. "Between us," said Gan Garrett, "we'll find out all there is to know. And I hope," he added, "that it is armslegging."

The girl was looking at his mascot now. "That's a nice thing. Kubicek, isn't it? I usually somehow don't think much of men who wear jewelry on their identification bracelets, but that's such a lovely swizard."

"A what?"

"That's what I used to call a plesiosaur when I saw pictures of them when I was little. They looked like part swan and part lizard, so I called them swizards. But what's it made out of? That isn't a natural stone, and it doesn't look like any of the usual carving plastics."

"It's lovestonite."

"Oh," said the girl.

"Odd stuff," Garrett went on. "Not much use for it ordinarily."

"Isn't there?" There was an odd tone of suggestion underlying her remark.

"Is there? I'd never heard of any."

"I don't know . . . I'm damned if I know," she said with quite disproportionate vigor. Her blue eyes flashed with puzzled irritation. "Damn lovestonite, anyway."

Gan Garrett held himself back. A technical authority on history should not be too pryingly eager with questions.

The girl changed the subject abruptly. "So you're an authority on the War of the Twentieth Century? That must be exciting, kind of. I haven't read so much serious history, but I know all the Harkaway novels. It must have . . . there was so much *to* living in those days."

Secretly Garrett almost agreed, but he replied in character. "Nonsense, my dear girl. Those were days of poverty and oppression, of want and terror. Science had turned only its black mask to us then; the greatness of man's intellect was expended on destruction."

"I know all that. But think how much more it meant to be alive when you were face to face with death."

"No. There is nothing glamorous about death from malnutrition, nor is there anything colorful about being blown to bits by a bomb."

"Don't be stuffy."

"I'm not being stuffy. We invest the past with glamour; we always have. We say, 'Mustn't it have been wonderful to be alive in the days of Elizabeth! Or Napoleon, or Hitler?' But the only good thing about the War of the Twentieth Century was its total badness. Only such complete evil could have prepared the world for the teachings of Devarupa."

The girl looked sobered for a moment. "I know. Devarupa was . . . well, wonderful. But I've never thought he meant peace quite like this. He must have meant a peace that was alive—that gave off sparks, that made music. Peace isn't just something to wallow in. Peace has to be fought for."

"You're Irish, aren't you?" said Gan Garrett dryly.

"Yes; why?"

"It takes the Hibernian to produce that kind of statement. An Irish bull, technically, is it not? It was an Irish scientist on our faculty who told me that microbes are tiny all right, but a virus is littler than a dozen microbes."

She laughed. "I know. I sound like the old Irish gag about 'There ain't gonna be no fightin' here if I have to knock the stuffin' out of every wan of yez.' I know; my dialect gets mixed. But the whole world's mixed now—and how is it we Irish still manage to stick out? Still, what I said is true, even if it does sound funny."

"It's been tried," said Garrett as historian. "The Pax Romana worked that way: Peace, ye underlings; or Rome will crush you to the ground. But the Empire weakened and was itself crushed, by its own chosen means of force. Peace has to be rooted in something deeper than fighting."

"Something deeper, yes. But you need the fighting, too. If people still had the guts to fight, we'd have a colony on Mars by now. But they'd sooner sit on their cushions and sew a fine seam. Maybe the world was better when there were weapons and—"

"The W.B.I. still has weapons."

"Those . . . those popguns?" The girl's eyes flashed, and she tossed her black hair. "And what do you know about the W.B.I., anyway, you . . . you academician?"

"Nothing, my dear," the W.B.I.'s most capable agent admitted gently.

"Then shut up!"

They traveled the next half hour in silence. The ship's windows proffered no view but a sea of clouds. Beneath those clouds, Garrett calculated from his watch, lay the opulence of the reclaimed deserts of the Southwest; a few more minutes and—

He turned again to the girl. Her reaction to lovestonite made it imperative that he keep in touch with her, even if other motives had not contributed their share to his desire. "You live in Sollywood?" he ventured.

"What do you care, you *historian?*"

"But do you?"

"Of course not!" she snorted. "I live in Novosibirsk and I'm flying out here for a beam test."

The ship dipped down through the clouds and emerged into rain. Fine drops streaked the window, but far below Garrett could glimpse some of the infinite variety of locations that comprise most of southern California, all dry and aglow with light under their vast domes.

The girl looked out at the rain. "Welcome to California," she said. "And I hope you drown."

Gan Garrett detached his identification plaque from its bracelet and placed it in the slot by the imposing entrance to Metropolis Solid Pictures, Inc. The beam filtered through his set of perforations, and the door dilated. No query; the combination must have been set to his perfs as soon as he was hired.

He stepped inside, apparently still in the open air but now out of the rain. Five moving sidewalks started off in different directions from this entrance, and he hesitated, studying the indicator.

A life devoted to all the works of the W.B.I., and especially to the suppression of armslegging, had heightened the rapidity of Garrett's reflexes. His movements were economical, but automatic and swift. Thus, he now found that he had, almost without knowing it, moved his body a few centimeters to the right and drawn what the black-haired girl had called his "popgun." Stuck fast in the center of the indicator quivered a knife.

Even Garrett could not repress a slight shudder at the narrow squeak. He whirled about, stooping and weaving as he did so with that skilled technique of his which disconcerted any but the finest marksman. There was not a soul in sight in this open area.

Calmly Garrett plucked and pocketed the knife and chose the proper sidewalk. The episode in one way had told him nothing. Anywhere but in Sollywood the very existence of a weapon would have had its significance, since the careful manufacturing regulations of the Department of Allocation permit no allotments of material for weapons save those such as Garrett now held in his hand. Even these are carefully controlled, and every one that has ever been manufactured is by now either outworn and destroyed or on the person of a W.B.I. man.

They are not lethal, these "popguns." They are compressed-gas pistols using carbon dioxide to fire a pellet filled with needlelike crystals of comatin, that most powerful and instantaneous of anaesthetics. They are, as is inevitable in a Devarupian world, purely a defensive weapon.

But the makers of sollies need to give the effect of lethal weapons in their historical epics; and they can secure permission from the Department for Metal to make plausible replicas. The weapons must by strict statute be nonlethal, blunt in the case of swords and daggers, the barrels blocked in the case of firearms; and rendering them lethal is an offense earning a one-way trip. But once the metal allocation has been secured, a desperate man will take his chance on lethalizing a prop weapon. So here the existence of a lethal dagger was no surprise.

He remembered stories of the past in which detectives examined weapons for fingerprints. They would be no help here, either; the criminal who neglected to use paraderm, so much more convenient than gloves, had been unheard-of for a century. The sole use of prints was no longer criminological, but in problems of civilian identification.

Still, he would keep the dagger; as evidence, he told himself, hardly daring admit that there was something consoling about carrying a forbidden weapon. For the one item of significance which the attack had revealed was this: There was a leak somewhere. Someone in Sollywood knew that he was more than a technical adviser. And that in turn meant that the lovestonite problem was quite as important as the secretary had feared.

Garrett fingered the lovestonite plesiosaur. Swizard, that girl had called it.

Sacheverell Breakstone, the great man of Metropolis, received Gan Garrett in person. He did not wear the usual native costume of the district—the slack trousers, the open shirt, and the colorful ascot which dated back to tradition long before the invention of solid pictures. His costume, Garrett realized, went back even further—the woven sheep's wool coat, the cloth headpiece with the rear projection, the leather leg casings. It was a curious anachronistic survival, but it was becoming to the short stock body of S.B., lending him a certain outrageous dignity.

"Welcome to Sollywood, Garrett," he began. "Hear you're the great man in your field. Well, we'll get on. I'm the great man in mine, and we'll understand each other. And this is going to be beyond any doubt the greatest epic ever beamed even by Metropolis. Even as a personally supervised Breakstone Production. Devarupa will be proud of us from wherever he's watching. And he'll be trusting us, trusting me and trusting you to tell the truth about his life and bring his super-

nal message afresh to all mankind as only the greatness of the greatest art form of
the centuries can bring it!"

"Yes, sir," said Gan Garrett. There seemed to be little else to say.

Sacheverell Breakstone needed no prompting. "Yes, my boy," he went on,
"truth is what we want from you. Truth and accuracy, but especially truth. Don't
spend too much worrying on niggling little details. Supposing—mind you, I'm
just thinking aloud—but supposing we put a woman in the picture. Now you and
I know that there wasn't any woman in Devarupa's life. That's accuracy. But he
loved all humanity, didn't he? And aren't women more than half of humanity? So
if we show him say loving a woman—you understand this is just groping with
words—isn't that truth in the deeper sense? You understand?"

"Yes, sir. I am here to give the cachet of academic authority to all the non-
academic changes you wish to ring on the story of Devarupa."

Breakstone hesitated, then burst out into a heavy laugh. "Good man. You do
understand me. No pretense about you. We'll get on, we will. You can understand
the creative mind. Because that's what I am, mind you. All this"—his broad gesture included every bit of Metropolis—"is my creation. And the creative mind
creates its own truth which is higher than facts. All my life I've wanted to do a life
of Devarupa—with all due reverence, you understand, but still showing he was a
real man. A man of and for men. And I'm the man to do. They don't call me the
Little Hitler of Sollywood for nothing."

Garrett smiled to himself. No one with any knowledge of twentieth-century
history could well consider a "Hitler" the ideal interpreter of that saint among
men, the great Devarupa. But the evil that conquerors do may often be interred
with their bones; he remembered from literary study how Caesar and Napoleon
had become just such metaphorical figures of power, with no allusion to their
manifold infamies.

"Well," Breakstone announced, "it's been wonderful having this talk with you,
Garner."

"Garrett."

"I said Garrett. It's been a pleasure to hear your ideas on Devarupa, and that's
a real suggestion of yours about the woman. You're no hidebound academician, I
can see that. Now if you'll take the left-hand walk for about two hundred meters,
you'll find Uranov's office. He's working on the script today—his third day, in
fact. He's lasting well. You talk it over with him. And enjoy yourself in Sollywood."

Garrett let the swizard jangle as he shook hands with his boss. Breakstone
glanced at it. "Hm-m-m. Nice thing. Dinosaur of some kind, eh? Odd material;
what's it made of?"

"Lovestonite."

"Lovestonite? Well, well. What next? The motto of Metropolis, by the way;
remember that. What next? You understand? Always something new. Come see
me any time you're in trouble, but you won't need to. We understand each other.
Good luck." Even as Garrett left, the Little Hitler of Sollywood had pulled several switches and begun dictating a letter to the Department of Allocation, giving
instructions to a set designer, and receiving from his Calcutta exhibitor.

The few people that Garrett passed on his way down the writers' corridor looked fretful and hagridden—almost like men from the Twentieth Century. The responsibility of turning out the major entertainment device of the world weighed heavily upon them. For though Breakstone's description of the "greatest art form of the centuries" might have been exaggerated, the solid picture was certainly the most widespread and important. With its own powerful impact, plus the freedom of a World State and the world-wide spread of Basic English, it had attained an influence that even the old two-dimensional pictures had never known.

Garrett heard a rich, deep voice behind the door as he knocked. There was a pause, and he held up his plaque for scrutiny through a one-way glass. The door dilated, and as he entered the room's occupant turned the switch on his dictotyper which altered it from recording to turning out a typed script.

"So!" said Hesekth Uranov. "You're S.B.'s newest find. You're the bright boy that's to ride herd on me, huh?"

Uranov represented the new interbred type that was rising to dominance in the world. It was rare by now, of course, to see any sample of such a pure racial type as the sheer Irishness of the black-haired, blue-eyed girl in the liner—doubtless a fortuitous throwback—but it was almost equally rare to see such a successful fusion as Hesketh Uranov. His skin was a golden brown, closest perhaps to the Polynesian, but not exactly that of any pure racial type. His aquiline nose, his thick lips, his slightly slanted eyes seemed not so much a heterogeneous collection of racial fragments as the perfectly right lineaments of a new race.

Garrett was still trying to find the friendly response to this unfriendly greeting when Uranov said, "You drink? I thought not. Historian— However." He up-ended the bottle. "Stay in Sollywood long enough and you'll learn worse than this, my boy. What're you sticking your hand out for? Can't wait to get your researcher's fingers on my script?"

"All I want," said Garrett patiently, "is that bottle." He took it.

After that swig, Uranov looked at him with new respect. "Maybe you're all right. But I doubt it. S.B. sent you."

"Look," said Gan Garrett. "I've seen S.B. for only five minutes. I've heard about you as Metropolis' ace writer for five years. So you have—sixty times twenty-four times three hundred and sixty-five—you have roughly half a million times as much cause to dislike him as I have. But I'll still enter the race with you."

"O.K.," said Uranov. "Don't mind if I bark. I just don't like anybody much these days, which is, of course, the perfect mood in which to approach a script on Devarupa."

"What're you doing to that script?" Garrett sat down, near the bottle. "S.B. babbled something about a woman."

Uranov groaned. "I know. These epics have the highest erotic value of any form of entertainment yet created. You probably know the old varieties of theater. Imagine how a burlesque audience would have reacted if its queen were ten times life size and visible in detail from the top of the gallery. Imagine how the flat film fan would have felt if his glamour girls had had three dimensions and the true color of flesh. So we musn't waste these possibilities and there's got to be a woman. I'm trying to tone her down; just a loyal disciple with a sort of hopeless spiritual love. But S.B.'s got his eye on Astra Ardless for it; and have you ever thought of what it'll be like to tone that last year's space-warmer down?" He took another drink and this time handed over the bottle unasked.

"Garrett," he said, "you're not going to believe this. But in some twisted, crazy, and very damned beautiful way I'm proud of this assignment. Sure, I know, I'm the guy that was going to write for posterity and here I am making a fortune under a dome in Sollywood and drinking my liver out of existence. But some things are still important to me, and Devarupa's one of them. People take him for granted now. They take for granted the whole state of peace that he created. They're forgetting that peace itself is the greatest of all battles. What I want to do—"

The dictotyper pinged. Uranov removed the finished copy, looked at it, and crumpled it up with a curse. Then he smoothed it out again and laid it on his desk. "It might do. I can't write this right; but I'm going to die trying. What I want to stress is his early years. Even before that. I want to show the false peaces in the War of the Twentieth Century, the '19 to '39 gap, for instance. The way the smug sat back and said 'Swell, it's peace, now there's nothing to worry about.' And you stop worrying and you cease to belong to mankind. Then I want to take some of Devarupa's own utterances—the Bombay Document, for example—and show the real fighting strength that's in them. I've got to make these dopes see that pacifism isn't passivism—while S.B.," he added despondently, "bewitches the whole thing up with our darling Astra."

Garrett drank. "I'm with you," he said simply.

"What I'd even like," Uranov went on heatedly, "is to work in a little propaganda at the end on this Martian business—show how a true living peace can function. You know, a sort of 'Join the space crews and see another world' whoozit. And, God, there is something you can get really excited about. To think of those—how many is it, near thirty now?—who've made the landing, accomplished man's impossible dream, and died there, on a bitterer one-way trip than any criminal ever made, all because this peaceful world—"

He broke off as Garrett was reaching for the bottle again. "Sorry. I talk too much. And in another minute you'll be asking me why I don't sign up myself if I feel so strongly. For the matter of that, why don't I? Nice swizard you're wearing there."

"Very. It's a Kubi— Hey! Did you say swizard? Then you know her?"

"Know who?"

"The girl who used to call them swizards when she was little. Black hair. Blue eyes. Funny little nose that tilts up. You know her?"

Uranov frowned. "I know her," he said abstractedly. "Works here in public relations. Fix you up any time, though how you— But what's your swizard made of? Lovestonite?"

"Yes."

"Funny use for it. Why, you don't maybe—" He killed the bottle. "If we're going to get together on this, comrade, you know what we need? A drink. Come on. We're going to paint Sollywood a bright magenta and end up seeing pink swizards. And maybe before the evening's over, we'll even have a talk about lovestonite."

"I should just warn you," said Gan Garrett. "Don't mind if a dagger hits you. It'll be meant for me."

But the next attack was not made with a dagger. It took place hours later when they were leaving the Selene, that resplendent night spot with its exact replica of its famous namesake in Luna City, even down to the longest bar in the universe— a safe enough statement so long as no spaceship had yet managed to return from another planet.

"In a way, you can't blame S.B.," Uranov was saying. This surprising tolerance was the only noticeable effect on him of the evening's liquor. "He's a frustrated creator. He'd flopped as a writer and as a musician before he discovered his executive talents. He hasn't a spark of the creative ability that I used to have or that a man like Mig Valentinez has; but he's got all the urge. And he takes it out in shoving around the ones who can create and then crying, 'Behold my creation!' In a way, it's sad rather than—"

The man appeared out of nowhere. He wore a heavy cloak and was only a black blob in the bright night. The flash came from the core of the blackness of his cloak, and there was no noise with it.

Gan Garrett's eyes blinked as he jumped, his popgun appearing automatically in his hand, and when they opened, the man was gone. Ten minutes of joint search failed to disclose him, though his cloak lay abandoned around the next corner.

"Did you see what he had in his hand?" Uranov asked. It looked like a prop pistol from an historical picture. But it didn't—" He stopped by the wall where the attack had happened, stared, and whistled.

Garrett looked at the charred xyloid.

"Could it—" Uranov groped. "It can't be that . . . that somebody really has found the power of disintegrator guns, like in that world-of-the-future epic I turned out last year?"

Garrett rubbed his cheek. "I felt something. I didn't dodge quite enough to—"

"Look, my boy." Uranov was serious. "I thought it was a gag when you babbled about daggers. I don't know what this lad was playing, but it wasn't nice games. You're the best drinking companion I've found since Schwanberg quit epics to make a hopeless try for Mars; but if I'm to see much more of you, I want to know who's trying to kill you and why."

"So do I," Garrett grunted. "But first"—he played with the swizard—"what do you know about lovestonite?"

"Just enough to worry a little. I know that there's an irrational amount of lovestonite processing going on, and I know Stag Hartle's mixed up in it which means no good. And I know that the . . . that some people I know are concerned about it."

"Can you tell me any more? Or can you put me in touch with anyone who can?"

"A, no. B, yes. This is, of course, all part of your technical-historical research?"

Garrett grinned. "I guess research workers don't go armed, do they? Nor have new lethal weapons tried out on them. Hardly much use to keep up the masquerade for you."

"W.B.I.?"

"Check."

"Come on home with me," Uranov decided suddenly. "God knows what kind of booby trap they may have rigged up where you're staying. You can explain it all right at the studio—we wanted to live together for closer collaboration on the epic. And tomorrow we'll see what we can do about more information. You know Mig Valentinez?"

"I know his work." Garrett sounded a little awed. "He's marvelous."

"I haven't seen him for a couple of months, but I know he was playing around with lovestonite. We can run down there and— But first, comrade, how about a nightcap?"

Garrett woke from a confused dream of a naked Irish girl who was riding tandem on a swizard with a man with a melancholy and wistful smile. The swizard was of the fire-breathing variety, and its breath was searing hot on Garrett's cheek. The cheek still burned when he was wideawake and looking up at the multiracial face of Hesketh Uranov.

"Sleep all right? No hangover?"

"None. But I've got the damnedest sensation here in my cheek—right where whatever it was missed me. Do you suppose it was an atomic weapon, and this is like a radium burn?"

Uranov bent over and stared at the cheek. When he rose he was half-laughing, half-worried. "I don't know what we're getting into," he said. "I should stick to my dictotyper and leave melodrama and lovestonite to the W.B.I. or to the . . . those friends I mentioned. Because this is nuts. Purely nuts."

"Yes? What goes?"

"What you received from the new lethal weapon, comrade, is nothing more nor less than a very nasty patch of sunburn."

II.

Uranov paused on their way to the research lab. "Want to watch 'em shooting? That's usually a thrill to the new visitor."

Garrett rubbed his salved but still burning cheek. "I've got thrills enough."

"Just for a minute. Then you can talk more plausibly when I tell S.B. I've just been showing you around."

A red light glowed in front of one of the studios. Their plaques admitted them to the soundproof observers' gallery. "This is an interior, of course," Uranov explained. "Exteriors are all shot outside under dome, some of them here at the main plant, most of them on the various locations. You probably saw them from the ship?"

Garrett nodded.

"California's amazing enough naturally, and after our landscapers went to work— It's really extraordinary. We can shoot any possible aspect of the world's surface, and we have a condensed replica of every city of any importance, from Novosibirsk to Luna City. Southern California is the world in miniature; destroy the rest of civilization, and an archaeologist could re-create it all from our locations." There was a certain possessive pride in his voice, despite his avowed contempt for Sollywood.

"All the shooting is under dome?"

Uranov nodded. "The cameramen say sunlight through dome is better than direct, and there are never any delays because of weather. The sky clouds over, and your artificial light comes on automatically at exactly the right strength."

Garrett looked down at the shooting interior. To judge from sets and costumes, it was a scene from a glamorous drawing-room comedy—probably the standard plot about the beautiful hostess on the lunar rocket who marries the son of the owner and longs fretfully for her exciting old life until she finds her true self in domesticity. There were only two actors in the scene. The man he recognized as that charmingly suave Eurasian Hartley Liu, but the woman— He glanced at Uranov questioningly.

"Astra Ardless," said Uranov. "Looks older, doesn't she? But wait till you see what those cameras make of her."

She did look older than Garrett had ever seen her on the beam. But that was not surprising; he had fallen adolescently in love with her when she first became famous, and that was almost fifteen years ago. She looked older and not nearly so glamorous, and yet in a strange way more beautiful. There was a quality of resigned sadness about her.

To fans all over the globe, only actors mattered. The heart that pounded at the thought of Astra Ardless or Hartley Liu would never have heard of a writer such as Uranov or even a producer-director such as S.B. And even Garrett, more intelligently perceptive than the average fan, had never realized how outnumbered the actors were on the set.

Two of them, and sixteen cameramen, to say nothing of the assistant technicians and prop men and the sound engineers dimly glimpsed in their niches in the opposite wall. The synchronized cameras all shot the scene at once from their sixteen different angles. Later those sixteen beams would be cast from sixteen similarly placed projectors onto a curtain of Cassellite, that strange, translucent, solid-seeming gas which had made the epics possible.

A slightly false inflection on the part of Astra Ardless' speaking voice, and perhaps one critic in Kamchatka or Keokuk might notice it and observe that Miss Ardless was slipping. One slightly false adjustment on the part of a single technician, and the entire scene would be so much junk.

"Actors don't really count for much, do they?"

"I don't know," said Uranov slowly. "Sometimes I think they're a bunch of built-up parasites, and yet— It's like wondering if an individual counts for much when the World State is so perfect. You get into trouble— But come on. You've seen enough to make talk with S.B. Now let's call on Doc Wojcek."

They had apparently interrupted a scene when they entered the laboratory. There was dead silence. The bald but sturdy-looking scientist fiddled uncomfortably with the articles on his desk, and seemed loath to raise his eyes to the newcomers. At last the sharp-faced man with the brilliant ascot—unusually brilliant even for Sollywood—said, "Hi, Hesky."

"Hi, Stag." There was no friendliness in Uranov's voice.

"S.B. wants to see you."

"I know. Be there in a minute. Just showing Garrett here around the works."

The sharp-faced man rose. His hand rested for a moment palm up on the table. "Well, Doc? All clear?"

"All clear," said Dr. Wojcek hesitantly.

"Then I'll be going. See you around, Hesky."

Something stayed in the room after his departure, an almost physical aura of oppression. "Who was that?" Garrett asked.

"Stag Hartle," Uranov explained. "One of our choicer jackals. Got his name because he started out in Sollywood bootlegging stag epics—you can see the possibilities in them? One of his actresses died of what he put her through—"

"And he never made a one-way trip?"

"Something happened. Strings— Nothing ever proved. Stag knows how to make himself useful. But he's theoretically leading a reformed life now."

Garrett could still see that hand palm up in the light of the laboratory. To the trained eye, the traces of paraderm on the fingers were clearly visible. Those who lead reformed lives do not usually need to conceal their fingerprints.

"I wonder—" said Dr. Wojcek.

"Sorry. I got sidetracked. Dr. Wojcek, this is Gan Garrett. New technical advisor on history. I'm showing him around the plant—thought he'd like to see your setup."

Wojcek nodded. He shrugged his shoulders as though to cast off the burden of Atlas. "Of course," he began, "we don't do any interesting theoretical work here—all purely practical study of needed technical developments. But still we have some odd angles. For instance—" As he spoke, his depression lifted. His absorption in his work outweighed his cares, and he was a brilliant and charming guide through the wonders of the laboratory.

At last, "Do you do much work with lovestonite?" Garrett asked casually.

"Not to speak of," said Dr. Wojcek.

Uranov made a curious gesture with two fingers.

Dr. Wojcek lifted one sparse eyebrow. "But a little," he added. "In fact, I've been carrying on some rather interesting experiments lately. Do you know much about the properties of lovestonite?"

"Very little. I gathered that it had practically none worth speaking about."

"From a commercial point of view, young man, that's true enough. But it does have one interesting characteristic." He led them over to a corner of the laboratory where a dark sheet of vitreous plastic, like the material of the swizard, stood in a frame. Wojcek stationed himself beside it like a lecturer in a class. "Now what, gentlemen, is the speed of light?"

"Three hundred thousand kilometers per second," Garrett answered automatically.

"True, but not wholly true. Three hundred thousand kilometers per second—in what?"

"In what? Why, in air, I suppose."

"To be precise, in a vacuum. For all practical purposes, it is the same in the ordinary atmosphere. And the speed of light is such a convenient constant in theory that we tend to think of it as a constant in fact. But in water, for instance, the speed of light is only two hundred thousand k.p.s., and in carbon disulphide, a mere hundred and twenty thousand."

"And in lovestonite?" Garrett asked.

"In lovestonite, normal untampered-with lovestonite, the speed of light is only seventy-five thousand kilometers per second. Now the differences in these speeds are not noticeable to the naked eye." He passed his arm behind the sheet of lovestonite. The plastic was dark but transparent, like smoked glass. "You perceive, of course, no difference between the parts of my arm behind and outside of this sheet, though actually you see one about one one-billionth of a second later than the other. The difference is large in theory, but negligible in fact.

"However, we have discovered one practical use for this difference. A lens made partly of normal glass and partly of lovestonite produces a very curious photographic effect. The result does not seem out of focus, but somehow just the least bit—how shall I put it—perturbing, *wrong*. We spent months on the exact structure of such a lens, and I think the results have been most satisfactory. You recall the supernatural scenes in 'The Thing from the Past'? Well, their incomparable eeriness which the critics praised so, was due to the use of part-lovestonite lenses." He paused.

"And that's all you know about lovestonite?"

Dr. Wojcek hesitated, and again Uranov gestured. "Well, I . . . I did make an interesting discovery quite by accident. My assistant was carrying on some other work near the lovestonite while I was engaged in some measurements, and we found that an electromagnetic field exerts a startling effect. It varies, of course, with the density of the field and the direction of the lines of force, and we have by no means exhausted our experiments as yet—" He stopped, with a sudden shock of realization.

"Go on."

"Yes— Yes— We have been able to increase the speed of light through lovestonite almost to the normal three hundred thousand, and to reduce it to as low as five thousand. The possibilities are—" He broke off again.

Garrett put his reaction together with the scene they had just interrupted. "So Stag Hartle has given you orders to lay off the lovestonite experiments?"

Dr. Wojcek did not reply with a direct yes or no. "What can I do?" he asked, expecting no answer. "Hartle has influence. My business here is to do what I am told, not to pursue promising lines of experimental theory."

Garrett frowned, thinking over this newest fact on lovestonite, and toyed with his swizard. "It still doesn't help," he thought aloud. "Not obviously. What do you think about these lovestonite mirrors?"

"I've heard they're being manufactured. I can't imagine why; the idea's ridiculous."

"Thanks," said Garrett. "Thanks a lot. This has been a most interesting—well, we'll say visitor's tour."

"And now," said Uranov, "we'll pay our respects to S.B., or he'll be wanting to know how we think we're earning our credits."

"Ah, boys," Sacheverell Breakstone greeted them. "Glad to see you. Getting acquainted with the place, Garrett? Coming to understand how we do things here?

Fine," he went on before Garrett could answer. "Glad to hear it. And now to business. You may have heard I'm going away for a while next week. We're shooting the big scenes in 'Lurazar' on location on the Moon. I think they need my personal supervision. Astra finishes her current epic today, and as soon as we can get under way— But what I wanted to say: I expect to see a shooting script when I get back. Stick close to him, Garrett. Don't let him idle. And I don't want either of you leaving Metropolis until then. You, Uranov, pay special attention to that suggestion of Garrett's about working in a woman—rather Astra's type as he described her. Maybe she could motivate him. Supposing—I'm just groping with words, you understand—she might be a Siberian general who—"

Hesketh Uranov listened patiently while S.B. twisted some of the most stirring events in history into a vehicle for Astra Ardless. Garrett frowned to himself. If his orders were to confine himself to the Metropolis lot, and he was bound to subordinate his real job to his apparent one, though he hardly needed to avoid suspicion any longer when knife throwers and practitioners with secret weapons—

"That'll be all," S.B. concluded. "I always find these conferences stimulating. You understand? Free interchange of minds. And I'll want that script when Astra and I get back from the Moon. Meanwhile, you stick here. Both of you."

"Mr. Breakstone," Garrett asked with academic diffidence, "who is designing the sets for the Devarupa epic?"

"Tentatively Benson." S.B. did not sound contented.

"If I may offer technical advice, it seems to me that Emigdio Valentinez's knowledge of the period and great artistic ability—"

"I know. I know. I'd mortgage half the studio to get Valentinez for the job. But he's gone hermit on us. He won't listen to—"

"He might listen to me," Garrett lied quietly. "We're old friends. Don't you think it might be worth our while for me to run down to his place? Uranov can drive me, and we can work on the way?"

Breakstone grunted. "Fine. Fine. But remember the deadline on that script."

Uranov's two-seater copter was laden with swank gadgetry, most of which served to indicate his position in Sollywood rather than any practical need. It rode well, however, and made the trip to Valentinez's beach retreat in about ten minutes.

"I hate to drop in on Mig announced," said Uranov, "but he hasn't a televisor or even a blind phone, and he won't open mail. He said he was coming out here to solve a problem—artistic, I think, rather than personal—and the hell with all the complications of progress. That was a month or two ago and nobody's heard a word from him since. Neat trick of yours, by the way, to get S.B. to turn us loose."

"We might bring it up at that," said Garrett. "Valentinez would be ideal to design that epic."

"Bring up your lovestonite problem first. If you mention S.B., he's apt to walk out on you flat. Temperamental, I suppose, but still a nice guy. I think Astra's still carrying a torch for him."

"So? That's a bit of Sollywood gossip that never got on the telecasts."

"Which reminds me: I haven't forgotten about your swizard girl. We're having dinner with her tonight, if we get through here in time."

"I wish you hadn't told me. I'll be thinking about that dinner instead of lovestonite. But what do you think Valentinez can tell us?"

"I don't know. I only know that it seemed to tie in somehow with this problem of his. And any lead that you can get—"

The copter dropped straight down onto the rolling dunes. It might have been a time machine that had carried them out of the reach of all signs of progress. Nothing but the ramshackle studio indicated the presence of man, and even that might have come bodily out of some far earlier century.

"Mig!" Uranov shouted. "Hi, Mig! Get out the glasses! Company!"

No answer came from the wind-worn wooden studio. Garrett and Uranov plowed up the hillock to the door and paused to empty sand from their shoes. Uranov beat a rhythmic tattoo on the weather-beaten door. There was still no answer.

Garrett pushed at the door, and old-fashioned hinged affair. It swung open. The only trace of progress inside the studio was the hundreds of microbooks and their projector. There were shelves upon shelves of the older paper books, too, and canvases and an easel and brushes and paint pots and rags and everything but Emigdio Valentinez.

He heard Uranov's puzzled voice from behind his shoulder. "We'd have heard about it if he'd come back to town. The man's news."

"He's probably out painting someplace. You're the one that knows him; you go scout around. I'll wait here in case you miss him and he comes back."

Uranov nodded. "I'll be glad to. I can see how Mig feels about this stretch of coast. You see nothing but sand and ocean and your soul begins to come back inside you. Maybe with a shack like this I could write the—" He shook himself and said, "See you later."

Garrett was glad to be rid of a witness. Even the cynical Uranov might not appreciate the ethics of W.B.I. work. To find what has to be found, that is the important thing. The moral problem involved in the guest's right to search his host's belongings is secondary. Supposing Valentinez, when he did appear, declined to talk of lovestonite? Best to forestall that by learning what one could to start with.

It was a distracting search. Valentinez's library was a great temptation, and his own canvases were an absolute barrier to serious detective work. In no gallery had Garrett ever seen a Valentinez exhibit like this, and everything from the hastiest sketches to a magnificent and carefully finished sandscape bore the complete authority of the master.

Two things especially Garrett could gladly have spent long hours contemplating. One was a very rough crayon sketch for a self-portrait; there was no mistaking the gentle melancholy of that smiling face. The other was a half-finished composition of sun and sea and rock and algae, which even in its imperfect state seemed to sum up all the beauty of a world without man's refinements—and yet a beauty that existed only because a great man could understand and perfect it.

But Garrett resolutely tore his eyes from these two fragmentary masterpieces and went on with his search. He had covered the whole studio when he realized what was wrong—terribly wrong. There was not the slightest hint of anything concerned with lovestonite.

His own swizard was the only bit of lovestonite in the room. The random notes and scribbled jottings filed haphazardly among canvases and furniture dealt with formulas for paint, possible new developments in epic sets, an essay on the problems of peace, the possibilities of revival of old-style cookery, the latest discoveries in radioactivity, revisions in the orbit calculations of the doomed Martian spaceships—everything under and around the sun—for Valentinez had the da Vinci type of creative mind—save lovestonite. Even the all-embracing library seemed to contain no books on the newer plastics, the clays of Australia, or the varying transmission speeds of light.

Yet Valentinez was said to have been working on lovestonite. And working where? There were no laboratory facilities here.

Then Garrett looked out of the rear window and noticed the blackening of the sand there. It had all been carefully raked over, but some large structure had been burned to the ground. A laboratory? A laboratory where Emigdio Valentinez had discovered—what?

His mind whirling with a half-resolved hypothesis, Garrett returned to contemplation of his two favorites among the pictures. That self-portrait was extraordinary. Partly in that it did not portray the artist as artist, no brush and palette to label it, partly in that it seemed so much freer, more unconstrained than a self-portrait generally managed to be.

He picked it up. On the reverse was marked in red crayon capitals LVSTITE.

Garrett clicked his tongue against his teeth. He went over to a pile of other sketches and found what he thought he'd remembered seeing—another self-portrait. Good—could a Valentinez help being good?—but far inferior—conventional in pose and somewhat stilted in treatment. He turned it over. On its reverse was crayoned MIRROR.

He sat down. With one flash, the whole business clicked into place. Everything fitted—for a start at least. Valentinez had come here to work on a problem and had thought to solve it with lovestonite. The speed of light in lovestonite is variable; Dr. Wojcek hoped eventually to reduce it almost to zero at will.

Suppose the problem was that of self-portraiture. Artist have previously worked with mirror arrangements. That has disadvantages. One, you have to paint yourself working; you model and paint the model at once. Two, either you see a mirror-image of yourself, which is not as others see you; or you use a complex arrangement of mirrors which gives you a direct as-seen-by-others image, but confuses your movements terribly. When you move your right hand, say, and your mirror image moves, not its left, but its own right, you grow so confused that it affects your muscular co-ordination.

But suppose you can at will vary the speed of light through lovestonite. You reduce the speed almost to zero. You stand in front of the lovestonite. Your image enters it, but is not visible yet on the other side; will not be visible for some indefinite length of time. Then reverse the slab of lovestonite. Control it with an electromagnet. Let that light, which is your image, come through to you under your control—

A brilliant solution of a technical problem of painting. Fully worthy of the

great Valentinez. But it did not explain the sudden increase in lovestonite manufacture. It did not explain why Valentinez's laboratory had been burned down and
all traces of his researches destroyed. It did not explain why someone wished to
wipe out Gan Garrett, nor why Uranov was so long finding the painter. Garrett
began to feel a terrible conviction that no one would ever find Emigdio Valentinez
alive. He began to fear the report that Uranov would bring back.

The door creaked open on its metal hinges. Garrett looked up reluctantly.
"You didn't find him," he started to say, but the words stopped short. For the
man in the doorway was not Uranov, but that notable jackal Stag Hartle.

A faint rising hum told of the departure of Uranov's copter.

"Nice of you to bring yourself down here," said Stag Hartle. In his hand was what
looked like a prop pistol. "It's been kind of difficult getting at you in Sollywood.
It's quiet and uninterrupted here since your friend cleared out."

"Friend," Garrett repeated bitterly. It hurt. In the past twenty-four hours he
had come to like the multiracial epic writer.

"He has good sense," said Hartle. "I gave him a hint of what we'd planned for
you and wondered did he want to be included in. He was a bright boy; he decided no."

Garrett let his hand rest in his pocket. The popgun which the girl had so de-
rided was reassuringly capable of putting this jackal instantly out of action. But
there were things to find out first. "So you're going to kill me, just as you killed
Emigdio Valentinez?"

"Not just the same. No. We've got our own plans for you."

"Then you admit killing the greatest painter of our day?"

"Why not?" Hartle asked casually. "You're not telling anybody." Then he added
more loudly, "Come on in, boys."

Garrett's cheek smarted; the effect of the ointment was wearing off. As his
night-acquired sunburn tingled, he glanced at Hartle's prop pistol. More of the
picture began to shape up as clearly as though beams were focusing on a Cassellite
screen in front of him. "Valentinez had perfected the control of lovestonite," he
said slowly. "He was fool enough to show his device to you."

A half dozen men filed into the room. They were a crummy lot—the scrapings
of the dives in Luna City, or those outcasts that gravitate to extra work in
Sollywood as they used to drift into the Foreign Legion. They all held pistols.

Garrett lounged back, both hands comfortably in his pockets. His left encountered the knife which had missed him on his entrance to Metropolis Pictures.
Yes, there was even that left if everything else failed him, though if he could bring
himself to use it— "Valentinez thought," he went on calmly, "that he had simply
invented a device for self-portraiture. You realized that what he had actually created was a gadget for storing sunlight and releasing it at will in any desired strength.
You—or someone behind you—began the processing of vast amounts of
lovestonite. Metal and explosives are unobtainable for weapons; but the mirrors
that you have manufactured, when the right electromagnetic hookup is attached
to them, will arm a host that can set a city ablaze and blind its every defender.
There are tiny lovestonite 'mirrors' in those pistols. They've been exposed to
sunlight; the trigger releases the stored energy."

"Smart, ain't he, boys?" Stag Hartle demanded. "Figured it out all by himself, too."

Garrett's hand was firm on his popgun. Uranov's copter was gone, but there must be another outside that had brought this crew. If he could keep talking, build to a moment of distraction— "But why?" he wondered aloud. "You've found a new weapon that can be manufactured without overt violation of the law. But why? The quantities you've been turning out—what mob are you arming, and for what purpose?"

"For a purpose that good little boys from the W.B.I. shouldn't ought to understand. Because you're the backbone of this cockeyed peace that's sapping the guts of the world. Hell, there ain't no fun in life now. But there will be, brother. Christmas on wheels, but there will be!"

A luxurious gloat spread over Hartle's narrow face. His self-satisfaction provided the one necessary instant of diversion. For the first time, his lovestonite pistol was not pointed in Garrett's face.

No frontiersman in an historical epic of the Old West was quicker on the draw than a good W.B.I. man. The anaesthetic gun was in Gan Garrett's hand now, and trained neatly on Hartle. "You realize," said Garrett with dry factuality, "that the comatin crystals would penetrate before you could raise your weapon. I've learned as much as I need at the moment, and thank you, Hartle. Now I'm leaving—and I wouldn't try to stop me."

His mind was clear and cool. He could even reflect that that last sentence of his was itself something of an Irish bull. He deliberately turned his back on Hartle; he was reasonably sure that a lovestonite blast would have little effect though thicknesses of clothing, and he felt that Hartle's mysterious "plans" for him did not include anything so direct as another dagger.

His trained muscles carried him with rapid deftness. He was past the crew while they still goggled at their leader's discomfiture. One remained. In the doorway stood a huge bulk of a man with a flowing blond beard. Gan Garrett squeezed his trigger. The pellet made a little plop as it penetrated clothing and skin. Blond Beard opened his mouth, half moved his own pistol hand, and then crumpled.

Seconds made the difference here, and the huge bulk of Blond Beard caused the seconds' delay. His body, even unconscious, still blocked the doorway, and Garrett had to pause, to gather himself for a leap. In that momentary pause, he felt a sharp burning pang in his right hand. He did not quite drop his popgun, but his hand sank. Wiry fingers clutched his wrist and forced it down still farther.

He twisted to glimpse his antagonist. It was a squat and extremely hairy oriental—probably an Ainu—whose sinewy arms were devoting their utmost effort to turning him to face Hartle.

Garrett's uninjured left hand drew out the knife. He still did not know within himself whether he could use it. But to free himself now, when so much, the very structure of the peace itself might depend on his use of what he had learned here—

He heard Hartle's sardonic laugh. "So the W.B.I. boys don't mind a little killing so long as their guys that do it. Garrett, you don't know how much easier you're making our job."

Garrett's body twisted with the Ainu's like one sculptural mass. The muscles of his left arm tightened. Then a sudden jerk brought him face to face with Hartle. He saw the flicker of pleasure on the man's face and the slight movement of his pistol hand.

The world exploded around him. The sight of his eyes flared up to searing incandescence and then went out. He was in blackness filled with red and green glints of chaotic vividness. The skin of his face ached with burning pain. His mind whirled, and he felt himself spinning into limitless space.

He could see again when he regained consciousness. It must have been a conservative release of sunpower; a lovestonite pistol could, he was sure, induce permanent blindness, and possibly much more. He was surprised that Stag Hartle had showed him such mercy. He was, in fact, surprised to find himself alive at all. But he was most surprised to find himself where he was.

He had seen these clean, sunny, and terrible empty white cells often enough before. A W.B.I. man makes arrests and often finds it necessary later to visit his prisoners. But he does not expect to find himself in prison.

The doctor said, "Conscious now? Good. Feeling better? No, don't touch your face. That's a nasty burn, but it'll heal up. In time for your one-way trip."

Gan Garrett gasped. For a minute he thought the red-and-green-speckled blackness was coming back. "One-way trip—" he fumbled out. "What—" But the doctor had already left.

Garrett knew the layout of these cells. He found his way to the tablet dispenser and swallowed a mouthful of condensed food. Damn these dispensers! No need now for a guard to bring meals. A guard could be questioned. But instead he must sit here wondering—

Had he indeed stabbed that Ainu? In some sort of muscular spasm after unconsciousness? If so— He straightened his shoulders and took a deep breath. The laws were good. Man must not kill man. If he had done so, no matter under what circumstances, then a one-way trip was his only possible reward. But if he had been somehow framed by Stag Hartle— Could that have been what the jackal had meant by "what we'd planned for you"—

There was the buzz which meant that the cell door was being dilated for an official visitor. The man who came in was very young, very alert, and very precise. He said, "Garrett?"

"I guess so. I'm not too sure of anything."

"Breckenridge. I've been appointed to defend you before the judicial council. I might as well warn you to start with that I have no hope whatsoever." He made the statement with efficient impartiality.

"That's cheery. But first of all—what are you defending me for?"

"Killing. It's a one-way trip for sure. But if you'll tell me your story—"

"First tell me the prosecution."

"Very simple. And I may add, convincing. One Stag Hartle—not too good a witness, I know, but plentifully corroborated—was worried about the continued silence of the painter Emigdio Valentinez and took a searching party down to his beach studio. They did not find Valentinez, but they did find an unidentified Ainu lying dead on the sand, stabbed through the back. You lay beside him; apparently you had fainted from the shock of killing him and lain on the beach long enough to acquire a startlingly severe sunburn. The prosecution's theory is that you disposed of Valentinez, perhaps into the ocean, and that this unknown was his bodyguard, or perhaps a mere tramp who saw you and so had to be finished off."

"Nuts," said Gan Garrett. "If that's all they've got—"

"The Ainu's blood was all over you—spurted out of his back when he was stabbed. Positions of stains indicate your left arm did the stabbing. Besides, there are your prints all over the knife handle. Why on earth couldn't you have had the sense to use paraderm?" the defense lawyer moaned sadly.

The trial took fifteen minutes. In the two days before it, Gan Garrett had worked harder than ever before in his life. He had managed to get an interview with the police chief himself, and spent an hour desperately trying to rip holes in the prosecution's case, with no success whatsoever. In all his cases, the chief had never had a murderer before; he was loath to relinquish this one. And if a man can't convince his own attorney of his of his innocence—

Through his lawyer he sent desperate but restrained appeals to Hesketh Uranov and Sacheverell Breakstone. He had no answer at all from the writer, which confirmed him in his growing belief that Uranov was a traitor rather than a weakling and had deliberately lured him down to the lonely beach studio. S.B. spent a half-hour with him, told him three new fictional sub-plots to the Devarupa epic—just groping with words, you understand—wondered if he could recommend another historical technician, regretted that he himself could not attend the trial because he'd be on the Moon by then, and heard not a word of Garrett's defense or his accusations against Hartle.

Garrett knew that there was no hope in appealing to the secretary who had sent him on this job or to the W.B.I. itself. The standing rule was "Get yourself out." At last a sort of stoic resignment settled on him. He spent the last twelve hours before the trial preparing a minute precis of everything he had learned about lovestonite, Valentinez, and Stag Hartle. His lawyer promised to see that it was forwarded to the Secretary of Allocation.

His trial began at 14:15, on a fine sunny California afternoon. At 14:30 it was over. At 15:45 he was looking at the one-man rocket through a hazy mist of the beginning effects of dormitol. By 16:00 the lid was down, the pressure screws turned, and Gan Garrett was ready to set out on the one-way trip.

Somewhere in Sollywood Stag Hartle was probably celebrating.

III.

The one-way trip is a form of punishment—or penalty is perhaps the better word—unique in the world's history. But it evolved logically and inevitably from the fact of a world at peace, even if the world itself had paradoxically evolved as a direct consequence of the War of the Twentieth Century.

At any time in the world's history before the year 2000, the voice of Devarupa would have gone unheard—unheard, that is, even as the voice of Christ went unheard by a nominally Christian world devoted to greed and murder. Only after the total destruction wrought by that world-wide and century-long war could man have listened seriously to the true message of peace.

The world had first heard of Devarupa when India was being overrun by both sides during the last vicious years of the German-Japanese War. The official Domei and DNB dispatches slurred over or perverted his acts; but the legend had seeped through somehow and spread over the world, the legend of that one province which had finally succeeded in practicing in its perfection the traditional doctrine of nonresistance, so successfully that each horde of invaders in turn at last drew back with almost supernatural awe.

But that was a minute island of success. Not until after the Revolt of the Americas, when a united North and South America arose in glorious daring to cast off and destroyed their masters—already weakened by their own Kilkenny-cattery—did the teachings of Devarupa begin to spread.

Who or what he was, it is impossible now to say. He was the second coming of Christ; he was a latter-day John the Baptist; he was a prophet of Allah; he was the Messiah; he was an avatar of Vishnu; he was an old god returned; he was a new god born; he was all the gods; he was no god.

All these things have been said, and all are still believed. For every religion accepted Devarupa, as god or as prophet; and Devarupa rejected none of them. To many of the irreligious he became a new religion; to others he represented only the deepest greatness of mankind, and as such was even more holy.

What religion he himself professed cannot now be historically determined; each church has certain proof that he belonged to it. But all churches, and all those without the churches, agree on the doctrines that he taught.

There was nothing novel about these. Christ or Buddha or Kung-fu-tse had said them all. But Devarupa was aided by the time in which he spoke; and by the fact that his own mixed heritage enabled him to fuse, as none other had ever done, the practical vigor and solemnity of western religion with the sublime mysticism of the Orient.

The weary world at last truly and sincerely wanted peace. The teachings of Devarupa showed it the way. And from this fortunate meeting of the time and the man came the World State, the world peace, and, inevitably, the one-way trip.

For if man may not kill man—and no Devarupian teaching is more basic than this—surely the State may not do so. And yet man is but slowly perfectible; even a weary and repentant world contains its individual fiends. There must be some extreme penalty for the most extreme offenses.

Life imprisonment, even when it came to be enforced literally, proved unavailing. The prisoner's mind inevitably grows to the shape of one purpose: to destroy his bars. Segregation, in something like a humane and idealized version of the old system of penal colonies without their imperialist element, seemed promising for a while. The independent state of segregates on Madagascar was apparently a complete success until that black year of '73 and the invasion of the African mainland.

Again the coincidence of time was fortunate, for the first rocket reached the Moon in '74, and in '75 Bright-Varney conceived the one-way trip.

The State may not kill, but it must dispose of certain individuals. Then ship them off into space. Put them in one-man nondirigible rockets, with a supply of condensed food and oxygen corresponding to their calculated normal life span, and send them forth on indeterminate journeys.

Most of these rockets became satellites of the Earth. Some chanced to enter the orbit of attraction of the Moon. And a few went off into the unknown reaches of space. Science-fiction writers were fond of the plot of a one-way tripper as the first man to set foot on an alien planet.

For, despite the discovery of the spaceship, the Solar System remained unexplored. Only the Moon and Mars had been reached, and only the Moon had been developed. For the exploratory voyages to Mars had themselves been one-way trips of the most fatal sort.

There had been five of these voyages, and thirty fine men had been lost on them in vain. The ships had landed; that much was almost certain from astronomical calculation and observation. But there had been no return. The ships could not carry enough fuel for a two-way trip; and a small crew could not maintain itself long enough on the planet to accumulate fuel from the known resources there present. Until ships could be built with greater fuel capacity, or enough men jolted themselves from their lethargy of peace, the farther reaches of space would be known only to those who never returned.

The possibility that a deliberately one-way rocket might find a strange landing place had been considered by the planners. As a result, the nose was equipped with repulsion jets which would function automatically upon sufficiently close contact with a larger body to effect a safe landing, and the equipment of the rockets included a pressure-regulating breathing suit and indestructible materials with which to leave a record for future explorers.

There were even microbooks in the rocket, with a small pocket-model viewer; there was hardly space for a projector. Every comfort of life, in fact, except companionship—which meant, to a man of a world believing so firmly and truly in the brotherhood of man, except life itself.

A nineteenth-century poet, still read not only by scholars, wrote of "the Nightmare Life-in-Death Who thicks man's blood with cold." And was this Life-in-Death who had replaced Death as the State's reward to malefactors.

Gan Garrett woke feeling as refreshed, after the dormitol, as a ten-year-old on a summer morning when school was over. He started to spring carefree to his feet, ready to begin a vigorous day, and only when his movements floated him about free of gravity did he realize his situation.

This brought gravity enough to his thoughts, if not to his body. The days before the trial had gone by too fast for him to attain any true perception of what was happening. And there had always been the hope that something—

But there was no hope now. Nothing at all forever any more. Nothing but coursing through space in this rocket until the carefully calculated end of his allotted days, a Vanderdecken of the spaceways.

There would be others out here, too, others sealed in their rocketlets, cut off forever from communication with each other, going their several courses, yes, even when the inhabitant lay—or rather floated—dead and the rocket moved on forever in whatever path the chance combination of forces had decreed for it. Space zombies, moving bodies with the souls dead within them.

These were not cheery thoughts for waking. He breakfasted off the proper average ration of concentrates, and washed them down—to his great surprise and pleasure—with a swig of first-rate brandy, which he was sure was not standard one-way equipment.

He wondered how long it had been since the take-off. Time obviously had no direct meaning for him any longer, but he still wondered. He did not know what the standard dose of dormitol for the occasion was; he might have been asleep anywhere from an hour to a week. He tried to judge by his unshaven cheeks; but his beard was so light and slow-growing that he could conclude nothing. Nor did he know the rate of the rocket. Had he already settled into a cirucumterrestrial orbit? Or was he one of the few who had excitingly escaped the Earth's grasp and shot onward into the unknown? Might he—

That was the one hope. The one notion to cling to, to make life valuable. He treasured it, but even a prospect as enthralling as that of being the Columbus of an alien planet must fight a losing battle against pure ennui.

His chronometer had run down during his sleep. (He might have deduced something from that, but he could not remember, in the recent confusion, when he had last wound it.) He did not bother to rewind it. What were hours and minutes in this temporal vacuum?

He ate when he was hungry, wondering if his stomach obeyed the calculated averages. Supposing he should overeat and be doomed to the death of starvation? But he ate by instinct nonetheless. He read occasionally, he maddened himself with the small stock of cards and puzzles, he slept when he wanted to—which was a great deal of the time. He constructed fantasies of how he would conquer the alien planet single-handed.

Finally, hours or days or weeks after he first awoke, he went back to the brandy bottle which he had hardly touched since that breakfast. He finished it almost at a gulp and threw a magnificent party in which he entertained in his narrow quarters all the most enjoyable people he had ever known and finally retired to the floating couch, where he made some momentously significant discoveries as to the erotic importance of gravity.

Then the repulsion jets automatically blasted and the rocket braked to a safe landing on the alien planet. He donned his breathing suit and, tenderly holding the hand of the swizard girl, he opened the lock and led her forth to be the queen of his alien empire.

The strong, pure oxygen of the suit, headier than the aërous mixture circulated in the rocket, sobered him. The swizard girl vanished, and so did his delusions of conquering magnificence. But drunk or sober, he was indisputably stepping forth from the one-way rocket onto the barren soil of an alien world.

It is reported by one of the older poets that stout Cortez—by whom he doubtless means stout Balboa—with eagle eyes stared at the Pacific, and all his men looked at each other with a wild surmise. This is a somewhat more plausible account of the discovery of a new world than that of a composer of much the same period, who represents Vasco da Gama, upon his discovery of India, as bursting into a meltingly noble tenor aria.

Words do not come, let alone song, even if your breathing suit permitted you to utter them. "A wild surmise" is the exactly right phrase for the magnificent bewilderment that seizes you.

Not quite consciously, Gan Garrett checked the readings of the various gauges on his arm. Gravity low, temperature very low, atmosphere nonexistent. He scanned the pitted desert on which he had landed, noted the curious, sharp outlines of the jagged rocks, the complete absence of erosion on an airless world. The bright cold light turned the desert scene into one of those vividly unreal landscapes which the closed eyes sometimes present to the half-sleeping mind, or into a painting by that eccentric twentieth-century master Salvador Dali.

The light—Gan Garrett tilted back his head, and the moon shone so brightly into his visioplate as almost to blind him. It was an enormous, titanic moon, of curiously familiar outlines, and its light, he calculated roughly, was a good twenty times as brilliant as earthly moonlight. He turned to the filing cabinet of his memory and tried to recall a planet that possessed a moon like that. Certainly none in the Solar System. And, therefore—

The thermocells of his suit did not prevent a chill from coursing along his spine. An extrasystemic planet— The men of Earth still wondered if they could accomplish translunar trips, if they could some day safely reach Mars. And he, the outcast, the one-way tripper—

He began the casting up of hasty plans, and wished that he had left just a little of that brandy. This sudden sobriety was uncomfortable.

He knew scientists who would tell him flatly that a planet without atmosphere is incapable of sustaining life, that he must be alone on this cold spinning desert world. But to say that life can only be the carbon-nitrogen-and-oxygen-sustained life which we know had always seemed to him anthropocentric stupidity. There might be intelligent life here which he could not even recognize as such—worse yet, which could not recognize him.

He would have to base himself on the rocket, and from there conduct carefully plotted tours of exploration until he could discover—what? At least he had many many Earth-years yet to do it in. Should he start now, or wait for the sun, which would reduce the wear on his thermocells? Now, at night, he could at least attempt to draw some conclusion as to his whereabouts from a study of the sky. He would need first of all to refresh his memory more accurately from a couple of microbooks. Then—

He was starting back for the lock of the rocket when he saw them. The suit was not wired for sound; he could not hear what must have been their heavily clumping approach. For they were in suits not basically dissimilar to his in principle, as best one could judge, though of fantastically cut design like nothing seen on Earth.

They, or their suits at least, were android. Bipeds with arms. They showed no signs of either hostility or friendliness. They simply advanced, and a detachment of two or three moved between him and the rocket.

His mind raced. Men—or things—in suits on an airless planet meant one of two things: survivors of an elder race, driven to an artificial underground or doomed existence by the deaëration of the planet and venturing forth thus protected on its surface; or explorers, rocket visitants like himself, but from what strange world? Here in the alien void to meet yet other aliens—

He was outnumbered. And worse, he was unarmed, without even his W.B.I. weapon; and it was doubtful if the alien explorers adhered to anything like the code of Devarupa.

But they made no move to harm him. They simply encircled him. Their heavy awkward bodies moved with surprising agility—a clue that they, too, came from a world of heavier gravity. They flowed about him in utter silence, like an ameba engulfing a meal. Then they flowed off again, away from the rocket, and Gan Garrett perforce flowed in their midst.

Garrett had once seen at the museum a showing of the silent flat pictures which were the seed from which epics were to grow. This procession was like that, save that the silent movement was smooth and unjerking, and as unreal as those relics of the past. It was like a continuation of his brandy dream, without its fine exaltation.

He flowed along lightly with the alien creatures, across the barren ground and on into an equally barren but more civilized region. There were roads here, and domes. Survivors of the elder race, then, in all probability, rather than explorers. Somehow that made them more reassuring. Aliens upon the alien world, alienness squared, so to speak, would be too much.

The men under the dome wore no suits. He had though "men" rather than "creatures" involuntarily. For they were exceedingly like men. Their costumes were strange, their hair was weirdly and—he guessed—symbolically arranged, and the tint of their skins ranged through half a dozen unearthly shades; but men they did seem to be. They talked to each other, and he wished he were adept at lip reading. The sounds looked not unlike earthly ones in formation.

Then he was led through a hall and into a small room, where only half a dozen of his captors followed. And there he decided that this was merely a continuation of the brandy dream after all.

For there, facing him, sat a woman identical in every feature with the girl who used to call them swizards.

She made a calmly efficient gesture and said something. His suited guards withdrew. Numbly, his mind aswirl, he snagged the ring of his right glove on the hook at his belt and jerked off the glove. Now with a hand capable of free manipulation he could undo his other vents.

The gesture had bared his identification bracelet, and the lovestonite plesiosaur dangling from it. His eyes had never left the woman, and now, even with his scant ability at lip reading, he could swear that she exclaimed, "The swizard! It's you!" and he thought she added, "Well, I'll be damned."

When he had got his helmet off, the girl was extending to him what looked like an ordinary bottle of terrene brandy, such as he had had on the trip. "Here," she said in perfectly familiar speech. "Hesketh said you like this. That's why he had one smuggled into the rocket for you. He tried to smuggle in one of your popguns,

but they're impossible to get hold of. Drink it up. And leave me a drop. But you—
I can't get over it. If it wasn't for the swizard I'd think you had a double. The nice
prim academician—"

"Look," said Gan Garrett. "This isn't real. It can't be." But the brandy undeniably was. "Will you tell me what's going on? And while you're at it, you might
please fix that screw at the back. I'm not used to these things."

"Sure," said the girl. Her hands were nimble. "Well," she said from behind his
back, "Hesketh told us that a W.B.I. man was being framed into a one-way trip
and there wasn't any legal hope of saving him. So we—"

"Wait a minute. Questions first. Where am I? Or before that—more important question—what's your name?"

She came back in front of him, and he shucked himself out of the suit. "Maureen
Furness. I'm in charge of public relations at Metropolis—and other things." The
skin crinkled around her blue eyes. "I'm glad it's important."

"Maureen .. I like it. We can discuss the Furness part later. Now where am I?"

"On the Moon, of course. Didn't you recognize it?"

Garrett kicked himself. The relative gravity, the absence of atmosphere, the
pitted desert— "But I've never been here before, and what with rockets and
dormitol and the vanishing of all sense of time, I—"

Maureen laughed. It was a good, clear laugh. "So you thought you were an
interplanetary discoverer? Fun. And what on Earth—or off it—did you think we
were?"

"Things," he confessed.

"Swell. Maw Riin, the Wicked Queen of Alpha Centauri. I love the role."

"But the Moon," he began. "The Moon doesn't have a satel— Oh—" he ended
lamely, remembering the familiar shape of its outlines.

"Of course. When we're facing away from the Sun, the Earth looks like an
enormous moon. Amazing effect, isn't it?"

"And how did I get here and what are you doing and— I never heard of a one-
way trip ending on the Moon before."

"It never did. This wasn't any accident. But the engineer who fires off the one-
way rockets is one of us. He aimed it here. We not only wanted to save you from
the frame-up. We thought a trained W.B.I. man might come in very useful in the
next few days on the Moon."

"You keep saying we. But just who are 'we'?"

Maureen's face grew grave. "We started out as a joke, and now it looks as
though we may mean the salvation of Earth. We . . . well, I guess you'd call us a
secret society. We don't have a name, and we don't have a ritual or fancy officers;
but that's what we are. I don't know if Hesketh ever mentioned or hinted at us?"

"No." But now Garrett understood Uranov's several cryptic allusions to "some
people he knew," and the signals with which he had induced Dr. Wojcek to speak
freely.

"It was Mig Valentinez who invented us, though he was usually too wrapped
up with some artistic or scientific project to take much part. But he felt that the
peace was going stale. That people were beginning to accept it as something to
wallow in rather than something to keep fighting for. So he founded his crusaders,

to keep fighting the little things, to keep alive against the small violations of Devarupa's thought, the petty inhumanities of man to man—maybe even do a little propaganda and build to where people could finally unite and fight in something like the Martian project.

"Then a little while after Mig went away to be a hermit, we stumbled on something big: the lovestonite business. Hesketh says that's where you come in, and you know a lot about it. Right?"

"I've gathered some. I know what the weapon is and how it works and what Stag Hartle is up to and why Valentinez was killed."

"You're sure he was?"

"Hartle admitted it."

"He was a good guy, that Mig—" Maureen said tenderly. "Well, anyway, you know enough for background now."

"Except what you're doing here. Oh, that's right. S.B. said something about coming up here with Astra Ardless and a shooting company."

"Yes." Maureen's voice was harsh. "And that didn't sound funny to you?"

"No. Should it have? Oh— What Uranov told me about locations—"

"Exactly. There are in California landscaped locations under dome for every possible type of setting, including lunar. So why should S.B. go to the expense of toting a vast number of extras and all his equipment up here to shoot the picture under less favorable conditions? Except for documentaries, nobody's made location trips in decades."

"Then you think—"

"We think this is what it's all been building up to. He's ready for his big coup. His first blow is going to be here on the Moon."

"Then Hartle's here?"

"Hartle, hell. S.B. Didn't you realize that Hartle was just a stooge? This whole lovestonite racket has been S.B. from the beginning."

Garrett took more brandy. "All right," he said. "S.B. is set to blow the top off of things, and we're going to stop him. Do I count as one of 'we' now?"

"You do," said Maureen.

"Then what's my first duty?"

"Look. This takes a little explaining. The boys that brought you in and the ones you saw outside are us. But there's a lot more extras here, and they're not here to function as extras. What they are is S.B.'s mercenaries.

"You noticed the fantastic make-up? They're all supposed to be natives of Mars when the first spaceship arrived, and nobody but a producer would think of shooting a Martian picture on a lunar landscape but the public'll never know the difference and that's hardly the point now, anyway. But in that getup there's no recognizing individuals, and we don't wear our bracelets most of the time. So a handful of us are going to slip into the dome where S.B. is staying—with Astra installed as empress-elect. We'll seem to be just part of his army."

"And then—"

"We'll have a council of war tonight and get that straight. Hesketh and I are in the party and two others. Want to make it five?"

"What do you think?"

"Good. That's settled. Now come and meet us."

As she rose, Garrett gently thrust her back into the chair. "Just a minute. The Secretary of Allocation gave me this swizard to use in starting conversations about lovestonite. I'm not apt to find that necessary any more. You like swizards. Want it?"

"A Kubicek? You're giving me a Kubicek swizard? And do I want it?"

He detached the swizard from his identification bracelet and fastened it onto hers. As he leaned over her, her lips met him halfway. There was a little more than gratitude in the kiss.

Maureen eventually leaned back and ran a straightening hand through her rumpled black hair. "And, by the way," she said, "what's *your* name?"

Gan Garrett listened to his fellow extras:

"He's what we've needed all along—one stong man to tell us what's what."

"Sure. That's the hell of the State. There's a lot of guys running it and who are they and who cares?"

"And what are they running it for? Peace—nuts!"

"What's peace? Blood and steel, that's what we need."

"You don't draw blood with these pistols, though."

"But have you ever got to use one full strength? Watch a face shrivel up and burn under it and the eyes go dead?"

"And blood or not, they kill if you use them strong enough. And there's no power without killing."

"Power— That's ours now."

"Ours under him."

"Yeah, sure. Under him—"

Hesketh Uranov listened to his fellow extras:

"But, my dear fellow, of course I welcomed this plan. I was simply so unutterably bored—"

"I know. If they want to maintain peace, they should never let us study the past. You read of all those thrilling events of history, and you begin to wonder. There's a strange sort of yearning goes through your muscles—"

"Of course the man's a fool. But if a fool chooses to provide us with weapons—"

"A world. A whole entire rounded world. The legions of Caesar never held anything like that. Even the Nazis never reached all the way into Asia. And we—"

"It's farewell to boredom now."

Maureen Furness listened to her fellow extras:

"—and the way it's changed the men! Why, everything's so different it doesn't feel like the same thing any more."

"A man really isn't a man unless he's killed somebody, I always say."

"But isn't that Ardless woman the lucky one, though? To be *his* woman—"

"When I think of my sister sitting at home with those three children and that wishywashy husband of hers, I could laugh in her face."

"You know, a friend of mine was studying the old dialects and there used to be a word for just what we are. There used to be women like us, and you know what they called them? Tramp followers."

They forgathered at the appointed meeting place—Garrett and Maureen and Uranov and the other one of "us," a dark intense young man named Loewe.

"It's astounding," the epic writer exclaimed. "There hasn't been anything like it since the twentieth century. And for a true analogy you've got to go back further than that—the European wars of the seventeenth, or even back to the Roman legions. This dome that's supposed to house a location company is an armed camp of mercenaries, ready to let loose rapine and destruction upon the world."

"They're mad," Maureen protested. They can do infinite harm for a little while, but what can this handful hope to accomplish in the long run?"

It was Garrett who answered. "You know from the old medical records what syphilis could do to an uncontaminated population, with no resistance to it? This scourge can act the same way. How much they'll gain for themselves is doubtful, but they'll spread the poison of hatred and killing. The world has almost forgotten that; but the memory will come back quickly enough."

"And still you know—" Maureen sounded ashamed of her own statement. "These people— I know they're terrible. But somehow they've come alive. There's something in their eyes, even if the sight of it terrifies you—"

Uranov laughed. "Still dreaming of the vigor of the olden days, Maureen? Well, we've space enough for vigor now. We've got to learn what their plans are specifically and circumvent them—very specifically. And first— But where's Wojcek? He ought to be here by now."

Loewe spoke. "I was with him. One of these . . . these killers had worked in the lab once. He recognized him in spite of the body tint and the wig. He got suspicious. They took him away. I don't think we'll see him again."

Garrett swore. Maureen gave a little stifled choking noise. Uranov said coldly, "That's a score to settle."

Garrett shook his head. "We can't talk of settling scores now. Private revenge— that belongs to *their* way of thought. We're working to frustrate this movement, and then comes our real job: to see to it that the peace never again breeds such a movement."

"But how?" Loewe protested. "Short of annihilating this entire camp. We're far too few to do that, and even if we could—"

"No. These men aren't lost to mankind. Remember they've grown up in a world conditioned to the ideals of Devarupa. They're revolting against those ideals now because they're under the domination of a strong leader who appeals to the worst in them; but that condition is still there, if we reawaken the ideals."

"But how?"

"One problem at a time. First to our current job: Did any of you find a way into S.B.'s quarters?"

Each answered in turn, but their answers amounted only to what Garrett had learned himself: that the sanctum sanctorum of the chief's high command was tightly, impenetrably guarded.

"And you didn't gather anything of what his first move is to be?"

"The men don't know, and they don't care. It's enough for them that a strong man is going to guide them to loot and slaughter and vivid excitement. They'll take what comes when he gives the orders."

"It all boils down to that, doesn't it? One strong man. If we can get at him, if we can weaken him in any way—"

"Such," Uranov suggested, "as killing him."

"There are other weapons that will not so surely turn against us. Maureen, what did you find out about Astra's quarters?"

"They adjoin S.B.'s, of course. That's only practical. She has a dozen ladies in waiting or harem slaves or whatever you want to call them; it's easy enough for a woman to slip in there. But the way through to S.B.'s is through her boudoir; you couldn't make it without—"

"—Without her help. Exactly. And that, my dear children, is what we are now going to obtain. Listen—"

"—And you never know what's going to happen to you next," said the woman who had learned she was a tramp follower. "Like last night, there I was walking along not bothering anyone unless, like Joe always tells me, I bother people just *by* walking along, only you can't believe a word Joe says, that Moon pilot, and all of a sudden this big hunky man appears out of nowhere and—"

She let out a little scream. She had not expected her narrative to be so appositely illustrated. This time there were three men, one for each of her friends, too. She held her breath and reminded herself that it was about time for her to be vaccinated again and she certainly mustn't forget, or else—"

When she let out her breath again it was in a sigh of anguish. "Of all the— To strip off your clothes and then . . . and then just take the clothes and vanish—" In dazed frustration, she clothed herself with the male garments which Gan Garrett had left behind.

The three female-clad figures followed Maureen unnoticed into Astra Ardless' apartment. Her ladies in waiting lolled about in provocative boredom, obviously longing for the coeducational life outside. Garrett looked at them, and began to understand why certain prerequisites were demanded of a male harem attendant. Maureen coolly walked on into the boudoir, and the three followed her.

Astra Ardless sat alone at her dressing table. Her face was in its natural state while she surveyed the array of cosmetics before her. Seen thus, it was a sad face, a lonely face, an old face, and in an odd way, a more beautiful face than she had ever displayed on the beams.

Maureen approached her. "Madame wish a massage?"

She started slightly. "No. Who told you— Or did I order . . . I don't remember— But, anyway, I don't want one now. Go away. No, not that way. That's—"

Maureen turned back from S.B.'s door—it had been a ridiculously long chance, but worth trying—and left the room. Two of her attendants followed.

Astra Ardless turned back to the dressing table. She picked up a graceful bottle, contemplated it, and set it down again. She looked at her naked face and shrugged. Then in the mirror she saw the remaining attendant, and turned. "I told you to go," she said imperiously and yet wearily.

"I cannot go until I have talked with you," said Gan Garrett softly.

Astra Ardless snatched up a robe. "A man! I'll have you blinded for this— burned to death even. I'll—" Her tone softened; there was, after all, something not unflattering in the situation. "Who are you?"

He held out his wrist in silence.

"Gan Garrett—" she read on the bracelet. "Garrett— But . . . but you—" She drew back, half trembling.

"Yes," he said quietly, "I made a one-way trip."

"But . . . but nobody ever came back alive from a one-way trip."

"No."

"Then you're . . . you're dead? You're a— No. No! Oh, I know the research societies say there's some evidence of— But it couldn't be. There aren't ghosts! There aren't!"

"I am here."

She held the robe tight about her and sought to control her shuddering body. "Why? What do you want of me?"

"I have a message for you. A message from Emigdio Valentinez."

"Migdito! No— He's not— He's not what you are, is he? *Is he?*"

The shrill tension of her voice, the hand that reached out to clutch him and yet was afraid to, the quivering of her lips left no doubt that Uranov's bit of gossip had been right; and on that Garrett had built his whole campaign. Now he said, "Valentinez is dead. Stag Hartle killed him."

Her lips quivered no longer. They tightened cruelly. "Hartle killed—" Her hands made a little wrenching motion. It seemed to say, "That settles Hartle."

"Stag Hartle killed him—for Breakstone."

Her eyes went blank. "Breaksone? You mean Sacha? He had Migdito killed by that jackal?"

"Do the dead come back to tell lies? Valentinez invented the new use of lovestonite. Breakstone and Hartle needed it. Valentinez died. Breakstone has the lovestonite weapons."

Astra Ardless said nothing. But her face was no longer old and sad. It had a new vigor in it, and the bitterness of the tragedy that is beyond mere sadness. She rose and moved toward the door of the adjoining apartment.

"No," said Garrett gently. "You can do nothing alone. You need helpers. I have brought them." He moved to the door of the anteroom and raised his arm in the prearranged gesture. The other three returned.

The face of Astra Ardless was the mask of Electra. Even that of Alecto. "You will help me?" she said simply, almost childishly.

"We will help you."

Then even as they approached the door, it dilated. Four guards entered, each with a pistol. The first, in a pure spirit of fun, discharged the full force of the weapon into the face of the young man named Loewe, whose shrieks were already dying into permanent silence when Sacheverell Breakstone followed his guards.

"*Tut,*" said S.B., looking down at the corpse. "Unnecessary. But harmless. And how nice of you, Astra, to collect this little group of traitors for me. It's a shame that you'll have to share their fate, which will probably be long and unpleasantly ingenious. Of course, I'm just groping with words, you understand."

Gan Garrett's hand twitched helplessly at the popgun that wasn't there.

IV.

"You surely didn't think, did you," S.B. went on with leisurely calm, "that a man of my creative ability could have been so careless as to leave Astra's room unwired? In an enterprise so daring and significant as mine, one must take all possible precautions. I have had two operatives on shifts regularly listening to this room—save, of course, when I was in it myself. And you"—he turned to Garrett—"you certainly do not expect me to swallow, like Astra, your folderol about being a ghost? How you escaped from a one-way trip, I have no notion, though I intend to learn such a useful secret before I am through with you; but I have no doubt that you are solid and corporeal and alive—for the time being."

Garrett answered him with equal calm. "It was a pretty frame, S.B., but the picture stepped out of it. Very pretty, and quite worthy of you. But I didn't expect to find you at the head of this lovestonite racket."

S.B. smiled his satisfaction. "So? You find that you had underestimated my abilities?"

"Not under. Over. I thought you were too clever to make such a fool of yourself. It smelled more like, say, Hartle's work to me."

"Hartle!" S.B. snorted. "That mercenary! That jackal! A man of action, yes, even of a certain contemptible ingenuity. But what creative power does he have? Do you think for a minute that he could conceive and carry out such a colossal undertaking as this?"

Garrett smiled. "You're doomed, S.B. You're damned. What can you accomplish with this devilish violence? Kill off a few hundred people—say even a few thousand. And then the millions of mankind will swallow up your little terrorists as though they had never been."

A trace of anger contorted S.B.'s face, then faded into a laugh. "Poor idealistic idiot! My dear Astra, before I dispatch you and your fumbling confederates to appropriate destinations, I should like to borrow your boudoir for a lecture hall. Sit down. Sit down, all of you. And you boys, keep your trigger fingers steady. Now Garrett, Uranov, Miss Furness, you are to have the privilege of hearing the functioning of a great creative mind."

Garrett sat down comfortably enough. He did not need the added illogical reassurance of Maureen's handclasp. Get S.B. talking, induce him to reveal of his own accord all they needed to know, and keep him talking until the opportune break presented itself. That had been his hastily contrived strategy, and it seemed to be working. The man was a frustrated creator; Uranov had told him that, and it was the key to the whole set-up. And the mediocre, the self-insufficient creator can never resist an audience which must perforce admire him.

"All Sollywood," Sacherverell Breakstone begain, "acknowledged my creative-executive supremacy. The Little Hitler, they called me. And I remember reading in a biography of that great man how he could have been a magnificent painter had he chosen to follow that line instead of creating in terms of maters and men. Even so, I could have been a great musician, but I instinctively turned away from the sterility of such purely artistic creation. I found my metier in Sollywood; but even there I was cramped, strangled by the limitations of peace. The man who would create with men needs weapons. The man who would create life must be able to mete out death.

"I had my plans for lethalizing the period weapons of Sollywood—filing the daggers, clearing the barrels, finding ammunition somehow through armsleggers— But it was a difficult project. You men of the W.B.I and the powers of the Department of Allocation— I could have done it. I should have created the means of frustrating you. But then, Hartle came to me with the inspired discovery of Emigdio Valentinez."

"You—" Astra Ardless' voice was harsh and toneless, hardly recognizable as human. "You did kill him—"

"Not quite. Hartle had forestalled me there. Valentinez was already dead, although I should surely have ordered his death if he had not been. But why are you so concerned, my dear? You were willing to accept a share in an empire founded on a thousand other deaths, and yet you boggle at that one as though you were the idiot Devarupa himself."

Astra Ardless said nothing. She looked as though only her own death interested her now.

"This is indeed," Breakstone went on, "a brilliant little weapon, which I think I may claim the credit of inventing, with the basis of the few hints of Valentinez and Hartle. This particular model," he brandished the one in his hand, "contains a disk of lovestonite a centimeter and a half in diameter and a centimeter thick. It was charged in direct sunlight, using a fifteen-centimeter burning glass focused on it. It contains approximately the solar energy of a full day.

The trigger releases that energy for one twenty-fifth of a second. This slide here controls the time of passage. At this end of the scale, the energy released in that twenty-fifth of a second is only enough to daze and blind momentarily. At this end—" He concluded the sentence by indicating the scorched face of the corpse of Loewe. "It is all weapons in one, from the gentle stunner to the conclusive killer. And by its power I shall create a new world."

He showed signs of pausing. Garrett spurred him on with a fresh laugh. "I'm still amazed at your stupidity, S.B. What can your few accomplish, even armed with that?"

"What could five serpents accomplish in a herd of five thousand rabbits? Especially if they had the certainty of winning many of those rabbits over to serpentry, and even of equipping them with fangs?"

"A nice metaphor. But, of course, you're only groping with words."

"I've gone beyond words now, Garrett. It's the deeds of Breakstone that will change the world."

"And they are—"

"Listen, you idiots. Understand how a man must act to create. Tomorrow we take over the Moon. That is simple. All the life, all the supplies and communications of the Moon center in Luna City. That we take over, and we need pay no further heed to the few isolated scientists and engineers and work crews that we cut off. Now we own a satellite. We take over the spaceport and the translunar experimental station. We control the spatial wireless and with forged messages lure most of Earth's spaceships here. We then control a space fleet.

"Then, at our leisure, we invade Earth. We have left enough men behind to be our helpful Quislings in this invasion. The W.B.I. can fight individual armsleggers, but it is not strong enough to combat my armed hundreds, who will soon be thousands. And there is no other physical force to resist us. Even those who are strong enough to resist will be sapped by their own idealistic beliefs. They will not dare to kill us until it is too late and they have themselves been killed.

"And then— You know that classic, 'The Count of Monte Cristo'? I produced an unimportant epic of it as one of my first creations. It reaches its high point when the hero says four words, which mean all of life to him, as they must to any man of creative genius. Four words that have never been true before in all history, but which will find truth at last when I utter them:

'The world is mine!'

Garrett was moved to shudder at the blazing light of S.B.'s eyes, as vivid and as murderous as a lovestonite flash. But he forced himself to go on scoffing. "And you expect your hundreds and thousands to follow you loyally? Can a man like you inspire love and loyalty?"

"Love! Loyalty! Say rather loot and laziness. They are offered the privilege of sacking the Earth, and their lazy souls are spared the necessity of ever thinking or acting for themselves."

"They'll never follow you. The risks are theirs and the glory is yours."

"You think not? Then come. Tonight I speak to them. For the first time I tell them a definite plan. I outline the assault upon Luna City. And you shall hear me speak, and you shall know for yourself if they will follow me. Boys," he said to the guards, "bring these carefully after me. They are to be honored guests at the foundation of the new world."

Outside , in the public square of this dome which Breakstone had filled with his army, the hordes were beginning to gather, the seething mass of these new Huns. Inside, in this upper room, S.B. waited patiently. As a producer-director, he had been noted for his sense of timing. Now with that same sense, he awaited the exact moment when he should go out on that balcony and address his followers.

The suppression of balconies, Gan Garrett reflected with bitter whimsicality, may be necessary in a world which wishes to prevent the rise of dictators.

A guard came in, saluted, and said, "Hartle."

Sacheverell Breakstone returned the salute and nodded. "Show him in."

Stag Hartle came in, wearing an ascot which was unusually brilliant even for him—so blinding as almost to eliminate the need for lovestonite weapons. "Hi, boss," he said casually. "Just wanted to—" His voice dropped as he spotted Garrett. "Christmas on wheels," he muttered. "Ain't it bad enough to see a ghost without him being in drag?"

"Mr. Garrett is no ghost," said S.B. "And the female garments are merely part

of a plot of his against me—a plot which miscarried as grievously as your attempt to railroad him on a one-way trip. Clumsy work, Hartle."

Hartle bridled. "My part of it was O.K. I'm reliable. And that's what a lot of
people are finding out now, boss."

"So? And what does that mean?"

"It means that when I tell 'em there's going to be loot and excitement, they
believe me. When you talk big, S.B., they begin to wonder what's in it for them, or
are they just all stooging for you?"

"So? Go on—"

"It means, S.B., that I've come here with a little proposition before you go out
on that balcony, and there's a lot of the boys'll back me up." Hartle's confidence
was growing even cockier. "It means it'd be a very wise idea to put me in command of this assault on Luna City. You can stick around with your big ideas, but
leave the practical stuff to me."

"So? You wish to relegate me to a figurehead? Like the ruler of the old constitutional monarchies, while you— This is a—shall we say a revolt? You understand
I—"

"Sure, you're just groping with words. Yeah, call it a revolt if you like. Words
don't count. That's what you've got to learn."

"And if I refuse, as I assuredly will?"

"Then—"

It happened almost too quickly to follow. Hartle's hand reached toward his
blouse, but before it had more than begun the movement there was a flash from
the hand of S.B. Something that had been Stag Hartle lay blasted on the floor. The
illegally sharpened knife clanked from his blouse; the sound of ringing metal was
clean against the anguished echo of his dying screams.

Sacheverell Breakstone walked over and picked up the knife. "A singularly
clumsy attempt at assassination," he observed. "The fool was hampered by his
old habits. Conventionally, he had prepared his fingers for the knife with paraderm;
that was enough to forewarn me. Now are you content, Astra? I have punished
the murderer of Valentinez." He spurned the body with his foot. "Outside, boys,"
he said, and gestured to the balcony.

Two guards carried the corpse of Stag Hartle and tossed it over into the
gathering throng. For a moment S.B. stood where he could be seen from below,
the knife in one hand, the lovestonite pistol in the other. The visual object lesson
was complete and succinct.

He turned back to the guests in the room. "You see, gentlemen and ladies,
how simple and effective is the true exercise of power?"

Maureen Furness had sat through all this in tense and shuddering silence. Now
at last she spoke. "I used to think that the old times were more alive, more exciting. That was before I ever saw a man die—"

Breakstone laughed. He seemed to swell physically to match his magniloquent
dreams. His short stocky body in its comically anachronistic costume dominated
the room. "Leave us," he said abruptly to his guards. Then as they hesitated incredulous, he roared: "Leave us. You heard me."

Hesitantly the men left.

The murmur of the gathering mob was loud from outside the balcony. "In a moment," said S.B., "I shall address my tools of creation. And in this guardless moment, you fools shall provide me with my final proof of power, my last touch of inspiration. I shall show you your own impotence and grow strong on it. There." He laid his lovestonite pistol and Stag Hartle's sharpened dagger on the floor. "I am here, unguarded. There are weapons. And I am safe because you—"

Astra Ardless sprang forward and siezed the pistol. With one almost careless blow, Breakstone knocked her aside. There was a flash as she fell, and she cried out in pain. S.B. glanced down at her incuriously. "I had forgotten her; she does not share your idealism. Only her dead lover moves her. But she has not had the courtesy to take care of herself."

Gan Garrett felt his muscles straining against his will. He could attack S.B. weaponless. He could beat him to a pulp; but to what avail? He could simply summon his guards back and— Destruction was the necessity. But can a man, conditioned from childhood to certain beliefs, beliefs moreover which he knows deep in his heart to be the lasting truth of mankind, can he sacrifice those beliefs even when they themselves seem to demand it?

His helplessness seemed to justify Breakstone's taunts. And yet would his action not justify Breakstone even more profoundly? And then abruptly he realized how futile even destruction would be. He needed something more, something—

"—and enterprises of great pith and moment," Uranov was muttering, "with this regard their currents turn awry, and lose the name of action—"

"Your moment is over," S.B. announced. "You have proved your spiritual castration, and from your impotence I have drawn fresh potency. Now I shall speak to my multitude, and within the hour we shall have begun our march upon Luna City. Our two-meter lovestonite disks—you did not know we had progressed to weapons of such size and power?—shall attack and melt down the dome of the city, turning the lunar night into the fatal glare of our new day, while—"

Both men seemed to move at once, so rapidly that Maureen Furness saw for a moment only a confused blur of movement. Hesketh Uranov had leaped for the knife, snatching it from the floor and driving it toward Breakstone's heart. But at the same instant, Gan Garrett sprang between. His right hand caught Uranov's, wrenched at the wrist, and forced the dagger down. His left connected squarely with the point of Breakstone's jaw.

Garrett stood looking down at the sprawled body of the producer-director-fuehrer. "Failing my popgun," he said, "my left is the best instantaneous anesthetic I know."

Uranov rubbed his aching wrist and grunted. "What good is that? Let me kill him. I know the consequences. I know your W.B.I. oath and I know you'll take me in and have me sent on a one-way trip. But my life doesn't count, and his death does.

"Uh-huh. So we kill Breakstone, and where are we? We've still got his henchmen to reckon with, his gauleiters. The late Mr. Hartle can't have been the only one. And there's still that mob outside, hungry for anything that isn't peace. No, Breakstone knew what he was doing when he made his big gesture."

"It was the gestrue of a megalomaniac fool. They'll all go too far and end by destroying themselves. This gesture was Breakstone's invasion of Russia."

"It's going to turn out that way, but he didn't see that far. It made sense to him—a psychological trick to bolster his own morale, and no danger attached. He knew we were sensible enough to see that his death couldn't possibly do any good." Garrett crossed to the unconscious Astra Ardless and picked up the pistol that had marred her vanishing beauty. "It seems like years I've been on the track of this lovestonite weapon, and this is the first time I've held one in my hand. Neat little gadget, isn't it?"

"But what are we going to do?" Maureen protested. "You say S.B.'s death couldn't do us any good. Then what do we gain by just knocking him out?"

"Listen. You heard him mention two-meter lovestonite weapons for attacking cities. I didn't know they were working on such a scale. I wonder . . . yes, they could be terrific. Use a huge aluminum-foil mirror for charging them . . . yes. All right. Remember what he said about turning the night into a new day? Remember what the men out there are rebelling against and what they want?"

The door dilated, and one of Breakstone's guards stepped in. He found himself looking straight into Garrett's lovestonite pistol.

"Come on in," Garrett urged politely. "Right this way. Take his pistol, Uranov, and keep him covered."

The man's eyes went to S.B.'s body, then to Garrett's face. His mouth half-opened, but his eyes shifted to Garrett's hand and he was silent.

"Good boy," Garrett commended him. "I've got a little job for you."

The man kept his eyes on the pistol and nodded. He had seen it work on Stag Hartle.

"And the first thing, if the lady will please turn away her eyes, is for you to strip."

Gan Garrett stood on the balcony, in the uniform of Breakstone's personal guard. His stolen female garments would not have become him in this crucial moment. Oratory, he felt, did not become him, either. But oratory was a necessary weapon of demagogy, and was demagogy at times perhaps a necessary weapon to bring him to his own higher aims?

The mob, long awaiting its leader, muttered restlessly. Garrett found the switch of the speaker, turned it, and began the most important words he was ever to say.

"Listen, men. You are gathered to hear your orders from your leader."

There was a roar of impatient agreement.

"Very well. I bring you your orders from your leader. But not from Breakstone. Breakstone is through."

There was a furious outcry of protest. The flash of a lovestonite pistol seared the wall just to Garrett's right. He stepped up to the speaker to dominate the crowd noise and spoke urgently: "Listen: Would I be here speaking to Breakstone's men from Breakstone's balcony if he hadn't been bested? And do you want a leader who can be bested? Then listen to me. Hear the new words, the new orders, the new war."

The murmur of the mob died down slowly, reluctantly. He could catch the dim echo of phrases: "—might as well—" "—got to find out what goes—" "—so what the hell; let's hear what he—"

"Breakstone," he repeated, "is through. He was a great leader, but a blind and foolish one. I offer you a greater. He planned to lead you on a great war, but a cruel and pointless one. I offer you a greater."

There began to be mutterings of welcome, almost approbation from the crowd.

Garrett found his mind unwontedly praying, praying that this idea would work and that he might be worthy to carry it out. "You came with Breakstone," he went on, "because you were not happy alone and in peace. Man demands more than that. He does not want to be his lonely self; he yearns for a great man, a great leader in whom he can put his trust. He does not want peace; he wants life and action and the great crusade of war."

There was a handful of scattered cheers from below.

"Let me tell you about the crusade I bring you. See how it dwarfs Luna City. There were always wars in the old world because man needed his crusade. Because in wartime there came new life and new vigor. Because the weak piping times of peace were not worthy of man. And now, for these same reasons, Breakstone was leading you to war in this new world. Peace was not worthy of man—nor was man worthy of peace. He made peace into something weary, stale, flat and unprofitable. While peace, true peace—

"We *fight* a war; but in peacetime we relax into stupid nothingness. We take what comes, we wallow in comfort, and we come alive only for the next war. We have not yet learned to *fight* a peace.

"Crusades do not die when the weapons of war crumble into silence. Every moment of the true life of man should be, must be a crusade. In Africa and in Australia there are black men who have not yet been brought to full membership in mankind; there is a crusade. In Europe and Asia and America, there are still injustices even under our economic dispensation; there is a crusade. Cancer is dead by now; but diabetes and tuberculosis and Kruger's disease still claim their thousands and their tens of thousands; there is a crusade."

He was losing the mob; he felt that. They talked among themselves in huddled groups. There were no more shouts of acclaim. He lowed his voice to a pitch of intense resolution and plunged on to the heart of his offer.

"But those crusades are for the stay-at-homes, the ones that haven't yet rebelled against this stagnant peace. You want more. You want fame and glory and wealth and excitement. You want a world to conquer. Well, it's yours for the fighting. I promise you a world. I promise you—Mars!"

He went on hastily, before they could react away from the novel idea. "Why have our trips to Mars failed? Because only a few brave men—warriors like yourselves—dared to make them. The ships cannot carry enough fuel to return, and much of what they carry must be wasted against the cold of the Martian night. A handful of men cannot do enough work to extract the fuel we know is there.

"You are brave, you are daring, and you are no mere handful. A fleet, an armada of spaceships can carry you to Mars. Lovestonite can ease the fuel problem, not in the ship itself, but against the Martian night. Your two-meter disks will turn that night into a new day. And there, in this new outpost of man, there you can fight. You can fight the cold and the hardships. You can fight God knows what dangers of nature lurking there. You will be the bravest, the most daring, the *fightin'est* of men.

"Man has not conquered Mars because he has been peace-loving and timorous and sheeplike. Men! *Are you these things?*"

There was a roar of *NO!* which must have drowned out the revelry in the night spots of Luna City if the airless moon could have carried sound outside the domes. Warmth flowed into Gan Garrett. The guess was working. He hastened on:

"I promised you a greater war. I also promised you a greater leader. You need him. You need the greater leader that bested Breakstone, because only he can make this new crusade real."

He saw their eyes raised to him, and he moved his hand in a gesture of disclaimer. "No. I am not that leader. But I speak for him now. There is a great man for you to follow. Greater than Caesar and Napoleon and Hitler, and immeasurably greater than Breakstone. Greater even than the infinitely different greatness of Devarupa. Follow him. Let him lead you to triumph in the new crusade."

He waited until there arose clamorous outcries for the new leader. Then he let his voice drop until the tuned-down speaker barely carried it, small and still, over the hushed crowd.

"That man is Man. He alone is the all-great leader. No single man, no world-conqueror, no saint, no genius of art or science, is important beside Man himself. And Man is all of you—and each of you. Look within that part of Man that is yourself, and find there that part of yourself that is Man. There is your great man, your strong leader. Follow him, and fight the crusade of Mars. Mars was the god of war. Now he leads the new war of peace!"

The balcony seemed upheld by a surging wave of jubilant noise.

"They didn't get the last of it," Gan Garrett said to his friends as he stepped back into S.B.'s chamber. "For them I'm the great man on the white horse. I've destroyed a fuehrer to become one. But they'll learn, and meanwhile I've set them on the right road. We've a new world before us."

Sacheverell Breakstone writhed, and grunted through the gag that was part of Garrett's female costume.

Uranov gestured to him. "I just thought of another blessing. As a W.B.I. man, you're arresting him?"

"Of course. He'll get a one-way trip for Hartle."

Uranov grinned. "Good. Now I can write the Devarupa epic without any words that he's groped with."

The Devarupa epic, generally accepted by now as the finest solly ever made, was released on the same day that the space armada left for Mars. Its fate, critical and commercial, did not concern its author. You don't worry about epics on a space crew.

Garrett and Maureen said good-by to him at the spaceport. "That's why I'm not going," Garrett said. "If I led this magnificent exhibition, if I was even on it, I'd be fixed forever as a great new fuehrer. I'm sinking back into the anonymity of a good W.B.I. agent."

Uranov glanced at the loading of the two-meter disks. "See you soon though. And I'm the first man ever leaving for Mars who's said that with any confidence."

"Here," said Maureen Garrett abruptly. She took a lovestonite figure from her recently altered identification bracelet. "Take him. He's been pretty good luck for us by and large so far. I want him to make the first two-way trip."

The loading was being speeded up. The crew was impatient for a new world, and for the new war of peace.

Man's Reach

He listened carefully to the baritone's opening phrases and after a moment jotted down the word *robust* on the pad in front of him. In another moment he added four letters to make it read *robustious*.

The voice rang big in the audition hall:

> To saddle, to saddle, to spur, and away
> In the gray of the glancing dawn,
> When the hounds are out with a treble shout
> And the whip and spur of the merry rout . . .

"A treble shout," he reflected, would nicely characterize that last dramatic soprano . . . The baritone sang on, as big as the hall itself; and as empty. Dear God, how long was it since anyone even here on Terra had indulged in the absurdity of fox hunting, and when would concert baritones stop singing about it?

An attendant was shoving a broom down the aisle, unperturbed by the baritone or anything else—even, apparently, by the fact that the aisle was perfectly clean. There was nothing to sweep away in front of his broom; yet oddly a scrap of paper remained behind it.

Jon Arthur was careful not to catch the attendant's eye as he let his hand slip down and gather in the scrap. He tucked it under the pad and resolutely kept his gaze on the baritone.

The hunting song ended. The baritone paused, made an effort to adjust himself to the logical fact that there is no applause at auditions, and launched into his second number.

Jon Arthur grinned. He had won a bet with himself; he knew that so robustious a man would be bound to select Rhysling's *Jet Song*. The familiar words boomed forth with that loving vigor of all baritones who have never seen deep Space.

> Feel her rise! Feel her drive!
> Straining steel, come alive . . .

It was safe to unfold the scrap of paper now. Arthur read the four simple words and knew that the pattern of his life was changed:

Kleinbach is at Venusberg

It was the finest rice paper, of course, and easy to swallow. Gulping, he looked at his fellow critics and wondered how many of them would vote in the election (the last election?) with one tenth of the care with which they were now considering their audition ballots. And whether, if he did not reach Kleinbach at Venusberg, it could possibly matter a damn how carefully they voted.

Jet Song was over, and it was clear from all expressions that this baritone, at any rate, would *not* get the scholarship to Mme. Storm's Resident Laboratory. There was one more contestant, and Arthur grudgingly cursed the waste of even that much time before he could get started.

The girl looked like nothing much. Nobody had explained to her how unfortunate this year's styles were for tall women. Then she began to sing.

Jon Arthur hastily consulted the audition list and noted the name Faustina Parva. He began to make a note on the pad, then let the pencil rest idle in his hand while his whole being lived in his ears.

The music was almost as inconsequential as the baritone's hunting song—an arrangement of one of the waltz-like Martian *kumbus*. But the voice . . .

It was not only the rich solidity of its lower notes, its ease in the upper register, the unbroken transition over what must be damned near two and a half octaves, but the absolute clarity and facility with which it handled every trick in the conceivable repertory of the voice. It was cold; you might even say it was mechanical; but it was, Jon Arthur realized, the first time in his life that he had heard absolutely perfect singing.

He looked at the faces of the other critics. Good, there'd be no time wasted in balloting. The audition was settled, and he could stop being a music critic and take up the more important (and, his observing mind could not help commenting, somewhat more absurd) task of striving single-handed to save man and his system.

He always thought of the penthouse in the Eighties, complete with view of the Hudson, as "Headquarters." It was another of the small touches of melodrama that he liked to insert to keep himself sane.

Steele Morrison maneuvered his pulleys and the outsize boatswain's chair swung across the room to greet him. "Sure," Morrison always answered the frequent protests, "I know with modern prosthetics I could walk as good as anybody. But then I'd get exercise and I'd lose weight; and every time I weighed in for spaceflight, I swore once I retired I'd be the fattest man in New York."

Jon Arthur shook the vast hand and marveled, as always, at the unflabbiness of its grip. "Somebody's tracked him down," he said without preamble. "He's at Venusberg."

"We do get some breaks, baby, don't we?" Morrison zoomed the boatswain's chair across its network to the bar. "Straight?"

"As usual."

"How soon you going?"

"This damned audition deal ties in like a dream. Since I was on the committee, it'll be a natural to sell the paper on a follow-up story on Mme. Storm's colony at Venusberg."

Morrison nodded as he traveled back with the drinks. You never went to the part of the room where Steele Morrison was; it hurt his feelings not to be able to zoom back at you. "Don't know why—had a hunch and did a little reading on Mme. Storm. Rumors of something nice and tender back in her great days between her and Kleinbach. Use it for what it's worth."

"She was a great singer. I've heard her tapes."

Morrison shrugged. "Something else too, I guess. Can a man fall in love with a voice, baby?"

Jon Arthur gave a little silent and serious consideration to his drink and (surprising himself) to the question.

"Matter? Did I say something?"

"No, just thinking. Making plans. The audition winner," Arthur carefully sounded as indifferent as though it had been the baritone, "leaves next Monday. I can set up the deal by then. Think it's worth one last crack at Weddergren in the meantime?"

Steele Morrison zoomed for a corner and traveled back with an election pamphlet in the familiar aseptic blue and white of the Academy. "Here's his latest, baby. It's out in the open now: no more elections, that's for sure. Antiquated and unscientific, seems as how. *The system is Man's laboratory,*" he read, "*in which he conducts the greatest of all his experiments: the shaping of his own destiny. To run this laboratory by democratic politics is as absurd as to base its experiments upon the 'laws' of alchemy and astrology.* That's what the man says."

"The worst of which is that it so damned near makes sense."

"Baby," said Morrison, "I've got kind of a vested interest in this system. With one leg buried on Mars and the other on Venus you might say I sort of straddle it. All our kind of people a hundred years ago, they thought once we forgot nationalism and got world government everything was going to be as easy as a high jump on Mars. Well, we've got world government, no phony league but an honest Federation based on the individual as a unit—and that Federation is smack up against the most important election in its history without any possibility of electing the right party. If the Academy wins, we're a laboratory—which I give maybe one generation before it becomes a technological autocracy. If the Populists win—and may their jets clog forever for stealing that fine old word—we'll have book burnings and lab smashings and a fine fast dive into the New Dark Ages. And in between are the guys who don't care, the guys who can't be bothered, the guys who'd like to *but . . .*"

"And us," Arthur concluded, "keeping underground so we won't wind up in the Belsens of either side . . . I'm seeing Weddergren tonight," he suddenly announced his decision. "We've got to make one more try."

The system's greatest scientist but one, the Academy's candidate for President of the World Federation, was surprisingly accessible to Jon Arthur. A technician (the Academy was firmly opposed to a servant class, but a man needs technical assistants) ushered Arthur into the study the moment he heard his name.

Dr. Weddergren advanced, white mane and all, to greet him warmly. "Delighted, my boy! I was hoping you'd come around in person to congratulate me on my pupil."

This seemed a peculiar gambit even for an Academy politician. "Your pupil?"

"The Parva. Faustina Parva. The contralto who—"

For a moment Arthur was distracted from his mission. "Phenomenal," he admitted. "The greatest voice, I swear, that I have ever heard. But your pupil . . . ?"

Dr. Weddergren allowed himself a patronizing smile. "So you didn't know? You're like the rest, eh? The Weddergren Drive . . . the Weddergren Orbit Calculator . . . The shoemaker should stick to his last, perhaps, as those unscientific Populists keep striving to assert?"

Arthur had never quit realized that *unscientific* could be the most obscene term of invective in the language. "I knew, of course, that you were fond of music . . ." he began.

"Fond?" There was a brief glimpse of a sincerity which the Weddergren features had never revealed on a telescreen. "You might say that. You might also, if you wish, say that it is my life—in a way that the Weddergren Drive or even the Academy can never be. And this part of my life," his features took on again their reasonable persuasiveness, "offers fresh evidence of the nature in which science can guide and mold life in any of its aspects. As a music critic, you are, I imagine, somewhat familiar with vocal training and its methods?"

"I am." Arthur smiled. "It is difficult to imagine a less scientific field."

"Precisely. And yet what is its objective? To enable a machine to produce optimum results. The nature of that machine is exactly and minutely known. There is not the slightest mystery attached to the functioning of any of its parts. Yet instead of feeding into that machine an accurately punched tape, furnishing it with complete instruction on the control and articulation of each of its parts for every specified result desired, what do vocal teachers do? They teach by example, by metaphor, by analogy, by feeling and intuition! It is as though, instead of allowing a calculator the normal functioning of its binary synapses, you read it a lecture on the mystique of the theory of numbers!"

"There's something in what you say," Arthur admitted, with an eerie echo of his partial agreement with the doctrine of the System as Laboratory.

"The Parva," Weddergren announced, "is my proof. A good vocal organ to start with, of course. One does not waste time on a shoddily constructed machine. Careful analysis of the precise physiology of the voice. A long and detailed course of training, on strictest scientific principles with no mystical flubdubbery. Intensive hypnopedagogy until the mind has learned in sleep every minutest aspect of the volitional control of the vocal apparatus. That is all, and the result you heard this afternoon."

Jon Arthur's mental ear heard again the beauty, the perfection . . . and the hint of coldness. It was that hint which enabled him to say, "Music is so often allied with science, isn't it? One has read of Einstein, and wasn't Kleinbach much interested too?"

Again Weddergren nearly forgot to be telegenic. "Kleinbach . . ." he said softly. "I studied under him, you know. I suppose if this century has produced a great man . . ."

"I've met others of his pupils, but they never could explain him to me. Perhaps you can, Dr. Weddergren. Do you understand why he did . . . what he did?"

"Vanish, you mean? Remove himself? To think we do not even know whether he is alive or . . . Frankly, I think I do. He understood the necessity for the Academy and for the steps that we shall take after the election. But he could not bring himself to face those steps in actuality. With all his greatness he was . . . a romantic, shall we say? Perhaps even an atavist. And yet I have sometimes thought . . . It was an equation of Kleinbach's, you know, that started me on the road to the Drive. And it was Kleinbach taking me to hear Storm that first aroused my interest in the voice. If I could talk to him, I've sometimes thought . . . If after the election he . . . My boy," Dr. Weddergren suddenly observed to a nonexistent telecamera, "I have no desire to talk anything but music with you. I so rarely have such an opportunity to indulge myself. You thought you heard something extraordinary this afternoon—as indeed you did. How would you like, now, to hear the only *perfect* voice in the world?"

Jon Arthur was all affable interest and musical companionship. He had learned what he needed to know.

It was as he left Weddergren's, still a little dazed by what the scientist had displayed, that the first attempt was made on his life.

It was a clumsy attempt and undoubtedly Populist in origin. An Academy assassin might simply have brushed against him and deposited a few bacilli; it was fortunate that the Populists' abhorrence of science extended even to its criminal uses.

The plan had obviously been to insert a knife between his ribs. The moment he sensed the rush of his attacker, he set his muscles in the Fifth Position of *juzor*— that extraordinary blend of Terran *judo* and Martian *zozor* on which he had spent so many months under Steele Morrison's eye, with Steele's sharp tongue keeping him going whenever he was tempted to point out the absurdity of a peace-loving music critic as a *juzor*-expert secret agent.

Somewhat to his amazement, the Fifth Position worked. The Populist lay sprawled on the sidewalk, looking like a not too bright but rather friendly young man who has just passed out amiably. Arthur did not stop to check if the skull was fractured in the precise spot indicated in the book of instructions; he simply pocketed the knife and, once he had convinced himself there was not another on his tail, hurried to "Headquarters."

"So now maybe you'll begin to think it's serious," Morrison grunted after the third drink, "Until you reach Kleinbach and get back with his message—if he'll give you one—your chances of enjoying good health are about as good as for a bonfire on an airless asteroid. Especially watch it on the liner; they're bound to have somebody aboard."

They did, but it was a week before Jon Arthur spotted him.

The liner was one of the new de luxe fleet, completely autogravitized and hyperjetted to the point where the trip to Venus was cut down to three months. With the election seven months off, a half-year's round trip left him one month to find Kleinbach and persuade him; that was timing it as fine as writing music for split-second telecast tapes.

But all the time-tension would come when they hit Venusberg. For three months on the liner there was nothing to do but enjoy himself—and, incidentally, stay alive.

The latter task seemed to offer no difficulties at the moment; certainly neither did the former, once he began to become really acquainted with Faustina Parva.

The audition winner had at first treated him merely with the courtesy due to a judge who had cast one of the votes that sent her to Venus. The slight coldness that he had detected in her singing was accentuated in her speaking personality, and he was more than willing now to believe that she was Dr. Weddergren's creation.

Then, one week out, came the episode of her practicing.

Whether it was consideration for others or the sense of relaxation that strikes all space voyagers, Jon Arthur was uncertain; the first seemed a little unlikely. But for a week she had refrained from practicing. Now she began.

The most beautiful voice in the world (which it was quite possible that the Parva possessed) is somewhat lacking in appeal when it practices scales, when it takes one single phrase of great technical difficulty and scant musical interest and repeats it, worries it, frets it until at last the phrase is perfect and the accidental listener is cutting out paper dolls.

No space crew in history has ever mutinied, but few space crews have traveled with a contralto whose tremendous voice can fill an amphitheater—or a space liner.

What made Jon Arthur pause in front of the captain's cabin was the unusual quality of intense emotion in the Parva's voice.

"You can't do this!" she was saying, toward the very top of her extensive range. "I *have* to practice. If I go three months without practicing, I'll land at Venusberg in such shape that Mme. Storm will wonder why they ever picked me!"

"If you go three months *with* practicing, my dear young lady," the captain announced, "there won't be a man on this liner capable of landing you at Venusberg!"

It was a pretty impasse, Arthur thought. Both parties were unquestionably right. It seemed a problem to which there was no key . . .

Key . . .

Key . . . !

Jon Arthur pushed open the door. "Pardon me, I couldn't help overhearing the discussion. Wouldn't it solve the problem," he hurried on before he could be interrupted, "if Miss Parva were assigned one hour a day in which she might practice in one of the air locks?"

Both captain and contralto stared at him, then turned to each other with broad smiles.

"So the key *was* the lock," Arthur was saying to the Parva later in the bar. "Vacuum-sealed, soundproof . . ."

"I'm afraid I'm very much indebted to you." She sounded as though she really regretted the fact. "First the audition, now this . . ."

"Honestly, I'm indebted to you." Why had he thought her plain at that audition? "Simply for existing with the voice that you have."

"Do you mind?" a man's voice asked. "Since we're all going to the same place, why not get acquainted now?"

The Parva seemed not to place him, but Arthur's mind rang instantly with sounds about saddles and hounds and the treble shout of the merry rout. The robustious baritone introduced himself as Ivor Harden, explained that though he'd lost out on the scholarship he had scraped up barely enough money to make it on his own, paid the Parva a pretty compliment on winning, and still without having allowed the interposition of a word ended with, "And what's that you're drinking, Mr. Arthur?"

"Bourbon over ice," said Arthur, thinking that the least the baritone could do to atone for his interruption was to buy a round.

But Harden simply beckoned the steward and ordered one bourbon over ice. Resignedly Arthur ordered another and a Deimos Delight for the girl, and hastily threw the conversation back to her with a reference to Dr. Weddergren.

For the first time he felt a warm devotion in her as she spoke of the scientist who had molded her voice. The transference with singer and vocal teacher is not unlike that with patient and psychiatrist, and even Weddergren's purely scientific method seemed to have evoked the same phenomenon.

"He's wonderful!" she said. "There isn't a man alive who understands the voice as he does—and can make you understand it too."

"*My* teacher," said Harden, "says it's bad to understand too much; you should *feel*."

"Nonsense!" Faustina Parva announced flatly. "You sound like a Populist!"

"That's bad?" the baritone snapped.

It was as well that the drinks arrived then; Populist-Academist arguments were never safe, and especially uncomfortable to Arthur in his loathing of both sets of extremists. By the time the drinks were signed for, the Parva was safely back on vocal training.

"And did Dr. Weddergren show you Marchesi?" she asked.

"He did—damnedest experience I've ever had, not even excepting," he added, "your audition." *(Was the corner of his eye tricking him, or had the baritone just dropped something into his own bourbon over ice?)*

"Please!" She was imperious. "Don't be gallant!"

"I'm not. Just factual." He looked at her for a moment with intense and concentrated devotion. *(Which allowed the move which he had next expected; with sleight of hand worthy of such legendary figures as Robert-Houdini or Rawson, the baritone had switched the two bourbons.)*

"Who is Marchesi?" Harden asked.

"You don't know the name?"

"Never heard it."

"That's odd." And it was, for a singer. "Considered the greatest vocal teacher of the late nineteenth and early twentieth century, and possibly of all time."

"Until now," the Parva interrupted.

"As you will. And Weddergren has his Marchesi too. Look over at the bar, Harden; you see that electronic mixer?" Harden looked. *(And the bourbons changed places again;* juzor *training develops one's aptitude for sleight of hand.)*

"What about it?" Harden asked.

"It's a fine example of a usuform robot, made to do one thing superlatively well. Weddergren has made a *singing* robot—a precise reproduction of the ideal human vocal apparatus, but incapable of human errors."

"Not quite precise," the girl corrected him. "It has a slightly larger uvula than any human being. Dr. Weddergren thinks that's important; one reason he chose me to train was my uvula. Look—it's extraordinarily well developed."

She opened her generous mouth. Now the face which had begun to seem oddly beautiful to Arthur was distorted into a comedy mask; he leaned forward and peered, honestly interested professionally in this odd physiological fact. *(For one instant even the corner of his eye was observing nothing but a singular uvula.)*

"And does this Marchesi sing well?" the baritone asked.

"Perfectly," said the Parva.

"I'll agree," Arthur added. "But I'm not sure that's a desideratum. The voice is free of human errors—and of humanity." *(If I were Harden . . . He could have switched them then; if he did I should switch back. But is he counting on that? Did he leave them alone so that I would switch them back and feed myself whatever he's slipped in there?)*

"Freedom from errors," the girl said a trifle sharply, "should be humanity's goal."

"Please! Let's stay away from politics and keep to music." *(Or is it indeed my turn to switch anyway? Where is it now ? First he . . . Then . . .)*

The girl's glass was empty. "Gentlemen, neither of you's even sipped his drink. And I shouldn't have had two Deimoses; they're too sweet. I want a taste of whisky to clean my mouth. Which of you will be so kind?"

(Which glass is it? Which was the last switch? And if it is mine and I offer it, will he let her . . . ?)

As if actuated by one control button, the two men rose, neatly upsetting the table. The two streams of bourbon, toxic and intoxicant, mingled on the floor.

It is not within the scope of this narrative to detail the three months of the trip. That scene in the bar was in its way typical enough.

Conversations, in and out of the bar, with Faustina Parva followed the same pattern. The two were drawn together by their common deep devotion to singing, and held apart by the difference in their attitudes. And at the moment when Arthur was struggling hardest to repress a sharp retort to some philosophical echo of Weddergren, he would find himself wondering why he had never noticed before that she had unusually deep dimples, which lent a curious softness to an otherwise almost severely carved face.

There was no doubt that Ivor Harden was a Populust agent, and that his singing career was a fraud. His inadequacy as a vocalist did not prove it; some of the least talented can be the most career-minded. But it was significant, for instance, that he bothered to avail himself of an air lock for practice only twice in the course of the trip.

It was also not without significance that the steward reported his presence in Arthur's corridor just before the incident of the Martian sand adder in the bedclothes, and that he had left his palmprints on the cargo box which so nearly decapitated Arthur when the captain (his warmest friend since the lock-solution) was showing him over the hold.

Typical Populist scorn of the methodology of any science—criminalistics, in this case—not to know that palmprints are as sure as fingerprints, nor to realize that Arthur would long ago have unobtrusively secured all the baritone's prints (smiling to himself with the pleasant notion that something might be solved by means of the big toe).

The last attack came on the night of the captain's dinner. In the concert that followed, Arthur heard Parva sing (other than in practice) for the first time since the audition. She did not choose to unleash her pyrotechnics for this somewhat indifferent audience. She merely sang a few popular songs, and the dark rich purity of her voice was as clean and deep as Space itself.

When Ivor Harden began (he had the incredible nerve to sing *Jet Song* to the spacemen who had grown up on it), Arthur slipped out to the smoking chamber. Parva's singing had stirred him deeply (what was it Steele had said about Kleinbach and Storm?), but that was partly because he was a specialist, a connoisseur. He had watched the unmoved faces of the average listener . . .

The attack came from a direction which indicated the defensive use of the Seventh Position of *juzor*—which was also advisable because it was reasonably certain to leave the attacker alive . . . and in no mood to argue.

Arthur retrieved the weapon—one of those damnable South Martian thorns, as long as your forearm and instant death once the bloodstream meets it—and looked down at the gasping understeward. The door was still open; Harden was off to hounds with a treble shout for an encore.

Arthur weighed the thorn suggestively and nodded toward the source of the voice. "He hired you to do it, didn't he? So he'd have an alibi from the whole ship's company."

Nerve-wrenched and feeble though he was, the steward protested. "He didn't have to hire me. I'm as good a Populist as he is any day! The hell with science! Let's be men again!"

"And all have a jolly time sticking thorns in each other . . . Get out! Tell him he'll have to try again—oh, and another message: Tell him he's still flatting on his G's."

Tomorrow they would land. Ivor's opportunities should be plentiful on a strange planet. Now to stay alive until he found Kleinbach . . .

Irita Storm had been (Arthur had seen early stereos) as enchanting a soubrette as ever graced operetta and opera, with a voice whose light brilliance had been supported by a strong lower register. Now at 65, she retained only her middle voice, but with so complete a command of style and musicianship that you hardly regretted the absence of necessary notes. And she had so perfected the soubrette's art of coquetry that you could enjoy it as an abstract technical triumph without concern over the more physiological aspects of the male-female relationship.

But there was little coquetry evident, even though she was alone with a man, when she talked with Jon Arthur after first hearing the Parva. Her professional concern was too strong.

"Of course you were right as a judge to select her," she pouted. "It's one of those voices that make legends. It's in the tremendous tradition—Pasta, Mantelli, Schumann-Heink, Geyer, Supervia, Pharris, Krushelnitsa . . . and now Parva. And she's trained to perfection—nothing for me to do there. But my dear young man, can you imagine the greatest voice in the world with the emotional and interpretive warmth of a carefully constructed robot?"

"I can," Arthur smiled, "because I've heard it. The robot, I mean, and I will say that Parva comes closer to humanity than that."

"I'm furious, do you hear me? There's never been a voice so perfected—and so wasted! It's high time she came here! Give me six months. That's all I ask, young man—six months, and you won't know her!"

Six months, Jon Arthur reflected as he left, and you may not know the system . . .

He had met one impasse after another since his arrival on Venus. He had expected to receive almost immediately one of the familiar rice-paper messages; he had received nothing. Even, in its way, more perturbing: he had expected the necessity of holding his guard high against Ivor Harden and his allies; he had moved unharmed through an apparently tranquil existence.

The cliff he was strolling along, the surf far below, reminded him of the Big Sur country in California. Venus had, in most respects, proved surprisingly Terra-like after the great project of the gyro-condensers had removed the vapor layer. But it was to him a Never-Never-Terra in which his tensions and problems seemed to have removed themselves—and thereby agonizingly increased his anxiety.

No clue anywhere to the retreat of Kleinbach, and yet the message had been so specific—and someone should have contacted him at once. There had been, he'd learned, two recent "accidental" deaths on the staff of the Storm Resident Laboratory. That might explain the lack of contact—but then what explained his own charmed life? Why not an "accident" to—

He heard a soft chuckle behind him and sprang around through one hundred and eighty degrees of arc so that he should be no longer between the sound and the cliff.

Ivor Harden smiled at him almost patronizingly. "These cliffs are dangerous," he observed. "You should be more careful." And he walked off with as strictly ham a laugh as any baritone ever emitted at the end of the creed in *Otello*.

Jon Arthur stared after him. In his preoccupation he had almost invited Harden to kill him. The opportunity had been perfect. But the baritone had declined it, and even made a point of stressing his forbearance.

Therefore . . .

"He's either dead or dying," he said flatly to Mme. Storm. "They don't even care now whether I reach him. But they're stupid—they may have guessed wrong; there may still be a chance. You *must* take me to him."

Mme. Storm fluttered her eyelashes with a skill rarely attained at an age when they are worth fluttering. "My dear boy," she murmured with the faintest hint of throatiness, "flattering though it is to be accused of having a lover hidden away . . ."

"You're the only one of his former intimates on Venus. He loved you once.

He'd turn to you when he was alone and dying. I've explained why I must see him. I'm forced to trust you. And you see what it can mean to—"

The deft gesture of Mme. Storm's right hand evoked a nonexistent fan, over which her old eyes shone with a far from old warmth. "Please, my dear. Don't make another noble speech. You see, you've done it. When you said he loved me *once*. I have to correct that: He still loves me."

"Then he *is* here!"

"Come," she said, and moved from the room like a bride.

The great and dying Kleinbach was trying to listen; Jon Arthur could see that. The mechanisms of bones and veins which had once been hands plucked senselessly at the covers, and the pallid eyes stared at the face of Mme. Storm (with the mouth of a coquette and the eyes of a widow) or at nothing at all. But Arthur could feel, almost extrasensorily, the desire to respond.

"You can save us," he insisted. "An authentic message from you—I'll take care of identity checks that will satisfy every expert. You're the man that they'll *all* listen to. To the Academy, you're the one man that even Weddergren feels damned near humble before. To the Populists—maybe not to their leaders, but to the millions who act and vote—you're a symbol, as Einstein was before you and as no Academist is: a symbol of something wonderful and strange but very human. You're the bridge, the link, the greatness that synthesizes opposites. A word from you—and the Center falls together behind that word, leaving the extremists where they belong, on the sidelines of man's march . . ."

"Shh!" Mme. Storm whispered. She had sensed the effort in the sunken face before Arthur could realize that the old man intended to speak.

The first words were in German: *"Es irrt der Mensch . . ."*

The emaciated voice dwindled to nothing. Arthur remembered the passage from *Faust;* something about how man must still strive and err as he strives . . .

The next words were in English, and were two: *"Man's reach . . ."*

Then there was silence in the little room. From some faraway world, certainly no nearer this than the orbit of Mercury, came sounds of scales and vocalizing, those jarring preliminaries to beauty which characterize a school of singing.

Arthur never knew how long the room was silent before he realized that it was too silent.

There had been three different rhythms of breathing. Now there were two.

Mme. Storm looked up at him, at once older and younger than he had yet seen her. "It's all right," she whispered. "Don't blame yourself. You didn't . . . It was only days, perhaps hours . . ."

He leaned over and kissed her on the thin roughed lips. " From him," he said. He looked at the dried thing on the bed. "Cover his face," he said gently. "He died old."

To musicians, artists, writers, Venusberg means The Colony; to spacemen it means the most wide-open port in the system.

The first aspect had afforded Jon Arthur his excuse for coming; the second provided oblivion against the tragic failure of a mission.

It was two weeks before he even attempted to sober up. It was another week before he emerged from the pea soup fog of his hangover.

He emerged to find a batch of cryptically phrased spacegrams from Steele Morrison, Morrison, whose general tenor was "any luck?" and another batch from his managing editor, whose general tenor was "Where the hell is the first article of the series on Storm?" He tore up both batches unanswered.

"The dark night of the soul" is a phrase invented by a great mystic to describe a certain indescribable and enviable state of mystic communion and dissolution, but it sounds as though it described what a less mystic religious writer called "the Slough of Despond."

It was night in Jon Arthur's soul, a night of blackest indifference. Not even despair, which implies a certain desperate striving; but a callous inability to sense the importance of anything now that the Great Importance had collapsed.

Weeks passed and the election was held on Terra and the Academy won and Dr. Weddergren became President and 720,000 people were killed on both sides (and on neither) in the Populist riots which the Academy's military technicians (the Academy did not believe in soldiers) finally quelled and Dr. Weddergren announced again that the system is Man's laboratory and as a token thereof canceled the municipal elections about to be held in Greater Hollywood and Jon Arthur did not give a damn.

More weeks passed and the spacegrams kept coming and the last one said it was the last one because music critic and correspondent Arthur was no longer employed and Jon Arthur did not give a damn.

He had a few hundred credits left and the abandoned hut on the beach cost nothing and the hangovers were relatively shorter when you timed the bouts more carefully and there was much to be said for simply watching the waves to pass the time while staying sober.

So many people had come and gone in the hut on one night or another—Parva, Steele Morrison (with both legs), Kleinbach (reading a volume of Browning), Ivor Harden, even Marchesi once—that Arthur felt little surprise to see Irita Storm standing before him.

"You placed the quotation of course?" he remarked, as though they had just been discussing that scene in the little room.

"Of course," she said. *"Ah, but a man's reach should exceed his grasp—"*

"—Or what's a heaven for? Good question, that. *Andrea del Sarto."*

"Very good question. Question that leads me, young man, to ask you to come to see me."

Jon Arthur decided that was permissible to leer at imaginary elderly coquettes. He did not feel it fair of imaginary elderly coquettes to deal him an almost convincingly unimaginary slap.

"When you're sober." There was no coquetry in the voice. "If ever. For one thing, I want you to hear Parva. I'd really value your opinion—when you think I can get it."

It took almost two days for Arthur to convince himself that the brief scene had really taken place. At the end of another two he was neither trembling nor thirsty . . . at least not very much.

But he was trembling a little when Mme. Storm came into the side room where she had placed him.

"I didn't want her to know you were here," she explained. "It might have made her either very much above or very much below her usual form."

"I don't see why," he asserted argumentatively.

"Don't *fish!*" snapped Mme. Storm—and then answered his fishing with an odd little smile that could have made her even greater than she was in her youthful career as soubrette. "But what did you think?"

"Astonishing," he answered soberly. "She's not only singing . . . she's living and feeling and . . . and *being*. She's cut the duralloy cord that tied her to Weddergren and Marchesi."

Mme. Storm looked smug. "I don't think," she said, "that the President is going to like me."

Gradually the night began to clear. Music meant something more than the surf. And there might be meaning even in a life without Kleinbach, even in a life under the Academy.

And there was Faustina.

Most of her nonworking time they now spent together. Casually they ignored the fact that he was no longer the Great Critic who could build her career. They talked as fellow workers in music, planning productions, discussing repertory, making notes on the new translations he would prepare for some of her roles.

He decided to move from the hut to the Resident Laboratory when Mme. Storm asked him to give her pupils a series of lectures in music history. It was by then quite natural that Faustina should help him move such few possessions as he had.

And afterwards when they were sitting on the cliff she said, "I listened today to some of the tapes I made when I first came here. You know, I don't think I like that girl."

"That's funny," he said. "I was in love with her, in a way."

"She's too much like Mar— You were what?"

"In love with her."

"I must say this is a fine time to mention it!"

"Hardly realized it myself till now. Of course it wasn't anything comparable to being in love with you."

She took both his hands in hers. "And you are, aren't you?" she said gravely. "You'd better be . . . It's ridiculous, I've learned so much from Mme. Storm, I think I've even learned how to be *me* from her, but I haven't learned how to flirt." He kissed her hands gently. "So I'd better," she went on, "just plain say I love you, and we'll both know where we are."

"We are," he said quietly, "on a cliff on Venus which might well be the Big Sur on that blue star up there. That far an Academist might go. But of course the correct answer is simply *We are*, period."

After a long time, when her mouth was finally not otherwise occupied, she began to sing. She started with *Plaisir d'amour*: "Love's pleasure lasts but an instant, love's regrets for a lifetime . . ."

There is such a voluptuous sweetness to sad songs when you are unbearably happy.

And she sang this and that, and *Greensleeves* and *Stardust*. And the beauty of her voice and the beauty of her body and the beauty of her love were one.

That night had ended the night.

The next day Jon Arthur knew what he must do, and it was not to give a series of lectures on the history of music.

Mme. Storm protested. "You, yes, young man. Do what you will. But not Parva. I'm not through; she's only great, she—" But she capitulated finally. "If you promise to bring her back—and as many other robots that well trained as you can find. I'll make wonderful people of them too." And the invisible fan bestowed a parting benediction.

The spaceliner office protested. "Last minute reservations are just impossible. Two cabins— We might be able to arrange one double . . ."

The captain protested. "Never heard of performing a ceremony on the first day out! I don't care if you can't go to your cabin without it . . . !" But he capitulated too, after a jocular suggestion that Faustina could stay respectable by occupying her old air lock.

They themselves protested, both of the Arthurs, against the inactive three months forced upon them by Space. But they too capitulated; a honeymoon is a honeymoon.

Steele Morrison protested, shooting himself around Headquarters like a schizophrenic yo-yo. "You'll never even get in to see him! And you'll do no good if you do. The idea's crazy; drop it and try to make the best of what we have!"

A series of domestic technicians and secretarial technicians protested. But once the message reached him, President Weddergren eagerly insisted on an immediate interview with Faustina Parva Arthur.

Excellent journalist though he was, Jon Arthur would never have attempted a description of the reactions of Weddergren as he listened to his pupil—for of course his first desire, before any such trifles as felicitations on marriage, was to hear her after her sojourn with Storm.

Surprise, resentment, perplexity—those were certainly, in order, the first reactions to this blend of Weddergren perfection with Storm humanity. After that the emotions were more complex . . .

At the end of the brief recital there was a pause. Then the President observed, "My dear, I sent you to Venus as the greatest *voice* in the system. You have returned as the greatest *singer*."

And that was all.

It was the next day that the letter came—addressed not to Faustina but to Jon Arthur.

Their tenth reading of it was to Steele Morrison, who actually hung immobile for its duration:

Dear Mr. Arthur:

You are indeed a clever man, to realize the one thing that means so much to me that I can even, in its terms, understand an allegory that goes against my beliefs.

Yes, your nonallegoric suggestion is agreeable to me. The pressures of my office leave me little time to participate in the work myself; but my technicians will instruct you fully in my theories of physiology, in the demonstrative uses of Marchesi, and in the methods of hypnopedagogy. With these you may return to Venusberg and aid in establishing the Venusberg school of singing, the Weddergren-Storm ["She'll never accept that billing," Arthur interpolated] method, in which each contributor has something uniquely valuable to impart.

As to your unstated but implicit allegorical suggestions:

I had known, of course, through our Academy agents, that you were working for some nebulous Third Force, and that you hoped to save the world with some message from Kleinbach. I knew even that you were present at Kleinbach's deathbed. (Did it never occur to you that that baritone was too typically Populist to be anything but an Academy agent among Populists?) I had not expected the message to come in this form, or with this, to me, peculiarly forceful impact.

Science and humanity have made of Parva something which she could never have become without science—and yet something which the more absolutely perfect Marchesi could never become at all.

The analogy may be worth pursuing.

Respectfully yours,
James Weddergren

As Arthur finished, Steele Morrison zoomed across to the unsorted welter of papers which he termed his filing cabinet.

"I got me a letter today too, babies," he stated, brandishing a leaf of the same official note paper. "At first—hell, I don't know—I thought it was a rib maybe. It's about would I consider a cabinet post—*me* yet! And would I call at my earliest convenience with any suggestions as to psychological methods of preparation for a possible reintroduction of elections . . ."

Faustina opened her mouth and her throat. A three-octave run was as good a comment as any.

"Damn it," Arthur exclaimed, "I feel like singing myself. Something great and stirring and human and free—*Battle Hymn of the Republic* or *Thaelmanns-Kolonne* or *La Marseillaise!*"

Faustina began it. Her voice *was* Man's freedom, technically freed by science, spiritually free in its own ardor. *"Allons, enfants de la patrie! . . ."*

"Hell!" shouted Steele Morrison, zooming toward the bar. "I know how to translate that: *Come on, kids, let's have a party!*"

So they did.

Mr. Lupescu

The teacups rattled, and flames flickered over the logs.

"Alan, I *do* wish you could do something about Bobby."

"Isn't that rather Robert's place?"

"Oh, you know *Robert*. He's so busy doing good in nice abstract ways with committees in them."

"And headlines."

"He can't be bothered with things like Mr. Lupescu. After all, Bobby's only his *son*."

"And yours, Marjorie."

"And mine. But things like this take a *man,* Alan."

The room was warm and peaceful; Alan stretched his long legs by the fire and felt domestic. Marjorie was soothing even when she fretted. The firelight did things to her hair and the curve of her blouse.

A small whirlwind entered at high velocity and stopped only when Marjorie said, "Bob-*by!* Say hello nicely to Uncle Alan."

Bobby said hello and stood tentatively on one foot.

"Alan . . ." Marjorie prompted.

Alan sat up straight and tried to look paternal. "Well, Bobby," he said. "And where are you off to in such a hurry?"

"See Mr. Lupescu 'f course. He usually comes afternoons."

"Your mother's been telling me about Mr. Lupescu. He must be quite a person."

"Oh gee I'll say he is, Uncle Alan. He's got a great big red nose and red gloves and red eyes—not like when you've been crying but really red like yours're brown—and little red wings that twitch only he can't fly with them cause they're ruddermentary he says. And he talks like—oh gee I can't do it, but he's swell, he is."

"Lupescu's a funny name for a fairy godfather, isn't it, Bobby?"

"Why? Mr. Lupescu always says why do all the fairies have to be Irish because it takes all kinds, doesn't it?"

"*Alan!*" Marjorie said. "I don't see that you're doing a *bit* of good. You talk to him seriously like that and you simply make him think it *is* serious. And you *do* know better, don't you, Bobby? You're just joking with us."

"Joking? About *Mr. Lupescu?*"

"Marjorie, you don't— Listen, Bobby. Your mother didn't mean to insult you or Mr. Lupescu. She just doesn't believe in what she's never seen, and you can't blame her. Now, suppose you took her and me out in the garden and we could all see Mr. Lupescu. Wouldn't that be fun?"

"Uh-uh." Bobby shook his head gravely. "Not for Mr. Lupescu. He doesn't like people. Only little boys. And he says if I ever bring people to see him, then he'll let Gorgo get me. G'bye now." And the whirlwind departed.

Marjorie sighed. "At least thank heavens for Gorgo. I never can get a very clear picture out of Bobby, but he says Mr. Lupescu tells the most *terrible* things about him. And if there's any trouble about vegetables or brushing teeth, all I have to say is *Gorgo* and hey presto!"

Alan rose. "I don't think you need worry, Marjorie. Mr. Lupescu seems to do more good than harm, and an active imagination is no curse to a child."

"You haven't *lived* with Mr. Lupescu."

"To live in a house like this, I'd chance it," Alan laughed. "But please forgive me now—back to the cottage and the typewriter . . . Seriously, why don't you ask Robert to talk with him?"

Marjorie spread her hands helplessly.

"I know. I'm always the one to assume responsibilities. And yet you married Robert."

Marjorie laughed. "I don't know. Somehow there's something *about* Robert . . ." Her vague gesture happened to include the original Degas over the fireplace, the sterling tea service, and even the liveried footman who came in at that moment to clear away.

Mr. Lupescu was pretty wonderful that afternoon, all right. He had a little kind of an itch like in his wings and they kept twitching all the time. Stardust, he said. It tickles. Got it up in the Milky Way. Friend of mine has a wagon route up there.

Mr. Lupescu had lots of friends, and they all did something you wouldn't ever think of, not in a squillion years. That's why he didn't like people, because people don't do things you can tell stories about. They just work or keep house or are mothers or something.

But one of Mr. Lupescu's friends, now, was captain of a ship, only it went in time, and Mr. Lupescu took trips with him and came back and told you all about what was happening this very minute five hundred years ago. And another of the friends was a radio engineer, only he could tune in on all the kingdoms of faery and Mr. Lupescu would squidgle up his red nose and twist it like a dial and make noises like all the kingdoms of faery coming in on the set. And then there was Gorgo, only he wasn't a friend—not exactly; not even to Mr. Lupescu.

They'd been playing for a couple of weeks—only it must've been really hours, cause Mamselle hadn't yelled about supper yet, but Mr. Lupescu says Time is funny—when Mr. Lupescu screwed up his red eyes and said, "Bobby, let's go in the house."

"But there's people in the house, and you don't—"

"I know I don't like people. That's why we're going in the house. Come on, Bobby, or I'll—"

So what could you do when you didn't even want to hear him say Gorgo's name?

He went into Father's study through the French window, and it was a strict rule that nobody *ever* went into Father's study, but rules weren't for Mr. Lupescu.

Father was on the telephone telling somebody he'd try to be at a luncheon but there was a committee meeting that same morning but he'd see. While he was talking, Mr. Lupescu went over to a table and opened a drawer and took something out.

When Father hung up, he saw Bobby first and started to be very mad. He said, "Young man, you've been trouble enough to your Mother and me with all your stories about your red-winged Mr. Lupescu, and now if you're to start bursting in—"

You have to be polite and introduce people. "Father, this is Mr. Lupescu. And see, he does too have red wings."

Mr. Lupescu held out the gun he'd taken from the drawer and shot Father once right through the forehead. It made a little clean hole in front and a big messy hole in back. Father fell down and was dead.

"Now, Bobby," Mr. Lupescu said, "a lot of people are going to come here and ask you a lot of questions. And if you don't tell the truth about exactly what happened, I'll send Gorgo to fetch you."

Then Mr. Lupescu was gone through the French window.

"It's a curious case, Lieutenant," the medical examiner said. "It's fortunate I've dabbled a bit in psychiatry; I can at least give you a lead until you get the experts in. The child's statement that his fairy godfather shot his father is obviously a simple flight mechanism, susceptible of two interpretations. A, the father shot himself; the child was so horrified by the sight that he refused to accept it and invented this explanation. B, the child shot the father, let us say by accident, and shifted the blame to his imaginary scapegoat. B has, of course, its more sinister implications: if the child had resented his father and created an ideal substitute, he might make the substitute destroy the reality . . . But there's the solution to your eyewitness testimony; which alternative is true, Lieutenant, I leave up to your researchers into motive and the evidence of ballistics and fingerprints. The angle of the wound jibes with either."

The man with the red nose and eyes and gloves and wings walked down the back lane to the cottage. As soon as he got inside, he took off his coat and removed the wings and the mechanism of strings and rubber that made them twitch. He laid them on top of the ready pile of kindling and lit the fire. When it was well started, he added the gloves. Then he took off the nose, kneaded the putty until the red of its outside vanished into the neutral brown of the mass, jammed it into a crack in the wall, and smoothed it over. Then he took the red-irised contact lenses out of his brown eyes and went into the kitchen, found a hammer, pounded them to powder, and washed the powder down the sink.

Alan started to pour himself a drink and found, to his pleased surprise, that he didn't especially need one. But he did feel tired. He could lie down and recapitulate it all, from the invention of Mr. Lupescu (and Gorgo and the man with the Milky Way route) to today's success and on into the future when Marjorie—pliant, trusting Marjorie—would be more desirable than ever as Robert's widow and heir. And Bobby would need a *man* to look after him.

Alan went into the bedroom. Several years passed by in the few seconds it took him to recognize what was waiting on the bed, but then, Time is funny.

Alan said nothing.

"Mr. Lupescu, I presume?" said Gorgo.

Balaam

"What is a '*man*'?" Rabbi Chaim Acosta demanded, turning his back on the window and its view of pink sand and infinite pink boredom. "You and I, Mule, in our respective ways, work for the salvation of *man*—as you put it, for the brotherhood of *men* under the fatherhood of God. Very well, let us define our terms: Whom, or more precisely *what,* are we interested in saving?"

Father Aloysius Malloy shifted uncomfortably and reluctantly closed the *American Football Yearbook* which had been smuggled in on the last rocket, against all weight regulations, by one of his communicants. I honestly like Chaim, he thought, not merely (or is that the right word?) with brotherly love, nor even out of the deep gratitude I owe him, but with special individual liking; and I respect him. He's a brilliant man—too brilliant to take a dull post like this in his stride. But he *will* get off into discussions which are much too much like what one of my Jesuit professors called "disputations."

"What did you say, Chaim?" he asked.

The rabbi's black Sephardic eyes sparkled. "You know very well what I said, Mule; and you're stalling for time. Please indulge me. Our religious duties here are not so arduous as we might wish; and since you won't play chess . . ."

". . . and you," said Father Malloy unexpectedly, "refuse to take any interest in diagraming football plays . . ."

"*Touché.* Or am I? Is it my fault that as an Israeli I fail to share the peculiar American delusion that football means something other than rugby and soccer? Whereas chess—" He looked at the priest reproachfully. "Mule," he said, "you have led me into a digression."

"It was a try. Like the time the whole Southern California line thought I had the ball for once and Leliwa walked over for the winning TD."

"What," Acosta repeated, "is *man?* Is it by definition a member of the genus *H. sapiens* inhabiting the planet Sol III and its colonies?"

"The next time we tried the play," said Malloy resignedly, "Leliwa was smeared for a ten-yard loss."

The two *men* met on the sands of Mars. It was an unexpected meeting, a meeting in itself uneventful, and yet one of the turning points in the history of *men* and their universe.

The *man* from the colony base was on a routine patrol—a patrol imposed by the captain for reasons of discipline and activity-for-activity's-sake rather than from any need for protection in this uninhabited waste. He had seen, over beyond the next rise, what he would have sworn was the braking blaze of a landing rocket—if he hadn't known that the next rocket wasn't due for another week. Six and a half days, to be exact, or even more exactly, six days, eleven hours, and twenty-three minutes, Greenwich Interplanetary. He knew the time so exactly because he, along with half the garrison, Father Malloy, and those screwball Israelis, was due for rotation then. So no matter how much it looked like a rocket, it couldn't be one; but it was something happening on his patrol, for the first time since he'd come to this God-forsaken hole, and he might as well look into it and get his name on a report.

The *man* from the spaceship also knew the boredom of the empty planet. Alone of his crew, he had been there before, on the first voyage when they took the samples and set up the observation autoposts. But did that make the captain even listen to him? Hell, no; the captain knew all about the planet from the sample analyses and had no time to listen to a guy who'd really been there. So all he got out of it was the privilege of making the first reconnaissance. Big deal! One fast look around reconnoitering a few googols of sand grains and then back to the ship. But there was some kind of glow over that rise there. It couldn't be lights; theirs was the scout ship, none of the others had landed yet. Some kind of phosphorescent life they'd missed the first time round . . . ? Maybe now the captain would believe that the sample analyses didn't tell him everything.

The two *men* met at the top of the rise.

One *man* saw the horror of seemingly numberless limbs, of a headless torso, of a creature so alien that it walked in its glittering bare flesh in this freezing cold and needed no apparatus to supplement the all but nonexistent air.

One *man* saw the horror of an unbelievably meager four limbs, of a torso topped with an ugly lump like some unnatural growth, of a creature so alien that it smothered itself with heavy clothing in this warm climate and cut itself off from this invigorating air.

And both *men* screamed and ran.

"There is an interesting doctrine," said Rabbi Acosta, "advanced by one of your writers, C. S. Lewis . . ."

"He was an Episcopalian," said Father Malloy sharply.

"I apologize." Acosta refrained from pointing out that Anglo-Catholic would have been a more accurate term. "But I believe that many in your church have found his writings, from your point of view, doctrinally sound? He advances the doctrine of what he calls *hnaus*—intelligent beings with souls who are the children of God, whatever their physical shape or planet of origin."

"Look, Chaim," said Malloy with an effort toward patience. "Doctrine or no doctrine, there just plain aren't any such beings. Not in this solar system anyway. And if you're going to go interstellar on me, I'd just as soon read the men's microcomics."

"Interplanetary travel existed only in such literature once. But of course if you'd rather play chess . . ."

"My specialty," said the man once known to sports writers as Mule Malloy, "was running interference. Against you I need somebody to run interference *for*."

"Let us take the sixteenth psalm of David, which you call the fifteenth, having decided, for reasons known only to your God and mine, that psalms nine and ten are one. There is a phrase in there which, if you'll forgive me, I'll quote in Latin; your Saint Jerome is often more satisfactory than any English translator. *Benedicam Dominum, qui tribuit mihi intellectum.*"

"*Blessed be the Lord, who schools me,*" murmured Malloy, in the standard Knox translation.

"But according to Saint Jerome: *I shall bless the Lord, who bestows on me*—just how should one render *intellectum?*—not merely intellect, but *perception, comprehension* . . . what Hamlet means when he says of *man: In apprehension how like a god!*"

Words change their meanings.

Apprehensively, one *man* reported to his captain. The captain first swore, then scoffed, then listened to the story again. Finally he said, "I'm sending a full squad back with you to the place where—maybe—you saw this thing. If it's for real, these mother-dighting bug-eyed monsters are going to curse the day they ever set a God-damned tentacle on Mars." The *man* decided it was no use trying to explain that the worst of it was it *wasn't* bug-eyed; any kind of eyes in any kind of head would have been something. And they weren't even quite tentacles either . . .

Apprehensively, too, the other *man* made his report. The captain scoffed first and then swore, including some select remarks on underhatched characters who knew all about a planet because they'd been there once. Finally he said, "We'll see if a squad of real observers can find any trace of your egg-eating limbless monsters; and if we find them, they're going to be God-damned sorry they were ever hatched." It was no use, the *man* decided, trying to explain that it wouldn't have been so bad if it *had* been limbless, like in the picture tapes; but just *four* limbs . . .

"What is a *man?*" Rabbi Acosta repeated, and Mule Malloy wondered why his subconscious synapses had not earlier produced the obvious appropriate answer.

"*Man,*" he recited, "*is a creature composed of body and soul, and made to the image and likeness of God.*"

"From that echo of childish singsong, Mule, I judge that is a correct catechism response. Surely the catechism must follow it up with some question about that likeness? Can it be a likeness in"—his hand swept up and down over his own body with a graceful gesture of contempt—"*this* body?"

"*This likeness to God is chiefly in the soul.*"

"Aha!" The Sephardic sparkle was brighter than ever.

The words went on, the centers of speech following the synaptic patterns engraved in parochial school as the needle followed the grooves of an antique record. "*All creatures bear some resemblance to God inasmuch as they exist. Plants and animals resemble Him insofar as they have life . . .*"

"I can hardly deny so profound a statement."

"*. . . but none of these creatures is made to the image and likeness of God. Plants and animals do not have a rational soul, such as man has, by which they might know and love God.*"

"As do all good *hnaus*. Go on; I am not sure that our own scholars have stated it so well. Mule, you are invaluable!"

Malloy found himself catching a little of Acosta's excitement. He had known these words all his life; he had recited them the Lord knows how many times. But he was not sure that he had ever listened to them before. And he wondered for a moment how often even his Jesuit professors, in their profound consideration of the x^n's of theology, had ever paused to reconsider these childhood ABC's.

"How is the soul like God?" He asked himself the next catechistic question, and answered, *"The soul is like God because it is a spirit having understanding and free will and is destined . . ."*

"Reverend gentlemen!" The reverence was in the words only. The interrupting voice of Captain Dietrich Fassbänder differed little in tone from his normal address to a buck private of the Martian Legion.

Mule Malloy said, "Hi, Captain." He felt half relieved, half disappointed, as if he had been interrupted while unwrapping a present whose outlines he was just beginning to glimpse. Rabbi Acosta smiled wryly and said nothing.

"So this is how you spend your time? No Martian natives, so you practice by trying to convert each other, is that it?"

Acosta made a light gesture which might have been polite acknowledgment of what the captain evidently considered a joke. "The Martian day is so tedious we have been driven to talking shop. Your interruption is welcome. Since you so rarely seek out our company, I take it you bring some news. Is it, God grant, that the rotation rocket is arriving a week early?"

"No, damn it," Fassbänder grunted. (He seemed to take a certain pride, Malloy had observed, in carefully not tempering his language for the ears of clergymen.) "Then I'd have a German detachment instead of your Israelis, and I'd know where I stood. I suppose it's all very advisable politically for every state in the UW to contribute a detachment in rotation; but I'd sooner either have my regular legion garrison doubled, or two German detachments regularly rotating. That time I had the pride of Pakistan here . . . Damn it, you new states haven't had time to develop a military tradition!"

"Father Malloy," the rabbi asked gently, "are you acquainted with the sixth book of what you term the Old Testament?"

"Thought you fellows were tired of talking shop," Fassbänder objected.

"Rabbi Acosta refers to the Book of Joshua, Captain. And I'm afraid, God help us, that there isn't a state or a tribe that hasn't a tradition of war. Even your Prussian ancestors might have learned a trick or two from the campaigns of Joshua—or for that matter, from the Cattle Raid on Cooley, when the Hound of Cullen beat off the armies of Queen Maeve. And I've often thought, too, that it'd do your strategists no harm to spend a season or two at quarterback, if they had the wind. Did you know that Eisenhower played football, and against Jim Thorpe once at that? And . . ."

"But I don't imagine," Acosta interposed, "that you came here to talk shop either, Captain?"

"Yes," said Captain Fassbänder, sharply and unexpectedly. "My shop and, damn it, yours. Never thought I'd see the day when I . . ." He broke off and tried another approach. "I mean, of course, a chaplain is part of an army. You're both army officers, technically speaking, one of the Martian Legion, one in the Israeli forces; but it's highly unusual to ask a man of the cloth to . . ."

"To praise the Lord and pass the ammunition, as the folk legend has it? There are precedents among my people, and among Father Malloy's as well, though rather different ideas are attributed to the founder of his church. What is it, Captain? Or wait, I know: We are besieged by alien invaders and Mars needs every able-bodied man to defend her sacred sands. Is that it?"

"Well . . . God damn it . . ." Captain Fassbänder's cheeks grew purple. ". . . YES!" he exploded.

The situation was so hackneyed in 3V and microcomics that it was less a matter of explaining it than of making it seem real. Dietrich Fassbänder's powers of exposition were not great, but his sincerity was evident and in itself convincing.

"Didn't believe it myself at first," he admitted. "But he was right. Our patrol ran into a patrol of . . . of *them*. There was a skirmish; we lost two men but killed one of the things. Their small arms use explosive propulsion of metal much like ours; God knows what they might have in that ship to counter our A-warheads. But we've got to put up a fight for Mars; and that's where you come in."

The two priests looked at him wordlessly, Acosta with a faint air of puzzled withdrawal, Malloy almost as if he expected the captain to start diagraming the play on a blackboard.

"You especially, Rabbi. I'm not worried about your boys, Father. We've got a Catholic chaplain on this rotation because this bunch of legionnaires is largely Poles and Irish-Americans. They'll fight all right, and we'll expect you to say a field Mass beforehand, and that's about all. Oh, and that fool gunner Olszewski has some idea he'd like his A-cannon sprinkled with holy water; I guess you can handle that without any trouble.

"But your Israelis are a different problem, Acosta. They don't know the meaning of discipline—not what we call discipline in the legion; and Mars doesn't mean to them what it does to a legionnaire. And besides a lot of them have got a . . . hell, guess I shouldn't call it superstition, but a kind of . . . well, reverence—awe, you might say—about you, Rabbi. They say you're a miracle-worker."

"He is," said Mule Malloy simply. "He saved my life."

He could still feel that extraordinary invisible power (a "force-field," one of the technicians later called it, as he cursed the shots that had destroyed the machine past all analysis) which had bound him helpless there in that narrow pass, too far from the dome for rescue by any patrol. It was his first week on Mars, and he had hiked too long, enjoying the easy strides of low gravity and alternately meditating on the versatility of the Creator of planets and on that Year Day long ago when he had blocked out the most famous of All-American line-backers to bring about the most impressive of Rose Bowl upsets. Sibiryakov's touchdown made the headlines; but he and Sibiryakov knew why that touchdown happened, and he felt his own inner warmth . . . and was that sinful pride or just self-recognition? And then he was held as no line had ever held him and the hours passed and no one on Mars could know where he was and when the patrol arrived they said, "The Israeli chaplain sent us." And later Chaim Acosta, laconic for the first and only time, said simply, "I knew where you were. It happens to me sometimes."

Now Acosta shrugged and his graceful hands waved deprecation. "Scientifically speaking, Captain, I believe that I have, on occasion, a certain amount of extrasensory perception and conceivably a touch of some of the other *psi* faculties. The Rhinists at Tel Aviv are quite interested in me; but my faculties too often refuse to perform on laboratory command. But 'miracle-working' is a strong word. Remind me to tell you some time the story of the guaranteed genuine miracle-working rabbi from Lwow."

"Call it miracles, call it ESP, you've got something, Acosta . . ."

"I shouldn't have mentioned Joshua," the rabbi smiled. "Surely you aren't suggesting that I try a miracle to win your battle for you?"

"Hell with that," snorted Fassbänder. "It's your men. They've got it fixed in their minds that you're a . . . a saint. No, you Jews don't have saints, do you?"

"A nice question in semantics," Chaim Acosta observed quietly.

"Well, a prophet. Whatever you people call it. And we've got to make men out of your boys. Stiffen their backbones, send 'em in there knowing they're going to win."

"Are they?" Acosta asked flatly.

"God knows. But they sure as hell won't if they don't think so. So it's up to you."

"What is?"

"They may pull a sneak attack on us, but I don't think so. Way I see it, they're as surprised and puzzled as we are; and they need time to think the situation over. We'll attack before dawn tomorrow; and to make sure your Israelis go in there with fighting spirit, you're going to curse them."

"Curse my men?"

"Potztausend Sapperment noch einmal!" Captain Fassbänder's English was flawless, but not adequate to such a situation as this. "Curse *them!* The . . . the *things,* the aliens, the invaders, whatever the *urverdammt* bloody hell you want to call them!"

He could have used far stronger language without offending either chaplain. Both had suddenly realized that he was perfectly serious.

"A formal curse, Captain?" Chaim Acosta asked. "Anathema maranatha? Perhaps Father Malloy would lend me bell, book, and candle?"

Mule Malloy looked uncomfortable. "You read about such things, Captain," he admitted. "They were done, a long time ago . . ."

"There's nothing in your religion against it, is there, Acosta?"

"There is . . . precedent," the rabbi confessed softly.

"Then it's an order, from your superior officer. I'll leave the mechanics up to you. You know how it's done. If you need anything . . . what kind of bell?"

"I'm afraid that was meant as a joke, Captain."

"Well, these *things* are no joke. And you'll curse them tomorrow morning before all your men."

"I shall pray," said Rabbi Chaim Acosta, "for guidance . . ." But the captain was already gone. He turned to his fellow priest. "Mule, you'll pray for me too?" The normally agile hands hung limp at his side.

Mule Malloy nodded. He groped for his rosary as Acosta silently left the room.

Now entertain conjecture of a time when two infinitesimal forces of *men*—one half-forgotten outpost garrison, one small scouting fleet—spend the night in readying themselves against the unknown, in preparing to meet on the morrow to determine, perhaps, the course of centuries for a galaxy.

Two *men* are feeding sample range-finding problems into the computer.

"That God-damned Fassbänder," says one. "I heard him talking to our commander. 'You and your men who have never understood the meaning of discipline . . . !'"

"Prussians," the other grunts. He has an Irish face and an American accent. "Think they own the earth. When we get through here, let's dump all the Prussians into Texas and let 'em fight it out. Then we can call the state Kilkenny."

"What did you get on that last? . . . Check. Fassbänder's 'discipline' is for peace—spit-and-polish to look pretty here in our sandy pink nowhere. What's the pay-off? Fassbänder's great-grandfathers were losing two world wars while mine were creating a new nation out of nothing. Ask the Arabs if have no discipline. Ask the British . . ."

"Ah, the British. Now *my* great-grandfather was in the IRA . . ."

Two *men* are integrating the electrodes of the wave-hurler.

"It isn't bad enough we get drafted for this expedition to nowhere; we have to have an egg-eating Nangurian in command."

"And a Tryldian scout to bring the first report. What's your reading there? . . . Check."

"'A Tryldian to tell a lie and a Nangurian to force it into truth,'" the first quotes.

"Now, brothers," says the *man* adjusting the microvernier on the telelens, "the Goodman assures us these monsters are true. We must unite in love for each other, even Tryldians and Nangurians, and wipe them out. The Goodman has promised us his blessing before battle . . ."

"The Goodman," says the first, "can eat the egg he was hatched from."

"The rabbi," says a *man* checking the oxyhelms, "can take his blessing and shove it up Fassbänder. I'm no Jew in his sense. I'm a sensible, rational atheist who happens to be an Israeli."

"And I," says his companion, "am a Romanian who believes in the God of my fathers and therefore gives allegiance to His state of Israel. What is a Jew who denies the God of Moses? To call him still a Jew is to think like Fassbänder."

"They've got an edge on us," says the first. "*They* can breathe here. These oxyhelms run out in three hours. What do we do then? Rely on the rabbi's blessing?"

"I said the God of my fathers, and yet my great-grandfather thought as you do and still fought to make Israel live anew. It was his son who, like so many others, learned that he must return to Jerusalem in spirit as well as body."

"Sure, we had the Great Revival of orthodox religion. So what did it get us? Troops that need a rabbi's blessing before a commander's orders."

"Many men have died from orders. How many from blessings?"

"I fear that few die well who die in battle ..." the *man* reads in Valkram's great epic of the siege of Tolnishri.

"... for how [the *man* is reading of the eve of Agincourt in his micro-Shakespeare] *can they charitably dispose of anything when blood is their argument? "*

"... and if these do not die well [so Valkram wrote] *how grievously must their bad deaths be charged against the Goodman who blesses them into battle ..."*

"And why not?" Chaim Acosta flicked the question away with a wave of his long fingers.

The bleep (even Acosta was not so linguistically formal as to call it a bubble jeep) bounced along over the sand toward the rise which overlooked the invaders' ship. Mule Malloy handled the wheel with solid efficiency and said nothing.

"I *did* pray for guidance last night," the rabbi asserted, almost as if in self-defense. "I ... I had some strange thoughts for a while; but they make very little sense this morning. After all, I am an officer in the army. 1 do have a certain obligation to my superior officer and to my men. And when I became a rabbi, a teacher, I was specifically ordained to decide questions of law and ritual. Surely this case falls within that authority of mine."

Abruptly the bleep stopped.

"What's the matter, Mule?"

"Nothing ... Wanted to rest my eyes a minute ... Why did you become ordained, Chaim?"

"Why did you? Which of us understands all the infinite factors of heredity and environment which lead us to such a choice? Or even, if you will, to such a being chosen? Twenty years ago it seemed the only road I could possibly take; now ... We'd better get going, Mule."

The bleep started up again.

"A curse sounds so melodramatic and medieval; but is it in essence any different from a prayer for victory, which chaplains offer up regularly? As I imagine you did in your field Mass. Certainly all of your communicants are praying for victory to the Lord of Hosts—and as Captain Fassbänder would point out, it makes them better fighting men. I will confess that even as a teacher of the law, I have no marked doctrinal confidence in the efficacy of a curse. I do not expect the spaceship of the invaders to be blasted by the forked lightning of Yahveh. But my men have an exaggerated sort of faith in me, and I owe it to them to do anything possible to strengthen their morale. Which is all the legion or any other army expects of chaplains anyway; we are no longer priests of the Lord, but boosters of morale—a type of sublimated YMCA secretary. Well, in my case, say YMHA."

The bleep stopped again.

"I never knew your eyes to be so sensitive before," Acosta observed tartly.

"I thought you might want a little time to think it over," Malloy ventured.

"I've thought it over. What else have I been telling you? Now please, Mule.

Everything's all set. Fassbänder will explode completely if I don't speak my curse into this mike in two minutes."

Silently Mule Malloy started up the bleep.

"Why did I become ordained?" Acosta backtracked. "That's no question really. The question is why have I remained in a profession to which I am so little suited. I will confess to you, Mule, and to you only, that I have not the spiritual humility and patience that I might desire. I itch for something beyond the humdrum problems of a congregation or an army detachment. Sometimes I have felt that I should drop everything else and concentrate on my *psi* faculties, that they might lead me to this goal I seek without understanding. But they are too erratic. I know the law, I love the ritual, but I am not good as a rabbi, a teacher, because . . ."

For the third time the bleep stopped, and Mule Malloy said, "Because you are a saint."

And before Chaim Acosta could protest, he went on, "Or a prophet, if you want Fassbänder's distinction. There are all kinds of saints and prophets. There are the gentle, humble, patient ones like Francis of Assisi and Job and Ruth—or do you count women? And there are God's firebrands, the ones of fierce intellect and dreadful determination, who shake the history of God's elect, the saints who have reached through sin to salvation with a confident power that is the reverse of the pride of the Lucifer, cast from the same ringing metal."

"Mule . . . !" Acosta protested. "This isn't you. These aren't your words. And you didn't learn these in parochial school . . ."

Malloy seemed not to hear him. "Paul, Thomas More, Catherine of Siena, Augustine," he recited in rich cadence. "Elijah, Ezekiel, Judas Maccabeus, Moses, David . . . You are a prophet, Chaim. Forget the rationalizing double talk of the Rhinists and recognize whence your powers come, how you were guided to save me, what the 'strange thoughts' were that you had during last night's vigil of prayer. You are a prophet—and you are not going to curse *men,* the children of God."

Abruptly Malloy slumped forward over the wheel. There was silence in the bleep. Chaim Acosta stared at his hands as if he knew no gesture for this situation.

"Gentlemen!" Captain Fassbänder's voice was even more rasping than usual over the telecom. "Will you please get the blessed lead out and get up that rise? It's two minutes, twenty seconds, past zero!"

Automatically Acosta depressed the switch and said, "Right away, Captain."

Mule Malloy stirred and opened his eyes. "Was that Fassbänder?"

"Yes . . . But there's no hurry, Mule. I can't understand it. What made you . . . ?"

"I don't understand it, either. Never passed out like that before. Doctor used to say that head injury in the Wisconsin game might—but after thirty years . . ."

Chaim Acosta sighed. "You sound like my Mule again. But before . . ."

"Why? Did I say something? Seems to me like there was something important I wanted to say to you."

"I wonder what they'd say at Tel Aviv. Telepathic communication of subconscious minds? Externalization of thoughts that I was afraid to acknowledge consciously? Yes, you said something, Mule; and I was as astonished as Balaam when his ass spoke to him on his journey to . . . Mule!"

Acosta's eyes were blackly alight as never before, and his hands flickered eagerly. "Mule, do you remember the story of Balaam? It's in the fourth book of Moses . . ."

"Numbers? All I remember is he had a talking ass. I suppose there's a pun on *Mule?*"

"Balaam, son of Beor," said the rabbi with quiet intensity, "was a prophet in Moab. The Israelites were invading Moab, and King Balak ordered Balaam to curse them. His ass not only spoke to him; more important, it halted and refused to budge on the journey until Balaam had listened to a message from the Lord . . .

"You were right, Mule. Whether you remember what you said or not, whether your description of me was God's truth or the telepathic projection of my own ego, you were right in one thing: These invaders are *men,* by all the standards that we debated yesterday. Moreover they are *men* suited to Mars; our patrol reported them as naked and unprotected in this cold and this atmosphere. I wonder if they have scouted this planet before and selected it as suitable; that could have been some observation device left by them that trapped you in the pass, since we've never found traces of an earlier Martian civilization.

"Mars is not for us. We cannot live here normally; our scientific researches have proved fruitless; and we maintain an inert, bored garrison only because our planetary ego cannot face facts and surrender the symbol of our 'conquest of space.' These other *men* can live here, perhaps fruitfully, to the glory of God and eventually to the good of our own world as well, as two suitably populated planets come to know each other. You were right; I cannot curse *men.*"

"GENTLEMEN!"

Deftly Acosta reached down and switched off the telecom. "You agree, Mule?"

"I . . . I . . . I guess I drive back now, Chaim?"

"Of course not. Do you think I want to face Fassbänder now? You drive on. At once. Up to the top of the rise. Or haven't you yet remembered the rest of the story of Balaam? He didn't stop at refusing to curse his fellow children of God. Not Balaam.

"He blessed them."

Mule Malloy had remembered that. He had remembered more, too. The phonograph needle had coursed through the grooves of Bible study on up to the thirty-first chapter of Numbers with its brief epilog to the story of Balaam:

So Moses ordered a muster of men sufficient to wreak the Lord's vengeance on the Midianites. . . . All the menfolk they killed, the chiefs of the tribe . . . Balaam, too, the son of Beor, they put to the sword.

He looked at the tense face of Chaim Acosta, where exultation and resignation blended as they must in a man who knows at last the pattern of his life, and realized that Chaim's memory, too, went as far as the thirty-first chapter.

And there isn't a word in the Bible as to what became of the ass, thought Mule Malloy, and started the bleep up the rise.

The Anomaly of the Empty Man

"This is for you," Inspector Abrahams announced wryly. Another screwy one."

I was late and out of breath. I'd somehow got entangled on Market Street with the Downtown Merchants' Association annual parade, and for a while it looked like I'd be spending the day surrounded by gigantic balloon-parodies of humanity. But it takes more than rubber Gullivers to hold me up when Inspector Abrahams announces that he's got a case of the kind he labels "for Lamb."

And San Francisco's the city for them to happen in. Nobody anywhere else ever had such a motive for murder as the butler Frank Miller in 1896, or such an idea of how to execute a bank robbery as the zany Mr. Will in 1952. Take a look at Joe Jackson's *San Francisco Murders,* and you'll see that we can achieve a flavor all our own. And when we do, Abrahams lets me in on it.

Abrahams didn't add any explanation. He just opened the door of the apartment. I went in ahead of him. It was a place I could have liked it if it hadn't been for what was on the floor.

Two walls were mostly windows. One gave a good view of the Golden Gate. From the other, on a fine day, you could see the Farallones, and it was a fine day.

The other two walls were records and a record player. I'd heard of the Stambaugh collection of early operatic recordings. If I'd been there on any other errand, my mouth would have watered at the prospect of listening to lost great voices.

"If you can get a story out of this that makes sense," the Inspector grunted, "you're welcome to it—at the usual fee." Which was a dinner at Lupo's Pizzeria, complete with pizza Carus's, tomatoes with fresh basil and sour French bread to mop up the inspired sauce of Lupo's special *calamari* (squids to you). "Everything's just the way we found it."

I looked at the unfinished highball, now almost colorless with all its ice melted and its soda flat. I looked at the cylindrical ash of the cigarette which had burned itself out. I looked at the vacuum cleaner—a shockingly utilitarian object in this set for gracious living. I looked at the record player, still switched on, still making its methodical seventy-eight revolutions per minute, though there was no record on the turntable.

Then I managed to look again at the thing on the floor.

It was worse than a body. It was like a tasteless bloodless parody of the usual

299

occupant of the spot marked X. Clothes scattered in disorder seem normal—even more normal, perhaps, in a bachelor apartment than clothes properly hung in closets. But this . . .

Above the neck of the dressing gown lay the spectacles. The sleeves of the shirt were inside the sleeves of the dressing gown. The shirt was buttoned, even to the collar, and the foulard tie was knotted tight up against the collar button. The tails of the shirt were tucked properly into the zipped-up, properly belted trousers. Below the trouser cuffs lay the shoes, at a lifelike angle, with the tops of the socks emerging from them.

"And there's an undershirt under the shirt," Inspector Abrahams muttered disconsolately, "and shorts inside the pants. Complete outfit: what the well-dressed man will wear. Only no man in them."

It was as though James Stambaugh had been attacked by some solvent which eats away only flesh and leaves all the inanimate articles. Or as though some hyperspatial suction had drawn the living man out of his wardrobe, leaving his sartorial shell behind him.

I said, "Can I dirty an ashtray in this scene?"

Abrahams nodded. "I was just keeping it for you to see. We've got our pictures." While I lit up, he crossed to the record player and switched it off. "Damned whirligig gets on my nerves."

"Whole damned setup gets on mine," I said. "It's like a strip-tease version of the *Mary Celeste*. Only the strip wasn't a gradual tease; just abruptly, *whoosh!*, a man's gone. One minute he's comfortably dressed in his apartment, smoking, drinking, playing records. The next he's stark naked—and where and doing what?"

Abrahams pulled at his nose, which didn't need lengthening. "We had the Japanese valet check the wardrobe. Every article of clothing James Stambaugh owned is still here in the apartment."

"Who found him?" I asked.

"Kaguchi. The valet. He had last night off. He let himself in this morning, to prepare coffee and prairie oysters as usual. He found this."

"Blood?" I ventured.

Abrahams shook his head.

"Visitors?"

"Ten apartments in this building. Three of them had parties last night. You can figure how much help the elevator man was."

"The drink?"

"We took a sample to the lab. Nothing but the best scotch."

I frowned at the vacuum cleaner. "What's that doing out here? It ought to live in a closet."

"Puzzled Kaguchi too. He even says it was still a little warm when he found it, like it had been used. But we looked in the bag. I assure you Stambaugh didn't get sucked in there."

"Motive?"

"Gay dog, our Mr. Stambaugh. Maybe you read Herb Caen's gossip column too? And Kaguchi gave us a little fill-in. Brothers, fathers, husbands . . . Too many motives."

"But why this way?" I brooded. "Get rid of him, sure. But why leave this hollow husk . . . ?"

"Not just why, Lamb. How."

"How? That should be easy enough to—"

"Try it. Try fitting sleeves into sleeves, pants into pants, so they're as smooth and even as if they were still on the body. I've tried, with the rest of the wardrobe. It doesn't work."

I had an idea. "You don't fit 'em in," I said smugly. "You take 'em off. Look." I unbuttoned my coat and shirt, undid my tie, and pulled everything off at once. "See," I said; "sleeves in sleeves." I unzipped and stepped out of trousers and shorts. "See; pants in pants."

Inspector Abrahams was whistling the refrain of *Strip Polka*. "You missed your career, Lamb," he said. "Only now you've got to put your shirt tails between the outer pants and the inner ones and still keep everything smooth. And look in here." He lifted up one shoe and took out a pocket flash and shot a beam inside. "The sock's caught on a little snag in one of the metal eyelets. That's kept it from collapsing, and you can still see the faint impress of toes in there. Try slipping your foot out of a laced-up shoe and see if you can get that result."

I was getting dressed again and feeling like a damned fool.

"Got any other inspirations?" Abrahams grinned.

"The only inspiration I've got is as to where to go now."

"Some day," the Inspector grunted, "I'll learn where you go for your extra-bright ideas."

"As the old lady said to the elephant keeper," I muttered, "you wouldn't believe me if I told you."

The Montgomery Block (Monkey Block to natives) is an antic and reboantic warren of offices and studios on the fringe of Grant Avenue's Chinatown and Columbus Avenue's Italian-Mexican-French-Basque quarter. The studio I wanted was down a long corridor, beyond that all-American bend where the Italian newspaper *Corriere del Popolo* sits cater-corner from the office of Tinn Hugh Yu, Ph.D. and Notary Public.

Things were relatively quiet today in Dr. Verner's studio. Slavko Catenich was still hammering away at his block of marble, apparently on the theory that the natural form inherent in the stone would emerge if you hit it often enough. Irma Borigian was running over vocal exercises and occasionally checking herself by striking a note on the piano, which seemed to bring her more reassurance than it did me. Those two, plus a couple of lads industriously fencing whom I'd never seen before, were the only members of Verner's Varieties on hand today.

Irma ah-ah-ahed and pinked, the fencers clicked, Slavko crashed, and in the midst of the decibels the Old Man stood at his five-foot lectern-desk, resolutely proceeding in quill-pen longhand with the resounding periods of *The Anatomy of Nonscience,* that never-concluded compendium of curiosities which was half Robert Burton and half Charles Fort.

He gave me the medium look. Not the hasty "Just this sentence" or the forbidding "Dear boy, this page *must* be finished"; but the in-between "One more deathless paragraph" look. I grabbed a chair and tried to watch Irma's singing and listen to Slavko's sculpting.

There's no describing Dr. Verner. You can say his age is somewhere between seventy and a hundred. You can say he has a mane of hair like an albino lion and a little goatee like a Kentucky Colonel who never heard of cigars. ("When a man's hair is white," I've heard him say, "tobacco and a beard are mutually exclusive vices.") You can mention the towering figure and the un-English mobility of the white old hands and the disconcerting twinkle of those impossibly blue eyes. And you'd still have about as satisfactory a description as when you say the Taj Mahal is a domed, square, white marble building.

The twinkle was in the eyes and the mobility was in the hands when he finally came to tower over me. They were both gone by the time I'd finished the story of the Stambaugh apartment and the empty man. He stood for a moment frowning, the eyes lusterless, the hands limp at his sides. Then, still standing like that, he relaxed the frown and opened his mouth in a resonant bellow.

"You sticks!" he roared. (Irma stopped and looked hurt.) "You stones!" (The fencers stopped and looked expectant.) "You worse than worst of those that lawless and uncertain thoughts" (Slavko stopped and looked resigned.) "imagine howling," Dr. Verner concluded in a columbine coo, having shifted in mid-quotation from one Shakespearean play to another so deftly that I was still looking for the joint.

Verner's Varieties waited for the next number on the bill. In majestic silence Dr. Verner stalked to his record player. Stambaugh's had been a fancy enough custom-made job, but nothing like this.

If you think things are confusing now, with records revolving at 78, 45, and $33\frac{1}{3}$ rpm, you should see the records of the early part of the century. There were cylinders, of course (Verner had a separate machine for them). Disc records, instead of our present standard sizes, ranged anywhere from seven to fourteen inches in diameter, with curious fractional stops in between. Even the center holes came in assorted sizes. Many discs were lateral-cut, like modern ones; but quite a few were hill-and-dale, with the needle riding up and down instead of sideways—which actually gave better reproduction but somehow never became overwhelmingly popular. The grooving varied too, so that even if two companies both used hill-and-dale cutting you couldn't play the records of one on a machine for the other. And just to make things trickier, some records started from the inside instead of the outer edge. It was Free Enterprise gone hogwild.

Dr. Verner had explained all this while demonstrating to me how his player could cope with any disc record ever manufactured. And I had heard him play everything on it from smuggled dubbings of Crosby blow-ups to a recording by the original *Floradora* Sextet—which was, he was always careful to point out, a double sextet or, as he preferred, a duodecimet.

"You are," he announced ponderously, "about to hear the greatest dramatic soprano of this century. Rosa Ponselle and Elisabeth Rethberg were passable. There was something to be said for Lillian Nordica and Lena Geyer. But listen!" And he slid the needle into the first groove.

"Dr. Verner—" I started to ask for footnotes; I should have known better.

"Dear boy . . . !" he murmured protestingly, over the preliminary surface noise of the aged pressing, and gave me one of those twinkles of bluest blue which implied that surely only a moron could fail to follow the logic of the procedure.

I sat back and listened. Irma listened too, but the eyes of the others were soon longingly intent on foils and chisel. I listened casually at first, then began to sit forward.

I have heard, in person or on records, all of the venerable names which Dr. Verner mentioned—to say nothing of Tebaldi, Russ, Ritter-Ciampi, Souez and both Lehmanns. And reluctantly I began to admit that he was right; this was *the* dramatic soprano. The music was strange to me—a setting of the Latin text of the *Our Father,* surely eighteenth century and at a guess by Pergolesi; it had his irrelevant but reverent tunefulness in approaching a sacred text. Its grave sustained lilt was admirable for showing off a voice; and the voice, unwavering in its prolonged tones, incredible in its breath control, deserved all the showing off it could get. During one long phrase of runs, as taxing as anything in Mozart or Handel, I noticed Irma. She was holding her breath in sympathy with the singer, and the singer won. Irma had let out an admiring gasp before the soprano had, still on one breath, achieved the phrase.

And then, for reasons more operatic than liturgical, the music quickened. The sustained legato phrases gave way to cascades of light bright coloratura. Notes sparkled and dazzled and brightness fell from the air. It was impeccable, inapproachable—infinitely discouraging to a singer and almost shocking to the ordinary listener.

The record ended. Dr. Verner beamed around the room as if he'd done all that himself. Irma crossed to the piano, struck one key to verify the incredible note in alt upon which the singer had ended, picked up her music, and wordlessly left the room.

Slavko had seized his chisel and the fencers were picking up their foils as I approached our host. "But Dr. Verner," I led with my chin. "The Stambaugh case . . ."

"Dear boy," he sighed as he readied the old one-two, "you mean you don't realize that you have just heard the solution?"

"You will have a drop of Drambuie, of course?" Dr. Verner queried formally as we settled down in his more nearly quiet inner room.

"Of course," I said. Then as his mouth opened, " 'For without Drambuie,' " I quoted, " 'the world might never have known the simple solution to the problem of the mislaid labyrinth.' "

He spilled a drop. "I was about to mention that very fact. How . . . ? Or perhaps I have alluded to it before in this connection?"

"You have," I said.

"Forgive me." He twinkled disarmingly. "I grow old, dear boy."

Ritualistically we took our first sip of Drambuie. Then:

"I well remember," Dr. Verner began, "that it was in the autumn of the year 1901 . . .

. . . that the horror began. I was then well established in my Kensington practice, which seemed to flourish as it never had under the ministrations of its previous possessor, and in a more than comfortable financial position. I was able at last to look about me, to contemplate and to investigate the manifold pleasures which a metropolis at once so cosmopolitan and so insular as London proffers to the unattached young man. San Francisco of the same period might perhaps compare in quality; indeed my own experiences here a few years later in the singular affair of the cable cabal were not unrewarding. But a man of your generation knows nothing of those pleasures now ten lustra faded. The humours of the Music Halls, the delights of a hot bird and a cold bottle shared with a dancer from Daly's, the simpler and less expensive delights of punting on the Thames (shared, I may add, with a simpler and less expensive companion)—these claimed what portion of my time I could salvage from my practice.

But above all I was devoted to music; and to be devoted to music meant, in the London of 1901, to be devoted to—but I have always carefully refrained from the employment of veritable and verifiable names in these narratives. Let me once more be discreet, and call her simply by that affectionate agnomen by which my cousin, to his sorrow, knew her: *Carina.*

I need not describe Carina as a musician; you have just heard her sing Pergolesi, you know how she combined nobility and grandeur with a technical agility which these degenerate days associate only with a certain type of light soprano. But I must seek to describe her as a woman, if woman she may be called.

When first I heard the tittle-tattle of London, I paid it small heed. To the man in the street (or even in the stalls) *actress* is still a euphemism for a harsher and shorter term, though my experience of actresses, extending as it has over three continents and more than my allotted three score and ten years, tends to lead me, if anywhere, to an opposite conclusion.

The individual who stands out from the herd is the natural target of calumny. I shall never forget the disgraceful episode of the purloined litter, in which the veterinarian Dr. Stookes accused me of—but let us reserve that anomaly for another occasion. To return to Carina: I heard the gossip; I attributed it to as simple a source as I have indicated. But then the evidence began to attain proportions which the most latitudinarian could hardly disregard.

First young Ronny Furbish-Darnley blew out his brains. He had gambling debts, to be sure, and his family chose to lay the stress upon them; but his relations with Carina had been common knowledge. Then Major MacIvers hanged himself with his own cravat (the MacIvers tartan, of course). I need hardly add that a MacIvers had no gambling debts. Even that episode might have been hushed up had not a peer of so exalted a name that I dare not even paraphrase it perished in the flames of his ancestral castle. Even in the charred state in which they were recovered, the bodies of his wife and seven children evinced the clumsy haste with which he had slit their throats.

It was as though . . . how shall I put it? . . . as though Carina were in some way a "carrier" of what we had then not yet learned to call The Death Wish. Men who knew her too well hungered no longer for life.

The press began to concern itself, as best it might with due regard for the laws of libel, with this situation. Leading articles hinted at possible governmental intervention to preserve the flower of England from this insidious foreigner. Little else was discussed in Hyde Park save the elimination of Carina.

Even the memorable mass suicides at Oxford had provided no sensation comparable to this. Carina's very existence seemed as much in danger as though Jack the Ripper had been found and turned over to the English people. We are firm believers in our English justice; but when that justice is powerless to act, the Englishman aroused is a phenomenon to fear.

If I may be pardoned a Hibernian lapse, the only thing that saved Carina's life was . . . her death.

It was a natural death—perhaps the first natural action of her life. She collapsed on the stage of Covent Garden during a performance of Mozart's *Così fan tutte,* just after having delivered the greatest performance of that fantastic aria, *Come scoglio,* that a living ear has heard.

There were investigations of the death. Even my cousin, with an understandable personal interest, took a hand. (He was the only one of Carina's close admirers to survive her infection; I have often wondered whether this fact resulted from an incredible strength or an equally incredible inadequacy within him.) But there was no possible doubt that the death was a natural one.

It was after the death that the Carina legend began to grow. It was then that young men about town who had seen the great Carina but once began to mention the unmentionable reasons which had caused them to refrain from seeing her again. It was then that her dresser, a crone whose rationality was as uncertain as her still persistent terror was unquestionable, began to speak of unspeakable practices, to hint at black magic as among milady's avocations, to suggest that her utterance (which you have heard) of flights of notes, incredibly rapid yet distinct, owed its facility to her control and even suspension of the mortal limitations of time.

And then began . . . the horror. Perhaps you thought that by *the horror* I meant the sequence of Carina-carried suicides? No; even that lay still, if near the frontier, within the uttermost bounds of human comprehension.

The horror passed those bounds.

I need not ask you to envision it. You have beheld it. You have seen clothing sucked dry of its fleshy tenant, you have seen the haberdasher's habitation sink flabbily in upon itself, no longer sustained by tissue of bone and blood and nerves.

All London saw it that year. And London could not believe.

First it was that eminent musicologist, Sir Frederick Paynter, FRCM. Then there were two young aristocrats, then, oddly, a poor Jewish peddler in the East End.

I shall spare you the full and terrible details, alluding only in passing to the Bishop of Cloisterham. I had read the press accounts. I had filed the cuttings for their very impossibility (for even then I had had adumbrations of the concept which you now know as *The Anatomy of Nonscience*).

But the horror did not impinge upon me closely until it struck one of my own patients, a retired naval officer by the name of Clutsam. His family had sent for me at once, at the same time that they had dispatched a messenger to fetch my cousin.

As you know, my cousin enjoyed a certain fame as a private detective. He had been consulted in more than one previous instance of the horror; but I had read little of him in the press save a reiteration of his hope that the solution lay in his familiar dictum: "Discard the impossible; and whatever remains, no matter how improbable, must be true."

I had already formulated my now celebrated counter-dictum: "Discard the impossible; then if *nothing* remains, some part of the 'impossible' must be possible." It was thus that our dicta and ourselves faced each other across the worn and outdated naval uniform on the floor, complete from the gold braid on its shoulders to the wooden peg below the empty left trouser leg, cut off at the knee.

"I imagine, Horace," my cousin remarked, puffing at his blackened clay, "that you conceive this to be your sort of affair."

"It is obviously not yours," I stated. "There is something in these vanishings beyond—"

"—beyond the humdrum imagination of a professional detective? Horace, you are a man of singular accomplishments."

I smiled. My cousin, as my great-uncle Etienne used to remark of General Masséna, was famous for the accuracy of his information.

"I will confess," he added, "since my Boswell is not within earshot, that you have occasionally hit upon what satisfies you, at least, as the truth in some few cases in which I have failed. Do you see any element linking Captain Clutsam, Sir Frederick Paynter, Moishe Lipkowitz and the Bishop of Cloisterham?"

"I do not." It was always discreet to give my cousin the answer which he expected.

"And I *do!* And yet I am no nearer a solution than . . ." His pipe clenched in his teeth, he flung himself about the room, as though pure physical action would somehow ameliorate the lamentable state of his nerves. Finally he paused before me, looked sharply into my eyes and said, "Very well. I shall tell you. What is nonsense in the patterns shaped by the reasoning mind may well serve you as foundation for some new structure of unreason.

"I have traced every fact in the lives of these men. I know what they habitually ate for breakfast, how they spent their Sundays, and which of them preferred snuff to tobacco. There is only one factor which they all possess in common: Each of them recently purchased a record of the Pergolesi *Pater Noster* sung by . . . Carina. And those records have vanished as thoroughly as the naked men themselves."

I bestowed upon him an amicable smile. Family affection must temper the ungentlemanly emotion of triumph. Still smiling, I left him with the uniform and the leg while I betook myself to the nearest gramophone merchant.

The solution was by then obvious to me. I had observed that Captain Clutsam's gramophone was of the sapphire-needled type designed to play those recordings known as hill-and-dale, the vertical recordings produced by Pathé and other companies as distinguished from the lateral recordings of Columbia and Gramophone-and-Typewriter. And I had recalled that many hill-and-dale recordings were at that time designed (as I believe some wireless transcriptions are now) for an inside start, that is, so that the needle began near the label and traveled outward to the rim of the disc. An unthinking listener might easily begin to play an inside-start record in the more normal manner. The result, in almost all instances, would be gibberish; but in this particular case . . .

I purchased the Carina record with no difficulty. I hastened to my Kensington home, where the room over the dispensary contained a gramophone convertible to either lateral or vertical recordings. I placed the record on the turntable. It was, to be sure, labeled INSIDE START; but how easily one might overlook such a notice! I overlooked it deliberately. I started the turntable and lowered the needle . . .

The cadenzas of coloratura are strange things in reverse. As I heard it, the record naturally began with the startling final note which so disheartened Miss Borigian, then went on to those dazzling *fioriture* which so strengthen the dresser's charge of time-magic. But in reverse, these seemed like the music of some undiscovered planet, coherent to themselves, following a logic unknown to us and shaping a beauty which only our ignorance prevents us from worshipping.

And there were words to these flourishes; for almost unique among sopranos, Carina possessed a diction of diabolical clarity. And the words were at first simply *Nema . . . nema . . . nema . . .*

It was while the voice was brilliantly repeating this reversed *Amen* that I became *literally* beside myself.

I was standing, naked and chill in the London evening, beside a meticulously composed agglomeration of clothing which parodied the body of Dr. Horace Verner.

This fragment of clarity lasted only an instant. Then the voice reached the significant words: *olam a son arebil des men . . .*

This was the Lord's Prayer which she was singing. It is common knowledge that there is in all necromancy no charm more potent than that prayer (and most especially in Latin) *said backwards*. As the last act of her magical malefactions, Carina had left behind her this record, knowing that one of its purchasers would occasionally, by inadvertence, play it backwards, and that then the spell would take effect. It had taken effect now.

I was in space . . . a space of infinite darkness and moist warmth. The music had departed elsewhere. I was alone in this space and the space itself was alive and by its very moist warm dark life this space was draining from me all that which was my own life. And then there was with me a voice in that space, a voice that cried ever *Eem vull! Eem vull!* and for all the moaning gasping urgency in that voice I knew it for the voice of Carina.

I was a young man then. The Bishop's end must have been swift and merciful. But even I, young and strong, knew that this space desired the final sapping of my life, that my life should be drawn from my body even as my body had been drawn from its shell. So I prayed.

I was not a man given to prayer in those days. But I knew words which the Church has taught us are pleasing to God, and I prayed with all the fervor of my being for deliverance from this Nightmare Life-in-Death.

And I stood again naked beside my clothes. I looked at the turntable of the gramophone. The disc was not there. Still naked, I walked to the dispensary and mixed myself a sedative before I dared trust my fingers to button my garments. Then I dressed and went out again to the shop of the gramophone merchant. There I bought every copy in his stock of that devil's *Pater Noster* and smashed them all before his eyes.

Ill though I could afford it, even in my relative affluence, I spent the next few weeks in combing London for copies of that recording. One copy, and one only, I preserved; you heard it just now. I had hoped that no more existed . . .

". . . but obviously," Dr. Verner concluded, "your Mr. Stambaugh managed to acquire one, God rest his soul . . . and body."

I drained my second Drambuie and said, "I'm a great admirer of your cousin." Dr. Verner looked at me with polite blue inquiry. "You find what satisfies *you* as the truth."

"Occam's Razor, dear boy," Dr. Verner murmured, associatively stroking his smooth cheeks. "The solution accounts economically for every integral fact in the problem."

"But look," I said suddenly. "It doesn't! For once I've got you cold. There's one 'integral fact' completely omitted."

"Which is . . . ?" Dr. Verner cooed.

"You can't have been the first man that thought of praying in that . . . that space. Certainly the Bishop must have."

For a moment Dr. Horace Verner was silent. Then he fixed me with the Dear-boy-how-idiotic! twinkle. "But only I," he announced tranquilly, "had realized that in that . . . space all sound, like the Our Father itself, was reversed. The voice cried ever *Eem vull!* and what is that phonetically but *Love me!* backwards? Only *my* prayer was effective, because only I had the foresight to pray in *reverse phonetics.*"

I phoned Abrahams to say I had an idea and could I do some checking in the Stambaugh apartment?

"Good," he said. "I have an idea too. Meet you there in a half hour."

There was no Abrahams in the corridor when I got there; but the police seal was broken and the door was ajar. I went on in and stopped dead.

For the first moment I thought it was still Stambaugh's clothes spread out there. But there was no mistaking Inspector Abrahams' neat gray plainclothes— with no Abrahams in them.

I think I said something about *the horror.* I draw pretty much of a blank between seeing that empty suit and looking up to the far doorway and seeing Inspector Abrahams.

He was wearing a dressing gown of Stambaugh's, which was far too short for him. I stared at his grotesque figure and at the android parody which dangled from his hand.

"Sorry, Lamb," he grinned. "Couldn't resist the theatrical effect. Go on. Take a good look at the empty man on the floor."

I looked. The clothes were put together with the exactly real, body-fitting, sucked-out effect which we had already decided was impossible.

"You see," Abrahams said, "I remembered the vacuum cleaner. And the Downtown Merchants' parade."

I was back at the studio early the next morning. There was nobody from Verner's Varieties there but Slavko, and it was so relatively quiet that Dr. Verner was just staring at the manuscript of *The Anatomy* without adding a word.

"Look," I said. "In the first place, Stambaugh's record player isn't equipped for hill-and-dale records."

"They can be played even on an ordinary machine," Dr. Verner observed tranquilly. "The effect is curious—faint and with an odd echoing overlap, which might even enhance the power of the cantrip."

"And I looked in his card catalog," I went on, "and he didn't have a recording of the Pergolesi *Pater Noster* by anybody."

Dr. Verner widened his overblue eyes. "But of course the card would vanish with the record," he protested. "Magic makes allowances for modern developments."

"Wait a minute!" I exclaimed suddenly. "Hey, I'm brilliant! This is one Abrahams didn't think of. It's *me,* for once, that solves a case."

"Yes, dear boy?" said Dr. Verner gently.

"Look: You *can't* play an inside-start record backwards. It wouldn't work. Visualize the spiraling grooves. If you put the needle in the outside last groove, it'd just stay there ticking—same like it would if you put it in the inside last groove of a normal record. To play it backwards, you'd have to have some kind of gearshift that'd make the turntable spin backwards."

"But I have," said Dr. Verner blandly. "It enables one to make extraordinarily interesting experiments in sound. Doubtless Mr. Stambaugh had too. It would be simple enough to switch over by mistake; he was drinking . . . Tell me. the spinning turntable that you saw . . . was it revolving clockwise or counterclockwise?"

I thought back, and I was damned if I knew. Clockwise, I took for granted; but if I had to swear . . . Instead I asked, "And I suppose Captain Clutsam and the Bishop of Cloisterham had alternate counterclockwise gearshifts?"

"Why, of course. Another reason why such a serious collector as Mr. Stambaugh would. You see, the discs of the Fonogrammia company, a small and obscure firm but one boasting a few superb artists under exclusive contract, were designed to be so played."

I stared at those pellucid azure eyes. I had no notion whether counterclockwise Fonogrammia records were the coveted objective of every collector or a legend that had this moment come into being.

"And besides," I insisted, "Abrahams has demonstrated how it was really done. The vacuum cleaner tipped him off. Stambaugh had bought a man-sized, man-shaped balloon, a little brother of those monster figures they use in parades. He inflated it and dressed it in his clothes. Then he deflated it, leaving the clothes in perfect arrangement with nothing in them but a shrunken chunk of rubber, which he could withdraw by unbuttoning the shirt. Abrahams found the only firm in San Francisco that manufactures such balloons. A clerk identified Stambaugh as a purchaser. So Abrahams bought a duplicate and pulled the same gag on me."

Dr. Verner frowned. "And the vacuum cleaner?"

"You use a vacuum cleaner in reverse for pumping up large balloons. And you use it normally for deflating them; if you just let the air out *whoosh!* they're apt to break."

"The clerk" (it came out *clark*, of course) "identified Stambaugh positively?"

I shifted under the piercing blueness. "Well, you know identifications from photographs . . ."

"Indeed I do." He took a deliberately timed pause. "And the record player? Why was its turntable still revolving?"

"Accident, I guess. Stambaugh must've bumped against the switch."

"Which projected from the cabinet so that one might well engage it by accident?"

I pictured the machine. I visualized the switch and the depth to which one would have to reach in. "Well, no," I granted. "Not exactly . . ."

Dr. Verner smiled down at me tolerantly. "And the motive for these elaborate maneuvers by Stambaugh?"

"Too many threatening male relatives on his tail. He deliberately staged this to look oh-so-mysterious nobody'd spot the simple fact that he was just getting the hell out from under. Abrahams has an all-points alarm out; he'll be picked up any time within the next few days."

Dr. Verner sighed. His hands flickered through the air in gesture of infinitely resigned patience. He moved to his record cabinet, took out a disc, placed it on the turntable, and adjusted certain switches.

"Come, Slavko!" he announced loudly. "Since Mr. Lamb prefers rubber balloons to truth, we are conferring a signal privilege upon him. We are retiring to the other room, leaving him here alone with the Carina record. His cocksure materialism will surely wish to verify the effect of playing it in reverse."

Slavko stopped pounding and said, "Huh?"

"Come, Slavko. But first say a polite good-by to Mr. Lamb. You may not be seeing him again." Dr. Verner paused in the doorway and surveyed me with what seemed like genuine concern. "Dear boy," he murmured, "you won't forget that point about the reverse phonetics . . . ?"

He was gone and so (without more polite good-by than a grunt) was Slavko. I was alone with Carina, with the opportunity to disprove Dr. Verner's fabulous narrative once and for all.

His story had made no pretense of explaining the presence of the vacuum cleaner.

And Inspector Abrahams' theory had not even attempted to account for the still-revolving turntable.

I switched on the turntable of the Verner machine. Carefully I lowered the tone-arm, let the oddly rounded needle settle into the first groove from the outer rim.

I heard that stunning final note in alt. So flawless was the Carina diction that I could hear, even in that range, the syllable to which it was sung: *nem*, the beginning of the reverse-Latin *Amen*.

Then I heard a distorted groan as the turntable abruptly slowed down from 78 to zero revolutions per minute. I looked at the switch, it was still on. I turned and saw Dr. Verner towering behind me, with a disconnected electric plug dangling from his hand.

"No," he said softly—and there was a dignity and power in that softness that I had never heard in his most impressive bellows. "No, Mr. Lamb. You have a wife and two sons. I have no right to trifle with their lives merely to gratify an old man's resentment of skepticism."

Quietly he lifted the tone-arm, removed the record, restored it to its envelope, and refiled it. His deft, un-English hands were not at their steadiest.

"When Inspector Abrahams succeeds in tracing down Mr. Stambaugh," he said firmly, "you shall hear this record in reverse. And not before then."

And it just so happens they haven't turned up Stambaugh yet.

The Ghost of Me

I gave my reflection hell. I was sleepy, of course. And I still didn't know what noise had waked me; but I told it what I thought of mysterious figures that lurked across the room from you and eventually turned out to be your own image. I did a good job, too; I touched depths of my vocabulary that even the complications of the Votruba case hadn't sounded.

Then I was wide awake and gasping. Throughout all my invective, the reflection had not once moved its lips. I groped behind me for the patient's chair and sat down fast. The reflection remained standing.

Now, it was I. There was no doubt of that. Every feature was exactly similar, even down to the scar over my right eyebrow from the time a bunch of us painted Baltimore a mite too thoroughly. But this should have tipped me off from the start: the scar was on the right, not on the left where I've always seen it in a mirror's reversal.

"Who are you?" I asked. It was not precisely a brilliant conversational opening, but it was the one thing I had to know or start baying the moon.

"Who are *you?*" it asked right back.

Maybe you've come across those cockeyed mirrors which, by some trick arrangement of lenses, show you not the reversed mirror image but your actual appearance, as though you were outside and looking at yourself? Well, this was like that—exactly, detailedly me, but facing me rightway round and unreversed. And it stood when I sat down.

"Look," I protested. "Isn't it enough to be a madhouse mirror? Do you have to be an echo too?"

"Tell me who you are," it insisted quietly. "I think I must be confused."

I hadn't quite plumbed my vocabulary before; I found a couple of fresh words now. "You think *you're* confused? And what in the name of order and reason do you think *I* am?"

"That's what I asked you," it replied. "What are you? Because there must be a mistake somewhere."

"All right," I agreed. "If you want to play games. I'll tell you what I am, if you'll do the same. You chase me and I'll chase you. I'm John Adams. I'm a doctor. I've got a Rockefeller grant to establish a clinic to study occupational disease among Pennsylvania cement workers—"

"—I'm working on a variation of the Zupperheim theory with excellent results, and I'm a registered Democrat but not quite a New Dealer," it concluded, with the gloomiest frown I've ever noted outside a Russian novel.

My own forehead was not parchment-smooth. "That's all true enough. But how do you know it? And now that I've told you I'm John Adams, will you kindly kick through with your half of the bargain?"

"That's just the trouble," it murmured reluctantly. "There must be a terrible mistake somewhere. I've heard of such things, of course, but I certainly never expected it to happen to me."

I don't have all the patience that a medical man really needs. This time when I said *"Who are you?"* it was a wild and ringing shout.

"Well, you see—" it said.

"I hardly know how to put this—" it began again.

"To be blunt about it," it finally blurted out, "I'm the ghost of John Adams."

I was glad I was sitting down. And I understood now why old Hasenfuss always recommended arms on the patient's chair to give him something to grab when you deliver the verdict. I grabbed now, and grabbed plenty hard.

"You're the—"

"I'm the ghost—"

"—the ghost of—"

"—of John Adams."

"But"—I held onto the chair even tighter—"I *am* John Adams."

"I know," my ghost said. "That's what's so annoying."

I said nothing. That was far too impressive an understatement to bear comment. I groped in the pocket of my dressing gown and found cigarettes. "Do you smoke?" I asked.

"Of course. If John Adams smokes, naturally I do."

I extended the pack.

He shook his head. "I'll have to dematerialize it. Put one on the table."

I obeyed and watched curiously. A hand that was not quite a hand but more a thin pointing shape stretched out and touched the cigarette. It lingered a moment, then came away holding a white cylinder. The cigarette was still on the table.

I lit it and puffed hard. "Tastes just like any other Camel."

"Of course. I took only the nonmaterial part. You wouldn't miss that any more than you miss . . . well, me."

"You mean you're smoking the ghost of a cigarette?"

"You can put it that way."

For the first five puffs it wasn't easy to get the cigarette into my mouth. My hand was more apt to steer it at nose or ear. But with the sixth puff I began to feel as normal and self-possessed as any man talking with his own ghost. I even got argumentative.

"This isn't possible," I protested. "You won't even come into existence until after I'm dead."

"Certainly," my ghost agreed politely. "But you see, you *are* dead."

"Now, look. That's nonsense. Even supernaturally. Because if I were dead . . . well, if I were dead, I'd be my own ghost. I'd be you. There wouldn't be two of us."

"I am glad that I had a clear and logical mind when I was alive. I didn't know but that might have come later; it sometimes does. But this way we can understand each other. What I meant is this: Where I come from, of course I am dead; or if you prefer, you are dead. It means the same thing. Also I am alive and also I am not yet born. You see, I come from outside of time. You follow?"

"I think so. Eternity embraces all time, so when you've gone over from time into eternity, all time coexists for you."

"Not too precise an expression, but I think you grasp the essentials. Then, perhaps you can see what's happened. I've simply come back into time at the wrong point."

"How—"

"Imagine yourself at large in three dimensions, facing a fence with an infinite series of two-dimensional slots. Think how easy it'd be to pick the wrong slot."

I thought a while and nodded. "Could be," I admitted. "But if it's that easy, why doesn't it happen more often?"

"Oh, but it does. You've heard of apparitions of the living? You've heard of *Doppelgänger?* You've even heard of hauntings before the fact? Those are all cases like this—just slipping into the wrong slot. But it's such a damned stupid thing to do. I'm going to take a terrible ribbing for this." My ghost looked more downcast and perplexed than ever.

I started to be consoling. "Look. Don't take it so— Hey!" The implication suddenly hit me. "You said haunting?"

"Yes."

"Is that what you're doing?"

"Well . . . yes."

"But you can't be haunting me?"

"Of course not."

"Then whom are you haunting in my room?"

My ghost played with his ghostly cigarette and looked embarrassed. "It's not a thing we care to talk about. Haunting, I mean. It's not much fun, and it's rather naïve. But after all, it's—well, it's expected of you when you've been murdered."

I could hear the right arm of the chair crack under my clutch. "When you've been—"

"Yes. I know it's ridiculous and childish; but it's such an old, established custom that I haven't the courage to oppose it."

"Then you've been murdered? And that means *I've* been murdered? I mean, that means I'm *going* to be murdered?"

"Oh, yes," he said calmly.

I rose and opened a drawer of the desk. "This," I prescribed, "calls for the internal application of alcoholic stimulants. Damn," I added as the emergency buzzer rang. All I needed was a rush operation now, with my fingers already beginning to jitter.

I opened the door and looked out into star-bright emptiness. "False alarm." I was relieved—and then heard the whiz. I ducked it just in time and got the door closed.

My ghost was curiously contemplating the knife where it stuck quivering in the wall. "Right through me," he observed cheerfully.

It was no sinister and exotic stiletto. Just a plain butcher knife, and all the more chillingly convincing through its very ordinariness. "Your prophecies work fast," I said.

"This wasn't it. It missed. Just wait."

The knife had stopped its shuddering, but mine went on. "Now I really need that stimulant. You drink rye? But of course. I do."

"You don't happen," my ghost asked, "to have any tequila?"

"Tequila? Never tasted it."

"Oh. Then I must have acquired the taste later, before you were murdered."

I was just unscrewing the bottle top, and jumped enough to spill half a jiggerful. "I don't *like* that word."

"You'll get used to it," my ghost assured me. "Don't bother to pour me one. I'll just dematerialize the bottle."

The rye helped. Chatting with your own ghost about your murder seems more natural after a few ounces of whiskey. My ghost seemed to grow more at ease too, and after the third joint bottle tilting the atmosphere was practically normal.

"We've got to approach this rationally," I said at last. "Whatever you are, that knife's real enough. And I'm fond of life. Let's see what we can do to stave this off."

"But you can't." My ghost was quietly positive. "Because I—or you—well, let's say *we*—already have been murdered."

"But not at this time."

"Not at this time yet, but certainly *in* this time. Look, I know the rules of haunting. I know that nothing could have sent me to this room unless we'd been killed here."

"But when? How? And above all, by whom? Who should want to toss knives at me?"

"It wasn't a knife the real time. I mean, it won't be."

"But why—"

My ghost took another healthy swig of dematerialized rye. "I should prefer tequila," he sighed.

"That's too damned bad," I snapped. "But tell me about my murder."

"Don't get into such a dither. What difference does it make? Nothing you can do can possibly affect the outcome. You have sense enough to understand that. Foreknowledge can never conceivably avert. That's the delusion and snare of all prophecy."

"All right. Grant that. Let's pretend it's just my natural curiosity. But *tell me about my murder.*"

"Well—" My ghost was hesitant and sheepish again. "The fact is—" He took a long time to swallow his dematerialized rye, and followed the process with a prolonged dematerialized burp. "To tell you the truth—I don't remember anything about it.

"Now, now!" he added hastily. "Don't blow up. I can't help it. It's dreadfully easy to forget things in eternity. That's what the Greeks meant by the waters of Lethe in the afterworld. Just think how easy it is to forget details in, say, ten years, when the years are happening only one at a time. Then try to imagine how much you could forget in an infinity of years when they're all happening at once."

"But our own murder!" I protested. "You couldn't forget our murder!"

"I have. I know we must have been murdered in this room because here I am haunting it, but I've no idea how or when. Excepting," he added reflectively, "that it must be after we acquired a taste for tequila."

"But you must at least know the murderer. You have to know the guy you're supposed to be haunting. Or do you just haunt a *place?*"

"No. Not in the strict rules. You merely haunt the place because the murderer will return to the scene of the crime and then you confront him and say, *Thou art the man!*' "

"And supposing he doesn't return to the scene?"

"That's just the trouble. We know the rules, all right. But the murderers don't always. Lots of times they never return at all, and we go on haunting and haunting and getting noplace."

"But look!" I exclaimed. "This one will *have* to return, because he hasn't been here yet. I mean, this isn't the scene of the crime; it's the scene set for a crime that hasn't happened yet. He'll have to come here to . . . to—"

"To murder us," my ghost concluded cheerfully. "Of course. It's ideal. I can't possibly miss him."

"But if you don't know who he is—"

"I'll know him when I see him. You see, we ghosts are psychic."

"Then if you could tip me off when you recognize him—"

"It wouldn't do you any— What was that?"

"Just a rooster. Dawn comes early these summer mornings. But if I knew who he was, then I—"

"Damn!" said my ghost. "Haunting must be so much simpler in winter, with those nice long nights. I've got to be vanishing. See you tonight."

My curiosity stirred again. "Where do you go when you vanish?" But he had already disappeared.

I looked around the empty consulting room. Even the dematerialized rye had vanished. Only the butcher knife remained. I made the natural rye vanish too, and staggered back to bed.

The next morning it all seemed perfectly simple. I had had one hell of a strange vision the night before; but on the consulting-room desk stood an empty pint which had been almost full yesterday. That was enough to account for a wilderness of visions.

Even the knife didn't bother me much. It would be accounted for some way— somebody's screwy idea of a gag. Nobody could want to kill me, I thought, and wasn't worried even when a kid in a back-lot baseball game let off a wild pitch that missed my head by an inch.

I just filed away a minor resolve to climb on the wagon if this sort of thing became a habit, and got through a hard day's work at the clinic with no worries beyond the mildest of hangovers. And when I got the X-rays on Nick Wojcek's girl with her lungs completely healed, and the report that she hadn't coughed for two weeks, I felt so gloriously satisfied that I forgot even the hangover.

"Charlie," I beamed at my X-ray technician, "life is good."

"In Cobbsville?" Charlie asked dourly.

I gloated over those beautiful plates. "Even in Cobbsville."

"Have it your way," said Charlie. "But it'll be better this evening. I'm dropping by your place with a surprise."

"A surprise?"

"Yeah. Friend of mine brought me a present from Mexico."

And even that didn't tip me off. I went on feeling as chipper and confident as ever all through the day's work and dinner at the Greek's, and walked home enjoying the freshness of the evening and fretting over a twist on a new kind of air filter for the factories.

That was why I didn't see the car. I was crossing the street to my house, and my first warning was a bass bellow of "John!" I looked up to see a car a yard away, rolling downhill straight at me. I jumped, stumbled, and sprawled flat in the dust. My knee ached and my nose was bleeding; but the car had missed me, as narrowly as the knife had last night.

I watched it roll on down the hill. There was no driver. It was an old junk heap—just the sort of wreck that would get out of control if carelessly left parked on a steep grade. It was a perfectly plausible accident, and still— The car hit the fence at the bottom of the hill and became literally a junk heap. Nobody showed up to bother about it. I turned to thank Father Svatomir for his shout of warning.

You've seen those little Orthodox churches that are the one spot of curious color in the drab landscape of industrial Pennsylvania? Those plain frame churches that blossom out on top into an exotic bloated spire topped by one of those crosses with an extra slantwise arm?

Father Svatomir was the priest from one of those, and his black garments, his nobly aquiline nose, and his beautifully full and long brown beard made him look as strange and Oriental as his own church. It was always a shock to me to hear his ordinary American accent—he'd been born in Cobbsville and gone to the Near East to study for the priesthood—and to realize that he was only about my age. That's thirty-two, for the record; but Father Svatomir seemed serenely ageless.

He waved away my thanks. "John, my son, I must speak with you. Alone and seriously."

"OK, Father"—and I took him around to the door into my own room. I somehow didn't want to go into the consulting room just yet. I was sure that there was nothing there; but night had fallen by now, and there was no telling.

I sat on the bed, and the priest pulled a chair up close. "John," he began quietly, "do you realize that you are in danger of your life?"

I couldn't help a glance at the door of the consulting room, but I said casually, "Nuts, Father. That little accident out there?"

"Accident? And how many other 'accidents' have befallen you recently?"

I thought of the butcher knife and the wild pitch, but I repeated, "Nuts. That's nonsense. Why should anybody want my life?"

"Because you are doing too much good. No, don't smile, my son. I am not merely indulging in a taste for paradox. I mean this. You are doing too much and you are in danger of your life. Martyrs are not found in the Church alone. Every field has its martyrs, and you are in most grievous danger of becoming a martyr to your splendid clinic."

"Bosh," I snorted, and wished I believed it.

"Bosh it is indeed, but my parishioners are not notably intellectual. They have brought with them from their own countries a mass of malformed and undigested superstitions. In those superstitions there is some small grain of spiritual truth, and that I seek to salvage whenever possible; but in most of those old-country beliefs there is only ignorance and peril."

"But what's all this to me?"

"They think," said Father Svatomir slowly, "that you are working miracles in the clinic."

"I am," I admitted.

He smiled. "As an agnostic, John, you may call them miracles and think no more of it. But my parishioners cannot see matters so simply. If *I,* now, were to work these wonders of healing, they would accept the fact as a manifestation of God's greatness; but when *you* work them— You see, my son, to these poor believing people, all great gifts and all perfect gifts are from above—or from below. Since you, in their sight, are an unbeliever and obviously not an agent of God, why, then, you must be an agent of the devil."

"Does it matter so long as I heal their lungs from the effects of this damned cement dust?"

"It matters very much indeed to them, John. It matters so much that, I repeat, you are in danger of your life."

I got up. "Excuse me a minute, Father . . . something I wanted to check in the consulting room."

It checked, all right. My ghost sat at the desk, large as death. He'd found my copy of *Fanny Hill,* dematerialized it, and settled down to thorough enjoyment.

"I'd forgotten this too," he observed as I came in.

I kept my voice low. "If you can forget our own murder, small wonder you'd forget a book."

"I don't mean the book. I'd forgotten the subject matter. And now it all comes back to me—"

"Look!" I said sharply. "The hell with your memories."

"They're not just mine." He gazed at me with a sort of leering admiration.

"The hell with them anyway. There's a man in the next room warning me that my life's in danger. I'll admit he just saved my life, but that could be a trick. Could he be the man?"

Reluctantly my ghost laid his book aside, came to the door, and peered out. "Uh-uh. We're safe as houses with him."

I breathed. "Stick around. This check-up system's going to be handy."

"You can't prevent what's happened," he said indifferently, and went back to the desk and *Fanny Hill.* As he picked up the book he spoke again, and his voice was wistful. "You haven't got a blonde I could dematerialize?"

I shut the consulting-room door on him and turned back to Father Svatomir. "Everything under control. I've got a notion, Father, that I'm going to prove quite capable of frustrating any attempts to break up my miracle-mongering. Or is it monging?"

"I've talked to them," the priest sighed. "I've tried to make them see the truth that you are indeed God's agent, whatever your own faith. I may yet succeed, but in the meanwhile—" He broke off and stared at the consulting room. "John, my son," he whispered, "what is in that room?"

"Nothing, Father. Just a file that I suddenly remembered needed checking."

"No, John. There's more than that. John, while you were gone, *something* peered at me through that door."

"You're getting jumpy, Father. Stop worrying."

"No. John, there is a spirit in this place."

"Fiddlesticks!"

"Oh, you may not feel affected; but after all, a man of my calling is closer to the spirit world than most."

"Father, your parishioners are corrupting you."

"No. Oh, I have smiled at many of their superstitions. I have even disbelieved in spirits. I knew that they were doctrinally possible and so to be believed; but I never believed in them personally, as an individual rather than a priest. But now— John, something peered at me."

I swore silently and said aloud, "Calm yourself, Father."

Father Svatomir had risen and was pacing the room, hands clasped like Felix the Cat. "John, my son," he said at last, "you have been a good friend to me and my parish. I have long been grateful to you, and never been able to prove that gratitude. I shall do so now."

"And how?" I asked, with a certain nervous foreboding.

"John," he paused in his pacing and laid a hand on my shoulder, "John, I am going to exorcise the spirit that haunts this place."

"Hey!" I gasped. "No, Father. Please!" Because, I reasoned hastily to myself, exorcising spirits is all very well, but when it's your own spirit and if that gets exorcised—well, what happens to you then? "No," I insisted. "You can't do that."

"I know, John," he went on in his calm, deep voice. "You think that this is more superstition, on a level with the beliefs of my parishioners. But though you do not sense this . . . this *thing* yet, you will in time. I shall save you much pain and discomfort. Wait here, John, while I go fetch some holy water and check up the formula for exorcism. I'm afraid," he added ruefully, "I haven't looked at it since my days in the seminary."

I seized his arm and opened my mouth in protestation too urgent for words.

"John," he said slowly and reproachfully, "are you willfully harboring a spirit?"

A knock on the door cut the scene short and gave me a breathing spell. I like Charlie, but I don't think I've ever before been so relieved to see him.

"Hi," he said, and "Hi," again to Father Svatomir. "That's the advantage of being celibate," he added. "You can grow a beard. I tried to once, but the waitress down at the Greek's didn't like it."

Father Svatomir smiled faintly.

"Three glasses, mine host," Charlie commanded, and produced from under his arm a tall bottle of greenish glass. "Told you I had a surprise."

I fetched three whiskey glasses and set them on the table. Charlie filled them with a flourish. "Noble stuff, this," he announced. "Want to hear what you gentlemen think of it. There's supposed to be a ritual goes with it, but I like it straight. Down the esophagus, boys!"

Was it Shelley who used the phrase "potable gold"? Whoever it was had surely tasted this liquor. It flowed down like some molten metal that had lost the dangerous power to scorch, but still glowed with rich warmth. While the subtle half-perceived flavor still clove to my mouth, I could feel the tingling heat reach my fingertips.

"By Heaven," I cried, "nothing like this has happened to the blood stream since Harvey discovered the circulation. Charlie, my lad, this is henceforth my tipple!"

Father Svatomir beamed and nodded. "I concur heartily. Tell us, Charles, what is this wondrous brew?"

"Tequila," said Charlie, and I dropped my glass.

"What is the trouble, my son? You're pale and trembling."

"Look, Johnny. I know it's high-proof stuff, but it hadn't ought to hit you like that."

I hardly heard them. All I knew was that the onetime barrier separating me from my murder was now removed. I had come to like tequila. I bent over to pick up the glass, and as I did so I saw a hand reach out from the consulting room. It touched the tequila bottle lightly and withdrew clutching a freshly dematerialized fifth.

Charlie refilled the three glasses, "Another one'll put you back on your feet, Johnny. It's swell stuff once you get used to it."

Father Svatomir was still concerned. "John," he insisted, "was it the tequila? Or did you . . . have you sensed what we were speaking of before?"

I gulped the second glass. "I'm all right," I protested. "A couple more of these and I'll— Was that a knock?"

Charlie looked around. "Consulting-room door, I think. Shall I go check?"

I slipped quickly between him and the door. "Never mind. I'll see."

"Had I better go with you?" the priest suggested. "If it were what I warned you of—"

"It's OK. I'll go."

My ghost was lolling back in my chair with his feet propped up on the desk. One hand held *Fanny Hill* and the other the tequila. "I got a good look at the guy that brought this," he volunteered without looking up. "He's all right."

"Fine. Now I have to let in a patient. Could you briefly disappear?"

"Uh-uh. Not till the cock crows."

"Then please hide. Try that cupboard—I think it's big enough."

He started for the cupboard, returned for book and bottle, and went back to shut himself up in comfort. I opened the outer door a very small crack and said, "Who is it?"

"Me, Dr. Adams. Nick Wojcek."

I opened the door without a tremor. Whatever Father Svatomir might say about the other inhabitants of Cobbsville, I knew I had nothing to fear from the man whose daughter was my most startlingly successful cure to date. I could still see the pitiful animal terror in his eyes when he had brought her to me and the pure joy that had glistened in them when I told him she was well.

"Come in, Nick. Sit down and be comfortable."

He obeyed the first half of my injunction, but he fidgeted most uncomfortably. Despite his great height and his grizzled hair, he looked like a painfully uncertain child embarrassed by the presence of strange adults. "My Ljuba," he faltered. "You got those pictures you tell me about?"

"I saw them today. And it's good news, Nick. Your Ljuba is all well again. It's all healed up."

"She stay that way now?"

"I hope to God. But I can't promise. So long as you live in this dump and breathe cement dust day in and day out, I can't guarantee you a thing. But I think she'll be well now. Let her marry some nice young man who'll take her away from here into the clean air."

"No," he said sullenly.

"But come, Nick," I said gently. It was pleasant to argue an old man's foibles for a moment instead of fretting over your approaching murder. "She has to lead her own life."

"You tell me what do? You go to hell!"

I drew back astounded. There was the sheer venom of hatred in that last phrase. "Nick!" I protested.

He was on his feet now, and in his hand was an ancient but nonetheless lethal-looking revolver. "You make magic," he was saying slowly and harshly. "God would let my Ljuba die. You make her live. Black magic. Don't want daughter from magic."

"Nick," I urged as quietly as I could, "don't be a damned fool. There are people in the next room. Suppose I call for them?"

"I kill you first," said Nick Wojcek simply.

"But they'll find you here. You can't get away. They'll burn you for this, Nick. Then what'll become of Ljuba?"

He hesitated, but the muzzle of the revolver never wavered. Now that I was staring my murderer right in the nose, I felt amazingly calm. I could see, in a clear and detached way, just how silly it was to try to avert the future by preknowledge. I had thought my ghost would warn me; but there he was in the closet, comfortably curled up with a bottle of liquor and a dirty book, and here I was, staring into Nick Wojcek's revolver. He'd come out afterward, of course, my ghost would; he'd get in his haunting and go home. While I . . . only then I'd be my ghost, wouldn't I? I'd go home too—wherever that was.

"If they get me," said Nick at last, "they get me. I get you first."

His grip tightened on the revolver. And at that moment my tardy ghost reeled out of the closet. He brandished the empty green tequila bottle in one hand, and his face was carefree and roistering.

My ghost pointed the bottle dramatically at Nick Wojcek and grinned broadly. *"Thou art the man!"* he thundered cheerily.

Nick started, whirled, and fired. For an instant he stood rooted and stared first at the me standing by the desk and then at the me slowly sinking to the floor. Then he flung the revolver away and ran terror-stricken from the room.

I was kneeling at my ghost's side where he lay groaning on the floor. "But what happened?" I gasped. "I don't understand."

"Neither do I," he moaned. "Got a little drunk . . . started haunting too soon—" My ghost's form was becoming indistinct.

"But you're a ghost. That knife went right through you. Nothing can wound you."

"That's what I thought. But he did . . . and here I am—" His voice was trailing away too. "Only one thing . . . could have—" Then there was silence, and I was staring at nothing but the empty floor, with a little glistening piece of light metal on it.

Father Svatomir and Charlie were in the room now, and the silence was rapidly crammed with questions. I scrambled to my feet and tried to show more assurance than I felt. "You were right, Father. It was Nick Wojcek. Went for me with that revolver. Luckily, he missed, got panicky, and ran away."

"I shall find him," said Father Svatomir gravely. "I think that after this fright I may be able to talk some sense into him; then perhaps he can help me convince the others." He paused and looked down at the gleaming metal. "You see, John? I told you they believed you to be a black magician."

"How so?"

"You notice that? A silver bullet. Ordinary lead cannot harm a magician, but the silver bullet can kill anything. Even a spirit." And he hastened off after Nick Wojcek.

Wordlessly, I took the undematerialized tequila bottle from Charlie and paid some serious attention to it. I began to see now. It made sense. My ghost hadn't averted my death—that had been an absurd hope—but he had caused his own. All the confusion came from his faulty memory. He was haunting not mine, but his *own* murderer. It was my ghost himself who had been killed in this room.

That was right. That was fine. I was safe from murder now, and must have been all along. But what I wanted to know, what I still want to know, what I have to find out and what no one can ever tell me, is this:

What happens after death to a man whose ghost has already been murdered?

Snulbug

"That's a hell of a spell you're using," said the demon, "if I'm the best you can call up."

He wasn't much, Bill Hitchens had to admit. He looked lost in the center of that pentacle. His basic design was impressive enough—snakes for hair, curling tusks, a sharp-tipped tail, all the works—but he was something under an inch tall.

Bill had chanted the words and lit the powder with the highest hopes. Even after the feeble flickering flash and the damp fizzling *zzzt* which had replaced the expected thunder and lightning, he had still had hopes. He had stared up at the space above the pentacle waiting to be awe-struck until he had heard that plaintive little voice from the floor wailing, "Here I am."

"Nobody's wasted time and powder on a misfit like me for years," the demon went on. "Where'd you get the spell?"

"Just a little something I whipped up," said Bill modestly.

The demon grunted and muttered something about people that thought they were magicians.

"But I'm not a magician," Bill explained. "I'm a biochemist."

The demon shuddered. "I land the damnedest cases," he mourned. "Working for that psychiatrist wasn't bad enough, I should draw a biochemist. Whatever that is."

Bill couldn't check his curiosity. "And what did you do for a psychiatrist?"

"He showed me to people who were followed by little men and told them I'd chase the little men away." The demon pantomimed shooing motions.

"And did they go away?"

"Sure. Only then the people decided they'd sooner have little men than me. It didn't work so good. Nothing ever does," he added woefully. "Yours won't either."

Bill sat down and filled his pipe. Calling up demons wasn't so terrifying after all. Something quiet and homey about it. "Oh, yes it will," he said. "This is fool-proof."

"That's what they all think. People—" The demon wistfully eyed the match as Bill lit his pipe. "But we might as well get it over with. What do you want?"

"I want a laboratory for my embolism experiments. If this method works, it's going to mean that a doctor can spot an embolus in the blood stream long before it's dangerous and remove it safely. My ex-boss, that screwball old occultist Reuben Choatsby, said it wasn't practical—meaning there wasn't a fortune in it for him—and fired me. Everybody else thinks I'm wacky too, and I can't get any backing. So I need ten thousand dollars."

"There!" the demon sighed with satisfaction. "I told you it wouldn't work. That's out for me. They can't start fetching money on demand till three grades higher than me. I told you."

"But you don't," Bill insisted, "appreciate all my fiendish subtlety. Look— Say, what is your name?"

The demon hesitated. "You haven't got another of those things?"

"What things?"

"Matches."

"Sure."

"Light me one, please?"

Bill tossed the burning match into the center of the pentacle. The demon scrambled eagerly out of the now cold ashes of the powder and dived into the flame, rubbing himself with the brisk vigor of a man under a needle-shower. "There!" he gasped joyously. "That's more like it."

"And now what's your name?"

The demon's face fell again. "My name? You really want to know?"

"I've got to call you something."

"Oh, no you don't. I'm going home. No money games for me."

"But I haven't explained yet what you are to do. What's your name?"

"Snulbug." The demon's voice dropped almost too low to be heard.

"Snulbug?" Bill laughed.

"Uh-huh. I've got a cavity in one tusk, my snakes are falling out, I haven't got enough troubles, I should be named Snulbug."

"All right. Now listen, Snulbug, can you travel into the future?"

"A little. I don't like it much, though. It makes you itch in the memory."

"Look, my fine snake-haired friend. It isn't a question of what you like. How would you like to be left there in that pentacle with nobody to throw matches at you?" Snulbug shuddered. "I thought so. Now, you can travel into the future?"

"I said a little."

"And," Bill leaned forward and puffed hard at his corncob as he asked the vital question, "can you bring back material objects?" If the answer was no, all the fine febrile fertility of his spell-making was useless. And if that was useless, heaven alone knew how the Hitchens Embolus Diagnosis would ever succeed in ringing down the halls of history, and incidentally saving a few thousand lives annually.

Snulbug seemed more interested in the warm clouds of pipe smoke than in the question. "Sure," he said. "Within reason I can—" He broke off and stared up piteously. "You don't mean— You can't be going to pull that old gag again?"

"Look baby. You do what I tell you and leave the worrying to me. You can bring back material objects?"

"Sure. But I warn you—"

Bill cut him off short. "Then as soon as I release you from that pentacle, you're to bring me tomorrow's newspaper."

Snulbug sat down on the burned match and tapped his forehead sorrowfully with his tail tip. "I knew it," he wailed. "I knew it. Three times already this happens to me. I've got limited powers, I'm a runt, I've got a funny name, so I should run foolish errands."

"Foolish errands?" Bill rose and began to pace about the bare attic. "Sir, if I may call you that, I resent such an imputation. I've spent weeks on this idea. Think of the limitless power in knowing the future. Think of what could be done with it: swaying the course of empire, dominating mankind. All I want is to take this stream of unlimited power, turn it into the simple channel of humanitarian research, and get me $10,000; and you call that a foolish errand!"

"That Spaniard," Snulbug moaned. "He was a nice guy, even if his spell was lousy. Had a solid, comfortable brazier where an imp could keep warm. Fine fellow. And he had to ask to see tomorrow's newspaper. I'm warning you—"

"I know," said Bill hastily. "I've been over in my mind all the things that can go wrong. And that's why I'm laying three conditions on you before you get out of that pentacle. I'm not falling for the easy snares."

"All right." Snulbug sounded almost resigned. "Let's hear 'em. Not that they'll do any good."

"First: This newspaper must not contain a notice of my own death or of any other disaster that would frustrate what I can do with it."

"But shucks," Snulbug protested. "I can't guarantee that. If you're slated to die between now and tomorrow, what can I do about it? Not that I guess you're important enough to crash the paper."

"Courtesy, Snulbug. Courtesy to your master. But I tell you what: When you go into the future, you'll know then if I'm going to die? Right. Well, if I am, come back and tell me and we'll work out other plans. This errand will be off."

"People," Snulbug observed, "make such an effort to make trouble for themselves. Go on."

"Second: The newspaper must be of this city and in English. I can just imagine you and your little friends presenting some dope with the Omsk and Tomsk *Daily Vuskutsukt*."

"We should take so much trouble," said Snulbug.

"And third: The newspaper must belong to this space-time continuum, to this spiral of the serial universe, to this Wheel of If. However you want to put it. It must be a newspaper of the tomorrow that I myself shall experience, not of some other, to me hypothetical, tomorrow."

"Throw me another match," said Snulbug.

"Those three conditions should cover it, I think. There's not a loophole there, and the Hitchens Laboratory is guaranteed."

Snulbug grunted. "You'll find out."

Bill took a sharp blade and duly cut a line of the pentacle with cold steel. But Snulbug simply dived in and out of the flame of his second match, twitching his tail happily, and seemed not to give a rap that the way to freedom was now open.

"Come on!" Bill snapped impatiently. "Or I'll take the match away."

Snulbug got as far as the opening and hesitated. "Twenty-four hours is a long way."

"You can make it."

"I don't know. Look." He shook his head, and a microscopic dead snake fell to the floor. "I'm not at my best. I'm shot to pieces lately, I am. Tap my tail."

"Do what?"

"Go on. Tap it with your fingernail right there where it joins on."

Bill grinned and obeyed. "Nothing happens."

"Sure nothing happens. My reflexes are all haywire. I don't know as I can make twenty-four hours." He brooded, and his snakes curled up into a concentrated clump. "Look. All you want is tomorrow's newspaper, huh? Just tomorrow's, not the edition that'll be out exactly twenty-four hours from now?"

"It's noon now," Bill reflected. "Sure, I guess tomorrow morning's paper'll do."

"OK. What's the date today?"

"August 21."

"Fine. I'll bring you a paper for August 22. Only I'm warning you: It won't do any good. But here goes nothing. Goodbye now. Hello again. Here you are." There was a string in Snulbug's horny hand, and on the end of the string was a newspaper.

"But hey!" Bill protested. "You haven't been gone."

"People," said Snulbug feelingly, "are dopes. Why should it take any time out of the present to go into the future? I leave this point, I come back to this point. I spent two hours hunting for this damned paper, but that doesn't mean two hours of your time here. People—" he snorted.

Bill scratched his head. "I guess it's all right. Let's see the paper. And I know: You're warning me." He turned quickly to the obituaries to check. No Hitchens. "And I wasn't dead in the time you were in?"

"No," Snulbug admitted. "Not *dead*," he added, with the most pessimistic implications possible.

"What was I, then? Was I—"

"I had salamander blood," Snulbug complained. "They thought I was an undine like my mother and they put me in the cold-water incubator when any dope knows salamandry is a dominant. So I'm a runt and good for nothing but to run errands, and now I should make prophecies! You read your paper and see how much good it does you."

Bill laid down his pipe and folded the paper back from the obituaries to the front page. He had not expected to find anything useful there—what advantage could he gain from knowing who won the next naval engagement or which cities were bombed?—but he was scientifically methodical. And this time method was rewarded. There it was, streaming across the front page in vast black blocks:

MAYOR ASSASSINATED
FIFTH COLUMN KILLS CRUSADER

Bill snapped his fingers. This was it. This was his chance. He jammed his pipe in his mouth, hastily pulled a coat on his shoulders, crammed the priceless paper into a pocket, and started out of the attic. Then he paused and looked around. He'd forgotten Snulbug. Shouldn't there be some sort of formal discharge?

The dismal demon was nowhere in sight. Not in the pentacle or out of it. Not a sign or a trace of him. Bill frowned. This was definitely not methodical. He struck a match and held it over the bowl of his pipe.

A warm sigh of pleasure came from inside the corncob.

Bill took the pipe from his mouth and stared at it. "So that's where you are!" he said musingly.

"I told you salamandry was a dominant," said Snulbug, peering out of the bowl. "I want to go along. I want to see just what kind of a fool you make of yourself." He withdrew his head into the glowing tobacco, muttering about newspapers, spells, and, with a wealth of unhappy scorn, people.

The crusading mayor of Granton was a national figure of splendid proportions. Without hysteria, red baiting, or strike-breaking, he had launched a quietly purposeful and well-directed program against subversive elements which had rapidly converted Granton into the safest and most American city in the country. He was also a persistent advocate of national, state, and municipal subsidy of the arts and sciences—the ideal man to wangle an endowment for the Hitchens Laboratory, if he were not so surrounded by overly skeptical assistants that Bill had never been able to lay the program before him.

This would do it. Rescue him from assassination in the very nick of time—in itself an act worth calling up demons to perform—and then when he asks, "And how, Mr. Hitchens, can I possibly repay you?" come forth with the whole great plan of research. It couldn't miss.

No sound came from the pipe bowl, but Bill clearly heard the words, "Couldn't it just?" ringing in his mind.

He braked his car to a fast stop in the red zone before the city hall, jumped out without even slamming the door, and dashed up the marble steps so rapidly, so purposefully, that pure momentum carried him up three flights and through four suites of offices before anybody had the courage to stop him and say, "What goes?"

The man with the courage was a huge bull-necked plain-clothes man, whose bulk made Bill feel relatively about the size of Snulbug. "All right, there," this hulk rumbled. "All right. Where's the fire?"

"In an assassin's gun," said Bill. "And it had better stay there."

Bullneck had not expected a literal answer. He hesitated long enough for Bill to push him to the door marked MAYOR—PRIVATE. But though the husky's brain might move slowly, his muscles made up for the lag. Just as Bill started to shove the door open, a five-pronged mound of flesh lit on his neck and jerked.

Bill crawled from under a desk, ducked Bullneck's left, reached the door, executed a second backward flip, climbed down from the table, ducked a right, reached the door, sailed back in reverse and lowered himself nimbly from the chandelier.

Bullneck took up a stand in front of the door, spread his legs in ready balance, and drew a service automatic from its holster. "You ain't going in there," he said, to make the situation perfectly clear.

Bill spat out a tooth, wiped the blood from his eyes, picked up the shattered remains of his pipe, and said, "Look. It's now 12:30. At 12:32 a redheaded hunch-back is going to come out on that balcony across the street and aim through the open window into the mayor's office. At 12:33 His Honor is going to be slumped over his desk, dead. Unless you help me get him out of range."

"Yeah?" said Bullneck. "And who says so?"

"It says so here. Look. In the paper."

Bullneck guffawed. "How can a paper say what ain't even happened yet? You're nuts, brother, if you ain't something worse. Now go on. Scram. Go peddle your paper."

Bill's glance darted out the window. There was the balcony facing the mayor's office. And there coming out on it—

"Look!" he cried. "If you won't believe me, look out the window. See on that balcony? The redheaded hunchback? Just like I told you. Quick!"

Bullneck stared despite himself. He saw the hunchback peer across into the office. He saw the sudden glint of metal in the hunchback's hand. "Brother," he said to Bill, "I'll tend to you later."

The hunchback had his rifle halfway to his shoulder when Bullneck's automatic spat and Bill braked his car in the red zone, jumped out, and dashed through four suites of offices before anybody had the courage to stop him.

The man with the courage was a huge bull-necked plain-clothes man, who rumbled, "Where's the fire?"

"In an assassin's gun," said Bill, and took advantage of Bullneck's confusion to reach the door marked MAYOR—PRIVATE. But just as he started to push it open, a vast hand lit on his neck and jerked.

As Bill descended from the chandelier after his third try, Bullneck took up a stand in front of the door, with straddled legs and drawn gun. "You ain't going in," he said clarifyingly.

Bill spat out a tooth and outlined the situation. "—12:33," he ended. "His Honor is going to be slumped over the desk, dead. Unless you help me get him out of range. See? It says so here. In the paper."

"How can it? Gwan. Go peddle your paper."

Bill's glance darted to the balcony. "Look, if you won't believe me. See the redheaded hunchback? Just like I told you. Quick! We've got to—"

Bullneck stared. He saw the sudden glint of metal in the hunchback's hand. "Brother," he said, "I'll tend to you later."

The hunchback had his rifle halfway to his shoulder when Bullneck's automatic spat and Bill braked his car in the red zone, jumped out, and dashed through four suites before anybody stopped him.

The man who did was a bull-necked plain-clothes man, who rumbled—

"Don't you think," said Snulbug, "you've had about enough of this?"

Bill agreed mentally, and there he was sitting in his roadster in front of the city hall. His clothes were unrumpled, his eyes were bloodless, his teeth were all there, and his corncob was still intact. "And just what," he demanded of his pipe bowl, "has been going on?"

Snulbug popped his snaky head out. "Light this again, will you? It's getting cold. Thanks."

"What happened?" Bill insisted.

"People," Snulbug moaned. "No sense. Don't you see? So long as the newspaper was in the future, it was only a possibility. If you'd had, say, a hunch that the mayor was in danger, maybe you could have saved him. But when I brought it into now, it became a fact. You can't possibly make it untrue."

"But how about man's free will? Can't I do whatever I want to do?"

"Sure. It was your precious free will that brought the paper into now. You can't undo your own will. And, anyway, your will's still free. You're free to go getting thrown around chandeliers as often as you want. You probably like it. You can do anything up to the point where it would change what's in that paper. Then you have to start in again and again and again until you make up your mind to be sensible."

"But that—" Bill fumbled for words, "that's just as bad as . . . as fate or predestination. If my soul wills to—"

"Newspapers aren't enough. Time theory isn't enough. So I should tell him about his soul! People—" and Snulbug withdrew into the bowl.

Bill looked up at the city hall regretfully and shrugged his resignation. Then he folded his paper to the sports page and studied it carefully.

Snulbug thrust his head out again as they stopped in the many-acred parking lot. "Where is it this time?" he wanted to know. "Not that it matters."

"The racetrack."

"Oh—" Snulbug groaned, "I might have known it. You're all alike. No sense in the whole caboodle. I suppose you found a long shot?"

"Darned tooting I did. Alhazred at twenty to one in the fourth. I've got $500, the only money I've got left on earth. Plunk on Alhazred's nose it goes, and there's our $10,000."

Snulbug grunted. "I hear his lousy spell, I watch him get caught on a merry-go-round, it isn't enough, I should see him lay a bet on a long shot."

"But there isn't a loophole in this. I'm not interfering with the future; I'm just taking advantage of it. Alhazred'll win this race whether I bet on him or not. Five pretty hundred-dollar parimutuel tickets, and behold: The Hitchens Laboratory!" Bill jumped spryly out of his car and strutted along joyously. Suddenly he paused and addressed his pipe: "Hey! Why do I feel so good?"

Snulbug sighed dismally. "Why should anybody?"

"No, but I mean: I took a hell of a shellacking from that plug-ugly in the office. And I haven't got a pain or an ache."

"Of course not. It never happened."

"But I felt it then."

"Sure. In a future that never was. You changed your mind, didn't you? You decided not to go up there?"

"O.K., but that was after I'd already been beaten up."

"Uh-uh," said Snulbug firmly. "It was before you hadn't been." And he withdrew again into the pipe.

There was a band somewhere in the distance and the raucous burble of an announcer's voice. Crowds clustered around the $2 windows, and the $5 weren't doing bad business. But the $100 window, where the five beautiful pasteboards lived that were to create an embolism laboratory, was almost deserted.

Bill buttonholed a stranger with a purple nose. "What's the next race?"

"Second, Mac."

Swell, Bill thought. Lots of time. And from now on— He hastened to the $100 window and shoved across the five bills that he had drawn from the bank that morning. "Alhazred, on the nose," he said.

The clerk frowned with surprise, but took the money and turned to get the tickets.

Bill buttonholed a stranger with a purple nose. "What's the next race?"

"Second, Mac."

Swell, Bill thought. And then he yelled, "Hey!"

A stranger with a purple nose paused and said, " 'Smatter, Mac?"

"Nothing," Bill groaned. "Just everything."

The stranger hesitated. "Ain't I seen you someplace before?"

"No," said Bill hurriedly. "You were going to, but you haven't. I changed my mind."

The stranger walked away shaking his head and muttering how the ponies could get a guy.

Not till Bill was back in his roadster did he take the corncob from his mouth and glare at it. "All right!" he barked. "What was wrong this time? Why did I get on a merry-go-round again? I didn't try to change the future!"

Snulbug popped his head out and yawned a tuskful yawn. "I warn him, I explain it, I warn him again, now he wants I should explain it all over."

"But what did I do?"

"What did he do? You changed the odds, you dope. That much folding money on a long shot at a parimutuel track, and the odds change. It wouldn't have paid off at twenty to one, the way it said in the paper."

"Nuts," Bill muttered. "And I suppose that applies to anything? If I study the stock market in this paper and try to invest my $500 according to tomorrow's market—"

"Same thing. The quotations wouldn't be quite the same if you started in playing. I warned you. You're stuck," said Snulbug. "You're stymied. It's no use." He sounded almost cheerful.

"Isn't it?" Bill mused. "Now look, Snulbug. Me, I'm a great believer in Man. This universe doesn't hold a problem that Man can't eventually solve. And I'm no dumber than the average."

"That's saying a lot, that is," Snulbug sneered. "People—"

"I've got a responsibility now. It's more than just my $10,000. I've got to redeem the honor of Man. You say this is the insoluble problem. I say there *is* no insoluble problem."

"I say you talk a lot."

Bill's mind was racing furiously. How can a man take advantage of the future without in any smallest way altering that future? There must be an answer somewhere, and a man who devised the Hitchens Embolus Diagnosis could certainly crack a little nut like this. Man cannot refuse a challenge.

Unthinking, he reached for his tobacco pouch and tapped out his pipe on the sole of his foot. There was a microscopic thud as Snulbug crashed onto the floor of the car.

Bill looked down half-smiling. The tiny demon's tail was lashing madly, and every separate snake stood on end. "This is too much!" Snulbug screamed. "Dumb gags aren't enough, insults aren't enough, I should get thrown around like a damned soul. This is the last straw. Give me my dismissal!"

Bill snapped his fingers gleefully. "Dismissal!" he cried. "I've got it, Snully. We're all set."

Snulbug looked up puzzled and slowly let his snakes droop more amicably. "It won't work," he said, with an omnisciently sad shake of his serpentine head.

It was the dashing act again that carried Bill through the Choatsby Laboratories, where he had been employed so recently, and on up to the very anteroom of old R. C.'s office.

But where you can do battle with a bull-necked guard, there is not a thing you can oppose against the brisk competence of a young lady who says, "I shall find out if Mr. Choatsby will see you." There was nothing to do but wait.

"And what's the brilliant idea this time?" Snulbug obviously feared the worst.

"R. C.'s nuts," said Bill. "He's an astrologer and a pyramidologist and a British Israelite—American Branch Reformed—and Heaven knows what else. He . . . why, he'll even believe in you."

"That's more than I do," said Snulbug. "It's a waste of energy."

"He'll buy this paper. He'll pay anything for it. There's nothing he loves more than futzing around with the occult. He'll never be able to resist a good solid slice of the future, with illusions of a fortune thrown in."

"You better hurry, then."

"Why such a rush? It's only 2:30 now. Lots of time. And while that girl's gone there's nothing for us to do but cool our heels."

"You might at least," said Snulbug, "warm the heel of your pipe."

The girl returned at last. "Mr. Choatsby will see you."

Reuben Choatsby overflowed the outsize chair behind his desk. His little face, like a baby's head balanced on a giant suet pudding, beamed as Bill entered. "Changed your mind, eh?" His words came in sudden soft blobs, like the abrupt glugs of pouring syrup. "Good. Need you in K-39. Lab's not the same since you left."

Bill groped for the exactly right words. "That's not it, R. C. I'm on my own now and I'm doing all right."

The baby face soured. "Damned cheek. Competitor of mine, eh? What you want now? Waste my time?"

"Not at all." With a pretty shaky assumption of confidence, Bill perched on the edge of the desk. "R. C.," he said, slowly and impressively, "what would you give for a glimpse into the future?"

Mr. Choatsby glugged vigorously. "Ribbing me? Get out of here! Have you thrown out— Hold on! You're the one—Used to read queer books. Had a grimoire here once." The baby face grew earnest. "What d'you mean?"

"Just what I said, R. C. What would you give for a glimpse into the future?"

Mr. Choatsby hesitated. "How? Time travel? Pyramid? You figured out the King's Chamber?"

"Much simpler than that. I have here"—he took it out of his pocket and folded it so that only the name and the date line were visible—"tomorrow's newspaper."

Mr. Choatsby grabbed. "Let me see."

"Uh-uh. Naughty. You'll see after we discuss terms. But there it is."

"Trick. Had some printer fake it. Don't believe it."

"All right. I never expected you, R. C., to descend to such unenlightened skepticism. But if that's all the faith you have—" Bill stuffed the paper back in his pocket and started for the door.

"Wait!" Mr. Choatsby lowered his voice. "How'd you do it? Sell your soul?"

"That wasn't necessary."

"How? Spells? Cantrips? Incantations? Prove it to me. Show me it's real. Then we'll talk terms."

Bill walked casually to the desk and emptied his pipe into the ash tray.

"I'm underdeveloped. I run errands. I'm named Snulbug. It isn't enough—now I should be a testimonial!"

Mr. Choatsby stared rapt at the furious little demon raging in his ash tray. He watched reverently as Bill held out the pipe for its inmate, filled it with tobacco, and lit it. He listened awe-struck as Snulbug moaned with delight at the flame.

"No more questions," he said. "What terms?"

"Fifteen thousand dollars." Bill was ready for bargaining.

"Don't put it too high," Snulbug warned. "You better hurry."

But Mr. Choatsby had pulled out his checkbook and was scribbling hastily. He blotted the check and handed it over. "It's a deal." He grabbed up the paper. "You're a fool, young man. Fifteen thousand! *Hmf!*" He had it open already at the financial page. "With what I make on the market tomorrow, never notice $15,000. Pennies."

"Hurry up," Snulbug urged.

"Goodbye, sir," Bill began politely, "and thank you for—" But Reuben Choatsby wasn't even listening.

"What's all this hurry?" Bill demanded as he reached the elevator.

"People!" Snulbug sighed. "Never you mind what's the hurry. You get to your bank and deposit that check."

So Bill, with Snulbug's incessant prodding, made a dash to the bank worthy of his descents on the city hall and on the Choatsby Laboratories. He just made it, by stop-watch fractions of a second. The door was already closing as he shoved his way through at three o'clock sharp.

He made his deposit, watched the teller's eyes bug out at the size of the check, and delayed long enough to enjoy the incomparable thrill of changing the account from William Hitchens to The Hitchens Research Laboratory.

Then he climbed once more into his car, where he could talk with his pipe in peace. "Now," he asked as he drove home, "what was the rush?"

"He'd stop payment."

"You mean when he found out about the merry-go-round? But I didn't promise him anything. I just sold him tomorrow's paper. I didn't guarantee he'd make a fortune off it."

"That's all right. But—"

"Sure, you warned me. But where's the hitch? R. C.'s a bandit, but he's honest. He wouldn't stop payment."

"Wouldn't he?"

The car was waiting for a stop signal. The newsboy in the intersection was yelling "Uxtruh!" Bill glanced casually at the headline, did a double take, and instantly thrust out a nickel and seized a paper.

He turned into a side street, stopped the car, and went through this paper. Front page: MAYOR ASSASSINATED. Sports page: Alhazred at twenty to one. Obituaries: The same list he'd read at noon. He turned back to the date line. August 22. Tomorrow.

"I warned you," Snulbug was explaining. "I told you I wasn't strong enough to go far into the future. I'm not a well demon, I'm not. And an itch in the memory is something fierce. I just went far enough ahead to get a paper with tomorrow's date on it. And any dope knows that a Tuesday paper comes out Monday afternoon."

For a moment Bill was dazed. His magic paper, his fifteen-thousand-dollar paper, was being hawked by newsies on every corner. Small wonder R. C. might have stopped payment! And then he saw the other side. He started to laugh. He couldn't stop.

"Look out!" Snulbug shrilled. "You'll drop my pipe. And what's so funny?"

Bill wiped tears from his eyes. "I was right. Don't you see, Snulbug? Man can't be licked. My magic was lousy. All it could call up was you. You brought me what was practically a fake, and I got caught on the merry-go-round of time trying to use it. You were right enough there; no good could come of that magic.

"But without the magic, just using human psychology, knowing a man's weaknesses, playing on them, I made a syrup-voiced old bandit endow the very research he'd tabooed, and do more good for humanity than he's done in all the rest of his life. I was right, Snulbug. You can't lick Man."

Snulbug's snakes writhed into knots of scorn. "People!" he snorted. "You'll find out." And he shook his head with dismal satisfaction.

Sanctuary

So there I was at dinner with a Gestapo chief.

It wouldn't be wise nor politic, not right now, to say where this took place. It wouldn't be wise nor possible, as you'll see later, to say when it took place. Temporally speaking, the events rambled. As to place, it should be enough to say that it was near the coast of quote unoccupied quote France, and I won't even say which coast. There's no point in tipping them off on where the new secret weapon is operating.

I'm afraid the names aren't true either, but that won't matter to you. One Gestapo chief is much the same as another to you, and you wouldn't know my Colonel von Schwarzenau from the Major Helm that they got in Zagreb the other day or the Erich Guttart who met up with his near Lublin. And you probably wouldn't have heard of Dr. Norton Palgrave under his real name either. Your grandchildren will, though, whether they're majoring in science or history.

I'm giving you my name straight, out of egotism, I suppose. You may have heard it—Jonathan Holding. No? Well, most of my stuff was privately printed in Paris. One volume in this country with new directions, "Apollo Mammosus." I was one of that crowd in Paris. The aesthetic Expatriate, that was me. I visited with Gertrude and Alice; I talked bullfighting with Ernest; I got drunk with Elliot; I sneered at everything American except the checks—you get the picture?

I wasn't in any hurry to get out of Paris even after the war started and the embassy began making noises about neutrals clearing out to where they belonged. What the hell, we had the Maginot Line between them and us, didn't we? And Paris could never be captured. Even in 1870 she held out, and from all I'd read of that siege it sounded like interesting raw material. She'd stick it out, and I'd stick it out with her.

And then came May, 1940, and I found out.

A lot of people found out a hell of a lot in the month or two following that May. I'll lay you whatever odds you want that there hasn't been such a period for taking stock of truth since the start of Western civilization. I found out things about the world and the people in it, and I found out things about myself.

I wasn't the same Jonathan Holding that wound up on this coast, which shall still be nameless but which was for me, in a very true sense, the seacoast of Bohemia. (I've still got my habit of allusive quotations, I see.) How I got there, why my left hand is a finger the poorer and my brain a great many thoughts the richer, how I saved Jeannot from the Little Massacre at Eaux-des-Anges and how I failed to save old Patelin, how I accidentally made contact with the Free French— or Fighting French, as they are now by name and have always been by spirit—by asking at a bakery for my own particular hard-to-get kind of croissant, all that's a long story and a different one. Just the end of it has to be mentioned here to explain why I wound up at the dinner table with Colonel von Schwarzenau and why Dr. Palgrave baffled the Gestapo by laying—and creating—a black-faced ghost.

"We can get you on a ship," de Champsfleuris told me. When I had last seen him he was some sort of an under-secretary in the foreign department. Now he looked as much at home in his crude fisher's garments and his stocking cap as ever he had in a white tie at a reception. "It is simple, that. Within eight days a fishing boat leaves which will not arrest itself until it has arrived at—" No, I'll x out that word; it would indicate the coast. Say England, Portugal, Africa, whatever strikes your fancy. "But you must live somewhere until then. The inn is not safe. An American—but, yes, you still retain the slightest of accents, my friend— living here to no purpose— We do not have tourists now. And still less safe to establish you with one of my friends, for I would imperil not only you but him." He mused, and then his eyes glinted as I had once seen them glint when he remembered that a Ruritanian Plyszt took diplomatic precedence over a Graustarkian Glagoltnik. "Dr. Palgrave," he said softly.

"Who's he?" I asked.

"You do not know of Dr. Palgrave, you an American? But then I ask myself how many Americans know of your fine surrealist work. Each man to his field, and the greatest in his field may be unknown save to himself. This Dr. Palgrave, he has a villa here, where his laboratory also finds itself."

"Research? What sort?"

De Champsfleuris's eyes twinkled. "Ah! That you will learn, my friend, do not fear. He is a strange one, that. I do not know myself, me, Henri-Marie de Champsfleuris, who can tell at a glance if a diplomat is authorized to make twice the concessions which he offers, I do not know if that one is one of the greatest men in the world or only one of the greatest fools. You are an artist; perhaps you will tell me."

"And he is—" I felt a little awkward as to how to put it. "He is one of us?"

"No— Alas, no. He has not awakened himself. He is as you were, my friend, a few short months ago. If he knew why you were here and what it is that you think to do when you leave here, I should not speak for his reception. But say only that you are an American from his old university. Say that you interest yourself— Are you acquainted with time theory?"

I nodded. "It's one of the few aspects of modern thought that we surrealists found material in."

"Good. Then talk to him of that. He will invite you to stay at the villa. Stay there, and do nothing until I send word to you through the postman Soisson."

It seemed a curious station on the underground railway, to spend a week in a luxurious villa talking time theory. But I had no suspicion then of how curious. I certainly never expected to meet, at my first dinner there, the head of the local Gestapo. Which brings us back now to when you came in.

Herr Oberst Heinz von Schwarzenau would be a fine name for one of the lean and leering Gestapo villains beloved of melodrama; but this jolly little man with the round, beaming face and the pudgy white hands hardly seemed at first glance to live up to his label. Dr. Palgrave wasn't too well cast as the Mad Scientist, either. His hair was neatly combed and his eyes were mildly blinking. His dinner jacket hung on his thin stooped shoulders about as gracefully as it might have decorated a scarecrow. There was nothing colorful or eccentric about him but his conversation. That was enough.

"You may define a dimension as you will, my dear colonel," he observed over the fish. "You may quite correctly term it the degree of manifoldness of a magnitude or any other proper terminological gibberish your methodical mind chooses to employ. But a dimension is basically a measure of extent; and if extent is measurable, then extension is possible."

The colonel beamed. "I am not sure if you are playing with ideas, or simply with words. What is your opinion, Mr. Holding?"

I had to fight to keep from jumping each time he addressed me. I had to remind myself that my exploits in the Little Massacre had been strictly anonymous and that the Gestapo, so far as I knew, had no more information on me than that I was a practitioner of degenerate art but otherwise harmless. I was, I kept saying to myself, far safer here, as a sort of purloined letter in person, than anywhere else. But I have since wondered how the purloined letter itself felt about the Minister D—'s brilliant ruse. "What are ideas themselves but playing with words?" I said casually. "Can a wordless idea exist?"

Colonel von Schwarzenau frowned. "That is loose thinking," he said severely, in that overperfect English of his. "Ideas can exist for instance as mathematical formulas, or even as an unformulated series of sensory images. Please, Mr. Holding, more discipline in your thought." Having put me in my decadent place, he turned back to his host as Antoine brought on the braised meat. "But granting, sir, your possibility of extension in the time dimension, to what practical purpose do you propose to apply this theory?"

I had my marked suspicion that the meat was horseflesh, but Antoine had accomplished such wonders with a sauce bordelaise that I didn't give a damn. That sauce would have been enough to distract my attention from most conversations, but Dr. Palgrave's next remark jerked me back.

"Propose to? But, my dear colonel, I have applied it. My time machine is already in operation."

All of the colonel's plump body shook with delight. "Ah, so? And what treasures do you bring us from the future, dear dcotor? Ray guns perhaps, to aid us in perpetuating the New Order?"

"I must confess that I have so far succeeded only with the past, but—"

"The past? But there are treasures there, too. Perhaps you could fetch back and restore the honor and glory of France?" He chuckled at this one.

"I . . . I have not as yet ventured into the machine myself. But I consider my efforts with the transportation of inanimate objects and of small animals to have proved my case completely. Iron sent into the past, left there for a year, and brought back has returned covered with rust, while it remained in the machine for only a minute of our time here. My first guinea pig died of old age through a mistake in my calculations. He was not yet adult when I put him in the machine; when I took him out thirty seconds later, he was dead of senile decay."

Colonel von Schwarzenau's chuckle became almost a giggle. "You are so symbolic, my dear doctor. It is you and not our friend here who should be the poet. Iron that rusts and guinea pigs that die of senile decay, always while seeking the past and ignoring the future. What better picture could you paint of the Third Republic?"

I held my temper. "And you offer—"

"Steel that never rusts and men who never age while their eyes remain fixed on the future, on the glory of the New Order. Steel and the bodies of men and always the future, the German future that must be the future of the world." For a moment he was in deadly earnest, but then the pudgy chuckle crept back into his voice. "Ah, it is good to be among representatives of your great democracy who still understand us. And such representatives. A scientist and a poet. A scientist who plays with time machines and a poet who plays with surrealism. There is your science and your art in a democracy. And yet you understand us, do you not, my friends? You are the admiring crowd who look up, the spiked wheels of the Juggernaut and cry, 'How beautiful is the goddess Kali today!' And because you see her beauty, she will spare you. Yes, you will be spared, and long may you be happy here in your haunted villa. Pursue your time machines and your surreal reality. *And do not interfere.*" There was a fleeting expression of grimness, then a broad beam.

Dinner went like that. We were treated like two not-too-bright but understanding Quislings who were fortunate to be in the good graces of the potent representative of the New Order. I boiled inside. I seethed so that I forgot the excellences of Antoine's miraculous makeshift cooking, even forgot the astonishing significance of Dr. Palgrave's claims. I wanted nothing but to kick out the Herr Oberst's shining white teeth, build them into a marimba, and play "The Battle Hymn of the Republic" on them.

But I had to be sensible. There was work for me to do. I had to put up with this until the fishing boat left. But Palgrave? He was staying here, living in the midst of this, putting up with it, liking it—

I couldn't help myself. I boiled over when Colonel von Schwarzenau made a regretfully early departure for an evening tour of inspection. "How can you tolerate that man as a guest?" I burst out, pouring myself an outsize dose of my host's notable brandy. "You, a free American, how can you listen to—"

Dr. Palgrave smiled calmly. "Why should it bother me? Much of what he says may be true. I don't know. Politics are no concern of mine. But if I listen to him politely, he lets me work in peace. What more should I ask?"

I took a deep breath. "Politics," I said slowly, "are no concern of yours. I never thought to hear those words again. I thought they were as dead as the grandfather of all dodos. Man, have you any notion of what your friend the colonel stands for?"

"Young man," Palgrave said, with a certain quiet dignity, "I am a scientist. The petty squabbles of men hold no meaning for me. I have my laboratory here. It is a valuable possession, expensive and difficult to reconstruct. I shall certainly not risk it by bothering my head about matters that do not concern me. Shall we have Antoine bring us some more—well, let us continue to call it coffee, in the living room?"

I changed the subject when the coffee came. I couldn't risk insulting my host. And a curious phrase of the colonel's had recurred to my mind. "Your friend wished us happiness in this 'haunted villa.' What did he mean by that? Surely this is too modern a place to have its ancestral specters?"

Outside the large windows of the living room we should have seen the terrace and the sea, but the blackout curtains shut us into our narrow personal cell. From outside a steady drumming noise beat into this cell, the percussive rhythm of machinery from the nearby Barras plant, origin of France's cheapest pleasure car in peace times and now given over to even de Champsfleuris knew not what. Dr. Palgrave hesitated before replying, and the steady thumps of manufactured death were loud in the room.

"Yes," he said at last. "This place is, by reliable reports, haunted. Or once was. One sole manifestation, which is, I gather from physical students, most unusual."

"Give," I said. "Or does your scientific mind reject it?"

"So many scientific minds have rejected what I have accomplished that I keep my own mind open, or try to. But this is a curious incident. It was before my tenancy, when the villa belonged to its original owner, the British novelist Uptonleigh. One day in 1937, I believe, in the midst of a house party, there suddenly appeared a ghost. A black-faced ghost, like a relic from one of the minstrel shows of my boyhood, clad in dirty dungarees and tattered tennis shoes. He spoke with an American accent and announced that he had just been treacherously murdered and had never expected heaven to be like this. The guests were sufficiently merry when he arrived, as was usually the case with Uptonleigh's guests, to enter into the spirit with the spirit, so to speak; if it chose to believe that heaven was one long party, they would give it one long party. The party lasted, I believe, for six weeks, almost equaling the record set by the wake which Uptonleigh held when his best novel was filmed. In that time the ghost assumed civilized attire, washed its face and grew a beard. The party might have gone on to a new record if the ghost had not vanished as abruptly as it appeared. It has never been seen since."

Dr. Palgrave related this preposterous narrative as calmly as he had told of his time machine, as calmly as he had accepted Colonel von Schwarzenau's manifestos of the New Order. I smiled politely. "Some drunken American who decided to crash a good party," I suggested.

Dr. Palgrave shook his head. "You do not understand. The ghost appeared suddenly from nowhere in the midst of them. One moment there was empty space, the next this black-faced intruder. All accounts allow of no rational explanation."

The Barras works thumped. I stared at the thin-bearded scientist. Did nothing interest him, nothing perturb him but his ventures into the past with senile guinea pigs and rusting iron? "It would be fun," I said, "to see your ghost meet your colonel."

Dr. Palgrave half smiled. "But we talk of these trivial matters when I have so much to show you, Holding. I want so very much to interest you in my experiments. I even dare hope that if I can convince you—"

There was an honest-to-God gleam in his eye. "Hold on," I said hurriedly. "You aren't aiming to graduate from guinea pigs to me, are you?"

"I should not have put it quite that way, but my thought was something of that nature."

"I'm afraid," I said politely, "I haven't any scientific aptitude. I'd never learn to handle the controls on a time machine. I can't even drive a car."

"Oh, that would be nothing. I have a remote-control panel so that I can operate the machine from such a distance that its field does not affect me. Contact with the field, you see, sets up a certain sympathetic parallel in the electronic vibrations of the blood stream; it is that that enables me to recall a living object from the past even if it has left the physical bounds of the machine."

"Then you have brought them back alive?"

"Guinea pigs, yes. But I have not had the opportunity to experiment with higher forms of life. How the field would affect the nervous system, whether there might be certain synaptic short circuits— Antoine refuses to make the attempt. And moreover he is so valuable a cook— But if I could interest you in the tremendous possibilities—"

I cursed Henri-Marie de Champsfleuris thoroughly up one side and down the other. It wasn't enough that he should play purloined letter with me under the nose of a Gestapo colonel. No; he has to expose me as guinea pig to a time-machine crackpot. I began to think it would have been a simpler and safer life to hide in hedges, sleep in haymows, and live off ditch water till that fishing boat sailed. I couldn't antagonize my host; but I was damned if I was going to have curious currents shot through me, whether they transported me in time or not. I was trying to frame a courteous excuse when I heard a thud that wasn't from the Barras works.

It was the steady rhythmic clump of trained marchers. They went to the back of the house first, and I heard sullen curses and a sharp scream that must have come from Antoine. Then they came back, thudding across the terrace.

The Barras works thumped out death for all men. The feet on the terrace thumped an unknown but far more immediate peril. And Dr. Palgrave talked about the effect of a temporomagnetic field on the ganglia of guinea pigs.

The French windows opened and a squad of four men came in, in gray uniforms with swastika brassards. A corporal saluted us and said nothing. His hand was an inch from his automatic as the men searched the room.

Dr. Palgrave paid no attention to them. I started to speak, but I thought better of it when I caught the corporal's hard eye and saw his fingers twitch. I sat there listening to the details of the Palgrave remote-control time mechanism while the four men completed their wordless search.

The corporal saluted again in silence, and the searchers filed out. I stared at Dr. Palgrave.

"It is nothing," he said calmly. "You see we are near the Barras works. Not infrequently saboteurs are spotted near here. Perhaps even a Commando. These searches are necessary. To protest would imperil my position. Antoine sometimes objects to the treatment he receives, but I give him a bonus."

I was speechless. But no speech from me was necessary. Dr. Palgrave's remark was answered by a new voice, a fresh crude voice with a vivid Americanism I hadn't heard in years of self-exile.

"Shut up, you guys," it said, "and stay shut. *Fermy le butch or cuppy le gorge,* get me?"

I turned to gape at the ghost of the villa—dirty dungarees, tattered tennis shoes, blackened face and all.

"Why, you're the ghost," Dr. Palgrave observed, as one who notes an interesting but insignificant fact.

"Brother, it's you that's slated to be the ghost if there's any trouble." There was the sheen of steel in the figure's hand—an efficient-looking blade about six inches long that seemed to be all cutting edge.

I got it. "You're a Commando," I said.

He snorted. "You civilians don't know from nothing. I'm a Commandoman." I was put in my place again. "But, look, boys. You talk English. You talk it kind of funny—classylike—but tell me: Are you Americans?"

I nodded.

"Is that a relief! I didn't do so good in French class; I was better at rough-and-tumble. And I guess I don't need this either, brothers." He sheathed the glinting six inches. "But get this: You've got to hide me."

"Why?" Dr. Palgrave asked imperturbably.

Blackened eyebrows lifted on the blackened face. The Commandoman jerked a thumb at Palgrave. " 'Why?' he says. Is he nuts?"

"He runs the joint," I said. "I'm just here pretty much the way you are."

"Look, brother," he addressed Dr. Palgrave. "I got cut off from the Commando. That patrol missed me by a flea's eyelash and I ducked in here after they'd gone. But they'll be back. They always search twice; it's a rule. And you've got to hide me."

"Why?" Dr. Palgrave repeated.

"Why? You're an American. Or are you?"

"I am, sir, a citizen of the world of science."

The distant thud of returning footfalls was barely audible over the Barras thumpings.

"Look." The Commandoman's hand rested on his sheath. "You listen to sense or you listen to Betsey. It don't make no matter if I get killed. What the hell, every time you black your face you say to yourself, 'Make-up for the last act.' But I'm the dope they made memorize the plans for sabotage at the works here. I've got to get through to a certain Frenchman with that message. And if they get me there's always the chance I'll crack under the games they play. So you've got to stall them and hide me some way."

The thudding steps were on the terrace now. I knew nothing of the house. I was helpless, but I spoke pleadingly to my host. "Dr. Palgrave, these men, these friends of yours, have declared war against citizens of your world of science as bitterly as against Poles or Czechs. This Commandoman is fighting your own scientific battle. You must—"

Dr. Palgrave indicated a small door across the room. "In there," he said tersely.

Herr Oberst Heinz von Schwarzenau was with the squad this time. He plumped his pudgy body into the most comfortable chair and came straight to the point. "My dear Dr. Palgrave, I assure you that I regret inconveniencing you. But I fear that this charming, if haunted, villa of yours is harboring a democratic dog of a Commandoman."

Dr. Palgrave said nothing. He sat at his desk and fiddled nervously with some gadgets in front of him. I spoke up. "Your men searched here once, Herr Oberst."

He glared at the men, and there was terror beneath their impassivity. "They did so. They searched badly. A loyal peasant has informed us, after only the slightest persuasion, that he saw the pig-dog enter this house."

I shrugged. "Dr. Palgrave and I have been sitting here, drinking our . . . coffee, and talking about the ghost. The only interruption was your searching squad." Dr. Palgrave still said nothing.

"So? I begin to understand now the purpose of that ghost legend. How was the ghost described? Black-faced and clad in dirty dungarees and tattered tennis shoes? So if a servant should see one of these Commando devils here he might think only, 'Aha! The ghost.' Most ingenious. Most ingenious. We have caught a glimpse of this man, and how well he would serve as your ghost— And you, Dr. Palgrave. I had thought you so faithful an adherent of the New Order."

Dr. Palgrave's fingers twitched at gadgets. You know me, colonel," he said, almost pitifully. "Can you imagine me a participant in a plot to give sanctuary to Commandos?"

"Frankly, no." The colonel smiled. "But once before in my life I misjudged a man. It can happen; I admit it. That one died slowly, and when he died he was no longer a man—" He chuckled. "But I could think of a more appropriate emasculation for you, dear doctor. If you do not reveal to us the hiding place of this Commando dog—I no longer trust the searching abilities of these dolts—I shall take great personal pleasure in slowly and thoroughly smashing every piece of scientific apparatus in this villa."

Dr. Palgrave started to his feet with a little choking gurgle of "No—"

"But, yes, I assure you. I shall give you fifteen seconds, dear doctor, to make up your mind. Then I shall proceed happily to the task of demolition. I tolerated your eccentric researches while they amused me and you were faithful. Now the devil take them."

"Fifteen seconds—"

Colonel von Schwarzenau glanced up from his wrist watch. "Five are gone."

The Barras thumping *rose crescendo* in the silence. If our Commandoman escaped, that lethal humming might stop forever. If he were taken—

"Ten are gone," the colonel announced.

Dr. Palgrave rapped nervously on his desk. He toyed with dials and verniers. He plucked at his lower lip.

"Fiftee—"

Silently, Dr. Palgrave rose and pointed to the small door. I started from my chair, then sank back as the armed squad passed me. I could do nothing. There was ashen dread on Dr. Palgrave's face, and a grin of ugly self-satisfaction on that of the colonel. The corporal jerked open the door.

A stranger stepped out. He was a good-looking young man with a curly red beard, faultlessly dressed in Savile Row white flannels, a subtly figured white shirt, and a professionally arranged ascot. His skin glowed with clean health.

Colonel Heinz von Schwarzenau stared speechlessly. The corporal peered into the room and made a flabbergasted announcement in German to the effect that there were no facilities there for washing or changing clothes, nor any sign of the Commando. One little glimmer of hope shone in von Schwarzenau's eyes. He stepped forward and tugged at the beard.

The stranger said, "Ouch!"

Dr. Palgrave smiled. "I could not resist the joke, my dear colonel. I happened to have another American guest whom you had not yet met. The temptation to build a dramatic introduction was too much for me. But now if you wish to search the house personally for your mythical Commandoman, I shall be glad to be of any assistance that I can. You know my loyalty to you and your friends."

The stranger and I sat silent under the watchful eyes of the corporal while von Schwarzenau searched the house. He returned glowering. "Pigs!" he snorted. "Weakling offspring of impure dogs! You bring me information and what is the result! You allow that one makes a fool of me!"

Not until the footsteps were dead in the distance did anyone speak. Then the stranger burst out, "What goes here, brothers? Where have I been and how did I get back here and— I thought I was dead and was that a heaven for you!"

I began to understand. "Then you—"

"Yes, Holding," Dr. Palgrave explained. "Our friend here is indeed the ghost. I realized that the exact description could not be coincidental. And if he was the ghost, then my time machine must be successful with a human traveler. It must be I who sent him back to Uptonleigh's classic party. And the ghost changed in those six weeks, you will recall, cleaned up and grew a beard. If I could bring him back, he would be completely unrecognizable to von Schwarzenau. So I sent him into my traveling cabinet."

"But how— You didn't go near it."

"I explained to you that it operated by remote control. I sent him on his journey and fetched him back under von Schwarzenau's very eyes, while he thought I was indulging in mere nervous twiddling."

"Brother," the Commandoman said, "I had you tagged all wrong. You're a right guy, after all, and I'm sorry I waved Betsy at you. You've done a good deed today for the United Nations."

"The United Nations?" Dr. Palgrave blinked. "Oh, yes. Yes— But what is important is that I have proved that my time machine is a practical device capable of carrying human life."

The Commandoman gulped. "You mean I was a guinea pig?" His hand sneaked toward Betsy, but he dropped it again. "Who cares? You saved me, that's the main thing."

"That colonel," Dr. Palgrave spoke reflectively, "he meant what he said—"

"They mostly do, them boys."

"He really meant that he would wantonly destroy all my invaluable apparatus merely to— And I thought he had a respect for science, an understanding of my—"

It was my chance to strike. "You get it now, Dr. Palgrave? You've been his dupe, his court jester. And when amusement palled, neither you nor your work meant a thing to him. All your research would have been wiped out without a moment's compunction."

"The . . . the devil—" Dr. Palgrave gasped.

I tried not to smile. "You've learned it now, sir. You've learned that your holy world of science isn't sacred to them, doesn't stand apart from the rest of the world. There are no islands any more. There never have been. No man is an island, entire of himself. And every man who is not a part of their black force is going to find himself and all that he holds holiest destroyed when it suits their convenience. One by one, we learn our lesson. Some of us had sense and soul enough to learn it as part of mankind from seeing the sufferings of others; some, like you and me, had to be pushed around personally to learn it. But every lesson learned, from whatever motive, is one more blow aimed at their heart."

"That's telling him, brother," said the Commandoman.

Dr. Palgrave stood erect, and his eyes did not blink. "Your next step, sir, I believe, will be to resume your former condition of grime. I shall aid you in any way possible. Consider this house your sanctuary, and inform those who follow after you, if you are fortunate enough to return, that this villa is theirs."

"Thanks, brother. I'll do that little thing."

"And tell your commander of this experience. He will doubtless not believe you, but insist that he communicate with the general staff. Take these formulas, and see that they reach the finest physicists in England. They will at least understand the possibility of what I am doing. Then we can arrange some communication and figure out a method for practical applications. I can already foresee, for instance, how futile would be advance secret-service notice of a Commando raid if the Commando moved back to do its damage the day *before* it landed here."

The Commandoman swung to his feet. "Me," he said, "I don't understand a word of this. I know something screwy has happened and I got away from the Gestapo, and was I ever on a sweet party! But I'll do what you say, brother." He raised two spread fingers.

My own part in the experiments for the next week and the details of my escape in the fishing boat are not essential to this narrative. I can best conclude it by a newspaper dispatch which I read when last in London, and the comment thereon by one of my friends in higher military circles.

VICHY, June 23.—The Vichy government announces the execution of twelve hostages for the recent sabotage at the Barras plant near *** and the murder of Colonel Heinz von Schwarzenau on June 12th. "The Jews and Communists involved in the treachery," the announcement reads, "have not yet been apprehended. It is believed that they were aided and reinforced by a party of Commando troops. Twelve more hostages will be shot daily until they are under arrest.

"But you know, old boy," young Wrothbottam insisted, "that's devilish peculiar. There was no Commando raid at *** on the twelfth. And what's odder yet, there was one on the thirteenth. Reported operations successful, but there hasn't been a word about it in the Vichy dispatches."

Transfer Point

There were three of them in the retreat, three out of all mankind safe from the yellow bands.

The great Kirth-Labbery himself had constructed the retreat and its extraordinary air-conditioning—not because his scientific genius had foreseen the coming of agnoton and the end of the human race, but quite simply because he itched.

And here Vyrko sat, methodically recording the destruction of mankind, once in a straight factual record, for the instruction of future readers ("if any," he added wryly to himself), and again as a canto in that epic of Man which he never expected to complete but for which he lived.

Lavra's long golden hair fell over his shoulders. It was odd that its scent distracted him when he was at work on the factual record, yet seemed at times to wing the lines of the epic.

"But why bother?" she asked. Her speech might have been clearer if her tongue had not been more preoccupied with the savor of the apple than with the articulation of words. But Vyrko understood readily; the remark was as familiar an opening as P-K4.

"It's my duty," Vyrko explained patiently. "I haven't your father's scientific knowledge and perception. Your father's? I haven't the knowledge of his humblest lab assistant. But I can put words together so that they make sense and sometimes more than sense, and I have to do this."

From Lavra's plump red lips an apple pip fell into the works of the electronic typewriter. Vyrko fished it out automatically; this too was part of the gambit, with the possible variants of grape seed, orange peel . . .

"But why," Lavra demanded petulantly, "won't Father let us leave here? A girl might as well be in a—a—"

"Convent?" Vyrko suggested. He was a good amateur paleolinguist. "There is an analogy—even despite my presence. *Convents* were supposed to shelter girls from the Perils of The World. Now the whole world is one Peril—outside of this retreat."

"Go on," Lavra said. She had long ago learned, Vyrko suspected, that he was a faintly over-serious young man with no small talk, and that she could enjoy his full attention only by asking to have something explained, even if for the *n*th time.

He smiled and thought of the girls he used to talk *with*, not *at*, and of how little breath they had for talking now in the world where no one drew an unobstructed breath.

It had begun with the accidental discovery in a routine laboratory analysis of a new element in the air, an inert gas which the great paleolinguist Larkish had named *agnoton,* the Unknown Thing, after the pattern of the similar nicknames given to others: *neon,* the New Thing; *xenon,* the Strange Thing.

It had continued (the explanation ran off so automatically that his mind was free to range from the next line of the epic to the interesting question of whether the presence of ear lobes would damage the symmetry of Lavra's perfect face), it had continued with the itching and sneezing, the coughing and wheezing, with the increase of the percentage of agnoton in the atmosphere, promptly passing any other inert gas, even argon, and soon rivaling oxygen itself.

And it had culminated (no, the lines were cleaner without lobes), on that day when only the three of them were here in this retreat, with the discovery that the human race was allergic to agnoton.

Now allergies had been conquered for a decade of generations. Their cure, even their palliation, had been forgotten. And mankind coughed and sneezed and itched—and died. For while the allergies of the ancient past produced only agonies to make the patient long for death, agnoton brought on racking and incessant spasms of coughing and sneezing which no heart could long withstand.

"So if you leave this sheller, my dear," Vyrko concluded, "you too will fight for every breath and twist your body in torment until your heart decides that it is all a little too much trouble. Here we are safe, because your father's eczema was the only known case of allergy in centuries—and was traced to the inert gases. Here is the only air-conditioning in the world that excludes the inert gases—and with them agnoton. And here—"

Lavra leaned forward, a smile and a red fleck of apple skin on her lips, the apples of her breasts touching Vyrko's shoulders. This too was part of the gambit.

Usually it was merely declined. (Tyrsa, who sang well and talked better; whose plain face and beautiful throat were alike racked by agnoton . . .) This time it was interrupted.

Kirth-Labbery himself had come in unnoticed. His old voice was thin with weariness, sharp with impatience. "And here we are! Safe in perpetuity, with our air-conditioning, our energy plant, our hydroponics! Safe in perpetual siege, besieged by an inert gas!"

Vyrko grinned. "Undignified, isn't it?"

Kirth-Labbery managed to laugh at himself. "Damn your secretarial hide, Vyrko. I love you like a son, but if I had one man who knew a meson from a metazoön to help me in the laboratory—"

"You'll find something, Father," Lavra said vaguely.

Her father regarded her with an odd seriousness. "Lavra," he said, "your beauty is the greatest thing that I have wrought—with a certain assistance, I'll grant, from the genes so obviously carried by your mother. That beauty alone still has meaning. The sight of you would bring a momentary happiness even to a man choking in his last spasms, while our great web of civilization—"

He left the sentence unfinished and switched on the video screen. He had to try a dozen channels before he found one that was still casting. When every gram of a man's energy goes to drawing his next breath, he cannot tend his machine.

At last he picked up a Nyork newscast. The announcer was sneezing badly ("The older literature," Vyrko observed, "found that comic . . ."), but still contriving to speak, and somewhere a group of technicians must have had partial control of themselves.

"Four hundred and seventy-two planes have crashed," the announcer said, "in the past forty-eight hours. Civil authorities have forbidden further plane travel indefinitely because of the danger of spasms at the controls, and it is rumored that all vehicular transport whatsoever is to come under the same ban. No Rocklipper has arrived from Lunn for over a week, and it is thirty-six hours since we have made contact with the Lunn telestation. Urope has been silent for over two days, and Asia for almost a week.

" 'The most serious threat of this epidemic,' the head of the Academy has said in an authorized statement, 'is the complete disruption of the systems of communication upon which world civilization is based. When man becomes physically incapable of governing his machines . . .' "

It was then that they saw the first of the yellow bands.

It was just that: a band of bright yellow some thirty centimeters wide, about five meters long, and so thin as to seem insubstantial, a mere stripe of color. It came underneath the back drop behind the announcer. It streaked about the casting room with questing sinuosity. No features, no appendages relieved its yellow blankness.

Then with a deft whipping motion it wrapped itself around the announcer. It held him only an instant. His hideously shriveled body plunged toward the camera as the screen went dead.

That was the start of the horror.

Vyrko was never to learn the origin of the yellow bands. Even Kirth-Labbery could offer no more than conjectures. From another planet, another system, another galaxy, another universe . . .

It did not matter. Kirth-Labbery was almost as indifferent to the problem as was Lavra; precise knowledge had now lost its importance. What signified was that they were alien, and that they were rapidly and precisely completing the destruction of mankind begun by the agnoton.

"Their arrival immediately after the epidemic," Kirth-Labbery concluded, "cannot be coincidence. You will observe that they function freely in an agnoton-laden atmosphere."

"It would be interesting," Vyrko commented, "to visualize a band sneezing . . ."

"It's possible," the scientist went on, "that the agnoton was a poison-gas barrage laid down to soften the Earth for their coming; but is it likely that they could *know* that a gas harmless to them would be lethal to other life? It's more probable that they learned from spectroscopic analysis that the atmosphere of this Earth lacked an element essential to them, which they supplied before invading."

Vyrko considered the problem while Lavra sliced a peach with delicate grace . . . then was unable to resist licking the rich juice from her fingers. "Then if the agnoton," he ventured, "is something that they imported, is it possible that their supply might run short?"

Kirth-Labbery fiddled with the dials under the screen. It was still possible to pick up occasional glimpses from remote sectors, though by now the heart sickened in advance at the knowledge of the inevitable end of the cast.

"It is possible, Vyrko. It is the only hope. The three of us here, where the agnoton and the yellow bands are alike helpless to enter, may continue our self-sufficient existence long enough to outlast the invaders. Perhaps somewhere on earth there are other such nuclei; but I doubt it. We are the whole of the future—and I am old."

Vyrko frowned. He resented the terrible weight of a burden that he did not want but could not reject. He felt himself at once oppressed and ennobled. Lavra went on eating her peach.

The video screen sprang into light. A young man with the tense lined face of premature age spoke hastily, urgently, "To all of you, if there are any of you . . . I have heard no answer for two days now . . . It is chance that I am here. But *watch,* all of you! I have found how the yellow bands came here. I am going to turn the camera on it now—*watch!*"

The field of vision panned to something that was for a moment totally incomprehensible. "This is their ship," the old young man gasped. It was a set of bars of a metal almost exactly the color of the bands themselves, and it looked in the first instant like a three-dimensional projection of a tesseract. Then as you looked at it your eye seemed to follow strange new angles. Possibilities of vision opened up beyond your capacities. For a moment you seemed to see what the human eye was not framed to grasp.

"They come," the voice panted on, "from—"

The voice and the screen went dead at once. Vyrko covered his eyes with his hands. Darkness was infinite relief. A minute passed before he felt that he could endure once more even the normal exercise of the optic nerve. He opened his eyes sharply at a little scream from Lavra.

He opened them to see how still Kirth-Labbery sat. The human heart, too, is framed to endure only so much; and, as the scientist had said, he was old.

It was three days after Kirth-Labbery's death before Vyrko had brought his prose and verse record up to date. Nothing more had appeared on the video, even after the most patient hours of knob-twirling. Now Vyrko leaned back from the keyboard and contemplated his completed record—and then sat forward with abrupt shock at the thought of that word *completed.*

For it was quite literally true. There was nothing more to write.

The situation was not novel in literature. He had read many treatments, and even written a rather successful satire on the theme himself. But here was the truth itself.

He was that most imagination-stirring of all figures, The Last Man on Earth. And he was bored.

Kirth-Labbery, had he lived, would have devoted his energies in the laboratory to an effort, even conceivably a successful one, to destroy the invaders; Vyrko knew his own limitations too well to attempt that.

Vrist, his gay wild twin who had been in Lunn on yet another of his fantastic ventures when the agnoton struck—Vrist would have dreamed up some gallant feat of physical prowess to make the invaders pay dearly for his life; Vyrko found it difficult to cast himself in so swashbuckling a role.

He had never envied Vrist till now. *Be jealous of the dead; only the living are alone.* Vyrko smiled as he recalled the line from one of his early poems; it had been only the expression of a pose when he wrote it, a mood for a song that Tyrsa would sing well . . .

It was in this mood that he found (the ancient word had no modern counterpart) the *pulps*.

He knew their history: how some eccentric of two thousand years ago (the name was variously rendered as Trees or Tiller) had buried them in a hermetic capsule to check against the future; how Tarabal had dug them up some fifty years ago; how Kirth-Labbery had spent almost the entire Hartl Prize for them because, as he used to assert, their incredible mixture of exact prophecy and arrant nonsense offered the perfect proof of the greatness and helplessness of human ingenuity.

But he had never read them before. They would at least be a novelty to assuage the ennui of his classically dramatic situation. And they helped. He passed a more than pleasant hour with *Galaxy* and *Surprising* and the rest, needing the dictionary but rarely. He was particularly impressed by one story detailing with the most precise minutiae the politics of the American Religious Wars—a subject on which he himself had based a not unsuccessful novel. By one Norbert Holt, he observed. Extraordinary how exact a forecast—and yet extraordinary too how many of the stories dealt with space- and time-travel which the race had never yet attained and now never would . . .

And inevitably there was a story, a neat and witty one by an author named Knight, about The Last Man on Earth. He read it and smiled, first at the story and then at his own stupidity.

He found Lavra in the laboratory, of all unexpected places.

She was staring fixedly at one corner, where the light did not strike clearly.

"What's so fascinating?" Vyrko asked.

Lavra turned suddenly. Her hair and her flesh rippled with the perfect grace of the movement. "I was thinking . . ."

Vyrko's half-formed intent permitted no comment on that improbable statement.

"The day before Father . . . died, I was in here with him and I asked if there was any hope of our escaping ever. Only this time he answered me. He said yes there was a way out but he was afraid of it. It was an idea he'd worked on but never tried. And we'd be wiser not to try it, he said."

"I don't believe in arguing with your father—even post mortem."

"But I can't help wondering . . . And when he said it he looked over at that corner."

Vyrko went to that corner and drew back a curtain. There was a chair of metal rods, and there was a crude panel, though it was hard to see what it was intended to control. He shrugged and restored the curtain.

For a moment he stood watching Lavra. She was a fool, and she was exceedingly lovely. And the child of Kirth-Labbery could hardly carry nothing but a fool's genes.

Several generations could grow up in this retreat before the inevitable failure of the most permanent mechanical installations made it uninhabitable. By that time the earth would be free of agnoton and yellow bands, or they would be so firmly established that there was no hope. The third generation would go forth into the world, to perish or . . .

He walked over to Lavra and laid a gentle hand on her golden hair.

Vyrko never understood whether Lavra had been bored before that time. A life of undemanding inaction with plenty of food may well have sufficed her. Certainly she was not bored now.

At first she was merely passive; Vyrko had always suspected that she had meant the gambit to be declined. Then as her interest mounted and Vyrko began to compliment himself on his ability as an instructor, they became certain of their success; and from that point on she was rapt with the fascination of the changes in herself.

But even this new development did not totally alleviate Vyrko's own ennui. If there were only something he could *do*, some positive, Vristian, Kirth-Labberian step that he could take! He damned himself for an incompetent esthetic fool who had taken so for granted the scientific wonders of his age that he had never learned what made them tick or how greater wonders might be attained.

He slept too much, he ate too much, for a brief period he drank too much—until he found boredom even less attractive with a hangover.

He tried to write, but the terrible uncertainty of any future audience disheartened him.

Sometimes a week would pass without his consciously thinking of agnoton or the yellow bands. Then he would spend a day flogging himself into a state of nervous tension worthy of his uniquely dramatic situation, and thereafter relapse.

Now even the consolation of Lavra's beauty was vanishing, and she began demanding odd items of food which the hydroponic garden could not supply.

"If you loved me, you'd find a way to make cheese . . ." or ". . . grow a new kind of peach . . . a little like a grape only . . ."

It was while he was listening to a wire of Tyrsa's (the last she ever made, in the curious tonalities of that newly-rediscovered Mozart opera) and visualizing her homely face made even less lovely by the effort of those effortless-sounding notes that he became conscious of the operative phrase. "If you loved me . . ."

"Have I ever said I did?" he snapped.

He saw a new and not readily understood expression mar the beauty of Lavra's face. "No," she said in sudden surprise. "No," and her voice fell to flatness, "you haven't . . ."

And as her sobs—the first he had ever heard from her—traveled away toward the hydroponic room, he felt a new and not readily understood emotion. He switched off the wire midway through the pyrotechnic rage of the eighteenth-century queen of darkness.

Vyrko found a curious refuge in the *pulps*. There was a perverse satisfaction in reading the thrilling exploits of other Last Men on Earth. He could feel through them the emotions that he should be feeling directly. And the other stories were fun too, in varying ways. For instance that astonishingly accurate account of the hairsbreadth maneuvering which averted what threatened to be the first and final Atomic War . . .

He noticed one oddity: Every absolutely correct story of the "future" bore the same by-line. Occasionally other writers made good guesses, predicted logical trends, foresaw inevitable extrapolations; but only Norbert Holt named names and dated dates with perfect historical accuracy.

It wasn't possible. It was too precise to be plausible. It was far more spectacular than the erratic Nostradamus so often discussed in certain of the *pulps*.

But there it was. He had read the Holt stories solidly through in order a half-dozen times without finding a single flaw when he discovered the copy of *Surprising Stories* that had slipped behind a shelf and was therefore new to him. He looked at the contents page; yes, there was a Holt and—he felt a twinge of irrational but poignant sadness—one labeled as posthumous. He turned to the page indicated and read:

> This story, we regret to tell you, is incomplete, and not only because of Norbert Holt's tragic death last month. This is the last in chronological order of Holt's stories of a consistently plotted future; but this fragment was written before his masterpiece, *The Siege of Lunn*. Holt himself used to tell me that he could never finish it, that he could not find an ending; and he died still not knowing how *The Last Boredom* came out. But here, even though in fragment form, is the last published work of the greatest writer of the future, Norbert Holt.

The note was signed with the initials M. S. Vyrko had long sensed a more than professional intimacy between Holt and his editor Manning Stern; this obituary introduction must have been a bitter task. But his eyes were hurrying on, almost fearfully, to the first words of *The Last Boredom*:

> There were three of them in the retreat, three out of all mankind safe from the yellow bands. The great Kirth-Labbery himself had constructed . . .

Vyrko blinked and started again. It still read the same. He took firm hold of the magazine, as though the miracle might slip between his fingers, and dashed off with more energy than he had felt in months.

He found Lavra in the hydroponic room. "I have just found," he shouted, "the damnedest unbelievable—"

"Darling," said Lavra, "I want some meat."

"Don't be silly. We haven't any meat. Nobody's eaten meat except at ritual dinners for generations."

"Then I want a ritual dinner."

"You can go on wanting. But look at this! Just read those first lines!"

"Vyrko," she pleaded, "I *want* it. Really."

"Don't be an idiot!"

Her lips pouted and her eyes moistened. "Vyrko dear . . . What you said when you were listening to that funny music . . . Don't you love me?"

"No," he barked.

Her eyes overflowed. "You don't love me? Not after . . . ?"

All Vyrko's pent-up boredom and irritation erupted. "You're beautiful, Lavra, or you were a few months ago, but you're an idiot. I am not given to loving idiots."

"But you—"

"I tried to assure the perpetuation of the race—questionable though the desirability of such a project seems at the moment. It was not an unpleasant task, but I'm damned if it gives you the right in perpetuity to pester me."

She moaned a little as he slammed out of the room. He felt oddly better. Adrenalin is a fine thing for the system. He settled into a chair and resolutely read, his eyes bugging like a cover-monster's with amazed disbelief. When he reached the verbatim account of the quarrel he had just enjoyed, he dropped the magazine.

It sounded so petty in print. Such stupid inane bickering in the face of— He left the magazine lying there and went back to the hydroponic room.

Lavra was crying—noiselessly this time, which somehow made it worse. One hand had automatically plucked a ripe grape, but she was not eating it. He went up behind her and slipped his hand under her long hair and began rubbing the nape of her neck. The soundless sobs diminished gradually. When his fingers probed tenderly behind her ears she turned to him with parted lips. The grape fell from her hand.

"I'm sorry," he heard himself saying. "It's me that's the idiot. Which, I repeat, I am not given to loving. And you're the mother of my son and I do love you . . ." And he realized that the statement was quite possibly, if absurdly, true.

"I don't want anything now," Lavra said when words were again in order. She stretched contentedly, and she was still beautiful even in the ungainly distortion which might preserve a race. "And what were you trying to tell me?"

He explained. "And this Holt is always right," he ended. "And now he's writing about us!"

"Oh! Oh, then we'll know—"

"We'll know everything! We'll know what the yellow bands are and what becomes of them and what happens to mankind and—"

"—and we'll know," said Lavra, "whether it's a boy or a girl."

Vyrko smiled. "Twins probably. It runs in my family—at least one pair to a generation. And I think that's it—Holt's already planted the fact of my having a twin named Vrist even though he doesn't come into the action."

"Twins . . . That *would* be nice. They wouldn't be lonely until we could . . . But get it quick, dear. Read it to me; I can't wait!"

So he read Norbert Holt's story to her—too excited and too oddly affectionate to point out that her longstanding aversion for print persisted even when she herself was a character. He read on past the quarrel. He read a printable version of the past hour. He read about himself reading the story to her.

"Now!" she cried. "We're up to *now*. What happens next?"

Vyrko read:

The emotional release of anger and love had set Vyrko almost at peace with himself again; but a small restlessness still nibbled at his brain.

Irrelevantly he remembered Kirth-Labbery's cryptic hint of escape. Escape for the two of them, happy now; for the two of them and for their . . . say, on the odds, their twins.

He sauntered curiously into the laboratory, Lavra following him. He drew back the curtain and stared at the chair of metal rods. It was hard to see the control board that seemed to control nothing. He sat in the chair for a better look.

He made puzzled grunting noises. Lavra, her curiosity finally stirred by something inedible, reached over his shoulder and poked at the green button.

"I don't like that last thing he says about me," Lavra objected. "I don't like anything he says about me. I think your Mr. Holt is nasty."

"He says you're beautiful."

"And he says you love me. Or does he? It's all mixed up."

"It's all mixed up . . . and I love you."

The kiss was a short one; Lavra had to say, "And what next?"

"That's all. It ends there."

"Well . . . Aren't you . . . ?"

Vyrko felt strange. Holt had described his feelings so precisely. He was at peace and still curious, and the thought of Kirth-Labbery's escape method nibbled at his brain.

He rose and sauntered into the laboratory, Lavra following him. He drew back the curtain and stared at the chair of metal rods. It was hard to see the control board that seemed to control nothing. He sat in the chair for a better look.

He made puzzled grunting noises. Lavra, her curiosity finally stirred by something inedible, reached over his shoulder and poked at the green button.

Vyrko had no time for amazement when Lavra and the laboratory vanished. He saw the archaic vehicle bearing down directly upon him and tried to get out of the way as rapidly as possible. But the chair hampered him and before he could get to his feet the vehicle struck. There was a red explosion of pain and then a long blackness.

He later recalled a moment of consciousness at the hospital and a shrill female voice repeating over and over, "But he wasn't there and then all of a sudden he was and I hit him. It was like he came out of nowhere. He wasn't there and then all of a sudden . . ." Then the blackness came back.

All the time of his unconsciousness, all through the semi-conscious nightmares while doctors probed at him and his fever soared, his subconscious mind must have been working on the problem. He knew the complete answer the instant that he saw the paper on his breakfast tray, that first day he was capable of truly seeing anything.

The paper was easy to read for a paleolinguist with special training in *pulps*—easier than the curious concept of breakfast was to assimilate. What mattered was the date. 1948—and the headlines refreshed his knowledge of the Cold War and the impending election. (There was something he should remember about that election . . .)

He saw it clearly. Kirth-Labbery's genius had at last evolved a time machine. That was the one escape, the escape which the scientist had not yet tested and rather distrusted. And Lavra had poked the green button because Norbert Holt had said she had poked (would poke?) the green button.

How many buttons could a wood poke poke if a wood poke would poke . . .

"The breakfast didn't seem to agree with him, Doctor."

"Maybe it was the paper. Makes me run a temperature every morning too!"

"Oh, Doctor, you do say the funniest things!"

"Nothing funnier than this case. Total amnesia, as best we can judge by his lucid moments. And his clothes don't help us—must've been on his way to a fancy-dress party. Or maybe I should say fancy-*un*dress!"

"Oh, Doctor . . . !"

"Don't tell me nurses can blush. Never did when I was an intern—and you can't say they didn't get a chance! But this character here—not a blessed bit of identification on him! Riding some kind of newfangled bike that got smashed up . . . Better hold off on the solid food for a bit—stick to intravenous."

He'd had this trouble before at ritual dinners, Vyrko finally recalled. Meat was apt to affect him badly—the trouble was he had not at first recognized those odd strips of oily solid which accompanied the egg as meat.

The adjustment was gradual and successful, in this case as in other matters. At the end of two weeks, he was eating meat easily (and, he confessed, with a faintly obscene nonritual pleasure), and equally chatting with nurses and fellow patients about the events (which he still privately tended to regard as mummified museum pieces) of 1948.

His adjustment, in fact, was soon so successful that it could not long endure. The doctor made that clear.

"Got to think about the future, you know. Can't keep you here forever. Nasty unreasonable prejudice against keeping well men in hospitals."

Vyrko allowed the expected laugh to come forth. "But since," he said, gladly accepting the explanation that was so much more credible than the truth, "I haven't any idea who I am, where I live, or what my profession is—"

"Can't remember anything? Don't know if you can take shorthand, for instance? Or play the bull fiddle?"

"Not a thing." Vyrko felt it hardly worth while to point out his one manual accomplishment, the operation of the as yet uninvented electronic typewriter.

"Behold," he thought, "the Man of the Future. I've read all the time travel stories. I know what should happen. I teach them everything Kirth-Labbery knew and I'm the greatest man in the world. Only the time travel never happens to a poor dope who took for granted all the science around him, who pushed a button or turned a knob and never gave a damn what happened, or why, between that action and the end result. Here they're just beginning to get two-dimensional black-and-white short-range television. We had (will have?) stereoscopic full-color world-wide video—which I'm about as capable of constructing here as my friend the doctor would be of installing an electric light in Ancient Rome. The Mouse of the Future . . ."

The doctor had been thinking too. He said, "Notice you're a great reader. Librarian's been telling me about you—went through the whole damn hospital library like a bookworm with a tapeworm!"

Vyrko laughed dutifully. "I like to read," he admitted.

"Ever try writing?" the doctor asked abruptly, almost in the tone in which he might reluctantly advise a girl that her logical future lay in Port Saïd.

This time Vyrko really laughed. "That does seem to ring a bell, you know . . . It might be worth trying. But at that, what do I live on until I get started?"

"Hospital trustees here administer a rehabilitation fund. Might wangle a loan. Won't be much, of course; but I always say a single man's got only one mouth to feed—and if he feeds more, he won't be single long!"

"A little," said Vyrko with a glance at the newspaper headlines, "might go a long way."

It did. There was the loan itself, which gave him a bank account on which in turn he could acquire other short-term loans—at exorbitant interest. And there was the election.

He had finally reconstructed what he should know about it. There had been a brilliant Wheel-of-If story in one of the much later pulps, on *If* the Republicans had won the 1948 election. Which meant that in fact they had lost; and here, in October of 1948, all newspapers, all commentators, and most important, all gamblers, were convinced that they must infallibly win.

On Wednesday, November third, Vyrko repaid his debts and settled down to his writing career, comfortably guaranteed against immediate starvation.

A half dozen attempts at standard fiction failed wretchedly. A matter of "tone," editors remarked vaguely, on the rare occasions when they did not confine themselves to the even vaguer phrases of printed rejection forms. A little poetry sold—"if you can call that selling," Vyrko thought bitterly, comparing the financial position of the poet with his own world.

His failures were beginning to bring back the bitterness of boredom, and his thoughts turned more and more to that future to which he could never know the answer.

Twins. It had to be twins—of opposite sexes, of course. The only hope of the continuance of the race lay in a matter of odds and genetics.

Odds . . . He began to think of the election bet, to figure other angles with which he could turn foreknowledge to profit. But his pulp-reading had filled his mind with fears of the paradoxes involved. He had calculated the election bets carefully; they could not affect the outcome of the election, they could not even, in their proportionately small size, affect the odds. But any further step . . .

Vyrko was, like most conceited men, fond of self-contempt, which he felt he could occasionally afford to indulge in. Possibly his strongest access of self-contempt came when he realized the simplicity of the solution to all his problems.

He could write for the science fiction pulps.

The one thing that he could handle convincingly and skillfully, with the proper "tone," was the future. Possibly start off with a story on the Religious Wars; he'd done all that research on his novel. Then . . .

It was not until he was about to mail the manuscript that the full pattern of the truth struck him.

Soberly, yet half-grinning, he crossed out *Kirth Vyrko* on the first page and wrote *Norbert Holt*.

Manning Stern rejoiced loudly in this fresh discovery. "This boy's got it! He makes it sound so real that . . ." The business office was instructed to pay the highest bonus rate (unheard of for a first story), and an intensely cordial letter went to the author outlining immediate needs and offering certain story suggestions.

The editor of *Surprising* was no little surprised at the answer:

. . . I regret to say that all my stories will be based on one consistent scheme of future events and that you must allow me to stick to my own choice of material . . .

"And who the hell," Manning Stern demanded, "is editing this magazine?" and dictated a somewhat peremptory suggestion for a personal interview.

The features were small and sharp, and the face had a sort of dark aliveness. It was a different beauty from Lavra's, and an infinitely different beauty from the curious standards set by the 1949 films; but it was beauty and it spoke to Norbert Holt.

"You'll forgive a certain surprise, Miss Stern," he ventured. "I've read *Surprising* for so many years and never thought . . ."

Manning Stern grinned. "That the editor was a surprise? I'm used to it—your reaction, I mean. I don't think I'll ever be quite used to being a woman . . . or a human being, for that matter."

"Isn't it rather unusual? From what I know of the field . . ."

"Please God, when I find a man who can write don't let him go all male-chauvinist on me! I'm a good editor, said she with becoming modesty (and don't you ever forget it!), and I'm a good scientist. I even worked on the Manhattan Project—until some character discovered that my adopted daughter was a Spanish War orphan. But what we're here to talk about is this consistent-scheme gimmick of yours. It's all right, of course; it's been done before. But where I frankly think you're crazy is in planning to do it *exclusively*."

Norbert Holt opened his briefcase. "I've brought along an outline that might help convince you . . ."

An hour later Manning Stern glanced at her watch and announced, "End of office hours! Care to continue this slugfest over a martini or five? I warn you—the more I'm plied, the less pliant I get."

And an hour after that she stated, "We might get someplace if we'd stay someplace. I mean the subject seems to be getting elusive."

"The hell," Norbert Holt announced recklessly, "with editorial relations. Let's get back to the current state of opera."

"It was paintings. I was telling you about the show at the—"

"No, I remember now. It was movies. You were trying to explain the Marx Brothers. Unsuccessfully, I may add."

"Un . . . suc . . . cess . . . fully," said Manning Stern ruminatively. "Five martinis and the man can say unsuccessfully successfully. But I try to explain the Marx Brothers yet! Look, Holt. I've got a subversive orphan at home and she's undoubtedly starving. I've *got* to feed her. You come home and meet her and have potluck, huh?"

"Good. Fine. Always like to try a new dish."

Manning Stern looked at him curiously. "Now was that a gag or not? You're funny, Holt. You know a lot about everything and then all of a sudden you go all Man-from-Mars on the simplest thing. Or do you? . . . Anyway, let's go feed Raquel."

And five hours later Holt was saying, "I never thought I'd have this reason for being glad I sold a story. Manning, I haven't had so much fun talking to— I almost said 'to a woman.' I haven't had so much fun talking period since—"

He had almost said *since the agnoton came.* She seemed not to notice his abrupt halt. She simply said, "Bless you, Norb. Maybe you aren't a male-chauvinist. Maybe even you're . . . Look, go find a subway or a cab or something. If you stay here another minute I'm either going to kiss you or admit you're right about your stories—and I don't know which is worse editor-author relations."

Manning Stern committed the second breach of relations first. The fan mail on Norbert Holt's debut left her no doubt that *Surprising* would profit by anything he chose to write about.

She'd never seen such a phenomenally rapid rise in author popularity. Or rather you could hardly say *rise.* Holt hit the top with his first story and stayed there. He socked the fen (Guest of Honor at the Washinvention), the pros (first President of Fantasy Writers of America), and the general reader (author of the first pulp-bred science fiction book to stay three months on the best-seller list).

And never had there been an author who was more pure damned fun to work with. Not that you edited him; you checked his copy for typos and sent it to the printers. (Typos were frequent at first; he said something odd about absurd illogical keyboard arrangement.) But just being with him, talking about this, that and those . . . Raquel was quite obviously in love with him—praying that he'd have the decency to stay single till she grew up and you know, Manningcita, I *am* Spanish; and the Mediterranean girls . . .

But there *was* this occasional feeling of *odd*ness. Like the potluck and the illogical keyboard and that night at FWA . . .

"I've got a story problem," Norbert Holt announced. "An idea, and I can't lick it. Maybe if I toss it out to the lions . . ."

"Story problem?" Manning said, a little more sharply than she'd intended. "I thought everything was outlined for the next ten years."

"This is different. This is a sort of paradox story, and I can't get out of it. It won't end. Something like this: Suppose a man in the remote year X reads a story that tells him how to work a time machine. So he works the time machine and goes back to the year X minus 2000—let's say, for instance, now. So in 'now' he writes the story that he's going to read two thousand years later, telling himself how to work the time machine because he knows how to work it because he read the story which he wrote because—"

Manning was starting to say "Hold it!" when Matt Duncan interrupted with "Good old endless-cycle gimmick. Lot of fun to kick around but Bob Heinlein did it once and for all in 'By His Bootstraps.' Damnedest tour de force I ever read; there just aren't any switcheroos left after that."

"Ouroboros," Joe Henderson contributed.

Norbert Holt looked a vain question at him; they knew that one word per evening was Joe's maximum contribution.

Austin Carter picked it up. "Ouroboros. The worm that circles the universe with its tail in its mouth. The Asgard Serpent, too. And I think there's something Mayan. All symbols of infinity—no beginning, no ending. Always out by the same door where in you went. See that magnificent novel of Eddison's, *The Worm Ouroboros;* the perfect cyclic novel, ending with its recommencement, stopping not because there's a stopping place but because it's uneconomical to print the whole text over infinitely."

"The Quaker Oats box," said Duncan. "With a Quaker holding a box with a Quaker holding a box with a Quaker holding a . . ."

It was standard professional shoptalk. It was a fine evening with the boys. But there was a look of infinitely remote sadness in Norbert's Holt's eyes.

That was the evening that Manning violated her first rule of editor-author relationships.

They were having martinis in the same bar in which Norbert had, so many years ago, successfully said *unsuccessfully.*

"They've been good years," he remarked, apparently to the olive.

There was something wrong with this evening. No bounce. "That's a funny tense," Manning confided to her own olive.

"I've owed you a serious talk for a long time."

"You don't have to pay the debt. We don't go in much for being serious, do we? Not so dead-earnest-catch-in-the-throat serious."

"Don't we?"

"I've got an awful feeling," Manning admitted, "that you're building up to a proposal, either to me or that olive. And if it's me, I've got an awful feeling I'm going to accept—and Raquel is *never* going to forgive me."

"You're safe," Norbert said dryly. "That's the serious talk. I want to marry you, darling, and I'm not going to."

"I suppose this is the time you twirl your black mustache and tell me you have a wife and family elsewhere?"

"I hope to God I have!"

"No, it wasn't very funny, was it?" Manning felt very little, aside from wishing she was dead.

"I can't tell you the truth," he went on. "You wouldn't believe it. I've loved two women before; one had talent and a brain, the other had beauty. I think I loved her. The damnedest curse of Ouroboros is that I'll never quite know. If I could take that tail out of that mouth . . ."

"Go on," she said. "Talk plot-gimmicks. It's nicer."

"And she is carrying . . . will carry . . . my child—my children, it must be. My twins . . ."

"Look, Holt. We came in here editor and author— remember back when? Let's go out that way. Don't go on talking. I'm a big girl but I can't take . . . everything. It's been fun knowing you and all future manuscripts gratefully received."

"I knew I couldn't say it. I shouldn't have tried. But there won't be any future manuscripts. I've written every Holt I've ever read."

"Does that make sense?" Manning aimed the remark at the olive, but it was gone. So was the martini.

"Here's the last." He took it out of his breast-pocket, neatly folded. "The one we talked about at FWA—the one I couldn't end. Maybe you'll understand. I wanted somehow to make it clear before . . ."

The tone of his voice projected the unspoken meaning, and Manning forgot everything else. "Is something going to happen to you? Are you going to— Oh my dear, no! All right, so you have a wife on every space station in the asteroid belt; but if anything happens to you . . ."

"I don't know," said Norbert Holt. "I can't remember the exact date of that issue . . ." He rose abruptly. "I shouldn't have tried a goodbye. See you again, darling—the next time round Ouroboros."

She was still staring at the empty martini glass when she heard the shrill of brakes and the excited upspringing of a crowd outside.

She read the posthumous fragment late that night, after her eyes had dried sufficiently to make the operation practicable. And through her sorrow her mind fought to help her, making her think, making her be an editor.

She understood a little and disbelieved what she understood. And underneath she prodded herself. "But it isn't a *story*. It's too short, too inconclusive. It'll just disappoint the Holt fans—and that's everybody. Much better if I do the damnedest straight obit I can, take up a full page on it . . ."

She fought hard to keep on thinking, not feeling. She had never before experienced so strongly the I-have-been-here-before sensation. She had been faced with this dilemma once before, once on some other time-spiral, as the boys in FWA would say. And her decision had been . . .

"It's sentimentality," she protested. "It isn't *editing*. This decision's right. I know it. And if I go and get another of these attacks and start to change my mind . . ."

She laid the posthumous Holt fragment on the coals. It caught fire quickly.

The next morning Raquel greeted her with, "Manningcita, who's Norbert Holt?"

Manning had slept so restfully that she was even tolerant of foolish questions at breakfast. "Who?" she asked.

"Norbert Holt. Somehow the name popped into my mind. Is he perhaps one of your writers?"

"Never heard of him," said Manning.

Raquel frowned. "I was almost sure . . . Can you really remember them all? I'm going to cheek those bound volumes of *Surprising*."

"Any luck with your . . . what was it? . . . Holt?" Manning asked the girl a little later.

"No, Manningcita. I was quite unsuccessful."

. . . *unsuccessful* . . . Now why, in Heaven's name, mused Manning Stern, should I be thinking of martinis at breakfast time?

Conquest

The cat was the first one out of the airlock—the first creature from Earth to touch the soil of a planet outside our system.

Laus was all against it, of course. He wanted out himself—not to get his name in the books for the Big Moment in History, but because it was his cat, and he'd sooner take a chance with his own body.

But Mavra made sense. "Eccentricity, yes," she said. "Stupidity, no. Bast's going." And Bast went.

She liked it, too. We could see that from the port. Hydroponic-cycle air is OK, and Bast has seemed as used to it as the rest of us; but lots of loose fresh oxygen hit her like a dose of catnip. Something too small for us to make out flew by just above her. She leaped and missed; but the leap was so pleasingly high ("Slightly less than Earth-gravity," Laus observed) that she kept repeating it, bouncing among the flowers of the meadow and into the dusty path.

Then abruptly she sat down and inspected herself. The ship was so automatically clean that she'd been spotless for weeks. I guess she was glad of this chance to resume a normal life. No sound came through to us, of course, but just looking at her you could hear the thunderous purr as she settled down to give herself a tail-tip-to-whiskers bath.

We were damned near purring ourselves. This was a livable world—at least as far as gravity and oxygen went. Which is doing all right for an emergency crash-landing.

It was our third trip into space, and the first time we'd found a star with planets—seven of them, no less, of which this one (with two moons) was the second. We found the system and overdrove back to Communications, that Earth-built satellite of Alpha Centauri, the poor sun that never spawned any planets of its own. Don't ask me why you can install overdrive in a scoutship, but not Faster than Light communication. All I know is it takes something the size of the Communications satellite to house FL transmitters and receivers, and we have to go there to clear with the red-tape boys back home.

So we got the clearance: No other scouts had reported our system, so go ahead and good luck. Find a habitable planet and you take the jackpot that's been accumulating compound interest for almost two centuries ever since the UN set it up just after the first moon flight.

So we overdrove back to our system . . . and crash-landed.

For a minute I thought we were through as a team. Laus kept looking back and forth between me and his smashed instruments, flexing his fingers and rubbing that damned bare chin of his. Any second he was going to go off with a Bikini burst. Even Mavra wasn't trining; she was withdrawn, off someplace of her own where she didn't have to look at a thing like me.

Then Bast decided that I was the best prospect to hit. She rubbed her order against my leg, looking up with a woebegone face whose big eyes plainly stated that nobody ever fed cats on this godforsaken spaceship—but if I acted fast I might be able to prevent a serious case of starvation.

Among our blessings, the reutilizer had sprung a leak. I didn't turn the spigot; I just put the dehydrated fish in a pan and held it under the leak. I mixed it, set it down, gave Bast a couple of little strokes behind the ears, and got out some plastiflux to stopper the leak. Bast looked at the pan dubiously, and I said, "Go on: Nice fish for fine cats." She hesitantly tried a mouthful, agreed, and made a brief remark of minimum gratitude.

"Well," I said, "somebody's speaking to me."

Mavra came back from wherever she'd been, and laughed. "Bast's right," she said. "You're still human. You're still useful. We're still alive. What more do we want?"

Laus still looked at the ruined instruments, as though it would take him a good hour to begin answering that question. But he looked at Bast too, and finally at me. "All right, Kip," he said. "Astrogation's a new science—"

"Science, hell!" I grinned at him. "It's an art. I don't know any more about the science of overdrive than the first airplane ace knew about the science of heavier-than-air flight. I fly with my synapses, if that's the word I want, and sometimes I guess they don't apse."

He was staring at my useless control dials. "I can see your problem. You're working in such incalculable distances that a relatively minute error is absolutely enormous. A miscalculation of 20,000 miles could be fatal in causing a crash-pull into a planet's gravity—and it would show up on that dial as .000,000,001 parsec." He seemed to feel better, as if stating our problem in decimal fractions he'd worked out in his head made it all a little more endurable.

"Well," said Mavra, "we're on a planet. The next test for the UN jackpot is the little word *habitable*. I don't suppose the atom-analyzer still . . . ?"

It didn't, and that's where the argument started about who was to be first guinea pig through the airlock.

Now we three watched Bast finish her bath, and knew that at least we could breathe here. There were little items like food and water still to worry about, but it was safe to leave the ship. I was just starting to open the lock when Mavra's cry called me back to the port. That was how we saw the first of the Giants.

It looked like an Earth meadow out there. The sun, we knew from our scouting tests, was a little colder than Sol, but the planet was closer in than Earth. The sunlight was about the same, and it was bright noon now. The grass was, so far as we could see, just plain grass, and if the flowers in the meadow and the trees beyond it looked unfamiliar, they didn't seem improbable—no more strange than Florida would look to a New Englander, or maybe not so much.

But the Giants . . . There were two of them, and they were of different sexes, if holding hands and looking (I guess the technical word is *gazing*) into each other's eyes, and not noticing where the hell you're going, have universal meaning. From which you'll gather they were humanoid—hands and eyes and all the other standard attributes so far as we could see, for they wore clothes—free-flowing garments which looked like woven cloth, implying some degree of civilization.

But there were three nonhumanoid things about them. A: they were both absolutely flat-chested, which sort of spoiled the picture. B.: they were both absolutely bald, which didn't help it any either. And C: they were both, as best we could judge using Bast as a measuring comparison, well over twelve feet tall and built (by humanoid standards) in proportion.

"It isn't possible . . . !" Mavra gasped. "This planet's Earth-size, Earth-gravity. They'd be bound to be . . ."

"Why?" Laus asked bluntly. "I've always doubted that point. Wrote a paper on it once. Earth has creatures every size from the ant to the elephant. Make it from the bacterium to the brontosaur. It's pure chance, aided by an opposable thumb, that of all living beings the medium-sized primates developed intelligence. Why should we expect the size-ratio aliens over us equals their planet over ours?"

"Shh!" said Mavra irrationally, as if the Giants might hear us.

We watched Bast's jump of astonishment as the four Giant feet pounded the soil near her. She looked at them curiously but without bristling, much as she had, from time to time, regarded the things that lived in the spaceship without our knowledge. As they sauntered along, lost in each other, Bast made up her mind. She stood up, leaned back on her hind feet, dug her foreclaws into the ground well in front of her, gave her vertebrae a thorough stretching, then recompacted herself and walked casually toward the Giants, her tail carried like a tall exclamation point over the round dot beneath.

She picked the larger and presumably male Giant for her rubbing post. When, for the first time since we'd seen him, he took his eyes from his companion, Bast rolled over in her extra-voluptuous pose, the one that suggests that there's a mirror in the ceiling.

They both stopped and bent over her. You could guess the dialogue from the humanoid gestures and expressions: *What on Earth's that? Never saw one before. Well, it seems friendly anyhow. And it's cute too. Look, it wants to be rubbed. See, it likes it. Especially right there . . .*

"She's a lucky Giantess," said Mavra. "Nothing like tactile intuition in a man."

"I hope you've noticed," I said, "that Bast likes me."

"*Shh!*" she said, having started the conversation.

The male fumbled in a sort of sporran and tossed something to Bast, who fielded it nicely. The lovers grinned and looked at each other and stopped grinning and went on looking. Their hands met again and they started to stroll away, in no condition to notice a trifle like a scoutship crashed in the bushes at the edge of the meadow.

Bast spent a minute using the Giant's gift as a toy, batting it along the grass and chasing it. Then her interest became more practical. She sniffed at it, turned it over once and crouched eying it, tail atwitch. When she finally ate it, it made three mouthfuls.

Laus and I each held one of Mavra's hands, but it was no such hand-holding as we'd been witnessing. It was just trine unification in the intensity of our suspense—suspense squared as Bast decided that now, in all this lovely sun, was just the time for a nap. But she had hardly curled up when one of the tiny flying things passed over her. She bounded up with another of those leaps, chased it vainly for a full minute, then abruptly stopped and trotted sedately back to the ship as though that was all she'd intended all along.

We all let out our breaths at once. Laus dropped Mavra's hand; I didn't. "So there's also food here," he said, "that's at least not immediately poisonous. If one food's edible, doubtless most are; it implies a reasonably similar metabolism. It's a habitable planet."

"Jackpot!" I said, and then felt like seventy-eight kinds of damned fool.

Mavra smiled at me. "The Giants seem not uncivilized. They might even be able to repair the ship. But whether the UN ever learns the fact or not, we can live here."

"If," said Laus, "we can communicate with the Giants."

He was flexing his fingers again and rubbing his bare chin, but this time I knew his concern was focused on himself. This was his job; would he do it better than I'd done mine?

We were a team of specialists:

Kip Newby, astrogator. I was deciding to invent a new slogan for the Service: "You can't call yourself an astrogator until you've had your first crash-landing." By which standard I would be the only astrogator in the Galaxy.

Dr. Wenceslaus Hornung, xenologist—even more untried in his job than I was in mine. For the Giants were the first Xenoids (aliens to you) that an Earth man had ever found. For more than two centuries we'd been developing what some of them called Contact-Theory. It had never proved necessary in the solar system, but the theoretical work went on. Of all the boys who'd ever taken the works in BLAM (Biology, Linguistics, Anthropology, Mathematics) Laus was reckoned the absolute tops in xenology——so damned good that he could even get away with eccentricities like taking a pet on a space trip or scraping the hair off his face like an ancient Roman or a Dawn-Atomic man.

Mavra Dario, co-ordinator. We haven't developed a good word yet for her specialty. I've known lads that called her a "neuro-sturgeon," which I'm told derives from an early investigator who discovered some of the principles of trine symbiosis. Her specialty is being unspecialized, being herself and thereby making each of us be more himself and at the same time more a part of the team. If you've never been on a team I couldn't make it clear to you; if you have I don't need to.

That was the team, plus—thank God for Laus's eccentricities—Bast. Laus has told me, more than once, all about the Egyptian goddess, but I still think of that name as an affectionate but not wholly inaccurate shortened form.

She was at the airlock now. I opened it. She seemed to think this was fine. It had been weeks since she'd had a door to decide whether or not to go through.

While she was making up her mind, Mavra spoke. "Don't rush it, Laus. There's no hurry for First Contact. If we're lucky, we can take a few days to size them up beforehand. And the first thing is to get busy with this shrubbery and try a reasonable job of camouflaging the ship. The next Giants may not be in love."

We were lucky. Our meadow was a mountain meadow; as we guessed then and later learned, it was used for pasturing and it wasn't quite the right time of the year yet to move the flocks up there. Nearby, the mountain ran up higher to a peak. With slightly lower gravity and slightly higher oxygen percentage, it was a pleasure to go in for a little mountain-climbing. And there in the valley on the other side was a city.

Our telefocals were among the very few surviving instruments. They were strong enough to give us a damned good idea of life in the city. We spent days of observation up there. Once Bast came along but it bored her. After that she would squat in the ship and peer after us through almost-shut eyes, regarding us somewhat as an idol might look upon a crowd of worshippers, who are necessary for existence, but whose departure leaves him in more peaceful possession of the temple.

One thing was for sure: The Giants were civilized, even highly so. Their architecture was (Mavra said) of exquisite if alien proportion. Their public statuary was good enough, by Earth standards, to hide away in a museum and not leave out, like the Hon. Rufus Fogstump in bronze, for the pigeons and the people. Their public life seemed peaceful and orderly, and largely centered around an enormous natural amphitheater, featuring what we interpreted to be plays and concerts and games. The games—Olympic-type contests of individuals rather than massed groups—gave us a chance to see the Giants practically naked in all their absolute hairlessness, and learn why a perfectly flat-chested girl could inspire passion. They were marsupials. I wondered if I would ever become a connoisseur of pouches.

We couldn't hear the music from the amphitheater, but once a group of picnickers made music of their own in our meadow. The instruments looked strange, though you could figure out familiar principles, but they listened good. There was one number especially that Laus described as "a magnificently improvised true passacaglia" and I (being something of a historical scholar myself in this field) called "jamming a real zorch boogie." Mavra said we were both right, and Bast implied we were both wrong but kept quiet about it.

A high civilization . . . but apparently not a mechanical one. Nothing visible beyond quadruped-power and simple applications of water wheels and windmills.

Help in repairing the ship began to look like an impossible dream. And supplies were running low. Water ran near us, but food . . .

"With civilization of this level," Laus pronounced confidently, "contact will be no problem." Bast shifted in his lap and indicated that she'd like a little more attention higher up the spine. "We've seen no evidence of armies or weapons, and the first Giants were friendly toward Bast even though she was, presumably, more alien to them than we shall seem."

I think Laus was set for a good half hour's discourse on why contact presented no problems, when Mavra pointed out the now always open airlock. "There's a Giant," she said. "I think it's the one Bast met first, and he's alone. How about now?"

If hand-holding and breath-holding had marked our watching of Bast's encounter with this Giant, it was nothing to our tenseness now. We knew what Laus was doing. God knows he'd told us all about it often enough, and especially why Mathematics was the all-important M in the BLAM courses.

He was proving to a civilized alien that he too was a civilized being, more than an animal. He was demonstrating by diagram that he knew that this was the second planet (with two moons yet) in a system of seven. He was teaching his system of numbers and doing simple arithmetical exercises. He was proving that the square on the hypotenuse of a right-angle triangle equals the sum of the squares on the other two sides. He was using prepared pieces of string to show that the circumference of a circle is three and (for simplicity) one-seventh times as long as its diameter.

That was what he was doing, in theory. What we saw was this:

The Giant looked first astonished, then amused. *A man runs into the damnedest things in this meadow!* He reached out a hand to stroke Laus's hair. Laus withdrew on his human dignity and began making marks on his pad. As he pointed from his drawing up to the sun, down to the planet itself, the Giant grinned, imitated the gestures, and then ran his large hand down Laus's back. He looked puzzled. *Feels more like cloth than fur.* Laus picked up a handful of pebbles to go into his counting routine. The Giant picked up a stone and threw it away, then looked a little resentful when Laus failed to chase it. Laus held up two pebbles and made a mark on his pad. The Giant rubbed his odd-feeling back again, then reassured himself by rubbing his hair. Laus shook his head indignantly and held up three pebbles. The Giant reached for them and tossed them in the air. He watched them, then looked back with some astonishment to see Laus still unmoved. He rubbed Laus's hair again, then jumped back at something he saw in Laus's eyes.

I don't know whether I heard Mavra say "Oh dear God . . . !" or felt it coming through our palms.

Laus had dropped the pebbles and got out his strings. As Laus spread the long one on the grass to make the circle, the Giant approached hesitantly. *I didn't get the other game, but this looks simple.* He lifted the string and held it at arm's length, above even his head and far out of Laus's grasp. He dangled it tantalizingly as Laus tried desperately to snatch it. The Giant began to smile. *Fine; this is what it likes.* He began backing away, Laus jumping and snatching after him. Then sharply Laus stopped and reached over for more pebbles.

Back to that routine, I thought; but Mavra was ahead of me. Her hand wasn't in mine, and when I turned she was half out of her workclothes.

"Look," I glugged. "I know I've been patient a long time, but is this quite the moment."

"Damn this zipper!" she said intently. "Give me a hand." And she went on peeling.

I needed two sets of eyes. Through the camouflage-bushes I could see that I'd been all wrong about Laus's use for the pebbles.

And him without even a slingshot.

The first stone smote the Giant in the forehead all right, but the rest of the sequence didn't follow. All it did was to irritate the hell out of him. He lashed out with one backhand blow and Laus was stretched on the grass.

Then the Giant backed away in consternation. My God! another one! But he didn't back fast, and Mavra's light on her feet. There she was, curving against him, looking up at him with soft wide eyes. And as his face relented and the old grin came back, he reached out for her and she dropped lithely, rolled over, and contemplated that mirror up there.

In vague general design, I suppose, she wasn't too different from his Giantess, but the size and the hair and the breasts would all be enough to keep any such thoughts out of his mind. Gently, soothingly, happily he stroked her, exactly as I was stroking Bast, who had just jumped into my lap with an ill-tempered remark about people who spend their time staring at unimportant things and neglect the comfort of cats.

It all seems obvious when you look back on it from the vantage of God knows how many years; and up till the day he died, some three *here*-years ago, Laus was always ready with a speech on why the BLAM boys should have foreseen it.

"The science fiction writers seemed to be a step ahead," he'd say, "and the scientists followed their line. It seemed so logical. This was how to communicate with any intelligent being. But practically it meant 'any intelligent being with a Copernican view of his own world and an understanding of the mathematical use of zero.' In other words, nobody in the highest civilizations of our own Earth up until only a few hundred years ago. The noblest Roman of them all couldn't have understood my planetary diagram. The finest Greek mind would have been confused by my system of numbers. From what we know now, the best men here would understand about pi and about the square of the hypotenuse; with such an architectural culture it's inevitable. But what chance contact would? Even in our own contemporary Earth?"

And Mavra would always cut him off, eventually, by saying, "But isn't it better this way? If you had made contact, we'd simply have been lost aliens, trapped in a civilization that could never help us home. As it is," and she'd yawn and stretch gracefully, "we've conquered the planet."

Which we have, of course. Like I said, I don't know how long it's been. At the rate my great-great-(I think)–grandchildren are growing up, I must be pushing a hundred, which is the expectancy the actuaries gave me when last heard from; but I feel good for maybe another fifty.

There are hundreds of us by now, and we're beginning to spread into the other continents. Give us another generation or two, and there'll be thousands. It isn't hard to teach the kids something that combines duty and pleasure to such an extraordinary degree as multiplying. (Though I always doubt that Laus had his proper share of descendants; he took his crash-landing harder than I did mine.) And we teach them other things too, of course, all that we can remember of what all three of us knew.

(Funny: it still seems trine even with Laus gone . . . and by now even I know a fair amount of BLAM to pass on.)

And we teach them what Bast knew, and never meant to teach us. We still miss her. It's sad that she had a much shorter lifespan and no mate. But then otherwise she and her tribe would have been competition—and pretty ruthless, considering how much their long training would make them better at it.

But we learned enough from her. We know how to make the Giants feel that it's a pleasure to give pleasure to us, and a privilege to provide us with food and shelter. No clothes, since we saw they puzzled the one I still think of as Our Giant (Mavra still lives in his home). We don't need them much in this climate (I wonder if we ever needed them as much as we thought we did on Earth?), and besides our genes seem to have learned something from Bast too. Our great-greats are hairier than the hairiest Earth man, even a white. (This was a blow to Laus; he never quite got over having to stop scraping his face.)

The Giants obey well, for a race new to the custom. (Oh, sure they had pets before, but the type of pets that obey *them*.) Their medical science isn't bad; they've been training special doctors for us for some time, and this year they're building a hospital. There are farmers making a good living out of foods which we like but which never had much market before. They've even started cultivating that weed I accidentally discovered which is so much like tobacco and makes such a fine chaw.

The camouflage-bushes have grown naturally (with a little irrigation and fertilization when there were no Giants around). They have no idea where we came from, and since they have no notion of evolution or the relation of species, they've decided it doesn't matter. When they do reach that point, their paleontologists can undoubtedly knock up a few fossil reconstructions near enough to suffice as our ancestors.

And meanwhile we're ready, whenever our people land, to hand over to them a ready-conquered planet.

But it's been a long time. In all these years, wouldn't a scoutship have . . . ?

Sometimes I can't help wondering:

Have Bast's people landed on Earth?

The First

"He was a bold man," wrote Dean Swift, "that first eat an oyster." A man, I might add, to whom civilization owes an enormous debt—were it not that any debt was quite canceled by that moment of ecstasy which he was first of all men to know.

And countless other such epic figures there have been, pioneers whose achievements are comparable to the discovery of fire and possibly superior to the invention of the wheel and the arch.

But none of these discoveries (save perhaps that of the oyster) could have its full value for us today but for one other, even more momentous instant in the early history of Man.

This is the story of Sko.

Sko crouched at the mouth of his cave and glared at the stewpot. A full day's hunting it had taken him to get that sheep. Most of another day he had spent cooking the stew, while his woman cured the hide and tended the children and fed the youngest with the breast food that took no hunting And now all of the family sat back there in the cave, growling with their mouths and growling with their bellies from hunger and hatred of the food and fear of the death that comes from no food, while only he ate the stewed sheep-meat.

It was tired and stale and flat in his mouth. He had reasons that made him eat, but he could not blame the family. Seven months and nothing but sheep. The birds had flown. Other years they came back; who knew if would this year? Soon the fish would come up the river again, if this year was like others; but who could be sure?

And now whoever ate of the boars or of the rabbits died in time, and when the Ceremonial Cuts were made, strange worms appeared inside him. The Man of the Sun had said it was now a sin against the Sun to eat of the boar and of the rabbit; and clearly that was true, for sinners died.

Sheep or hunger. Sheep-meat or death. Sko chewed the tasteless chunk in his mouth and brooded. He could still force himself to eat; but his woman, his children, the rest of The People . . . You could see men's ribs now, and little children had big eyes and no cheeks and bellies like smooth round stones. Old men did not live so long as they used to; and even young men went to the Sun without wounds from man or beast to show Him. The food-that-takes-no-hunting was running thin and dry, and Sko could easily beat at wrestling the men who used to pound him down.

The People were his now because he could still eat; and because The People were his, he had to go on eating. And it was as if the Sun Himself demanded that he find a way to make The People eat too, eat themselves back into life.

Sko's stomach was full but his mouth still felt empty. There had once been a time when his stomach was empty and his mouth felt too full. He tried to remember. And then, as his tongue touched around his mouth trying for that feeling, the thought came.

It was the Dry Summer, when the river was low and all the springs had stopped living and men went toward the Sun's birth and the Sun's death to find new water. He was one of those who had found water; but he had been gone too long. He ate all the dried boar-meat he carried (it was not a sin then) and he shot all his arrows and still he was not home and needed to eat. So he ate growing things like the animals, and some of them were good. But he pulled from the ground one bulb which was in many small sections; and one of those sections, only one, filled his mouth with so much to taste so sharply that he could not stand it and drank almost all the water he was bringing back as proof. He could taste it still in his mind.

His hand groped into the hole at the side of the cave which was his own place. He found there the rest of that bulb which he had brought as a sign of the far place he had visited. He pulled the hard purple-brown skin off one yellow-white section and smelled it. Even the smell filled the mouth a little. He blew hard on the coals, and when the fire rose and the stewpot began to bubble, he dropped the section in with the sheep-meat. If one fills the stomach and not the mouth, the other the mouth and not the stomach, perhaps together . . .

Sko asked the Sun to make his guess be right, for The People. Then he let the pot bubble and thought nothing for a while. At last he roused and scooped a gobbet out of the stewpot and bit into it. His mouth filled a little, and something stirred in him and thought of another thing that filled the mouth.

He set off at a steady lope for the Licking Place which the tribe shared with the sheep and the other animals. He came back with a white crystal crust. He dropped this into the stewpot and stirred it with a stick and sat watching until he could not see the crust any more. Then he bit into another gobbet.

Now his mouth was indeed full. He opened it and from its fullness called into the cave the sound that meant *Food*. It was his woman who came out first. She saw the same old stewpot of sheep and started to turn, but he seized her and forced her mouth open and thrust in a gobbet of the new stew. She looked at him for a long silence. Then her jaws began to work fast and hard and not until there was nothing left to chew did she use the *Food* sound to call out the children.

There are other Licking Places to use, Sko thought while they ate; and runners can fetch more of the bulbs from where this one grew. There will be enough for The People . . . And then the pot was empty, and Sko Fyay and his family sat licking their fingers.

After a thousand generations of cooks, hunger and salt and garlic had combined to produce mankind's first chef.

The Greatest Tertian [*]

One of the outstanding characteristics of the culture of the third planet from the Sun is, as I have stressed earlier, the tendency toward onomatolatry, the worship of great names all but divorced from any true biographical or historical comprehension.

Many of these names, employed with almost magical significance, must be investigated in later chapters; they include (to give approximate phonetic equivalents) Linkn, Mamt, Ung Klsam, Staln, Ro Sflt (who seems to have appeared in several contradictory avatars), Bakh, Sokr Tis, Mi Klan Jlo, Me Uess-tt, San Kloss, and many others, some of them indubitably of legendary origin.

But one name appears pre-eminently in every cultural cache so far investigated. From pole to pole and in every Tertian language, we have yet to decipher any cultural remains of any sizable proportion that do not contain at least a reference to what must have been unquestionably the greatest Tertian of all time: Sherk Oms.

It is well at this point to settle once and for all the confusion concerning the two forms of the name: Sherk Oms and Shek Sper. A few eccentric scholars, notably Shcho Raz in his last speech before the Academy,[†] have asserted that these names represented two separate individuals; and, indeed, there are small items in which the use of the two forms does differ.

Sherk Sper, for instance, is generally depicted as a writer of public spectacles; Sherk Oms as a pursuer of offenders against society. Both are represented as living in the capital city of the *nation*[**] of In Glan under the unusual control of a female administrator; but the name of this female is generally given, in accounts of Sherk Sper, as Li Zbet; in accounts of Sherk Oms, as Vi Kto Rya.

The essential identity of these female names I have explained in my *Tertian*

---

[*] Excerpt from Rom Gul's *Tertian History and Culture.* Translated by Anthony Boucher. 12 vols. Kovis, 4739.

[†] See my refutation in *Academy Proceedings,* 2578: 9, 11/76.

[**] For a full discussion of this extraordinary word, meaning a group of beings feeling themselves set apart from, and above, the rest of the same type of beings (a peculiarly Tertian concept), *vide infra,* Chapter 127.

Phonology[*]. The confusion of professions is more apparent than real; the fact of the matter is that Sherk Oms (to use the more widespread of the two forms) was both a writer and a man of action and tended to differentiate the form of his name according to his pursuit of the moment.

Clinching evidence exists in the two facts that:

(1) While we are frequently told that Sherk Oms wrote extensively, no cultural cache has turned up any fragment of his work, aside from two accounts in his personal adventures.

(2) While we know thoroughly the literary work of Sherk Sper, no cultural cache has revealed the slightest reliable biographical material as to his life.

One characteristic, it may be added, distinguished the great Sherk under both names: his love for disguise. We possess full details on the many magnificently assumed characterizations of Sherk Oms, while we also read that Sherk Sper was wont to disguise himself as many of the most eminent writers and politicians of his ear, including Bekn, Ma Lo, Ok Sfud, and others.

Which aspect of the great Sherk was it, you may well ask, which so endeared him to all Tertians? This is hard to answer. Aside from religious writings, there are two items which we are always sure of discovering in any Tertian cultural cache, either in the original language of In Glan or in translation: the biographical accounts[†] of the crime-hunter Sherk Oms, and the *plays* (to use an untranslatable Tertian word) of Sherk Sper.

Both contributed so many phrases to the language that it is difficult to imagine Tertian culture without them:

The dog did nothing in the nighttime (a proverb equivalent to our: While nature rests, the wise chudz sleeps).

Friends, Romans, countrymen, lend me your ears (indicating the early Tertian development of plastic surgery).

The game is a foot (a baffling reference, in that no cultural cache has yet yielded evidence of a sport suitable to monopods).

To bee or not to bee (an obvious reference, though by Sherk Sper, to Sherk Oms' years of retirement).

Difficult though it is to estimate the relative Tertian esteem for the Master in his two guises, we certainly know, at least, from our own annals, which aspect of the great Sherk would in time have been more valuable to the Tertians—and it was perhaps a realization of this fact that caused the dwellers in Ti Bet to address their prayers to him in the form: *Oms mani padme Oms*[**].

The very few defeats which Sherk Oms suffered were, as we all know, caused by us. Limited as even he was by the overconventional pattern of Tertian thought, he was quite unable to understand the situation when our advance agent Fi Li Mor was forced to return to his house for the temporospatial rod that Wa Tsn thought to be a rain shield. Our clumsy and bungling removal of a vessel for water trans-

---

[*] Pp. 1259 ff.

[†] Principally by Wat Tsn, though also by Start, Pa Mr, Smit, Dr Leth, etc.

[**] The meaning of the middle words is lost.

port named, I believe, A Li Sha was still sufficiently alien to perplex him; and he never, to we must thank the Great Maker, understood what we had planted on his Tertian world in what he thought to be a matchbox.

But in time, so penetrating a mind as he reveals under both guises would have understood; and more than that, he might have developed methods of counterattack. We owe our thanks to the absurd brevity of the Tertian life span that he, considered long-lived among his own people, survived fewer than a hundred orbital cycles of the third planet.

If Sherk Oms, most perceptive and inventive of Tertians, had still been living, the ultimate conquest of the third planet by the fourth might well have been foiled, and his planet might even today still swarm with pullulating Tertians, complete with their concepts of *nations*, *wars,* and *races,** rather than being the exquisitely lifeless playground for cultural researchers which today it offers to us, the inhabitants of that neighboring planet which, as best our phoneticists can make out, the Tertians knew as Marz.

---

* For these peculiarly Tertian words, again see Chapter 127.

Expedition

The following is a transcript of the recorded two-way messages between Mars and the field expedition to the satellite of the third planet.

First Interplanetary Exploratory Expedition to Central Receiving Station:
What has the Great One achieved?

Murvin, Central Receiving Station, to First Interplanetary Exploratory Expedition:
All right, boys. I'll play games. What *has* the Great One achieved? And when are we going to get a report on it?

Falzik, First Interplanetary Exploratory Expedition, to Murvin, Central Receiving Station:
Haven't you any sense of historical moments? That was the first interplanetary message ever sent. It had to be worthy of the occasion. Trubz spent a long time working on the psychology of it while I prepared the report. Those words are going to live down through the ages of our planet.

Murvin to Falzik:
All right. Swell. You'll be just as extinct while they live on. Now, how's about that report?

Report of First Interplanetary Exploratory Expedition, presented by Falzik, specialist in reporting:
The First Interplanetary Exploratory Expedition has landed successfully upon the satellite of the third planet. The personnel of this expedition consists of Karnim, specialist in astrogation; Halov, specialist in life sciences; Trubz, specialist in psychology; Lilil, specialist in the art; and Falzik, specialist in reporting.

The trip itself proved unimportant for general reporting. Special aspects of difficulties encountered and overcome will appear on the detailed individual report of Karnim after the return of the expedition. The others, in particular Trubz and Lilil, were largely unaware of these difficulties. To anyone save the specialist in astrogation, the trip seemed nowise different, except in length, from a vacation excursion to one of our own satellites.

The majority theory is apparently vindicated here on this satellite of the third

planet. It does not sustain life. According to Halov, specialist in life sciences, it is
not a question of cannot, since life of some strange sort might conceivably exist
under any conditions save those of a perfect vacuum. But so far as can be ascertained there is no life of any remotely recognizable form upon this satellite.

This globe is dead. It is so dead that one may say the word without fear. The
euphemism *extinct* would be too mild for the absolute and utter deadness here. It
is so dead that the thought of death is not terrifying.

Trubz is now working on the psychology of that.

Observation checks the previous calculations that one face of this satellite is
always turned toward its world and one always away from it, the period of rotation coinciding exactly with the orbital period. There seems to be no difference in
nature between the two sides; but obviously the far side is the proper site for the
erection of our temporary dome. If the hypothetical inhabitants of the third planet
have progressed to the use of astronomical instruments, we do not wish to give
them warning of our approach by establishing ourselves in the full sight of those
instruments.

The absence of life on this satellite naturally proved a serious disappointment
to Halov, but even more so to Lilil, who felt inspired to improvise a particularly
ingenious specimen of his art. Fortunately, the stores of the ship had provided
for such an emergency, and the resultant improvisation was one of the greatest
triumphs of Lilil's great career. We are now about to take our first rest after the
trip, and our minds are aglow with the charm and beauty of this exquisite work.

Murvin to Falzik:

All right. Report received and very welcome. But can't you give us more color?
Physical description of the satellite—minerals present—exploitation possibilities—anything like that? Some of us are more interested in those than in Trubz's
psychology or even Lilil's practice of the art.

Falzik to Murvin:

What are you asking for? You know as well as I do the purpose of this expedition: to discover other intelligent forms of life. And you know the double purpose behind that purpose: to verify by comparison the psychological explanation
of our race-dominant fear of death (if this were a formal dispatch I'd censor that
to "extinction"), and to open up new avenues of creation in the art.

That's why the personnel of this expedition, save for the astrogator, was chosen for its usefulness *if* we discover life. Until we do, our talents as specialists are
wasted. We don't know about minerals and topography. Wait for the next
expedition's report on them.

If you want color, our next report should have it. It will come from the third
planet itself. We've established our temporary base here easily and are blasting
off very soon for what our scientists have always maintained is the most probable
source of life in this system.

Murvin to Falzik:

All right. And if you find life, I owe you a sarbel dinner at Noku's.

Falzik to Murvin:

Sarbel for two, please! Though what we've found, the Great One only—but go on to the report.

Report of First Interplanetary Exploratory Expedition, presented by Falzik, specialist in reporting:

The site of the Expedition's landing on the third planet was chosen more or less at random. It is situated on the third in size of the five continents, not far from the shore of the largest ocean. It is approximately indicated by the coordinates — and —* in Kubril's chart of the planet.

In the relatively slow final period of our approach, we were able to observe that the oceans of the third planet are indeed true liquids and not merely beds of molten metal, as has been conjectured by some of our scientists. We were more elated to observe definite signs of intelligent life. We glimpsed many structures which only the most unimaginative materialist could attribute to natural accident, and the fact that these structures tend to cluster together in great numbers indicates an organized and communal civilization.

That at least was our first uplifting emotional reaction, as yet not completely verified. The place of our landing is free of such structures, and of almost everything else. It is as purely arid a desert as the region about Krinavizhd, which in some respects it strongly resembles.

At first we saw no signs of life whatsoever, which is as we could have wished it. An exploratory expedition does not want a welcoming committee, complete with spoken speeches and seven-string sridars. There was a sparse amount of vegetation, apparently in an untended state of nature, but nothing to indicate the presence of animal life until we saw the road.

It was an exceedingly primitive and clumsy road, consisting of little more than a ribbon of space from which the vegetation had been cleared; but it was a sign, and we followed it, to be rewarded shortly by our first glimpse of moving life. This was some form of apodal being, approximately one-fifth of the length of one of us, which glided across the road and disappeared before we could make any attempt at communication.

We continued along the road for some time, suffering severely from the unaccustomed gravity and the heavy atmosphere, but spurred on by the joyous hope of fulfilling the aim of the expedition. Lilil in particular evinced an inspired elation at the hope of finding new subjects for his great compositions.

The sun, markedly closer and hotter here on the third planet, was setting when at last we made our first contact with third-planet life. This being was small, about the length of the first joint of one's foreleg, covered with fur of pure white, save for the brown dust of the desert, and quadrupedal. It was frisking in a patch of shade, seeming to rejoice in the setting of the sun and the lowering of the temperature. With its forelegs it performed some elaborate and to us incomprehensible ritual with a red ball.

---

*The mathematical signs indicating these coordinates are, unfortunately, typographically impossible to reproduce in this publication.—EDITOR.

Halov approached it and attracted its attention by a creaking of his wing rudiments. It evinced no fear, but instantly rolled the red ball in his direction. Halov deftly avoided this possible weapon. (We later examined it and found it to be harmless, at least to any form of life known to us; its purpose remains a mystery. Trubz is working on the psychology of it.) He then—optimistically, but to my mind foolishly—began the fifth approach, the one developed for beings of a civilization roughly parallel to our own.

It was a complete failure. The white thing understood nothing of what Halov scratched in the ground, but persisted in trying to wrench from his digits the stick with which he scratched. Halov reluctantly retreated through the approaches down to approach one (designed for beings of the approximate mental level of the Narbian aborigines), but the creature paid no heed to them and insisted upon performing with the moving stick some ritual similar to that which it had practiced with the ball.

By this time we were all weary of these fruitless efforts, so that it came as a marked relief when Lilil announced that he had been inspired to improvise. The exquisite perfection of his art refreshed us and we continued our search with renewed vitality, though not before Halov had examined the corpse of the white creature and determined that it was indubitably similar to the mammals, though many times larger than any form of mammalian life has ever become on our planet.

Some of us thought whimsically of that favorite fantasy of the science-fiction composers, the outsize mammals who will attack and destroy our race. But we had not yet seen anything.

Murvin to Falzik:

That's a fine way to end a dispatch. You've got me all agog. Has the Monster Mammal King got you in his clutches?

Falzik to Murvin:

Sorry. I didn't intend to be sensational. It is simply that we've been learning so much here through—well, you can call him the Monster Mammal King, though the fictionists would be disappointed in him—that it's hard to find time enough for reports. But here is more.

Report of First Interplanetary Exploratory Expedition, presented by Falzik, specialist in reporting:

The sun was almost down when we saw the first intelligent being ever beheld by one of our race outside of our planet. He (for we learned afterward that he was male, and it would be unjust to refer to an intelligent being as *it*) was lying on the ground in the shade of a structure—a far smaller structure than those we had glimpsed in passing, and apparently in a sad state of dilapidation.

In this posture the fact was not markedly noticeable, but he is a biped. Used as we are on our own planet to many forms of life—octopods (though the Great One be thanked that those terrors are nearly wiped out), ourselves hexapods, and the pesky little mammalian tetrapods—a biped still seems to us something strange and mythical. A logical possibility, but not a likelihood. The length of body of this one is approximately that of a small member of our own race.

He held a container apparently of glass in one foreleg (there must be some other term to use of bipeds, since the front limbs are not used as legs) and was drinking from it when he spied us. He choked on his drink, looked away, then returned his gaze to us and stared for a long time. At last he blinked his eyes, groaned aloud, and hurled the glass container far away.

Halov now advanced toward him. He backed away, reached one forelimb inside the structure, and brought it out clasping a long metal rod, with a handle of some vegetable material. This he pointed at Halov, and a loud noise ensued. At the time some of us thought this was the being's speech, but now we know it came from the rod, which apparently propelled some form of metal missile against Halov.

The missile, of course, bounced harmlessly off Halov's armor (he prides himself on keeping in condition), and our specialist in life sciences continued to advance toward the biped, who dropped the rod and leaned back against the structure. For the first time we heard his voice, which is extraordinarily low in pitch. We have not yet fully deciphered his language, but I have, as instructed, been keeping full phonetic transcriptions of his every remark. Trubz has calculated psychologically that the meaning of his remarks must be:

"Ministers of the Great One, be gracious to me!"

The phonetic transcription is as follows: *

AND THEY TALK ABOUT PINK ELEPHANTS!

He watched awestruck as Halov, undaunted by his former experience, again went directly into the fifth approach. The stick in Halov's digit traced a circle in the dirt with rays coming out of it, then pointed up at the setting sun.

The biped moved his head forward and back and spoke again. Trubz's conjecture here is:

"The great sun, the giver of life."

Phonetic transcription:

BUGS THAT DRAW PRETTY PICTURES YET!

Then Halov drew a series of concentric ellipses of dotted lines about the figure of the sun. He drew tiny circles on these orbits to indicate the first and second planets, then larger ones to indicate the third and our own. The biped was by now following the drawing with intense absorption.

Halov now pointed to the drawing of the third planet, then to the biped, and back again. The biped once more moved his head forward, apparently as a gesture of agreement. Finally Halov in like manner pointed to the fourth planet, to himself, and back again, and likewise in turn for each of us.

The biped's face was blank for a moment. Then he himself took a stick and pointed from the fourth planet to Halov, saying, according to Trubz:

"This is really true?"

Transcription:

YOU MEAN YOU'RE MARTIANS?

---

* For the convenience of the reader, these transcriptions have been retranscribed into the conventional biped spelling.—EDITOR

Halov imitated the head movement of agreement. The biped dropped his stick and gasped out sounds which Trubz is sure were the invocation of the name of a potent deity. Transcription:

ORSON WELLES!

We had all meanwhile been groping with the biped's thought patterns, though no success had attended our efforts. In the first place, his projection was almost nil; his race is apparently quite unaccustomed to telepathic communication. In the second place, of course, it is next to impossible to read alien thought patterns without some fixed point of reference.

Just as we could never have deciphered the ancient writings of the Khrugs without the discovery of the Burdarno Stone which gave the same inscription in their language and in an antique form of our own, so we could not attempt to decode this biped's thought patterns until we knew what they were like on a given known subject.

We now began to perceive some of his patterns of the Solar System and for our respective worlds. Halov went on to the second stage of the fifth approach. He took a group of small rocks, isolated one, held up one digit, and drew the figure one in the dirt. The biped seemed puzzled. Then Halov added another rock to the first, held up two digits, and drew the figure two, and so on for three and four. Now the biped seemed enlightened and made his agreement gesture. He also held up one digit and drew a figure beside Halov's.

His *one* is the same as ours—a not too surprising fact. Trubz has been working on the psychology of it and has decided that the figure one is probably a simple straight line in any numerical system. His other figures differed markedly from ours, but his intention was clear and we could to some extent follow his patterns.

Using both forelegs, Halov went on to five, six, and seven, with the biped writing down his number likewise. Then Halov held up all his digits and wrote a one followed by the dot which represents zero and is the essence of any mathematical intelligence. This was the crucial moment—did these bipeds know how to calculate or was their numerical system purely primitive?

The biped held up eight digits and wrote a new figure, a conjoined pair of circles. Halov, looking worried, added another rock to his group and wrote down two ones. The biped wrote a circle with a tail to it. Halov added another rock and wrote a one followed by a two. The biped wrote a one followed by a circle.

Then Halov understood. We have always used an octonary system, but our mathematicians have long realized the possibility of others: a system of two, for instance, in which 11 would mean three, a system of four (the folk speech even contains survivals of such a system) in which 11 would mean five. For 11 simply means the first power of the number which is your base, plus one. This system of the bipeds obviously employs a decimal base.

(Trubz has been working on the psychology of this. He explains it by the fact that the bipeds have five digits on each forelimb, or a total of ten, whereas we have four each, a total of eight.)

Halov now beckoned to Karnim, who as astrogator is the best mathematician among us, and asked him to take over. He studied for a moment the biped's numbers, adjusted his mind rapidly to the (for the layman) hopeless confusion of a decimal system, and went ahead with simple mathematical operations. The biped followed him not unskillfully, while the rest of us concentrated on his thought patterns and began to gather their shape and nature.

The growing darkness bothered the biped before it incommoded Karnim. He rose from his squatting position over the numerals and went into the structure, the interior of which was soon alight. He came back to the doorway and beckoned us to enter. As we did so, he spoke words which Trubz conjectures to mean:

"Enter my abode and stay in peace, O emissaries from the fourth planet."

Phonetic transcription:

YOU'LL BE GONE IN THE MORNING, AND WILL I HAVE A HEAD!

Murvin to Falzik:

What a yarn! A planet of intelligent beings! What a future for the art! Maybe I never was sold on this expedition, but I am now. Keep the reports coming. And include as much phonetic transcription as you can—the specialists are working on what you've sent and are inclined to doubt some of Trubz's interpretations. Also tell Trubz to get to work as soon as possible on the psychological problem of extinction. If this being's a mammal, he should help.

[Several reports are omitted here, dealing chiefly with the gradually acquired skill of the expedition in reading a portion of the biped's thought patterns and in speaking a few words of his language.]

Report of First Interplanetary Exploratory Expedition, presented by Falzik, specialist in reporting:

Halov and Trubz agree that we should stay with this *man* (for such we have by now learned is the name of his race) until we have learned as much from him as we can. He has accepted us now and is almost at ease with us, though the morning after our arrival, for some peculiar reason, he seemed even more surprised to see us than when we first appeared.

We can learn much more from him, now that he is used to us, than we could from the dwellers in the large massed structures, and after we are well versed in his civilization we stand much more chance of being accepted peaceably.

We have been here now for three of the days of this planet, absorbed in our new learning. (All save Lilil, who is fretful because he has not practiced his art for so long. I have occasionally seen him eyeing the *man* speculatively.) By using a mixture of telepathy, sign language, and speech, we can by now discuss many things, though speech comes with difficulty to one who has used it only on formal and fixed occasions.

For instance, we have learned why this *man* lives alone, far from his fellows. His speciality is the making of pictures with what he calls a *camera,* a contrivance which records the effect of differing intensities of light upon a salt of silver—a far more complex method than our means of making pictures with photosensitized elduron, but one producing much the same results. He has taken pictures of us, though he seems doubtful that any other *man* will ever believe the record of his *camera.*

At present he is engaged in a series of pictures of aspects of the desert, an undertaking that he seems to regard not as a useful function but as an art of some strange sort. Trubz is working on the psychology of it and says that a reproductive and imitative art is conceivable, but Lilil is scornful of the notion.

Today he showed us many pictures of other *mans* and of their cities and structures. *Man* is a thin-skinned and almost hairless animal. This *man* of ours goes almost naked, but that is apparently because of the desert heat. Normally a *man* makes up for his absence of hair by wearing a sort of artificial fur of varying shapes known as *clothes*. To judge from the pictures shown us by the *man*, this is true only of the male of the species. The female never covers her bare skin in any way.

Examination of these pictures of females shown us by our *man* fully confirms our theory that the animal *man* is a mammal.

The display of pictures ended with an episode still not quite clear to us. Ever since our arrival, the *man* has been worrying and talking about something apparently lost—something called a *kitten*. The thought pattern was not familiar enough to permit us to gather its nature, until he showed us a picture of the small white beast which we had first met, and we recognized in his mind this *kitten*-pattern. He seemed proud of the picture, which showed the beast in its ritual with the ball, but still worried, and asked us, according to Trubz, if we knew anything of its whereabouts. Transcription:

YOU WOULDN'T ANY OF YOU BIG BUGS KNOW WHAT THE DEVIL'S BECOME OF THAT KITTEN, WOULD YOU?

Thereupon Lilil arose in his full creative pride and led the *man* to the place where we had met the *kitten*. The corpse was by now withered in the desert sun, and I admit that it was difficult to gather from such a spectacle the greatness of Lilil's art, but we were not prepared for the *man*'s reaction.

His face grew exceedingly red, and a fluid formed in his eyes. He clenched his digits and made curious gestures with them. His words were uttered brokenly and exceedingly difficult to transcribe. Trubz has not yet conjectured their meaning but the transcription reads:

YOU DID THAT? TO A POOR, HARMLESS LITTLE KITTEN? WHY, YOU—*

His attitude has not been the same toward us since. Trubz is working on the psychology of it.

Murvin to Falzik:
Tell Trubz to work on the major psychological problem. Your backers are getting impatient.

Falzik to Murvin:
I think that last report was an aspect of it. But I'm still puzzled. See what you can make of this one.

---

* The remainder of this transcription has been suppressed for this audience.—EDITOR

Report of First Interplanetary Expedition, presented by Falzik, specialist in reporting:
Tonight Halov and Trubz attempted to present the great psychological problem to the *man*. To present such a problem in our confusion of thoughts, language, and gesture is not easy, but I think that to some extent they succeeded.

They stated it in its simplest form: Our race is obsessed by a terrible fear of extinction. We will each of us do anything to avoid his personal extinction. No such obsession has ever been observed among the minute mammalian pests of our planet.

Now, is our terror a part of our intelligence? Does intelligence necessarily imply and bring with it a frantic clinging to the life that supports us? Or does this terror stem from our being what we are, rather than mammals? A mammal brings forth its young directly; the young are a direct continuation of the life of the old. But with us a half dozen specialized individuals bring forth all the young. The rest of us have no part in it; our lives are dead ends, and we dread the approach of that black wall.

Our psychologists have battled over this question for generations. Would another—say, a mammalian—form of intelligent life have such an obsession? Here we had an intelligent mammal. Could he answer us?

I give the transcription of his answer, as yet not fully deciphered:
I THINK I GET WHAT YOU MEAN. AND I THINK THE ANSWER IS A LITTLE OF BOTH. OK, SO WE'RE INTELLIGENT MAMMALS. WE HAVE MORE FEAR OF DEATH THAN THE UNINTELLIGENT, LIKE THE POOR LITTLE KITTEN YOU BUTCHERED; BUT CERTAINLY NOT SUCH A DOMINANT OBSESSION AS I GATHER YOUR RACE HAS.

Trubz thinks that this was an ambiguous answer, which will not satisfy either party among our specialists in psychology.

We then proposed, as a sub-question, the matter of the art. Is it this same psychological manifestation that has led us to develop such an art? That magnificent and highest of arts which consists in the extinction with the greatest aesthetic subtlety of all other forms of life?

Here the *man*'s reactions were as confusing as they had been beside the corpse of the *kitten*. He said:
SO THAT'S WHAT HAPPENED TO SNOWPUSS? ART . . . ! ART, YOU CALL IT, YET! AND YOU'VE COME HERE TO PRACTICE THAT ART ON THIS WORLD? I'LL SEE YOU FRIED CRISP ON BOTH SIDES ON HADES' HOTTEST GRIDDLE FIRST!

Trubz believes that the extremely violent emotion expressed was shock at realization of the vast new reaches of aesthetic experience which lay before him.

Later, when he thought he was alone, I overheard him talking to himself. There was something so emphatically inimical in his thought patterns that I transcribed his words, though I have not yet had a chance to secure Trubz's opinion on them. He beat the clenched digits of one forelimb against the other and said:
SO THAT'S WHAT YOU'RE UP TO! WE'LL SEE ABOUT THAT. BUT HOW? HOW . . . ? GOT IT! THOSE PICTURES I TOOK FOR THE PUBLIC HEALTH CAMPAIGN . . .

I am worried. If this attitude indicated by his thought patterns persists, we may have to bring about his extinction and proceed at once by ourselves. At least it will give Lilil a chance to compose one of his masterpieces.

Final Report of the First Interplanetary Exploratory Expedition, presented by Falzik, specialist in reporting:

How I could so completely have misinterpreted the *man*'s thought patterns I do not understand. Trubz is working on the psychology of it. Far from any hatred or enmity, the *man* was even then resolving to save our lives. The First Interplanetary Exploratory Expedition owes him a debt that it can never repay.

It was after sunup the next day that he approached us with his noble change of heart. As I describe this scene I cannot unfortunately give his direct words; I was too carried away by my own emotions to remember to transcribe. Such phrases as I attribute to him here are reconstructed from the complex of our intercourse and were largely a matter of signs and pictures.

What he did first was to show us one of his pictures. We stared at it and drew back horrified. For it represented a being closely allied to us, almost to be taken for one of us, meeting extinction beneath a titanic weapon wielded by what was obviously the characteristic five-digited forelimb of a *man*. And that forelimb was many, many times the size of the being resembling us.

"I've been keeping this from you," he informed us. "I'll admit I've been trying to trap you. But the truth is: I'm a dwarf *man*. The real ones are as much bigger than me as you are bigger than the *kitten*. More, even. And their favorite pastime—only they call it a sport, not art—is killing bugs like you."

We realized now what should have struck us before—the minute size of his structure compared with those which we had seen before. Obviously he spoke the truth—he was a dwarf specimen of his race.

Then he produced more pictures—horrible, terrifying, monstrous pictures, all showing something perturbingly like us meeting cruel extinction at the whim of a *man*.

"I've just been keeping you here," he said, "until some real members of my race could come and play with you. They'd like it. But I haven't got the heart to do it. I like you, and what you told me about your art convinces me that you don't deserve extinction like that. So I'm giving you your chance: Clear out of here and stay away from this planet. It's the most unsafe place in the universe for your kind. If you dread extinction, stay away from the third planet!"

His resolve to spare our lives had made him happy. His face kept twisting into that grimace which we had learned to recognize as a sign of *man*'s pleasure. But we hardly watched him or even listened to him. Our eyes kept returning with awful fascination to those morbidly terrifying pictures. Then our thoughts fused into one, and with hardly a word of farewell to our savior we sped back to the ship.

This is our last report. We are now on the temporary base established on the satellite and will return as soon as we have recovered from the shock of our narrow escape. Lilil has achieved a new composition with a captive pergut from the ship which has somewhat solaced us.

Murvin to First Interplanetary Exploratory Expedition:

You dopes! You low mammalian idiots! It's what comes of sending nothing but specialists on an expedition. I tried to convince them you needed a good general worker like me, but no. And look at you!

It's obvious what happened. On our planet, mammals are minute pests and the large intelligent beings are arthropodal hexapods. All right. On the third planet things have worked out the other way round. *Bugs*, as the *man* calls our kin, are tiny, insignificant things. You saw those pictures and thought the *mans* were enormous; actually they meant only that the *bugs* were minute!

That *man* tricked you unpardonably, and I like him for it. Specialists . . . ! You deserve extinction for this, and you know it. But Vardanek has another idea. Stay where you are. Develop the temporary base in any way you can. We'll send others to help you. We'll build up a major encampment on that side of the satellite, and in our own sweet time we can invade the third planet with enough sensible ones to counteract the boners of individual specialists.

We can do it, too. We've got all the time we need to build up our base, even if that *man* has warned his kind—who probably wouldn't believe him anyway. Because remember this always, and feel secure: *No being on the third planet ever knows what is happening on the other side of its satellite.*

Public Eye

The great criminal lawyer had never looked so smugly self-satisfied, not even just after he had secured the acquittal of the mass murderer of an entire Martian family.

"Yes, gentlemen," he smirked, "I will gladly admit that this century has brought the science—one might almost say the art—of criminalistics to its highest peak. Throughout the teeming billions of the system, man continues to obey his primal urge to murder; yet for fifty years your records have not been blotted, if I may indulge in such a pen-and-ink archaism, by one unsolved murder case."

Fers Brin shifted restlessly. He was a little too conscious of the primal urge to murder in himself at the moment. It was just as well that Captain Wark chose that point to interrupt the florid speech.

"Mr. Mase," the old head of the Identification Bureau said simply, "I'm proud to say that's true. Not one unsolved murder among damned near seventy billion people, on nine planets and God knows how many satellites and asteroids; but I'd hate to tell you how many unconvicted murderers."

"Who needs to tell him?" Brin grunted.

"Oh come now," Dolf Mase smiled. "I'm hardly responsible for *all* of them. Ninety per cent or so, I'll grant you; but there are other lawyers. And I'm not at all sure that any of us are responsible. So long as the system sticks to the Terran code, which so fortunately for criminals was modeled on Anglo-American concepts rather than on the Code Napoléon . . ."

Captain Wark shook his grizzled head. "Uh-uh. We'll keep on sticking to the idea that if justice is bound to slip, it's better to free the guilty than convict the innocent. But it kind of seems to us, Mr. Mase, like you've been pushing this 'free the guilty' stuff a little far."

"My dear Captain!"

The patronizing tone was too much for Brin. "Let's cut the politeness, Mase. This is a declaration of war. Let's have it out in the open. Captain Wark represents everything that's official and sound and inescapable. And me—well, as the best damned public eye in the business, I represent everything that's unofficial and half-jetted and just as inescapable. And we're feeding it to you straight. Your quote legal unquote practice amounts to issuing a murder license to anybody with enough credits. You've got three choices: A, you retire; B, you devote that first-rate mind of yours to something that'll benefit the system; C, the Captain and I are going to spend every minute off duty and half of 'em on hunting for the one slip you've made some time that'll send you to the asteroid belt for life."

Dolf Mase shrugged. "I wish you a long life of hunting. There's no slip to find. And no!" he protested as Captain Wark began to speak. "Spare me the moral lecture which I can already read, my dear captain, in those honest steely eyes of yours. I have no desire to devote myself to the good of the system, nor to the good of anyone save Dolf Mase. Such altruism I leave to my revered if somewhat, as you would say, Mr. Brin, 'half-jetted' brother. I suffered enough from his starveling nobility in my younger days—I too declared war, first on him and then on the rest of the seventy billion . . . Good day, gentlemen—and may tomorrow find waiting in my office a sextuple sex slayer!" With this—and a gust of muted laughter—Dolf Mase left the Identification Bureau.

"You've got to hand it to him," Fers Brin chuckled in spite of himself, as he contemplated the closing panel. "He picked the most unpronounceable damned exit line I ever heard."

"And he pronounced it," the Captain added morosely.

"He never slips," Fers murmured.

The phone buzzed and Captain Wark clicked his switch.

The face on the screen bore an older gentler version of the hawk-beaked, crag-browed Mase features which had so recently been sneering at them. The voice too had the Mase resonance and formality, without the oversharp bite.

"Thank you, gentlemen," said Lu Mase. "Deeply though I regret what I heard, I confess that I needed to hear it."

"It's like I told you, Professor," said the Captain. "He's always hated you and the cream of it all, to him, was making you think that he did his job for the sake of justice."

Fers moved into phone range. "And now that you know, what follows?" he demanded. "There's bound to be something somewhere. The devil himself isn't perfect in deviltry."

On the screen Professor Mase's eyes seemed to stare unseeing at the infinite array of microbooks which lined his study. "There was that time when Dolf was young . . . He'd convinced me that he'd changed . . . And of course you'd have to study the statute of limitations."

"We'll have the best men in the system on it tomorrow," Wark assured him hastily. "Just a minute. I'll turn on the scriber and you can give me the details."

"He's my brother, Captain," Mase said softly.

"Which means how much to him?" Fers snapped.

"Still . . . I'll be in your office tomorrow at nine, Captain."

The screen went dark.

Fers began a little highly creative improvisation in the way of cursing, not unaided by his habit of drinking with space pilots.

But Captain Wark was more sanguine. "What's another day, Brin, when we've got the war launched at last? That was a first-rate job you did of fast-talking the Professor into listening in—and the brilliant Dolf Mase fell into the good old trap of thinking a phone's off when its screen's dead."

"He didn't fall," Fers corrected. "He didn't care. He's so proud of what a big bad villain he is, he's glad to tell the world—but he forgot we might pipe it through to the one man whose opinion of him mattered. There was the slip; now when we learn this past secret . . . Hell!" he remarked to the clock. "I'm on another of those damned video interviews in fifteen minutes. See you tomorrow—and we'll start cleaning up the system."

The interviewer, Fers observed regretfully, should have had better sense than to succumb to this year's Minoan fashions, especially for broadcast. But maybe it was just as well; he could keep his mind on her conversation.

"Now first of all, Mr. Brin, before you tell us some of your fascinating cases—and you don't know how thrilled I am at this chance to hear all about them—I'm sure our watchers would like to hear something about this unusual job of yours. Just what *is* a public eye?"

Fers began the speech he knew by heart. "We aren't so uncommon; there must be a hundred of us here on Terra alone. But we don't usually come into the official reports; somehow lawyers and judges are apt to think we're kind of—well, unconventional. So we dig up the leads, and the regular boys take over from there."

"Has this system been in use long?"

"About a hundred years or so. It got started in sort of a funny way. You probably know that the whole science of crime detection goes back only a few centuries—roughly to about the middle of the Nineteenth. By around another century, say in Nineteen Fifty, they knew scientifically just about all the basic principles we work on; but the social and political setup was too chaotic for good results. Even within what was then the United States, a lot of localities were what you might call criminalistically illiterate; and it wasn't until the United Nations got the courage and the sense to turn itself into the World Federation that criminalistics began to get anywhere as the scientific defense-weapon of society. After the foundation of the W.F.B.I., man began to be safe, or nearly so, from the atavistic wolves—which, incidentally, are something I don't think we'll ever get rid of unless we start mutating."

"Oh, Mr. Brin, you *are* a cynic. But how did the public eyes start? You said it was funny."

"It was. It all came out of the freak chance that the head of W.F.B.I. a hundred years ago—he was the legendary Stef Murch—had started out in life as a teacher of Twentieth Century literature. He wrote his thesis on what they used to call *whodunits*—stories about murder and detectives—and if you've ever read any of that damned entertaining period stuff, you know that it was full of something called *private eyes*—which maybe stood for private investigator and maybe came from an agency that called itself The Eye. These characters were even wilder than the Mad Scientists and Martians that other writers then used to dream up; they could outdrink six rocketmen on Terra-leave and outlove an asteroid hermit hitting Venusberg. They were nothing like the real private detective of the period—oh yes, there were such people, but they made their living finding men who'd run out on their debts, or proving marital infidelity."

"I'd like to ask you to explain some of those words, Mr. Brin, but I'm sure our watchers want to get on with the story of *your* life as a public eye."

"Sorry; but it's a period you've got to use its own words for. Anyway, Stef Murch saw that detectives like these *private eyes,* even if they never existed, could be a perfect adjunct to official scientific criminalists and solid trained policemen. We don't wear uniforms, we don't keep office hours, we don't always even make reports or work on definite assignments. Our job's the extras, the screwball twists, the— Look: If you wanted an exact statement of a formula you'd have it written by a Mark, wouldn't you? But suppose you wanted a limerick? We take the cases that have the limerick-type switch to them. We do what we please when and where we please. We play our hunches; and God knows it's scientific heresy to say so, but if you don't get hunches you won't last long at the—"

Suddenly, Brin's image had vanished mysteriously from the screen.

"Mr. Brin! Where are you? Mr. Brin, we're still on the air!"

"Sorry," said Fers Brin off-camera. "Tell your watchers they've had a rare privilege. They've just seen a public eye get a hunch and he's acting on it right now!"

His hunch was, Fers realized later, like most hunches: a rational piecing together of known facts by the unconscious mind. In this instance the facts were that Professor Mase was a just and humane man, and that his life-long affection for his brother—quite possibly wilful self-delusion—could not vanish overnight. Conclusion: he would give the lawyer one last chance before turning evidence over to Captain Wark, and there was only one way Dolf Mase would react in self-protection.

Resultant hunch: Murder.

The helicab made it from the casting station to the Professor's quiet Connecticut retreat in record time; but the hunch had come too late. It might even have been too late the moment when the screen had gone dark during the earlier conversation with the Professor. For, as the prosecution was to reconstruct the case, Dolf Mase had already remembered where there was evidence of his one slip and was on his way.

It wasn't usual for a public eye to find a body; the eyes were generally called into the case later. It wasn't usual for any man to find the body of a man whom he had liked and respected—and whom he might possibly, with a faster-functioning hunch, have kept alive.

Professor Lu Mase had been killed very simply. His skull had been crushed by a Fifth Dynasty Martian statuette; and long after the bone splinters had driven life from the brain tissue, the killer had continued to strike, pounding with vicious persistence at what he could not make dead enough to satisfy him.

A shard of the statuette had broken off and pierced the throat. A red fountain had spurted up in the room.

It was an old-fashioned, even an archaic murder, and Fers Brin found his mind haunted by a half-remembered archaic line. Something about being surprised that the old man had so much blood . . .

Another level of his mind registered and filed the details of the scene. Another level took him to the phone for the routine call to the criminalistics squad. But the topmost conscious level held neither observation nor reason, but only emotion—grief for the too trusting Professor, rage at Dolf Mase, who had crowned a career of licensing murderers by becoming a murderer himself.

By the time the squad arrived, the Brin emotions were under control, and he was beginning to realize the one tremendous advantage given him by the primitive brutality of the killing. Dolf Mase had forgotten himself—his life-long hatred of his brother and all he represented had boiled over into unthinking fury.

Now, if ever in his life, Dolf Mase must have slipped—and the Professor's death, if it resulted in trapping this damnable sponsor of murder, would not be in vain.

Within an hour Fers knew the nature of the slip.

It was a combination of an old-fashioned accident and the finest scientific techniques of modern criminalistics that forged the perfect evidence against Dolf Mase.

A man was fishing in a rowboat in the Sound. And it was precisely over his boat that the escaping murderer decided he could safely jettison the coat he had worn. The weighted coat landed plump at the fisherman's feet. When he saw the blood he hastily rowed ashore and reported it. The laboratories did the rest.

"You ever read about Alexander Wiener, Fers?" Captain Wark asked later that night. "He damned near invented the whole science of serology. Now he'd be a happy man if he could see how we've sewed up this whole case on this one piece of serological evidence. The blood on the coat is the Professor's; the sweat stains on the collar check with all the clothing we found in Mase's empty apartment. And there's the case in one exhibit."

"It's hard to believe," Fers said, "but only eighty years ago a judge threw out a case that depended strictly on serological identity."

"Sure, and five hundred years ago Faurot had a hell of a time making fingerprint evidence stick. But now we've got, as Wiener foresaw that long ago, enough identifiable type-factors in blood, sweat, mucus, semen, and the rest to establish exact personal identity with as much mathematical certainty as a fingerprint. Mase has made his getaway and is lying low for the moment; but the dragnet's out and once we've got him, he's going to face a prosecution case he can't get out of—not even if he gets Dolf Mase for his lawyer!"

It was the bright eyes of a passport inspector, three days later, that spotted the forgery and caused Dolf Mase to be jerked at the last minute, in the guise of a traveling salesman for extra-terrestrial insect sprays, off the Venus rocket. He had shed the salesman's extroverted bonhomie for his normal self-confident arrogance by the time he was booked for murder.

"I'm reserving my defense," was his only remark to everyone from Captain Wark to the Intersystem News Service.

That's where the case should have ended. That way it would have been nice and simple and eminently moral: villainy detected, guilt punished, and science—for there seemed no doubt that Mase's reserved defense was a bluff—triumphant.

Only this was precisely the point at which the case skipped right out of its orbit.

Fers was puzzled by Captain Wark's face on the phone. He'd never seen the rugged old features quite so weirdly taut. He didn't need the added note of urgency in the voice to make him hyperjet himself down to the Identification Bureau.

All that the Captain said when he arrived was "Look!" and all that he did was to hand Fers a standard fax-floater on a criminal suspect.

This one was from Port Luna. Jon Do, wanted for burglary in hotel. Only identification, one fingerprint lifted from just-polished shoes of victim, who had the curious habit of tucking spare credits away in his footwear for the night.

"So?" Fers asked. "Don't know as I ever saw a fax-floater on a more uninteresting crime."

The third time Captain Wark opened his mouth he managed to speak. "You know it's routine to send all stuff like that here; we've got the biggest file of single prints in the system."

"Yes, daddy," said Fers patiently. "I've heard rumors."

"So I punched the data on a card and put it through, and I got an answer. Know whose print that is?"

Fers looked again at the date of the hotel theft—November nineteenth, the same day his hunch had taken him to Connecticut. "If you're going to say what I'm afraid you are, I'll tell you right now I don't believe it."

"It's a fact. That is the print of the middle finger, left hand, of Dolf Mase! On the day of the murder he was looting a hotel room in Port Luna."

"Look," said Fers. "We live in an Age of Marvels, sure—and I wonder what age Man's ever lived in that he hasn't thought that—but I've got a funny way of only believing what's possible. And our Marvels just plain flat do not God-damned well include being in Connecticut and on the moon within the span of a couple of hours."

"It's the perfect alibi in history, Brin. Alibi means elsewhere, or used to—"

"And how elsewhere can you get? But hell, Captain, we didn't see the murder; but we did see Dolf Mase here in this office just an hour before it. According to your fingerprint, that's equally impossible."

"Mase won't say so. He'll say we never saw him; that we're trying to frame him."

"Which is an idea at that," Fers mused. "Is there any real reason why the defense—"

The Captain smiled grimly. "I was afraid you'd try a little temptation, Brin. And I wasn't sure how well I'd resist. So before I phoned you I sent a spacegram to the Chief of Port Luna."

Fers exploded. "You idiot! You half-jetted hypomoronic—"

"Hold it, Brin. Identification's my job. It's what I know and what I'm good at. If I get a request to identify a print, I damned well identify it."

"Even when you know there must be something phony?"

"There isn't. I know the Port Luna chief. He's a good man. There isn't a known method of forging a print that could get by him. This is for real."

"But we saw Mase here!"

The Captain sighed. "You know, Brin, I'm beginning to wonder . . ."

Brin's temperament is a mercurial one. Suddenly the public eye snapped his fingers and beamed. "The serological evidence! We've got him cold on that coat!

And you yourself said blood-typing and sweat-typing are as certain identity evidence now as fingerprints."

"And you yourself said it was only eighty years since a court threw out serology. Which evidence will it believe now? The new-fangled proof, or the fine old proof that ninety per cent of all identity work is based on?"

Fers slumped again. "It *has* to be some kind of gimmick of Mase's. The only other possibility—"

"The only other possibility," said Captain Wark flatly, "is that the whole foundation of the science of identification is one vast lie."

The public eye rubbed his red pate and frowned. "And the only way to find out which," he said softly, "would seem to be at Port Luna . . ."

Port Luna was erected as the first great non-terrestrial city. It was intended as the great pleasure dome of Man, the dream city of everyone from the millionaire to the stenographer saving up for her vacation by skipping lunches.

But rocket travel developed so rapidly that pleasure-planning Man said to himself, "What's the moon? It's nice to be under; but what do I get out of being *on* it? Let's go to Venus, to Mars—"

And the pleasure dome became the skid road of the system, untended, unrepaired, unheeded. The observatory crew lived under a smaller dome of their own. So did the crews of the space strip. Passengers were rushed from space liners to the Terra Shuttle without even seeing the city of Port Luna. And in the city were the bars and stereos and other needful entertainment for the barracked crews and all the shattered spacemen who drifted back this far but could not quite bring themselves to return to Terra.

It would take a good man, Fers reflected, to be Police Chief in Port Luna.

"The Chief left on the last shuttle," a uniformed sergeant told him. "You must've crossed him. He's gone to Terra to pick up a hotel sneak thief—and say: Guess who our little old Port Luna sneak thief turned out to be?"

Fers sighed, but not audibly. He registered proper amazement when the sergeant revealed the startling news, registered it so satisfactorily that from then on, as far as the sergeant went, Port Luna was his.

But even the confidential files on the case were no help. The victim was a salesman from Venus, ostensibly traveling in microbooks but suspected—according to a note in the dossier—of peddling Venusian pictures on the side. The amount stolen was approximately what Dolf Mase might charge for five minutes of consultation in his office.

"I'm beginning to get an idea," Fers said slowly. "I don't like it, and I can't get rid of it. Sergeant, I want you to do something for me."

"Sure. I got a kid who's crazy about public eyes. He's gonna get a big blast out of this. What you want I should do?"

"Got some omnidetergent here? Good. Now watch me wash my hands."

"Huh?"

Very carefully Fers scrubbed, rinsed, and dried his hands. "Now write down that you saw me do that, and put it through the time stamper. Then lock it in your safe."

"I don't get it."

"I'm not too damned sure I do myself. But I've got to try. Now which way's that hotel?"

The Luna Palace was at the corner of Tsiolkovsky and Oberth, only a short walk from the station. Fers was relieved, both because he hated to walk wearing gravity soles and because he loathed these streets of cut whisky and tenth-run stereos, of cheap beds and cheap bedmates.

The Palace was a barely perceptible cut above the other hives of bedding-cells, exactly right both for the Venusian peddler—who wanted to display a touch of swank to his customers—and for the sneak thief—who would find the pickings too slim elsewhere.

The girl behind the desk might have been the model for whom Minoan designs were revived. Fers was pleased; it was easier to work among attractive surroundings.

"My name's Bets," she stated.

"That's nice," said Fers. "Is the manager in?"

"I get off at five o'clock," Bets announced.

"If that means that he comes on then, maybe I better stick around. Mind if I linger over the desk?"

"Nobody comes in here much," Bets revealed.

"Good place for a spot of quiet brooding then. Bets, I've got me a problem—one they can't solve by criminalistics. One that maybe disproves criminalistics."

"Not even in the lobby," Bets further disclosed.

"And I think I've got the answer," Fers went on. "I'm almost sure I've got it if I can find out how to prove it. Did you ever read a *whodunit,* Bets?"

"I get kind of hungry around five," Bets admitted.

"I like that period—the Twentieth Century, not around five—partly because of Stef Murch, I guess, and partly because I had a great-great-grandfather who was a *private eye.* I've read a lot and they keep saying they couldn't write a detective story about the 'future'—meaning, say, now—because everything would be different and how could you be fair?"

"I like steaks," Bets proclaimed.

"And the answer I've got is one you could have figured out even in the Twentieth Century. It's a problem that couldn't happen till now, but the answer was in their knowledge. They had a writer named Quinn or Queel or something who used to issue a challenge to the reader, and this would be the place to do it."

"The best steaks are at the Jet," Bets explained.

"Challenge," Fers mused. "What brought Dolf Mase's left middle finger to the Luna Palace? And how am I going to prove it?"

"Only lately," Bets annotated, "there's too many crooks hanging around the Jet so I go to the Spacemen's Grotto."

Fers leaned over the desk and bussed her warmly. "Bless you, Bets," he said. "I knew our conversations were bound to meet eventually! And if this works, you get the biggest steak on the whole damned moon!"

The sergeant looked with some dubiety at the public eye, who held on to a chair to steady himself with his right hand while keeping his left hand carefully in the air.

"I don't think," Fers observed, "that I could pass a sobriety test. Call of duty. Got me into a little drinking more along the standards of a *private eye.* But I've got some jobs for you. Got an ultraviolet light, first of all?"

The baffled sergeant followed instructions. Perplexedly he assembled the dossier on the sneak-thief, the time-marked slip from the safe, the ultra-violet lamp.

He flashed the lamp, at Fers' behest, on the public eye's left palm, and stared at the fine set of hitherto invisible fingerprints.

"Notice the middle one," said Fers. "Now look at the sneak-thief's."

After a full minute of grunting study, the sergeant looked up. He might have been staring at a Venusian swamp-doctor in the flesh.

"And remember," Fers went on, "that my hands were scrubbed with omnidetergent three hours ago. I shook hands with that man and got his prints on this invisible fluorescent film some time in the last three hours. Therefore he's on Luna. Therefore he isn't Dolf Mase, whom your Chief is probably still interviewing on Terra."

"Then—then there's two guys with the same print!" The sergeant looked as if his world were collapsing around him.

"It makes sense," said Fers. "It's crazy but it makes sense. And don't worry—you're still in business. And I wonder whether another drink would save my life or kill me?"

Doggedly the sergeant had fought his way through his bewilderment to the immediate problem. "Where is he? If he's here, I gotta arrest him."

"How right you are. He's at the Jet and his name's Wil Smit."

"That son-of-a-spacesuit! We been trying to pin something on him for years!"

"I thought so. It had to be somebody you'd never actually arrested and printed, or you'd have had him on file and not needed to send out a fax-floater. So when I learned that the Jet was in favor with the criminal set this season, I wandered around there—if you can call it wandering in these damned gravity-soles. I threw around the names of some criminals I know on Terra—little enough to be in his league but big enough to be familiar names out here. I said I needed a guy for a hotel job only it had to be somebody with a clean record. It was around the seventh drink that I met Wil Smit. When we shook on the deal I got all drunk and obstinate and, by God, if I was left-handed, he was going to shake left-handed too."

"But you ain't left-handed. Or are you?" added the sergeant, to whom nothing was certain any longer in a system in which the same print belonged to two different guys.

"Right-handed as a lark," said Fers airily, and then paused to contemplate his statement. He shook his head and went on, "You go get Smit. Suspicion of theft. Book him, print him, and then you'll have him cold. About that time I'll be back and we'll take the next shuttle. Meantime, I've got a date with a couple of steaks at the Spacemen's Grotto."

An urgent spacegram had persuaded the Port Luna Chief to stay on Terra with his presumptive prisoner until the public eye arrived.

"Of course," that prisoner was remarking once again, "I shall refuse to disclose the reason for my presence on Luna, the name under which I traveled thither, or the motive for my invasion of the picture-peddler's room. I shall merely plead guilty and serve my sentence on Luna, while you, my dear Captain Wark, continue to prosecute here on Earth the search for the abominable murderer of my beloved brother."

The Lunar Chief gave his old friend a yes-but-what-can-I-do? look.

"Nothing." Captain Wark answered his unspoken query. "You've got your evidence; you have to prosecute. But Brin's spacegram hinted—"

"The public eye," Dolf Mase stated, "is a vastly overrated character. The romantic appeal of the unconventional—"

At this point the nascent lecture was interrupted by the entrance of a public eye and a Lunar sneak-thief.

And in another five minutes there occurred one of the historical moments in the annals of criminalistics: the comparison of two identical prints made by two different men.

Wark and the Chief were still poring over the prints, vainly striving to find the faintest classifiable difference, when Fers addressed the lawyer.

"War's over," he said. "And I think it's unconditional surrender for Mase. You try to bring up this Lunar 'alibi' in court and we'll have Smit shuttled down here and produced as a prosecution exhibit. Unless you force us to that, we'll just forget the whole thing; no use announcing this identity-problem until we've adjusted our systems to it. But either way we've got you cold."

"I still," said Dolf Mase smugly, "reserve my defense."

Hours later, Fers Brin was delivering his opinion over a beer.

"Only this time," Fers said, "we know it's a bluff. This fingerprint gimmick was a gift from his own strange gods—he never could have counted on it. All he has left now is some kind of legalistic fireworks and much damned good it'll do him."

"You've done a good job, Brin," Captain Wark said glumly. "We've got Mase nailed down—only . . ."

"Only you can't really rejoice because you've lost faith in the science of identification? Brighten up, Captain. It's OK. Look: it's all because we forgot one little thing. Fingerprint identification worked so beautifully for so many centuries in so many million cases that we came to believe in it as a certainty. We took it as an axiom: There are no identical fingerprints. And we missed the whole point. There never was any such certainty. There were only *infinitely long odds*."

Captain Wark sat up slowly and a light began to gleam in his eyes.

But the Chief said, "Odds?"

"Galton," Fers went on, "is the guy who started it all on a serious criminalistic level. Sir Francis Galton, English anthropologist. It's all in your office; I looked it up again while you were disposing of our print-twins. Quite a character, this Galton; practically founded meteorology and eugenics too. And he figured that the odds on any two fingerprints coinciding on all the points we used in classification was one in sixty-four billion. For his time this was fine; it was just about the same, for practical police work, as saying one in infinity. But what's the population of the system now?"

"The whole system?" The Chief's eyes were boggling. "Damned near—*seventy billion!*"

"So by now," the Captain exclaimed, "it just about *had* to happen sooner or later!"

"Exactly," said Fers. "From now on a *single* print is *not* identification. It's strong presumptive evidence, but that's all. And it'll usually be enough. Just remember never to feed the defense ammunition by trying to claim that an odds-on chance is an unshakable fact. And you've still got the best possible personal identification in two or more prints. You noticed that all the other fingers on those two men were completely different. Chances on two prints coinciding are about one in forty quadrillion, which is good enough for us. For a while. And we don't have words for the chances on all ten matching up. That works out to the sixtieth power of two times the eightieth power of ten—if you want to see what it looks like, put down a one and write ninety-eight zeroes after it."

Captain Wark looked like himself again. Happily he raised his beer mug in a toast. "I propose we drink to the identification man of the future Inter-Galactic Empire," he proclaimed, "who first discovers two sets of ten matching prints!"

Secret of the House

Of course no one realized in advance what would be, ounce for ounce, the most valuable return cargo of the Earth-Venus spaceships, even though the answer should have been obvious to anyone with the faintest knowledge of historical patterns.

Rare metals? With the cost of fuel to lift them out of Venus' almost-Earth gravity making them even costlier than on Earth itself? No, the answer was the obvious but overlooked one: What did Marco Polo bring back from China and Vasco da Gama from India? Why was Columbus seeking a new route to the Indies?

In one word: *spices.*

Man's palate needs occasional rejuvenation. One of the main purposes of exploration, intercontinental or interplanetary, is the restimulation of jaded taste buds. And in addition to the new spices there were new methods of cooking, such as that wonderful native Venusian quick passing through live steam, which gave the startling effect of sizzling hot crisp rawness; or *balj,* that strange native dish which was a little like a curry and a little like a bouillabaisse, but richer and more subtle than either. There was *sokalj,* or Venusian swamphog, the most delicately delicious meat on three planets—not that anything Martian would ever be considered by the true gourmet . . .

This was the speech that Kathy listened to regularly once a week for the first year of her marriage. For she had married not only a prominent and successful man, she soon realized, but one who had been bitten at a susceptible age by the word *gourmet.*

It was fun while they were courting. It was fun, anyway, for a video network receptionist to be taken to good restaurants by the top interplanetary commentator. It was especially fun to watch him go through the masculine production number of conferring with the headwaiter, sending his compliments (and instructions) to the chef, and exchanging views with the *sommelier,* as Kathy quickly learned to call the-man-with-the-wine. Wine did not ship well interplanetarily; acceleration over one *g,* in the term of the cognoscenti, "bruised" it. In this domain, the French still reigned supreme, and stressed their superiority to mask their natural jealousy of the upstart Venusian colonists.

In every American city—with a few exceptions in New Orleans and San Francisco—former "French" restaurants had become "Venusian" and even in Paris *cuisine vénérienne* marked some of the most highly esteemed establishments.

But the entertainment value of a gourmet exhibitionist decreased as courtship progressed logically into marriage, and being wined and dined gave place to the daily problem of feeding the man. Quick freezing had, of course, made the bride's problems simple compared to those of earlier centuries. But George, completely in character, insisted on a high percentage of personally prepared meals—and was shrewd enough to spot any substitute makeshifts via the deep freeze and the electronic oven.

Not even the apartment on the very top level of Manhattan, where you could still see the Hudson, not even the charge accounts at shops she'd never dared enter, not even the wondrous fact that she loved George with an intensity which she had always considered just an unlikely convention of the women's minimags—none of these could quite reconcile Kathy to life with a man who could down three bowls of your best hand-made oyster stew without interrupting his speech on the glories of authentic *balj à la* Venusberg, who could devour enough of a prime rib roast to throw the whole week's budget out of joint while expatiating on the absurdity of the legend that Earth cooks in general, and the Anglo-Saxons in particular, did at least understand beef.

Kathy toyed with the idea of hiring a cook, not so much to satisfy George as to divert his inevitable reproaches to someone else. But aside from the fact that a cook's salary would turn her charge accounts anemic, Kathy knew that her mother, both her grandmothers, and undoubtedly all four of her great- and all eight of her great-great-grandmothers had fed their men and kept them happy. This was a matter of family pride.

Then came the awful day when George brought José Lermontov home to dinner. Kathy's younger sister was also dining with them that night, and wrinkled her nose after George's face faded from the visiphone.

"These revolting Venus colonial diplomats," said Linda. "He'll have a swamp-beard and a paunch and a wife and six children at home. Kathy, why doesn't George ever meet anybody newsworthy who's—well, worthy?"

"He's a very fine young man, I hear," Kathy muttered distractedly. "Guerrilla leader against the dictatorship, wrote a fine book about its overthrow. What worries me is the paunch—and what I'm going to put into it."

Five minutes after meeting the Venusian, Linda slipped into the kitchen to whisper, "Sister . . . please . . . can I have that in my stocking for Christmas?" But even this pleasing reversal did not divert Kathy from the task of preparing to fill the, as it turned out, non-existent paunch.

Dinner, she thought a little later, was going surprisingly well, especially between José and Linda. But then George, having speared and destroyed the last pork chop, cleared his throat.

"You must make allowances, Lermontov. Mere pork to a man accustomed to *sokalj* . . ."

"Mean swamphog?" José asked politely, with the usual clipped Venusian avoidance of pronouns and articles.

"And," George added commiseratingly, "this so-called 'country gravy'—rather a shock to a man from a planet where they think, thank God, not in terms of gravies, but of sauces."

"Very good gravy," said José, mopping up the last of his with a slice of Kathy's own bread. "Imagine 'so-called' because first made by those who live in country?"

"Even granting that," George persisted, "can't you picture what just a pinch of *balj*-powder would have done for it? Or perhaps a hint of *tinilj?*"

"Myself," José replied gravely, "prefer one of your Earth herbs—dash of oregano, bit of savory. Summer savory, of course."

George gave the matter serious thought. "Possibly. Very possibly. But in either case it demonstrates the pitiful lack of imagination of the average Earth housewife."

It is conceivable that Kathy made too obvious a clatter in stacking and removing the dinner dishes. In any event, Linda followed her hastily into the kitchen.

"Please, Kathy angel, don't explode, not just yet. I know George is asking for it, but *he's* probably been told already that all Earth-women are shrews and I *don't* want . . ."

Kathy controlled herself until the one agreeable result of the evening was reached when José asked if he might see Linda home. To her surprise, she went right on controlling herself even after they had left, because by then she had thought of The Plan.

The very next morning, The Plan was well under way.

A: Kathy invaded her favorite bookshop and bought every book in stock on Venusian spices and cooking, and even added such pre-Venusian classics of culinary perception as Brillat-Savarin, Escoffier, and M. F. K. Fisher.

B: She enrolled herself for daily lessons at the Uya Rulj School of Venusian Cookery (formerly the École de Cuisine Cordon Bleu).

C: Knowing that George had a luncheon date in Chicago with his sponsor, she visited the restaurant where her husband normally lunched. It was an unobtrusive chop house in the thirties, far down on Manhattan's base-level, and the excellent lunch she enjoyed there confirmed her darkest suspicions.

For two weeks she read her books and took her lessons without trying out what she learned except for lunches by herself. And she did learn things. George's school of thought had its points. For Kathy's cooking, like that of her eight great-great-grandmothers, had been not only Earthly but plain American.

There was a fresh delight in learning that the Architect of all things had established on this planet a certain inevitable relationship between tomatoes and sweet basil, and had ordained that caraway seeds should fulfill the destiny of red cabbage—even as on another planet, He had sown *tinilj* so that the flesh of the swamphog might be even sweeter. And who was to anticipate the masterfully predestined interplanetary blends? The inescapable kinship of garlic and lamb Kathy had long known, but her eyes opened wide on discovering how a pinch of *balj*-powder completed the trinity.

But these discoveries did not weaken The Plan. And that same Architect smiled upon The Plan by allowing the network's robowaxer to deposit a minutely over-sufficient flow upon the floor of the corridor in front of George's office. On that wax, George slipped and broke his leg.

George probably never admitted, even to himself, that he enjoyed being bedridden: the visiphone calls, the miniscript couriers from the network, the bedside microphone and cameras. But he did begin to admit that he was enjoying Kathy's cooking.

Where once she might have served steak, she now brought forth *grenadine de boeuf à la vénérienne.* Where once she might have served her asparagus with melted butter, she now ventured on a hollandaise (with five grains of *balj*-powder replacing the cayenne of ancient recipes). Where once she might have served left-overs simply reheated, she now masked them with a sauce which would cause the recumbent George to smack his lips, roll his eyes, and murmur, "*Silj,* of course, and chives . . . and a hint of *tinilj* . . . possibly a whisper of *pnulj,* probably Earth-grown? Yes, I thought so . . . and . . . what *is* that?"

"Chervil, darling," Kathy would say, and he'd answer, "Of course, of course. I would have had it in a minute. You know, Katherine my dear, you are developing an imagination!"

When it was announced that George's plasticast was to come off that Thursday, Kathy decided it was time for the denouement of The Plan. As she was painstakingly making up her shopping list on Thursday morning, the visiphone rang and it was, miraculously, not the network for George.

"Oh, Kathy!" Linda burbled. "I've got one of those nice let's-see-what-happens dates with *him* tonight and could you possibly ask us both to dinner? Because he likes you and he's really just about almost *there* and if we were . . . you know, all in the family and everything, I think it might *just—*"

"José?" Kathy asked, knowing the answer. She grinned and doubled the quantities on the list.

The worst of the preparations for dinner were over when Linda arrived, carrying, to Kathy's surprise, a weekend case. The girl devoted only the necessary minimum of time to admiring George's knitted leg, then dragged her sister into the bedroom.

"Kathy. I've got *such* a problem. He's known so many women . . . all over two planets and at embassies and maybe even *spies.* I told you tonight I think he *will;* only I don't know what lipstick to use, what perfume, anything. I've got to make myself *interesting;* but I don't want to overdo it. So I just brought everything I have. You tell me."

Kathy looked at the array. She thought of her dinner and The Plan and she began giving Linda her advice.

It was the same cast that had attended the awful dinner which inspired The Plan, but they were different people. José, no longer the visiting colonial, was a gentleman at home among friends; Linda was radiant in the glow of simplicity and a well-scrubbed face; and George was praising the food.

He praised the green peas. He praised the mashed potatoes. And above all he praised the fried chicken.

"I can't quite analyze it," he kept saying. "There's a touch there I can't quite get. You've brought out the flavor miraculously. It wouldn't," he demanded suspiciously, "be that new powder Köenigsberg claims he found among the natives at the tip of the southern continent? I thought they hadn't shipped any of that in yet."

"They haven't, darling," said Kathy.

"Perhaps the tiniest pinch of *balj* with a little freshly ground celery seed?"

"No."

"Then what in two planets—"

"A woman must have some secrets, George. Let's just say this is . . . a secret of the house."

At this point Kathy happened to catch José's eye and hastily looked away. It was impossible that a Venusian diplomat would be winking at his hostess!

George was still pursuing his questions over brandy in the living room. José, also possibly (Kathy prayed) in a question-asking mood, had led Linda out onto what the architect called the sun-area, though Kathy persisted in thinking of it, more romantically, as the balcony. As she saw the two turn to come back in, Kathy headed for the kitchen, an immemorial spot for sisterly confidences.

But it was not Linda who followed her in. It was José. He leaned casually against the door jamb and told her, "Know secret of house."

"Yes?" said Kathy casually. "Oh, I mean—you *do?* Sometimes I have to stop and reread you, like a telegram. Well?"

"Bought food of highest quality, cooked it extremely well, relied on nothing but natural flavor, probably little salt. Good old George always wanted so much seasoning, this strikes him as new and revolutionary taste sensation. Right?"

Kathy grinned. "I'll go quietly," she said. "I thought it would work and I was sure of it when I ate at his regular lunch place. That's just what they do; but because it's a chop house with a reputation, he thinks it's magic. Except I've learned things his way, too. From now on, George gets variety at home—and I think he'll like all of it without ever knowing why he likes which."

"Simplicity also magic," José observed. "Your idea—clean, fresh simplicity of Linda that accounts for fact am going to be your brother-in-law. Correct?"

"Correct? Hell, it's *perfect!*" Impulsively, Kathy kissed him. "Oh, my!" she said as she drew back. "Now you've got lipstick after coming off the balcony spotless!"

"Variety," said José approvingly. "Still wonder one thing, Kathy. Those mashed potatoes—extraordinary. If secret of house, there's where. Confide in me?"

"Now that you're part of the family, sure."

"Yes?"

"The secret is this: I take lots of butter and cream—read cow-stuff, no syntho —and I beat the living bejeepers out of 'em."

When they returned to the living room, it was obvious that Linda had told George the news. Using his newly recovered leg with as ostentatious pride as a year-old toddler, George advanced paternally upon José Lermontov.

"Let tonight's dinner be a marital lesson to you, my boy. Remember the last time you ate here, and realize that there's no fault in a wife that a little husbandly persistence can't cure."

This time there was no doubt whatsoever that the gentlemanly Venusian diplomat was winking at his hostess.

The Scrawny One

The old magician had only one arm.

"That is why," he explained, "I now employ the fuse. It is dangerous to reach any part of your body inside the pentacle when you light the powder. They are hungry, these ones that we call up, and our flesh is to their taste."

John Harker watched the old man lead the fuse from the powder-heaped center of the pentacle to a safe distance from its rim. He watched him lean over and strike a match on the cement floor, watched the sudden flame disquiet the shadows of the deserted warehouse, watched the fuse begin to sputter.

Then John Harker struck. The knife pierced easily through the soft flesh of the old back. His other hand came up to keep the magician from falling across the fuse. He hurled the dying body back, safely away from fuse and pentacle, and thrust it from his mind as his eyes followed the sputtering sparks.

John Harker was unconcerned with fingerprints and clues. After tonight no man could touch him, not even for the most easily proved murder.

He had built to this carefully. Six months of research in the role of a freelance writer, investigating the multitudinous magic cults of Southern California. A meticulous screening of frauds, fakes and phonies, and finally the discovery of this one-armed man of undeniable powers. The arrangements for this instant of ultimate truth, the calling up of a demon . . .

The hissing boom within the pentacle drowned out the last grating rattle of the old man's voice. John Harker looked at what he had caused to be summoned.

The first word that came to him was *scrawny*. Which is a peculiar word to apply to something not of our flesh, nor shaped in any way conceivable to us; but there was that in what passed for its eyes that told of endless deprivation, insufficiency, hunger.

It spoke, though no sound waves disturbed the stillness of the warehouse. It said, "You called me. I can grant you one wish. Make up your mind."

John Harker smiled. "Are your customers usually so irresolute? I have made up my mind."

The scrawny one's eyes fed on him. "What can you want?" it said, and there was hatred and envy in its soundless words. "What can any *man* want when you have the one thing to be prized above all others . . . *flesh?*"

"How fortunate," Harker observed, "that you are not empowered to call us up. But little though you may believe it, we have our hungers too, and largely because of this so enviable flesh. And my own hungers I am resolved to end now."

"Your wish!" The scrawny one writhed in impatience.

Harker deliberately dawdled, savoring this little moment of power, this curtain-raiser to the ultimate power. "In the opera," he began, "Mephisto, when summoned, proffers Faust first gold, then glory, then power. But that prime idiot the learned Doctor Faust replies, 'I want a treasure that contains them all! . . . I want youth!'" Harker laughed and hummed a snatch of the tripping tune to which Faust expresses his senile desire. "But I know better."

"Your wish!" the scrawny one insisted.

"I know that power and wisdom and strength and honor and glory and blessing can all be summed up, in this most worldly of all possible worlds, in one word: wealth. My wish is simple: You will make me the richest man in the world. From that all else will follow."

The scrawny one made a sign of agreement, while darting hunger glimmered in several of its eyes. Then it added, "You must release me from the pentacle before I can accomplish that."

John Harker hesitated. "I know that you are bound to truth while you are contained there. You swear to me that if I release you you will do no harm to me in soul or body?"

"I swear."

"You swear that if I release you you will, immediately, make me the richest man in the world?"

"I swear. You must cut the pentacle with cold steel."

John Harker nodded and jerked the knife from the dead magician's back. As he extended the bloody knife toward the pentacle there was a flicker of the scrawny shape, and that part of the blade which protruded beyond the rim was licked clean of blood.

The cold steel descended and scraped across the cement floor.

The pentacle was empty and the scrawny one was beside John Harker.

"Now!" he commanded.

But the scrawny one flashed the thought that it had something to do first.

When there was no trace left of the magician's body (and how convenient that was, even when you were unconcerned about damaging evidence), the not quite so scrawny one ceased its intricate vibrations and stood all but motionless beside John Harker.

"Are you ready for your wish?" it asked.

John Harker smiled and nodded.

That is, he lowered his chin in assent. A nod is usually concluded by bringing the chin back to its normal position. But his muscles would not obey and his chin remained sunk on his breastbone.

There was trouble with his eyes too. He did not remember closing the lids, but closed they were and obstinately so.

His ears functioned. They brought a sound of music totally unfamiliar to him who had casually prided himself on his knowledge of music. And mingled with the wailing of unknown pipes was the wailing of hundreds of unknown voices. And mingled with the plunking of strings and the thumping of drums was the plunking thump of hundreds of small hard objects, like the rattle of hail close to his ears.

His other senses functioned, too. One told him that he lay suspended on some flat metal surface, that he did not rest in one position, but slowly kept floating higher in the air. And another told him that there was not a fiber of his body that did not ache with a pain so exquisitely refined as to be almost beyond the limits of conscious endurance.

And yet another sense informed him that he was surrounded by a stench of decay, an aura of charnel rot so strong, so intimate, that he could not long resist the conclusion that it rose from his own vile body.

The upward movement had stopped, and he floated in equipoise as the music and the rattle ceased and a shout went up from the hundreds of voices. Now at last his eyes half-opened, and he could see his vast bloated bulk swaying in one pan of a tremendous gold balance, while in the other pan hung his weight in precious stones.

The sight of his wealth gave him a last flash of strength. He was able to move his hand close enough to his eyes for their half-parted slits to watch his little finger slowly detach itself and drop, leaving a ragged stump of corruption. Through the eyes that had once been John Harker's, the once scrawny one read the newspaper story:

RICHEST MAN DYING
Annual gem rite held

RAVENPORE, India (UP).— The Djatoon of Khot, reputedly the wealthiest man in the world, lay dying here today of an obscure disease; but his loyal subjects still performed the traditional annual ceremony in which the Djatoon is presented with his weight in precious stones.

The greatest physicians of three continents profess themselves baffled by the degenerative malignancy which has attacked the wealthy potentate, and express no hopes for his recovery.

The once scrawny one used John Harker's features to shape a satisfied smile. Then it used John Harker's muscles to propel his body and went out into the streets of the city, there to accomplish at its leisure those delightful undertakings which would enable it, in time, quite to forget its starved and scrawny past.

Star Bride

I always knew, ever since we were in school together, that he'd love me some day; and I knew somehow too that I'd always be in second place. I didn't really care either, but I never guessed then what I'd come second to: a native girl from a conquered planet.

I couldn't guess because those school days were before the Conquest and the Empire, back in the days when we used to talk about a rocket to a moon and never dreamed how fast it would all happen after that rocket.

When it did all begin to happen I thought at first what I was going to come second to was Space itself. But that wasn't for long and now Space can never take him away from me and neither can she, not really, because she's dead.

But he sits there by the waters and talks and I can't even hate her, because she was a woman too, and she loved him too, and those were what she died of.

He doesn't talk about it as often as he used to, and I suppose that's something. It's only when the fever's bad, or he's tried to talk to the Federal Council again about a humane colonial policy. That's worse than the fever.

He sits there and he looks up at her star and he says, "But damn it, they're *people*. Oh, I was like all the rest at first; I was expecting some kind of monster even after the reports from the Conquest troops. And when I saw that they looked almost like us, and after all those months in the space ship, with the old regulation against mixed crews . . ."

He has to tell it. The psychiatrist explained that to me carefully. I'm only glad it doesn't come so often now.

"Everybody in Colonial Administration was doing it," he says. "They'd pick the girl that came the closest to somebody back home and they'd go through the Vlnian marriage rite—which of course isn't recognized legally under the C. A., at least not where we're concerned."

I've never asked him whether she came close to me.

"It's a beautiful rite, though," he says. "That's what I keep telling the Council: Vln had a much higher level of pre-Conquest civilization than we'll admit. She taught me poetry and music that . . ."

I know it all by heart now. All the poetry and all the music. It's strange and sad and like nothing you ever dreamed of . . . and like everything you ever dreamed.

"It was living with her that made me know," he says. "Being with her, part of

413

her, knowing that there was nothing grotesque, nothing monstrous about green and white flesh in the same bed."

No, that's what he used to say. He doesn't say that part any more. He does love me. "They've got to understand!" he says, looking at her star.

The psychiatrist explained how he's transferring his guilt to the Council and the Colonial policy; but I still don't see why he has to have guilt. He couldn't help it. He wanted to come back. He meant to come back. Only that was the trip he got space fever, and of course after that he was planet-bound for life.

"She had a funny name," he says. "I never could pronounce it right—all vowels. So I called her Starbride, even though she said that was foolish—we both belonged to the same star, the sun, even if we were of different planets. Now is that a primitive reaction? I tell you the average level of Vlnian scientific culture . . ."

And I still think of it as her star when he sits there and looks at it. I can't keep things like that straight, and he does call her Starbride.

"I swore to come back before the child was born," he said. "I swore by her God and mine and He heard me under both names. And she said very simply, 'If you don't, I'll die.' That's all, just 'I'll die.' And then we drank native wine and sang folksongs all night and went to bed in the dawn."

And he doesn't need to tell me about his letter to her, but he does. He doesn't need to because I sent it myself. It was the first thing he thought of when he came out of the fever and saw the calendar and I wrote it down for him and sent it. And it came back with the C. A. stamp: *Deceased* and that was all.

"And I don't know how she died," he says, "or even whether the child was born. Try to find out anything about a native from the Colonial Administrator! They've got to be made to realize . . ."

Then he usually doesn't talk for a while. He just sits there by the waters and looks up at the blue star and sings their sad folksongs with the funny names: *Saint Louis Blues* and *Barbara Allen* and *Lover, Come Back to Me.*

And after a while I say, "I'm not planet-bound. Some day when you're well enough for me to leave you I'll go to Vln—"

" 'Earth,' " he says, almost as though it was a love-word and not just a funny noise. "That's their name for Vln. She called herself an earth woman, and she called me her martian."

"I'll go to Earth," I say, only I never can pronounce it quite right and he always laughs a little, "and I'll find your child and I'll bring it back to you."

Then he turns and smiles at me and after a while we leave the waters of the canal and go inside again away from her blue star and I can stand coming second even to a dead native white Starbride from the planet Earth.

The Way I Heard It

They were telling ghost stories. It was an odd assortment of guests; but then, you expected that at Martin's. There were an actress and a reporter and a young doctor who made amateur films and an elderly professor of English and several just plain people. Martin finished the one about the female medical student, and they were all duly horrified, even though you couldn't call it a ghost story proper. Somebody threw another log on the fire, and there was a pause for refilling glasses.

Then the actress spoke. "Now I know this one is true," she said, "because the girl who told it to me heard it from a man who knew the cousin of one of the people it happened to. So there."

"What you call direct evidence," the reporter murmured.

The actress didn't hear him. "It happened in Berkeley," she went on. "It seems these people were driving up in the hills on a dark, dark night, when all of a sudden they heard—only I ought to tell you about the car first of all. You see, it was a two-door sedan—you know, where you can't get out of the back without climbing over the people in front."

A man who worked in a travel office interrupted her. "Sorry, but I know this one. Only it happened in New Orleans. A friend of mine who's a steward on a boat—"

"That must be something else. I tell you I know this happened in Berkeley."

"I heard it in San Francisco," the reporter put in. "A friend of mine tried to run the story down, but he didn't get anywhere."

"Don't quarrel, children," Martin said. "It is a Berkeley legend; I've heard it a dozen times up there. And I don't know where else it might be current. Let's go on to a new story."

The doctor objected. "But I don't know it. And besides, I'm looking for something for a short supernatural picture. Would this do, do you think?"

"It might at that."

"Then somebody tell it."

"Yes," said the professor of English. "By all means tell it."

The actress unruffled herself. "All right. Now please be quiet, everybody. These people were driving up in the hills—"

"A doctor and his wife," the reporter added.

"I've heard a clergyman," Martin said.

"I don't think that matters. Anyway, they heard these moans, so they stopped the car. And there under a hedge—"

"The way I heard it," the travel man protested, "she was standing on the curb."

"But don't you see, she has to be lying down, because she's really— But that would spoil the story, wouldn't it? I'm sorry. So they go over to her and help her into the car . . ."

"Don't forget the suitcase."

"What suitcase?"

"But she *has* to have a suitcase, because—"

"I don't see why."

The doctor was getting impatient. "For the Lord's sake, will somebody tell this story? I don't give a hang about suitcases. I want to hear what happened."

Three people started at once. The actress won out and went on. "So they ask her where they can take her, and she says she doesn't know."

"She doesn't know! But that kills the whole—"

"Of *course,* how can you—"

"Please," said the professor quietly.

"She doesn't know then," the actress continued calmly. "She tells them later. Oh, I should say that they put her in the back seat. You have to know that. Then she tells them where to take her—she's very pale, of course, and beautiful and sad—and they take her there. And when they drive up to the house—"

"Only first they notice—"

"No, not till they get there."

"Well, the way I heard it . . .'"

"Let's hear her version first," Martin suggested. "Then you can argue."

"So they look around, and she isn't there anymore. And you see, there isn't any way she could have got out without their knowing it, because the car was a two-door thing. That's why I had to tell you about that. And it looks impossible, and they're worried; but they go up to the house anyway. And a man answers the doorbell, and he asks what the matter—"

"No!" the reporter broke in sharply. "He says, 'I know why you have come.' "

The actress thought. "Yes. I guess you're right. He says, 'Don't tell me why you've come.' Only they tell him anyway, which is just what people always do. And he says, 'Yes. You're the tenth people'—that sounds silly, doesn't it?—you're the tenth people who've brought her here.' "

"Only what he *really* said," the travel man explained, "is, 'She's come here every night for a month now.' "

"But why?" the doctor asked. "What's it all about? You'd have to know the story back of it to do anything with it."

"Don't you see? It was his wife that he'd murdered."

"That's screwy," said the reporter. "It was his daughter. She was coming home from school and was killed in an accident at that spot and was trying to finish her journey home. That's why the suitcase."

"It was his daughter all right," the travel man said, "but the way I heard it, she'd taken poison and then changed her mind and tried to get home, only she was dead."

"Humph," the doctor said.

"You see," Martin explained, "you've got your choice. Anything will do for your picture. That's the way with legends."

"It is indeed a curious legend," the professor observed, "and one deserving scholarly study. Mr. Woollcott, I believe, dealt with it on the air, and I happen to have given it some further attention myself. I think I might be able to reconcile your variant versions."

"Ooh," said the actress. "Go on."

The fire crackled and shone on the glasses. "It is basically a Berkeley legend," the professor said, "though it seems to have spread far from there. In the original form, the suitcase is correct, and so is the girl's lying down. The people in the car are variously described—I think because it occurred to various people."

The actress gave a stage shudder. "You mean it's *real?*"

"He means it may have several independent sources," Martin enlightened her.

"Of the explanations, yours, sir, is the most nearly accurate," the professor continued, nodding to the travel man. "It was the suicide of a daughter. She had been driven from her home because of the father's madly melodramatic suspicions of her affair with his assistant—which proved to have been quite innocent, if terribly sincere. She had loved her father dearly. Sorrow overcame her, and she took poison. But afterwards, she wanted to get home—to tell her father that he was forgiven."

"And did she ever tell him, if she never got there?"

"The visitations ceased," the professor said pedantically.

"And you found out all this from your researches?"

"Yes"—in a toneless voice.

The fire had almost died down. Now it flared up brightly and for a moment Martin could see the professor's face. He saw . . . and sat in shocked silence. He should have realized it before. There was no other way a man could know so much about it. Through the darkness, he could half see a smile on the old man's lips now. The old man was remembering that, after all, his daughter had forgiven him.

"It's a fair enough story," the doctor said at last. "But I still can't see it as a picture."

The Star Dummy

"... It's something—outside of me," Paul Peters found himself saying. "I've read stories, Father, about ... losing control. It sounded absurd. But this is real. It ... he talks to me."

It was close and dark in the booth, but Paul could almost see the slow smile spreading from the Paulist priest. "My son, I know that anonymity is usual in the confessional booth. But since there is only one professional ventriloquist in this parish, it's a little hard to maintain in this case, isn't it? And knowing you as I do outside of the confessional, Paul, does make a difference in advising you. You say that your dummy—"

"Chuck Woodchuck," Paul muttered venomously.

"Chuck talks back to you, says things not in your mind?"

"Yes."

"Not even in your subconscious mind?"

"Can my conscious mind answer that?"

"Question withdrawn. Paul, to certain souls I might say simply fast and pray. To others I might suggest consulting with the Archbishop for permission for a formal exorcism. To you, however, I think I might make a more materialistic recommendation: see an analyst."

Paul groaned in the darkness. "It's more than that. It's something *outside* of me ..."

"Occam's razor," the Paulist murmured. "With your fondness for science fiction, you'll appreciate that. See if the simplest answer works. If it doesn't, we can discuss less materialistic causes. See an analyst. And perhaps you needn't offend the good doctor by telling him that I also advise prayer along with his treatment."

"... and I see no reason," the eminent analyst concluded, "why we should not dispel your demon in a relatively brief time. In fact, young man, we'll leave you in better shape than when you started having these hallucinations. Your choice of profession is of course highly symptomatic. A predilection for ventriloquism clearly indicates a basically schizoid personality, which chooses to externalize one portion of itself."

Paul brought his attention back from the splendid view of the Bay. "And you'll fix that up?"

The analyst deigned to smile. "Easily, I hope."

"I don't know," Paul ventured, "if you've heard of a friend of mine named Joe Henderson? Writes science fiction?"

"That escapist dianetics-spawning rubbish?" the analyst exclaimed, as if each word were spelled with four letters.

"As you say. My friend went to an analyst, and in the course of the first interview mentioned his profession. 'Aha!' said the doctor gleefully. 'We'll soon put a stop to that nonsense!' "

"Sound attitude," the analyst agreed.

"Only it occurred to Joe that then how was he going to pay his bills—including, of course, the doctor's. So somehow Joe never did get himself analyzed . . ."

Paul got up hesitantly. "I'm a professional ventriloquist, Doctor. I'm a good one. I make good money. At least, I used to when . . ." his voice became a little unsteady for a trained ventriloquist, or even for a normal man . . . "when Chuck was nothing more than an amusingly carved piece of wood. It's the only business I know. If you 'cure' me of it, well—Othello's occupation's gone."

"This Othello." The analyst's eyes sharpened. "Another externalization? Does he speak to you too?"

"Tell you what," said Paul. "I'll send Chuck in to see you. He'll tell you more about me than I can."

Which was perfectly true, Paul thought as he rode down fifteen stories. Could anyone, even the psychiatrist—even the priest—imagine what it was like to sit there awake all night in the dark room with the carved wood telling you all about yourself? All the little indecencies, the degradations of humanity hidden deep under your thoughts. Taunting you with the baseness of your flesh viewed with a cold contempt which only wood could feel. Sitting there listening, listening and feeling the contempt probe ever more deeply, ever more accurately.

Somehow he was on the sidewalk in front of the office building, shaking so violently that he suddenly had to force his hands around the standard of a No-Parking sign to keep himself erect.

Fortunately, this was San Francisco, where no one is ever far from a bar. When he was capable again of freeing one hand from the standard, he made the sign of the cross and moved off. A brief wordless prayer and two wordless straight bourbons later he knew, since he could not return to the room where the wood lay, the best place for him that afternoon.

The zoo is a perfect place for relaxation, for undoing internal knots. Paul had often found it so when baffled by script problems, or by the idiosyncrasies of agencies and sponsors. Here are minds of a different order, a cleaner, freer creation to which you can abandon yourself, oblivious of human complexities.

He knew most of the animals by sight as individuals, and he had even acquired a better-than-nodding acquaintance with many of the attendants. It was one of these who literally bumped into him as he stood in front of the parrot cage, and proceeded to make the afternoon far more distracting than he had ever anticipated.

"Tim!" Paul exclaimed. "Where on earth are you running to? Or from? Lion escaped or what?"

"Mr. Peters!" the attendant gasped. "I been chasing all over the place making phone calls to God knows who all. There's something screwy going on over in the wombats'."

"It couldn't pick a better place," Paul smiled. "Catch your breath a minute and tell me what gives."

"Got a cigarette? Thanks. Well, Mr. Peters, I'll tell you: Couple of times lately some of the boys they say they see something funny in one of the cages. Somebody checks up, it's always gone. Only today it's in there with the wombats and everybody's looking at it and nobody knows what—"

Paul Peters had always had a highly developed sense of curiosity. (Schizoid externalization? he reflected. No, cancel that. You're forgetting things. This may be fun.) He was already walking toward the wombats' enclosure as he asked. "This thing. What does it look like?"

"Well, Mr. Peters, it's pretty much like a koala," Tim explained, "except for where it's like an anteater."

Paul was never able to better that description. With the exception, of course, that neither koalas nor anteaters have six-digited forepaws with opposing thumbs. But that factor was not obvious on first glance.

He could see the thing now, and it was in body very much like an outsize koala—that oddly charming Australian eucalyptus-climber after whom the Teddy bear was patterned. It had no visible pouch—but then it might be a male—and its ears were less prominent. Its body was about two feet long. And its face was nothing like the flat and permanently startled visage of the koala, but a hairless expanse sloping from a high forehead, past sharp bright eyes, to a protracted proboscis which did indeed resemble nothing so much as the snout of an anteater.

The buzz through which they pushed their way consisted chiefly of "What *is* that?" and "I don't know," with an occasional treble obbligato of "*Why* don't you know, Daddy?"

But it was not what it was so much as what it was doing that fascinated Paul. It concentrated on rubbing its right forepaw in circles on the ground, abruptly looking up from time to time at the nearest wombat, while those stumpy marsupials either stared at it detachedly or backed away with suspicion.

"When the other boys saw it," Paul asked, "what was it doing then?"

"It's funny you ask that, Mr. Peters, on account of that's one of the things that's funny about it. What it was doing, I mean. One time when it was in with the llamas it was doing like this, just playing in the dirt."

"Playing?" Paul wondered softly.

"Only when it was in with the monkeys it was chattering at them something fierce, just like a monkey too, this guy said. And when it was in with the lions, well I'm not asking you to believe this and God knows I didn't yesterday and I don't know as I do now, but this other guy says it gives a roar just like a lion. Only not *just* like, of course, because look at it, but like as if you didn't have your radio turned up quite enough."

"Wombats don't make much noise, do they? Or llamas?" All right, Paul said to himself. You're crazy. This is worse than wood talking; but it's nicer. And there *is* a pattern. "Tim," he said abruptly, "can you let me in the wombat enclosure?"

"Jeez, Mr. Peters, there's bigshots coming from the University and . . . But you did give us that show for free at the pension benefit and . . . And," Tim concluded more firmly as he tucked the five unobtrusively into his pocket, "can do, I guess. O.K., everybody! Let's have a little room here. Got to let Dr. Peters in!"

Paul hesitated at the gate. This was unquestionably either the most momentous or the most ridiculous effort he had made in a reasonably momentous-ridiculous life. "Joe Henderson, thou shouldst be with me at this hour!" he breathed, and went in.

He walked up to where the creature squatted by its circles.

He knelt down beside it and pointed his forefinger, first at the small central circle with the lines sticking out all around it, then up at the sun. Next he tapped his finger insistently on the unmarked ground, then thrust it at the large dot on the third of the bigger concentric circles.

The creature looked up at him, and for the first time in his life Paul understood just what Keats had meant by a *wild surmise*. He saw it on the creature's face, and he felt it thrill through his own being.

An animal who can draw, an animal who can recognize a crude diagram of the solar system, is rational—is not merely a beast like the numbly staring wombats.

Hastily the creature held up a single digit of one forepaw and then drew a straight line in the dirt. Paul did the same, with an amused sudden realization of the fact that the figure *one* is probably a straight line in almost any system.

The creature held up two fingers and made an odd squiggle. Paul held up two fingers and made our own particular odd squiggle which is shaped 2. They almost raced each other through the next three numbers.

At the squiggle shape 5, the creature looked at Paul's five fingers, hesitated, then advanced by a daring step. It held up both its hands, each with its six digits, and made a straight line followed by an *S*-shaped curve.

Paul thought frantically, and wished that he had majored in mathematics. He held up his ten fingers, then marked down a straight line followed by a circle. The creature paused a moment, as if rapidly calculating. Then it nodded, looked carefully at Paul's 2 squiggle, held up its own twelve fingers again, and wrote down *12*.

Paul sank back on his heels. This twelve-fingered being had, as was plausible, a duodecimal system, based on twelve as our decimal system is on ten. And it had almost instantaneously grasped the human ten-system so well as to write down its *twelve* in our method.

"Friend," said Paul softly, pitching his voice too low for the crowds outside the enclosure, "you can't understand my language; but in the name of God and Man, welcome to Earth."

"Oh dear," said the creature, "you communicate only by speech! And otherwise you seem such a highly rational being."

Paul gulped. "That's an accusation I haven't had leveled against me recently."

"I never dreamed," it went on, "that the beings shaped like you were the rational ones. I couldn't get any waves from them. I can from you, though, even enough to pick up the language."

"And you got waves from the other animals," Paul mused. "That's why you chattered like a monkey and roared like a lion-not-turned-up-enough. Only they didn't understand your diagrams, so you knew they weren't high enough for you to deal with."

"But why do you have waves and not the others?"

"I am not," said Paul hastily, "a mutant. We can figure out why later. The trouble right now, if I know anything about the people-without-waves, is that nobody's going to believe a word of this scene. As if indeed I did. But it's nicer than wood . . ."

The creature shuddered, then apologized. "I'm sorry. Something I touched in there . . ."

"I know," said Paul, abruptly grave and humble. "Maybe we can help each other. God grant. I'm taking a chance—but I think the first thing is to get you out of here before Tim's 'bigshots from the University' show up and maybe decide to dissect you. Will you trust me?"

The pause was a long one—long enough for Paul to think of all the vile weakness of his humanity and know his infinite unworthiness of trust. He could hear the words pouring forth from the wood—and then the creature said simply, "Yes."

And the wood was silent even in memory.

Never, Paul felt, had he invested twenty dollars more wisely. And never had he discovered such unsuspected inborn acting talent as Tim's. There was something approaching genius, in a pure vein of Stanislavsky realism, in Tim's denunciation of Paul as a publicity-seeker—in his explanation to the crowd that the koala-like object was a highly ingenious mechanical dummy planted here by a venal ventriloquist who had planned to "discover" it as some strange being and trade on the good name of the Zoo itself for his own selfish promotional advancement. Bitter lashings of denunciation followed Paul and the creature as they departed—a matter of minutes, Tim confessed *sotto voce,* before the professors from across the Bay were due.

Now they were parked by the beach in Paul's convertible. Sensibly, he felt he should head for home and privacy; but he still could not quite bring himself to enter that room where Chuck Woodchuck waited.

"First of all, I suppose," he ventured, "comes: what's your name?"

"The nearest, my dear Paul, that your phonetics can come to it is something like *Tarvish.*"

"Glad to meet you. Now—how did you know mine? But of course," he added hastily, "if you can read . . . Well, next: where are you from? Mars?"

Tarvish thought. "Mars . . . Ah, you mean the fourth planet? All that sand . . ." He shuddered as if at a memory of infinite boredom. "No. I'm from a planet called Earth, which revolves around a star called the sun."

"Look!" Paul exclaimed. "Fun's fun, but isn't this a little too much of a muchness? This is Earth. That ball getting low over there is the sun. And you—"

"Don't you understand?" The tip of Tarvish's nose twitched faintly. "Then ask me what kind of a creature I am, what race I belong to."

"All right, Mr. Bones, I'm asking."

"I," said Tarvish, twitching violently, "am a man."

It took Paul a minute to interpret; then his laugh, his first free laugh in days, was as loud as Tarvish's twitching was vigorous. "Of course. Everybody has a name for everything in the universe—everything *else*. But there aren't names for your own race or your own planet or your own star. You're *men*, you're *people*, you live on the *Earth*, you're warmed by the *sun*. I remember reading that some Indian languages were like that: the name for the tribe meant simply *the people* and the name for their country was just *the land*. We've smiled at that, and interplanetarily we're doing the same damned thing. All right—where is *your* sun?"

"How can I tell you? You don't know our system of spatial coördinates. I don't understand what I find in your mind about 'constellations,' meaningless pictures which look different from any two points in space, or 'lightyears,' because your *year* doesn't convey a time-meaning to me."

"It's three hundred and sixty-five days."

"And what is a *day?*"

"Twenty-four—no, skip it. I can see that this is going to be a lot tougher than Joe Henderson and his friends think. Let's start over again. How did you get here?"

Two minutes later Paul repeated the question.

"I've been thinking," said Tarvish. "Trying to find the words in your mind. But they aren't there. Your words make too sharp a distinction between matter and energy. If I say 'a spaceship,' you will think of a metal structure. If I say 'a force field,' you will picture me traveling in something immaterial. Both are wrong."

"Let's try again. Why did you—" Paul stopped abruptly.

The nose twitched. "No," said Tarvish gently, "I am not the advance guard of an invasion and you are not betraying your race by being human to me. Please forget your science-fiction friends. We men of Earth have no desire to take over any of the planets of this star; ever since our terrible experience with the—" it sounded a little like *Khrj* "—we have made it a firm rule never to land on an inhabited planet."

"Then what are you doing here?"

"Because . . ." Tarvish hesitated. A faint blue colored the root of his nose. "Because my girl is here."

"I'm improving," Paul said. "It took me only five seconds to adjust to that *girl*. You're in love?" Oddly, he didn't even feel like smiling.

"That's why I had to land. You see, she went off by herself in the . . . I think if I invent the word 'space dinghy' it will give you the idea. I warned her that the . . . well, an important part was defective; but we had just had a small quarrel and she insisted on spiting me. She never came back. That's why I had to make contact with intelligent life to learn something of the planet which I have to search."

"Only the intelligent life doesn't have waves. Except me because, God help me, I expect strange things to speak. You need a combination of Sherlock Holmes and Frank Buck, and you're stuck with a possibly not quite sane ventriloquist."

"You will help me? When you see her!" Tarvish was almost rapturous. "The most beautiful girl, I swear, on the whole earth. With," he added reminiscently, "the finest pair of ears in the universe." On the word *ears* his voice sank a little, and the blue tinge deepened at the root of his proboscis.

The universe, Paul smiled to himself, must provide a fascinating variety of significant secondary sexual characteristics. "If I can help you," he said sincerely, "I'll try. I'll do my best. And in the meantime we've the little problem of feeding you. I'll have to take you—" he tensed a little "—home. I suppose, that is, you *do* eat?"

"So far as we have observed," Tarvish pronounced solemnly, "all races of rational beings eat and sleep and . . ." The blue was again intensified.

"And relish a fine pair of ears," Paul concluded for him. "Definition of rationality." He started the car.

By the next morning Paul Peters had learned a number of things.

He had learned that men of Tarvish's race are, as they choose, bipeds or quadrupeds. When they entered the Montgomery Block, that sprawling warren of odd studios where Paul lived, Tarvish had trotted behind him on all fours "because," he said, "it would be less conspicuous," as indeed was true. He was only by a small margin the most unusual of the animal and human companions whom Montgomery Block denizens had brought home, few of whom—including the humans—were at the moment functionally bipedal. But once inside the studio apartment, he seemed to prefer the erect posture.

Between them they had worked out the problem of feeding. The proboscidiferous Tarvish was of course edentate, and accustomed to subsisting on liquids and pap. Milk, raw eggs, and tomato juice sufficed him for the time being—a surprisingly simple diet to contain most of the requisite vitamins and proteins. Later Paul planned to lay in a supply of prepared baby foods, and looked forward to the astonishment of the clerk at the nearby chain store who knew him as a resolute bachelor.

Paul had also learned an astonishing amount, considering the relative brevity of the conversation, concerning the planet which was to Tarvish *the Earth*—from its socio-economic systems to the fascinating fact that at present fine full, ripe ears were, as any man would prefer, in style, whereas only a generation ago they had been unaccountably minimized and even strapped down. Paul's amused explanation of the analogy on this Earth served perhaps as much as anything to establish an easy man-to-man intimacy. Tarvish went so far as to elaborate a plan for introducing gradually inflatable false earlobes on his Earth. It was never quite clear to Paul how an edentate being could speak so easily, but he imagined that the power resembled his own professional skill.

All of these strange thoughts coursed through Paul's head as he lay slowly waking up the next morning; and it was only after several minutes of savoring them that he perceived the wonderful background note that served as their ground-bass. Not since the first difficult instant of entering the apartment had he so much as thought of the corner of the main room in which Chuck Woodchuck lay.

"You know, Tarvish," Paul said as they finished breakfast, "I like you. You're easy to be with."

"Thank you, Paul." The root of the proboscis blushed faintly blue. "I like you too. We could spend happy days simply talking, exchanging, learning to know. . . But there *is* Vishta."

"Vishta?"

"My girl. I dreamed about her last night, Paul . . ." Tarvish gave a little sigh, rose, and began bipedally to pace the room. "Your Earth is enormous, even though the figures you tell me convey no meaning to me. Whatever a square mile means, one hundred and ninety-seven million of them must represent quite an area. There must be some way . . ."

"Look," Paul said. "Before we tackle the problem again, let's try restating it. (A), we must find Vishta. But that doesn't necessarily mean literally, physically, Dr. Livingstone-I-presume *find*, does it? She'll be over the lovers' quarrel by now; she'll want to get back to the—you'll pardon the expression—spaceship. If we can let her know where you are, that's enough, isn't it?"

Tarvish rubbed the tip of his large nose. "I should think so."

"All right. Restate the restatement. (A), get word to Vishta. (B), without revealing your interplanetary presence to the world at large. Both because it's against your mores and because I think it'll cause just too damned much trouble. Agreed?"

"Agreed."

The two sat in silence for perhaps five minutes. Paul alternately cudgeled his brains, and addressed brief prayers to the Holy Ghost for assistance in helping this other creature of God. Meanwhile, his eyes drifted around the apartment, and for a moment rested on the noble two-volume Knopf edition of Poe.

"My God in Heaven!" he exclaimed. The most devout could not have considered this a violation of the decalog. "Look, Tarvish. We have in our literature a story called 'The Purloined Letter.' Its point is that the most over-obvious display can be the subtlest concealment."

"The point occurs in our folklore as well," said Tarvish. "But I don't—" Suddenly he stopped.

Paul grinned. "Did you get a wave? But let me go on out loud—this race is happier that way. Yes, we had it all solved yesterday and let it slip. The lie we bribed Tim to tell—"

"—that I am your new dummy," Tarvish picked up eagerly.

"The act'll be sensational. Because you can really talk, I can do anything. Eat soda crackers while you're talking—it won't make any difference. And you—I hate like hell to say this to any man, but from an audience viewpoint it's true—you're *cute*. You're damned near cuddly. They'll love you. And we bill you with the precise truth: you're a visitant from outer space. It ties a ventriloquism act into the science-fiction trend in TV. You're THE STAR DUMMY. We'll make a fortune—not that I'm thinking of that—"

"Aren't you?" Tarvish asked dryly.

Paul smiled. "Can anyone be a hypocrite in a telepathic civilization?"

"It's been known to happen."

"Well, anyway, I'm not thinking *primarily* of the fortune. We'll get publicity we couldn't buy. And wherever she is, unless it's in Darkest Africa or behind the Iron Curtain, Vishta'll learn where you are."

"Paul," said Tarvish solemnly, "you're inspired. On that I could use a drink."

"Another custom of all rational races?"

"Nearly all. But just a moment: I find in your mind the concept *alcohol*. I'm afraid that doesn't convey much."

Paul tried to think back to his high-school chemistry. Finally he ventured, "C_2H_5OH. That help any?"

"Ah, yes. More correctly, of course, CH_3CH_2OH. You find that mild fluid stimulating? We use it somewhat in preparing food, but . . . Now, if I might have a little $C_8H_{10}N_4O_2$?"

Paul rubbed his head. "Doesn't mean a thing to me. Sounds like some kind of alkaloid. It's the touch of nitrogen that does it with you people?"

"But indeed you do know it. You were drinking it at breakfast. And I must say I admired the ease with which you put away so much strong liquor so early in the day."

Hastily Paul checked in a dictionary. *"Caffeine,"* he groaned. "And what do you use to sober up? A few cups of good straight alcohol, no cream?"

And in copious shots of C_2H_5OH and $C_8H_{10}N_4O_2$ the two men pledged the future of THE STAR DUMMY.

So now you see at last to what this story has been leading. What began in a confessional and passed through an analyst's office to a zoo—all symbolism is read into the sequence at your own peril—is in actuality the backstage story of the genesis of your own favorite television program.

Most of the rest of that genesis you know from a thousand enthusiastic re-countings, from John Crosby's in the *Herald Tribune* to Philip Hamburger's in the *New Yorker:* how network producers at first greeted Paul Peters skeptically when he returned to show business, after a mysterious absence, with a brand-new type of act; how THE STAR DUMMY was at first somewhat hesitantly showcased on *San Francisco Presents;* how the deluge of fan mail caused that first showing to be kinnied all over the country, while the next week a live performance shot over the nation on a microwave relay; how the outrageous concept of a cuddlesome dummy from Outer Space managed unbelievably to combine the audiences of Charlie McCarthy and *Space Cadet;* how Star Dummies outgrossed the combined total sales of Sparkle Plenty Dolls and Hopalong Cassidy suits.

But there are a few untold backstage scenes which you should still hear.

Scene: Station KMNX-TV. Time: the morning after the first Star Dummy broadcast. Speaker: a vice-president.

"But my God, M.N., there's all hell popping. That was Hollywood on the phone. They've got the same damned show lined up for show-casing next week. Same format—identical dummy—only maybe theirs has bigger ears. The property owner's flying up here and our lawyers had better be good!"

Scene: Same. Time: that afternoon.

"I think," Paul had said, "that we might be able to reach a settlement out of court." The vice-presidents had filed out eagerly, the lawyers somewhat reluctantly.

Once he had been introduced to Vishta (and so close had he come, in weeks of preparing the show, to Tarvish's ways of thinking that he found her enchantingly lovely), it would have been inconceivably rude and prying to do anything but turn his back on the reunion of the lovers. Which meant that he had to keep his eyes on Marcia Judd, property owner of the Hollywood show.

"I'm not a professional ventriloquist like you, Mr. Peters," she was saying. "I couldn't do a thing without Vishta. But when we talked about it, it seemed the most logical way to let Tarvish know where she was. You know, like 'The Purloined Letter.' "

"And you have waves?" Paul marveled. It was about the only thing which she did not obviously have on first glance.

"I guess maybe it's because I write fantasy and s.f. Oh, I don't sell much, but a little. And I'm not too sure that there's *anything* that can't happen. So when I was walking through the San Diego zoo and I saw something in with the koalas that was making diagrams . . . Well, I couldn't help remembering Joe's story about intercultural communication—"

"Joe Henderson? You know old Joe?"

"He's helped me a lot. I guess you'd sort of say I'm his protege."

"So long," Paul smiled, "as he isn't your protector. But tell me, does Joe still . . ."

And one half of room was as happy in the perfect chatter of a first meeting as was the other half in the perfect silence of a long-delayed reunion.

Truth had shifted again, and THE STAR DUMMY was in fact a dummy—a brilliantly constructed piece of mechanism which had eaten up the profits of the three shows on which Tarvish himself had appeared. But the show was set now, and Paul's own professional skill could carry it from this point on. And the highly telegenic presence of Marcia Judd did no harm.

Paul's car stopped by a lonely stretch of beach south of the city.

"We can find what you like to call the spaceship from here," said Tarvish. "I'd sooner you didn't see it. I think it would only confuse you."

"We love you both," said Vishta gently. "God bless you."

"God!" Marcia exclaimed. "Don't tell me people with a science like yours believe in God!"

Paul sighed. "I hope you don't mind too much that I'm such a barbarian."

"It's your conditioning," said Marcia. "But with them . . . !"

"And *your* conditioning, Marcia," Tarvish observed, "has driven you the other way? Yes, I do believe in God in a way—if less devoutly than Paul, or at least than Paul being devout. Many do on our Earth; not all, but many. There was once a man, or possibly more than a man. We argue about that. His name was Hraz, and some call him the Oiled One." Marcia smiled and Tarvish added, "It refers to a ceremony of honor. I am not quite a follower of Hraz, and yet when I pray—as I did, Paul, shortly before you found me—it is in words that Hraz taught us."

"Which are?"

"We'll say them together," said Vishta. "It makes a good good-bye."

And the lovers recited:

Lifegiver over us, there is blessing in the word that means you. We pray that in time we will live here under your rule as others now live with you there; but in the meantime feed our bodies, for we need that here and now. We are in debt to you for everything, but your love will not hold us accountable for this debt; and so we too should deal with others, holding no man to strict balances of account. Do not let us meet temptations stronger than we can bear; but let us prevail and be free of evil.

Then they were gone, off down the beach.

Marcia sniffled away a tear. "It is *not* the prayer," she protested indignantly. "But they were so *nice* . . ."

"Yes," said the Paulist at Old St. Mary's, "you may tell your fiancée to come in next Thursday at three to start her pre-marital instruction."

"You'll find her a tartar, Father," Paul grinned.

"Atheism can be the most fanatical of religions. Thank Heaven my duty is only to inform, not to convert her. I'm glad you're getting married, Paul. I don't think anything inside or outside of you will denounce the flesh so violently again. Did the analysis help you?"

"Somehow I never got around to it. Things started happening."

"Now this . . . ah . . . document," the Paulist went on. "Really extraordinary. *Lifegiver over us* . . . Terribly free, of course, but still an unusually stimulating, fresh translation of the *Pater Noster*. I've shown it to Father Massini—he was on the Bishops' Committee for the revised translation of the New Testament—and he was delighted. Where on earth did you get it?"

"Father, you wouldn't believe me if I told you."

"No?" asked the priest.

Review Copy

The only light in the room was the flame burning inside the pentacle.

The man who kept his face in the shadows said, "But why do you want to kill him?"

The customer said, "What's that to you?"

"Let us put it this way," the man said persuasively. "In order to establish the psychic rapport necessary for the success of our . . . experiment, I need a full knowledge of all the emotional factors involved. Only complete knowing can compel the Ab." He hoped it sounded plausible

The customer said, "Once he gave me a mortal wound. I need to kill him too."

"And why this method? Why not something more direct?"

"I can't cross the continent. I can't leave New York. As soon I cross the river— I don't know, it's like breath going out of me . . ."

Compulsion neurosis, the man thought; form of agoraphobia. "But men have been murdered by mail?" he suggested.

"Not this one. He's too smart. He writes mystery novels; you don't think he'll open unexpected parcels, eat chocolates from strangers—why is it always chocolates?—he's too smart, the devil."

"But surely it should be possible to—"

The customer sprang to his feet and his shadow wove wildly in the light from the pentacle. "I'm paying you; isn't that enough? A body'd think you're trying to talk me out of it."

"Nonsense," said the man in the shadows. Though it was true. He knew that he had powers and that he could make good money from their use. But he knew too how unpredictable they were, and he always experienced this momentary desire to talk the customer out of it. "But if you'd tell me your reason . . . ?" There was method to that insistence too. When sometimes things failed and the customer turned nasty, a bit of private knowledge could often keep him from demanding his money back.

The customer settled down again. "All right," he said. "I'll tell you." The light from the pentacle shone on his bared teeth and glistered off the drop of saliva at the corner of his mouth. "He reviewed my book. It was a clever review, a devilish review. It was so damnably wittily phrased that it became famous. Bennett Cerf and Harvey Breit quoted it in their columns. It was all anybody heard about the book. And it killed the book and killed me and he has to die."

The man in shadow smiled unseen. One review out of hundreds, and in an out-of-town paper at that. But because it had been distinctively phrased, it was easy to make it a scapegoat, to blame its influence alone for the failure of a book that could never have succeeded. His customer was crazy as a bed-bug. But what did that matter to him, whose customers always were as mad as they were profitable?

"You realize," he said, "that the blood must have fire?"

"I've learned a lot about him. I know his habits and his reactions. There will be fire, and he'll use it." The customer hesitated, and a drop of saliva fell, luminous in the flame from the pentacle. "Will I . . . will I know about it? As though I were there?"

"It's your blood, isn't it?" the man said tersely.

He said nothing more while he arranged the customer inside the pentacle. At his side he set the container of thick black stuff and propped the customer's wrist over it so that the blood dripped in as he made the incision. Then he tossed a handful of powder onto the flame and began to chant.

The book came into the office of the San Francisco *Times* in a normal and unobtrusive manner. It was in a cardboard box wrapped in brown paper and bore postage at the proper book-rate. The label was plain, bearing no information other than the typed address, which read:

> Book department
> San Francisco Times
> San Francisco, California

Miss Wentz opened the package and discarded the wrappings. She glanced at the oddly figured jacket, opened the book, and read the printed slip.

> We take pleasure in sending you this book for review and we shall appreciate two clippings of any notice you may give it.

She muttered her opinion of publishers who give neither price or publication date, and turned to the title page. Her eyes popped a little.

THE BLOOD IS THE DEATH
being a collection of arcane matters
demonstrating
that in the violence of death
lies the future of life
assembled by
Hieronymus Melanchthon

New York
The Chorazin Press
1955

She had never heard of Hieronymus Melanchthon nor The Chorazin Press; but anything comes to a newspaper. In a book-review department, incredulity is a forgotten emotion. Miss Wentz shrugged and soberly set to making out a card for the files, just as though the thing were really a book.

She was interrupted by the arrival of The Great Man, as she (in private) termed The Most Influential Bookpage Editor West of the Mississippi. He breezed in, cast a rapid eye over the pile of new arrivals, and hesitated as he looked at *The Blood Is the Death.*

"What now?" he said. He picked it up, held it in one hand, and let the pages riffle past his thumb. Malicious people said he could turn out an impeccable 250-word review after such a gesture. "Crackpot," he said tersely. "Over on the left." He picked up his mail and headed for the inner office. But he stopped a minute and looked at his thumb, then took out his handkerchief and rubbed at an ink smudge. He looked hurt, as a biologist might if a laboratory guinea pig turned on him and scratched him.

Miss Wentz put *The Blood* on the left. One wall of the office was a tall double bookcase. On the right were current books to be reviewed, from which the staff reviewers made their selections. On the left was a hodge-podge of rental romances, volumes of poetry printed by the author, secrets of the Cosmos published in Los Angeles, and other opera considered unworthy even of a panning. *The Blood* went in among them, between *Chips of Illusion* and *The Trismegist of the Count St. Germain.*

Miss Wentz went back to her typewriter and to her task of explaining to the usual number of eager aspirants that The Great Man did not read unsolicited manuscripts. In a moment she looked up automatically and said "Hello," but there was no one there. Reviewers were always in and out all day Monday; she was sure she had heard, seen, *felt* somebody . . .

She tried to type and wished the phone would ring or The Great Man would decide to dictate or even a screwball author would wander in. Anything rather than this room that was not quite empty . . .

She was very warm in her welcome of The Reverend, as she mentally labeled him—so warm as thoroughly to disconcert the *Times*'s reviewer of religious books. He was a young man still in his diaconate—not a year out of the seminary yet, but already realizing the nets and springes that are set for an unmarried clergyman. He was slowly becoming not so much a misogynist as a gynophobe, and found himself reading Saint Paul more and more often. He had always thought of the *Times* office as a haven of safety, but if even here— He turned away his face, which was reddening embarrassingly, and devoted himself to serious study of the books on the right.

He took down the letters of a Navy chaplain, a learned thesis on contemplation, and a small book in large type with the peppy title *Prayer Is the Payoff.* He set them on the table with a sigh of resignation (at that, there might be a sermon idea in them somewhere) and looked idly at the shelves again. With half a smile he reached for *The Blood Is the Death.*

"Such a sacrilegious title!" he observed, paging through it. "I imagine this might fall into my province at that?"

"What? Oh." Miss Wentz looked at *The Blood.* "That's supposed to be over on the other side. He doesn't want anything on that."

"I found it here," he protested mildly.

"I'd swear I put it over with the rejects." She rose and thrust it in its proper place. "Well, it's there now."

The Reverend frowned at his finger. "What frightful ink in that odd book! Look how it comes off."

Miss Wentz reached in the drawer. "Here's a Kleenex."

But rub though he would, the stain persisted. He was still at it, and rather wishing that he might revert to the vocabulary of his undergraduate days, when Mark Mallow came in.

The word usually used for Mark Mallow was clever, or sometimes even brilliant. People always said how much they admired his work, or how entertaining he was. They were never heard to say anything so simple as "Mallow? Yeah, a swell guy." Mallow wore, among other necessary items, a trim Van Dyke and a jaunty hat and a bright bow tie. You had a feeling that he might have added spats and a cane if that had not been a little too much for San Francisco. There was a spring to his step and a constant smile on his lips, which were thus always parted to show his teeth.

This was fair warning; for though Mark Mallow never barked, his bite was an essential part of his life. Few people ever questioned his judgment in his chosen field of criticism; Starrett and Queen and Sandoe were in constant correspondence with him and respected his taste; but no one had ever accused him of immoderate softheartedness. He was honest, and he wrote a rave review when necessary; but the words sounded forced and compelled. His pannings, on the other hand, were gems of concise assassination, surgically accurate scalpel work that drew life blood.

He had fun.

Mallow nodded to The Reverend, smiled at Miss Wentz, and groaned at the weekly stack of whodunits set aside for him. Then he looked over the general section on the right, picked out a couple of works that bordered on his interests, and paused with a whistle of amazement. He took down a book, stared at its title page, and said, "I'll be damned! If you'll pardon me, Reverend?"

The Reverend, who had long concurred in the opinion, said "Quite."

"Jerome Blackland, or I'll be several things I shouldn't mention here. Jot me down for this, Miss Wentz, if you please; this ought to be good clean sport."

Miss Wentz looked up automatically and then made a sharp little noise of exasperation. "How did *that* get back there?"

"It was right here," Mallow said.

"I know . . . and I'll take my oath on a stack of Bibles that I put it over on the left not once but twice. Didn't I?"

The Reverend nodded. "I saw you."

"And now it's . . . Oh well. He doesn't want it reviewed, but if it interests you especially . . ."

"Why?" The Reverend asked.

Mallow extended the book open at its mad title page. "You see that unbelievable name, Hieronymus Melanchthon?"

"A pseudonym, of course. So much of that quasi-mystical literature is pseudonymous."

"Like the man who wrote under the name of St. John a century or so later?"

Mallow asked slyly. "Well, I know who's back of this pseud. Translate it, and what do you get?"

The Reverend summoned up his seminarian Greek. "Jerome Black . . . land, would it be?"

"Exactly. Rich screwball New Yorker. Got all tangled up with black magic and stuff and turned out an amazing opus, half-novel, half-autobiography, that made William Seabrook and Montague Summers look like skeptics. I had fun with it. I think I'll have fun with this, too— Damn!" He broke off and stared at his thumb. "I'm bleeding. Did this infernal opus up and take a nip at me? No . . . I'm not bleeding. It's off the book. What the devil kind of ink *is* this?"

The Reverend looked—and was—perplexed. On his own hand the smudge from that strangely printed volume was black. On Mark Mallow's it was blood-red. It seemed perverse. Doubtless some simple explanation—some chemical salt present in Mallow's body secretions and not in his which acted as reagent . . . Nevertheless he was nervous, and found an occasion promptly to leave the office.

Mallow went on into the inner office to confer with The Great Man, leaving *The Blood* behind him. This time it stayed put, waiting for him. Miss Wentz tried to type again, but still the room was unempty. Not until Mallow and his book-crammed briefcase had departed did the room feel ordinary again.

Mark Mallow settled himself comfortably on the Bridge train. It was the commuters' hour and the train was packed; but experience and ingenuity always combined to get him a seat. When he had finished a cursory examination of the afternoon newspaper, he spread it over his trouser legs, hoisted his briefcase up onto his lap, and began rummaging among the week's stock. The paunchy businessman occupying the other half of the seat needed more than a half for his bulk; but Mallow's muscles, skilled in this form of civilian commando, unconsciously fended off his encroachment.

The ride over the Bay Bridge, even by train (which operates on a lower and less scenic level than motor traffic), is beautiful and exciting the first time. But habitués never glance out the window unless to attempt to draw deductions from ships in port at the moment. Mark Mallow saw nothing of the splendor of the bay as he selected the latest Simenon to enjoy on the trip. (For Mallow did enjoy reading a good whodunit; he merely hated to write about any but the stinkers.)

He read the first page over three times before he realized that the endeavor was vain. Something urged him to replace the Simenon in the briefcase and extract another volume, the one with the oddly figured jacket. His hand seemed to move of itself, and at the same time his muscles announced the surprising fact that there was no longer a pressure from the businessman. In fact, he seemed to be edging away.

Mallow smiled as he opened the book. The pretentious absurdity of the title page delighted him, and the text more than lived up to it. (The businessman did not look the type who would give his seat to a lady.) It is, I suppose, inevitable, Mallow reflected, that those who seek to express the inexpressible should have no talent for expression. (The lady did not look the type to refuse a seat either.) Surely worth a choice stabbing little paragraph for the column. A joy, if only it weren't for this damned ink . . . (The seat remained vacant, in that crowded car, for the whole of the trip. Mallow did not notice it; it seemed as though there were some one there.)

The Reverend was still a trifle perturbed. It was ridiculous that one should worry about such a nothing as a minor chemical oddity. Had he not in fact prepared a sermon for next Sunday decrying the modern materialists who reduce everything to a series of chemical reactions?

But there was always one source of peace and consolation. The Reverend took down his Bible, intending to turn to the psalms—the ninety-first, probably. But he dropped the Book in astonishment.

It had happened so quickly it could scarcely be believed.

The smudge on his thumb had been black. In the instant that it touched the Bible it turned blood-red, exactly like the stain on Mark Mallow's hand. Then there was a minute hissing noise and an instant of intense heat.

There was no smudge at all on his thumb now.

There was no one in Dr. Halstead's office. The Reverend took up the phone hastily and dialed the number of the *Times*. He said "Book department," and a moment later demanded urgently, "Miss Wentz? Can you give me Mallow's home address?"

Mark Mallow ate well, as he always did when he felt inclined to cook for himself. The dinner was simple: a pair of rex sole, boiled rice (with a pinch of saffron), and a tossed salad; but it could not have been satisfactorily duplicated even in San Francisco, the city of restaurants.

A half bottle of decent Chablis with dinner and a brandy after (both from California vineyards, but nowise despicable) had made Mallow mellow, as he thought to himself with perverse delight in the jarring phrase. Now the insight of Simenon would add pleasurably to his glow.

He settled himself in front of the fireplace. It was quiet up there in the Berkeley hills. No, quiet was too mild a word. It was still—no, stronger yet—it was stilled. Hushed and gently frozen into silence.

There was nothing in the world but the fire and his purring digestive system and the book in his hand . . . The book was *The Blood Is the Death* and the fire shone on his reddened hand.

Mark Mallow swore to himself, but he was too post-prandially lazy to move from the chair. He opened the book and read on a little. His eyes half-closed; high-flown gibberish is one of the finest soporifics. They jerked open and he sat up with a start to greet the unexpected visitor.

The room was empty.

He swore again, in a half-hearted way. He turned his attention to those exquisitely satisfactory digestive processes and noticed that they had reached a point demanding some attention. He rose from the chair, carried *The Blood* over to the current-review bookcase, replaced it there, and took out the Simenon and laid it on the arm of the chair. Then he went to the bathroom, looking, for no good reason, over his shoulder as he left the room.

*   *   *

The Reverend had stout legs. He needed them as he toiled up the hills beyond the end of the bus line.

What are you going to say? The Reverend asked himself. What are you going to do? He couldn't answer his questions. He knew only that he had encountered a situation where his duty demanded action.

In the Roman Church, he believed, one of the lower orders of the priesthood was known by the title of Exorcist. He wondered if the Roman clergy were taught the functions of that order, or was the name merely an archaic survival? Shame-facedly he let his fingers steal into his pocket and touch the bottle nestling there—the tiny bottle which he had filled with holy water as he passed a Roman church.

The lights ahead must be those of Mark Mallow's house. From the front window came a glow which seemed to be that of a reading lamp combined with a wood fire. The lighted window was peaceful and of good omen.

The redness came then—the vast redness that filled the room and the window and both The Reverend's eyes.

When Mark Mallow came back from the bathroom, he almost hesitated before entering the room. He felt an absurd impulse to retreat, lock the door, and go to bed. He smiled at himself (a rare phenomenon) and proceeded resolutely to the chair. He sat back, picked up the Simenon . . . and its print came off red on his fingers. He stood up in wrath and hurled the crackpot volume into the fire.

In the instant before he hurled it, the room gathered itself up into expectation. The shadows quivered, knowing what manner of light was about to dispel them. The flames of the fireplace shrank back to receive their fierce fresh fuel. For an instant there was no time in this space.

That tick that was eternity passed and time rushed back into the room. The book found the flames and the flames found the blood and the blood found the death that is the life and the life that is death. The shadow went from infra-visibility to blinding sight and it was one with flames and blood and book and the one thing that was shadow and flames and blood and book leapt.

The room was dark when The Reverend entered. There had been too much light there for an instant; the balance of the sane universe demanded blackness.

The light came on without his touching it when the balance hung even again. He did not blink because it was necessary that he should see this sight. He saw the body of Mark Mallow and he saw the blood of Mark Mallow and another.

The Reverend knew what to do. He opened the phial of holy water and started to pour it on the blood. Instead, the blood ran toward him, but he did not flinch. He stood his ground and watched as the water and the blood commingled and were one, and that one was the water. He recorked the phial, and in it was only water and around the body of Mark Mallow was only the blood of one man.

He left the house. He understood a little. He understood that human reason cannot accept a corpse which sheds twice its amount of blood, and that his presence had enabled him to redress the balance. Now Mallow's death would be only a terrible and unsolved murder, while it might have opened to man a knowledge which he could not bear. He found it harder to understand why he had been permitted to arrive only *after* the . . . happening. He guessed that in some way the small petty comfortable evils of Mark Mallow had made him vulnerable to a larger evil.

He did not know. He did not know if he himself could bear the knowledge which he had shouldered. He knew only that he could pray for Mark Mallow's soul—and probably for that of a man named Blackland.

The man who usually kept his face in the shadow had the decency to attend Jerome Blackland's funeral. He always did this for his clients. It was a sort of professional ethics.

A purist of professional ethics might suggest that he should have warned Blackland of the dangers inherent in bestowing the vital virtues of one's blood to animate printer's ink. But why? Half the time the charms worked imperfectly if at all; and you do not wantonly frighten away customers.

He too said prayers, of his sort, for the souls of Blackland and Mallow.

A Kind of Madness

In 1888 London was terrified, as no city has been before or since, by Jack the Ripper, who from April through November killed and dissected at least seven prostitutes, without leaving a single clue to his identity. The chain of murders snapped abruptly. After 1888 Jack never ripped again. Because on 12th July, 1889 . . .

He paused on the steps of University College, surrounded by young ladies prattling the questions that were supposed to prove they had paid careful attention to his lecture-demonstration.

The young ladies were, he knew as a biologist, human females; dissection would establish the fact beyond question. But for him womankind was divided into three classes: angels and devils and students. He had never quite forgiven the college for admitting women nine years ago. That these female creatures should irrelevantly possesss the same terrible organs that were the arsenal of the devils, the same organs through which the devils could strike lethally at the angels, the very organs which he . . .

He answered the young ladies without hearing either their questions or his answers, detached himself from the bevy, and strolled towards the Euston Road.

For eight months now he had seen neither angel nor devil. The events of 1888 seemed infinitely remote, like a fever remembered after convalescence. It had indeed been a sort of fever of the brain, perhaps even—he smiled gently—a kind of madness. But after his own angel had died of that unspeakable infection which the devil had planted in him—which had affected him so lightly but had penetrated so fatally to those dread organs which render angels vulnerable to devils . . .

He observed, clinically, that he was breathing heavily and that his hand was groping in his pocket—a foolish gesture, since he had not carried the scalpel for eight months. Deliberately he slowed his pace and his breathing. The fever was spent—though surely no sane man could see anything but good in an effort to rid London of its devils.

"Pardon, m'sieur."

The woman was young, no older than his students, but no one would mistake her for a female of University College. Even to his untutored eye her clothes spoke of elegance and chic and, in a word, Paris. Her delicate scent seemed no man-made otto but pure *essence de femme*. Her golden hair framed a piquant face, the nose slightly tilted, the upper lip a trifle full—irregular, but delightful.

"Ma'm'selle?" he replied, with courtesy and approbation.

"If m'sieur would be so kind as to help a stranger in your great city . . . I seek an establishment of baggages."

He tried to suppress his smile, but she noticed it, and a response sparkled in her eyes. "Do I say something improper?" she asked almost hopefully.

"Oh, no. Your phrase is quite correct. Most Englishmen, however, would say 'a luggage shop.'"

"Ah, *c'est ça*. 'A luggage shop'—I shall remember me. I am on my first voyage to England, though I have known Englishmen at Paris. I feel like a small child in a world of adults who talk strangely. Though I know"—his gaze was resting on what the French politely call the throat—"I am not shaped like one."

An angel, he was thinking. Beyond doubt an angel, and a delectable one. And this innocently provocative way of speaking made her seem only the more angelic.

He took from her gloved fingers the slip of paper on which was written the address of the "establishment of baggages."

"You are at the wrong end of the Euston Road," he explained. "Permit me to hail a cab for you; it is too far to walk on such a hot day."

"Ah, yes, this is a July of Julys, is it not? One has told me that in England it is never hot, but behold I sweat!"

He frowned.

"Oh, do I again say something beastly? But it is true: I do sweat." Tiny moist beads outlined her all but invisible blonde moustache.

He relaxed. "As a professor of biology I should be willing to acknowledge the fact that the human female is equipped with sweat glands, even though proper English usage would have it otherwise. Forgive me, my dear child, for frowning at your innocent impropriety."

She hesitated, imitating his frown. Then she looked up, laughed softly, and put her small plump hand on his arm. "As a token of forgiveness, m'sieur, you may buy me an ice before hailing my cab. My name," she added, "is Gaby."

He felt infinitely refreshed. He had been wrong, he saw it now, to abstain so completely from the company of women once his fever had run its course. There was a delight, a solace, in the presence of a woman. Not a student, or a devil, but the true woman: an angel.

Gaby daintily dabbed ice and sweat from her full upper lip and rose from the table. "M'sieur has been most courteous to the stranger within his gates. And now I must seek my luggage shop."

"Mademoiselle Gaby—"

"Hein? Speak up, m'sieur le professeur. Is it that you wish to ask if we shall find each other again?"

"I should indeed be honored if while you are in London—"

"Merde alors!" She winked at him, and he hoped that he had misunderstood her French. "Do we need such fine phrases? I think we understand ourselves, no?

There is a small bistro—a pub, you call it?—near my lodgings. If you wish to meet me there tomorrow evening . . ." She gave him instructions. Speechless, he noted them down.

"You will not be sorry, m'sieur. I think well you will enjoy your little tour of France after your dull English diet."

She held his arm while he hailed a cab. He did not speak except to the cabman. She extended her ungloved hand and he automatically took it. Her fingers dabbled deftly in his palm while her pink tongue peered out for a moment between her lips. Then she was gone.

"And I thought her an angel," he groaned.

His hand fumbled again in his empty pocket.

The shiny new extra large trunk dominated the bedroom.

Gabrielle Bompart stripped to the skin as soon as the porter had left (more pleased with her wink than with her tip) and perched on the trunk. The metal trim felt refreshingly cold against her flesh.

Michel Eyraud looked up lazily from the bed where he was sprawled. "I never get tired of looking at you, Gaby."

"When you are content just to look," Gaby grinned, "I cut your throat."

"It's hot," said Eyraud.

"I know, and you are an old man. You are old enough to be my father. You are a very wicked lecherous old man, but for old men it is often hot."

Eyraud sprang off the bed, strode over to the trunk, and seized her by her naked shoulders. She laughed in his face. "I was teasing you. It *is* too hot. Even for me. Go lie down and tell me about your day. You got everything?"

Eyraud waved an indolent hand at the table. A coil of rope, a block and tackle, screws, screwdriver . . .

Gaby smiled approvingly. "And I have the trunk, such a nice big one, and this." She reached for her handbag, drew out a red-and-white girdle. "It goes well with my dressing gown. And it is strong." She stretched it and tugged at it, grunting enthusiastically.

Eyraud looked from the girdle to the rope to the pulley to the top of the door leading to the sitting-room, then back to the trunk. He nodded.

Gaby stood by the full-length mirror contemplating herself. "That silly bailiff, that Gouffé. Why does he dare to think that Gaby should be interested in him? This Gaby, such as you behold her . . ." She smiled at the mirror and nodded approval.

"I met a man," she said. "An Englishman. Oh, so very stiff and proper. He looks like Phileas Fogg in Jules Verne's *Le Tour du Monde*. He wants me."

"Fogg had money," said Eyraud. "Lots of it."

"So does my professor . . . Michi?"

"Yes?"

Gabrielle pirouetted before the mirror. "Am I an actress?"

"All women are actresses."

"Michi, do not try to be clever. It is not becoming to you. Am I an actress?"

Eyraud lit a French cigarette and tossed the blue pack to Gaby. "You're a performer, and entertainer. You have better legs than any actress in Paris. And if you made old Gouffé think you love him for his fat self . . . Yes, I guess you're an actress."

"Then I know what I want." Gaby's eyelids were half closed. "Michi, I want a rehearsal."

Eyraud looked at the trunk and the block and tackle and the red-and-white girdle. He laughed, heartily and happily.

He found her waiting for him in the pub. The blonde hair picked up the light and gave it back, to form a mocking halo around the pert devil's face.

His fingers reassured him that the scalpel was back where it belonged. He had been so foolish to call "a fever" what was simply his natural rightful temperature. It was his mission in life to rid the world of devils. That was the simple truth. And not all devils had cockney accents and lived in Whitechapel.

"Be welcome, m'sieur le professeur." She curtseyed with impish grace. "You have thirst?"

"No," he grunted.

"Ah, you mean you do not have thirst in the throat. It lies lower, hein?" She giggled, and he wondered how long she had been waiting in the pub. She laid her hand on his arm. The animal heat seared through his sleeve. "I go upstairs. You understand, it is more chic when you do not see me make myself ready. You ascend in a dozen of minutes. It is on the first floor, at the left to the rear."

He left the pub and waited on the street. The night was cool and the fog was beginning to settle down. On just such a night in last August . . . What was her name? He had read it later in The Times. Martha Tabor? Tabby? Tabbypussydevil.

He had nicked his finger on the scalpel. As he sucked the blood he heard a clock strike. He had been waiting almost a half hour; where had the time gone? The devil would be impatient.

The sitting-room was dark, but subdued lamplight gleamed from the bedroom. The bed was turned down. Beside it stood a huge trunk.

The devil was wearing a white dressing-gown and a red-and-white girdle that emphasized its improbably slender waist. It came towards him and stroked his face with hot fingers and touched its tongue like a branding iron to his chin and ears and at last his lips. His hands closed around its waist.

"Ouf!" gasped the devil, "You may crush me, I assure you, M'sieur. I love that. But please to spare my pretty new girdle. Perhaps if I debarrass myself of it . . ." It unclasped the girdle and the dressing-gown fell open.

His hand took a firm grip on the scalpel.

The devil moved him towards the door between the two rooms. It festooned the girdle around his neck. "Like that," it said gleefully. "There—doesn't that make you a pretty red-and-white cravat?"

Hand and scalpel came out of his pocket

And Michel Eyraud, standing in the dark sitting-room, fastened the ends of the girdle to the rope running through the block and tackle and gave a powerful jerk.

The rope sprang to the ceiling, the girdle followed it, and the professor's thin neck snapped. The scalpel fell from his dead hand.

The rehearsal had been a complete success.

Just as they planned to do with the bailiff Gouffé, they stripped the body and plundered the wallet. "Not bad," said Eyraud. "Do actresses get paid for rehearsing?"

"This one does," said Gaby. And they dumped the body in the trunk.

Later the clothes would be disposed of in dustbins, the body carried by trunk to some quiet countryside where it might decompose in naked namelessness.

Gaby swore when she stepped on the scalpel. "What the hell is this?" She picked it up. "It's sharp. Do you suppose he was one of those types who like a little blood to heighten their pleasures? I've heard of them but never met one."

Gaby stood pondering, her dressing-gown open . . .

The first night, to the misfortune of the bailiff Gouffé, went off as smoothly as the rehearsal. But the performers reckoned without the patience and determination and génie policier of Marie-François Goron, Chief of the Paris Sûreté.

The upshot was, as all aficionados of true crime know, that Eyraud was guillotined, nineteen months after the rehearsal, and Gaby, who kept grinning at the jury, was sentenced to twenty years of hard labor.

When Goron was in London before the trial, he paid his usual courtesy call at Scotland Yard and chatted at length with Inspector Frederick G. Abberline.

"Had one rather like yours recently ourselves," said Abberline. "Naked man, broken neck, left to rot in the countryside. Haven't succeeded in identifying him yet. You were luckier there."

"It is notorious," Goron observed, "that the laboratories of the French police are the best in the world."

"We do very well, thank you," said Abberline distantly.

"Of course." The French visitor was all politeness: "As you did last year in that series of Whitechapel murders."

"I don't know if you're being sarcastic, Mr. Goron, but no police force in the world could have done more than we did in the Ripper case. It was a nightmare with no possible resolution. And unless he strikes again, it's going to go down as one of the greatest unsolved cases in history. Jack the Ripper will never hang."

"Not," said M. Goron, "so long as he confines his attention to the women of London." He hurried to catch the boat train, thinking of Gabrielle Bompart and feeling a certain regret that such a woman was also such a devil.

Nellthu

Ailsa had been easily the homeliest and the least talented girl in the University, if also the most logical and level-headed. Now, almost twenty-five years later, she was the most attractive woman Martin had ever seen and, to judge from their surroundings, by some lengths the richest.

". . . so lucky running into you again after all these years," she was saying, in that indescribably aphrodisiac voice. "You know about publishers, and you can advise me on this novel. I was getting so tired of the piano . . ."

Martin had heard her piano recordings and knew they were superb—as the vocal recordings had been before them and the non-representational paintings before *them* and the fashion designs and that astonishing paper on prime numbers. He also knew that the income from all these together could hardly have furnished the Silver Room in which they dined or the Gold Room in which he later read the novel (which was of course superb) or the room whose color he never noticed because he did not sleep alone (and the word *superb* is inadequate).

There was only one answer, and Martin was gratified to observe that the coffee-bringing servant cast no shadow in the morning sun. While Ailsa still slept (superbly), Martin said, "So you're a demon."

"Naturally, sir," the unshadowed servant said, his eyes adoringly upon the sleeper. "Nellthu, at your service."

"But such service! I can imagine Ailsa-that-was working out a good spell and even wishing logically. But I thought you fellows were limited in what you could grant."

"We are, sir. Three wishes."

"But she has wealth, beauty, youth, fame, a remarkable variety of talents—all on three wishes?"

"On one, sir. Oh, I foxed her prettily on the first two." Nellthu smiled reminiscently. " *Beauty*'—but she didn't specify, and I made her the most beautiful centenarian in the world. *Wealth beyond the dreams of avarice*'—and of course nothing is beyond such dreams, and nothing she got. Ah, I was in form that day, sir! But the third wish . . ."

"Don't tell me she tried the old *For my third wish I want three more wishes*'! I thought that was illegal."

"It is, sir. The paradoxes involved go beyond even our powers. No, sir," said

445

Nellthu, with a sort of rueful admiration, "her third wish was stronger than that. She said: *'I wish that you fall permanently and unselfishly in love with me.'*"

"She was always logical," Martin admitted. "So for your own sake you had to make her beautiful and . . . adept, and since then you have been compelled to gratify her every—" He broke off and looked from the bed to the demon. "How lucky for me that she included *unselfishly!*"

"Yes, sir," said Nellthu.

Rappaccini's Other Daughter

For of course that sinister Paduan precursor of Mad Scientists, whose story has been so ably if incompletely related by Mr. Hawthorne, was, though mad, enough of a scientist to keep a control. While he gave out that the beauteous Beatrice, of the loving soul and envenomed breath, was his only daughter, he was rearing in seclusion the equally beauteous Laura.

And that is why our time machines are not permitted to travel back farther than the middle of the twentieth century.

It had taken Dr. Giacomo Rappaccini some 16 years to rear Beatrice to toxic perfection, nurturing her on lethal vegetable extracts until the rich balsam of her breath was itself a poison. By the time of her regrettable death, this incunabular toxicologist had learned more rapid methods; was he not able to produce the same condition in her lover Giovanni in a matter of months? It took even less time to elevate Laura from her position as control to the focal role in the great (if mad) experiment; soon she, who had ever been as beautiful as Beatrice, was now also as deadly.

That shallow youth Giovanni Guasconti found himself as facilely and superficially in love with one baleful beauty as with the other—indeed, with yet greater ease on this second occasion, since he had been wondering, ever since he knew himself to be a victim of the Rappaccini method, how he was to discharge the normal impulses of youth upon a living object.

All the wedding guests agreed that never had there been a more handsome couple nor a more splendid wedding, even though the bride's father eccentrically enjoined the use of masks by all—through which, however, all could still faintly perceive the dulcet and balsamous breath of the pair.

Laura and Giovanni were, though the term was not yet in vogue, the guinea pigs of Dr. Rappaccini. They were also young and eager and Mediterranean, and like guinea pigs they bred—if not indeed like hurkles.

After a quarter of a millennium had passed, in the first half of the twentieth century, the pure Rappaccini-Guasconti strain (under a score of advisable pseudonyms) had spread throughout the earth in such numbers that the problem of integration with ordinary, unscented, non-lethal humanity was an acute one. During the eighteenth century the women had passed unnoticed by attaching breath-filters to their face masks; in the nineteenth, the men had inserted filters in their

447

beards. But the barefaced twentieth century posed a dilemma: Live in undesired obscurity, or risk killing off the rest of the race.

The dilemma was solved by a Rappaccini in whom Dr. Giacomo's brilliance was reborn. Ordinary humanity had always shown a liking for the sweet Rappaccini breath, which was dulcet in contagion. The twentieth century possessed the means of converting this liking into envy and hunger: the power of advertising.

The device succeeded by its own momentum; once it was launched, few Rappaccinis needed to participate in the campaign to make people despise their own living exhalations (as they had already learned to detest their sweat and certain areas of their hair) and to long instead for venomous fragrance. But it did of course take a Rappaccini to introduce, after several decades of preparation, the final touch: Dr. Giacomo's secret ingredient, derived from plants, which had altered Beatrice and Giovanni and Laura, known to its discoverer as *chiorofile* and now modernized as chlorophyll.

Today, in this late twenty-first century, we are all balsamous products of the Rappaccini method. The normal population was simply converted, without its knowledge and without undue loss of life (despite minor unexplained epidemics, unexpected failures of medicines, ungrounded charges of germ warfare), by its advertising-induced absorption of the key Rappaccini ingredient. We are harmless to each other, we adorn the very air we respire, and we do not use our time machines beyond 1950.

The first visit of our time travelers was to London in the fall of 1664, a date familiar to readers of Daniel Defoe's *Journal of the Plague Year.* It needed but a few more such visits, particularly those to the fourteenth century and the descent upon the camp of Sennacherib, to cause the World Senate of Scientists to pass stringent laws fixing a chronokinetic barrier at 1950.

This brief report is submitted for what guidance it may provide in the current WSS debate upon travel beyond the already sterile planets of this solar system.

Khartoum: A Prose Limerick

The last man and the last woman on Earth sat on the edge of the last bed.

Somewhere the Arcturians were watching them, gloating over having found at last two specimens, and with marked sexual differences. But both were inured by now to this benevolent scrutiny.

The figure in the shaggy tweeds stirred restlessly. "You're pretty," the gruff voice rasped as one hand out to touch a silk-sheathed knee. "The Arcturians did O.K. by me."

The improbably jutting breasts rose and fell rapidly. "I like *you*, too," the pouting lips admitted. "And of course we *are* going to have all kinds of *fun* . . . But when it comes to Perpetuating the Race—well, I'm afraid the Arcturians are in for an *awful* shock," he giggled as he reached in, detached one improbably jutting breast, and playfully tossed it to his companion.

The powerful masculine hands half fondled the conical object, then embarrassedly discarded it. The lean rangy body rose from the bed and began shedding the tweed coat. "It's against all my principles and probably yours; but it's been a long time and at least it'll be a novelty . . . I guess," she grunted as she freed her own quite probable breasts from their overtight bra, "the Arcturians knew what they were doing after all."

A Shape in Time

Temporal Agent L-3H is always delectable in any shape; that's why the Bureau employs her on marriage-prevention assignments.

But this time, as she reported to my desk, she was also dejected. "I'm a failure, Chief," she said. "He ran away—from *me*. The first man in twenty-five centuries . . ."

"Don't take it so seriously," I said. She was more than just another Agent to me; I was the man who'd discovered her talents. "We may be able to figure out what went wrong and approach it on another time line."

"But I'm no good." Her body went scrawny and sagging. Sometimes I wonder how people expressed their emotions before mutation gave us somatic control.

"Now there," I said, expanding my flesh to radiate confidence, "just tell me what happened. We know from the dial readings that the Machine got you to London in 1880—"

"To prevent the marriage of Edwin Sullivan to Angelina Gilbert," she grimaced. "Time knows why."

I sighed. I was always patient with her. "Because that marriage joined two sets of genes which in the course of three generations would produce—"

Suddenly she gave me one of her old grins, with the left eyebrow up. "I've never understood the time-results of an assignment yet, and don't try to teach me now. Marriage-prevention's fun enough on its own. And I thought it was going to be extra good this time. Edwin's beard was red and *this* long, and I haven't had a beard in five trips. But something went— The worst of it is, it went wrong when I was naked."

I was incredulous, and said so.

"I don't think even you really understand this, Chief. Because you are a man—" her half-smile complimented me by putting the italics of memory under *man* "—and men never have understood it. But the fact is that what men want naked, in any century, in any country, is what they're used to seeing clothed, if you follow me. Oh, there are always some women who have to pad themselves out or pull themselves in, but the really popular ones are built to fit their clothes. Look at what they used to call feelthy peectures; any time, any place, the girls that are supposed to be exciting have the same silhouette naked as the fashion demands clothed. Improbable though it seems."

452   Anthony Boucher

"L!" I gasped. She had suddenly changed so completely that there was hardly more than one clue that I was not looking at a boy.

"See?" she said. "That's the way I had to make myself when you sent me to the 1920s. And the assignment worked; this was what men wanted. And then, when you sent me to 1957 . . ."

I ducked out of the way as two monstrous mammae shot out at me. "I hadn't quite realized—" I began to confess.

"Or the time I had that job in sixteenth-century Germany."

"Now you look pregnant!"

"They all did. Maybe they were. Or when I was in Greece, all waist and hips . . . But all of these *worked.* I prevented marriages and improved the genetic time-flow. Only with Edwin . . ."

She was back in her own delectable shape, and I was able to give her a look of encouraging affection.

"I'll skip the build-up," she said. "I managed to meet Edwin, and I gave him *this* . . ." I nodded; how well I remembered *this* and its effects. "He began calling on me and taking me to theaters, and I knew it needed just one more step for him to forget all about that silly pink-and-white Angelina."

"Go on," I urged.

"He took the step, all right. He invited me to dinner in a private room at a discreet restaurant—all red plush and mirrors and a screen in front of the couch. And he ordered oysters and truffles and all that superstitious ritual. The beard was even better than I'd hoped: crisp and teasing, ticklish and . . ." She looked at me speculatively, and I regretted that we've bred out facial follicles beyond even somatic control. "When he started to undress me—and how much trouble that was in 1880!—he was delighted with *this.*"

She had changed from the waist up, and I had to admit that *this* was possibly more accurate than *these.* They were as large as the startling 1957 version, but molded together as almost one solid pectoral mass.

"Then he took off my skirts and . . ." L-3H was as near to tears as I had ever known her. "Then he . . . *ran.* Right out of the restaurant. I would've had to pay the check if I hadn't telekinned the Machine to bring me back to now. And I'll bet he ran right to that Angelina and made arrangements to start mixing genes and I've ruined everything for you."

I looked at her new form below the waist. It was indeed extraordinary and hardly to my taste, but it seemed correct. I checked the pictures again in the Sullivan dossier. Yes, absolutely.

I consoled and absolved her. "My dear L, you are—Time help me!—perfectly and exactly a desirable woman of 1880. The failure must be due to some slip on the part of the chronopsychist who researched Edwin. You're still a credit to the bureau, Agent L-3H!—and now, let's celebrate. No, don't change back. Leave it that way. I'm curious as to the effects of—what was the word they used for it in 1880?—of a woman's *bustle.*"

Summer's Cloud

Can such things be,
And overcome us like a summer's cloud,
Without our special wonder?
—Macbeth, act III, scene 4

Walter Hancock was not superstitious. He said so to his wife when they walked on either side of a post on their way from the little Italian pension to the railway station. And he said so to his table companion at dinner that evening, when he had drunk a glass more than usual to prove that he was a bachelor for the night. This, of course, was why he had spilled the salt—or perhaps it was because his table companion spoke with a strange accent and wore a low-necked gown. He could not decide which intrigued him the more, and took another glass of wine to find out. He decided upon the gown, or at least . . . Well, yes— the gown.

Giuseppe, proprietor of the pension, looked surprised and not altogether pleased when Mr. Hancock danced with his table companion after dinner. The proprietor was talking excitedly with his wife Maria when the two guests came off the balcony out of the Italian moonlight. Maria passed near to them and looked at Mr. Hancock very closely. Especially at his throat.

Giuseppe was still displeased when Mr. Hancock ordered brandy. But Mr. Hancock was very well pleased indeed when the brandy came. The growth of his familiarity with his companion's accent kept even pace with the alcoholic dulling of his perceptions, so that her speech still remained vague but fascinating. The movements of the dance had made her other fascination much more clear to him.

It was in the dark hall that she told him she would leave her door open. He was not quite sure of what she said, but the welcome which his lips and hands received reassured him.

Nor was his assurance shaken when he met Maria at the head of the stairs. But he was puzzled. Even his slight knowledge of Italian sufficed to make clear that she was delivering a physical warning, not a moral reprimand. The morals of her lodgers were none of her affair, she kept saying; or were the repetitions merely within his brain? That was nonsense, but it was what she said. At least he thought so; *la morta* was "death," wasn't it?

He was still puzzled when she went away, and looked curiously at the little gold cross which she had pressed into his hand with such urgent instructions.

Giuseppe and Maria were not puzzled when Mr. Hancock's companion was not in her room the next morning. She was, in fact, nowhere in the pension; and Giuseppe advanced the theory, with which Maria agreed, that she was nowhere in Italy.

They were only slightly puzzled when they found Mr. Hancock's body on her bed. There were no clothes outside his flesh, and no blood inside. Nor was there a trace of blood anywhere in the room.

Although they jointly resolved that even her liberal payments could not induce them to accept Mr. Hancock's companion as a guest again, Maria's conscience felt clear when she found the small gold cross in the hall where Mr. Hancock had obviously tossed it in scorn.

You see, he was not superstitious.

The Tenderizers

It was the Pernod, of course. It must have been the Pernod.

Much though I have come to love that greenish-milky potable gold, I am forced to put the responsibility upon the Pernod, or to believe

Let me first make it clear (to myself) that I am not writing this to tell it to anyone, and above all not for sale and publication. I am simply setting this down to make it all clear to myself *(hypocrite lecteur)* and above all to convince myself that it was the Pernod.

Not when I was drinking the Pernod, certainly. Not there in the bright promenade deck bar with the colored lights behind the bottles and the bartenders playing cribbage with each other between orders and a ship's officer and a girl trying to pick out singable show tunes on the piano. But the Pernod was (well, then, the Pernods were) in me later on that isolated deck in the thick fog when the voice that I should not have recognized

To be sure, there had been queer moments before on the trip—that trip so nicely combining tourism with occasional business with editors and publishers in such a manner as to satisfy the Internal Revenue Service.

There was that room far down in the Paris Opera—Charles Garnier's masterpiece—which so surpasses in opulence and eeriness even *The Phantom of the Opera*. A room that I stumbled on, that nobody seemed to visit during intermissions, a big small room that would have seemed a ballroom in a lesser edifice, where some of the walls were walls and some were mirrors. And I walked toward a mirror and saw myself advancing toward myself and then realized that this could be no mirror. The advancing man resembled me strongly; but I was in a tourist's ordinary best dark suit and he was in white tie and tails, with a suggestion of the past *(la belle epoque?* Garnier's Second Empire?) in his ruffled shirt and elegant sash. I moved toward him, smiling to acknowledge our odd resemblance; and then I was facing myself and it was a mirror and the bell rang and in the second intermission I could not find that room.

And there was that moment in the Wakefield Tower, that part of the Tower of London which houses the Regalia of the Kings and Queens of England. I was marveling at the Stars of Africa and realizing for the first time the true magic of diamonds (which exists in those that only potentates may own) when I felt the beads of a rosary gliding between my fingers. I knew a piercing pain, and as 1 all but lost consciousness, I heard a grating croak of which I could make out only the words ". . . *aspiring blood* . . ." Then I was calmly looking at diamonds again and stepping back to read the plaque stating that tradition says that here the devout Henry VI was slain at his orisons in fourteen blankty-blank. With my ears still feeling the rasp of the words which Shakespeare attributed to his murderer, I prayed for his gentle soul.

And these episodes were without Pernod (brandy at the Opera, tea at the Tower), but there is no denying the Pernod (the Pernods) when I visited, late at night, the sports deck of R.M.S. *Queen Anne* in mid-Atlantic.

The deck was deserted. I like the open decks at night, in any weather save the most drenching; but the average passenger (wisely? I now wonder) huddles by the bar or the dance orchestra or the coffee-and-sandwiches or the bingo.

The deck and I were the nucleus of a cocoon of fog, opaque and almost colorless—white, one might say, in contrast to the soiled fog/smog of a city, but more of an intensely dense absence of color. Absence of form, absence of movement—a nothing that tightly enswathed.

We could be in the midst of a story by William Hope Hodgson, I thought, recalling with a pleasant shudder some of the tales by that master of horror of the sea.

I settled myself in a deck chair. Even with my eyes closed I could sense the fog pressing in, ever narrowing the limits of my little universe.

My first awareness of the other was through my nose. A lifetime of respiratory illnesses has left me with a deficient sense of smell normally roused only by, say, a fine cognac; but this was a smell that even I could notice. Prosaically, it suggested to me a badly refrigerated fish-market—which would have been horror enough for H. P. Lovecraft, who found (almost comically, I once thought) something profoundly horrible in the very notion of fish.

"We could be in the midst of a story by William Hope Hodgson," said a voice that I almost recognized.

I could not see him clearly, though he was sitting in the next deck chair. I started to say, "You took the words—"

"—From the same source as you," he concluded. "They used Hodgson. He was one of the first of us. Still the best, perhaps, on the sea, though I had my own touch in the air."

"Ev!" I exclaimed, and turned to him with that warmth one feels toward a colleague who is a genuine professional.

You will remember Everard Wykeham. (And to whom am I speaking? *Hypocrite écrivain* . . .) Wrote a little for *Weird Tales* back in the Lovecraft days, then went to England and developed quite a reputation in the *Strand* and British *Argosy*. Much good general fiction, including Buchanesque adventure, but what one particularly recalls (and so vividly!) are his horror stories, perfect capsules of grisly suggestion, mostly dealing with the unsuspected and chilling implications, psychological and metaphysical, of man's flight in the air. It was true: in the domain of the horror story, the air was Wykeham's as the sea was Hodgson's; and rarely had I flown without a twinge of grue as I recalled one or another of the Wykeham stories collected as *The Arrow That Flies*.

Wykeham and I had never been intimate; but we had met occasionally at conventions or at publishers' parties and had (I think) liked and respected each other. Now he grunted a reply to my greeting and muttered, "Wish I could remember things better. I—I'm not quite all there. Nor all here either. There's a long speech by the Ghost in *Hamlet* explaining just how and why the hell he got back to . . . well, call it 'earth.' Look it up and take it for read."

"I don't think I've seen you," I said, "since *Playboy* published that beautiful chiller about—"

"I haven't much time." His voice was flat and toneless. "The Ghost puts it better but that's the trouble, you have to say so much and there just isn't time. And *you* don't remember things too damn well either, for that matter."

I paused, and then I made a speech that I have cut out of a large number of manuscripts, by myself and others. I made the half-strangled noise that is indicated by "you" followed by a dash. Like this:

"You—"

I could dimly see a nod. "Yes. Off the *Queen Anne* on her maiden voyage. Never recovered. Oh, they arrange fancy ends for some of us. Look at Ambrose Bierce. And wait till you see what they have cooked up for Ray Bradbury. But look: The glowworm gins to glimmer like the fretful porpentine or something. I have to make this clear."

There was a licorice backwash of Pernod in my mouth. I tried to play it straight. "Make what clear?"

"What they're doing. What they're making *us* do. Can't you see?"

I could see nothing but the cocooning fog and the shape in the next deck chair. In some kind of glimmer against all laws of optics I could sometimes catch a glimpse of the face, and it was not always Everard Wykeham's. The Wilkes Booth tragic mask of Poe was there and the arrogant white mane of Bierce. And hints of other faces, living faces that I knew and loved, the gentle-satyr glint of Theodore Sturgeon, the warm japery of Robert Bloch, the ageless eagerness of Ray Bradbury . . .

"We're all one to them," he/they/something said. "We're what they use. To soften the people up and make them *fear*. You can't really make people fear real things. Look at Britain under bombardment. Oh, they have used killers. They had a good run of fear in London in the 1880's and Cleveland in the 1930's. But mostly they use *us,* the writers, the ones that can suggest the unspeakable, that can put the very essence of fear, like the old boy from Eton, into a bundle of dirty linen."

"They . . ." I said slowly, and thinking of a hundred science fiction stories. "They *live* off of these—these sweats of fear?"

"I don't know. Not for sure. I think it's more like—well, an aperitif, like your Pernod. (No, I'm not mind-reading; I can smell it.) It's something that they . . . *savor.* So they let us have hints and glimpses, just a touch of the way their world impinges on ours. Where time and space are—well, not quite so disciplined as we like to think. And we use these hints and build them and—"

The fog was thicker. So was his speech, almost to being unintelligible. I caught something about the glowworm and the porpentine again, and then something about impinges and the Opera and the Tower and then the deck was silent.

Then it was as if a sudden wind roared about my head and shouted *god help me the damned thing is of such a color nervous very dreadfully nervous I am and have been a negotio perambulante in tenebris oh whistle and I'll come to you peter quint the ceremony of innocence ibi cubavit lamia now we're locked in for the night but who is that on the other side of you?*

The deck was empty. The fog had thinned to admit a moon pouring its fecund gold down on the Danae sea.

I went below.

Sometimes I think I remember words from that thick unintelligibility, words that must have been answers to questions I cannot recall asking.

"Why do we serve them even when we know? (And most of us do know.) There are so many reasons, especially for an author in middle life. The children, medical expenses, maybe the cost of a divorce—who turns down a fast check?"

And:

"Where am I now? Put 'where' in quotes. And 'when.' (See Rodgers and Hart.) And look up that Ghost speech again. And there's something in Matthew, I think. One of the parables—about the unjust steward and how it's a good idea to make friends out of wicked powers. Because . . ."

It was the Pernod. And whatever the—the Pernod said about middle-aged reasons, I shall not sell this story. I checked the parable of the unjust steward.

. . . for they shall receive you into their everlasting dwellings.

They Bite

There was no path, only the almost vertical ascent. Crumbled rock for a few yards, with the roots of sage finding their scanty life in the dry soil. Then jagged outcroppings of crude crags, sometimes with accidental footholds, sometimes with overhanging and untrustworthy branches of greasewood, sometimes with no aid to climbing but the leverage of your muscles and the ingenuity of your balance.

The sage was as drably green as the rock was drably brown. The only color was the occasional rosy spikes of a barrel cactus.

Hugh Tallant swung himself up onto the last pinnacle. It had a deliberate, shaped look about it—a petrified fortress of Lilliputians, a Gibraltar of pygmies. Tallant perched on its battlements and unslung his field glasses.

The desert valley spread below him. The tiny cluster of buildings that was Oasis, the exiguous cluster of palms that gave name to the town and shelter to his own tent and to the shack he was building, the dead-ended highway leading straightforwardly to nothing, the oiled roads diagramming the vacant blocks of an optimistic subdivision.

Tallant saw none of these. His glasses were fixed beyond the oasis and the town of Oasis on the dry lake. The gliders were clear and vivid to him, and the uniformed men busy with them were as sharply and minutely visible as a nest of ants under glass. The training school was more than usually active. One glider in particular, strange to Tallant, seemed the focus of attention. Men would come and examine it and glance back at the older models in comparison.

Only the corner of Tallant's left eye was not preoccupied with the new glider. In that corner something moved, something little and thin and brown as the earth. Too large for a rabbit, much too small for a man. It darted across that corner of vision, and Tallant found gliders oddly hard to concentrate on.

He set down the bifocals and deliberately looked about him. His pinnacle surveyed the narrow, flat area of the crest. Nothing stirred. Nothing stood out against the sage and rock but one barrel of rosy spikes. He took up the glasses again and resumed his observations. When he was done, he methodically entered the results in the little black notebook.

His hand was still white. The desert is cold and often sunless in winter. But it was a firm hand, and as well trained as his eyes, fully capable of recording faithfully the designs and dimensions which they had registered so accurately.

Once his hand slipped, and he had to erase and redraw, leaving a smudge that displeased him. The lean, brown thing had slipped across the edge of his vision again. Going toward the east edge, he would swear, where that set of rocks jutted like the spines on the back of a stegosaur.

Only when his notes were completed did he yield to curiosity, and even then with cynical self-reproach. He was physically tired, for him an unusual state, from this daily climbing and from clearing the ground for his shack-to-be. The eye muscles play odd nervous tricks. There could be nothing behind the stegosaur's armor.

There was nothing. Nothing alive and moving. Only the torn and half-plucked carcass of a bird, which looked as though it had been gnawed by some small animal.

It was halfway down the hill—hill in Western terminology, though anywhere east of the Rockies it would have been considered a sizable mountain—that Tallant again had a glimpse of a moving figure.

But this was no trick of a nervous eye. It was not little nor thin nor brown. It was tall and broad and wore a loud red-and-black lumberjacket. It bellowed, "Tallant!" in a cheerful and lusty voice.

Tallant drew near the man and said, "Hello." He paused and added, "Your advantage, I think."

The man grinned broadly. "Don't know me? Well, I daresay ten years is a long time, and the California desert ain't exactly the Chinese rice fields. How's stuff? Still loaded down with Secrets for Sale?"

Tallant tried desperately not to react to that shot, but he stiffened a little. "Sorry. The prospector getup had me fooled. Good to see you again, Morgan."

The man's eyes narrowed. "Just having my little joke," he smiled. "Of course you wouldn't have no serious reason for mountain climbing around a glider school, now, would you? And you'd kind of need field glasses to keep an eye on the pretty birdies."

"I'm out here for my health." Tallant's voice sounded unnatural even to himself.

"Sure, sure. You were always in it for your health. And come to think of it, my own health ain't been none too good lately. I've got me a little cabin way to hell-and-gone around here, and I do me a little prospecting now and then. And somehow it just strikes me, Tallant, like maybe I hit a pretty good lode today."

"Nonsense, old man. You can see—"

"I'd sure hate to tell any of them Army men out at the field some of the stories I know about China and the kind of men I used to know out there. Wouldn't cotton to them stories a bit, the Army wouldn't. But if I was to have a drink too many and get talkative-like—"

"Tell you what," Tallant suggested brusquely. "It's getting near sunset now, and my tent's chilly for evening visits. But drop around in the morning and we'll talk over old times. Is rum still your tipple?"

"Sure is. Kind of expensive now, you understand—"

"I'll lay some in. You can find the place easily—over by the oasis. And we ... we might be able to talk about your prospecting, too."

Tallant's thin lips were set firm as he walked away.

The bartender opened a bottle of beer and plunked it on the damp-circled counter. "That'll be twenty cents," he said, then added as an afterthought, "Want a glass? Sometimes tourists do."

Tallant looked at the others sitting at the counter—the red-eyed and unshaven old man, the flight sergeant unhappily drinking a Coke—it was after Army hours for beer—the young man with the long, dirty trench coat and the pipe and the new-looking brown beard—and saw no glasses. "I guess I won't be a tourist," he decided.

This was the first time Tallant had had a chance to visit the Desert Sport Spot. It was as well to be seen around in a community. Otherwise people begin to wonder and say, "Who is that man out by the oasis? Why don't you ever see him anyplace?"

The Sport Spot was quiet that night. The four of them at the counter, two Army boys shooting pool, and a half-dozen of the local men gathered about a round poker table, soberly and wordlessly cleaning a construction worker whose mind seemed more on his beer than on his cards.

"You just passing through?" the bartender asked sociably.

Tallant shook his head. "I'm moving in. When the Army turned me down for my lungs, I decided I better do something about it. Heard so much about your climate here I thought I might as well try it."

"Sure thing," the bartender nodded. "You take up until they started this glider school, just about every other guy you meet in the desert is here for his health. Me, I had sinus, and look at me now. It's the air."

Tallant breathed the atmosphere of smoke and beer suds, but did not smile. "I'm looking forward to miracles."

"You'll get 'em. Whereabouts you staying?"

"Over that way a bit. The agent called it 'the old Carker place.'"

Tallant felt the curious listening silence and frowned. The bartender had started to speak and then thought better of it. The young man with the beard looked at him oddly. The old man fixed him with red and watery eyes that had a faded glint of pity in them. For a moment, Tallant felt a chill that had nothing to do with the night air of the desert.

The old man drank his beer in quick gulps and frowned as though trying to formulate a sentence. At last he wiped beer from his bristly lips and said, "You wasn't aiming to stay in the adobe, was you?"

"No. It's pretty much gone to pieces. Easier to rig me up a little shack than try to make the adobe livable. Meanwhile, I've got a tent."

"That's all right, then, mebbe. But mind you don't go poking around that there adobe."

"I don't think I'm apt to. But why not? Want another beer?"

The old man shook his head reluctantly and slid from his stool to the ground. "No thanks. I don't rightly know as I—"

"Yes?"

"Nothing. Thanks all the same." He turned and shuffled to the door.

Tallant smiled. "But why should I stay clear of the adobe?" he called after him.

The old man mumbled.

"What?"

"They bite," said the old man, and went out shivering into the night.

The bartender was back at his post. "I'm glad he didn't take that beer you offered him," he said. "Along about this time in the evening I have to stop serving him. For once he had the sense to quit."

Tallant pushed his own empty bottle forward. "I hope I didn't frighten him away."

"Frighten? Well, mister, I think maybe that's just what you did do. He didn't want beer that sort of came, like you might say, from the old Carker place. Some of the old-timers here, they're funny that way."

Tallant grinned. "Is it haunted?"

"Not what you'd call haunted, no. No ghosts there that I ever heard of." He wiped the counter with a cloth and seemed to wipe the subject away with it.

The flight sergeant pushed his Coke bottle away, hunted in his pocket for nickels, and went over to the pinball machine. The young man with the beard slid onto his vacant stool. "Hope old Jake didn't worry you," he said.

Tallant laughed. "I suppose every town has its deserted homestead with a grisly tradition. But this sounds a little different. No ghosts, and they bite. Do you know anything about it?"

"A little," the young man said seriously. "A little. Just enough to—"

Tallant was curious. "Have one on me and tell me about it."

The flight sergeant swore bitterly at the machine.

Beer gurgled through the beard. "You see," the young man began, "the desert's so big you can't be alone in it. Ever notice that? It's all empty and there's nothing in sight but, there's always something moving over there where you can't quite see it. It's something very dry and thin and brown, only when you look around it isn't there. Ever see it?"

"Optical fatigue—" Tallant began.

"Sure. I know. Every man to his own legend. There isn't a tribe of Indians hasn't got some way of accounting for it. You've heard of the Watchers? And the twentieth-century white man comes along, and it's optical fatigue. Only in the nineteenth century things weren't quite the same, and there were the Carkers."

"You've got a special localized legend?"

"Call it that. You glimpse things out of the corner of your mind, same like you glimpse lean, dry things out of the corner of your eye. You encase 'em in solid circumstance and they're not so bad. That is known as the Growth of Legend. The Folk Mind in Action. You take the Carkers and the things you don't quite see and you put 'em together. And they bite."

Tallant wondered how long that beard had been absorbing beer. "And what were the Carkers?" he prompted politely.

"Ever hear of Sawney Bean? Scotland—reign of James First, or maybe the Sixth, though I think Roughead's wrong on that for once. Or let's be more modern—ever hear of the Benders? Kansas in the 1870s? No? Ever hear of Procrustes? Or Polyphemus? Or Fee-fi-fo-fum?

"There are ogres, you know. They're no legend. They're fact, they are. The inn where nine guests left for every ten that arrived, the mountain cabin that sheltered travelers from the snow, sheltered them all winter till the melting spring uncovered their bones, the lonely stretches of road that so many passengers traveled halfway—you'll find 'em everywhere. All over Europe and pretty much in this country too before communications became what they are. Profitable business. And it wasn't just the profit. The Benders made money, sure; but that wasn't why they killed all their victims as carefully as a kosher butcher. Sawney Bean got so he didn't give a damm about the profit; he just needed to lay in more meat for the winter.

"And think of the chances you'd have at an oasis."

"So these Carkers of yours were, as you call them, ogres?"

"Carkers, ogres—maybe they were Benders. The Benders were never seen alive, you know, after the townspeople found those curiously butchered bones. There's a rumor they got this far west. And the time checks pretty well. There wasn't any town here in the eighties. Just a couple of Indian families, last of a dying tribe living on at the oasis. They vanished after the Carkers moved in. That's not so surprising. The white race is a sort of super-ogre, anyway. Nobody worried about them. But they used to worry about why so many travelers never got across this stretch of desert. The travelers used to stop over at the Carkers', you see, and somehow they often never got any farther. Their wagons'd be found maybe fifteen miles beyond in the desert. Sometimes they found the bones, too, parched and white. Gnawed-looking, they said sometimes."

"And nobody ever did anything about these Carkers?"

"Oh, sure. We didn't have King James Sixth—only I still think it was First—to ride up on a great white horse for a gesture, but twice Army detachments came here and wiped them all out."

"Twice? One wiping-out would do for most families." Tallant smiled.

"Uh-uh. That was no slip. They wiped out the Carkers twice because, you see, once didn't do any good. They wiped 'em out and still travelers vanished and still there were gnawed bones. So they wiped 'em out again. After that they gave up, and people detoured the oasis. It made a longer, harder trip, but after all—"

Tallant laughed. "You mean to say these Carkers were immortal?"

"I don't know about immortal. They somehow just didn't die very easy. Maybe, if they were the Benders—and I sort of like to think they were—they learned a little more about what they were doing out here on the desert. Maybe they put together what the Indians knew and what they knew, and it worked. Maybe Whatever they made their sacrifices to understood them better out here than in Kansas."

"And what's become of them—aside from seeing them out of the corner of the eye?"

"There's forty years between the last of the Carker history and this new settlement at the oasis. And people won't talk much about what they learned here in the first year or so. Only that they stay away from that old Carker adobe. They tell some stories— The priest says he was sitting in the confessional one hot Saturday afternoon and thought he heard a penitent come in. He waited a long time and finally lifted the gauze to see was anybody there. Something was there, and it bit. He's got three fingers on his right hand now, which looks funny as hell when he gives a benediction."

Tallant pushed their two bottles toward the bartender. "That yarn, my young friend, has earned another beer. How about it, bartender? Is he always cheerful like this, or is this just something he's improvised for my benefit?"

The bartender set out the fresh bottles with great solemnity. "Me, I wouldn't've told you all that myself, but then, he's a stranger too and maybe don't feel the same way we do here. For him it's just a story."

"It's more comfortable that way," said the young man with the beard, and he took a firm hold on his beer bottle.

"But as long as you've heard that much," said the bartender, "you might as well— It was last winter, when we had that cold spell. You heard funny stories that winter. Wolves coming into prospectors' cabins just to warm up. Well, business wasn't so good. We don't have a license for hard liquor, and the boys don't drink much beer when it's that cold. But they used to come in anyway because we've got that big oil burner.

"So one night there's a bunch of 'em in here—old Jake was here, that you was talking to, and his dog Jigger—and I think I hear somebody else come in. The door creaks a little. But I don't see nobody, and the poker game's going, and we're talking just like we're talking now, and all of a sudden I hear a kind of a noise like *crack!* over there in that corner behind the juke box near the burner.

"I go over to see what goes and it gets away before I can see it very good. But it was little and thin and it didn't have no clothes on. It must've been damned cold that winter."

"And what was the cracking noise?" Tallant asked dutifully.

"That? That was a bone. It must've strangled Jigger without any noise. He was a little dog. It ate most of the flesh, and if it hadn't cracked the bone for the marrow it could've finished. You can still see the spots over there. The blood never did come out."

There had been silence all through the story. Now suddenly all hell broke loose. The flight sergeant let out a splendid yell and began pointing excitedly at the pinball machine and yelling for his payoff. The construction worker dramatically deserted the poker game, knocking his chair over in the process, and announced lugubriously that these guys here had their own rules, see?

Any atmosphere of Carker-inspired horror was dissipated. Tallant whistled as he walked over to put a nickel in the jukebox. He glanced casually at the floor. Yes, there was a stain, for what that was worth.

He smiled cheerfully and felt rather grateful to the Carkers. They were going to solve his blackmail problem very neatly.

Tallant dreamed of power that night. It was a common dream with him. He was a ruler of the new American Corporate State that would follow the war; and he said to this man, "Come!" and he came, and to that man, "Go!" and he went, and to his servants, "Do this!" and they did it.

Then the young man with the beard was standing before him, and the dirty trench coat was like the robes of an ancient prophet. And the young man said, "You see yourself riding high, don't you? Riding the crest of the wave—the Wave of the Future, you call it. But there's a deep, dark undertow that you don't see, and that's a part of the Past. And the Present and even your Future. There is evil in mankind that is blacker even than your evil, and infinitely more ancient."

And there was something in the shadows behind the young man, something little and lean and brown.

Tallant's dream did not disturb him the following morning. Nor did the thought of the approaching interview with Morgan. He fried his bacon and eggs and devoured them cheerfully. The wind had died down for a change, and the sun was warm enough so that he could strip to the waist while he cleared land for his shack. His machete glinted brilliantly as it swung through the air and struck at the roots of the brush.

When Morgan arrived his full face was red and sweating.

"It's cool over there in the shade of the adobe," Tallant suggested. "We'll be more comfortable." And in the comfortable shade of the adobe he swung the machete once and clove Morgan's full, red, sweating face in two.

It was so simple. It took less effort than uprooting a clump of sage. And it was so safe. Morgan lived in a cabin way to hell-and-gone and was often away on prospecting trips. No one would notice his absence for months, if then. No one had any reason to connect him with Tallant. And no one in Oasis would hunt for him in the Carker-haunted adobe.

The body was heavy, and the blood dripped warm on Tallant's bare skin. With relief he dumped what had been Morgan on the floor of the adobe. There were no boards, no flooring. Just the earth. Hard, but not too hard to dig a grave in. And no one was likely to come poking around in this taboo territory to notice the grave. Let a year or so go by, and the grave and the bones it contained would be attributed to the Carkers.

The corner of Tallant's eye bothered him again. Deliberately he looked about the interior of the adobe.

The little furniture was crude and heavy, with no attempt to smooth down the strokes of the ax. It was held together with wooden pegs or half-rotted thongs. There were age-old cinders in the fireplace, and the dusty shards of a cooking jar among them.

And there was a deeply hollowed stone, covered with stains that might have been rust, if stone rusted. Behind it was a tiny figure, clumsily fashioned of clay and sticks. It was something like a man and something like a lizard, and something like the things that flit across the corner of the eye.

Curious now, Tallant peered about further. He penetrated to the corner that the one unglassed window lighted but dimly. And there he let out a little choking gasp. For a moment he was rigid with horror. Then he smiled and all but laughed aloud.

This explained everything. Some curious individual had seen this, and from his accounts had burgeoned the whole legend. The Carkers had indeed learned something from the Indians, but that secret was the art of embalming.

It was a perfect mummy. Either the Indian art had shrunk bodies, or this was that of a ten-year-old boy. There was no flesh. Only skin and bone and taut, dry stretches of tendon between. The eyelids were closed; the sockets looked hollow under them. The nose was sunken and almost lost. The scant lips were tightly curled back from the long and very white teeth, which stood forth all the more brilliantly against the deep-brown skin.

It was a curious little trove, this mummy. Tallant was already calculating the chances for raising a decent sum of money from an interested anthropologist—murder can produce such delightfully profitable chance by-products—when he noticed the infinitesimal rise and fall of the chest.

The Carker was not dead. It was sleeping.

Tallant did not dare stop to think beyond the instant. This was no time to pause to consider if such things were possible in a well-ordered world. It was no time to reflect on the disposal of the body of Morgan. It was a time to snatch up your machete and get out of there.

But in the doorway he halted. There, coming across the desert, heading for the adobe, clearly seen this time, was another—a female.

He made an involuntary gesture of indecision. The blade of the machete clanged ringingly against the adobe wall. He heard the dry shuffling of a roused sleeper behind him.

He turned fully now, the machete raised. Dispose of this nearer one first, then face the female. There was no room even for terror in his thoughts, only for action.

The lean brown shape darted at him avidly. He moved lightly away and stood poised for its second charge. It shot forward again. He took one step back, machete arm raised, and fell headlong over the corpse of Morgan. Before he could rise, the thin thing was upon him. Its sharp teeth had met through the palm of his left hand.

The machete moved swiftly. The thin dry body fell headless to the floor. There was no blood.

The grip of the teeth did not relax. Pain coursed up Tallant's left arm—a sharper, more bitter pain than you would expect from the bite. Almost as though venom—

He dropped the machete, and his strong white hand plucked and twisted at the dry brown lips. The teeth stayed clenched, unrelaxing. He sat bracing his back against the wall and gripped the head between his knees. He pulled. His flesh ripped, and blood formed dusty clots on the dirt floor. But the bite was firm.

His world had become reduced now to that hand and that head. Nothing outside mattered. He must free himself. He raised his aching arm to his face, and with his own teeth he tore at that unrelenting grip. The dry flesh crumbled away in desert dust, but the teeth were locked fast. He tore his lip against their white keenness, and tasted in his mouth the sweetness of blood and something else.

He staggered to his feet again. He knew what he must do. Later he could use cautery, a tourniquet, see a doctor with a story about a Gila monster—their heads grip too, don't they?—but he knew what he must do now.

He raised the machete and struck again.

His white hand lay on the brown floor, gripped by the white teeth in the brown face. He propped himself against the adobe wall, momentarily unable to move. His open wrist hung over the deeply hollowed stone. His blood and his strength and his life poured out before the little figure of sticks and clay.

The female stood in the doorway now, the sun bright on her thin brownness. She did not move. He knew that she was waiting for the hollow stone to fill.

The Model of a Science Fiction Editor

I am the very model of a modern s f editor.
My publisher is happy, as is each and every creditor.
I know the market trends and how to please the newsstand pur-
    chaser;
With agents and name authors my relations can't be courteouser.
I've a clever knack of finding out what newsmen want to write about
And seeing that their stories spread my name in black and white
    about.
I've a colleague to be blamed for the unpleasant sides of bossery,
And I know the masses never quite get tired of flying saucery.
In short, in matters monetary, social, and promotional,
I am the very model of a pro s f devotional.

I've a pretty taste in literature and know the trends historical
From Plato down to Bradbury in order categorical.
I can tell a warp in space from one that's purely in chronology,
And every BEM I publish has his own strange teratology.
I make my writers stress the small scale human problems solely
Because the sales are better and you might be picked by Foley.
I can stump the highbrow critics with allusions to Caractacus,
A ploy that I've perfected by a plentitude of practicus.
In short, in matters cultural, esthetical and liter'y
I run the very model of a true s f outfittery.

Now if I had a smattering of knowledge scientifical,
If I were certain "terrene" didn't simply mean "terrifical,"
If I could tell a proton from a neutron or a neuron,
How your weight on Mars will vary from the planet that now
    you're on,
If I knew enough to know why Velikovsky is nonsensic
And why too close a Shaver can make even hardened fen sick,
If I'd read what men have learned from other planets' spectranalysis,
In short, if I could tell the future Wonderland from Alice's,
I might in logic, insight and inspired extrapolation
Produce the very model of ideal s f creation.

We Print the Truth

"All right, then, tell me this: If God can do anything—" Jake Willis cleared his throat and paused, preparatory to delivering the real clincher.

The old man with the scraggly beard snorted and took another shot of applejack. "—can He make a weight so heavy He can't lift it? We know that one, Jake, and it's nonsense. It's like who wakes the bugler, or who shaves the barber, or how many angels can dance how many sarabands on the point of a pin. It's just playing games. It takes a village atheist to beat a scholastic disputant at pure verbal hogwash. Have a drink."

Jake Willis glared. "I'd sooner be the village atheist," he said flatly, "than the town drunkard. You know I don't drink." He cast a further sidewise glare at the little glass in Father Byrne's hand, as though the priest were only a step from the post of town drunkard himself.

"You're an ascetic without mysticism, Jake, and there's no excuse for it. Better be like me: a mystic without ary a trace of asceticism. More fun."

"Stop heckling him, Luke," Father Byrne put in quietly. "Let's hear what if God can do anything."

Lucretius Sellers grunted and became silent. MacVeagh said, "Go ahead, Jake," and Chief Hanby nodded.

They don't have a cracker barrel in Grover, but they still have a hot-stove league. It meets pretty regularly in the back room of the *Sentinel*. Oh, once in a while someplace else. On a dull night in the police station they may begin to flock around Chief Hanby, or maybe even sometimes they get together with Father Byrne at the parish house. But mostly it's at the *Sentinel*.

There's lots of spare time around a weekly paper, even with the increase in job printing that's come from all the forms and stuff they use out at the Hitchcock plant. And Editor John MacVeagh likes to talk, so it's natural for him to gather around him all the others that like to talk too. It started when Luke Sellers was a printer, before he resigned to take up drinking as a career.

The talk's apt to be about anything. Father Byrne talks music mostly; it's safer than his own job. With John MacVeagh and Chief Hanby it's shop talk: news and crime—not that there's much of either in Grover, or wasn't up to this evening you're reading about.

But sometime in the evening it's sure to get around to Is there a God? And if so why doesn't He— Especially when Jake Willis is there. Jake's the undertaker and the coroner. He says, or used to say then, that when he's through with them, he knows they're going to stay dead, and that's enough for him.

So here Jake had built up to his usual poser again. Only this time it wasn't the weight that Omnipotence couldn't lift. Everybody was pretty tired of that. It was, "If God can do anything, why doesn't he stop the war?"

"For once, Jake, you've got something," said John MacVeagh. "I know the problem of Evil is the great old insoluble problem; but Evil on a scale like this begins to get you. From an Old Testament God, maybe yes; but it's hard to believe in the Christian God of love and kindness permitting all this mass slaughter and devastation and cruelty."

"We just don't know," Chief Hanby said slowly. "We don't understand. 'For my thoughts are not your thoughts, neither are your ways my ways, saith the Lord. For as the Heavens are higher than the earth, so are my ways higher than your ways, and my thoughts than your thoughts.' Isaiah, fifty-five, eight and nine. We just don't understand."

"Uh-uh, Chief," MacVeagh shook his head. "That won't wash. That's the easy way out. The one thing we've got to know and understand about God is that He loves good and despises evil, which I'll bet there's a text for, only I wouldn't know."

"He loves truth," said Chief Hanby. "We don't know if His truth is our 'good.' "

Lucretius Sellers refilled his glass. "If the Romans thought there was truth in wine, they should've known about applejack. But what do you say, Father?"

Father Byrne sipped and smiled. "It's presumptuous to try to unravel the divine motives. Isaiah and the Chief are right: His thoughts are not our thoughts. But still I think we can understand the answer to Jake's question. If you were God—"

They never heard the end to this daring assumption; not that night, anyway. For just then was when Philip Rogers burst in. He was always a little on the pale side—thin, too, only the word the girls used for it was "slim," and they liked the pallor, too. Thought it made him look "interesting," with those clean, sharp features and those long dark eyelashes. Even Laura Hitchcock liked the features and the lashes and the pallor. Ever since she read about Byron in high school.

But the girls never saw him looking as pale as this, and they wouldn't have liked it. Laura, now, might have screamed at the sight of him. It isn't right, it isn't natural for the human skin to get that pale—as though a patriotic vampire had lifted your whole stock of blood for the plasma drive.

He fumbled around with noises for almost a minute before he found words. The men were silent. Abstract problems of evil didn't seem so important when you had concrete evidence of some kind of evil right here before you. Only evil could drain blood like that.

Finally one of his choking glurks sounded like a word. The word was "Chief!"

Chief Hanby got up. "Yes, Phil? What's the matter?"

Wordlessly, Luke Sellers handed over the bottle of applejack. It was a pretty noble gesture. There were only about two drinks left, and Phil Rogers took them both in one swallow.

"I thought you'd be over here. Chief," he managed to say. "You've got to come. Quick. Out to Aunt Agnes'."

"What's the matter out there? Burglary?" Chief Hanby asked with an optimism he didn't feel.

"Maybe. I don't know. I didn't look. I couldn't. All that blood— Look. Even on my trousers where I bent down— I don't know why. Any fool could see she was dead—"

"Your aunt?" Chief Hanby gasped. Then the men were silent. They kept their eyes away from the young man with blood on his trousers and none in his face. Father Byrne said something softly to himself and to his God. It was a good thirty seconds before the professional aspects of this news began to strike them.

"You mean murder?" Chief Hanby demanded. Nothing like this had ever happened in Grover before. Murder of H. A. Hitchcock's own sister! "Come on, boy. We won't waste any time."

John MacVeagh's eyes were alight. "No objections to the press on your heels, Chief? I'll be with you as soon as I see Whalen."

Hanby nodded. "Meet you there, Johnny."

Father Byrne said, "I know your aunt never quite approved of me or my church, Philip. But perhaps she won't mind too much if I say a mass for her in the morning."

Jake Willis said nothing, but his eyes gleamed with interest. It was hard to tell whether the coroner or the undertaker in him was more stirred by the prospect.

Lucretius Sellers headed for the door. "As the only man here without a professional interest in death, I bid you boys a good night." He laid his hand on the pale young man's arm and squeezed gently. "Sorry, Phil."

Father Byrne was the last to leave, and Molly bumped into him in the doorway. She returned his greeting hastily and turned to John MacVeagh, every inch of her plump body trembling with excitement. "What's happening, boss? What goes? It must be something terrific to break up the bull session this early."

MacVeagh was puffing his pipe faster and hotter than was good for it. "I'll say something's happened, Molly. Agnes Rogers has been killed. Murdered."

"Whee!" Molly yelled. "Stop the presses! Is that a story! Is that a— Only you can't stop the presses when we don't come out till Friday, can you?"

"I've got to talk to Whalen a minute—and about that very thing—and then I'll be off hotfooting it after the chief. It's the first local news in three years that's rated an extra, and it's going to get one."

"Wonderful!" Her voice changed sharply. "The poor crazy old woman— We're vultures, that's what we are—"

"Don't be melodramatically moral, Molly. It's our job. There have to be . . . well, vultures; and that's us. Now let me talk to Whalen, and I'll—"

"Boss?"

"Uh-huh?"

"Boss, I've been a good girl Friday, haven't I? I keep all the job orders straight and I never make a mistake about who's just been to the city and who's got relatives staying with them and whose strawberry jam won the prize at the Fair—"

"Sure, sure. But look, Molly—"

"And when you had that hangover last Thursday and I fed you tomato juice all morning and beer all afternoon and we got the paper out OK, you said you'd do anything for me, didn't you?"

"Sure. But—"

"All right. Then you stay here and let me cover this murder."

"That's absurd. It's my job to—"

"If you know how much I want to turn out some copy that isn't about visiting and strawberry jam— And besides, this'll be all tied up with the Hitchcocks. Maybe even Laura'll be there. And when you're . . . well, involved a little with people, how can you be a good reporter? Me, I don't give a damn about Hitchcocks. But with you, maybe you'd be in a spot where you'd have to be either a lousy reporter or a lousy friend."

MacVeagh grinned. "As usual, Friday, you make sense. Go on. Get out there and bring me back the best story the *Sentinel* ever printed. Go ahead. Git."

"Gee, boss—" Molly groped for words, but all she found was another and even more heartfelt *"Gee—"* Then she was gone.

MacVeagh smiled to himself. Swell person, Molly. He'd be lost without her. Grand wife for some man, if he liked them a little on the plump side. If, for instance, he had never seen the superb slim body of Laura Hitchcock—

But thoughts of Laura now would only get in the way. He'd have to see her tomorrow. Offer his condolences on the death of her aunt. Perhaps in comforting her distress—

Though it would be difficult, and even unconvincing, to display too much grief at Agnes Rogers' death. She had been Grover's great eccentric, a figure of fun, liked well enough, in a disrespectful way, but hardly loved. A wealthy widow— she held an interest in the Hitchcock plant second only to H. A.'s own—she had let her fortune take care of itself—and of her—while she indulged in a frantic crackpot quest for the Ultimate Religious Truth. At least once a year she would proclaim that she had found it, and her house would be filled with the long-robed disciples of the Church of the Eleven Apostles—which claimed that the election by lot of Matthias had been fraudulent and invalidated the apostolic succession of all other churches; or the sharp-eyed, businesslike emissaries of Christoid Thought—which seemed to preach the Gospel according to St. Dale.

It was hard to take Agnes Rogers' death too seriously. But that ultimate seriousness transfigures, at least for the moment, the most ludicrous of individuals.

Whalen was reading when John MacVeagh entered his cubbyhole off the printing room. One of those books that no one, not even Father Byrne, had ever recognized the letters of. It made MacVeagh realize again how little he knew of this last survival of the race of tramp printers, who came out of nowhere to do good work and vanish back into nowhere.

Brownies, he thought. With whiskey in their saucers instead of milk.

Not that Whalen looked like any brownie. He was taller than MacVeagh himself, and thinner than Phil Rogers. The funniest thing about him was that when you called up a memory image of him, you saw him with a beard. He didn't have any, but there was something about the thin long nose, the bright deepset eyes— Anyway, you saw a beard.

You could almost see it now, in the half-light outside the circle that shone on the unknown alphabet. He looked up as MacVeagh came in and said, "John. Good. I wanted to see you."

MacVeagh had never had a printer before who called him by his formal first name. A few had ventured on "Johnny," Luke Sellers among them, but never "John." And still, whatever came from Whalen sounded right.

"We've got work to do, Whalen. We're going to bring out an extra tomorrow. This town's gone and busted loose with the best story in years, and it's up to us to—"

"I'm sorry, John," Whalen said gravely. His voice was the deepest MacVeagh had ever heard in ordinary speech. "I'm leaving tonight."

"Leaving—" MacVeagh was almost speechless. Granted that tramp printers were unpredictable; still after an announcement such as he'd just made—

"I must, John. No man is master of his own movements. I must go, and tonight. That is why I wished to see you. I want to know your wish."

"My wish? But look, Whalen: We've got work to do. We've got to—"

"I must go." It was said so simply and sincerely that it stood as absolute fact, as irrevocable as it was incomprehensible. "You've been a good employer, John. Good employers have a wish when I go. I'll give you time to think about it; never make wishes hastily."

"But I— Look, Whalen. I've never seen you drink, but I've never known a printer that didn't. You're babbling. Sleep it off, and in the morning we'll talk about leaving."

"You never did get my name straight, John," Whalen went on. "It was understandable in all that confusion the day you hired me after Luke Sellers had retired. But Whalen is only my first name. I'm really Whalen Smith. And it isn't quite Whalen—"

"What difference does that make?"

"You still don't understand? You don't see how some of us had to take up other trades with the times? When horses went and you still wanted to work with metal, as an individual worker and not an ant on an assembly line— So you don't believe I can grant your wish, John?"

"Of course not. Wishes—"

"Look at the book, John."

MacVeagh looked. He read:

> At this point in the debate His Majesty waxed exceeding wroth and smote the great oaken table with a mighty oath. "Nay," he swore, "all of our powers they shall not take from us. We will sign the compact, but we will not relinquish all. For unto us and our loyal servitors must remain—"

"So what?" he said. "Fairy tales?"

Whalen Smith smiled. "Exactly. The annals of the court of His Majesty King Oberon."

"Which proves what?"

"You read it, didn't you? I gave you the eyes to read—"

John MacVeagh looked back at the book. He had no great oaken table to smite, but he swore a mighty oath. For the characters were again strange and illegible.

"I can grant your wish, John," said Whalen Smith with quiet assurance.

The front doorbell jangled.

"I'll think about it," said MacVeagh confusedly. "I'll let you know—"

"Before midnight, John. I must be gone then," said the printer.

Even an outsider to Grover would have guessed that the man waiting in the office was H. A. Hitchcock. He was obviously a man of national importance, from the polished tips of his shoes to the equally polished top of his head. He was well preserved and as proud of his figure as he was of his daughter's or his accountant's; but he somehow bulked as large as though he weighed two hundred. The top of his head was gleaming with unusual luster at the moment, and his cheeks were red. "Sit down, MacVeagh," he said, as authoritatively as though this was his own office.

John MacVeagh sat down, said, "Yes, Mr. Hitchcock?" and waited.

"Terrible thing," Mr. Hitchcock sputtered. "Terrible. Poor Agnes— Some passing tramp, no doubt."

"Probably," John agreed. Inhabitants of Grover were hard to picture as murderers. "Anything taken?"

"Jewelry from the dressing table. Loose cash. Didn't find the wall safe, fortunately. Chief Hanby's quite satisfied. Must have been a tramp. Sent out a warning to state highway police."

"That was wise." He wondered why H. A. Hitchcock had bothered to come here just for this. Molly would bring it to him shortly. He felt a minor twinge of regret—passing tramps aren't good copy, even when their victim is a magnate's sister.

"Hanby's satisfied," Mr. Hitchcock went on. "You understand that?"

"Of course."

"So I don't want you or your girl reporter questioning him and stirring up a lot of confusion. No point to it."

"If the chief's satisfied, we aren't apt to shake him."

"And I don't want any huggermugger. I know you newspapermen. Anything for a story. Look at the way the press associations treated that strike. What happened? Nothing. Just a little necessary discipline. And you'd think it was a massacre. So I want a soft pedal on poor Agnes' death. You understand? Just a few paragraphs—mysterious marauder—you know."

"It looks," said MacVeagh ruefully, "as though that was all it was going to be worth."

"No use mentioning that Philip and Laura were in the house. Matter of fact, so was I. We didn't see anything. She'd gone upstairs. No point to our evidence. Leave us out of it."

MacVeagh looked up with fresh interest. "All of you there? All of you downstairs and a passing tramp invades the upstairs and gets away with—"

"Damn clever, some of these criminals. Know the ropes. If I'd laid my hands on the— Well, that won't bring Agnes back to life. Neither will a scare story. Had enough unfavorable publicity lately. So keep it quiet. Don't trust that reporter of yours; don't know what wild yarns she might bring back to you. Thought I'd get it all straight for you."

"Uh-huh." MacVeagh nodded abstractedly. "You were all together downstairs, you and Laura and Philip?"

"Yes," said Mr. Hitchcock. He didn't hesitate, but MacVeagh sensed a lie.

"Hm-m-m," was all he said.

"Don't you believe me? Ask Laura. Ask Philip."

"I intend to," said John MacVeagh quietly.

Mr. Hitchcock opened his mouth and stared. "There's no need for that, young man. No need at all. Any necessary facts you can get from me. I'd sooner you didn't bother my daughter or my nephew or the chief. They have enough trouble."

MacVeagh rose from behind his desk. "There's been a murder," he said slowly. "The people of Grover want to know the truth. Wherever there's an attempt to cover up, you can be pretty sure that there's something to cover. Whatever it is, the *Sentinel*'s going to print it. Good night, Mr. Hitchcock."

With the full realization of what MacVeagh meant, Mr. Hitchcock stopped spluttering. There was nothing of the turkey cock about him now. He was quiet and deadly as he said, "I'll talk to Mr. Manson tomorrow."

"Sorry to disappoint you. My debt to Manson's bank was paid off last month. We haven't been doing badly since the influx of your workers doubled our circulation."

"And I think that our plant's printing will be more efficiently and economically handled in the city."

"As you wish. We can make out without it." He hoped he sounded more convincing than he felt.

"And you understand that my daughter will hardly be interested in seeing you after this?"

"I understand. You understand, too, that her refusal to see the press might easily be misconstrued under the circumstances?"

Mr. Hitchcock said nothing. He did not even glare. He turned and walked out of the room, closing the door gently. His quiet exit was more effectively threatening than any blustering and slamming could have been.

MacVeagh stood by the desk a moment and thought about Rubicons and stuff. His eyes were hard and his lips firmly set when he looked up as Whalen entered.

"It's almost midnight," the old printer said.

MacVeagh grabbed the phone. "Two three two," he said. "You're still bound to walk out on me, Whalen?"

"Needs must, John."

"OK. I can make out without you. I can make out without H. A. Hitchcock and his— Hello? Mrs. Belden? . . . MacVeagh speaking. Look, I'm sorry to wake you up at this hour, but could you go up and get Luke Sellers out of bed and tell him I want him over here right away? It's important . . . Thanks." He hung up. "Between us, Molly and I can whip Luke back into some sort of shape as a printer. We'll make out."

"Good, John. I should be sorry to inconvenience you. And have you thought of your wish?"

MacVeagh grinned. "I've had more important things on my mind, Whalen.

Go run along now. I'm sorry to lose you; you know that. And I wish you luck, whatever it is you're up to. Goodbye."

"Please, John." The old man's deep voice was earnest. "I do not wish you to lose what is rightfully yours. What is your wish? If you need money, if you need love—"

MacVeagh thumped his desk. "I've got a wish, all right. And it's not love nor money. I've got a paper and I've got a debt to that paper and its readers. What happened tonight'll happen again. It's bound to. And sometime I may not have the strength to fight it, God help me. So I've got a wish."

"Yes, John?"

"Did you ever look at our masthead? Sometimes you can see things so often that you never really see them. But look at that masthead. It's got a slogan on it, under where it says 'Grover Sentinel.' Old Jonathan Minter put that slogan there, and that slogan was the first words he ever spoke to me when he took me on here. He was a great old man, and I've got a debt to him too, and to his slogan.

"Do you know what a slogan really means? It doesn't mean a come-on, a bait. It doesn't mean Eat Wootsy-Tootsie and Watch Your Hair Curl. It means a rallying call, a battle cry."

"I know, John."

"And that's what this slogan is, the *Sentinel*'s battle cry: *'We print the truth.'* So this is my wish, and if anybody had a stack of Bibles handy I'd swear to it on them: May the *Sentinel* never depart from that slogan. May that slogan itself be true, in the fullest meaning of truth. May there never be lies or suppression or evasions in the *Sentinel,* because always and forever *we print the truth.*"

It was impossible to see what Whalen Smith did with his hands. They moved too nimbly. For a moment it seemed as though their intricate pattern remained glowing in the air. Then it was gone, and Whalen said, "I have never granted a nobler wish. Nor," he added, "a more dangerous one."

He was gone before MacVeagh could ask what he meant.

II

Wednesday's extra of the Grover *Sentinel* carried the full, uncensored story of the murder of Agnes Rogers, and a fine job Molly had done of it. It carried some filling matter too, of course—much of it mats from the syndicate—eked out with local items from the spindles, like the announcement of Old Man Herkimer's funeral and the secretary's report of the meeting of the Ladies' Aid at Mrs. Warren's.

There was no way of telling that one of those local items was infinitely more important to the future of John MacVeagh and of Grover itself than the front-page story.

MacVeagh woke up around two on Wednesday afternoon. They'd worked all night on the extra, he and Molly and Luke. He'd never thought at the time to wonder where the coffee came from that kept them going; he realized now it must have been Molly who supplied it.

But they'd got out the extra; that was the main thing. Sensationalism? Vultures, as Molly had said? Maybe he might have thought so before H. A. Hitchcock's visit. Maybe another approach, along those lines, might have gained Hitchcock's end. But he knew, as well as any man can ever know his own motives, that the driving force that carried them through last night's frantic activity was no lust for sensationalism, no greed for sales, but a clean, intense desire to print the truth for Grover.

The fight wasn't over. The extra was only the start. Tomorrow he would be preparing Friday's regular issue, and in that—

The first stop, he decided, was the station. It might be possible to get something out of Chief Hanby. Though he doubted if the chief was clear enough of debt to Manson's bank, to say nothing of political obligations, to take a very firm stand against H. A. Hitchcock.

MacVeagh met her in the anteroom of the station. She was coming out of the chief's private office, and Phil Rogers was with her. He had just his normal pallor now, and looked almost human. Still not human enough, though, to justify the smile she was giving him and the way her hand rested on his arm.

That smile lit up the dark, dusty little office. It hardly mattered that she wasn't smiling at MacVeagh. Her smile was beauty itself, in the absolute, no matter who it was aimed at. Her every movement was beauty, and her clothes were a part of her, so that they and her lithe flesh made one smooth loveliness.

And this was H. A. Hitchcock's daughter Laura, and MacVeagh was more tongue-tied than he usually was in her presence. He never could approach her without feeling like a high school junior trying to get up nerve to date the belle of the class.

"Laura—" he said.

She had a copy of the extra in one hand. Her fingers twitched it as she said, "I don't think there is anything we could possibly say to each other, Mr. MacVeagh."

Philip Rogers was obviously repressing a snicker. MacVeagh turned to him. "I'm glad to see you looking better, Phil. I was worried about you last night. Tell me: how did you happen to find the body?"

Laura jerked at Philip's arm. "Come on, Phil. Don't be afraid of the big, bad editor."

Philip smiled, in the style that best suited his pallid profile. "Quite a journalistic achievement, this extra, Johnny. More credit to your spirit than to your judgment, but quite an achievement. Of course, you were far too carried away by it all to do any proofreading?"

"Come *on*, Phil."

"Hold it, Laura. I can't resist showing our fearless young journalist his triumph of accuracy. Look, Johnny." He took the paper from her and pointed to an inside page. "Your account of Old Man Herkimer's funeral: 'Today under the old oaks of Mountain View Cemetery, the last rites of Josephus R. Herkimer, 17, of this city—' " He laughed. "The old boy ought to enjoy that posthumous youth."

"Seventeen, seventy-seven!" MacVeagh snorted. "If that's all that's gone wrong in that edition, I'm a miracle man. But, Laura—"

"You're quite right, Mr. MacVeagh. There are far worse things wrong with that edition than the misprint that amuses Philip."

"Will you be home tonight?" he said with harsh abruptness.

"For you, Mr. MacVeagh, I shall never be home. Good day."

Philip followed her. He looked over his shoulder once and grinned, never knowing how close his pallid profile came to being smashed forever.

Chief Hanby was frowning miserably as MacVeagh came into the office. The delicate smoke of his cigar indicated one far above his usual standard—it was easy to guess its source—but he wasn't enjoying it.

" 'Render therefore unto Caesar,' " he said, " 'the things which are Caesar's; and unto God the things that are God's.' Matthew, twenty-two, twenty-one. Only who knows which is which?"

"Troubles, Chief?" MacVeagh asked.

Chief Hanby had a copy of the extra on his desk. His hand touched it almost reverently as he spoke. "He went to see you, John?"

"Yeah."

"And still you printed this? You're a brave man, John, a brave man."

"You're no coward yourself, Chief. Remember when Nose O'Leary escaped from the state pen and decided Grover'd make a nice hide-out?"

The chief's eyes glowed with the memory of that past exploit. "But that was different, John. A man can maybe risk his life when he can't risk— I'll tell you this much: I'm not talking to you, not right now. Nothing's settled, nothing's ripe, I don't know a thing. But I'm still groping. And I'm not going to stop groping. And if I grope out an answer to anything—whatever the answer is, you'll get it."

MacVeagh thrust out his hand. "I couldn't ask fairer than that, Chief. We both want the truth, and between us we'll get it."

Chief Hanby looked relieved. "I wouldn't blame H. A. too much, John. Remember, he's under a strain. These labor troubles are getting him, and with the election coming up at the plant—"

"And whose fault are the troubles? Father Byrne's committee suggested a compromise and a labor-management plan. The men were willing enough—"

"Even they aren't any more. Not since Bricker took over. We've all got our troubles. Take Jake Willis, now— Why, speak of the devil!"

The coroner looked as though he could easily take a prize for worried expressions away from even MacVeagh and the chief. The greeting didn't help it. He said, "There's too much loose talk about devils. It's as barbarous as swearing by God." But his heart wasn't in his conventional protest.

"What is the matter, Jake?" the chief asked. "You aren't worried just on account of you've got an inquest coming up, are you?"

"No, it ain't that—" His eyes rested distrustfully on MacVeagh.

"Off the record," said the editor. "You've my word."

"All right, only— No. It ain't no use. You wouldn't believe me if I told you . . . Either of you going back past my establishment?"

The chief was tied to his office. But John MacVeagh went along, his curiosity stimulated. His questions received no answers. Jake Willis simply plodded along South Street like a man ridden by the devils in which he refused to believe.

And what, MacVeagh asked himself, would Jake think of a tramp printer who claimed to grant wishes? For the matter of that, what do I think— But there was too much else going on for him to spare much thought for Whalen Smith.

Jake Willis led the way past his assistant without a nod, on back into the chapel. There was a casket in place there, duly embanked with floral tributes. The folding chairs were set up; there was a Bible on the lectern and music on the organ. The stage was completely set for a funeral, and MacVeagh remembered about Old Man Herkimer.

"They're due here at three thirty," Jake whined. "And how'll I dare show it to 'em? I don't know how it happened. Jimmy, he swears he don't know a thing neither. God knows!" he concluded in a despairing rejection of his skepticism.

"It is Old Man Herkimer?"

"It ought to be. That's what I put in there yesterday, Old Man Herkimer's body. And I go to look at it today and—"

The face plate of the coffin was closed. "I'm going to have to leave it that way," he said. "I can't let 'em see— I'll have to tell 'em confidential-like that he looked too— I don't know. I'll have to think of something."

He opened up the plate. MacVeagh looked in. It was a Herkimer, all right. There was no mistaking the wide-set eyes and thin lips of that clan. But Old Man Herkimer, as the original copy for the item in the extra had read, was seventy-seven when he died. The boy in the coffin—

"Don't look a day over seventeen, does he?" said Jake Willis.

"Father Byrne," said John MacVeagh, "I'm asking you this, not as a priest, but as the best-read scholar in Grover: Do miracles happen?"

Father Byrne smiled. "It's hard not to reply as a priest; but I'll try. Do miracles happen? By dictionary definition, I'll say yes; certainly." He crossed the study to the stand that held the large unabridged volume. "Here's what Webster calls a miracle: 'An event or effect in the physical world beyond or out of the ordinary course of things, deviating from the known laws of nature, or,' and this should be put in italics, *'or transcending our knowledge of those laws.'* "

MacVeagh nodded. "I see. We obviously don't know all the laws. We're still learning them. And what doesn't fit in with the little we know—"

" 'An event,' " the priest read on, " 'which cannot be accounted for by any of the known forces of nature and which is, therefore, attributed to a supernatural force.' So you see, miraculousness is more in the attitude of the beholder than in the nature of the fact."

"And the logical reaction of a reasonable man confronted with an apparent miracle would be to test it by scientific method, to try to find the as yet unknown natural law behind it?"

"I should think so. Again being careful not to speak as a priest."

"Thanks, Father."

"But what brings all this up, John? Don't tell me you have been hearing voices or such? I'd have more hope of converting an atheist like Jake to the supernatural than a good hard-headed agnostic like you."

"Nothing, Father. I just got to thinking— Let you know if anything comes of it."

*   *   *

Philip Rogers was waiting for MacVeagh at the *Sentinel* office. There was a puzzling splash of bright red on his white cheek. Molly was there, too, typing with furious concentration.

"I want to talk you alone, Johnny," Rogers said.

Molly started to rise, but MacVeagh said, "Stick around. Handy things sometimes, witnesses. Well, Phil?"

Philip Rogers glared at the girl. "I just wanted to give you a friendly warning, Johnny. You know as personnel manager out at the plant I get a pretty good notion of how the men are feeling."

"Too bad you've never put it over to H. A., then."

Philip shrugged. "I don't mean the reds and the malcontents. Let Bricker speak for them—while he's still able. I mean the good, solid American workers, that understand the plant and the management."

"H. A.'s company stooges, in short. OK, Phil, so what are they thinking?"

"They don't like the way you're playing up this murder. They think you ought to show a little sympathy for the boss in his bereavement. They think he's got troubles enough with Bricker and the Congressional committee."

MacVeagh smiled. "Now I get it."

"Get what?"

"I'd forgotten about the committee. So that's what's back of all the hush-hush. A breath of scandal, a suspicion that there might be a murderer in the Hitchcock clan—it could so easily sway a congressman who was trying to evaluate the motives behind H. A.'s deals. He's got to be Caesar's wife. Above suspicion."

"At least," Philip said scornfully, "you have too much journalistic sense to print wild guesses like that. That's something. But remember what I said about the men."

"So?"

"So they might decide to clean out the *Sentinel* some night."

MacVeagh's hand clenched into a tight fist. Then slowly he forced it to relax. "Phil," he said, "I ought to batter that pallor of yours to a nice, healthy pulp. But you're not worth it. Tell the company police I'm saving my fists for their vigilante raid. Now get out of here, while I've still got sense enough to hold myself back."

Philip was smiling confidently as he left, but his face was a trifle paler even than usual.

MacVeagh expressed himself with calculated liberty on Philip Rogers' ancestry, nature, and hobbies for almost a minute before he was aware of Molly. "Sorry," he broke off to say, "but I meant it."

"Say it again for me, boss. And in spades."

"I should have socked him. He—" MacVeagh frowned. "When I came in, it looked as though someone might already have had that pious notion." He looked at Molly queerly. "Did you—"

"He made a pass at me," Molly said unemotionally. "He thought maybe he could enlist me on their side that way, keep me from writing my stuff up. I didn't mind the pass. Why I slapped him was, he seemed to think I ought to be flattered."

MacVeagh laughed. "Good girl." He sat down at the other typewriter and rolled in a sheet of copy paper. "We'll hold the fort." He began to type.
Molly looked up from her own copy. "Get any new leads, boss?"
"No," he said reflectively. "This is just an experiment." He wrote:

A sudden freakish windstorm hit Grover last night. For ten minutes windows rattled furiously, and old citizens began to recall the Great Wind of '97. The storm died down as suddenly as it came, however. No damage was done except to the statue of General Wigginsby in Courthouse Square, which was blown from its pedestal, breaking off the head and one arm. C. B. Tooly, chairman of the Grover Scrap Drive, expressed great pleasure at the accident. Members of the Civic Planning Commission were reportedly even more pleased at the removal of Grover's outstanding eyesore.

He tore the sheet out of the typewriter. Then a perversely puckish thought struck him and he inserted another page. He headed it:

WHAT PEOPLE ARE SAYING
Coroner Jake Willis has apparently abandoned his thirty-year stand of strict atheism. "In times like these," he said last night, "we need faith in something outside of ourselves. I've been a stubborn fool for too long."

Molly spoke as he stopped typing. "What kind of experiment, boss?"
"Let you know Friday," he said. "Hold on tight, Molly. If this experiment works—"
For a moment he leaned back in his chair, his eyes aglow with visions of fabulous possibilities. Then he laughed out loud and got on with his work.

III

No paper was ever gotten out by a more distracted editor than that Friday's issue of the Grover *Sentinel*.
Two things preoccupied John MacVeagh. One, of course, was his purely rational experiment in scientific methods as applied to miracles. Not that he believed for an instant that whatever gestures Whalen Smith had woven in the air could impart to the *Sentinel* the absolute and literal faculty of printing the truth—and making it the truth by printing it. But the episode of the seventeen-year-old corpse had been a curious one. It deserved checking—rationally and scientifically, you understand.
And the other distraction was the effect upon Grover of the murder.
Almost, John MacVeagh was becoming persuaded that his crusading truthfulness had been a mistake. Perhaps there was some justice in the attitude of the bluenoses who decry sensational publishing. Certainly the town's reaction to the sensational news was not healthy.
On the one hand, inevitably, there was the group—vocally headed by Banker

Manson—who claimed that what they called the "smear campaign" was a vile conspiracy between MacVeagh and labor leader Tim Bricker. That was to be expected. With Manson and his crowd, you pushed certain buttons and you got certain automatic responses. But MacVeagh had not foreseen the reverse of the coin he had minted: the bitterness and resentment among the little people.

"Whatddaya expect?" he overheard in Clem's barber shop. "You take a guy like Hitchcock, you don't think they can do anything to him, do you? Why, them guys can get away with—" The speaker stopped, as though that were a little more than he had meant to say.

But there were other voices to take up his accusation.

"Go ahead, Joe, say it. Get away with murder."

"Sure, who's gonna try to pin a rap on the guy that owns the town?"

"What good's a police chief when he's all sewed up pretty in Hitchcock's pocket?"

"And the *Sentinel* don't dare print half it knows. You all know the editor's got a yen for Hitchcock's daughter. Well—"

"Somebody ought to do something."

That last was the crystallized essence of their feeling. Somebody ought to do something. And those simple words can be meaningful and ugly. They were on many tongues in Germany in the twenties.

John MacVeagh thought about the sorcerer's apprentice, who summoned the powers beyond his control. But, no, that was a pointed but still light and amusing story. This was becoming grim. If he and Molly could only crack this murder, cut through to the solution and dispel once and for all these dissatisfied grumblings—

But how was that to be done? They had so few facts, and nothing to disprove the fantastic notion of a wandering tramp invading the upper story of a fully occupied house without disturbing a soul save his victim. If some trick of psychological pressure could force a confession—

MacVeagh mused on these problems as he walked back to the office after dinner on Thursday, and came regretfully to the conclusion that there was nothing to do but go on as per schedule: print Friday's regular edition with what follow-up was possible on the murder story, and dig and delve as best they could to reach toward the truth.

He frowned as he entered the office. Sidewalk loafers weren't so common on Spruce Street. They hung out more on South, or down near the station on Jackson. But this evening there was quite a flock of them within a few doors of the *Sentinel*.

Lucretius Sellers was chuckling over the copy he was setting up. "That sure is a good one you've got here on Jake, Johnny. Lord, I never did think I'd see the day— Maybe pretty soon we'll see that ascetic atheist taking a drink, too. Which reminds me—"

He caught MacVeagh's eye and paused. "Nope. Don't know what I was going to say, Johnny." He had been sober now since Whalen Smith's departure had caused his sudden drafting back into his old profession. And he knew, and MacVeagh knew, that the only way for him to stay sober was to climb completely on the wagon.

"Making out all right, Luke?" MacVeagh asked.

"Swell, Johnny. You know, you think you forget things, but you don't. Not things you learn with your hands, you don't. You ask me last week could I still set type and I'd say no. But there in my fingers—they still remembered. But look, Johnny—"

"Yes?"

"This item about the Wigginsby statue. It's a swell idea, but it just hasn't happened. I was past there not an hour ago, and the old boy's as big and ugly as ever. And besides, this says 'last night.' That means tonight—how can I set up what hasn't happened yet?"

"Luke, you've been grand to me. You've helped me out of a spot by taking over. But if I can impose on you just a leetle bit more—please don't ask any questions about the general's statue. Just set it up and forget about it. Maybe I'll have something to tell you about that item tomorrow, maybe not. But in any case—"

His voice broke off sharply. He heard loud thumping feet in the front office. He heard Molly's voice shrilling. "What do you want? You can't all of you come crowding in here like this!"

Another voice said, "We're in, ain't we, sister?" It was a calm, cold voice.

"We've got work to do," Molly persisted. "We've got a paper to get out."

"That," said the voice, "is what *you* think." There was a jangling crash that could be made only by a typewriter hurled to the floor.

MacVeagh shucked his coat as he stepped into the front office. No time for rolling up sleeves. He snapped the lock on the door as he came through; that'd keep them from the press for a matter of minutes, anyway. He felt Luke at his heels, but he didn't look. He walked straight to the towering redhead who stood beside Molly's desk, the wrecked typewriter at his feet, and delivered the punch that he had neglected to give Phil Rogers.

The redhead was a second too late to duck, but he rolled with it. His left came up to answer it with a short jab, but suddenly he staggered back. His face was a dripping black mess, and he let out an angry roar. He charged in wide-open fury, and this time MacVeagh connected.

He'd recognized the redhead. Chief of Hitchcock's company police. He'd heard about him—how he had a tough skull and a tougher belly, but a glass chin. For once, MacVeagh reflected, rumor was right.

It was the silent quickness of the whole episode that impressed the other Hitchcock men and halted them for a moment. MacVeagh blessed Molly for her beautifully timed toss with the ink bottle. He glanced at her and saw that she now held her desk scissors ready in a stabbing grip. Luke Sellers held a wrench.

But they were three, and there were a dozen men in the room besides the fallen redhead. One of them stepped forward now, a swarthy little man whose face was stubbled in blue-black save for the white streak of an old knife scar.

"You shouldn't ought to of done that," he said. "Red didn't mean you no harm, not personal. No roughhouse, see? And if you listen to reason, why, OK."

"And if I don't?" MacVeagh asked tersely.

"If you don't? Well, then it looks like we're going to have to smash up that pretty press of yours, mister. But there don't nobody need to get hurt. You ain't got a chance against the bunch of us. You might as well admit it if you don't want us to have to smash up that pretty puss of yours too."

"What can we do?" Molly whispered. "He's right; we can't stand them all off. But to smash the press—"

Luke Sellers waved his wrench and issued wholesale invitations to slaughter.

Scarface grinned. "Call off the old man, mister. He's apt to get hurt. Well, how's about it? Do you let us in nice and peaceable or do we smash down the door?"

MacVeagh opened a drawer of the desk and put his hand in. "You can try smashing," he said, "if you don't mind bullets."

"We don't mind bluffs," said Scarface dryly. "OK, boys!"

MacVeagh took his empty hand from the drawer. There was only one thing to do, and that was to fight as long as he could. It was foolish, pointless, hopeless. But it was the only thing that a man could do.

The men came. Scarface had somehow managed wisely to drop to the rear of the charge. As they came, MacVeagh stooped. He rose with the wreck of the typewriter and hurled it. It took the first man out and brought the second thudding down with him. MacVeagh followed it with his fists.

Luke Sellers, as a long-standing authority on barroom brawls, claimed that the ensuing fight lasted less than a minute. It seemed closer to an hour to MacVeagh, closer yet to an eternity. Time vanished and there was nothing, no thinking, no reasoning, no problems, no values, nothing but the ache in his body as blows landed on it and the joy in his heart as his own blows connected and the salt warmth of blood in his mouth.

From some place a thousand light-years away he heard a voice bellowing, "Quit it! Lay off!" The words meant nothing. He paid no more attention to them than did the man who at the moment held his head in an elbow lock and pummeled it with a heavy ring-bearing fist. The voice sounded again as MacVeagh miraculously wriggled loose, his neck aching with the strain, and delivered an unorthodox knee blow to the ring wearer. Still the voice meant nothing.

But the shot did.

It thudded into the ceiling, and its echoes rang through the room. The voice bellowed again, "Now do you believe I mean it? Lay off. All of you!"

The sound and smell of powder wield a weighty influence in civilian reactions. The room was suddenly very still. MacVeagh wiped sweat and blood from his face, forced his eyes open, and discovered that he could see a little.

He could see a tall gaunt man with crudely Lincolnian features striding toward him. He recognized the labor leader. "Sergeant Bricker, I presume?" he said groggily.

Bricker looked his surprise. "Sergeant? MacVeagh, you're punchy."

"Uh-huh." MacVeagh cast dim eyes on the two armed bodyguards at the door and at the restlessly obedient men of the company's police. "Don't you know? You're the U. S. Marines."

Then somebody pulled a blackdotted veil over the light, which presently went out altogether.

At first John MacVeagh thought it was a hangover. To be sure, he had never had a hangover like this. To be equally sure, he resolved that he never would again. A convention of gnomes was holding high revels in his skull and demonstrating the latest rock-drilling gadgets.

He groaned and tried to roll over. His outflung arm felt emptiness, and his body started to slip. A firm hand shoved him back into place.

He opened his eyes. They ached even more resolutely when open, and he quickly dropped his lids. But he had seen that he was on the narrow couch in the back office, that Molly's hand had rescued him from rolling off, and that it was daylight.

"Are you OK, boss?" Molly's voice was softer than usual.

"I'll be all right as soon as they shovel the dirt in on me."

"Can you listen while I tell you things?"

"I can try. Tell me the worst. What did I do? Climb chandeliers and sing bawdy ballads to the Ladies' Aid?"

He heard Molly laugh. "You weren't plastered, boss. You were in a fight. Remember?"

The shudder that ran through him testified to his memory. "I remember now. Hitchcock's little playmates. And Bricker showed up and staged the grand rescue and I passed out. Fine, upstanding hero I am. Can't take it—"

"You took plenty. Doc Quillan was worried about a concussion at first. That's why he had us keep you here—didn't want to risk moving you home. But he looked at you again this morning and he thinks you'll be OK."

"And I never even felt it. Exalted, that's what I must've been. Wonderful thing, lust of battle. This morning! Sunlight." He forced his eyes open and tried to sit up. "Then it's Friday! The paper should be—"

Molly pushed him back. "Don't worry, boss. The *Sentinel* came out this morning. Everything's hunky-dory. Bricker lent us a couple of men to help, and it's all swell."

"Bricker— Where'd we be without him? A god out of the machinists' union. And the paper's out . . ." Suddenly he tried to sit up again, then decided against it. "Molly!"

"Yes, boss?"

"Have you been in Courthouse Square this morning?"

"No, boss. Doc Quillan said I ought to— I mean, there's been so much to do here in the office—"

"Have you seen Jake?"

"Uh-huh. That was funny. He dropped in this morning. I think he heard about the ruckus and wanted to see was there anything in his line of business. And has he changed!"

"Changed?" What voice MacVeagh had was breathless.

"He practically delivered a sermon. All about what a fool he's been and man cannot live by bread alone and in times like these and stuff. Grover isn't going to seem the same without Jake's atheism."

"Scientific method," said MacVeagh.

"What do you mean, boss?"

"Molly, there's something I've got to tell you about the *Sentinel*. You'll think I'm crazy maybe, but there's too much to disregard. You've got to believe it."

"Boss, you know I believe every word you say." She laughed, but the laugh didn't succeed in discounting her obvious sincerity.

"Molly—"

"Hi, MacVeagh. Feeling fit again? Ready to take on a dozen more finks?"

MacVeagh focused his eyes on the gangling figure. "Bricker! I'm glad to see you. Almost as glad as I was last night. I don't feel too bright and loquacious yet, but when I do, consider yourself scheduled for the best speech of gratitude ever made in Grover."

Bricker waved one hand. "That's OK. Nothing to it. United front. We've got to gang up—victims of oppression. Collective security."

"Anything I can do for you—"

"You're doing plenty." Bricker pulled up a chair and sat down, his long legs sprawling in front of him. "You know, MacVeagh, I had you figured wrong."

"How so?"

"I thought you were just another editor. You know, a guy who joins liberal committees and prints what the advertisers want. But I had the wrong picture. You've got ideas and the guts to back 'em."

MacVeagh basked. Praise felt good after what he'd been through. But Bricker's next words woke him up.

"How much did *you* try to shake Hitchcock down for?"

"How much— I— Why— Look, Bricker, I don't get you."

Bricker eased himself more comfortably into the chair and said, "He don't shake easy. Don't I know! But a tree with them apples is worth shaking."

"You mean you're . . . you've been blackmailing Hitchcock?"

"I can talk to you, MacVeagh. Nobody else in this town has got the guts or the sense to see my angle. But you've got angles of your own; you can understand. Sure I've been shaking him down. Before I moved in on that local, it sounded like a Socialist Party pink tea. 'Better working conditions. A living wage. Rights of labor.' " He expressed his editorial comment in a ripe raspberry. "I saw the possibilities and I took over. Old Hasenberg and the rest of those boys—they don't know from nothing about politics. A few plants, a little pressure, and I was in—but for good. Then I put it up to H. A.: 'How much is it worth to you to get along without strikes?' "

MacVeagh opened his mouth, but the words stuck there.

"So you see?" Bricker went on calmly. "We can work together. The more pressure you put on Hitchcock with this murder scandal, the more he can't afford to risk labor trouble. And vice, as the fellow says, versa. So you can count on me any time you need help. And when this blows over— There's lots more can happen, MacVeagh, lots more. Between us, we can wind up owning this town.

"Keep the murder story running as long as you can. That's my advice. If it begins to look like a solution that'll clear Hitchcock and his family, keep it quiet. Keep the pressure on him, and he'll kick through in the end. I know his type . . . What is it you're really after, MacVeagh? Just cash, or the daughter?"

MacVeagh was still speechless. He was glad that Luke Sellers came in just then. It kept him from sputtering.

Luke was fair-to-middling speechless himself. He nodded at Bricker and Molly, and finally he managed to say, "Johnny, if I hadn't been on the wagon for two days I swear I'd go on and stay there!"

Bricker looked interested. "What's happened?"

"You were in Courthouse Square," said John MacVeagh.

"That's it, all right. I was in Courthouse Square. And General Wigginsby has enlisted in the scrap drive. Funny freak wind last night, the boys at Clem's say. Didn't do any other damage. But, Johnny, how you knew—"

"What is all this?" Bricker broke in. "What's the angle on the statue, Mac-Veagh?"

The editor smiled wearily. "No angle, Bricker. Not the way you mean. Nothing you'd understand. But maybe something that's going to make a big difference to you and your angles."

Bricker glanced at Molly and touched his head. "Still don't feel so good, huh? Well, I've got to be getting along. I'll drop in again off and on, MacVeagh. We've got plans to make. Glad I helped you last night, and remember: keep up the good work."

Luke Sellers looked after the lean figure. "What's he mean by that?"

"Not what he thinks he means," said John MacVeagh, "I hope. Out of the frying pan—"

Molly shuddered. "He's as bad as H. A. Hitchcock."

"Just about. And if I hush up the murder, I'm playing H. A.'s game, and if I give it a big play, I'm stooging for Bricker's racket. I guess," he said thoughtfully, "there's only one thing to do. Molly, Luke! We're getting out another extra."

"Life," said Luke Sellers, "used to be a sight simpler before I went and got sober. Now nothing makes any sense. An extra? What for?"

"We're going to get out another extra," MacVeagh repeated. "Tomorrow. And the banner head is going to be: MURDERER CONFESSES."

"But, boss, how do we know—"

Luke Sellers was thinking of General Wigginsby. "Hush, Molly," he said. "Let's see what happens."

IV

MURDERER CONFESSES

At a late hour last night, the murderer of Mrs. Agnes Rogers walked into the Grover police station and gave himself up. Police Chief J. B. Hanby is holding him incommunicado until his confession has been checked.

The murderer's identity, together with a full text of his confession, will be released in time for a further special edition of the *Sentinel* later today, Chief Hanby promises.

This story was set up and printed in the Grover *Sentinel* late Friday night and was on sale early Saturday morning. At eleven fifty-five P.M. Friday, Neville

Markham, butler to Mrs. Agnes Rogers, walked into the police station and confessed to the murder.

" 'The butler did it,' " said Molly between scornful quotation marks.

"After all," said John MacVeagh, "I suppose sometime the butler must do it.
Just by the law of averages."

It was Saturday night, and the two of them were sitting in the office talking
after the frantic strain of getting out the second extra of the day. Luke Sellers had
gone home and gone to bed with a fifth.

"A man can stay a reformed character just so long," he said, "and you won't
be needing me much for a couple of days. Unless," he added, "you get any more
brilliant inspirations before the fact. Tell me, Johnny, how did you . . . ?" But he let
the query trail off unfinished and went home, clutching his fifth as though it were
the one sure thing in a wambling world.

The second extra had carried the butler's whole story: how he, a good servant
of the Lord, had endured as long as he could his mistress' searching for strange
gods until finally a Voice had said to him, "Smite thou this evil woman," and he
smote. Afterward he panicked and tried to make it look like robbery. He thought
he had succeeded until Friday night, when the same Voice said to him, "Go thou
and proclaim thy deed," and he went and proclaimed.

MacVeagh wished he'd been there. He'd bet the butler and Chief Hanby had
fun swapping texts.

" 'The butler did it,' " Molly repeated. "And I never so much as mentioned the
butler in my stories. You don't even *think* of butlers—not since the twenties."

"Well, anyway, the murder is solved. That's the main thing. No more pressure
from either Hitchcock or Bricker. No more mumbling dissension in Grover."

"But don't you feel . . . oh, I don't know . . . cheated? It's no fun when a murder
gets solved that way. If you and I could've figured it out and broken the story, or
even if Chief Hanby had cracked it with dogged routine . . . But this way it's so
flat!"

"Weary, flat, and stale, Molly, I agree. But not unprofitable. We learned the
truth, and the truth has solved a lot of our problems."

"Only—"

"Yes, Molly?"

"Only, boss— How? I've got to know how. How could you know that the
butler was going to hear another Voice and confess? And that isn't all. Luke told
me about General Wigginsby."

Molly had never seen John MacVeagh look so serious. "All right," he said.
"I've got to tell somebody, anyway. It eats at me . . . OK. You remember how
Whalen left so abruptly? Well—"

Molly sat wide-eyed and agape when he finished the story. "Ordinarily," she
said at last, "I'd say you were crazy, boss. But Old Man Herkimer and General
Wigginsby and the butler . . . What *was* Whalen—"

MacVeagh had wondered about that too. Sometimes he could still almost feel
around the office the lingering presence of that gaunt old man with the books you
couldn't read and the beard that wasn't there. What had he been?

"And what're you going to do, boss? It looks like you can do practically anything. If anything we print in the paper turns out to be the truth— What *are* you going to do?"

"Come in!" MacVeagh yelled, as someone knocked on the door.

It was Father Byrne, followed by a little man whose blue eyes were brightly alive in his old, seamed face. "Good evening, John, Molly. This is Mr. Hasenberg— you've probably met him. Used to head the union out at the Hitchcock plant before Tim Bricker moved in."

"Evening, folks," said Mr. Hasenberg. He tipped his cap with a hand that was as sensitive and alive as his eyes—the hardened, ready hand of a skilled workman.

MacVeagh furnished his guests with chairs. Then he said, "To what am I indebted and such?"

"Mr. Hasenberg has a problem, John, and it's mine too. And it's yours and everybody's. Go on, sir."

Mr. Hasenberg spoke in a dry, precise tone. "Bricker's called a strike. We don't want to strike. We don't like or trust Hitchcock, but we do trust the arbitration committee that Father Byrne's on. We've accepted their decision, and we still hope we can get the management to. But Bricker put over the strike vote with some sharp finagling, and that'll probably mean the Army taking over the plant."

"And I know Bricker . . ." said MacVeagh. "But where do I come in?"

"Advice and publicity," said Father Byrne. "First, have you any ideas? Second, will you print the statement Mr. Hasenberg's preparing on the real stand of the men, without Bricker's trimmings?"

"Second, of course. First—" he hesitated. "Tell me, Mr. Hasenberg, if you were free of Bricker, do you think you could get the management to come to terms?"

"Maybe. They ain't all like Hitchcock and Phil Rogers. There's some of them want to get the stuff out and the war won as bad as we do. Now, ever since Mathers went to Washington, the post of general manager's been vacant. Suppose, now, Johansen should get that appointment—he'd string along with the committee's decision, I'm pretty sure."

MacVeagh pulled a scratch pad toward him. "Johansen— First name?"

"Boss! You aren't going to—"

"*Sh,* Molly. And now, Father, if you could give me an outline of the committee's terms . . ."

So Ingve Johansen became general manager of the Hitchcock plant, and Mr. Hasenberg resumed control of the union, after evidence had been uncovered which totally discredited Tim Bricker, and the arbitrated terms of the committee were accepted by labor and management, and the joint labor-management council got off to a fine start—all of which the burghers of Grover read with great pleasure in the *Sentinel.*

There was another important paragraph in that Friday's issue: an announcement that starting in another week the *Sentinel* was to become a daily.

"We've got to, Molly," MacVeagh had insisted. "There's so much we can do for Grover. If we can settle the troubles at Hitchcock, that's just a start. We can make this over into the finest community in the country. And we haven't space in one small weekly edition. With a daily we can do things gradually, step by step . . ."

"And what, boss, do we use for money? That'll mean more presses, more men, more paper. Where's the money coming from?"

"That," said John MacVeagh, "I don't know."

And he never did. There was simply a small statement in the paper:

ANONYMOUS
BENEFACTOR
ENDOWS *SENTINEL*

Mr. Manson was never able to find a teller who remembered receiving that astonishingly large deposit made to the credit of the *Sentinel*'s account; but there it was, all duly entered.

And so the Grover *Sentinel* became a daily, printing the truth.

V

If it's all right with you, we'll skip pretty fast over the next part of the story. The days of triumph never make interesting reading. The rise and fall—that's your dramatic formula. The build-up can be stirring and the letdown can be tragic, but there's no interest in the flat plateau at the top.

So there's no need to tell in detail all that happened in Grover after the *Sentinel* went daily. You can imagine the sort of thing: How the Hitchcock plant stepped up its production and turned out a steady flow of war matériel that was the pride of the county, the state, and even the country. How Doc Quillan tracked down, identified, and averted the epidemic that threatened the workers' housing project. How Chief Hanby finally got the goods on the gamblers who were moving in on the South Side and cleaned up the district. How the Grover Red Cross drive went a hundred percent over its quota. How the expected meat shortage never materialized . . . You get the picture.

All this is just the plateau, the level stretch between the rise and the fall. Not that John MacVeagh expected the fall. Nothing like that seemed possible, even though Molly worried.

"You know, boss," she said one day, "I was reading over some of the books I used to love when I was a kid. This wish—it's magic, isn't it?"

MacVeagh snapped the speaking box on his desk and gave a succinct order to the assistant editor. He was the chief executive of a staff now. Then he turned back and said, "Why, yes, Molly, I guess you might call it that. Magic, miracle—what do we care so long as it enables us to accomplish all we're doing?"

"I don't know. But sometimes I get scared. Those books, especially the ones by E. Nesbit—"

MacVeagh grinned. "Scared of kids' books?"

"I know it sounds silly, boss, but kids' books are the only place you can find out about magic. And there seems to be only one sure thing about it: You can know there's a catch to it. There's always a catch."

MacVeagh didn't think any further about that. What stuck in his mind were phrases like those he heard down at Clem's barber shop:

"Hanged if I know what's come over this burg. Seems like for a couple of months there just can't nothing go wrong. Ever since that trouble out at the plant when they got rid of Bricker, this burg is just about perfect, seems like."

Those were fine words. They fed the soul. They made you forget that little, nagging, undefined discontent that was rankling underneath and threatening to spoil all this wonderful miracle—or magic, if you prefer. They even made you be polite to H. A. Hitchcock when he came to pay his respects to you after the opening of the new *Sentinel* Building.

He praised MacVeagh as an outstanding example of free enterprise. (A year or so ago he would have said rugged individualism, but the phrase had been replaced in his vocabulary by its more noble-sounding synonym.) He probed with man-to-man frankness trying to learn where the financial backing had come from. He all but apologized for the foolish misunderstanding over the butler's crime. And he ended up with a dinner invitation in token of reconciliation.

MacVeagh accepted. But his feelings were mixed, and they were even more mixed when he dropped into the office on the night of the dinner, resplendent in white tie and tails, to check up some last-minute details on the reports of the election for councilman. He had just learned that Grizzle had had some nasty semi-Fascist tie-ups a year earlier, and must not be allowed to be elected.

"I don't know what's the matter," he confided to Molly after he'd attended to business. "I ought to be sitting on top of the world, and somehow I'm not. Maybe I almost see what the trouble is: No heavy."

"What does that mean, boss?"

"No opposition. Nothing to fight against. Just wield my white magic benevolently and that's that. I need a black magician to combat me on my own level. You've got to have a heavy."

"Are you so sure," Molly asked, "that yours is white magic?"

"Why—"

"Skip it, boss. But I think I know one thing that's the matter. And I think, God help me, that you'll realize it tonight."

Molly's words couldn't have been truer if she had printed them in the *Sentinel.*

The party itself was painful. Not the dinner; that was as admirable as only H. A. Hitchcock's chef could contrive. But the company had been carefully chosen to give MacVeagh the idea that, now that he was making such a phenomenal success of himself, he was to be welcomed among the Best People of Grover.

There were the Mansons, of course, and Phil Rogers, and Major General Front, U.S.A., retired, and a half dozen others who formed a neat tight little society of mutual admiration and congratulation. The only halfway human person present seemed to be the new general manager of the plant, Johansen; but he sat at the other end of the table from MacVeagh, in the dominating shadow of Mrs. Manson's bosom.

MacVeagh himself was loomed over by Mrs. Front, who gave her own interpretation of the general's interpretation of the plans of the High Command. He nodded dutifully and gave every impression of listening, while he saw and heard and felt nothing but Laura Hitchcock across the table.

Every man dreams of Helen, but to few is it ever given to behold the face that can launch a thousand ships. This is well. Life is complicated enough, if often pleasantly so, when we love a pretty girl, a charming girl, a sweet girl. But when we see beauty, pure and radiant and absolute, we are lost.

MacVeagh had been lost since he first arrived in Grover and old Jonathan Minter sent him to cover Laura's coming-out party. After that she had gone east to college and he had told himself that it was all the champagne. He couldn't have seen what his heart remembered.

Then she came back, and since then no moment of his life had ever seemed quite complete. He never knew how he stood with her; he never even knew what she was like. He would begin to get acquainted with her, and then she would be off to visit her aunt in Florida or her cousins, before the war, in France. Since the war she had stayed in Grover, busy with the various volunteer activities entailed by her position as H. A. Hitchcock's daughter. He was beginning to know her, he thought; he was beginning to reach a point where—

And then came the murder and the quarrel with Hitchcock. And this was the first time that he had seen her since then.

She smiled and seemed friendly. Evidently, like her father, she looked upon MacVeagh with a new regard since he had begun his mysteriously spectacular climb to success.

She even exchanged an intimate and shuddering glance with him after dinner, when Mrs. Manson began to sing American folk ballads in the drawing room. MacVeagh took courage and pointed to the open French window behind her.

His throat choked when she accepted the hint. He joined her on the lawn, and they strolled quietly over to the pond, where the croaking monotone of the frogs drowned out the distant shrilling of Mrs. Manson.

"What gets me," MacVeagh grunted, "is the people that call all that wonderful stuff 'ballads.' They're just plain songs, and good ones. And where they belong is a couple of guys that love them trying them out with one foot on the rail and the barkeep joining in the harmony. When the fancy folk begin singing them in drawing rooms with artistically contrived accompaniments—"

"I guess I'll just have to do without them then," said Laura. "I can't see myself in your barroom."

"Can't you?" There must have been something in the moon that stirred MacVeagh's daring. "Why not? There's a good, plain, honest bar not a mile from here that I like. Why don't we ditch the party and go—"

"Oh, John. Don't be silly. We couldn't. We're not bright young people, and it isn't smart to be like that any more. Everybody's serious now; this is war. And besides, you know, you have to think more of the company you're seen in now."

"Me?"

"Of course, John. Father's been telling me how wonderfully you're coming on. You're getting to be somebody. You have to look out for appearances."

"I'm afraid"—MacVeagh grinned—"I have congenitally low tastes. Can't I be a big-shot editor and still love the riff and the raff?"

"Of course not." She was perfectly serious, and MacVeagh felt a twinge of regret that such perfection of beauty was apparently not compatible with the least trace of humor. "You have to be thinking about settling down now."

"Settling down—" he repeated. This was so pat a cue, if he could get that lump out of his throat and go on with it. "You're right, Laura. At my age—" His voice was as harsh a croak as the frogs'.

"What's the matter, John?"

He harrumphed. "Something in my throat. But it's true. A man needs a wife. A man—"

"Marriage is a wonderful thing, isn't it? I've only just lately been realizing how wonderful."

He leaned toward her. "Laura—"

"John, I feel like telling you something, if you'll promise not to go printing it."

"Yes—"

"It's a secret yet, but—I'm going to be married."

There was a distant patter of applause for Mrs. Manson, and the frogs croaked louder than ever. These were the only noises that accompanied the end of the world.

For a moment there was a blankness inside John MacVeagh. He felt as though he had received a harder blow than any taken in the fight with Hitchcock's stooges. And then came the same reaction as he had known to those blows: the lust for battle. The lump in his throat was gone and words were pouring out. He heard the words only half-consciously, hardly aware that his own brain must be formulating them. He heard them, and was aghast that any man could lay bare his desires so plainly, his very soul.

They were pitiful words, and yet powerful—plaintive, and yet demandingly vigorous. And they were finally stopped by Laura's voice cutting across them with a harsh "John!"

"John," she said again more softly. "I— Believe me, I never knew you felt like this. I never would have— You're nice. You're sweet, and I like you. But I couldn't ever love you. I couldn't ever possibly marry you. Let's go back inside, John. Mrs. Manson must be through by now. What's the matter? Aren't you coming? John. Please."

But John MacVeagh stood motionless by the pool while Laura went on back to the big house. He listened to the frogs for a while and then he went to the good, plain, honest bar not a mile away and listened to some "ballads."

After the third whiskey the numbness began to lift. He began to see what he had to do. It must be Phil Rogers she was marrying. But he was her cousin, wasn't he? Oh, no—he was her aunt's husband's nephew. That made it all right.

But there was a way out. There was the one sure way. All right, so it was selfish. So it was abusing a great and mysterious power for private ends. But the custodian of that power had some privileges, didn't he? And if he had one and only one prayer on earth—

After the seventh whiskey he went back to the office. It took him three tries to turn out legible copy. He hadn't written a word for the Social Notes since Molly had joined the staff, and besides, the machine seemed to resent the drunken pawing of his fingers.

But he made it at last, and it appeared in the next day's *Sentinel,* and H. A. Hitchcock said to his daughter, "Wish you'd told me, first, Laura. But I must say I think it's a fine idea. He's a comer, that boy. And maybe if you can use a little influence with him— Useful thing, having a newspaper editor in the family. You can keep him in hand."

What came next is more plateau that we don't need to examine in detail. At least, apparently plateau; a discerning eye might see the start of the fall already. Because lives don't make nice, clear graphs. The rise and the fall can be going on at once, and neither of them noticeable.

So we can accept as read all the inevitable preparations for such an event as the wedding of H. A. Hitchcock's daughter to the most promising young man in Grover. We can pass over the account of the white splendor of the wedding day and the curiously anticlimactic night that followed.

That was the night, too, when Molly, who never drank anything but beer, brought two fifths of whiskey to Luke Sellers' boardinghouse and sat up all night discussing them and other aspects of life. But the scene would be difficult to record. Most of what she said wouldn't make any sense to a reader. It didn't make much sense to Luke, nor to Molly herself the next morning.

We can skip by the details of how Grover solved the manpower shortage in the adjacent farming territory, and of how liberalism triumphed in the council election. We can go on to a Saturday night three months after Whalen Smith departed, leaving a wish behind him.

John MacVeagh had been seeing quite a bit of Ingve Johansen since the Hitchcock dinner party. He was a man you kept running into at the luncheons you had to attend, and as your father-in-law's general manager he was a man you had to have to dinner occasionally.

And MacVeagh's first impression was confirmed: he was a good guy, this Johansen. A guy you'd be happy to have in a cracker-barrel session, only those sessions never seemed to come off any more. Running a daily was a very different job from being editor of the old weekly *Sentinel.* And when so much responsibility rested on your slightest word—you didn't have time for a good bull session any more.

But Johansen would have belonged, just as Mr. Hasenberg would. Sometime he must get the two of them together away from the plant. For an executive like Johansen no more deserved to be judged by H. A. than Mr. Hasenberg did to be rated like Bricker.

Besides all the lines of race or religion or country or class, MacVeagh was beginning to feel, there was another basic dividing line among men: There are the good guys, the Men of Good Will, if you want to be fancy about it, and there are—others.

Ingve Johansen was of the first; and that's why it hurt MacVeagh, when he dropped in that Saturday at his good, plain, honest bar for a quick one, to find Johansen reduced to telling the bartender the story of his life.

MacVeagh stayed in the bar longer than he'd intended. He steered the manager over to the corner table and tried gently to find out what was eating him. For this was no ordinary drinking, but some compelling obsession.

"Look," MacVeagh said finally, "I know it's none of my business, and if you want to tell me to go jump in a lake I'll try and find one. But you've got something gnawing inside you, and if there's anything I can do to help you—" You can't tell men that you have the power to ease their troubles, but if you can once learn the troubles . . .

Johansen laughed. His heavy shock of blond hair bobbled with his laughter. He said, "How do you expect me to feel after you stole my girl?"

MacVeagh sat up straight. "Your girl? You mean you're the one that she—"

"We were going to be married. Hadn't sounded out H. A. yet, but it was all set. And first thing I know I read that piece in your paper—"

There was nothing to say. MacVeagh just sat there. He'd been sure it was the contemptible Phil Rogers. His conscience had felt clear. But now, watching the man she should have married . . .

"The worst thing," Johansen added, "is that I like you, MacVeagh. I don't even want to wring your neck for you. But Laura'd better be happy."

"She will be," said MacVeagh flatly. He rose from the table stiffly, made arrangements with the bartender about getting Johansen home, and walked out. There was nothing he could do.

No, he couldn't even be generous and give her back. The scandal of a divorce . . . Magic doesn't work backward. Was this the catch that Molly talked about?

The second thing that happened that night was unimportant. But it makes a good sample of a kind of minor incident that cropped up occasionally on the plateau.

On his way to the office, MacVeagh went past the Lyric. He absently read the marquee and saw that the theater was playing *Rio Rhythm*, Metropolis Pictures' latest well-intentioned contribution to the Good Neighbor Policy. There were no patrons lined up at the box office—no one in the lobby at all save Clara in her cage and Mr. Marcus, looking smaller and unhappier than ever.

He took the usual huge stogie out of his mouth and waved a despondent greeting to MacVeagh. The editor paused. "Poor house tonight?" he asked sympathetically.

"Poor house, he says!" Mr. Marcus replaced the cigar and it joggled with his words. "Mr. MacVeagh, I give you my word, even the ushers won't stay in the auditorium!"

MacVeagh whistled. "That bad?"

"Bad? Mr. MacVeagh, *Rio Rhythm* is colossal, stupendous, and likewise terrific. But it smells, yet."

"I don't get it."

"Stink bombs, Mr. MacVeagh. Stink bombs they throw, yet, into the Lyric. A strictly union house I run, I pay my bills, I got no competitors, and now comes stink bombs. It ain't possible. But it's true."

MacVeagh half guessed the answer even then. He got it in full with Molly's first speech when he reached the office.

"Boss, you've got to look after things better yourself. I don't know how the copy desk let it get by. Of course, that kid you put onto handling movie reviews is green; he doesn't know there's some things you just don't say in a paper, true though they may be. But look!"

MacVeagh looked, knowing what he would see. The movie review, a new department added experimentally since the *Sentinel* had expanded so, stated succinctly: "*Rio Rhythm* stinks."

John MacVeagh was silent for a long count. Then he said wryly, "It's quite a responsibility, isn't it, Molly?"

"Boss," she said, "you're the only man in the world I'd trust with it."

He believed her—not that it was true, but that she thought it was. And that was all the more reason why . . .

"You're kidding yourself, Molly. Not that I don't like to hear it. But this is a power that should never be used for anything but the best. I've tried to use it that way. And tonight I've learned that—well, I'll put in *inadvertently* to salve my conscience—that I'm ruining one man's business and have destroyed another's happiness.

"It's too much power. You can't realize all its ramifications. It's horrible—and yet it's wonderful, too. To know that it's yours—it—it makes you feel like a god, Molly. No, more than that: Like God."

There was an echo in the back of his mind. Something gnawing there, something remembered . . .

Then he heard the words as clearly as though they were spoken in the room. Father Byrne's unfinished sentence: "If you were God—" And Jake Willis' question that had prompted it: "Why doesn't God stop the war?"

Molly watched the light that came on in the boss's eyes. It was almost beautiful, and still it frightened her.

"Well," said John MacVeagh, "why don't I?"

It took a little preparing. For one thing, he hadn't tried anything on such a global scale before. He didn't know if influence outside of Grover would work, though truth should be truth universally.

For another, it took some advance work. He had to concoct an elaborate lie about new censorship regulations received from Washington, so that the tickers were moved into his private office and the foreign news came out to the rewrite staff only over his desk.

And the public had to be built up to it. It couldn't come too suddenly, too unbelievably. He prepared stories of mounting Axis defeats. He built up the internal dissension in Axis countries.

And it worked. Associated Press reports from the battlefields referred to yesterday's great victory which had been born on his typewriter. For one last experiment, he assassinated Goering. The press-association stories were crowded the next day with rumors from neutral countries and denials from Berlin.

And finally the front page of the Grover *Sentinel* bore nothing but two words:

WAR ENDED

MacVeagh had deleted the exclamation point from the proof. There was no need for it.

VI

Excerpts from the diary of Hank Branson, FBI:

Washington, June 23.

This looks to be the strangest case I've tackled yet. Screwier than that Nazi ring that figured out a way to spread subversive propaganda through a burlesque show. The chief called me in this morning, and he was plenty worried. "Did you ever hear of a town called Grover?" he asked.

Of course I had. It's where the Hitchcock plant is. So I said sure and waited for him to spill the rest of it. But it took him a while. Almost as though he was embarrassed by what he had to say.

At last he came out with, "Hank, you're going to think I'm crazy. But as best we can figure it out, this is the situation: All this country is at war with the Axis— excepting Grover."

"Since when," I wanted to know, "do city councils have to declare war?"

So he tried to explain. "For two weeks now, the town of Grover has had no part in the war effort. The Hitchcock plant has stopped producing and is retooling for peace production. The Grover draft board hasn't sent in one man of its quota. The Grover merchants have stopped turning in their ration stamps. Even the tin-can collections have stopped. *Grover isn't at war.*"

"But that's nuts," I said.

"I warned you. But that's the case. We've sent them memoranda and warnings and notifications and every other kind of governmental scrap paper you can imagine. Either they don't receive them or they don't read them. No answers, no explanations. We've got to send a man in there to investigate on the spot. And it's got to be from our office. I don't think an Army man could keep his trigger finger steady at the spectacle of a whole community resigning from the war."

"Have you got any ideas?" I asked. "Anything to give me a lead."

The chief frowned. "Like you say, it's nuts. There's no accounting for it. Unless— Look, now you'll really think I'm crazy. But sometimes when I want to relax, I read those science-fiction magazines. You understand?"

"They're cheaper than blondes," I admitted.

"So this is the only thing that strikes me: some kind of a magnetic force field exists around Grover that keeps it out of touch with the rest of the world. Maybe even a temporal field that twists it into a time where there isn't any war. Maybe the whole thing's a new secret weapon of the enemy, and they're trying it out there. Soften up the people for invasion by making them think it's all over. Go ahead. Laugh. But if you think my answer's screwy—*and* it is—just remember: it's up to you to find the right one."

So that's my assignment, and I never had a cockeyeder one: Find out why one town, out of this whole nation, has quit the war flat.

Proutyville, June 24.

At least Proutyville's what it says on the road map, though where I am says just MOTEL and that seems to be about all there is.

I'm the only customer tonight. The motel business isn't what it used to be. I guess that's why the garage next door is already converted into a blacksmith's job.

"People that live around here, they've got to get into town now and then," the old guy that runs it said to me. "So they're pretty well converted back to horses already."

"I've known guys that were converted to horses," I said. "But only partially."

"I mean, converted to the use of horses." There was a funny sort of precise dignity about this correction. "I am pleased to be back at the old work."

He looked old enough to have flourished when blacksmithing was big time. I asked, "What did you do in the meanwhile?"

"All kinds of metal trades. Printing mostly."

And that got us talking about printing and newspapers, which is right up my alley because Pop used to own the paper in Sage Bluffs and I've lately been tied up with most of the department's cases involving seditious publications.

"A paper can do a lot of harm," I insisted. "Oh, I know it's been the style to cry down the power of the press ever since the 1936 and 1940 elections. But a paper still has a lot of influence even though it's hard to separate cause and effect. For instance, do Chicagoans think that way because of the *Tribune,* or is there a *Tribune* because Chicagoans are like that?"

From there on we got practically philosophical. He had a lot of strange ideas, that old boy. Mostly about truth. How truth was relative, which there's nothing new in that idea, though he dressed it up fancy. And something about truth and spheres of influence—how a newspaper, for instance, aimed at printing The Truth, which there is no such thing as, but actually tried, if it was honest, to print the truth (lower case) for its own sphere of influence. Outside the radius of its circulation, truth might, for another editor, be something quite else again. And then he said, to himself like, "I'd like to hear sometime how that wish came out," which didn't mean anything but sort of ended that discussion.

It was then I brought up my own little problem, and that's the only reason I've bothered to write all this down, though there's no telling what a crackpot blacksmith like that meant.

It's hard to get a clear picture of him in my mind now while I'm writing this. He's tall and thin and he has a great beak of a nose. But what I can't remember is does he have a beard? I'd almost swear he does, and still—

Anyway, I told him about Grover, naming no names, and asked him what he thought of that set-up. He liked to speculate; OK, here was a nice ripe subject.

He thought a little and said, "Is it Grover?" I guess some detail in my description of the plant and stuff tipped it off. I didn't answer, but he went on: "Think over what I've said, my boy. When you get to Grover and see what the situation is, remember what we've talked about tonight. Then you'll have your answer."

This prating hasn't any place in my diary. I know that. I feel like a dope writing it down. But there's a certain curious compulsion about it. Not so much because I feel that this is going to help explain whatever is going on in Grover, but because I've got this eerie sensation that that old man is like nothing else I've met in all my life.

It's funny. I keep thinking of my Welsh grandmother and the stories she used to tell me when I was so high. It's twenty years since I've thought of those.

Grover, June 25.

Nothing to record today but long, tiresome driving over deserted highways. I wonder what gas rationing has done to the sales of Burma Shave.

The roads were noticeably more populated as I got nearer Grover, even though it was by then pretty late. Maybe they've abolished that rationing, too.

Too late to do any checking now; I'll get to work tomorrow, with my usual routine of dropping in at the local paper first to gather a picture.

Grover, June 26.

Two of the oddest things in my life with the FBI have happened today. One, the minor one, is that I've somehow mislaid my diary, which is why this entry is written on note paper. The other, and what has really got me worried, is that I've mislaid my job.

Just that. I haven't the slightest idea why I am in Grover.

It's a nice little town. Small and cozy and like a thousand others, only maybe even more pleasant. It's going great guns now, of course, reveling, like everyplace else, in the boom of postwar prosperity.

There's a jiggy, catchy chorus in *The Chocolate Soldier* that goes, "Thank the Lord the war is over, tum-tee-tum tee-tum tee-tover—" Nice, happy little tune; it ought to be the theme song of these times. It seems like only yesterday I was stewing, and all the rest of the department with me, about saboteurs and subversive elements and all the other wartime problems.

Only now I've got something else to stew about, which is why I'm here.

I tried to get at it indirectly with John MacVeagh, a stolid sort of young man with heavy eyebrows and a quiet grin, who edits the Grover *Sentinel*—surprisingly large and prosperous paper for a town this size. Daily, too.

I liked MacVeagh—good guy. Says he didn't serve in the war because a punctured eardrum kept him out, but says he tried his best to see Grover through it on the home front. We settled down to quite a confab, and I deliberately let it slip that I was from the FBI. I hoped that'd cue him into, "Oh, so you're here on the Hungadunga case, huh?" But no go. No reaction at all, but a mild wonder as to what a G-man was doing in Grover.

I didn't tell him.

I tried the same stunt on the chief of police, who kept quoting Bible texts at me and telling me about a murder they had a while back and how he solved it. (Would you believe it? The butler did it! Honest.) Nothing doing on the reaction business. Grover, ever since the famous murder, has had the most crime-free record in the State. Nothing in my line.

Nothing to do but sleep on it and hope tomorrow turns up either my diary or my memory.

Grover, June 27.

I like Grover. Now that the war's over, the department'll be cutting down on its staff. I might do worse than resign and settle down here. I've always wanted to try some pulp writing to show up the guys that write about us. And in a few years Chief Hanby'll be retiring, and if I'm established in the community by then—

And I'm going to have to get out of the department if things go on like this. Had a swell day today—visited the Hitchcock plant and saw their fabulous new work with plastics in consumer goods, had dinner at MacVeagh's and went out to a picture and a bar on a double date with him and his wife—who is the loveliest thing I ever saw, if you like icicles—and a girl from the paper, who's a nice kid.

But I still don't know from nothing.

I sent a wire back to the chief:

WIRE FULL INSTRUCTIONS AT ONCE MY MISSION LOCAL POLICE CHIEF WANTS FORMAL OK.

I know, I know. It's a thin story, and it probably won't work. But I've got to try something.

Grover, June 28.

I got an answer:

YOUR QUOTE MISSION UNQUOTE ALL A MISTAKE. RETURN WASHINGTON.

I don't get it. Maybe when I see the chief again—

So now, regretfully, we bid farewell to the sunny, happy town of Grover, nestling at the foot—

Proutyville, June 29.

As you—whoever you are and whatever you think you're doing reading other people's diaries—can see, my diary's turned up again. And that I am, as they say in the classics, stark, raving mad seems about the only possible answer.

Maybe I thought the chief was crazy. What's he going to call me?

I read over again what the old guy with—or without—the beard said. Where he said I'd find the answer. I didn't.

So I went over to see him again, but he wasn't there. There was a fat man drinking beer out of a quart bottle, and as soon as he saw me he poured a glassful and handed it over unasked.

It tasted good, and I said, "Thanks," and meant it. Then I described the old boy and asked where was he.

The fat man poured himself another glass and said, "Damfino. He come in here one day and says, 'See you're setting up to shoe horses. Need an old hand at the business?' So I says, 'Sure, what's your name?' and he says, 'Wieland,' leastways that's what I think he says, like that beer out in California. 'Wieland,' he says. 'I'm a smith,' so he goes to work. Then just this morning he up and says, 'I'm needed more elsewhere,' he says, 'I gotta be going,' he says, 'now you been a swell employer,' he says, 'so if you—' " The fat man stopped. "So he up and quit me."

"Because you were a swell employer?"

"That? That was just something he says. Some foolishness. Hey, your glass is empty." The fat man filled my glass and his own.

The beer was good. It kept me from quite going nuts. I sat there the most of the evening. It wasn't till late that a kind of crawly feeling began to hit me. "Look," I said. "I've drunk beer most places you can name, but I never saw a quart bottle hold that many glasses."

The fat man poured out some more. "This?" he said, offhand-like. "Oh, this is just something Wieland give me."

And I suppose I'm writing all this out to keep from thinking about what I'm going to say to the chief. But what can I say? Nothing but this:

Grover isn't at war. And when you're there, it's true.

Washington, June 30.

I'm not going to try to write the scene with the chief. It still stings, kind of. But he softened up a little toward the end. I'm not to be fired; just suspended. Farnsworth's taking the Grover assignment. And I get a rest—

Bide-a-wee Nursing Home, July 1.

VII

It was hot in the office that June night. John MacVeagh should have been deep in his studies, but other thoughts kept distracting him.

These studies had come to occupy more and more of his time. His responsibilities were such that he could not tolerate anything less than perfection in his concepts of what was the desirable truth.

Ending the war had been simple. But now the *Sentinel* had to print the truth of the postwar adjustments. Domestically these seemed to be working fine, at the moment. Demobilization was being carried out smoothly and gradually, and the startling technological improvements matured in secrecy during wartime were now bursting forth to take up the slack in peacetime production.

The international scene was more difficult. The willful nationalism of a few misguided senators threatened to ruin any possible adjustment. MacVeagh had to keep those men in check, and even more difficult, he had to learn the right answers to all the problems.

The eventual aim, he felt sure, must be a world state. But of what nature? He plowed through Clarence Streit and Ely Culbertson and everything else he could lay hands on, rejecting Culbertson's overemphasis on the nation as a unit and Streit's narrow definition of what constitutes democracy, but finding in each essential points that had to be fitted into the whole.

MacVeagh's desk was heavy with books and notes and card indexes, but he was not thinking of any of these things. He was thinking of Laura.

The breaking point had come that night they went out with Molly and the G-man. (Odd episode, that. Why a G-man here in peaceful Grover? And so secretive about his mission and so abrupt in his departure.) It might have been the picture that brought it on, a teary opus in which Bette Davis suffered nobly.

It was funny that he couldn't remember the words of the scene. According to all tradition, they should be indelibly engraved on the tablets, et cetera. But he didn't remember the words, just the general pain and torture.

Laura crying, crying with that helpless quiet desperation that is a woman's way of drowning her sorrows. Himself, puzzled, hurt, trying to help and comfort her. Laura shuddering away from his touch. Laura talking in little gasps between her sobs about how he was nice and she liked him and he was so good to her, but she didn't understand, she never had understood how she made up her mind to marry him and she would try to be a good wife, she did want to, but—

He remembered those words. They were the only ones that stayed indelible: "—I just don't love you."

He had quieted her finally and left her red-eyed but sleeping. He had slept that night, and all the nights since then, in the guest room that some day was to be converted into a nursery.

Was to have been converted.

There's a catch, Molly said. Always a catch. You can make your marriage true, but your wife's love—

A man isn't fit to be God. A woman who cannot love you is so infinitely more important than the relation of Soviet Russia to Western Europe.

MacVeagh almost barked at Lucretius Sellers when he came in. The old printer was a regular visitor at the *Sentinel*. He wasn't needed any longer, of course, with the new presses and the new staff that tended them. But he'd appointed himself an unofficial member of the *Sentinel*'s forces, and MacVeagh was glad, though sometimes wondering how much of the truth about the truth Luke Sellers might guess.

Tonight Luke glanced at the laden desk and grinned. "Hard at it, Johnny?" He was sober, and there was worry in his eyes behind the grin.

MacVeagh snapped his thoughts back from their desolate wanderings. "Quite a job I've got," he said.

"I know. But if you've got a minute, Johnny—"

MacVeagh made a symbolic gesture of pushing books aside. "Sure, Luke. What's on your mind?"

Luke Sellers was silent a little. Then, "I don't like to talk like this, Johnny. I wouldn't if I wasn't afraid you'd hear it somewhere else. And Molly, even she thinks I ought to tell you. It's getting her. She slapped Mrs. Manson's face at the Ladies' Aid last meeting. Not but what that's sensible enough, but she's generally acting funny. Sometimes I'm almost afraid maybe—"

He bogged down.

"That's a heck of a preamble, Luke. What's it leading up to? Here—want to oil up your larynx?"

"Thanks, Johnny. Haven't had a drink all day—wanted to have my head clear to— But maybe this might help— Well, peace forever! Thanks."

"OK. Now what?"

"It's— Johnny, you're going to kick me out of this office on my tail. But it's about Mrs. MacVeagh."

"Laura?"

"Now, hold on, Johnny. Hold your horses. I know there's nothing in it, Molly knows there's nothing in it, but it's the way people around town are talking. She's been seeing a lot of that manager out at the plant, what's-his-name, Johansen. You work here late at nights, and— Phil Rogers, he saw them out at Cardotti's road-house. So did Jake Willis another night. And I just wanted— Well, Johnny, I'd rather you heard it from me than down at Clem's barber shop."

MacVeagh's face was taut. "It's no news to me, Luke. I know she's lonely when I work here. Fact is, I asked Johansen to show her a little fun. He's a good guy. You might tell that to Mrs. Manson and the boys at Clem's."

Luke Sellers stood looking at MacVeagh. Then he took another drink. "I'll spread it around, Johnny."

"Thanks, Luke."

"And I hope I can make it sound more convincing than you did."

He left. John MacVeagh sat silent, and the room was full of voices.

"How does it feel, MacVeagh? What's it like to know that your wife— No, MacVeagh, don't rub your forehead. You'll prick yourself on the horns—"

"Don't listen, MacVeagh. It's just people. People talk. It doesn't mean anything."

"Where there's smoke, MacVeagh— Remember? You didn't think there was any fire in Laura, did you? But where there's smoke there's—"

"You could fix it, you know. You could fix it, the way you fix everything. Something could happen to Johansen."

"Or if you haven't the heart for that, MacVeagh, you could send him away. Have him called to Washington. That'd be a break for him too."

"But it wouldn't solve the problem, would it, MacVeagh? She still wouldn't love you."

"You don't believe it, do you, MacVeagh? She can't help not loving you, but she wouldn't deceive you. You trust her, don't you?"

"MacVeagh."

It was some seconds before John MacVeagh realized that this last voice was not also inside his head. He looked up to see Phil Rogers, the perfect profile as hyperpale as it had been on the night of his aunt's murder. His white hand held an automatic.

"Yes?" MacVeagh asked casually. He tensed his body and calculated positions and distances with his eyes, while he wondered furiously what this meant.

"MacVeagh, I'm going to send you to meet God."

"My. Fancy talk." It was difficult. MacVeagh was hemmed in by files and a table of reference books. It would be next to impossible to move before Phil Rogers could jerk his right index finger. "And just why, Phil, should you take this job on yourself?"

"Maybe I should say because you stole Laura, and now she's making a fool of herself—and you—with that Johansen. I wanted her. I'd have had her, too. H. A. and I had it all fixed up."

It wasn't worth explaining that MacVeagh and Rogers had equally little just claim on Laura. "Noble," said MacVeagh. "All for love. You'd let them stretch your neck for love, too?"

Rogers laughed. "You know me, huh, MacVeagh?"

Play for time, that was the only way. "I know you enough to think there's a stronger motive—stronger for you."

"You're right there is. And you're going to hear it before you go. Go to meet God. Wonder what He'll think—of meeting another god."
This was more startling than the automatic. "What do you mean by that, Phil?"
"I've heard Luke Sellers talking when he was drunk. About General Wigginsby and the butler's confession. Everybody thought he was babbling. But I got it. I don't know how it works, but your paper prints true. What you print happens." MacVeagh laughed. "Nonsense. Listen to Luke? You must've been tight yourself, Phil. Go home."
"Uh-uh." Rogers shook his head, but his hand didn't move. "That explains it all. All you've done to me. You took Laura. You shoved that softie Johansen into the general manager's job I should have had. You got that sniveling, weak-kneed labor agreement through. You— MacVeagh, I think you ended the war!"
"And you'd hold that against me?"
"Yes. We were doing swell. Now with retooling, new products, trying to crash new markets, everything uncertain— I inherited my aunt's interest in the company. MacVeagh, you did me out of two–three years of profits."
"Do you think anybody'd believe this wild yarn of yours, Phil?"
"No. I don't. I was tight, just tight enough so things made sense. I wouldn't swallow it sober myself. But I know it's true, and that's why I've got to kill you, MacVeagh." His voice rose to a loud, almost soprano cry.
The white hand was very steady. MacVeagh moved his body slowly to one side and watched the nose of the automatic hold its point on him. Then, with the fastest, sharpest movement he'd ever attained in his life, he thrust his chair crashing back and dropped doubled into the kneehole of his desk. The motion was just in time. He heard a bullet thud into the plaster of the wall directly behind where he'd been sitting.
His plans had been unshaped. It was simply that the desk seemed the only armor visible at the moment. And to fire directly into this kneehole would mean coming around and up close where he might possibly grab at Rogers' legs. The wood between him and Rogers now should be thick enough to—
He heard a bullet plunk into that wood. Then he heard it go past his ear and bury itself in more wood. His guess was wrong. He could be shot in here. This bullet had gone past him as knives go past the boy in the Indian basket trick. But Phil Rogers was not a magician slipping knives into safe places, and no amount of contortion could save MacVeagh from eventually meeting one of those bullets.
He heard scuffling noises. Then he heard a thud that was that of a body, not a bullet, and with it another shot.
MacVeagh crawled out from under the desk. "Undignified posture," he said, "but what would you do if you were hemmed in and this maniac started— Is he hurt?"
It took a while for exchange of information, MacVeagh giving a much-censored version which made it seem that Phil Rogers was suffering a motiveless breakdown of some sort, the other telling how he'd been waiting outside, heard Phil's denunciations—though not their words—and then the shots, and decided to intervene. Rogers was so intent on his victim that attack from behind was a snap. The last shot had gone into Rogers' own left shoulder as they struggled. Nothing serious.

"Don't know how I can ever thank you, Johansen," said John MacVeagh.

"Any time," said his wife's lover. "It's a pleasure."

Rogers was on his feet again now. MacVeagh turned to him and said, "Get out. I don't care what you do or how you explain that bullet wound. I'm not bringing any charges. Get out."

Rogers glared at them both. "I'll settle with you, MacVeagh. You too, Johansen."

"Uh-uh. You're having a nervous breakdown. You're going to a sanitarium for a while. When you come out you'll feel fine."

"That's what you say."

"Get out," MacVeagh repeated. And as Rogers left, he jotted down a note to print the sanitarium trip and the necessary follow-ups on convalescence.

Without a word he handed a bottle to Johansen, then drank from it himself. "Thanks," he said. "I can't say more than that."

The tall blond man smiled. "I won't ask questions. I've had run-ins with Rogers myself. The boss's sister's nephew— But to tell the truth, John, I'm sorry I saved your life."

MacVeagh stiffened. "You've still got his gun," he suggested humorlessly.

"I don't want you to lose your life. But I'm sorry *I* saved it. Because it makes what I have to say so much harder."

MacVeagh sat on the edge of his desk. "Go on."

"Cold, like this? I don't know how I thought I was going to manage to say this— I never expected this kind of a build-up— All right, John, this is it:

"I told you once that Laura had better be happy. Well, she isn't. I've been seeing her. Probably you know that. I haven't tried to sneak about it. She doesn't love you, John. She won't say it, but I think she still loves me. And if I can make her happy, I'm warning you, I'll take her away from you."

MacVeagh said nothing.

Johansen went on hesitantly. "I know what it would mean. A scandal that would make Laura a fallen woman in the eyes of all Grover. A fight with H. A. that would end my job here and pretty much kill my chances in general. I'll make it clear to Laura—and I think she'll be as willing to risk it as I am.

"But I'm giving you your chance. If you can make her love you, make her happy, all right. It's Laura that counts. But if in another month there's still that haunted emptiness in her eyes—well, John, then it's up to me."

The two men stood facing each other for a moment. There were no more words. There was no possibility of words. Ingve Johansen turned and left the room.

If you can make her love you— Was this the limit to the power of the god of the *Sentinel*? You can't print EDITOR'S WIFE LOVES HIM. You can't—or can you?

Numbly MacVeagh groped his way to the typewriter. His fingers fumbled out words.

"Women have a double task in this new peace time," Mrs. John MacVeagh, president of the Volunteer Women Workers, stated when interviewed yesterday.

"Like all other citizens, women must take part in the tasks of reconstruction," said the lovely Mrs. MacVeagh, nee Laura Hitchcock. "But woman's prime job in reconstruction is assuring happiness in the home. A man's usefulness to society must depend largely on the love of his wife. I feel that I am doing good work here with the VWW, but I consider the fact that I love my husband my most important contribution to Grover's welfare."

MacVeagh sat back and looked at it. His head ached and his mouth tasted foul. Neither a pipe nor a drink helped. He reread what he'd written. Was this the act of a god—or of a louse?

But it had to be. He knew Laura well enough to know that she'd never stand up under the scandal and ostracism that Johansen proposed, no matter how eagerly she might think she welcomed them. As Ingve had said, it's Laura that counts.

It is so easy to find the most flattering motives for oneself.

He wrote a short item announcing I. L. Johansen's resignation as manager of the Hitchcock plant and congratulating him on his appointment to the planning board of the new OPR, the Office of Peacetime Reconstruction. He was typing the notice of Philip Rogers' departure for a sanitarium, phrased with euphemistic clarity, when Luke Sellers came back.

Luke had been gone an hour. Plenty had happened here in that hour, but more where Luke Sellers had been. The old printer had aged a seeming ten years.

He kept twitching at his little scraggle of white beard, and his eyes didn't focus anywhere. His lips at first had no power to shape words. They twisted hopefully, but what came through them was just sound.

"Molly—" Luke said at last.

John MacVeagh stood up sharply. "What is it? What's wrong?"

"Molly— Told you I was worried about her—"

"She— No! She hasn't! She couldn't!"

"Iodine. Gulped it down. Messy damned way. Doc Quillan hasn't much hope—"

"But why? Why?"

"She can't talk. Vocal cords— It eats, that iodine— Keeps trying to say something. I think it's— Want to come?"

MacVeagh thought he understood a little. He saw things he should have seen before. How Molly felt about him. How, like Johansen with Laura, she could tolerate his marriage if he was happy, but when that marriage was breaking up and her loss became a pointless farce—

"Coming, Johnny?" Luke Sellers repeated.

"No," said MacVeagh. "I've got to work. Molly'd want me to. And she'll pull through all right, Luke. You'll read about it in the *Sentinel.*"

It was the first time that this god had exercised the power of life and death.

VIII

The next morning, Laura looked lovelier than ever at breakfast as she glanced up from the paper and asked, "Did you like my interview?"

MacVeagh reached a hand across the table and touched hers. "What do you think?"

"I'm proud," she said. "Proud to see it there in print. More coffee?"
"Thanks."
She rose and filled his cup at the silver urn. "Isn't it nice to have all the coffee
we want again?" As she set the cup back at his place, she leaned over and kissed
him. It was a light, tender kiss, and the first she had ever given him unprompted.
He caught her hand and held it for a moment.
"Don't stay too late at the office tonight, dear," she said softly.

"Most amazing recovery I ever saw," Doc Quillan mumbled. "Take a while for
the throat tissues to heal; but she'll be back at work in no time. Damned near
tempted to call it a miracle, MacVeagh."

"I guess this OPR appointment settles my part of what we were talking about,"
Ingve Johansen said over the phone. "It's a grand break for me—fine work that
I'm anxious to do. So I won't be around, but remember—I may come back."

"Gather Phil made a fool of himself last night," said H. A. Hitchcock. "Don't
worry. Shan't happen again. Strain, overwork— He'll be all right after a rest."

Father Byrne dropped in that morning, happily flourishing a liberal journal which
had nominated Grover as the nation's model town for labor relations.
    Chief Hanby dropped in out of pure boredom. The Grover crime rate had
become so minute that he feared his occupation was all but gone. "The crooks are
all faded," he said. " 'The strangers shall fade away, and be afraid out of their
close places.' Psalms, eighteen, forty-five. Grover's the Lord's town now."
    John MacVeagh stood alone in his office, hearing the whir of presses and the
rushing of feet outside. This was his, the greatest tool of good in the world's
history.
    "And God saw everything that he had made, and, behold, it was very good."
Genesis, as Chief Hanby would say, one, thirty-one.

He did not stay too late at the office that night.

John MacVeagh reached over to the night table for a cigarette. There are times
when even a confirmed pipe smoker uses them. In the glow of the match he saw
Laura's face, relaxed and perfect.
    "Want one?"
    "No thanks, dear."
    He took in a deep breath of smoke and let it out slowly. "Do you love me?"
he asked gently.
    "What do you think?" She moved closer and laid her head on his shoulder.
    He felt a stirring of discontent, of compunction. "But I— Do you really love
me? Not just because of that interview—what I made you say, but—"
    Laura laughed. "You didn't make me say it. Except that your being you is what
makes me love you, and that's what made me say it. Of course I love you. I know
I've been frightfully slow realizing it, but now—"

"I want you to love me. I want you really to love me, of your own self—"
But even as he spoke, he realized the hopelessness of his longing. That could
never be now. He had forcibly made her into a thing that loved him, and that
"love" was no more like true love than the affection of a female robot or—he
shuddered a little—the attentions of the moronic ghost that brought love to Professor Guildea.

He could not even revoke this forced love, unless by figuring some means of
printing that she did not love him. And that then would be true, and forbid all
possibility of the real love that she might eventually have felt for him.

He was trapped. His power and his ingenuity had made him the only man on
earth who had not the slightest chance of ever feeling the true, unfeigned, un-
forced love of his wife.

It was this that brought it all into focus. MacVeagh understood now the nagging
discontent that had been gnawing at him. He looked at everything that he had made,
and behold, he felt only annoyance and impatience.

He tried to phrase it once or twice:

"Jake, supposing you knew it was only a trick, this change in your beliefs. It
was just a hoax, a bad practical joke played on you."

"How could it be? I used to have crazy ideas. I used to think I was too smart to
believe. Now I know different. That's no joke."

"Father Byrne, do you think this labor agreement could have been reached
without outside pressure? That men and management really could have got together like this?"

"They did, didn't they, John? I don't understand what you mean about outside
pressure—unless," the priest added, smiling, "you think my prayers were a form
of undue influence?"

MacVeagh did not try to explain what God had answered those prayers. Even
if you could persuade people of the actual state of things, that he and the *Sentinel*
had made them what they were, the truth would remain the truth.

He realized that when Molly came back to the office. For Molly knew the
whole story and understood. She understood too well. Her first words when they
were alone were, "Boss, I'm really dead, aren't I?"

He tried to pretend not to understand. He tried to bluff through it, pass it off
as nothing. But she was too sure. She insisted, "I died that night." Her voice was a
rough croak. He had forgotten to specify a miraculous recovery of the iodine-
eaten vocal cords.

At last he nodded, without a word.

"I suppose I ought to thank you, boss. I don't know if I do— I guess I do,
though Laura came to see me in the hospital and talked. If she loves you, you're
happy. And if you're happy, boss, life's worth living."

"Happy—" Then his words began to tumble out. Molly was the first person,
the only person that he could talk to about his new discovery: the drawback of
omnipotence.

"You see," he tried to make it clear, "truth has a meaning, a value, only because it's outside of us. It's something outside that's real and valid, that we can

reckon against. When you make the truth yourself it doesn't have any more meaning. It doesn't feel like truth. It's no truer than an author's characters are to him. Less so, maybe; sometimes they can rebel and lead their own lives. But nothing here in Grover can rebel, or in the world either. But it's worst here. I don't know people any more."

"Especially me," said Molly.

He touched her shoulder gently. "One thing I didn't make up, Molly. That's your friendship for me. I'm grateful for that."

"Thanks, boss." Her voice was even rougher. "Then take some advice from me. Get out of Grover for a while. Let your mind get straightened out. See new people that you've never done anything to except end the war for them. Take a vacation."

"I can't. The paper's such a responsibility that—"

"Nobody but me knows about it, and I promise to be good. If you're away, it'll run just like any other paper. Go on, boss."

"Maybe you're right. I'll try it, Molly. But one thing."

"Yes, boss?"

"Remember: this has got to be the best-proofread paper in the world."

Molly nodded and almost smiled.

For an hour after leaving Grover, John MacVeagh felt jittery. He ought to be back at his desk. He ought to be making sure that the Senate didn't adopt the Smith amendment, that the Army of Occupation in Germany effectively quashed that Hohenzollern Royalist putsch, that nothing serious came of Mr. Hasenberg's accident at the plant—

Then the jitters left him, and he thought, "Let them make out by themselves. They did once."

He spent the night at the Motel in Proutyville and enjoyed the soundest sleep he had known in months. In the morning he went next door to chat with the plump garage proprietor, who'd been good company on other trips.

He found a woman there, who answered his "Where's Ike?" with "Ain't you heard? He died last week. Too much beer, I guess."

"But Ike lived on beer."

"Sure, only he used to drink only as much as he could afford. Then for a while seems like there wasn't no limit to how much he had, and last week he comes down with this stroke. I'm his daughter-in-law; I'm keeping the joint going. Not that there's any business in times like these."

"What do you mean, in times like these?"

"Mister, where you been? Don't you know there's a war on?"

"No," said John MacVeagh dazedly. The daughter-in-law looked after him, not believing her ears.

MacVeagh hardly believed his, either. Not until he reached the metropolis of Zenith was he fully convinced. He studied newspapers there, talked with soldiers and defense workers.

There was no doubt at all. The world was at war.

He guessed the answer roughly. Something about relative truths and spheres of influence. He could work it out clearly later.

His head was spinning as he got back to his parked car. There was a stocky young man in a plain gray suit standing beside it, staring at the name plate GROVER attached to the license.

As MacVeagh started to get in, the young man accosted him. "You from Grover, Mac?"

MacVeagh nodded automatically, and the man slipped into the seat beside him. "We've got to have a talk, Mac. A long talk."

"And who are you?"

"Kruger. FBI." He flashed a card. "The Bureau is interested in Grover."

"Look," said MacVeagh, "I've got an appointment at the Zenith *Bulletin* in five minutes. After that, I'm at your disposal. You can come along," he added as the G-man hesitated.

"OK, Mac. Start thinking up answers."

Downtown traffic in Zenith was still fairly heavy, even in wartime. Pedestrian traffic was terrific. MacVeagh pulled his car up in the yellow zone in front of the *Bulletin* Building. He opened his door and stepped out. Kruger did the same. Then in an instant MacVeagh was back in the driver's seat and the car was pulling away.

He had the breaks with him. A hole opened up in the traffic just long enough to ensure his getaway. He knew there were too many bystanders for Kruger to risk a shot. Two blocks away, he deliberately stalled the car in the middle of an intersection. In the confusion of the resulting pile-up he managed to slip away unnoticed.

The car had to be abandoned anyway. Where could he get gas for it with no ration coupons? The important thing was to get away with his skin.

For he had realized in an instant that one of Kruger's first questions would be, "Where's your draft card, Mac?" And whatever steps he had to take to solve the magnificent confusion which his godhead had created, he could take none of them in Federal prison as a draft evader.

Molly stared at the tramp who had forced his way into the *Sentinel* office. "Well," she growled, "what do you want?"

"Molly, don't you know me?"

"Boss!"

The huskies on either side of him reluctantly relaxed their grips. "You can go, boys," she said. They went, in frowning dumbness.

MacVeagh spoke rapidly. "I can't tell it all to you now, Molly. It's too long. You won't believe it, but I've had the Feds on my tail. That's why this choice costume, mostly filth. The rods were the only safe route to Grover. And you thought I should take a vacation—"

"But why—"

"Listen, Molly. I've made a world of truth, all right. But that truth holds good only where the *Sentinel* dominates. There's an imaginary outside to go with it, an outside that sends me dispatches based on my own statements, that maintains banking relations with our banks, that feeds peacetime programs to our radios, and so on, but it's a false outside, a world of If. The true outside is what it would be without me: a world at war."

For a moment Molly gasped speechlessly. Then she said, "Mr. Johansen!"

"What about him?"

"You sent him to the Office of Peacetime Reconstruction. That's in your world of If. What's become of him?"

"I never thought of that one. But there are problems enough. It isn't fair to the people here to make them live in an unreal world, even if it's better than the real one. Man isn't man all by himself. Man is in and of his time and the rest of mankind. If he's false to his time, he's false to himself. Grover's going to rejoin the world."

"But how, boss? Are you going to have to start the war all over?"

"I never stopped it except in our pretty dream world. But I'm going to do more than that. I'm going to reveal the whole fake—to call it all a fake *in print*."

"Boss!" Molly gasped. "You . . . you realize this is suicide? Nobody'll ever read the *Sentinel* again. And suicide," she added with grim personal humor, "isn't anything I'd recommend."

"I don't count beside Grover. I don't count beside men. 'For God,' " he quoted wryly, " 'so loved the world—' "

"This is it," said John MacVeagh much later.

That edition of the *Sentinel* had been prepared by a staff of three. The large, fine new staff of the large, fine new *Sentinel* had frankly decided that its proprietor was mad or drunk or both. Storming in dressed like a bum and giving the craziest orders. There had been a mass meeting and a mass refusal to have anything to do with the proposed all-is-lies edition.

Luke Sellers had filled the breach again. He read the copy and nodded. "You never talked much, Johnny, but I had it figured pretty much like this. I was in at the start, so I guess it's right I ought to be in at the end."

This was the end now. This minute a two-sheet edition, its front page one huge headline and its inside pages containing nothing but MacVeagh's confession in large type, was set up and ready to run.

The confession told little. MacVeagh could not expect to make anyone believe in Whalen Smith and wishes and variable truths. It read simply like the story of a colossal and unparalleled hoax.

"There won't be enough rails in town for the guys that'll want to run you out on one, Johnny," Luke Sellers warned.

"I'm taking the chance. Go ahead: print it."

The presses clanked.

There was a moment of complete chaos.

Somewhere in that chaos a part of MacVeagh's mind was thinking. This was what had to happen. You gave your wish an impossible problem: to print that its truth is not truth. Like the old logical riddle about how you cannot say, "I am lying." If you are, it's the truth, and so you're not. Same in reverse. And when the wish meets the impossible—

The wish gave up. It ceased to be. And in the timeless eternity where all magic exists, it ceased ever to have been.

Anthony Boucher

IX

"All right then, tell me this: If God can do anything—" Jake Willis cleared his throat and paused, preparatory to delivering the real clincher.

The old man with the scraggly beard snorted and took another shot of apple-jack. "Why doesn't He end the war? I'm getting tired of that, Jake. I wish you'd go back to the weight He can't lift. Father's explained this one before, and I'm willing to admit he makes a good case."

"I don't see it," said Jake stubbornly.

Father Byrne sighed. "Because man must have free will. If men were mere pawns that were pushed around by God, their acts would have no merit in them. They would be unworthy to be the children of God. Your own children you love even when most they rebel. You do not love your chessmen. Man must work out his own salvation; salvation on a silver platter is meaningless."

John MacVeagh stirred restlessly. This idea seemed so familiar. Not from hearing Father Byrne expound it before, but as though he had worked it out for himself, sometime, in a very intimate application.

"But if there is a God—" Jake went on undisturbed.

MacVeagh caught Ingve Johansen's eye and grinned. He was glad Johansen had joined the crackerbarrel club. Glad, too, that Johansen's marriage with Laura Hitchcock was working so well.

The man with the tired face was playing with the black Scottie and trying to think of nothing at all. When he heard footsteps, he looked up sharply. The tiredness was automatically wiped from his face by a grin, which faded as he saw a stranger. "How did you get in here?" he demanded.

The stranger was an old man with a beaked nose. In the dim light it was hard to tell whether or not he wore a beard. He said, "I've been working for you."

The man with the Scottie looked at the defense worker's identification card which said

WHALING, SMITH

He resumed the grin. "Glad to see you. Fine work they've been turning out at your plant. You're a delegate to me?"

"Sort of. But just for me. You see, I'm quitting."

"You can't. Your job's frozen."

"I know. But that don't count. Not for me. But it's this way: Since the Army took over the plant, looks like you're my employer. Right?"

The man seemed puzzled as he fitted a cigarette into a long holder. "I guess so. Smoke?"

"No, thanks. Then if you're my employer, you've been a good one. You've got a wish coming to you."

The man with the holder peered at the other. It was hard to make him out. And he'd come in so silently, presumably through the guards.

The grin was crooked as he said, "I don't think you're even here. And since you aren't, there's no harm in playing the game. A wish—" He looked at the globe on the table and at the dispatches beside it. "Yes," he said finally, "I have a wish—"

John MacVeagh paused beside the Gypsy's booth at the Victory Garden Fair. "Want to have your fortune told, Molly?"

Molly shuddered. "Maybe I'm silly. But ever since I was a child I've been scared of anything like magic. There's always a catch."

The Scottie had been trying to gather courage to bark at the stranger. Now he succeeded. "Be quiet, Fala," his owner ordered. "Yes, Whaling, I wish—"

Mary Celestial

[with Miriam Allen deFord]

Xilmuch was discovered—once. It was discovered in 3942 by Patrick Ostronsky-Vierra, a Two Star Scout of the Galactic Presidium.

It is easy to find—it is in fact Planet IV of Altair. If it were not a little off the beaten track it would have been discovered long before. It is almost precisely the size of our Earth, has similar atmosphere, rotation, gravity, and climatic conditions. It is two-thirds land surface, and in every way is admirably adapted to human habitation. It has been the home of beings indistinguishable from humans, and was once the seat of a high civilization very like our own of the 40th century, except in minor details. There are no noxious animal forms (the only beasts are herbivorous and inoffensive), and there are no human inhabitants who would resist colonization.

And yet, no matter how overcrowded the colonized planets may become, Xilmuch (that was its name in the dominant native language) will never be discovered again. It will never be colonized.

Not after the report Patrick Ostronsky-Vierra brought back in 3942.

He landed in what seemed to be its largest city, after a preliminary survey of the entire planet in his little one-man scout ship. There was a beautiful airport, equipped for planes of every description. It was not in good repair. Squirrel-like animals infested the hangars full of grounded atmosphere-ships. Grass was growing between cracks in the wide runways. A storm had leveled what had been a huge neo-neon beacon.

Patrick spent two days exploring the city on foot. There were multitudes of parked surface cars and of helicopter-like planes, some of which had crashed and were piles of junk. All had been propelled by some fuel unknown to him, all the tanks were empty, and he could not find any stores of fuel that he could recognize. A good many of the main streets had moving sidewalks under plastic roofs, and some were still operating by remote control. It was the sort of civilization which in his experience implied the services of robots, but no robots of any kind were visible.

He explored systematically, starting at one end of the city and circling closer and closer to the center, which appeared to be a huge civic or control area, with overgrown parks, large imposing buildings, and a forest of tri-dimensional televiz

517

masts. The city itself stood on the banks of a wide river, an arm of which had been diverted to run in a circle around this Civic Center, with numerous bridges between.

He went in and out of private houses, what seemed to be hotels, stores, warehouses, schools, halls, factories, and one building apparently a center of worship. Not one solitary human being met him, nor any other living creature higher in the scale of evolution than the equivalent of a cow. The cow-like creatures were not abundant, but they looked well fed; apparently they browsed on the vegetation of the many parks and gardens. It was unthinkable that they could be the dominant race. This civilization had been built by animals with developed cortices and opposable thumbs.

The planet was as advanced artistically as it was scientifically. In the homes, under thick layers of dust, were delicate jewels and piles of beautiful thin coins engraved in strange designs. The walls of the larger buildings were all carved in bas-relief, in a manner nearer to ancient Mayan art than to any other Patrick knew. Demonology must have played a large part in the religion, for there were numerous carvings of small winged beings with long Grecoesque features and what looked like lightning-bolts for arms and legs. In the temple, a grotesque and horrible statue, a hundred feet high, filled most of the great nave.

There were no libraries or museums, no books, no paintings, no musical instruments, no microfilm. Yet the inhabitants must have had some means of visual and auditory public communication, judging by the televiz masts at the Civic Center.

Patrick camped for his first two nights in the nearest house, spreading his blanket on a rug because the beds were too thick in dust. He had his own food supplies in a knapsack, but the stores were full of shelves of metal containers obviously (though he could not understand the drawings on the labels) with edible contents. He sampled one or two, after testing them for harmlessness, and found one to'be a preserved fruit with a pleasant subacid flavor, another a sort of paste resembling *pâté de foie gras* mixed with caviar. There was also a pale pink liquid in a plastic bottle which turned out to be a delicate wine somewhat like *vin rosé*.

He felt like a cross between Goldilocks and Alice.

On the third day he passed over a bridge to the Civic Center. The buildings in their disheveled parks were grouped around a spreading stone edifice with a dome, which he took to be the City Hall. It was morning, a beautiful sunny summer day in the bluish whiteness of Altair. The ragged trees, something like oaks, were full of white and green birds, all singing their little hearts out. A metal fountain, carved in the likeness of a spreading tree, was spouting water from the tips of its branches into a little pond. The grass was covered with myriads of low-growing, velvety purple flowers run wild. Patrick took the broad road, whose ornamental green and brown tiles showed wide gaps through which grassy blades grew thickly, that led to the central building. A long flight of steps ended at a massive bronze-like door, heavily and intricately carved.

Before his eyes, the door opened. A man stood for a second in the doorway, then dashed down the steps toward him.

Patrick braced himself and reached for his raygun. But the man's arms were opened wide, his mouth was stretched in an ecstatic smile, and tears were running down his cheeks.

He was a tall, burly man, seemingly in late middle age; his hair was white but his movements were lithe and supple. He was clean-shaven, and was dressed in a sort of overall made of a grey fabric which looked both soft and durable. He called out something in a harsh guttural tongue. The scout shook his head.

"Welcome, welcome to Xilmuch!" cried the man then in perfect Standard Galactic. "Who are you? How did you get here? Where are you from? I was never so glad to see anyone in all my life!"

He gave Patrick no time to answer. Seizing him by the arm, he hustled him inside.

It had been an official building all right, Patrick could see that. There was a great lobby rising unimpeded to the dome, with an enormous wasteful central staircase. There were banks of levescalators on either side, and wide hallways led to ground-floor offices with transparent plastic doors running from floor to ceiling.

But half the rooms to the right had been transformed into a dwelling place. Patrick was hurried into a living-room whose stone floors were covered with thick grey rugs into which his boots sank. There were couches and low chairs, heavy cream-colored curtains at all the tall windows, long tables of a dark gleaming wood, their legs carved in flowers and birds.

An inner door opened, revealing a corner of a white shining room that must be a kitchen. A woman burst through it and ran to them.

She was about as old as the man, sturdy also, but too plump, with grey hair elaborately curled. She too was dressed in an overall, but hers was bright purple and over it she wore a fancy apron of lace with pink bows at its corners. She had been pretty once, in a vapid way—probably a piquant blonde of the buttercup-and-daisy variety.

She burst into excited chatter in the unknown tongue, clutching at the man's hand. Her voice was high and twittering, with a whine beneath it. The man answered her, and though Patrick could not understand the words, the contemptuous tone was clear enough. The scolding ran off her like water; she gazed at the man meltingly, then turned to stare angrily at the Terran.

The man disengaged himself from her. In Galactic he said to the scout:

"Oh, this is wonderful! A visitor—a visitor at last!

"We must celebrate. We will have a feast. The last case of *rexshan* I could find—I must open it now. Tell me what you want: if there is any of it left, it is yours.

"Oh, what a miracle! Somebody to talk to after so terribly long!"

The woman had sidled up and cuddled against the man, holding his hand to her cheek. He jerked away impatiently, and barked what must have been an order, for she nodded brightly and trotted back to the kitchen, throwing a kiss as she went. The man shrugged as if throwing off a weight and turned to Patrick with undisguised relief.

"Sit here," he said. "It is the most comfortable. And now tell me who you are, my friend, and how you found me."

Patrick showed his credentials. The stranger shook his head. He explained them in words. The man nodded sagely.

"I understand. I had never dared to hope for a visitor from beyond Xilmuch. But I have heard of space travel, though we never attained it."

"And yet you speak Galactic."

"Is that what it is? That is one of my— But tell me first—"

"No, *you* tell *me*. Who are you? What happened to this city? Why did I see nobody in three days, until I found you and—and the lady? Is all your world like this?"

"My name is Zoth—Zoth Cheruk, but you must call me Zoth, and I shall call you Patrick. All the rest you ask—I shall be glad to tell you everything, but we have plenty of time. We'll talk and talk! But first I want to know all about *you,* your world, how you all live, your own life—everything. I have been so starved for conversation—you can't imagine how much, or how long!"

"But oughtn't we to be helping the lady?" Patrick asked uneasily.

"Her name is Jyk. She is my wife." He scowled. "She can manage. She cooks well, at least. It will take her hours; I have ordered all the best for us. Meanwhile, we will drink while we wait."

He opened a tall cabinet with carved doors and took out goblets and a squat yellow bottle.

"Not *rexshan*—we shall have that at dinner. But almost as good; it is pure *stralp* of a very good year."

He poured an iridescent liquid.

"You smell it for a few minutes, then you sip, then you smell it again," he explained.

"Like brandy," Patrick agreed.

"That I do not know. But that is as good a place to start as any. Tell me of your foods and drinks."

There was no help for it. This guy was going to give in his own good time only. Planet scouts are trained in diplomacy. Patrick settled down to being a vocal encyclopedia attached to a question-machine.

Twice they were interrupted by calls from the kitchen. Each time Zoth rose reluctantly and went out, first replenishing Patrick's goblet; he could be heard lifting and setting down some heavy object, his annoyed voice interrupted by his wife's cooing tones. The relation between the two puzzled Patrick as much as anything else he had chanced upon in this strange world, this seeming *Mary Celeste* of the space-seas.

Several hours and several glasses of the iridescent *stralp* later, he was feeling only relaxed and very hungry. Zoth's wife appeared in the kitchen door, rosy and dimpling. This time Zoth beamed. "Now we shall eat," he said. "We are having a tender young *ekahir* I had been saving in the freezing-box. I shall bring it in."

Jyk—what ought he to call her? Mrs. Cheruk—cleared one of the long tables and from the lower part of the cabinet took dishes of some transparent plastic, golden yellow and delicately etched. She drew from a drawer knives and spoons—there were no forks—of a metal that looked like steel. Patrick hurried to help her. Her manner was distrait, and she kept glancing yearningly toward the kitchen. Presently Zoth entered, bearing a large tray heaped with steaming food.

The *ekahir* turned out to be a crisply roasted bird, its flesh tasting like a combination of turkey and duck. Zoth carved it adroitly, using a long thin knife with a carved metal handle, while his wife piled the plates high with unknown but interesting-looking vegetables. The *rexshan,* poured into tall slender glasses, proved to be a cool bubbling wine, with a warm aftertaste and an insidious effect.

The food was delicious, the drink delightful, and the Terran's appetite sharp; but after his first hunger was satisfied, Patrick found himself increasingly disquieted.

Something he could not understand was very wrong between these two. He didn't need to comprehend the words they exchanged to realize that Zoth loathed his wife, and that she worshiped him. There was scorn in every harsh command he gave her, and to each she hastened to respond with servile promptness. It got on Patrick's nerves, until at last Zoth himself noticed, and made an obvious effort to restrain himself.

The climax came when Jyk, watching her husband's plate with anxious solicitude, suddenly jumped from her seat, carried a dish of tart blue jelly to Zoth's place, placed a portion of it on his plate, and caressingly threw her other arm around his neck just as he was raising a spoonful of *ekahir* to his mouth.

The meat fell from his jostled arm to the table, and he leapt to his feet. The angry syllables he shouted were unmistakably a curse.

Then suddenly, before Patrick could take in what was happening, Zoth seized the long knife with which he had carved the bird—and plunged it full into his wife's breast.

Patrick dived and caught him by the arm before he could strike again. Shaking with horror, he turned his eyes to the victim.

She was not dead, she had not fallen, she was not even bleeding. With a gay laugh she plucked the knife from her flesh, chirped a few words in a tone of affectionate teasing, patted her husband's cheek, and returned amiably to her place at the foot of the table, where she calmly helped herself to more of the jelly.

Patrick's hand fell. He stood staring in paralyzed astonishment. Zoth laughed then too—but his laugh was half a groan.

"Forgive me for interrupting our meal so impolitely, my friend," he said. "Sometimes this woman exasperates me beyond endurance—but, as you see, it does her no harm."

Patrick could only continue to stare, as he slowly resumed his seat.

As for Jyk, she sat drinking *rexshan,* and smiling at her husband as a mother smiles at her naughty child.

Patrick's appetite was gone; he sat uncomfortably waiting for an explanation that did not come. Zoth cleaned the last scrap from his plate, drained the last drop of *rexshan,* and only then addressed a few curt remarks to his wife. She rose quickly and began removing the dishes. The host turned to his guest.

"Exercise is good after a full meal, Patrick. Let us walk for a while around the city, and I will show you how I get our food and all our supplies. There is still much I have not yet asked you about your world."

"There is much *I* want to know also, Zoth," the Terran reminded him.

"Later; there is no hurry. When it is dark I shall send the woman off to bed alone, and then we shall sit over glasses of *stralp* and you may ask me anything you wish to know. But now you must tell me more of this Galactic Presidium, and how it operates. You say there is an agreement by which hitherto undiscovered planets are opened for colonization by whatever life-form is best adapted to them? You may imagine how much this interests me, since I can detect no difference whatever between your form and mine—we are *akkir* together."

"*Akkir*—that means human?"

"Yes. And here is a whole empty world, with all the foundations of civilization already laid."

"I am only a scout, you understand," said Patrick. "I have no authority."

"I understand. But your recommendation would have great influence. I am only wondering how long it would take. Perhaps it would be better . . . However, all that we can discuss later. Now I want to ask you—"

Patrick turned again into a vocal encyclopedia.

Their walk took them to a large warehouse. Zoth opened the door.

"Here, you see," he explained, "are stored garments made of furs—furs of the carnivorous animals which no longer exist on Xilmuch. When it is cold, and we need warm clothing, we have only to take our pick. In the same way, all the stores and warehouses of the city are open to us to obtain whatever we desire in the way of food, clothes, furniture, ornaments—anything at all. There is only one real scarcity: *rhaz*, the fuel by which we run our planes and cars. I have stored all of that I could find in our house, which was once the City Hall, and I use a vehicle only when it is necessary to carry heavy loads. Otherwise, I walk. One man cannot operate the *rhaz* supplier, though when mine is gone I shall have to find some way."

"What about public utilities?" Patrick asked. "Water, lights, things like that?"

"Enough is still operating automatically to serve us. Much, of course, has failed. If, before I—if we of Xilmuch had only learned to split the atom, as you say your world has done— But we hadn't, and so, you will understand, there is great deterioration in such things, though they could be easily rehabilitated with sufficient manpower. After all, it has been fifty years."

"Fifty years since what?"

"Shall we turn back now? I don't want to tire you, and the sun will be setting soon. There are no street lights any more, and I shouldn't like you to stumble in our ruts and gullies in the darkness. Besides, I'm thirsty again, and so must you be. The woman will have finished cleaning up; I shall have her set out some refreshment for us and send her off."

They had walked farther than Patrick had realized; it was twilight before they crossed the bridge to the Civic Center where the great dome dominated the skyline. A glow of lights came from the right-hand windows on the first floor, and as they mounted the steps they found Jyk pacing up and down before the bronze door.

As soon as she glimpsed them, she ran toward them and threw her arms around her husband with a babble of speech. Zoth pulled away impatiently.

"The fool thought she had lost me," he said with a wry grin. "This is the first time I have been this long out of her sight in fifty years. She insists on following me everywhere I go, and it's not worth the trouble to get rid of her when I have no other companion—but today, when I have you—today I ordered her to stay at home and leave me free. She has been weeping. I am glad of it. Let her weep."

Pretty cool, thought Patrick, for a man who had just tried to murder his wife in cold blood, and had failed to do so only by a miracle!

The big municipal-office-turned-living-room was aglow with tubes of soft neo-neon light, and he sank wearily into one of the soft chairs. The cream-colored curtains were drawn, but through a gap he could see the dark sky. This world, he had found, had no moon; and since the city lay near the equator, twilight and dawn were very brief.

He could have done with some sleep; but after all, a scout is a sort of diplomat: if his host were looking forward to a long evening, there was nothing to do but acquiesce. Besides, curiosity was scratching at him; he could make nothing at all of the personal situation here, and it was time for Zoth to talk.

Zoth addressed his wife in a series of staccato remarks. She bustled obediently into the kitchen, while her husband laid out the goblets and fresh bottles of the *stralp*. In a few minutes she returned, bearing a plate heaped with strips of some crisp white substance glistening with what looked like salt. She threw her arms around her husband's neck, and, standing on tiptoe, pressed kisses on his unresponsive face. Patrick looked about him nervously, but this time Zoth stood uncomplainingly like a statue, his fists clenched. He said a few curt words, and Jyk disentangled herself and with a rebellious pout bowed unsmilingly to Patrick, making no attempt to dissemble her jealousy. She departed slowly through another door.

"Ah!" said the host, stretching luxuriously. "She will not dare to trouble us again tonight." He poured the glasses full. "You cannot imagine what this means to me! At last—an evening of social conversation with a congenial friend! I have waited so long—I had almost ceased to hope."

"I think it is your turn to talk now," said the scout coldly.

"I know. You are right. And I can see that you are displeased with me. You think me rude and brutal, you think I abuse a poor woman whose only fault is that she adores me too much. But when you have heard—"

"You tried to kill her, at dinner."

"Precisely: she angered me beyond endurance . . . and I *tried*. You observed that I did not succeed."

Patrick recovered his aplomb.

"I apologize," he said. "It is not my business to judge what I cannot understand. But you will realize I must be puzzled."

"I do indeed. And you are my friend—my first friend in fifty years. I will tell you everything you want to know. Only, it is hard to know how to start.

"Tell me: in your world, are there . . . beings . . . persons that are not human?"

Patrick smiled indulgently. "Some people in my world believe so. Everybody believed so once."

"Here also. Only, I have proved that they are real."

Oh, come now! Patrick thought. *Fairy tales at this point?* "You have?" he said in his best diplomatic manner.

"As you see about you . . . Then, have you a story that one may force such a being to do one's will?"

"We do have a myth—a symbol which has inspired some of our greatest artists—about selling one's soul to the devil—"

"Oh, as with the Nameless!" Zoth turned pale and raised his arms high, the thumbs and forefingers firmly pressed together. "Do not speak of Him!"

Patrick remembered the terrifying hundred-foot statue in the nave of the great temple. Unreasoningly, he knew that this was the Nameless; and for a moment he felt less scornful of the fairy tale.

"No," Zoth went on; "what I mean is closer to the simple *akkir* plane. These are lesser beings, but powerful enough. If one of them can be brought into your power, he can be compelled to grant you five wishes. You have such?"

"Fairies, leprechauns, demons . . . I see what you mean. But on Earth it is, according to legend, only three wishes that he grants. "

"You are luckier than we."

So Zoth's Standard Galactic, the scout thought with amusement, was not so altogether perfect as he had assumed—*luckier* when he meant *less lucky*. Patrick hid a smile as Zoth refilled their goblets.

"I shall tell you the whole story. It is the easiest way to make it clear."

. . . *if not necessarily convincing*, Patrick thought. *And yet*, he asked himself, *have you, my bright Galactic scout, found any normal rational method of accounting for this deserted planet, this celestial* Mary Celeste?

"Fifty years ago I was twenty-three years old. You look surprised. I can age like other *akkir*, but I can never be senile.

"I was young. I was poor. I had a mean job I hated. I was lonely, with no close friends—I, so gregarious a man—and I was madly in love with a girl who would not even look at me. I was in despair.

"How the *grosh* was summoned to me and how he came under my power I shall not tell you. It would be too hard to make it plain, and besides, these are secret things better not told. But he came, and I did subdue him to my will."

"The *grosh*—that's the demon?"

"You may call him so; he is in any event a being like neither you nor me, nor any material creature. I may tell you that my own grandfather was a *vardun*—a priest in the great temple of the Nameless in this city—and from him, though I myself was not chosen to be a *vardun*, I had learned many things in my boyhood."

He repeated the propitiatory gesture—the arms raised and the thumbs and forefingers pressed together.

"So there I was, with five wishes at my disposal. Even then—though I never guessed"—Zoth shuddered—"I thought it wise not to use up all of them at once, but to keep one at least in reserve. You will see how wise that was—but still not wise enough.

"What does anyone want? Long life, health, wealth, love, fame perhaps, though that I did not care about: and if one's heart is good, one wants also good fortune for others as well. I was canny; I had speculated long, to get into small compass as much as possible of the things I craved and had never had."

"Understandably," Patrick nodded. "We are of different worlds, Zoth, but of the same nature."

"So I wished, first, to live to a hundred years at least, and always in good health and strength, without injury or illness. 'Granted,' said the *grosh*.

"Then I wished, not for great wealth which may be a burden, but that I should never lack for any comfort or luxury I might desire. And, since I am one who loves my fellow-beings, loves company and good talk—I, who for fifty years have spoken only to that silly creature in there!—I specified that among these comforts and luxuries must be the ability to converse freely with every person I ever met. You must realize that in Xilmuch at that time there were different communities, all equal, but speaking different tongues—"

"You mean, different nations?"

"Of course; that is your word for them. I intended to travel much, and I wanted to be able to associate with all whom I met. So this, I stipulated, must be part of my second wish."

"So that's how you speak Standard Galactic, is it? That's puzzled me a lot."

"That is how. And if you had spoken any other language, I could have understood and spoken it just as well."

"And what was your third wish?" Patrick began to see a pattern forming—and wished that he did not.

Zoth paced the room, his glass of *stralp* in his hand. He glanced furtively at the door through which Jyk had vanished. Then he said in a shaking voice:

"I told the *grosh*—the Nameless forgive me!—that I wished that the girl with whom I was then so madly in love should love me in return, as madly and forever. I wished that she might be willing to marry me at once. And I wished that she should never leave me, but would live exactly as long as I did myself.

"And the *grosh* said, 'Granted.' "

"That's three wishes." Patrick hesitated. "Did you make any more?"

"One more. Do you know what a war is?"

"Certainly. It has been centuries since there has been a war on Earth, but in the past they were only too common. Even now, we must guard vigilantly against hostility and conflict between rival groups."

"We had not progressed so far. At one time or another, all of our various—nations, as you call them—on Xilmuch had been at one another's throats. We had torn one another almost to pieces, and as our science advanced our wars grew still more terrible. And at that very moment there was threat of a new war that would have advanced my own people, here in this city.

"I was an idealistic young man, who hated bloodshed. So for my fourth wish, I wished that everywhere on Xilmuch there should be complete and perpetual peace.

" 'Granted,' said the *grosh*.

"These were my four wishes. And I told the *grosh* that when I was ready to make the fifth, I would summon him: these beings are immortal, you know. I have still not made it."

"But I don't understand," Patrick objected. "It seems to me that those were all practicable wishes. And you say you had the—the *grosh* in your power. Didn't he really grant them?"

"He granted them all," said Zoth.

"As for the first, I am as you see me. I shall live at least 27 years more, and I shall never know illness or bodily pain. That wish I have no doubt the *grosh* granted me with pleasure—knowing that long before the end I should yearn in vain for death.

"And I have, as you observe, every comfort and luxury I could desire. I live in a palace, and I have at my disposal the food, the clothing, the furniture, all the paraphernalia of life of a great city. The supply, easily obtained, will certainly outlast my lifetime. As for the ability to converse with my fellow-beings in their own tongues, it is only today that I have had occasion to test it—and that with an *akkir* from a world of outer space. But you see it was granted to me."

"But the third wish? What went wrong about the girl you loved? How did the demon get out of really granting you that?"

"He didn't . . . It was Jyk."

"Oh."

"I had thought my heart was broken when she spurned every advance I made. Now of her own accord she came to me: she loved me wildly, as she always will. I was in ecstasy. We were married at once. I was the happiest man on Xilmuch.

"How could I foresee that my own love would turn to loathing? But against my will, it did: first she bored me, then she disgusted me, now I hate her with all my heart.

"And she will be with me all my life. She will live exactly as long as I."

"So that's why—" Patrick exclaimed.

"Yes, that is why no knife, nor any other means, can ever rid me of her.

"I am ashamed that you saw that scene; it does not happen often. But can you imagine what it must be like to have someone, someone you detest, pester you with constant worship? Sometimes I think I shall go mad: nothing, nothing will ever offend or alienate her, and she clings to me every minute. I know she is not sleeping now; she will do whatever I tell her, but she is waiting for me right now with open arms; if I did not go to her eventually, she would seek me out, wherever I might be. And for fifty years there has been no *akkir* on Xilmuch but her and me!"

He paused, fighting for self-control.

"I don't want you to think I am naturally cruel," he went on in a calmer voice. "If I had pity left for anyone but myself, I should pity her. But I need not; she is happy just to be with me, however I treat her. Nearly always I can pretend patience. It was only today, when your coming had so excited me—"

The scout averted his eyes. Quickly, to change the subject, he asked:

"But your fourth wish? Did the demon grant you that?"

"Is there not peace on Xilmuch?" asked Zoth simply.

The Terran was silent. *Demons indeed! But this planet . . . the pattern . . .*

"Yes," his host went on, "the *grosh* knew. We *akkir* are not made by nature for perpetual peace—or we were not so made fifty years ago. The animals also . . .

There is no animal on this planet now which fights with others for its mate, or kills others for its food.

"And there is great and lasting and perpetual peace today on Xilmuch."

Patrick said nothing. His host filled their glasses.

Finally the Terran broke the silence.

"Is there no way," he said hesitantly, "by which, with the wisdom you have acquired, you could use the fifth wish still at your disposal to undo some of the evil the demon did you?"

You might wish, Patrick thought, *to return your wife's love once more, and salvage that much out of the mess; but probably it's too late for that now.*

Zoth shook his head.

"Do you think I haven't worn myself out trying to find some way? The truth is, Patrick, I've been afraid to wish again—afraid he will twist that also to his own evil advantage. And then I should be completely defenseless, at his mercy.

"It is only today, my friend, that a bit of hope has come to me. How could even a *grosh,* I wonder, spoil so modest a wish? It is little enough to ask—I've been so horribly lonely—"

He looked long and speculatively at the Terran.

Patrick drained the last of his *stralp* and stood up. He felt himself trembling.

"Zoth," he said apologetically, "I hate to break this up, but I'm afraid I'm asleep on my feet. Let's go to bed now, shall we? Tomorrow's another day."

"Oh, my friend, forgive me! Of course—you must be worn out! What a way to treat a guest—and a guest who means so much to me! You must excuse an old man who has half a century of conversation to make up! I'll show you where you are to sleep."

He led the way through still a third door to another huge room, a corner of which had been screened off to hold a low couch covered with some soft woolly fabric.

"My guestroom," he smiled. "You are the first ever to occupy it. I hope you will find it comfortable. Right through here you will find the toilet facilities. You turn the light off thus.

"Sleep well, my friend. I shall be sleeping late in the morning myself—I don't often keep such hours as this. When you wake, come to the living hall, and a meal will be ready for you."

Patrick was alone at last.

He made no attempt to undress or go to bed. He had brought his knapsack in with him, and he checked its contents. Then he sat quietly on the edge of the couch, thinking.

He sat there for two solid hours, until there was no glimmer of light anywhere and from a distant room came the sound of faint but steady snoring.

The tall windows opened outwards, and this was the ground floor. Outside, he put on his boots.

It was very dark. No one could have seen him as he crept from tree to tree, in the shadow of the overgrown ornamental bushes, to the nearest bridge.

Once across, he set out at as rapid a pace as possible. Even so, it took three hours, and the sky was beginning to gray, before he reached his ship.

An hour later, well beyond the orbit of Xilmuch, he began to wonder if he had made a fool of himself.

... Who ever heard of the entire population of a planet's being wiped out, just to grant somebody's wish for worldwide peace? Space knew, there were enough other roads to devastation! Wasn't the reasonable conclusion that in some entirely natural way, some epidemic or other frightful catastrophe on Xilmuch, only this man and his wife had survived? Wouldn't it be logical that such a shock would have crazed them both? Hadn't he spent a day and a night listening to the tale of a lunatic?

It was obvious that the man was desperately lonely, and would have kept his chance guest just as long as he could; but did it make sense that he could have done so by merely uttering an unused wish? Wasn't Patrick Ostronsky-Vierra just as crazy as Zoth Cheruk to swallow such a story, even late at night and full of *rexshan* and *stralp?*

... But then why were there no carnivorous animals on Xilmuch, but plenty of herbivorous ones and every sort of vegetation? Catastrophes were not quite so selective as that.

And how ... how else could Zoth have plunged a knife deep into his wife's breast—Patrick's horror-stricken eyes had seen the blade go in to the handle— and draw not a single drop of blood, elicit no sign of pain?

Xilmuch would be a wonderful planet for colonization. Its discovery would be the climax of his career as a scout; there would be no limit to his rise in the profession after that.

And how Zoth would welcome the colonists!

... And what unguessed harm he could do them unwittingly by that fifth wish of his!

In twenty-seven years or so Zoth and Jyk would both be dead. Zoth could do no harm then. But what would the Galactic Presidium think if a scout should announce that here was a perfect colonization-point—only it must not be approached while an old man was still alive who might jinx them?

And with or without Zoth, how about a planet evidently full of mischievous, rancorous, double-crossing *grosh,* with who knew what bags of tricks in their possession?

To say nothing of the Nameless, that distinctly unpretty god or devil whose image Patrick had seen for himself.

Patrick Ostronsky-Vierra, trusted and dedicated Two Star Scout, decided deliberately to violate his sacred oath of office.

When he returned to the headquarters of the Galactic Presidium, his report read:

"I visited Planet IV of Altair, which has been hitherto undiscovered, and which on first approach appeared to be suitable for colonization. On further investigation I found that the atmosphere consists mostly of methane. The planet itself is still in a semi-molten state, with incessant volcanic eruptions and violent windstorms of ethane gas.

"I advise that the planet be given a wide berth—permanently. It is completely unfit for human habitation."

But there was another report: a private one. It was found among Ostronsky-Vierra's effects after his death in 4009. It was in a plastic closure marked: *For the Sealed Files of the Galactic Presidium. To Be Opened 50 Years after Receipt.*

In it was this complete narrative as I, Mari Swenskold-Wong, Secretary of the Presidium in this year 4060, read it to the entire Presidium at its meeting upon February 30.

We are still, as everyone knows, in great need of more living-space in the colonized planets. There has been much discussion of the possibility of colonizing Xilmuch, and there will be much more discussion, perhaps even insistence upon the part of the Opposition.

But the majority opinion, in which I concur, is that no foreseeable Galactic situation, even the mounting pressure of expansion, can justify sending colonists to what Ostronsky-Vierra justly labeled the *Mary Celeste* of space. Empty of Zoth Cheruk and his Jyk it must be by now, but not of its Nameless and its *grosh* (and who can say what powerful type of unknown life-form hides behind these supernatural masks?).

Superstitious, I hope I may safely say, we surely are not; but neither are we, in our Chairman's ringing words, "reckless damn fools." There are other worlds.

Recipe for Curry De Luxe

Anthony Boucher loved to cook. Poul Anderson says that he had considered an Anthony Boucher Cookbook. *The following recipe was one of the ones that his widow,
Phyllis White, gave to Anne McCaffrey for* Cooking Out of This World. *We
present it here to give you a sampling of yet another side of Anthony Boucher*

1 tbsp. curry powder	1 green pepper
¼ tsp. anise or fennel	1 apple
¼ tsp. paprika	1 clove garlic
¼ tsp. chili powder	(2 tbsp. raisins or chopped dates)
¼ tsp. turmeric	1 tbsp. Worcestershire sauce
¼ tsp. mace	2 lbs. lean stewing lamb
¼ tsp. cumin	1 bouillon cube
¼ tsp. ground cloves	1 cup boiling water
1/8 tsp. cardamom	2 tbsp. tomato paste
1 lime or small lemon	1 tbsp. sherry
5 tbsp. (1/3 cup) olive oil	1 tbsp. milk
1 large onion	1 egg

Make a powder of the first group of nine ingredients (curry, anise, paprika,
chili powder, turmeric, mace, cumin, cloves, and cardamom). Grind the whole
spices in a mortar, add the others, and mix thoroughly. Chop the vegetables and
fruit coarsely and sauté them in the oil with Worcestershire and ½ the powder
mixture. Add the meat and brown it with the rest of the powder. Dissolve the
bouillon cube and paste in the water and pour over all. Let simmer for 1¼ hours.
Remove the meat to a serving platter. Add the sherry and the juice of the lime or
lemon to the curry in the pan. Beat an egg lightly in the milk, add this, and cook,
stirring, about another minute, or until it begins to thicken. Pour over the meat,
and serve with rice and chutney. This should serve four, but two can make a
terrible hole in it.

This book was printed in Adobe Garamound for the text, with Book Antiqua for the titles. It was entered and set on a Gateway 486/66 in Microsoft Word 95 and PageMaker 6.0. It was printed on an HP LaserJet 4. The dust jacket was produced on a Macintosh PowerBook using PageMaker 6.0. It was printed by BookCrafters of Chelsea, Michigan.

Special Note

Despite several attempts, we were unable to track down the agent for the estate of Miriam Allen deFord. If the agent for the estate reads this, please contact us. We will be glad to pay standard royalties for the story co-authored by her.